P9-DNE-229

Praise for *Beyond the Tether*

"There may be no joy in "Mudville" where Casey struck out, but former minor league ballplayer turned author Bruno G. Botti hit a homerun with *Beyond the Tether* – a family's adoring and adventuresome relationship with their dying Siberian Husky Tasha who captured their mending hearts."

Paul A Sciria
La Gazzetta Italiana Editor

"A brilliant story with powerful illuminative writing about a man and his dog expressing their devotion and reverence to each other as they confront the torment of mortality."

Anthony Zampino
Surgeon and freelance writer

"Bruno Botti has captured the graceful power of animals that influences so much of our lives. He brings us into this magical relationship between animals and pet owners in a very entertaining way. This profound relationship with animals greatly affects who we are – not only bringing out the compassion that makes us better people, but also gives a healing process."

Teka Ludovico
Animal Behavior Specialist

"This is a wonderful story of an extraordinary dog who touched everyone that crossed her path. She had me laughing and crying."

Amy Cohen, Producer
Los Angeles, Ca.

"It's a truly amazing story that captures your mind and heart from page one. Bruno G. Botti completely understands the human-canine bond. *Beyond the Tether* is a wonderful read."

Tiff Gravel, Director, Producer
Los Angeles, Ca.

"I recommend this book to anyone who has ever been blessed by having a dog as a member of the family. Bruno G. Botti's novel tells the story of Tasha, an extraordinary Husky who adopted her humans as her "pack." She teaches them, and us, that true love transcends this lifetime."

Barbara Niven, Actress
Los Angeles, Ca.

Beyond
- the -
Tether

Beyond the Tether

- Bruno G. Botti -

Tate Publishing & *Enterprises*

Tate Publishing & Enterprises

Beyond the Tether

Cover design by Lynly D. Taylor
Interior design by Melanie Harr-Hughes

Published in the United States of America

ISBN: 1-5988646-3-7
07.01.17

Dedication

For Tasha, whose life's remembrances are threaded throughout the fabric of this novel, insuring her loving recall today, and years after her death.

For Phyllis whose love and affection for Tasha continue just as intensely for an abused and abandoned mix breed Shepherd. Against all odds of success, Phyllis resurrects her adopted Duchess, coaxing beyond fear and rejection, a responding show of love and dependency.

Preface

Tethered the dictionary defines in part as a rope, a chain or the like by which beings are fastened to a fixed or following object so as to limit its range or movement.

Beyond the Tether tells the story of a dog named Tasha, characteristically an Alpha sublimating those instincts to the strong leadership of George Staves whom she entrusts as her new provider until sadly her approaching death. Assimilated, within her new pack demonstrating in a series of defining events how extraordinarily gifted she is. With the tragic circumstance of her approaching death, she becomes a willing partner in an attempt to extend her biological clocks windings. When veterinarian treatments, including the most advanced prove unsatisfactory, desperation forces an accommodation with the mysterious incorporeal: which finds Tasha to be the one selectively anointed. Illuminated she decides to sacrifice herself. Experiencing an epiphany Tasha separates herself, her dedication re-prioritized, accepting her increasing pain before relieved by Euthanasia. In self baptismal, cleansed spiritually contrarily presenting herself to her Alpha with a new purpose; an awakened fulfillment. It's consequence, severing their cure searching alliance. Extending her longevity, no longer her preoccupation; her calling, an eternity of her choice gifted magically to continue to serve beyond her earthly being… her new allegiance. During her amazing lifetime: a Husky of unique persuasion, who when motivated demonstrated mysterious expansiveness of instincts. Demonstrating an intellect always unfolding and responsive, almost human in it's elevation. Displaying powers of the surreal, befitting the occasion, ultimately a precursor for joining the supernatural. *Beyond the Tether* is a novel permeating with experiences of fact leading to exploring and envisioning. Its blend; a provocative thesis in need of opportunity, so say the believers of animals unlimited capabilities; joyous in the books license that demonstrates that man is not exclusively cognizant. The novel also credits Tasha with surreal powers when all other of her extraordinary instincts fail. Baffled by it's source, the phenomenon's explanation left to burden the highest levels of developing science. Confounding, the division of the startling known, and the mystique of the unknown. The novels license during the surreal depictions, believed to be by advocates a forerunner of events of future discovery. Perhaps not of this world, but in the eternity that awaits us all; revealing, a late truth to skeptics, that dogs are instinctive with reasoning powers. Anthropomorphism would be the indictment voiced by dissenters crying out formidable arguments of nature and nurture influences; criticizing the rabid steadfastness of supporters. The critics uncompromising position exposed as flawed as evidence continues to mount. Characterized with those influences, Tasha was given license within the novel as the possessor of powers of other dimensions in life and death, whose plane, remains undiscovered by mankind. Meaningful references to authoritative factual studies are quoted in the novel. Birthing the expansiveness of the author's license to provoke debate.

As a result of Tasha's death, the bonds of the mourning pack members are severed, creating a slow to heal scaring during recovery of their wounds, testing their learning to live with only memories of their venerated and prized physical connection – *Beyond the Tether.* In life death would extinguish her radiance but not the monolith that was her memory.

The consequence of losing Tasha was an internal upheaval within George Staves. He tested his life's commitment to reasonableness. His usual philosophy analogous to the pragmatism of an ombudsman, an impossible outlook in Tasha's case. Ceding her prognosis as fatalistic – an expediency betraying trust and devotion that was their relationship. Unrelenting for the first time, creating a fissure in his granite wall of reality. Emotions venting a defiance, George rejecting Tasha's path to death as unalterable. While devastated he would not allow himself and his family a defeatist resignation. He accepted her death without an extraordinary and far reaching challenge. Impassioned, he marshals his family from paralyzing submission to search for credible hope, joining in optimism to support his aggressive response.

Driven, not accepting the limitations of conventional veterinary medicine: ministrations providing temporary and declining relief from insufferable pain. He eagerly solicits alternate treatments, encouraged by the evolving, the revolutionary as salvation. George Staves committed with every beat of his heart, faced condemnation and questions if after prolonged treatment any success proved fleeting, returning to the pitiful sight of Tasha losing mobility, her pain increasing, torturing all. To be criticized by the more pragmatic, indicting his pursuit "as beyond reason for personal reasons." The weight of that possible haunt not deterring him. Judgments of his motives to be rendered by a jury he would be part of, voiceless until the final reckoning.

Yet showing his feelings; wearing the unmistakable mask of the emotionally drained as Tasha's seeker – finding her savior from an imminent death sentence, continuing his extraordinary relationship. His conscience cleared by erasing thoughts of couching self-interest until circumstances reawakened him – the Hydra hypocrisy uncoiling in an alarming reappraisal. Until that moment, their dedication assumed a life of its own. Its blood components: his force of will and Tasha clearly signaling, in her special way, her want to live longer in her role, continuing as a member of his pack. Searching in alliance for a reversal of her fate – death a certainty for Tasha's corporeal being. Nether one of them anticipating, either individually, or in consort, of setting the pledge aside. Tested during their pursuit of ad hoc ministrations disappointingly proved unsuccessful.

Tasha's life's curtain in a downward fall, forced him to cross the surreal divide into a dimension that is amorphous. It's remarkable physics demonstrating unaccountable power, seeking acceptance they sought out initiation through out of body experience. His wife Rose acutely sensitive and distrustful, reluctantly succumbed, prayerfully becoming tolerant of his plan to seek an accommodation with his God to explore the occult. A mysterious world of the 'ancients' whose spectral beings still prowl the earth. Borderline as an adjunct to religion, held by believers as empowered to heal with God's oversight.

With the prospect of success within their immediate reach Tasha breaks their alliance, ending it's purpose in the interest of greater good, willingly a sacrifice to the pain ridden final hours of her lifetime. Shocked by her rejecting salvation in the offering, remorsefully abiding her wishes.

Chagrined at the turn of events, George still hopeful, along with others whose pets were of the same circumstances, seeks the miracle of the church, celebrating it's namesakes birth and gift of sainthood. Silent in prayer, self absorbed, circumventing her wishes invited intervention in the inevitability of Tasha's death. Denied, all his efforts spent, he is compelled to recognize her pain wracked body as fateful, knowing he will play a role in her euthanasic death, haunting him with guilt.

Prologue

George Staves, a lead character created by the author, lamenting the loss of Tasha, did not want her memory diminished by the passing of time. Her powerful impact on his and other's lives obligated him to securing a necessary and appropriate tribute. Initially he leaned in favor of a journal, a series of vignettes starting from the day they met each other, whence a leadership challenge developed. Bringing together a dominant Alpha canine and a countervailing human's purposeful strong will, in a confrontation that had to be waged before adoption was accomplished by the participants. The contesting finally reconciled, it set the stage for Tasha's devotion over her cherished lifetime. Circumstances warranted, demonstrating magical responses and instincts in a range of situations including crime prevention, improbable recoveries, and a climaxing episode with the surreal. Her differentiating accomplishments doubtful to most humans as unbelievable for canines unless gifted beyond what is known, a central thesis in distinguishing and separating.

After Tasha's death, her Alpha, George Staves considered as a proper tribute a journal to house a collection of remembrances impacting moments. The dated time frame of such events would succeed in arbitrating fading memories and miscalculations of time. A literal blueprint, offering not-to-scale measurements of the width and breadth of Tasha's intelligence and emotional attachments during her lifetime.

He wanted an expansion of opportunity for her appreciation-a tribute for the most wonderful dog that God ever provided to accompany man. George Staves, became convinced, the more connected writings of a book, would be a greater accurate tribute rather than sketches, serving as a memorial to her honor by readers, introduced to a wondrous visit.

He would choose this venue, using the unleashed, unconstrained power of a books written word to capture the full essence of her lifetime. Supplemented with revering family photo albums abounding with Tasha's pictures – an assist capturing only a moment in time: single dimensioned, impersonal and glossy silent, remaining so until given meaning by his fashioned words-enhancing them to three dimensional; her true substance.

The writing would weave a story of their magical bonding and her influence, being never apart until death pronounced the imminence of separation. His world, privileged to own this remarkable dog was facing an unprepared ending, drove him to the uncompromising passion of protection, no matter where it took him.

Together they were passionately driven for a longer biological clock if not a cure, partnering in pursuit. With the prospect of success within their immediate reach, Tasha broke their alliance, willingly sacrificing herself, relinquishing the searched for gift bestowed, to the excruciating pain of her final hours. The finality of her decision not without resistance from her Alpha, his concession not until the last possible tearful moment – precluded, he remorsefully, painfully abiding her wishes; his best possible reverence.

With her final moments bearing down on him, George would not abide the retaining of Tasha's ashes in a urn positioned on the mantel of their brick fireplace, suggestive of a revering alter, ostensibly suggesting prayer appropriate.

He was equally resistant to burial at a local pet cemetery, expressing scorn for the trappings of a commercial enterprise, profiting from the grief of the elderly or the impressionable youth whose world of dependency had ended. Equally disdaining; the prospect of a burial plot with a headstone, its inscription scribed in factual cold brevity: name, a perfunctory devotion, and the two fateful dates… birth and death – sure to be viewed with indifference by the casual visitor.

Assured a planned written tribute would better serve than a burial plots disheartening headstone overlooking dying grass; a chiseled inscription the only truth of her existence in the years to come.

The book, would be a factual testament of significant happenings in detail, re-acquainted by the turning of a page, recreating a mirror whose reflections bear none of the inaccuracies that aging can misrepresent. The record of the written word accurately describing passions a better venue; providing escape from the inevitable loneliness of a gravesite.

Tasha would convey to him, she wished cremation of her remains. Her ashes distributed amongst the freedoms of her chosen outdoors.

His original plan, the manuscripts charter; for family members only, in a closed circle of privileged joy, recalling from the pages; events empirically lived or shared. That conviction weakened as the books limited distribution began to draw his doubts. He now questioned whether familial appreciation was enough of a tribute. True, it would be enthusiastically accepted by family members, but her accomplishments, its message and acknowledgment deserved an expanded venue he proudly believed in – stimulating his growing enthusiasm for wider distribution. *It would be fitting to make her memory available throughout the world, he thought, even in novel form.* He was optimistic, envisioning Tasha gracing the pages, her remarkable achievements relived by all readers, sharing in the love and devotion she gave and received. Her characterization in novel format would frame literary license, foundational by actual events, easily recognized by those who knew her.

His new plan, use the draft of the journal as the building block, appreciating it's breath and depth, growing beyond the vignette. The novel medium would credential his freedom to expand and be more detailed, more descriptive of actual events. *A welcomed and easier task,* he thought affectionately, not so the commercially important invented characters, their dialogue and situations more daunting.

A book, he enthused confidently, would most assuredly be a challenge to his writing ability, burdening his unknown acumen for literate expansion of detail; hopefully rewarded with appreciation beyond the parochial offerings of a familial journal. The expanded exposure in novel form would ask readers to determine intermeshed fact from fantasy with no hint from the writer, challenging the imaginative reader, to make those judgments along the way or in post-mortem, while easily distinguished by those who bore witnesses.

He welcomed the challenge as an opportunity to share Tasha's incredible life. Perhaps in sharing, he thought, a sense of ownership would grow, of belonging to her spiritual being, denied the opportunity while she lived. A magnificent achievement, if the writings capture the hearts and minds of readers with age appreciation.

The evolved storyline would not go begging for the critical. While anticipated, it did not dissuade him. George Staves committed to write her story as a hybrid, a blend of occurrences; expectations influenced by selected authority, her real life extraordinary abilities in manufactured or anticipated circumstances. Interspersed with biographical accomplishments written as she lived them, leaving the separation up to the reader; the books cornerstone. Purchasing, challenge by frothing animal behavioral scientists, as prejudicial and debatable, the licensed as well as the actual occurrences. Contending that the sponsors emotional attachment shaped his advocacy disqualifying him as an authority in spite of his living through the experiences. Further contending only a scientist could make the judgments necessary in accessing Tasha's extraordinary behavior as conscious acts -elevating without prejudice… the authors heart obviously captivated – being unable to distinguish.

"Rote imbred reactions," their scholarly disclaimer, prefacing, "it is well known that animals lack emotional and cognitive thought processes. The author guilty of projecting his prejudiced judgments upon his dog, giving it human like characteristics. While a comforting haven for his imagination, resisting reality is hardly the position of science," was their sanctimonious conclusion. Ignored and weakening their sermonesque assessment, their conclusions predicated on the limitations of controlled rigid laboratory work, not the openness and the natural environment of field work. Where animal freedom of expression is given, not coerced or bribed or enslaved to a nurturing repetitive routine. Evidence exists that in its natural environment, animal reactions are much different than when in captivity, displaying unexpected instinctive and intuitive responses. Putting into question the whole issue of man as the only earthly being designate capable of cognitive response. Secular science holding only the human species can display a high degree of intellect and the full range of emotion. Finding otherwise would shake the foundation in the field of academia. Indicting years of acclaimed study as prejudicial and faulted.

It is certain that this writing will provoke debate and controversy; in some quarters, spawning charges of heresy. Indicting George Staves as guilty of "all God's children" anthropomorphism; the elevation of the attributions of human characteristics to non-humans. The writing would challenging the scientific community, deemed as doctrinaire. Still it hoped the book's license would give critics pause at a minimum, the thought provoking central thesis, excluding the imaginative, is well-founded and not without its unsolicited supporters as the following reference context could suggest:

Behaviorist John S. Kennedy laments, "The scientific study of animal behavior was inevitably marked from birth by its anthropomorphic parentage and to a significant extent still is. Anthropomorphism is much more a problem than animal neo-behaviorists believe. If the study of animal behavior is mature as a science the process of liberation from the delusions of anthropomorphism must go on."

The book, *When Elephants Weep* by Jeffrey Moussaieff Mason and Susan McCarthy, offers another cogent hypothesis. "While emotions cannot be simply a blend of hormones, to whatever hormones contribute to emotional states in humans, they probably also do so in animals. Substances like oxytocin, epinephrine, serotonin, and testosterone all are thought to affect human actions and feelings," continuing they go on to say, "The capacity to experience (emotions) them crosses cultures… if the feeling can cross cultures it seems like they can cross species," adding, "Most people, the authors of this book among them, have always believed animals love and suffer, cry and laugh; their hearts rise up in anticipation and fall in despair. They are lonely, in love, disappointed or curious. They look back in nostalgia and anticipate future happiness. They feel. Quite obvious to some of us."

"Enormous claims," say the disputing wing of the scientific community. Not wanting to be accused of anthropomorphism, distancing themselves and when pressed exhort, "Animals are instinct driven and survival oriented – lack complex emotions, like love, sadness, despair, jealousy, and sympathy. Nurture and nature's instincts drive their reactions," countering claims of extraordinary behavior in animals as fragmented and anecdotal, choosing to await a preponderance of evidence before reconsidering their on the record position.

Unfortunately, relationships with animals have always been uncomfortable to avoid, retarding its evolution. Historical and religious traditions prevented embracing the ideas that while humans are different, the chasm of differences is not beyond a leap of faith. The elitist Behavioral Scientist would have you believe establishing a dualism between us and them is sacrosanct. Whenever an animal's ability approaches humans, the fear of being charged with anthropomorphism, a scientific blasphemy, is so compelling as to bring furious responses, so strong is their disconnect.

Introduction

It had been days since Tasha's death. Adjustments to her being gone continue to be difficult. Reminders are everywhere, squirrels, birds and rabbits, with her threatening presence lacking, visit freely. Her distinguishingly scented blown hair, mixed with the grass cuttings, lacks intimidation; a fading memory. Needing substance in his treasured memories, George Staves sat in his lawn chair, wanting escape that only solitude can bring. To be selfishly alone. To allow his thoughts to wander… sharing with no one… private.

The quietude, stage set, he begins searching within the confines of his impatient mind. Reflections take him upward to the heavens above for additional stimulus, clear of clouds the vast color of blue is overwhelming. Enraptured George becomes philosophical: the sky, a member of his universe in folklore proclaiming it a religious heaven for the spirits. In science yielding elements that sustain life in all its forms. He visualizes the world as a worshiping satellite alternating it's rotating position to receive the energy bearing the sun's seeds of growth from millions of brilliant nuclear explosions seen today. Continuing life's accommodation spawned on the surfaces of the sun; cataclysmic upheavals releasing gases to nurture everything living… or transforming them into elements of a denser substance as they gain cooling distance.

"Go higher," George demanded of himself, releasing his mind to travel further. Beyond the ionosphere where there is no light, where there is no color. Beyond the deep black holes of astronomers. Beyond the lightless photosphere to the deepest impenetrable black where one finds the surface that magnetically repels, allowing no further passage of all energies. A barrier between universes where images and sounds of the ancient past traveling at warp speeds can go no further, held by it's tether of magnetism; at it's boundary, perpetually in motion. Followed by those most recent energies still in free flight, years away from the magnetic top of their world is where his mind wished to search the past. That of Einstein's theory of relativity bringing space and time together in a single four dimensional arrangement he called Spacetime. Where one can travel forward, backwards, and sideways in space. "Take me on this journey," he demanded of his transporter, "where my minds kaleidoscope can sort through and recapture… Present to me those moments."

George released his warp speed transporter, braking when the images and sounds that lived in the moment in time he wished to visit appeared;

prioritized moments of their lives together, not necessarily chronological. Another time and travel would be used to visit other periods not in his present port of calls. His mind configuring him as a trackless passenger train powered by anti-matter; he the sole passenger. His own kaleidoscope was focusing through the many windows featuring Tasha's life. There are no exhaust fumes announcing its movement, no currents of moving air resisting passage of this monolith. It moves freely, the jumbled pictorial presentation lasting seconds, his kaleidoscope functioning, sorting – the transporter coming to a complete halt. His sheer will is all that is needed to give the picture temporary leave from the caravan passing him by.

Where should he start amongst such a bounty of events? His original plan was to defer her most recent period in favor of only reliving those moments of happiness selected from his playbill. He would decide against this approach of selectivity as not measuring her accurately, lessening her substance by skipping those moments that tested everyone's character, that which brought so much pain to all. Influencing that decision, the shared purpose he had to fulfill: the ambitious task of writing a book in her honor. With notepad and pencil in hand to make the necessary notes as he traveled her history, starting with his first encounter with Tasha, the beginning of their relationship until her death.

one

They were sitting at the kitchen table, George Staves and his wife Rose relaxing over a cup of coffee after spending literally the last hour on their hands and knees searching the tufted carpeting of their den for one of her pearl earrings. Planning to look elsewhere, their efforts unsuccessful, they brushed their trousers and slacks, freeing them of the loose hairs attracted from deep within the carpet's pile.

"It's been six months since we lost her and we still find traces of her," he said sadly in reflection.

"She's everywhere," sadness overtaking Rose. Uncritically she said, "You should see what still comes out of the bag after vacuuming, although it's considerably less." Pausing to reflect, "I still miss her."

"We all do," George responded.

"Our kids feel we should get another dog. They keep bringing it up."

"Their intentions are good," he said. "But as you and I have talked, pets demand so much time, a factor to keep in mind in any decision. Frankly, I'm not sure I want to go through that all over again. And, besides, Zuni was a pet for all of us; the kids growing up taking a very active role. They'll not be as involved the next time, if there is a next time."

"I didn't mind the inconvenience," Rose said. "Missed vacation trips were a small price to pay for the joy she brought as she and the kids grew up together."

"I know, I know," George said. "Rosanne and Edward, married, and Phyllis, soon to be on her own; it's essentially you and me in this house, quiet of youthful activity. Everything we've done in the last six months is organized and planned around the two of us. Everything scheduled and predictable. No routine breakers. That's a comforting lifestyle but I have to admit, with little challenge."

"George," Rose said with a surprise in her voice, "you sound like you want another dog."

"Not at this moment. It's too soon. But down the road, maybe."

The doorbell rang, interrupting their thoughts. It was their daughter Rosanne and son-in-law Bill. Both seemed unexpectedly uncomfortable, as if still in the aftermath of a serious dispute. Rosanne's usual happy face a forced portrayal, with Bill visible nervousness beading perspiration on his upper lip.

"How nice of you to stop by. Were you out shopping? Take off your coats and have coffee with us." Rose said.

Their immediate response was not to move as if frozen, looking evasively at each other, inviting the other to speak. The ensuing silence exaggerating their discomfort. Exasperation prompted Rosanne step forward, take command, an action their son-in-law was obviously reluctant to take, saying, "Mom and Dad, we've brought you something you need," as if implying they had been denying themselves, her reawakened assertiveness not in the least surprising.

Rose and George looked at each other quizzically until their intuitiveness took hold and ciphered what they were about to be told. They awaited confirmation.

The answer to be given was hidden from view beneath their uncomfortable son in law Bill's jacket. Rosanne a force not easily deterred once decided, had plotted furtively, disregarding her parents reluctance, deciding now was the time to replace the beloved Husky Zuni, who mercifully died in her sleep after a long illness.

Their daughter reasoned the passing of more time, as her parents had claimed, was not needed to prepare them for another dog. Hers was an expedient to accomplish what they both truly wanted – Zuni's loss therapeutically to be more manageable, her image, her memory in their hearts assured, in spite of ongoing obvious comparisons. The remnants of grieving time giving way to full recovery: hastened by a new era. Their heaviness with sorrow would be replaced by the ebullient joy of renewal by a surrogate of her breed. Rosanne concluding it would be the best medicine.

Nodding in the direction of his wife, their flustered son-in-law said, "This was her idea. I reminded her of your feelings but she insisted," he continued defensively, still undecided as to his father-in-law's reaction as he began to unbutton his jacket.

"Mom, Dad," Rosanne said pleadingly, "it's time that you had another dog. And further," gaining confidence in her message by the shocked but sympathetic look on her parents' faces, interpreting it as rapidly falling resistance, "this is our gift to you. You can't refuse."

Whatever reluctance they had was archived immediately as history as the beautiful puppy of six weeks pushed her snout between the open buttons of Bill's jacket, entering George and Rose's world for the first heartfelt memorable time.

She peered out, blinking as she adjusted from the darkness of her concealment, quickly focusing her eyes to view them quizzically. Dressed by nature with the furtive bandit's mask of early age framing her excited eyes, one brown, the other blue, creating a contrary sinister illusion. She saw them for the first time bewildered by the strangeness; unfamiliar humans who now fawned over her.

"Where are my brothers and sisters?" the confusion in her expressive eyes asked. "Where is my mother who nursed and taught me? Where are my siblings who were just beginning to recognize me as their leader?"

Small enough to hold in his hands, delight glowing on his face, fending off a rapidly growing suspicion expressed in his wife's contacting eyes, George countering jocularly, "I was not part of any conspiracy," responding smiling defensively. His deferred accommodation not an early arrival – admitting time already passed psychologically prepared him for this very day – sure his wife had joined him. He marveled at the textbook coloring of the dog's pedigree, covered with an outer coat of black-and-white richness, to be complimented by warming coats evolving close to her body. Furry growth of soft cold insulating Down nature had in store for her, the continuing protection from the elements, purposeful for other latitudes and longitudes, to be more frequently blown in less severe climates.

She wasn't perfect in color. The quirks in the evolutionary process preventing any dog show consideration. She would have been judged "faulted" in overall appearance once past her beautiful conformation, blemished as she was by a trace of rouge whispering on her rear flanks. This the only sign she was kin to her siblings' red-and-white coloring mirroring that of their mother. She bore the coloring of her black-and-white father; her mother's coupling only hinted at.

George sensed an instant bonding take place as she, squirming in his hands, quieted, responding to his soothing and calming voice, recognized as signs that they would be good to her… that they would become companions for as long as God willed. Yes, they as strangers did remove her from her pack but she need not fear being alone and lost. They would comfort her as she howled those first nights as she learned to be separated from her mother's, sisters' and brothers, until it was George and Rose she looked forward to seeing.

Rosanne and Bill were pleased with themselves, overjoyed that their gift was greeted with little resistance. The tenseness in their faces softening, the thought they had made a mistake faded, their parents bearing the visage of being blessed as proud owners, smitten after the initial shock. Not a factor as they were easily captives, Rose and George perfunctory asked of her lineage. Her pedigree A.K.C. papers were presented by Rosanne, establishing a family tree connection to champion show dogs. That theatrical venue they knew would not be pursued, ruled out by her coloring imperfection. They would be of one voice, dismissing as inconsequential, so captivated, "let her siblings continue the tradition of being put on awarded display." Her destiny; their growing adoration equivalent to judged ribbons and medals as an assimilated member of her new family, her new pack.

"She looks like she can use some water," Rose commented as she took her into her arms, where she was instantly set upon by delighted lavishing squeals and kisses. Rose's pearl earring missing its mate caught the dog's attention and curiosity, sniffing and licking it profusely, the pearl and Rose's ear glistening with wetness, the sensation tickling. Laughing in delight, Rose laid her down before a dish that Rosanne had prepared. The dog's rapid lapping of the water caused as much spillage as she drank. When finally satiated, she turned her attention to the new surroundings, recognizing exploring the unfamiliar as an adventure. As Rose reached down to retrieve her, she bolted as fast as her little legs would carry her toward the living room. A panicky Rose Staves led the others in a charge to attempt to recapture her. Crafty and mischievous, she, one step ahead of them, easily avoided grasps, out of fear of hurting her, too delicate for the purpose. Exhausted from their chase, their concerns for her relieving herself waning, they stopped their futility, laughing at how ridiculous they each looked, a chase rivaling a Mac Sennet Keystone Cops comedy.

Unsure of why they had stopped chasing her, halted, she dropped down on the joints of her forelegs. Peering upward, her eyes twinkling in glee at her victory behind the bandit mask, her tail wagging from her raised hindquarters. She taunted them with yips of encouragement, wanting the game of play to continue.

Rose was enjoying the sight of the little puppy mischievously holding four adults at bay with her quick silver movements. Her concern returning that she would have an accident on the living room carpet as notice was given that the puppy's focus shifted to sniffing along the carpet. On a mission adroitly beyond their grasp, they frantically shouted for her return. Ignored she continued to sniff her way under the coffee table. Finally emerging, chewing on a unknown in her mouth. This time the puppy responded to Rose's concern for her safety by moving directly into her grasp. When picked up she responded with a grunt as she was brought up to Rose' bosom. Without hesitation or direction, she opened her mouth to reveal Rose's missing pearl earring.

"It's my earring," Rose shouted, clearly astounded. "We searched for it all morning. She knew it belonged to me. Why else would she give it to me? She sensed it was mine, knowing from her nuzzling that I was wearing another one. You all saw how she brought it right to me without hesitation. A display of such intelligence at this young age is remarkable. She's a winner," Rose added with growing affection.

"Amazing, quite amazing," George Staves said, adding his excited voice to Rosanne's and Bill's who were just grasping the implications.

The yet-to-be-named dog captured their mending hearts that memorable day and all the days that followed. George and Rose would subsequently name her Natasha, contracted to Tasha as they would call her from that day forward. She was not initially a one-man dog as is her breed's nature, receiving and giving affection equally. An alpha in her species that would have to adjust to a new social order within her new human pack.

Tasha's first view of them was not timid or subdued in spite of what appeared to be imposing human monoliths that came into her focus. She quickly distinguished herself as different as she ranged from welcoming kisses to playful excited biting with her razor sharp teeth, considered at her early age as one and the same – a greeting. While she, when fully matured would cease this habit, as a puppy it would be a consistent part of her acknowledgment when excited. The fixing of her razor sharp teeth around a hand was never done with the intention to harm. It was a form of play, a test to see how far she could go before responding to a chastising stop command. Strong willed and determined, this method of showing affection, always testing, was slow to leave her. It was in her early years that excitement drove this display, painful at times never construed as an act not connected to being lovingly. In her mature years if not interested, she would remain aloof and independent, in need of a stimuli.

The breed's bi-eyed presentation and false inference, wrongfully depicting them as menacing, when in fact, while they have no fear of strangers, they do not have the temperament for being watchdogs, although they may be perceived as threatening. Their true nature is hospitable in spite of their intense personality. Extremely loyal, they would die protecting you.

In it's early youth, Tasha was developed from a clumsy adorable puppy prancing about, to a maturity still looking for challenges or play. Housebroken in a relatively short period of time, she almost immediately recognized the purpose of yesterday's newspaper. In use during her housebreaking was a hastily constructed roofless wire cage that served as her sleeping quarters positioned by the patio door, the shortest distance to enable her when alerting the household to do her business in the backyard.

Huskies by nature need lots of room to exercise as their metabolism dictates, to move openly, driven by the free spirit to run, run, and run some more, almost indefatigable. Given the opportunity of no constraints, huskies would emancipate themselves by running free, resisting all calls to return, instinctive by the genetics of their ancestry whose penchant to run freely had not been bred out of them, doubtless that it ever would. Willful to run freely, curious to new sounds and sights for exploration.

She grew to the outer size range of the female of her working class species. Tasha grew extremely strong as she achieved adulthood, powerful enough to break her collar and chain on numerous occasions to wander for hours. Fortunately, usually close to home until bored, she was then ready to return.

As is her breed, she was extremely intelligent, graceful and comparatively easy to care for. Her temperament is affection with some conditions: when of want; solicitous, but shuns being fawned over, particularly by strangers. Her independence bred purposefully, bringing stubbornness and determination, challenging your ingenuity in dealing with her specific characteristics that must be willingly accommodated in some manner. Unless this commitment was made, first time dog owners should not consider this breed.

The whole family, captivated by the charm and personality, quickly adopted the new puppy as their own. The devotion was sure to create learning problems as expectations and demands varied amongst family members. It was obvious to George Staves, the lessons of Zuni still fresh in his mind, that a strict training regimen was necessary in order to change her behavior patterns. Changing an Alpha to a follower required constant reinforcement as to who would provide leadership.

Staves counseled, "Tasha is a pack animal that had achieved certain ranking expectations from her pack. Our family is her new pack. She must not dominate in a new environment. We must help her with her new identity by imposing certain guidelines that must be religiously enforced by all of us." George advised his family, what it would take to be successful substitute parents.

Recognizing Tasha as "different and unusual," they all agreed that commands from all family members had to be uniform and forceful. Commands of sit, stop, down, come, stay; must have the same meaning no matter which family used them. It would be preferable, George advised, not to repeat commands where practical- physically helping her carry them out.

"Tasha, as you can see, is without discipline, poking her nose into everything, ignoring us," George said. While her free spirit is cute and pleasurable to watch, George reminded everyone, "It only lasts while she is a puppy. We'll all grow tired of her being undisciplined as she gets older. She has to be reigned in without destroying her character," George Staves said in all seriousness.

He knew the men would be the enforcers. The women of his family would be more mellow in their approach, more conciliatory, needing more convincing of his regimen. Avoiding the hard and fast tactics, they would continue to downplay Tasha's poor behavior as fun loving mischief, making no connection with the future.

"She sure is cute and curious," a worshipping Phyllis said.

"Adorable," a completely captivated Rose would say.

Rosanne would just smile and plead for her father's understanding, her heart already stolen when she and her husband Bill selected her.

"Her breed," George Staves proclaimed, his emphasis for the women, "more than most others are organizationally structured, demanding a stability that only comes from social order ranking amongst den mates. It's obvious from what Bill and Rosanne learned from the breeder we have the dominating Alpha cavorting around us setting her own rules."

"We can't let that continue. Otherwise, having her as a pet will be brief," he said directly to the women, trying to look forceful, and knowing his threat would never happen, being hopelessly smitten.

"While you may think it's cruel to expect so much from a puppy, let me assure you even her natural mother who gave and showed a lot of attention and caring still had certain expectations of her puppies. We must be prepared to do the same thing if we wish her to develop into a pet everyone will be proud of. If persistent, we'll hopefully gain her understanding and attention, directing her rather than correcting unwanted behavior. It won't be easy. Her breed, as we all know from our experience with Zuni, practices dominance hierarchies. Tasha's already an Alpha." George paused in consternation at what appeared to be women's indifference to his comments. They sat looking glowingly at Tasha asleep in her cage; she could do no wrong in their eyes.

Exhorting them for attention, George continued, "That won't fly in this house. She'll have to learn that I'm the higher authority around here."

"Without appeal, with no options." he declared. His harshness unexpected by the startled looks of the women, he had made his point. Softening his intensity he said, "I'll need everyone's cooperation, including Tasha."

Smiles appeared on everyones face, including George's, at the realism of his qualifier, knowing Tasha's independence would be hard to counter, demand or no demands. He also knew he would inspire resistance from the women in spite of their assurances, having to tolerate sympathies, commiserating, ignoring enforcement. Occasional departures he could live with he thought understandingly, perfectly acceptable as long as he had gained their attention for the need.

George began implementing his researched program promoting an Alpha association by his presence. He knew it would be difficult as she had recognition, being seeded an Alpha by the capitulation of her siblings. Her mind and status committed to her successfully waged structuring, herself the leader, reluctant to concede otherwise as an adopted member of a human pack. Demanding a strong response to counter Tasha's self-coronation, a literal test of wills. Vesting to the victor the leadership role George was determined to win.

Principal to the success was the distasteful but necessary requirement that he treat Tasha as a subordinate, ignoring her family pet status. This was vitally important at her young age when molding is easier and recommended. Nonetheless, it remained a formidable task as Tasha already had an established the highest ranking. To gain dominance, George had to earn her obedience, meaning during this period of assimilation he would rank her without privilege starting with the "right of passage," at no time would he allow her to go through doors or passageways first. He would, if necessary, forcefully move her if she were blocking his path, never going around her. Subordinate animals he had learned instinctively move for the Alpha. Punitive as it seems during this period of transformation, he never moved to pet her, always calling her to his side for her to display affection, the only time allocated in his regimen. Tasha realized after a few episodes of not yielding, had to show response motivation to be rewarded. She learned when playing together, her chasing after and returning with his thrown ball proudly displayed in her mouth, she had to relinquish it to receive a rewarding treat. At the end of play he always made sure he ended up with the ball or toy, thereby gaining the necessary association.

Resisting temptation, it was equally important during his climb to Alpha status to never let her sleep with him. It was permissible with the children. In fact, he encouraged it, knowing his connection and status with the children would not go unnoticed. Once his identification was fixed in Tasha's mind, assured no regression would take place, he planned to depart from his many restrictions. But only when circumstances warranted.

Tasha was fed once a day at the family's dinner time. Nothing but water in-between. The setting for dinner would be artificially regimented. No one was to eat before he sat down in his chair at the head of the table, he being served first while she watched attentively. Only then would he personally fill her dish with dog food.

Going on Sunday drives was also a means of conveying his leadership role. His was the only "Want to go for a ride, Tasha?" invitation. Ecstatic, she would leap with squealing excitement, remembering the cooling pleasures of putting her head out the car window and being greeted by the rushing air. This invitation for a ride in the car was exclusively his as agreed upon until the assimilation was complete.

It was important when correcting her to make direct eye contact and speak assertively so she understood the authority was his, resisting with great difficulty as she tried to make amends by licking his hand seeking forgiveness. Disarmingly cute, George would never allow her to lick his hand, warding her off physically distancing himself to show superiority. Allowing her to "kiss" during disciplining loses the message. Establishing himself as her Alpha, he must use every opportunity to prove himself worthy of her trust and respect in all situations including providing for her needs from the day she acknowledged him as her leader forward.

After that day came, she still reserved herself private moments of independence, selecting on her own without direction or coercion a place out of the way of the flow of family. She chose the downstairs bathroom as her retreat, her sanctuary to be alone as she wished when she wished. The Staves family, learning the hard way to respect her wishes, were greeted with growling annoyance if intruded upon. Becoming accommodating, allowing her that space, her sanctuary without interference, while waiting patiently for her to rejoin them.

With success at hand, George and his family noted the evolving of unforced ground giving in his presence, final proof that Tasha had elevated him to Alpha ranking. Her concession did not exhaust or break her spirit, remaining independent when not answering to him, still in search of adventure and new challenges.

two

George Staves sent his powered transporter into motion again, his search a kaleidoscope sorting through events as jig saw puzzled pieces. Imagery rushing past... Tasha being housebroken... of wooden baby proofing gates blocking off stairways, carpeted rooms and other restricted areas. He saw flashes of the endless nights of yelping as she became accustomed to her new family, her pack and surroundings. Visions of trying to ease the absence of her mother and her siblings at nighttime, leaving a hot water bottle and a ticking clock attempting a folk law remedy was his only response. The initial successes short-lived as she resorted to a new wave of nighttime crying, this time for being separated from her new pack – sleeping alone. Disregarding other family members impassioned pleas to sooth her with their presence, he would deny as indulging, citing the importance of building her independence.

Nanosecond views of George responding to criticism of indifference, countering her loneliness by secretly leaving his T-shirt with his body scent, a reminder of his nearness and protection, proving successful. The first to awaken in the morning provided opportunity to protect his secret, avoiding his family's scoffing at being indulgent.

Surely if he had blinked during the early chronology of rapidly parading events he would have missed seeing Tasha sleeping comically with her legs splayed apart.

Quickly flashing images not given a priority, would be welcomed at a later time. The chapter in Tasha's life he wished to visit at this time coming into focus.

three

The characteristics of Tasha's independent attitude, constantly on the lookout for challenges to avoid boredom, were never more evident, taking on added meaning as George Staves remembered an incident when she broke free of her restraints permitting a search for adventure.

In reconstructing events he learned she was missing for approximately five hours. Tasha never missed during the attention diverting baby shower taking place at home. The realization she was gone came when George Staves called from his country club inquiring of his wife:

"How's the baby shower going?"

His wife Rose commented, "Everyone's having a wonderful time. Beautiful gifts are being given."

Other chit chat concluded, he inquired, "How's Tasha behaving?"

Rose, secure in the belief that all was well, answered, "She's resting under the shade of her favorite Crabapple tree. I can still hear the next door neighbor's children squealing – as usual holding her attention. She has behaved remarkably well, perfectly content to remain outside in spite of all the activity going on in the house."

Being suspicious of Tasha's newfound passivity he asked that, since Rose could not see her from her position, she physically check on her well-being.

Returning quickly to the phone, Rose said in a trembling voice of fright, failing in her wishes to whisper in deference to her house guests, "Tasha has broken through a chain link. She's gone." Frantic she could not say how long she was missing.

As he hung up the phone, planning to immediately leave, George asked of his wife to be outside the front door of the house to signal as he approached whether Tasha had returned before starting his search of where he suspected she might have gone. As he slowed to pass the house he saw his wife standing out front, her face distraught as she shook her head from side to side, confirming Tasha was still missing.

His search of near neighborhood streets as well as inquiries of neighbors failed to give her up. He drove slowly by the homes that had dogs, hoping she might have been lured there. Again, his results were without success. He repeated his search route a number of times, each time slower than the last, still no Tasha. With all his efforts turning up nothing, panic began building. He imagined the worst scenario: Tasha lying in the street, her body broken after being run over by a passing car. Sweating profusely he chastised his doom and gloom, replacing that catastrophe from his mind with the possibility that she had been picked up by the animal warden, or as had happened in the past, a recognizing neighbor. Mindful it only a possibility among varying scenarios George continued his search. With each passing fruitless moment added, the lack of cell phone contact from his wife, the weight of negative thoughts tipped the scale of possibilities away from optimism. Losing confidence that she would be found, he expanded the radius of his search.

He returned to where he had started, making a quick stop at his house to relate his lack of success to his visibly upset wife. Continuing, he went back to the neighboring streets. On one of the streets he noticed children at play. Pulling the car over and rolling down the window, he asked whether any of them had seen a black-and-white Husky. After looking at one another, they all responded, "No." He wrote down his address and phone number and gave it to one of the boys, telling them there would be a reward if they spotted her. Just as he was about to pull away, a police car with its lights flashing pulled directly behind him. As he remained in his car awaiting the approaching policeman, his thoughts turned to recent newspaper articles alerting parents of reports of adult strangers trying to induce children into their cars. He realized his actions could be viewed as suspicious, but under the circumstances had no choice. The children stopped their play to watch in curiosity.

"What can I do for you, officer?" an anxious George Staves asked of the policeman as he approached the car.

"Your license and registration," the officer demanded.

George quickly complied.

"What are you doing here?" the officer asked as he carefully viewed the documents.

As George was explaining his situation, an adult watching the proceedings approached them, having recognized Staves. "Can I be of help?" he asked the policeman.

"Not really unless you know this man," nodding in Staves' direction, his face hardened and alert.

"I certainly do. My name is Bill Grant. I live right across the street. I'm a member of the neighborhood watch committee- aware of reports of a child molester in our neighborhood. I know this man well. He's George Staves from this neighborhood. He and I have been on a number of neighborhood committees together. Both of us serving on the school board."

"Hi, Bill," Staves acknowledged, feeling relieved. "I'm trying to find my dog."

"She run away again?"

"I'm afraid so."

The policeman, taking in there exchange, coupling the answers he received from the witnessing children, satisfied him. No longer gruff, he softened considerably and offered to help.

"I'll call back to the dispatcher and alert her of your missing dog."

He returned shortly, advising George Staves and the growing number of onlookers that all patrol cars would be on the lookout for Tasha and apologized for delaying his search. Smiling, he returned Staves' license and registration.

"I understand, Officer Blanchard," Staves said, turning to thank Bill Grant; reiterating to the children a reward was being offered for Tasha's return.

The confrontation with officer Blanchard, while alerting him of how he could be perceived, did not lesson his necessity to return to patrolling the streets. After repeated passes through the streets, a somber George Staves was nearing a point where he would have to admit Tasha had ventured beyond her usual routes return home, and sit and wait; depending on police cognizance or a good Samaritan prayerfully finding her without injury. The information of ownership stamped on her collar.

An inner voice told him to try one more time, this time going well beyond his immediate neighborhood. Approaching the end of his expanded search area he spotted Tasha crossing a busy intersection. She appeared thoroughly confused and haggard, not recognizing the imminent threat to her well-being the heavy traffic posed. Without hesitation, with no regard for his own safety, George leaped from his stopped car, abandoning it in the middle of the street. Of no consequence the cars behind having to maneuver in infuriated caution to get around his driverless car. Waving off traffic, he rushed wildly to reach her in time. Interrupting his prayers with screams of her name, he rushed to save her from deaths jaws. His voice, his scent, his sight momentarily pushed aside her confusion, stopped her in her tracks.

Thanking God, she began moving toward him as angry impatient drivers pulled out of the line of stopped cards to drive around them, narrowly missing them both. Tasha now cognizant of her Alpha, the protection he would give her from the strange sounds and smells that accompanied the moving monoliths, quickened her tail wagging pace to reach him. A loud blast of a truck's horn changed things in an instant, returning her to her tail-between-the-legs fear and disorientation. Traumatized, not heeding George's shouts, Tasha unwittingly turned to return to the heavily trafficked intersection, momentarily miraculously escaping death. Frantic, he ran tight-roping the middle of the thoroughfare, viewed by pedestrians awaiting a signal change to cross the thoroughfare as a ranting, deranged, wild man, gave him a wide birth. The motorists, also responding to his attention getting tactics slowed; horror and shock greeting them as they saw Tasha. Reacting quickly they came to a screeching stop or swerved to avoid her.

Trapped momentarily in the maze of stopped cards, his pleas to Tasha to come to him were ignored, she began to move again towards certain death. Sweating profusely, mouth agape sucking in air, his voice hoarse from his frantic repeated calls, his face reflective of the horror he was certain would happen. All appeared lost until a young man in a convertible spotted Tasha. Pleasuring in being seen with a lady friend, his impulse bravado, he stepped from his car onto the roadway.

Knowing this would be the last opportunity before the horror of her death, "Grab her please," Staves pleaded to the young man. "She won't come to me." Sensing his reluctance, his voice piercing and elevated, "Don't worry. She won't bite."

In spite of assurances, the young man reached down with trepidation while grabbing Tasha by her collar as she moved close enough to be caught. She was stopped short of crossing the road's dividing lines, moving into the traffic flow on the north side, a consequence of confusion that would have ended Tasha's young life.

The young man held her until Staves could wrap his sweaty eager arms around her, bringing a squirming Tasha to his chest. He did this freely, unconcerned with her muddied coat and paws that quickly soiled his shirt. In his protection, his eyes freed of fright, his emotions moved one hundred and eighty degrees. He reflected on what might have been the consequences of her escapade, lovingly chanting, "Tasha, Tasha, we almost lost you."

Tasha, quieting at his comforting voice, began feverishly to lick his face.

"I can't thank you enough," George exclaimed, unable to extend a handshake as Tasha required both of his arms to hold.

"Glad to help," the young man said, getting back into his car, hurried by the blaring of car horns impatient with the delay.

"Thanks again," Staves said as he carried Tasha in his arms dodging between stopped cars and slowly moving rubberneckers.

During his maneuvering, he noted the varying reactions of the motorists-the drivers showing mixed emotions. Some, angry at being inconvenienced, he could almost hear their words of condemnation for not taking better care of Tasha. Others, pleased at his life-saving action, applauded him enthusiastically, relieved and grateful they had not witnessed the horrific sight of Tasha being run over, particularly those cars with children. The outcome avoiding sleep disturbing nightmares.

With Tasha weighing heavily within the safety of his arms, he slowly made his way back to his car. He found the driver's side door as open as he had hastily left it. The traffic, impeded by what was perceived as a stalled automobile moved slowly around Staves's car casting critical looks, the concluded drama beyond their vision. Tasha, recognizing the car, gained full recognition that she was safe in a familiar environment, continued to overwhelm him with slobbering kisses.

Driving back to their home with Tasha still panting from thirst and the exhaustion of her ordeal, George's euphoria left him as he was overcome with the thought of Tasha's narrow escape from death. Dominated emotionally, driving competently any further impossible in his frame of mind – pulled the car curbside. Leaving the engine running he composed himself, taking deep breaths to relieve his anxiety. It wasn't until Tasha moved to his side nudging him with her moistened muzzle, her sign of gratitude, did he realize how fortunate they both were. Tragedy had been averted. Their lives would continue together for as long as nature and circumstances would allow. Thankful for his perseverance… Thankful for God's will, a tragedy had been avoided. The incident furthering the bond that would carry them for the rest of their lives.

He directed his mind's eye, his authority the fidelity of his kaleidoscope. Under his direction sorting through a myriad of the mundane events over Tasha's lifetime: His priority, the search for that fateful day of Sunday, February 17. To re- witness the truth of a day ending incident that would test the continuation of their relationship – challenging it's progress. The occurrence placing George Staves at a cross roads. To continue development as each others guardians or concede assimilation defeated, ending her membership, and social alignment within the pack. The decision making stalled until determining whether Tasha had a hostile side; endangering his family. Displaying overly aggressive behavior characteristics neither expected nor to be tolerated, placing in jeopardy her suitability.

The day starting tranquil enough as he heard the shrieking pleasures of his daughter Phyllis playing with the family's new Husky puppy. Tasha was on the floor of the carpeted den, the venue being deliberately chosen by Phyllis. As playmates lessening the temptation of Tasha jumping up on the couch to join her mother. A "no, no" in her discipline development; an edict of his leadership. In the eventuality the women of the house's reprimand would be token; understandingly sympathetic. Tasha's behavior influenced by a level field of play. Considered any elevated position, even the height of a couch as minimizing her presence and stature. Alpha characteristics on display. George knew this with certainty. The taken women's adoration of Tasha, causing the bending of rules in his absence as Tasha gained parity. Scowling for effect when coming upon Tasha on the den counch, her status equal as she sat with the women at rest He secretly withholding finding limited harm in it, as long as it was not invited in his presence.

George Staves was sitting on the living room couch reading the Sunday paper, his eyes tiring from the sheer volume of his reading. Reacting he placed his eyeglasses on the end table, preparatory to laying down for a nap; the joy of the excited play in the den joined by his wife. Relaxed he laid down, a satisfied smile on his face.

Everyone is safe at home, waiting for the snowfall to end, he said to himself shutting his eyes to invite sleep; hearing once again the rumblings of the city's snowplows make another pass on his street.

"A lake effect snow fall," the newspaper meteorologists reported, "numerous lines of snow storms moving west to east would deposit snow intermittingly in the infamous Snow Belt girding the city. The fortunate townships to the south and west of it's affect missing the heavy accumulation. In spite of pauses in the line of tandem fronts, the undisturbed blanketing snow a picturesque continuous layer. In truth deceptive, the depth ever changing, the snow resuming after a teasing pause. The borderline temperatures preventing the formation of surface ice, the follow on snow crystals embracing each other. The unsophisticated recording as one snowfall deposited over days for its final tally.

"No change should be expected, this second day of snowfall," the meteorologist would convey. The word *should* an open admission that weather patterns that move over large bodies of water were almost impossible to predict accurately as was his city, fated to be within the lake affect. Most residents, enjoying the seasonal changes of their latitude and longitude took no exception to the heavy accumulation restricting commerce, having learned to live with the monastic living that it wrought. There were however, people who disdained the harsh winters, essentially becoming depressed shut in's, whose chafed skin and chapped lips resisted the best of lotions, the result of days of winter incompatibility, preferencing the warming environs of Florida or California. One such person was Staves's daughter Phyllis, whose physicality was just not suited for extreme climate changes. Harboring her secret, from her family that she had accepted a job in California, reuniting with encouraging friends. A decision reached with great difficulty, costing her wishes to remain physically near her family and experiencing further her special relationship with Tasha.

It was remarkable how much Phyllis resembled her mother. Physically they could be seen as sisters until closer scrutiny revealed one in the metamorphosis of maturity, the other needing more pages of the calendar to be turned. Their height and weight the same, both wearing glasses, clones, including favoring fun loving at the slightest opportunity; the standout feature of their common personalities. Responsive and pliable to a fault with only those willing to take advantage. True friends recognizing as traits of the simpatico, from which to draw comforting needed understanding in hours of disappointment and frustration. Mother and daughter willing to accommodate others at the sacrifice of their own interests. Sensitive to the criticism of those thought to be friends, displaying unwarranted loyalty until the end as they were sacrificed by the self-serving. Misguided yes, but not of weak character, willing to fight for what was believed in, with a *dam* the consequences forcefulness. Their visage, in spite of strong attempts to disguise, was easily recognizable.

Both Rose and Phyllis were animal lovers before it became fashionable as a noble cause to defend and protect them. Belonging to organizations that condemned the use of animals in laboratory experimentation… strongly refuting their claims that mankind was benefiting. Equally repulsed by the indiscriminate use of euthanasia as a means of controlling animal over population. Their ire raised, they would petition for the benefits of spaying and neutering as the more humane solution.

An adult Phyllis fully vested with her mothers characteristics, at an early age, showed unusual concern for stray or lost domestic animals. Becoming of her notice they would soon find safety in her arms as she carried them out of harm's way. In most cases, they fortunately were neighborhood pets easily identified by their licensed and tagged collars A quick phone call bringing the anxious owners in short order. Those without identification… "Truly lost," a sympathetic Phyllis would say, adding tears to supporters and anyone who would listen, "Stray animals rarely survive for long on their own. They die of disease, poisoning, starvation or are stolen by unscrupulous suppliers of sacrificed animals to laboratories, in the name of science. That is, if they survived not being run over in the streets."

Phyllis finding stray's not identifiable, would file notice with animal shelters within a five-mile radius of where she found it, knowing that strays often travel great distances from their homes. She would also call the newspapers, taking advantage of a free lost-and-found animal notice. Local radio stations were also very cooperative, making public service announcements. Phyllis and her friends bound together in common cause would put up signs on utility poles as well as trees, listing enough descriptive detail for the owners to come forward but withholding enough characteristics of her street find to defeat the devious.

The strays wearing tags made Phyllis' job easier, her joy; bringing the pet and owner together again. But when they weren't wearing tags, she suspected capricious owners interest had waned, the pet too burdensome, *losing* them to the streets after removing their identification; not caring about the animal's fate. Rescued, Phyllis would provide temporary quarters in one of her group's garages: halfway house's until exhausting all possibilities for adoption. Failing to do so would be emotionally painful for Phyllis and her friends, knowing failure would mean turning the animal over to animal shelters where, failing to arrange adoption, had no option but to euthanize the animal. Her failed efforts depressing her until the next stray was found, becoming her latest cause *celebré.*

With tiring eyes, George Staves smiled at the reflections of his daughter championing animal rights, bearing an almost mystical aura about her that brought immediate trust that animals felt in her presence.

"Everyone is at home safe and secure," he repeated, comforted. "The place to be riding out the storm."

The sounds of the city's snowplows rumbling through the streets now joined by his neighbors efforts offered encouragement that the storm was subsiding. The continuing vocal pleasures of Phyllis encouraging Tasha's antics, along with her mother's half-hearted admonishments for quiet, parceling her interests with the music of Puccini's *Madame Butterfly.* The scene presenting a cozy picture worthy of being depicted in Norman Rockwell's notable Americana paintings. The only thing missing was lighting the fireplace. He would do that later, he promised as he fell asleep, at peace with the world.

Tasha, tiring of play, curled herself into a furry ball fast asleep, her chest rising and falling to her exhausted snoring.

Phyllis, continuing to sit on the floor, adoringly watched Tasha, trying to anticipate her breathing pattern and wondering how much bigger she would get.

Phyllis, possessor of a life changing secret, reflected on the fact she would soon be absent of future moments; her mother at her side and Tasha, the love of her life, asleep within arms length, she became teary eyed, lessening her enthusiasm.

Putting down the cup of coffee her mother had given her, she returned to her thoughts of the soundly sleeping Tasha. In a moment of nostalgia, with heavy heart, needing to express the love she felt… that she would miss her terribly… she instinctively and without thought; violating a cardinal rule, leaned over and kissed Tasha adoringly between the eyes on her bandit mask. An action under normal circumstances welcomed, but not on this occasion.

Awakened with such suddenness, perceiving imminent danger, Tasha reacted instinctively as if threatened. Eyes not quite opened and focused, scent recognition lagging, she snapped at the perception of a menacing shadowy presence hovering over her, holding her razor sharp puppy teeth fast until she opened her eyes and saw it was Phyllis, a trusted member of her pack. Immediately she released her bite, her eyes tortured with sadness, her body language a cower, pleading for understanding that her response was instinctive; survival her motivation. Expressing intelligence beyond expectation, cognitive of the human's complex menu of reactions to which she was appealing.

Tasha knew Phyllis was hurt, sharing her pain as she cried out, the blood trickling onto Phyllis's lips from a bite inflicted to her nostril. She reacted to the sight by crawling submissively, head down, tail between her legs, bringing her forelegs and hindquarters together, reducing her size; a response of miniaturization. Her body parts bunched together, she approached the living room where George Staves was fast asleep, proceeding to lay before him on her back, her legs splayed apart in contrition.

Moving quickly, Rose, who watched the episode's consequences, tried desperately not to panic, to remain under control in spite of the blood oozing from Phyllis' open wound. Aghast, pale with worry, quickly telling Phyllis to apply pressure with her handkerchief to slow the flow of blood, as they prepared to leave for the hospital. Thankful in checking that her husband was still asleep. The circumstances could be explained after their return from emergency admissions at the local hospital. Deeply asleep the sound of the garage door opening did not waken her husband, the fallen snow on the ground and in the air muffling their departure. George Staves remained sound asleep, oblivious to what was happening around him.

As required by law, a hospital handling a dog bite of a human was mandated to notify the police, who would conduct an investigation as to the circumstances of the incident. Of significant impact of the course of action to be taken was the domesticated dog's prior history.

Rose and Phyllis were still at the hospital as George Staves was awakened by the stubborn ringing of the doorbell, Tasha barking joining in the jolting din. Removed from his deep sleep by the unwelcome sounds, he called out for his wife and daughter not expecting a lack of response. Exasperated, he approached the front door with retreating grogginess, the dullness in his head beginning to clear, bringing forth a mood of impatience his visitor would be subjected to. His response if he determined the Sunday intrusion that of a campaign for petition signing, preachers of religious awakening, or local politicians seeking support. Normally solicitous this day he would be intolerant of the visitors indiscretion, he would automatically reject the solicitation, his reprisal no matter how noble the cause. Dismissing the petitioner with the admonition, "contact him by mail," a more propitious means.

As he approached the door, his minds dullness dissipated, Rose and Phyllis' absence re-presented itself. "Where could they have sneaked off to?" he asked himself. His annoyance not hidden, he aggressively opened the front door. The sight greeting him was completely unexpected, standing before him, disarming him of annoyance was the imposing figure of a policemen of serious countenance – strongly indicative that his purpose was official. George Staves quickly adjusted his demeanor from criticism of Sunday solicitations to one more amenable.

"What can I do for you, officer?" he asked, holding back Tasha with a restraining leg.

"We have a report that a dog called Tasha residing at this address was involved in a biting incident," he responded, wary of Tasha's presence.

Astounded and incredulous, George defended, "That's impossible, officer. As you can see, my dog is right here. She is not allowed to leave the house and property unattended. She's always walked under leash control. There must be some kind of mistake."

The officer, trained to be patient, waited out his expected response of repeated denials, experience telling him owner attitude was typically denial.

"The person who was bitten is at the hospital as we speak."

Incredulity reigning, sure there was a mistake said, "Who?"

The policeman reading directly from the filed report answered, "A Phyllis Staves."

George Staves was taken aback. Shocked, he began to comprehend. "That's my daughter," he answered as if the policeman was not aware. "How?" he flustered. "Where is she? What hospital?" he questioned with concerned rapidity, the reason for his wife and daughter's absence confronting him.

"Hillcrest Emergency," the policeman responded, his official notice not complete. "You are required to quarantine your dog for seven days, even if she has had all of her shots. I must tell you that a second incident would require possession by the authorities."

"Do you have any questions?" he asked, impatient that this assignment took him from his preferable, more crediting law enforcement responsibilities.

"No," George responded, shaking his head from side to side, "I can't comprehend Tasha bitting my daughter let alone anyone else," acknowledging that he would do all that was required, thanking the policemen as he departed.

Immediately following the policeman's departure, he rushed to the phone and called the emergency room at the hospital, reaching a receptionist. Tasha, during his exchange with the policeman, seeing Staves' penetrating glares, sensing his angst and displeasure as she heard her name called out, left his side to sequester herself in the downstairs bathroom.

"I'm sorry, sir, we can't page or attempt to locate someone for you. We are quite busy. The emergency room is overflowing with people who need emergency attention," the receptionist bordering on insipidness said, elevating her importance and underestimating his determination.

"Look," he said his voice noticeably excited, "this is also an emergency. My daughter is being treated. I must know the seriousness of her injuries. If you can't help me then get me the head nurse or the treating physician," he demanded, his voice rising with every word.

Not expecting his audacity in challenging her, she considered hanging up the phone, claiming a loss of connection if later challenged. Deciding instead the potential risk of a reputation damaging confrontation to high a price to pay. Instead, she choose awarding herself a victory by having him wait. "Hold the line." she said to her demanding caller.

After what seemed like an eternity, his sweating frustrations keeping him on edge, he heard his wife Rose speak into the phone. Her voice steady and factual, right to the point, meant to reassure him, "It's not very serious. She has a tear on her nostril. We've called for a plastic surgeon. He's with her right now about to administer four stitches. He assured me that in time you won't be able to notice it," in spit of her resolve to display confidence, the incident affects caused her to speak in nervous rapidity.

Breathing easier, yet not completely relieved, a calmer George asked that she slow down and explain what had happened.

Knowing she had defused him, Phyllis's situational report out of the way, Rose slowed to speak with the authority of an unimpeachable witness, carefully and certain. She summed up the circumstances, emphatically concluding, "It wasn't Tasha's fault. It was an accident."

Rose's explanation, relieved him of his major concern, Phyllis's well being. The issue of Tasha's aggressive tendencies toward Phyllis remained a serious concern. Despite his wife's assurances he decided he would hear from Phyllis directly before judging.

"When will you be home?" he asked his tone significantly tempered, but not conciliatory.

"In about an hour," she replied.

He hung up the phone felling considerably unburdened, calling Tasha to his side, aware that she had sequestered herself after receiving body language alien to him. Coming to him when called obviously distraught, searching his countenance with woeful eyes for signs that she would regain her family stature. His patting superficial, his words that she was not to be blamed missing, not quite ready to give her absolution from her guilt.

When Rose and Phyllis arrived home her condition was not what he was prepared for. Aghast by Phyllis's appearance her heavily swollen nose not concealed by her bandage, the closest eye to the injury discolored. Her eyes were not tearing from her injury but of concern for the consequences to Tasha as she measured her fathers response.

"How do you feel, Phyllis?" her father asked his hands on her shoulders.

Seeing deep concern on his face, Phyllis assured, "It looks worse than it is."

"Once the swelling goes down, it will be as good as new," Rose interjected in an effort to lighten his concern.

His smile forced as he checked his daughters injury closely.

"It was all my fault, Dad," she said protectively, "I scared her." She then reiterated what had happened.

Her responsibility admitted; relieving the atmosphere of tension, Tasha exhibited sorrow that touched everyone. The effects of her behavior exhibited in her bowed head, pulled back ears almost flat against her head. Contrite, she moved across the floor awkwardly, her stomach almost touching the floor, deliberately reducing her size and stature, humbling herself as she approached Phyllis.

Phyllis, teary eyed, exuding love spoke to her softly, almost whispering to ease her tension, apologizing for her role. In revealing body language; a mutual confessional had been undertaken. The torture of both ameliorated by the penance expressed from each other.

Rose watched tearfully as they were reunited. George, his throat constricted, found the truth in their submission to one another; Tasha's absolution complete. Phyllis's forgiving words cathartic, Tasha's self-diminished physicality spurred to growth, energizing her defeated lifeless presence. Her full size recovered, ears erect, her plumed tail curled and centered on her back, her proud magnificence once again on display.

The tension of the moment fully gone, their electronic energies of reconciliation, traveling in space, sensed but not seen interacting with one another. Tasha and Phyllis had released invisible circuitries to flow from out of focus eyes fixed on one another – bridging the species separation. Aura's connecting forever... The interaction empowering Phyllis to be a source of relief in time of Tasha's need. Joyful of the expansion of their special bond, Tasha in celebration stood on her hind legs, her forelegs on Phyllis' chest presenting a sign of their compatibility. Phyllis, evoking a knowing smile, her bandaged nose interfering, still managed to kiss Tasha between the eyes. The moment gave special recognition to their relationship; no matter the passing of time and period of separation.

The incident revisited by the unscrambling kaleidoscope of George Staves, everyone would agree, the incident the hallmark of Tasha's final adjustment, conceding her dominant role to become George Staves's follower. The passing of time, this recalled period from the past, had not reduced the intensity of his amazement at Tasha's reaction. At her young age, during this challenging episode, she had shown uncanny instincts and understanding; befitting a truly an exceptional dog. He sat there remembering that he had thankfully shown restraint, the moments of justification to come. Turning his attention from that period of time, he allowed his transporter full throttle forward, the next stop he would select from the myriad of those rushing by, his only criteria this moment that it be very telling.

four

By nature Tasha was fastidiously clean. Self-cleaning, rivaling the combative cat, pruning herself clean no matter how dirty or muddied by her inclination to dig or bury prizes in the backyard. George knew that her breed's self-cleaning habits, under normal circumstances being free of the usual odors wafting from canines, not requiring assisted bathing of more than once a year. As long as not fragranced by her penchant to roll in the grass or hedges where strays, during passage, had marked or deposited.

Unlike most dogs at this early age, Tasha had a frightening aversion toward water. Heartbreaking howling and cry's like a baby was her response, during her terror taking a bath. The unacceptable telling smell of her recent foraging, dictated the need was immediate. Sensing a baths imminence, reacting instinctively she retreated to hide under beds. Fearfully whimpering as no other in his pet ownership lifetime. Her fright was unrelenting until she stood away from the laundry room sink with her fur flattened with wetness; her paining ordeal over.

George Staves would never have guessed that dogs had water phobias if not his experience with Tasha. With that fact a given in Tasha's case, he was baffled to explain her inconsistency while on walks experiencing sudden downpour's. Not panicking, attempting as he would have expected, to shield herself under a parked car, or freezing under the protection of a tree. Her only discernible reaction, with Staves without an umbrella, was to match his retreating pace, occasionally pausing as the rain pelting her body, making inconsequential attempts to shake off her wetness.

Gaining knowledge from the first time that happened, in deference to her great fear of bathing, he committed, if he could avoid it to never attempt to bathe her again, relying on natures convenient solution of rain. Prepping her coat with dry shampoo; grateful for the fulfilling rainfall he completed his opportunity, purposely avoiding that which terrorized her. While he remained protected under an umbrella, his walking pace deliberately slow, the rain his co-conspirator achieving the necessary results. Witnessed by neighbors in passing cars, sure to have evoked either thoughts of his mental retardation or deep commitment to walking his dog regardless of weather conditions. He preferred the latter characterization, thankful that the shampoo was without suds. Accepting the neighbors' whispered wonderment, at his lunacy, a small price to pay for freeing her coat of odors of corruption. Nature and a fragranced salvation a response to Tasha's hygienic dilemma. However, an unusual circumstance developed, that required of him to regrettably withdraw his disinclination to bathe her. Situationally, he had no choice, so compelling were the conditions, expanding upon his previous innovation that was timely successful, the price: whispered aberrant behavior by witnesses.

It began with Tasha scratching at the patio door, something he had come to expect from her, announcing she needed to relive herself. He tethered her to a leash that had twenty feet of length, enough to reach an area that would induce her to relieve herself. Always a challenge avoiding becoming entangled around her favorite Crabapple tree. With her business finished, she would position herself on the patio lording over her property, sniffing the air for strangers who would dare to challenge her reign. Her visible presence intimidating enough to dissuade other animals from infringing on her property. Tasha would bait, with lack of sudden movement, any animal that would risk their well-being. Intruded upon, Tasha, a bundle of pent up energy, would assume the stealth crouch of a hunter, keeping still until judged appropriate to move noiselessly; hoping to catch the intruder off guard. Fortunately they usually were just beyond the length of the chain, out of reach as Tasha sprung for the capture. Most times she fell short, as if calculated purposefully to continue the game. Sometimes she so abruptly stopped in mid-air it flung her backward violently. They were her play: the roaming squirrels in search of acorns, the importuning big black crows, looking to steal Tasha's treats carried from the house for her to bury. The intruders always on guard of Tasha tiring of play, the game ending abruptly, now she waited patiently for a death dealing mistake. Having learned just how far Tasha was restrained, her aware playmates avoided becoming victims. This was not always the case as demonstrated by Tasha's trophies, the less clever, deposited proudly on the patio.

Consequences kept visiting animals at a distance as Tasha camped herself majestically in the grass, cooled by the nights' lowering temperatures, or the morning moisture, nodding herself to sleep; bored by the lack of challenges. When they came, she would raise herself from her grass throne, alerted by a sound or scent that she needed to identify or sort out. Unless called she would sit or lay for hours, enjoying the cool breezes rippling through her coat. Breaking from her sentry duties only to quench her thirst from a bowl of water the family set out for her.

This evening was hot and humid, a prelude to expectant rain. George Staves alone, his wife Rose visiting friends, was watching television seated in the den that overlooked the patio and the surrounding backyard. Tasha, her chain stretched taunt, was out of his sight where she camped and ruled. The hour well after night took control of daylight, the relative passivity of darkness interrupted by Tasha's threatening growls; its ferocity feral.

Its threatening tone was easily heard, overwhelming the volume setting of the television set, spurring George to move quickly to investigate. The growling which had become more of an agitation, suddenly ceased. With blinds withdrawn and the light turned on, Staves peered from behind the partially open door, searching the illuminated patio and backyard. He saw no movement. In the absence of anything suspicious, his a reasonable guess; Tasha had been aroused by a passing dog under leash restraint by the owner. That perception was momentary, logic dismissing, Tasha's disturbance would have provoked aggressive barking and not combative growling. Becoming anxious to sight her, he opened the patio door and was immediately assaulted by the unmistakable fetid odor of skunk penetrating the night air, alerting him of another scenario, one not so pleasant.

Concerned, he called out, "Tasha!"

Her growling continued, her nearby location identified.

"Tasha, come here girl," he called again, more anxious, her being beyond his sight was troublesome.

Responding this time, she revealed herself from the side of the house. As she got closer to him, the reality set in. His worst fears were realized. She had been skunked, literally from head to paw and everywhere in between. Backing away with disgust as she neared him, speaking invectives for what had befallen her, realizing the abhorrent task that lay before him. Frantic that she would attempt to enter the house, he retreated quickly shutting the door just as she began to climb the patio steps. Staves voiced displeasure at what had to be done. He was limited by being alone, he awaited Rose's return. Together they could easily de-skunk her, dreading Tasha's reaction for what must be done.

He left the house, re-entering the fetid gagging atmosphere; quickly moving past her to the side of the house to what he hoped he would not find. An excited Tasha sped past him to stand proudly over the stilled body of a rather large skunk, her intruder meeting an unexpected death in pursuit of a nightly meal of grubs. The relative safety of nightfall and the skunk's repugnant odoriferous weaponry failing, as it had wandered within the radius of Tasha's tether, finding confrontation instead; this time nocturnal feeding not keeping it from discovery. Tasha had not been repelled by the skunk's fetid spray defense; her captive in vice-like jaws, unleashing a strength to shake violently, breaking the skunks spine, bringing instant death.

He stood there with mixed emotions at the scene before him, disturbed by the death of the careless skunk while in head shaking awe. He knew most dogs would have turned tail and run, losers in a testing meeting. Not so with Tasha, determined, her attack continuing through the stinging sensation to her eyes and the vomiting inducing taste in her mouth.

His approval was what a panting Tasha sought, standing proudly over the broken body of the skunk, posturing, demonstrating worthiness; anxious to hear his praise.

It began to rain. Determined to keep her from entering the house as he returned, quickly closing the door behind him. It was without question she could not enter the house smelling as she did; envisioning her instinctively rolling on the carpeting to rid herself of the offensive odor, a response that had to be prevented at all costs. His options limited, George had opted to await Rose's return, to assist him in the distasteful job of cleaning Tasha. Initially, it was a good plan until Tasha, her interest in the skunk lost, determined to get back into the house, repeatedly leaped against the closed patio door; yelping to have her way. As difficult as it was, he ignored her cries, hoping she would tire. As time passed it became evident she would not be deterred. The disturbance she was creating forced him to scrub his initial plan.

The onset of rain, prescribed he change tactics. He would dare to take drastic action, one that would prove most embarrassing if discovered. His resorting act in the middle of a rainstorm tending to an animal in need; an eccentricity by his viewers.

Amid Tasha's cries for attention, he rushed to gather everything needed. Arms full, he emerged from the door to stand with her on the steps of the patio. Thankfully the light falling rain continued – executing his response still doable.

He had changed to bathing trunks, shoed with an old pair of gym shoes he regularly used to wash his car. Holding his foot on the chain to keep Tasha from moving, he poured a copious amounts of tomato juice all over her. Vigorously rubbing the home remedy beyond her surface coat, beyond her down winter fur, into her very skin. The skunk spray in her mouth fouling her breath was his next attention, pulling back her lips, tomato juice cupped in his hand, he proceeded to rub it against her teeth. Tasha growled rejection, coughing and choking, breaking free she stooped to drink from a puddle of accumulating rain on the patio; returning to eye him warily.

The first part of her treatment complete, George holding her leash, moved her from the partially effective protection of the roof overhang. Her leash in hand they moved into the drenching rain, his hair flattening against his head, rivulets of water streaming from his face, his bathing trunks soaking wet clinging to his body as he watched the tomato juice slowly washing away. All the while Tasha squirmed and yelped in annoyance, not heeding his call to stay, the scene absurd to anyone watching.

Retreating to the steps and the roofs overhang, he bent down to smell her, and determined another application was needed. After repeating he walked back into the rain which was now falling at a torrential rate, effectively inundating Tasha in a shorter time. Returning to his washing station a second sniffing told him he had maximized the tomato juice purge; the last part of her treatment remaining. Liberally applying scented shampoo; rubbing it in deeply, lathering her from head to paws with suds, the scene bizarre as he saw an approaching flashlight scanning the backyard and the rear of the house. Behind the flashlight beam was a policeman, his protective rain gear glistening as was his angered face not wanting this assignment, his anger turning to shock, not comprehending what he was witnessing. He did, however, recognize the participants.

"What's going on, Mr. Staves? We've received repeated calls of a disturbance coming from your home," the heavy rain running off his protected policeman's cap, his wet forehead furrowed as he awaited an answer to the burlesque scene.

"Officer, I know it looks ridiculous but I had no choice. My dog has been skunked," pointing to the skunk lying dead in the grass. "I'm all alone. I couldn't allow her in that condition to enter the house. I'm sure my neighbors would understand if they knew the circumstances. I'm almost through."

Impatient and intolerant of Staves's reason, unhappy that it fell upon him to respond to his dispatcher's call, and putting him out in the rain on this miserable night, the officer said curtly, "Speed it up for everyone's sake."

"I'll do that, officer, as fast as she'll let me."

The officer left, still shaking his head in disbelief at what he had witnessed. "One for the books," he would tell his sergeant and fellow officers.

The ordeal over, Staves changed back to his blue jeans. Recovering from his unpleasant task, he sat at the kitchen table. Tasha's damp coat retained a hint of the skunks weaponry, lay curled around in her special place, the downstairs bathroom commode, her coat's contamination would dissipate to a musty odor when completely dry. After his shower, he repeated washed his bathing suit, the transferred skunk smell remaining after a soaking in tomato juice. Having failed at recovery, guessing it would prove insignificant, he flung it out into the nights heavy rain, a last attempt at purging the odor, the likelihood high that he would be discarding it the next morning at the city dump, bagged with the dead skunk.

When Rose finally got home the scene was no longer hectic. "There's a terrible skunk odor outside. Don't you smell it?" she said in disgust.

Smiling, George Staves said, "Yes, I noticed." He then proceeded to tell her the events of the night. Rose interrupted him repeatedly, commenting incredulously, "I don't believe it," while sniffing him and the air around her

"You missed all the fun," he said jokingly.

~

The unfortunate skunks death aside he smiled at the humorous aspects of the incident, willing his transporter remain idle… his kaleidoscope presentation at a standstill. His travel halted, to reflect on everyone's reaction, concluding as he had done then, his chosen course of action appropriate. While the policeman was aggrieved, his astonished look painting him over indulging Tasha's eccentricities. Unappreciative that George Staves, in his role, took seriously the mandate of an Alpha; providing leadership responding to threat, whether a perception or not. Additional exposure to Tasha's lifetime trace, had it been possible for the policeman would show Tasha equally expressive, protectively.

five

Never more evident of Tasha's assimilation into her new pack and the growing dependency she held for each member of the Staves family was her reaction to being boarded. Since she was a vital part of their lives, they avoided housing her, the threat of kennel cough and lack of attention enough discouragement. Further, all the literature available on the subject warned that Huskies do not adapt very well to strange confinements or extended periods of separation from their families. George Staves had heard stories of unhappy mature Huskies posing a constant threat to escape from separation. Given the slightest opportunity they would leave behind their bewildering isolation in search of a reunion. They just didn't handle being apart from their family's very well, removed from their comfort zone they would become resistant not willing to bond or relate to surrogates, showing their fangs if pushed by someone part of a scenario absenting their family-strangers perceived as enforcing their seclusion. In those circumstances dejectedly independent their preference, no matter the inducement. Dominating their thinking, the opportunity for escape.

As a result, the Staves were, as well they should be, very concerned for her well-being and adaptability. They pledged to be very selective and careful of their boarding choice; needing a high degree of confidence before entrusting her to someone else. Shocked and completely unexpected was the reaction of the first five kennels contacted who showed no willingness to board Tasha, tactfully withdrawing the availability of the facilities when they learned that Tasha was a Husky, never giving the Staves an opportunity to pass judgement on suitability. Uniform in their rejecting accommodation- all huskies being a disruptive breed – of one owner attachment; constantly seeking to escape by whatever means available to them. A further truth that had to be accommodated; their response to confinement; expressing their displeasure by howling throughout the night and disturbing all the other dogs under care to a frenzied cacophony of barking.

"Their beauty is unparalleled, strongly independent, motivated only by their owners. I'm afraid they are just too much trouble. We're just not equipped to handle her breed," the discriminating kennel owners would say politely in rejection.

Chagrined and anticipating further rejection, not willing to consider kennels that lacked recommendations or reputations, they began to consider canceling their trip. Time was running short. Rose expanded the search by contacting other acquaintances known to have boarded their dogs; seeking their recommendation. It was during one of these calls she learned of a woman who, along with her husband, owned a farm in Amish country. She and her husband enthusiasts in living off the land for their food supply, had a great love for animals of all descriptions, and cohabited not only with the typical farm and domestic animals but unusual and exotic ones as well. As an animal lover it was easy to understand her willingness to board dogs, possessing two dogs of their own; it also added to their farm income. She an ex-librarian presently managing and tended to the farm and animals and her boarding enterprise.

Rose Staves called the woman at the boarding farm the next morning citing her friend's reference and recommendation. After the usual exchange of pleasantries, Rose quickly made arrangements for a visit that very afternoon.

It took over an hour for Rose and George to drive there with Tasha in the backseat content to put her head out the window; serenely letting the rushing wind occupy her. They watched the landscape change from residential, to rural, to country farms as they drove the forty miles to the small farm located on fifty acres of land. Although troubled by the distance, they soon lessened it as a concern as they drove up the dirt road to the house. A perfect setting forming in their minds as they passed four attention commanding draft horses, one an obvious colt amidst his behemoth protectors. Magnificent Clydesdales, the backs of their legs featuring the feathery growth of long hairs, pulling their heads up from grazing peacefully in the fenced in meadows as they drove by; their stalls located conveniently nearby the barn.

"They certainly have enough room," Rose remarked, obviously pleased.

"I'll say," her husband responded. "Plenty of grounds for Tasha to be walked and find interesting."

Tasha, having climbed into the front seat between the two of them, put her head behind George's neck; eyes fixed not knowing what to make of the equine giants.

The woman was waiting for them at the head of the road which was really a driveway to the house.

"Welcome," she smiled, holding out her hand. "I'm Mrs. Joseph. And you are Mr. and Mrs. Staves," she asked with some uncertainty, "who called earlier? I'm expecting other boarders around the same time. I wasn't sure who was arriving first. But how foolish of me," she chastised herself, "the others have other breeds."

"How do you do?" George Staves said offering his hand.

"This is Tasha," he continued who at that moment was preoccupied with sniffing the surroundings, trying to identify all the animal scents that permeated the air. Responding favorably to Mrs. Joseph's petting by wagging her tail appreciably; a positive sign that pleased them both.

Mrs. Joseph then took them on a tour of the kennel area. It's income bearing while supplemental was intended as a bi-product of personal fulfillment, limited as she was by the number of dogs she could accommodate, farming to defer the cost of sustenance her primary purpose. The kennel was freshly painted and clean, the smell of recently applied disinfectant hanging in the air. The dogs' sleeping area under roof, was separated from individual runs of four feet by fifteen feet, accessed through a doored passageway secured with a six-foot high hurricane fence at its border. Visions of Tasha trying to climb it entered George's mind, temporarily distracting him; dissuaded as Tasha seemed genuinely taken by Mrs. Joseph.

She then took them through the barn, showing insight, she purposely asked for Tasha's leash, a successful approach in establishing command and furthering the building bond. Within the barn were six stalls, each occupied by cows that Mrs. Joseph personally milked every morning. Chicken coops were also visible, the newly laid eggs having already been harvested. Just as they were ready to leave the barn, a pot bellied pig appeared from one of the open stalls.

"This is Chang," Mrs. Joseph said. "He's a family pet along with my two shepherds. They get along famously," she added. Tasha and the pot bellied pig locked in wary eye contact. Chang, whose curiosity was aroused at this new stranger responding to Mrs. Joseph's call, joined them.

Rose and George Staves looked down at Tasha for her reaction which at the moment was nothing more than assessing this mud covered oddly shaped animal.

The pig's response was cautious and hesitant, having received a satisfying petting from Mrs. Joseph hurriedly turned and trotted away, aware that Tasha's shackles became extended; going unnoticed by Mrs. Joseph.

"Tasha doesn't seem bothered by Chang," Mrs. Joseph commented. "I have a feeling they'll get along fine."

The two Shepherds commanded to stay nearby, alert to the visitors, responding to Mrs. Joseph's call, joined them; completely ignoring Chang as they passed by. Introduced as King and Queenie, as Mrs. Joseph lustily and affectionately patted them.

After an introductory sniffing of one another, the Shepherds backed away giving Tasha, who had lost interest in their introduction, a wide birth; sensing that Tasha was asserting herself. The new border, not to generate their jealously, it's expression of independence, would preclude being a competitor for Mrs. Joseph's affection.

Clearly the Staves's were impressed with Mrs. Joseph's animal handling abilities, feeling comfortable with what she made available to Tasha… the location, the atmosphere of a farm and her obvious devotion to animals, all mitigating in her favor. Pleased with her responses covering feedings and the frequency of exercising and relieving walks swayed them, deciding Tasha's welfare and safety would not be better served anywhere else.

"I've never boarded Huskies before," she admitted, "but I'm aware of their characteristics. Tasha appears to offer no more than a normal challenge.

"Most kennels won't take Huskies," George Staves admitted honestly. "Of course, you have the room and can accommodate her need for exercise."

"I don't anticipate or expect any problems as she seems well-adjusted with an excellent temperament," Mrs. Joseph said. Rose and George Staves agreeing with her assessment.

Their eyes meeting in silent confirmation, George said, "We're satisfied. We don't have any further questions. Just one reminder that when she is outside of her cage she must always be under the control of a leash or tether."

"I'm clear on that," Mrs. Joseph acknowledged.

They then concluded the arrangements with a handshake. Her fee would also include home delivery of Tasha after her stay which pleased the Staves's. The dates for the week that they would be gone were reserved and held with a down payment. They felt very comfortable with Mrs. Joseph, confident Tasha would handle their separation quite well.

The day of the boarding, satisfaction was reconfirmed as they drove up the roadway to Mrs. Joseph's house. Nothing had changed, the facilities remained appealing. Their only concern was Tasha's reaction when she would finally realize they were leaving without her. Unsuspecting, Tasha's continuing curiosity in the unfamiliar landscape, pleased them, suggesting she would enjoy the adventure ahead. She would adapt after a minimal adjustment period, accepting being temporarily quartered in new surroundings, signaled, so they thought by the demonstrated budding attachment to her temporary guardian. As planned, their daughter Rosanne's phone number would be left in case of an emergency.

They left feeling confident they had made the best arrangements for Tasha, so reassured that they began looking forward to their trip. As they moved toward their car, Tasha, whose leash was in Mrs. Joseph's hand, realized she would be left behind. She pulled forcefully against her restraint, whimpering. Believing Tasha's reaction was only temporary, George and Rose left, not daring to look back for fear of changing their plans. Confident, their concerns minimal, released they would welcome the enjoyment of their planned trip.

They deliberately left early the day of their return in order to be home in plenty of time for Tasha's return. The absence of Tasha at home becoming more pronounced, her anticipated return eagerly awaited. Their excitement changed to concern when Mrs. Joseph was late by over half an hour. George was about to call the farm when Mrs. Joseph's station wagon came into view from the driveway where they waited. The first thing that struck them was that Tasha, as anticipated, was not in the holding cage in the back of the wagon. She was surprisingly in the front seat alongside Mrs. Joseph.

Mrs. Joseph got out of the station wagon with an excited Tasha in tow. Her demeanor while pleasant seemed mechanical, the countenance of the defeated fulfilling her surrender. Under siege emotionally, she watched Tasha rain kisses upon Rose and George Staves, the reuniting scene touching her, diminishing her previous disposition.

"As you can see, she absolutely missed you both," she said shaking her head from side to side at the display of devotion. She began to have second thoughts, to think it best not to be revealing of Tasha's stay at the farm.

"Why was Tasha riding up front with you?" George Staves asked finally, the greeting exchange over.

"She refused to be caged, growling and showing her teeth when I tried," she responded in exasperation, "She just wasn't responsive to me," her disappointment clearly showing.

Troubled, he asked, "How did she react during the trip? Was she aggressive toward you while you were driving?"

Regrouped she said, "No, not at all. Once the matter of being caged was settled. As a matter of fact she was quite loving, kissing my hands in approval and becoming more excited as we neared your house."

His relief was not complete, sensing Mrs. Joseph was holding back. "You look troubled," George Staves said solicitously, looking up while scratching Tasha's belly as she lay on her back delighted.

Rose joining George in uneasiness, sensed something was troubling Mrs. Joseph. Their frowning visage inquiring, urged her to speak openly. Drawing a deep breath, emboldened to speak just as Rose further encouraged, "What's wrong?"

"I didn't want to spoil your reunion. I wasn't going to say anything but your sincerity and your right to know changed my mind." Her internal conflict over, she smiled freely for the first time. She went on to say without bitterness, "Tasha added to my education, proving to be a very complex animal, showing very differing personality traits depending on the circumstances. That dichotomy urges me to speak." She paused to reflect momentarily, before proceeding, "I'm not suggesting she's neurotic but she requires special consideration." She paused again as if reconsidering, "I know what I'm about to tell you will be very upsetting. The easy way out would be to remain quiet and not hurt your feelings, turning you away the next time you called to board her, claiming I had no available space. That would have been dishonest and counterproductive. While I expect some situations where dogs in my charge become difficult which I know goes with the territory, it becomes another matter when one becomes as disruptive and threatening as to put the rest of my animals at great emotional risk."

Rose and George Staves were equally dumbfounded at what they were hearing, aghast at what could have precipitated such a damaging assessment – an overreaction on Mrs. Joseph's part, or traits of Tasha heretofore unseen running counter to everything that they had learned about Tasha and her breed. Waiting to make that judgment, they were nonetheless on guard, prepared for additional criticism.

Her inner conflict resolved, Mrs. Joseph went ahead and described the events of the past week. "When you left that day you dropped her off, she became unglued and began immediately to pull on the leash with such force I had trouble holding her back. I had no idea how much strength she had. With your car out of sight, she stopped dead in her tracks, threw back her head and howled balefully like a wolf mourning over its dead mate. I tried to comfort her to no avail. My Shepards who had responded to her howling were viciously turned upon. I dared not pet her while she was in such a state. Forcefully she turned away from me and pulled me toward the highway. I couldn't get her to turn back toward the barn area. Resisting every effort I made, while continuing her heartbroken howling. After what seemed an eternity, her throat sore from forceful lunging against her restraining choke collar, her howls became unsteady and cracking. Disconsolate, she turned and began to move in the direction of the kennel and what I sensed was a need for water... her cage having been made ready for her. Once inside the cage I removed the leash. Having her fill of water, she returned to the now closed cage door. Barred from leaving, in exhaustion, she laid on the ground on all fours, her head between her forepaws, her eyes forlorn but expectant... waiting."

Downcast, Rose and George, laden with guilt, murmured, "The poor dog."

"That's just the beginning," Mrs. Joseph said, "I thought that would be the worst of her reactions. I soon learned otherwise. When I tried to get back in her cage to fill her food bowl with the dog food you brought with you, she responded by growling and baring her teeth. The hair of her shackles stood straight up as if electrified, I being perceived as her enemy, showing aggression toward me. I backed off knowing this was not the right time to attempt to feed her, choosing instead to try later when she would be hungrier and tolerant of my presence. After an hour's wait it was more of the same, only this time she leaped against the cage in snarling fury. She wasn't about to let me into her cage or anywhere near her food bowl. Intimidated, I decided to wait for my husband and his thoughts on her hostility toward me. During my wait she renewed her baleful heart wrenching howling, repeatedly flinging herself against the cage stunning herself. When my husband arrived, seeing how unnerved I was, and hearing the sounds of disturbance, which now involved all of my farm animals, counseled after my explanation."

"It sounds like she's holding you responsible for her owner's absence," my husband reasoned.

"That's ridiculous," I told him. "Dog intelligence does not include reasoning powers. That's reserved for human."

"Nonetheless, let's operate on that premise. She has to eat."

With me hidden from Tasha's view, my husband approached her cage. She immediately faced him, sniffing as he approached her. "Good girl, Tasha, good girl," he said. She immediately calmed down becoming responsive to him. She was unquestionably committed to male association. Seeking his approval, she pushed her muzzle through an opening in the wire cage allowing him to pet her, not a growl, no baring of teeth. With confidence, my husband opened the cage door with just enough room to reach the food bowl and remove it for filling outside the cage, returning it quickly. Blocking the possibility of escape from the slightly open cage door with his body, keeping her from bolting. My husband then joined my side, chagrined as we watched her nibble at her food with little enthusiasm. I knew that huskies were not big eaters for their size; something to do with their metabolism, but eating so little was abnormal, her appetite obviously leaving with your departure.

" What will I do?" I asked of my husband. "You work; I run the farm and the kennel. She's in my charge. She must respond to me."

He agreed. "But we must change her attitude toward you," he said.

"How will we do that?" I asked.

"In stages with me chaperoning. You and I will walk her, then you alone when she readily accepts you."

"When the time came, sensing, she stood awaiting us. Wary of my presence but not displaying any aggressiveness toward me, a concession of tolerance after making a male connection to my husband. Her bond to you is strong, Mr. Staves" Mrs. Joseph paused to acclaim.

George Staves nodded but said nothing.

"With leash in hand, which I deliberately rattled for her attention, my husband opened the cage door as I blocked the opening. Successfully fixing her leash to her collar we started walking the property's periphery together. Comfortable that she had acclimated herself, he then handed me the leash to continue walking her as he stood fast leaving her view. Calling out, he regained Tasha's attention, announcing that he was returning to the barn. Tasha, watching him all the way, moved to follow him. Once there she allowed me to unleash her and guide her back into her cage, allowing me to refill her water bowl.

"I had passed the first test my husband concluded."

"She obviously has a male association predisposition but smart enough to recognize our social structure. She'll be fine with you as long as you don't attempt to lead her. To prove I'm right, tomorrow morning you'll be the one that responds to her needs," he said.

"She howled all through the night, her soulful entreaty to be retuned to her pack."

"Upon arising the next morning I learned firsthand the extent to which she would go to free herself from strangers. I did not see her in her cage but knew she had to be in her run, which is where I found her. Witnessing something I had heard of, but never believed possible, I watched aghast, incredulous as Tasha jumped onto the six-foot high wire fence in an attempt to scale it to freedom. Time after determined time she tried, only to fall back to the ground, suggesting she wouldn't succeed. A bi-product of her failure I hoped; would be a tempering effect of our relationship for the remainder of her stay. Undaunted and determined, her deterrent not conceded to, only temporary in her eyes, somehow it would be solved and her purpose succeeding. Her challenge teaching her with each jump to put her now bloodied paws through the square openings in the woven pattern of the wire fence gaining much needed support and leverage. This obviously painful technique showing progress as she fell back to the ground from greater heights. I waited silently for her, paws bloodied and exhausted to concede failure right up to the moment when she didn't fall back and made it to where she straddled the top of the fence. In satisfaction she perched haltingly before making her escape, jumping to the rain softened ground. I was frozen in disbelief, unable to stop her or sound a warning alarm to my husband. The last I saw of her she was running toward the divided highway."

"Oh, my God," Rose gasped, breaking her in awe silence, her hand to her mouth. Trembling, she managed to say, "What happened then?"

"Panicking, I rushed back towards the house, my arms waiving frantically at my husband, he startled, worriedly running towards me trying to decipher my screaming signals -finally realizing what had happened."

"We called the Highway Patrol. Sheriff Dallas, a good friend, promised to put all available patrol cars on the search. After three hours, the animal warden's truck pulled up to our house followed by the sheriff's car. A muzzled Tasha, led by the warden, emerged from one of the cages.

"Smiling, Animal Warden Siminski said, 'She's a tough one. She gave all of us a run for our money. We were finally able to snare her when she stopped to drink water from a sprinkler system in a fenced-in backyard. Before she knew it we had her boxed in. Snared, she put up a hell of a fight. We finally were able to muzzle her to keep from getting bitten.'

"Extremely grateful, I showed the warden where Tasha's cage was, the run area sealed off to her until I could figure out what to do. With his assistant holding her firmly by the tail, a heavily gloved Warden Siminski was able to remove her muzzle. Surprising everyone she entered the cage voluntarily."

Walking to their cars, the sheriff said, 'I kept getting reports from people who had spotted her. We finally caught up with her, tracking her until the warden arrived. It was absolutely amazing. She knew instinctively to stay on the berm or the median, recognizing the danger around her. She wouldn't cross the highway until she was sure it was free of traffic, even as we chased her.'

"What direction was she headed?" I asked.

"West, toward the city, the sheriff answered."

"She was heading home… Amazing," I commented, shaking my head in disbelief. "Improbable as it seems she probably could have made it. Forty miles is nothing as determined as she is."

"I can't believe she climbed that fence." The sheriff commented still astonished as he got into his car. "Ever see anything like that before," he asked Warden Siminski.

"I've heard stories. Always thought they were exaggerations. I know better now," he said as he got into his truck and drove away following the sheriff's car.

Mrs. Joseph paused, watching their faces of disbelief. Rose finally said, "I can't believe she did that. She could have been killed," then adding solemnly, "and it wouldn't have been anyone's fault."

"I doubt that would have happened as smart as she is avoiding traffic," Mrs. Joseph commented.

"Nonetheless, she was in a danger of her own making," Rose answered.

George Staves, knowing Mrs. Joseph had more to say, interrupted, "What did you do after that incident to prevent it from happening again?"

"My husband bolted on sheets of plywood, raising the fence height to eleven feet, presenting her with a surface that gave her no traction or support. But even that impossible challenge didn't stop her from trying."

"What do you mean?" Rose asked, her face pale with dread.

"Our experience kept us alert. We soon learned of another one of her talents – digging her way free. On one of my many checks I spotted her just as she was emerging from a hole she had dug underneath the extended fence, covered with dirt, the ring in her collar pulled apart, the failed restraining leash left behind in her cage. I was fortunate my husband was with me. He quickly tied a rope to her collar as she attempted to climb out of the hole."

"You mean she almost escaped again?" Rose moaned.

"She tried the very next day while we were still recovering from her last episode." To head off any criticism of negligence, Mrs. Joseph, making everyone mindful, pointedly offered, "Can you believe the strength it took for her to spread that holding ring?"

Silence and shaking heads of disbelief answered her.

"My husband and I decided since it was impractical to stand constant guard while she was in her cage or her run, that we try something different, give her more space and a sense of greater freedom, in an attempt to placate her. After welding the collar's holding ring, reattaching her leash with added length of tether, we staked the open end so deep into the ground only a tractor could pull it free. Positioning it outside of her open cage, giving her thirty feet of play, plenty of room to roam – having access to her open cage, and it's food and water."

"Did that solve the problem?" George Staves asked.

"As far as escaping we had no other incidences or attempts after testing her restraints, realizing it would be fruitless. But the repercussions of her stay at my kennel are still being felt," she responded wearily.

"What do you mean?" he asked pointedly. "Was she aggressive toward the other dogs?"

"Under competitive situations she would growl them into disassociation. My fearless shepherds wouldn't have anything to do with her. They sensed desperation in her primitive plaintive howling. Being of a purpose unfulfilled, and inconsolable, Tasha became highly agitated, encouraging they give her a wide berth," Mrs. Joseph continued.

"When the other owners came to pick up their pets they expressed concern over how little they had eaten of the food they had brought with them. Never buying into my explanation of 'adjustment effects.' Dismissing that explanation out of hand as my kennel was not their first experience. Suspecting that something was terribly wrong, I knew I would not be seeing them again."

"I'm sorry that happened, truly sorry," Rose commiserated.

"I knew you both would be. I wish that were the worst of it."

"No?" Rose stammered. "You mean something else happened?"

"From the first night the measure of her stay impacted all of us. The adjustments we made handled the problem of escape but there wasn't anything we could do to stop her grating howl that was a continuing to upset the other animals. My chickens are usually very productive but egg laying dropped off considerably. Tasha's wolf like howling destroying the passive setting. Not a conducive atmosphere necessary for contented chickens. Don't let anyone tell you that chickens can't fly. Fearful that Tasha was a predator, in spite of a contenting fattening diet, they put to use their wings and flight feathers, flying to the upper rafters of the barn – their above ground security. They'll return to their normal lives once they recognize the quite- regaining a sense of security."

"Furthering her impact, the cow's milk was not as plentiful, they too were concerned about their safety, their genetics warned them they were prey to a marauding wolf. Unwilling to leave the barn to graze in the meadow, I had to bring feed to the barn in order that they eat, and even then their appetites were down from fear. And then there were my horses, fearful in spite of their size, snorting and whinnying, banding together at the opposite end of the meadow away from Tasha. Interpreting the pandemonium as a threat, influenced them to defensive tactics, shielding the most vulnerable colt, determined to fend off an expected attack from wolves, being signaled by their leader's howl."

Mrs. Joseph continued: "My pot bellied pig Chang developed such a bad case of diarrhea she messed up everywhere she went when in earshot of Tasha's howling. Dragging her hind end behind her, putting out the fire, its eyes bulging in fear of an imminent attack by wolves. It was too much for her panicked digestive system."

"That's the scene I left, all hurtful situations bearing Tasha's imprint."

"All will recover in time I'm sure. In fact, my farm animals probably sense that Tasha is gone, normal conditions returning," Mrs. Joseph said.

She was finished with her discourse, hoping it didn't come across as a diatribe. Noticeably relieved that the unpleasant task was completed.

"I'm sorry things turned out so poorly for Tasha during her stay at my kennel," Mrs. Joseph offered, her tone conciliatory, a concession of forgiveness for her ordeal.

"So are we," George Staves said apologetically. "Understand I'm not defending her actions as brought upon by unfamiliarity. But certainly it was a factor. I suspect that even with familiar surroundings, in our absence she would have reacted the same way."

"Without a doubt." Mrs. Joseph responded

Concluding, their talk over, he said, "We appreciate your candidness. You can be sure we won't put anyone in that position again. Our apologies for all you've gone through."

With everything said that should have been said, the balance of her fee received, additional discussion was unnecessary. With the scene becoming awkward, Mrs. Joseph got back into her station wagon, waving goodbye as she left. Tasha, having left the scene, watched Mrs. Joseph leave from the top step leading from the garage, leaping upon the door, wanting to be let back into the house – her final assurance that she was home to stay.

As they sat around the kitchen table, Tasha, in her familiar position of security and independence curled around the bathroom commode. George Staves said to his wife, "As I think about this whole situation, while I am regretful, amongst those feelings, I must confess is a greater appreciation of Tasha's strong ties to our family- risking death to rejoin us. We have to consider ourselves blessed that nothing devastating happened during her escape. Setting that aside, not to be cruel and unsympathetic, I'm finding it difficult not to find humor amongst all the confusion. The vision of Mrs. Joseph's animals running around in panic over a solitary lonely Husky could be described as comedic. Don't you agree?" he asked

"I'm grateful that nothing regretful had happened." Rose answered.

"That's my point. Nothing really bad happened – the situations that developed could be easily described as humorous."

"Only to outsiders," was her feigned critical response, turning from him so that he wouldn't see her slight smile.

The transporter startup began soundlessly, his need to release it's powering energy source to search further. Having made copious book notes, of the time period visited, he readied himself for the next part of his journey, sure to present scarred emotions; passions under siege. Nonetheless he had committed to revisit all incidents including those that would relive his sorrow, to find reflections of some of his persuasions now judged self serving or experiences of heart quickening endeavors. The trappings of a modern day Greek tragedy laying before him, those prospecting pain not deterring him in its self-confessional, believing it would be a further cleansing experience. Reliving chronologically provided an escape of compartmentalizing; if only temporary. Recognizing separation could be fleeting as Tasha's ending time line approached, paying a price in the inevitable composite.

six

George always drew pleasure from her reaction when he announced their planned walks, exclaiming, "Want to go for a walk, Tasha girl?" as if she had to be asked.

Seeming to read his mind, she stood in readiness in front of him, attentive as a soldier awaiting orders, not moving, eyes alert and fixed. Her body language silent most times, not anxiously pleading for comprehension. Not reluctant at other times to bark vociferously if she felt she was being ignored. His words were eagerly awaited, signaling the same excited response no matter how often repeated. Running at great speed to the front door; her scraping paws no match for the tiled floor would comically slip from underneath her. Righting herself in time to leap upon the front door with such force to test its resiliency. Recoiling from her unyielding barrier, she would return excitedly to him for assurance that he was close behind, returning with added excitement to shudder the door again with a short distanced assault. Her excitement, in anticipation of the opening of the door, brought challenges, new adventures and opportunities for discovery. After sniffing for intruders that may have preceded her, she would re-spot her territory, covering their scent in challenge. With her leash fixed to her choke collar just long enough to allow her stealth movement to sniff at every hedge for hidden sparrows, she would leap as they took flight, their resting place no longer safe.

They walked the streets proudly, displaying manicured lawns on both sides. Occasionally squirrels in their stop and go search of buried nutritional treasures; tails fluttering, front paws digging, noses sniffing, would abandon their search for food as Tasha approached, climbing to safety and refuge within the branches of a nearby tree. Peering down, tails flicking nervously, they waited patiently for Tasha's passage; the threat of serious consequences ending. Looking back Tasha taunted as they resumed their hunt, strained against her collar.

Pesky brazen blackbirds in nearby trees squawked warnings to others hopping along the freshly cut lawns for disturbed insects, sounding the alarm that an enemy was approaching. Tasha largely ignored the irritating disjointed symphony of the wizened birds in recognition that they were out of reach, not near enough to surprise and negate their ability to gain flight quickly, a dimension she knew she was not gifted to travel.

Tasha when distracted would lapse into role reversal. In a burst of strength, would pull George until commanded to "heel." Repeating the infraction when hurrying her selection for scenting a site; staking a territorial claim. When outdoors, Tasha's size and magnificence became more noticeable or so it seemed. Perhaps a rationale; the indoors is by itself a containment, a sanctuary, connoting a certain tranquility; bodies at rest in seemingly inert surroundings tending to stay at rest, influencing thoughts that time and change were at a standstill. As opposed to the openness and dynamics of the outdoors where change is expected and ongoing. The reduced or of limited sights while indoors no longer a factor, horizons of greater appreciation presenting it's self, satiating and influencing An environment freed from containment, enhancing the notice of all change, even the subtle. Beauty becoming more magnificent, nearer – growth more discerning… related to. Exuberance more telling. So it was with Tasha in this venue, George Staves proudly pleased as strangers openly marveled at her beauty and conformation freely noticed in the dynamics of the outdoors.

His response was to adoringly look down on her powerful body producing a smooth effortless gait; characteristic of her breed. Continuing his pleasure he now focused on her head, well-proportioned to her body, well-rounded with a gently tapered muzzle. Ready to please, her Almond shaped eyes watched him, their configuration mirroring the same traits her beginning ancestry possessed- spaced moderately and set somewhat obliquely; one brown, one blue, bi-eyed expressions ranging from interested, to mischievous. How misinformed of the uninitiated, he said to himself, to find her countenance threatening, her naturally smiling face displaying keenness; usually friendly but independent. Reaching down, George Staves rubbed her distinct ears; medium sized, triangular in shape but rounded and set majestically high on her head. Thick and well furred, slightly arched at the back and strongly erect, tips pointed straight up. Again he reached down to pat her appreciatively. This time it was her neck: medium in length arched and carried proudly erect when standing tall. Her hallmark plumed long tail, was carried centrally over her back in a sickle curve when at attention, bred not to curl to either side of her body; lowered when in repose, extending from her body.

Her magnificent coat, double-coated actually, with the usual white undercoat, woolly and down-like, was covered by the longer guard hairs that contained her coloring.

It was this living pronouncement of beauty that George shared with the public on their daily walks theatre. It was not conceit but pride that he was the proud owner, sharing her beauty for all willing to behold her without prejudice.

He remembered an incident that occurred during one of their walks to a site they had not visited recently. It was one of a dozen that awaited development: a full acre, excavated, foundation poured and skeletal framing underway,. Progress was well along as the new house took shape. As they approached the site the workers that were huddled over the site plans became wary of Tasha's presence, backing off as she got near; misreading her intent; judging her aggressive; misreading the expression in her eyes.

"Is she friendly?" one of the workers asked from his retreated position.

"As long as I'm with her she's very friendly," George Staves responded. "Independent yes but in spite of her looks, not threatening."

"Can we pet her?" the reassured spokesman said, obviously the group leader.

"Sure you can. Her name is Tasha. Call her. She'll come to you." George said.

"Come, Tasha," another one of the workers said, their confidence increasing.

Sure enough without hesitation, she joyously moved toward them, her tail waving in anticipation for the petting and scratching that she was sure to receive.

"What a beautiful dog," another worker called out. "A Husky isn't it?"

"Yes," George responded. "Purebred," he said proudly. "She comes from a long line of champions."

"She's really quite friendly," the lead worker said as Tasha, lowering her head to receive his friendly petting, raised it to lick the hand that was delighting her.

Tiring of the admiration she strained against the leash, anxiously intent to seek out and mark the territory that was under attack by the shovels and earthmovers, effectively changing the landscape.

"This lot was a place for her to roam," George continued, "part of a chain of vacant land that she liked to visit. The few remaining acres of land are rapidly disappearing as this area is highly desirable for homesites. We're being evicted," he said smilingly. "You guys wouldn't mind if I continued to use this site for Tasha to visit? I assure you, you won't have to worry where you step. She'll be away from where you will be working."

"No problem," assured the leader. "It's all right by us but I'm not sure what response you'll get from the woman who bought the property and the house that's being built. She's either a widow or a divorcée and very particular," he continued, nodding his head affirmatively as if to remind himself. "She's been here almost every day checking our progress. She even carries a copy of the blueprints for reference, questioning this and that, wanting to know every detail of the ongoing construction."

George thanked him for the warning and the endorsed invitation and turning to leave said, "See you again," and began walking toward the newly paved street.

A luxury car turned the street corner and began heading in their direction.

"As a matter of fact, there she is," the foreman warned, still within hearing distance. "I suppose she'll be asking us for a progress report."

Walking away from the property, the start of their return trip home, Tasha unexpectedly stopped in her tracks holding fast. An odd reaction, he thought as Tasha to his knowledge was not normally fascinated by cars but for some reason that he couldn't fathom, held her ground, awaiting the car to pull to the curb.

It was a situation he hoped to avoid. The opportunity to leave had vanished. The possibility of confrontation loomed. He and Tasha had obviously been seen by the approaching visitor, not knowing what to expect. She could display outrage claiming Tasha was despoiling her property, demanding their trespassing end, or if hospitable accept George's assurances that the privileges if allowed to continue would cease and desist once the house was completed and ready for her occupancy, by far the remotest of possibilities he expected after the warnings of the foreman.

George, in a search to read this tall scholarly looking woman, found a countenance that while determined was not severe. Countering effectively was the obvious delighted sparkle in her eyes kindling her warmth, thawing her mindset; a relieving smile emerged.

Tasha became transfixed, sphinx-like, not moving, muscles taunt as he stroked her neck trying to read what she sensed. The unknown causing him reflexively to tighten his grip on the leash proved unnecessary, Tasha suddenly soothed to relaxation as the woman neared. Just as suddenly, Tasha heightened to unexpected joy, as she drew closer. Staves was flabbergasted by Tasha's reaction to this strange woman. Tasha's eyes communicated that she was someone special. A sixth sense on display? A mind-reading capacity?

Tasha acted like she knew this woman without ever having met her, knowing that the shadow she cast, her energies and vibrations, her effusing body chemistry, all signaled goodness to Tasha's receptor.

"How lovely she is," the woman said softly as she smiled. "How old is she?"

"Three years old" George answered. "We call her Tasha, short for Natasha. She seems taken by you. Have we met before?"

"No. I would have remembered this beauty," she answered, extending her hand. "Are you and your Husky my neighbors?"

"Within a few blocks," George replied, taking her hand. "I'm George Staves. You've already met Tasha. Welcome to the neighborhood."

"The neighborhood just got better," she said warmly. "My name is Elizabeth Springer." Completely disarmed and mesmerized with Tasha' presence, adding openly, "I'm a widow returning to my roots. My husband and I grew up in this area. All of my family is buried in the surrounding cemeteries." Her eyes saddened, "I just recently buried my husband of fifty years. His last wish was to be buried where we both grew up."

Tasha's nose was glued to Mrs. Springer's slacks. Finally moving away without a command from Staves, completing her investigation. Strangely and uncharacteristically, she sat down deliberately blocking Mrs. Springer's path, playfully raising her right then her left paw, moving her head to the side of the paw being offered to complete her ritual of introduction.

"It's amazing how she has taken to you," George said. Then adding upon reflection, "Do you own a dog?"

"As a matter of fact, I do, a Husky just like yours," she smiled.

"You do?" George said excitedly, Tasha's strange behavior no longer a mystery. "I should have guessed as much they way she reacted to you."

"You know that Huskies can distinguish their breed from all other species of dog, reacting very differently to each other when meeting."

"Yes. I knew that," George responded, "but your dog is not with you."

"It's his scent that I was carrying. They discriminate each other's scents from other canines," Mrs. Springer answered proudly.

"That would explain things. Tasha had on many occasions met other dog owners drawing nothing more than a cursory interest, nothing like today where she reacted to you before you got out of your car."

"Olfactory prowess," Mrs. Springer answered.

"That may be," he answered, "but it border's on the mystical."

Mrs. Springer said smilingly, "They are an unusual animal. I've seen similar behavior with my Husky Norse." Then adding reflectively, "He's older than your Tasha; twelve years old," her tone saddening.

"Wouldn't it be wonderful if they could meet?" he offered.

"I'm afraid that's not possible. He's deathly ill." Her eyes glazing over, "He's become frail and lethargic, the result of Cushing's disease in its late stages. I don't take him out away from the house any more. It's too tiring for him."

"I'm so sorry to hear that," he said sympathetically. "Perhaps when you're settled in your new house we could come by and they can see one another." He read by her reaction that if that happened, it would be a miracle as Cushing's disease is without recovery.

Choking back tears she marshaled her strength to face the unfolding day, giving Tasha a goodbye pat, saying:

"You and Tasha can walk here anytime. It would be nice if you can plan it about this time of day so I might see and pet her," she said hopefully.

Responding, George assured her he would when possible. Consoled, her eyes were thankful, she turned and walked to the wooden skeleton of her emerging house and the awaiting foreman.

George kept his promise to Mrs. Springer, planning Tasha's walks to coincide with her on-site inspections.

Their meetings provided a spiritual uplifting for Mrs. Springer, the appreciation of Tasha, a stimulant at least for those soothing moments that they shared contact, proving antidotal in relieving her of the sadness. Encouraging reliving the comparison flashback imagery of her companion of thirteen years, spry and healthy; a welcomed departure from the heart wrenching reality of today, a pitying agonizing sight; her beloved Norse's life helplessly slipping away.

Having shared years of memories they now faced dreaded separation, the canine component of mutual dependency in their later years to cease. A life ending, leaving behind a despaired life emptied of purpose and will, living a nothingness in a environment difficult for the aging alone – her only sanctuary, within sight of death.

Tasha, providing a needed lift in her accommodating presence, displaying to Mrs. Springer a demonstrable show of affection. Giving pause to her despair, encouraging her spirits to raise up from the crestfallen, if only for moments. Bringing her life a temporary respite from sadness, a reprise of earlier happier days.

This time her countenance was different. While it was a longed for reunion, a torture manifested, her hands trembled as she stroked Tasha, betraying her. Her demeanor, veiled protectively in public was gone, lines of fatigue frozen and shadowed by sleeplessness were apparent. Her despairing world now off its axis, imbalanced, its rotational spin skewed, void of any brightening sunlight; her perceptions dark and ominous.

Tasha whose excited response usually never wavered, upon seeing Mrs. Springer, sensed the difference, she being downtrodden. Instead of sitting before her obediently, offering up her paws, she chose to lie at her feet subdued, her body language supplicating, a silent communiqué of sensitivity to the obvious pain that Mrs. Springer was experiencing.

"What's wrong?" a troubled George Staves asked.

"Norse had a difficult night," a sleep deprived Mrs. Spring responded, her lips quivering as her weakened resiliency threatened to leave her entirely. Recovering, showing embarrassment, she apologized, "I'm sorry."

"No need to apologize I understand," a commiserating George Staves responded.

"He's getting progressively worse, I'm afraid. The vet and the specialist can do no more for him," tears welled in her blood-stained eyes, she bit her lip to control her emotions. Again she recovered. Saying, "I have to make a decision, the time almost now." Trembling to get the words out she gasped, "To euthanize Norse. I just can't do it. It keeps me awake at night. Just the thought of me being responsible for ending his life traumatizes me. I'll never be able to do it. I can't imagine a life without Norse after all these years," she sobbed.

George empathized with her situation, "You'll make the right decision when the time is right. Lord knows he is enduring a declining physical entity because of his love to please you with his presence, you'll respond, reacting to his needs by bringing him peace, his wish to stay alive for your sake taken from him."

Her eyes brimming with tears she said, "You're right. I'll not be selfish. We'll both share in the decision for what's best. If he tells me it's time than I'll act. If he wants to be with me until the painful end then I'll nurse him until his last breath." Bringing her handkerchief to her eyes, breathing deeply she choked off any further sobs. Adding, "Please continue to come by, you and Tasha are such a comfort to me." Turning she approached the construction crew foreman of the almost completed house who, at that moment, was overseeing a contracted landscaper planting trees, bushes and hedges around the perimeter of the property to ensure the privacy and independence requested by Mrs. Springer was achieved in all directions.

George Staves, in real time, thought back now as he watched the imagery. He brought back to life from his events menu of how he had reacted under similar circumstances. His words of guidance to Mrs Springer were fittingly appropriate, late in his discovery.

As circumstances would have it, he didn't see Mrs. Springer again for over a month during which time the house was completed and ready for occupancy. Final cleanup and last minute touchups were being completed along with the remaining planting of trees selectively positioned around the property.

The lawn grass was fully grown covering the unsightly mud, their roots firmly housed in the yielding soil ready for its first mowing.

Their approach to the house became labored as Tasha stalled to search the air for the scent that was disturbing her. After a lengthy pause she reacted by ignoring George's urgings to continue, repeatedly trying to turn away from the house. Her tail tucked between her legs, she panted feverishly in wary apprehension. A shocked abandonment of her expected enthusiasm. He knew his dog, her sensitivities, her intuitiveness- something was distressing her. It was then that Mrs. Springer, who was temporarily hidden stepped between her car and an open-ended flatbed truck parked at the curb fronting the house, the truck containing a number of maturing trees whose bindings were being retightened by the landscapers. His eyes searching could find no influence to Tasha's behavior beyond Mrs. Springer. It had to be her effusing a message that sensitized Tasha

As they arrived, Mrs. Springer greeted them. He was disturbed at her appearance. She seemed to have surrendered to the aging process overnight.

Her once carefully made-up face was ignored, presenting a countenance drained of color. Her expression temporarily recovering, showing pleasure in seeing them but not nearly enough to hide and override the deep lines of melancholy. Her sunken blood-stained eyes, shrouded in darkened shadows squinted against the sunlight, reluctantly met his.

"I had Norse euthanized, he told me it was time – that he could no longer bear the pain," she cried out emotionally staring at an out-of-reach Tasha. Mrs. Springer's head moved up and down, her silent gesture of acknowledging, motioning affirmation. "Tasha's a worthy replica of my beloved Norse. It's been difficult letting go, dealing with his loss. I see him everywhere. I've caught myself about to call him, expecting his wagging tail to respond, not realizing he's gone."

"I feel terrible for you. I know he meant so much to you," George said sympathetically, extending his hands to her shoulders in consoling contact. "What can I do to help?"

Tasha, watching intently, had sensed Norses death, mourning her breeds loss showed by her initially standing apart from Mrs. Springer in a private observance, recognizing she emotionally in a state of a inevitable resurrection of Norse in her embrace of Tasha, credited characteristics belonging to the bereaved while emotionally uplifting, was an invention prompted by kindred looks. Staves reading her reacting body language, overcoming her trepidation, she came within her reach, readily accepting her tearful praised petting. As Tasha and Staves had anticipated Mrs. Springer's association, voicing:

"She reminds me so much of Norse, his reincarnation " adding forlornly, "Tasha is young. You'll have many years of her pleasure to look forward to."

"Perhaps you'll consider getting another Husky. Not now, but in the future," he said in kindness.

"I could never have another dog," she said in solemn resignation. "I prefer to live out the rest of my life for whatever time has been decided by the good Lord- remembering him. I plan to memorialize his life's meaning to me by planting a tree in his honor, watching it grow and flourish under my care, a place for me to visit and Norse to visit me spiritually. You must see it. The landscapers have just finished planting it. I selected a Dogwood, not coincidentally- it's name therapeutic."

"I think that's an excellent idea," he said. "It will help you deal with his loss. A transference to something alive, vibrant, responding to your care with it's bloom"

"I feel that way. Thanks for supporting a fanaticizing tired old lady. I have more to tell you," she said secretly as she watched the landscaping crew finish their cleanup. "They'll be gone in a few minutes," she said looking at the workers directly.

When they finally left she went to the car, opened the trunk teary-eyed and withdrew a box tied with heavy twine fixed with a handle for ease in carrying, placing it carefully before them. Almost immediately a watchful Tasha rose from her seated position and walked slowly to the box, nostrils working furiously. Suddenly as if repelled, she threw her head back, eyes skyward, throating a long mournful wail until her lungs were exhausted. She returned her baleful eyes to the box once again shrilly piercing the unknowing silence.

"Tasha knows," Mrs. Springer said.

Confused, George retorted, "Knows what?"

"She knows I have Norse's ashes in the box. Her howling is her expression of grief for the passing of one of her breed."

He was flabbergasted, not because of Norse's ashes but of Tasha's response. As he now knew in totality why Tasha displayed reluctance earlier.

"I wouldn't have believed it if I hadn't witnessed it," he said to himself in continuing amazement. "It's absolutely unbelievable and uncomprehending that a dog has that sense, that it can show and communicate sorrow. Those emotions are supposed to be beyond the intelligence capabilities of dogs. It has to be true. How else could Tasha's actions be explained? "

Mrs. Springer, tears still streaming down her face, did what she planned to do. With hands shaking she found the strength to untie the box and take out the urn containing Norse's remains, solemnly, almost religiously distributing the ashes through out her property.

George Staves watched, his mind liberally drawing a parallel, equating a priest spreading holy water in a blessing – Mrs. Springer's property accommodating Norse's ashes. George watched the solemn ritual, Tasha her wailing sorrow a mourning background.

George Staves did not see much of Mrs. Springer after that fateful day. Frightened and alone, she preferred the safety of a monastic existence, reclusive and invisible most of the time except for the meticulous tending of her flower beds and in particular the dogwood tree. On rare occasions when he did see her busy with tending her garden, she would wave passively as he and Tasha passed the house, pausing briefly to admire Tasha, forlorn but smiling almost imperceptive, then biting her lower lip before returning to her task at hand. Consistent, she would never show them a hint of encouragement to move closer, always waving acknowledgment but dropping her hand quickly least it be misunderstood. Turning back to her work, effectively dissuading any move in her direction, effectively shutting off any further communication; signaling preferring to be alone.

She appeared to have aged significantly, her shoulders stooped as if weighted down invisibly. Her once proud body now frail and weakened by weight loss. George watched in sorrow as Mrs. Springer walked haltingly, uncertain of her next step.

He could only conclude that her strange behavior toward him and Tasha meant they represented too painful a reminder of what her life was once like, preferring solitude as she neared the end of her life cycle. Pitying her irrationality for willing her Norse not dead, as she honored his ashes, rationalizing only his physical being was temporarily taken from her. Finding the alternate and surrogate opportunities to communicate with him the better option than the painful physical presence of another dog, its life expressing a breathing and panting reality, battling her for attention to replace a Norse that was gone, she would never subscribe to. She knowingly chose this path, circumventing the wisdom to accept his death, and her opportunity for recovery. It was her will that found this other world where she could communicate spiritually. In it's serving causing no harm to others. Protective of her envisioning she discouraged any interference; discouraging a continuing relationship even from George Staves and Tasha who had befriended her. Her pain, her mission, not to be denied wherever it led.

He would later learn from her neighbors her only sighting was when she spent hours in her garden, the envy of the neighborhood, flourishing under her talented care. Which, according to them, also included her audible conversations with the plants and trees she walked among, encouraging their life in progress. She was thought of as peculiar by her neighbors. They did not know what to make of her showing no willingness to understand, choosing instead to ignore her, leaving her alone with her eccentricities and they with their intolerance.

New construction was proceeding at a feverish pace, gobbling up Tasha's walk sites, forcing George to find new routes that took them away from Mrs. Springer's home. Occasionally without her notice he would drive by and see her contributing to the marathon hours she spent amongst her flowers, plants and trees, knowing she was communicating her devotion.

The weather had changed far too early. A meandering jet stream the National Weather Bureau factually advised, or as some opportune *celebré* environment groups would indict, "Man influencing nature, polluting the atmosphere affecting seasonal change." The temperate days of fall prematurely ending and in full retreat from the distancing parenting sun. The scent of flowers carried by whispering balmy breezes a memory – blustery vacant winds replacing them, moving chilling air flushing through the trees. Detaching weakened nourishment starved leaves, in presentation of their final hurrah – a magnificent color epitaph proclaiming their seasonal demise. Left behind was the skeletal remains of bare branch limbs forever reaching skyward, their growth on hold, the muted beginning of the annual retreat to hibernation. The once colorful leaves separated from their life support, lay strewn about victims. In death stiffening and shriveling, awaiting movement by man or sudden gusts of wind, their resting place, bagged as unsightly litter, or dispatched as mulch during the summer season ending lawn mowing.

Ominous signs of a season being hurried heralding an early arrival of winter, George thought as he drove down Mrs. Springer's street after these many months. Approaching the house he saw unfamiliar faces walking around the property with a confidence belying the conclusion that they were visitors surveying. Alarmed by his perception and what it portended, he pulled to the curb in front of the house. Exiting his car he approached the man and woman. Both appeared to be in their late sixties, obvious retirees from business and parenting.

"Hello," he said. "I live on Lander Road, not far from here. I'm George Staves."

Having watched the car pull to the curb, hearing his declaration of who he was they acknowledged him as if already introduced, silently pitying his tone of alarm as they awaited his closing of the distance that separated them.

"Are you relatives of Mrs. Springer?" George questioned.

Their immediate reaction was to look at one another before returning their full attention to him.

"No," the man said, solemnly.

"We're not," the wife accentuated, equally as solemn as her husband "We're the new owners. I'm Faith Schindler and this is my husband Jim. I'm sorry to tell you that we have bad news. Mrs. Springer passed away a month ago."

His shock to the news gave way to overwhelming sorrow, he felt his throat tighten. His voice tremulous, he said, "How did it happen?"

Reacting to how affected he was, respectful yet resolute, Mrs.Schindler responded, "It seems one of her neighbors missed seeing her tending to her garden. Not knowing whether she might be out of town, the neighbor checked her mail and newspaper boxes and found they had not been emptied for days. He then rang the door bell and got no response. It was then he called the police who upon entering the house found her in bed just barely alive. The summoned emergency service rushed her to the hospital but it was too late to save her. She died within hours of her arrival. Reposed at DeCamps funeral home, she so instructed her lawyer for one day, receiving few visitors."

"How sad," an emotive George Staves offered. "In life and in death few reached out to her."

Empathizing, Mrs. Schindler paused, a melancholy expressed in her eyes. Her husband intervened giving her respite from her distress, "She also had written her own obituary notice, published at behest of her lawyer. I remember clearly, stating simply: 'Remembered by few, loved by those who preceded me. In passing I leave this earth willingly to join my beloved husband Kenneth and dog Norse in Gods Kingdom.' Her remains as requested of her attorney were cremated."

Agonized by the news, George Staves's mind momentarily departed the scene becoming critical of himself for not staying in touch with Mrs. Springer. That lonely depressed woman, he sorrowed, whose life she was shortening by reliving her grief daily. Perhaps, he chastised himself, he could have helped her more, telling himself he should have persisted and not backed away when she did not encourage continuing a friendship. He persisted with his self-criticism until the reality of their relationship gained greater focus, acknowledging he didn't turn his back on her. She chose the life she wanted to live. No amount of his well-intentioned pleading to join a pet loss support group would have succeeded. Remembered clearly; she quickly brushed aside any thoughts of surrounding herself with other pet mourners. Her memories and grief were personal and hers alone, the pain and pleasure of them were hers to recall and relive in private. Equally rejected was his suggestion that she seek professional third-party intervention. Misreading his intentions; resenting the suggestion of instability. Her emotions ruled, unfairly criticizing him as lacking understanding of her pledge and it's fulfillment. Wanting to continue her worship in a monastic setting as a devotional tribute to Norse; not wanting to escape from it.

Purged of personal guilt he returned his attention to the Schindler's, his eyes no longer vacant of their presence. "It's been months since I last saw her. While she was frail, I never realized that she was ill. We were friends," he continued sadly. "We both shared a common bond of love for Siberian Huskies."

"I knew she was an animal lover," Faith Schindler said, nodding her head knowingly. "When we were first shown the house we saw many photographs, all of a man we assumed to be her husband and a dog, or just of the dog, all over the house, in every room. The dog humorously wearing ties and baseball caps."

"That's not surprising, it reflects her devotion." George said sadly.

"What surprised me," Faith continued, "is that I saw no evidence of a dog living in the house. You know the usual things – dog hair, food dish, its scent."

"No, you wouldn't have. Her dog, she called him Norse, died before she could move in. It was such a pity. Her choice, to be left alone in this world with memories and a religiosity she wished to observe at home. A monastic self-imposed retreat the only setting she wanted to awake to, if not called by her maker."

"The pain of her broken heart in a narrowing life was soothed somewhat as she meticulously tended her lawn, her flowers and trees, the darkness of her disconsolation on leave during those moments she was amongst beauty she cultivating." George said in sorrow, stopping short of revealing the secret of her shrine.

"My husband and I are devotees of horticulture," Mrs. Schindler said. "That preoccupation sold us on the house. It's wonderful how much care and attention she gave. It shows in how beautiful everything is."

There was a lull in the conversation as Mrs. Schindler looked toward her husband for support to continue. Cleared by his understanding nod, she said, "Mr. Staves, why don't we go into the house and talk? We have so much more to tell you."

Surprised by the invitation, he nonetheless accepted, anxious and curious for what they were going to add, intuitively hopeful that it would ease his pain.

They sat in the well-appointed living room, the newness of the furniture's distinct smell still fresh.

Continuing she said, "We found out from the real estate agent who was handling the sale for the estate trustee that Mrs. Springer had one living relative, a Mrs. Gloria Bowers, a cousin living in Florida. Mrs. Springer's will left half of her estate to her cousin and the other half to the Humane Society. Her cousin, receiving notification from Mrs. Springer's attorney, Robert Mercer, chose not to attend the funeral, only finding reason to travel here to finalize the sale of all Mrs. Springers dutifully catalogued assets, including the household furnishings."

George immediately recognized Robert Mercer's name, recalling all his experiences and unpleasantness in dealing with him, cautiously alert he kept his thoughts to himself, as he had no reason to believe he would be in contact with him again.

Mr. Schindler continued, "Mrs. Springer's lawyer granted permission to allow the cousin to conduct daily announced asset sales until the house furnishings were sold," Pausing in disgust in the recollection, he then continued, "the cousin showed no emotion for her benefactor. Indifferent, considering it a bother to be here, her interest solely on her half of the monetary value of the estate. Once completed rushed to return to her life in Florida.Where she complained bitterly that the sale of the house along with the probate process, was to slow moving."

"I'm sure this unendearing women was joyous when she found out the house had been sold, our written bid accepted along with our binding down payment. It would be ours once probate was cleared. While probate was still an issue and the house not officially ours, Mr. Mercer gave us the keys allowing us to visit the house as often as we wished to make furnishing and paint color judgments."

Mrs. Schindler interjected, "Mrs. Bowers continued her relentlessness in pursuing her cousins benevolence, arrogantly displeasing in the wake of every phone contact with the real estate agent, she a vulture squawking over remains as sacrificing inconvenience, when events moved too slowly for her. Never once appreciating her surprised beneficiary status from a relative she openly stated she avoided 'because of her strangeness.' Attacking Mrs. Springer in death she complained of having to share the estate with the Humane Society all because of a dog. 'Can you imagine that? A dog,' Mrs. Bowers would rant in disgust to whom ever would listen."

Continuing their shared criticism Mr. Schindler said. "There was no limit to her brashness, being very critical of the federal and state tax obligations the estate was subject to. 'Blood suckers' she called them, never mindful or caring who she spoke to or concern for being labeled greedy."

In obvious contempt of her, Mr. Schindler, his anger growing, said, "A very unpleasant person. I'm glad not to be dealing with her anymore."

Mrs. Schindler listening to her husband's angry words brought closure to their angry reflections, insisting they get the conversation back to the reason for their invitation, her tone and calm having a quieting effect on her husband's angst.

"We learned that the police found her will, on her bureau. Very telling evidence that she judged her time as short. You would think that if she was lucid enough to plan for the will's convenient discovery, that she might have thought to save herself by calling for help, instead of laying their unattended gasping her final breaths. It sounds like she gave up."

George Staves didn't offer an opinion, silently having to agree with Mrs. Schindler's assessment of the final days.

Mrs. Schindler continued, "The police notified Robert Mercer, the creator and administer of the will. He in turn notified the Humane Society, Mrs. Gloria Bowers and the Probate Court."

Mr. Schindler fully recovered, his countenance at peace said, "A tax creditor obligation sale was held. We were fortunate enough to be the successful bidder on the house, and the car and some of the furnishings. The photographs, being of no sentimental value to Mrs. Bowers, served only to embitter her further, damming the will's division. Unconscionably asking that we destroy the photos. Instead we decided to send them to her after returning to Florida, antagonizing her our only weapon, a minor payback on our part for her unsavory behavior was our message; yet we knew it would be a short lived inconvenience to this women who was possessed by self interest- incapable of deliverance."

George Staves was expectant, eager for them to continue. Instead, a noticeable pause followed, each reconfirming to each other the need to continue, affirming that he correctly share their discovery of Mrs. Springers painful disclosure.

Mrs. Schindler continued, "While we were assembling the photographs

Mrs. Bowers had left behind we found a letter among them. We considered also sending it to the cousin. We changed our minds. Certain she had already read it during her search of Mrs. Springers possessions. Leaving it behind not interested in keeping it, and since the addressee; a general "To Whom It May Concern," we held it as caretakers for the appropriate.

"A letter?" George said his emotions mixed.

" Under the circumstances we felt obligated to hold it, as it was intended to be a open communiqué to those connected to her, a correspondence meaningful to those in her final days. Your association with Mrs. Springer is mentioned in the letter, you are entitled to read it," Mrs. Schindler revealed.

Nodding understanding. He felt reasonable certain, since it hadn't been brought up Mrs Springers letter did not reveal the secret they shared. If he was wrong; would the Shindlers show understanding for his involvement by circumstance – the confidence and burden it imposed? The guardianship of Norses ashes imposed upon them.Their demeanor of reaching out to him, sharing, indicated they would. Nonetheless he was prepared.

Mrs. Schindler then left the living room, returning moments later handing George Staves an envelope. After removing the letter, his visage solemn, and apprehensive for it's portent, shaped by the situational occasion, read it in silence, Mrs. Springer's letter in an unsteady hand, her tears bleeding the ink, the spacing inconsistent:

"To you who cared," it began simply, those words supportive enough to satisfy the Schindler's qualifying him. "I'll be gone when you read this letter, having departed a life that in it's final years severely tested me. Burdening years that led to my questioning my observance of my religious faith. My disassociation developing over time of continuing personal hurt. Finding it unbearable, succumbing to abandon my daily prayers, the written word of the scriptures. I recovered more passionate than ever as a believer, the power of the Jesus's forgiving words during the horrific pain of crucifixion, diminishing mine in comparison – removing doubts. Fervent I voiced my entreaty to enter the realm of my Maker, where the only currency to spend is his earned blessings, reunited in joining the spirituality of my awaiting family."

"I would have lived in this house for only a very short time. The house still new, as are my selected appointments. Unremarkable was my short stay; not enough to culture the life of my own persona in the furnishings, overlaying the designer's creations, with representation of my own personality."

Those words gave George Staves pause, imperceptible to the Schindlers watching him read in silence, judging the sadness of his facial expressions. He visualizing she lacked the needed time for her to body imprint and scent the couch pillows, or finalize the change in the color of paint from her original selections, nor the bothersome length of the window drapes that she would change more to her liking, never having happened.

His assessment consequence would also be true of the newly exposed materials used in the building of the house, time preventing the character building enhancement qualities of weathering that can't be rushed from immaturity. His imagination froze at her image of many hours seated at the kitchen table looking out the window at her thriving dogwood tree and lush green lawn. That somber image bringing him back from his journey, rejoining the Schindler's. Sadly, his eyes moistened by her vision, straining his continuing reading of Mrs. Springer's letter:

"The house's comforting pleasures made almost invisible by the great sadness I bore. Not blessed with the ability to have children, I shared most of my adult life with my devoted husband, content to live out our remaining time together committed to pleasing one another. Our marriage was never under strain for not having our own family. We did not feel vacant. We had each other. Everything we did, we did together. We weren't arrogant or aloof, finding our needs fulfilled by each other. So many satisfying years of happiness blessed with good health lulled us into believing we were invincible, that the vulnerability of age happened to others, not us. Neither one of us gave much thought to infirmity or survivorship. Genetics had served and continued to serve us well; we playfully teased one another. A change in our lifestyle was necessary, we finally did admit as we had noticeably slowed down, our desire and ambition to travel, as had been our preoccupation, was not as often- becoming more selective.

"Tragedy struck my devoted Kenneth. A severe stroke with cerebral hemorrhaging paralyzed him. No longer ambulatory, he was confined to a wheelchair. Helpless, he was tearfully cognizant of what had happened to him, distraught, becoming bewildered and confused by his short term memory loss.

"Proudly an excellent speaker, his speech now came hesitatingly from drooling distorted lips. While his consequences were devastating to both of us. I would learn to provide for his every need. I was of one mind: to minister to him myself, to maintain his companionship living off my strength. My marriage vows I held sacred. I knew that things would never be the same but I was committed to handle any situation. I would not forsake him. We were allied forever. Nothing would break that alliance.

"What I didn't foresee was his lack of will to live. He was not a "Type A" personality. He provided leadership by example and consensus building to complement his high intelligence. A strong and robust man, he delighted in serving all when asked. He would welcome the opportunity to challenge his intellect and physical prowess. His psychological reaction to his debilitating handicap was anguish, his pride ripped from his psyche as he watched me relegated to wet nursing him. Likening his circumstance to a near vegetative state was more than he was willing to bear."

"On more than one occasion as I tended to his incontinence, his eyes shedding tears, the words, 'I don't want to live anymore' would be spit from his mouth twisted into sneering distortion. No amount of pleading or teary impassioned assurances that I still loved him, or my chastisement for giving up would convince him he still had a place in our lives. He would hardly eat, just sitting there staring at me, eyes tearful. Stuttering forced fragmented words, "Le eet me ee d d die," was his wishes as I watched him deteriorate before my eyes.

"I was beside myself, the doctors offering little help, clearly distancing themselves with, 'He's lost his will to live. He's better off in a home.'

'But he will truly die there,' I pleaded. 'He's getting better care with me at home. There must be something that can be done to give him something to live for.'

"They would only shake their heads pityingly, their Hippocratic Oath satisfied. 'Make sure he keeps taking his medicine,' would be their only comments.

"Thankful for television, I turned the set on before him, hopeful each night to stir his interest. I, with the remote control at hand, sat browsing through a magazine ready to read to him when television no longer interested him. This our usual evening regimen."

"A ray of hope, a potential to break through – I marveled at an article describing patients in hospitals receiving a psychological boost toward recovery or becoming more reasonable in accepting the limitations of their illnesses by the introduction of animals in their lives. Encouraged, I made up my mind right then and there, ignoring my husband's pleas and protestations, preferring his death be expedited. The following day I went to a breeder and bought a Siberian Husky who I named Norse. His impact on my husband was immediate and remarkable, confirming the positive effects on human health an animal connection forges.

"I had given my husband a reason to live. He was no longer hesitant and embarrassed to be seen. Now he looked forward to spending hours, with me close by, sitting in the backyard watching Norse playfully chase everything that moved or flew. It was an amazing turnaround, the doctors acknowledged, his downward spiral ending, figuratively climbing his mountain. He had returned from his consignment of an empty death, a respondent to Norse's bonding, who sensed his need. No longer morose and dispirited over his dependent handicap, no longer bitterly claiming his immobility gave him no productive role in whatever years ahead of us. No longer citing dispirited: his best years, our best years, history. No longer wanting his life to be over… Accepting that he was of diminished capacity, wholly receiving care. Now tolerant of a relationship that he once saw as a undeserved burden on me. His handicap; no longer tendrils suffocating me – destroying him. Norse was responsible for the transformation. Now he had a purpose, a reason to live in spite of his limitations for whatever years God would keep us together–a life accommodating his handicap, one he could subsist in."

At this point he noticed the handwriting became more unsteady, misspelling lined out – envisioning her needing composure. On the verge of being overcome by what would follow, struggling to find the determination to continue her labored writing. "It would last until June fifteenth of the third year we had Norse. I came home early from shopping to find my husband in his wheelchair slumped over taken from me, that terrible stroke producing sneer of his mouth unfrozen. In death God returned his ability to smile, it telling that Norse was his last vision before his sight ended forever, having only known to embrace Norse as only the paralyzed can, with his eyes. Norse, his head anchored in my husband's lap, silently grieving him. I believe my husband died peacefully knowing I would not be alone, that Norse he helped nurture would represent his continuation."

"We had discovered that during our three years together sharing Norse, we could not imagine life without him. All those years prior we now measured insignificant, so profoundly had he impacted our lives. While the passing of my husband was a sad moment in my life, during the last three years of his devastating illness, the three of us were a family. A triumvirate giving me strength to face my husbands death, reconciled as always nearby. In his death we were not alone, Norse and I comforted one another in our grief, to draw strength from the remainder of our union."

"Since we always intended to move back to this area, I had his body interred in nearby Calvary Cemetery. The purposefully selected gravesite was close to one of the many access roads that weave throughout the cemetery, making it easier for me to smuggle Norse in to visit the gravesite, arriving just before closing. While it was against the rules, the workers turned their heads when they realized that Norse came to mourn, placing his head at the base of the gravestone, moaning almost imperceptibly while I lay flowers, talked and prayed."

"And now my beloved Norse, my dearest companion of over twelve years, is no longer with me. While I do have a cousin who discouraged my attempts for closer ties, preferring phone calls that I always initiated, visiting on my part never an offered invitation, her schedule to busy to accept mine. I remain not critical. I prefer to bear my pain alone."

"While my physical shortcomings prevented me from bearing children, it did not prevent me from returning love and affection. My ability to love deeply was not forsaken because I was made barren and could not conceive a being of my biology. I could still feel the joy of loving another God-created living being. God would not deny me such an association. I having the bounty, an energy that needed an outlet, he in his infinite wisdom choosing

Norse for me. God created dogs to be human companions in life and in the afterlife; in his kingdom for all living creature's spiritual being. He has ordained that death be not a permanent separation, reuniting awaits believers, a rewarding promise. I look forward to the day when I can join my husband and my Norse for eternity."

George Staves's outer reaches of his vision recognized his name amongst the upcoming words in the letter. He quickened his reading pace to learn the essence of him being referenced

"With the exception of George Staves, my newly found neighbor who shared my passion for Huskies, I now ask for understanding. You the bearer of intentions that you felt would be therapeutic, had I been amenable. I forced avoidance, to deter you. Sacrificing a friendship, so determinedly committed was I to my choice of seclusion with only my memories surrounding me while I awaited God to call me. It was my wish, I thank you now for your well intentioned attempts to bring Tasha into my time limited life. Forgive me, for resisting bringing into my heart a surrogate – It could only house my Norse.

"I suffered great prejudice and disdain for my devotion to my Norse from people who chose to lack understanding. They failed to understand how enriched I was by this sweet unselfish dog whose constant dedication was to please, never deterred if ignored. A weakness of self-absorption faulting our human psyche, gratefully omitted in dogs' genetic makeup. No matter how many times they may be summarily dismissed, even cruelly, dogs remain on alert for a show of affection."

"'Senility, lost her perspective,' they surely concluded amongst themselves, prompted by what they believed was my irrational devotion. Never venturing close enough to express neighborly acknowledging nods, as if to avoid a contagion – shutting me out of their world, no room for me and my chosen life"

"I felt it necessary to chronicle these events as my life nears it's end. I recognize my words may never reach the eyes and ears of those who were insensitive to me, nonetheless I must try. Hopefully to be given opportunity for redemption hearing of it's reading, to seek open forgiveness amongst themselves, or pride accommodating travel within their consciousness, to cleanse of guilt, the injurious thoughtless words and inactions inflicted on me."

"Find in my words no animosity for those who ignored, whose ridicule of insinuation kept my wounds open and bleeding. Lacking understanding of the strength and comfort Norse and I choose to bring to one another. Not tolerant of my selection."

"I go to my Maker forgiving. I know that most acted out of ignorance and selfishness, refusing to see a material or spiritual worth in a human/animal relationship. They who continually chose to ignore this blessing, visible before their eyes, preferring the ease of ridicule rather than a deeper understanding. Redemption, if granted the opportunity, will be theirs when called away from their earthly possessions in the sheer nakedness of their spirit. Their eternity to be salvaged when seeing the joy of our earthly bond continuing as ordained by God in the hereafter. I forgive you as you did not sin but unto yourself, not knowing the beauty and peace of accommodation when alive – for your not understanding that all God's creatures can feel. That one must have an opportunity to express. Should I have turned from fulfilling communiqués to a mode more conventional? Ignoring an outlet restoring to me what God had bestowed then taken, glorying in the memories."

"This path I chose, eased the despair and pain of barrenness that crowds my interrupted sleep. In noiseless darkness, empty of shape, character, panic reigns in it's frightening abyss. During this interminable period I do not pray for the medicinal powers of sleep as I would fall prey to dreams that would truly haunt me. My labored breathing breaking the silence my only companion during my intermittent sleep. Deprived, I anticipated being taken before the sunlight of morning illuminates the room. At the benevolence of my God, I am still earth bound my soul still within me presenting the time once again to make visible all of my cherished photographs.

"It is Norse's photo's depicting various representations that transports him to live again his dual role, appearing not only as himself to give us stolen time together, his death to soon, but representations of my husband, who having lived a full life soul awaits us in Gods kingdom. My programmed Norse images him as I encouraged – a symbolic representation, whose spiritual presence approves the portrayal. I and Norse are together again. The energies of the photo's fulfilling – I am no longer alone. His protecting companionship present again, his scent real and permeating. Familiar is his soft kiss to my longing hands and face. Soothing is his expressive stare of love as his photographs become alive; joining me. I fight hard to keep this image foremost in my thoughts exempting the reality of his passing. I draw back the sun blocking drapes to see the morning sunlight highlighting, glistening the trees and flowers still wet from the morning dew. I accept the new day as Gods will, my visualizations flourishing. My biological clock continuing it's final unwinding until spent of motion, my Gods decision.

With trepidation George Staves slowed to read Mrs. Springer's words, it's current path suggesting she would reveal the presence of Norse's ashes resting within the lawn. Continuing he was relieved it was not her admission.

"I went amongst my garden to reflect, to tend to it's needs, my remaining life's devotion during the hours of daylight. Uneasiness began to grip me as the days grew shorter, facing me with greater periods of terrifying darkness. Narrowing those sustaining illuminating periods, where I can culture representations of my loved ones during the nutrient of natural light, relishing the story of the photographs, until the arrival of darkness of night and fatiguing intermittent sleep that brings forth periods of time that terrify the fragile living. I am ready and pray for my makers deliverance"

Expectantly the writing which had become more sporadic ended. George Staves acknowledging in her death, her letter one of reconciliation, communicating on her terms, asking for no pardons for her remaining life of separation. The rest of the paper was blank, the author's disclosure losing it's written life. It wasn't coincidental that the last words she gave voice to was fatalistic, she was contributing to her death, making it imminent her wishes, leaving one life's form for another. For a place deeply believed to hold the promise that it is timeless for a being in spiritual form.

Sorrow dominated George Staves at the abrupt ending of her letter. Symbolic, the finality of her death he believed coming with her last chronicled words.

"She died with a broken heart," George Staves said in sadness. "She couldn't deal with her loss; a willing participant, almost suicidal in bringing about her demise. She had no earthly reason to live proceeding unhesitatingly toward her fate, guided by her belief she would rejoice in another world with her family once lost, but now found in death, for eternity."

He turned to face the Schindlers saying, "Thank you for letting me read the letter."

"Even though you said your relationship with Mrs. Springer was relatively new, the letter was essentially written to you," Mr. Schindler said.

George nodded in agreement. "It provided some answers for me and others."

Mr. Schindler agreed, "I could tell from your facial expressions that her words had an effect on you."

Again he nodded.

"My wife and I, complete strangers to Mrs. Springer, are moved every time we read it. It is so sad, so tragic, capturing your sympathy. While it is in some sense a letter for the general, she did mention your name, no others, except her niece but only in reference as having kin, not in name. She showing no interest ignored her chance to take possession of the letter earlier. For that reason we would like you to take the letter rather than send it to her uncaring relative."

Noticing George's reluctance, Mrs. Schindler added quickly, "It really belongs with you. Somehow I believe she knew it would wind up in your hands. Please take it."

Still he hesitated, briefly trying to gather his thoughts. What would I do with it, he asked himself. Still uncertain, he replied, "I will but only with your understanding that I might find another home for it, one that is more fitting."

They agreed, handing him the letter which he pocketed.

"Before you leave, Mr. Staves," Mr. Schindler said, "we would like to share something with you."

He followed them to the back of the house to the flowering dogwood tree. George stood there uncertain, not knowing their purpose, controlling his suspicions. Still confused he offered, "What a beautiful tree. It shows a lot of care."

"Yes, the tree is beautiful," Mrs. Schindler said, "but look closely to where I'm pointing."

George followed the direction of her pointing finger, finally spotting what she was asking that he acknowledge. A piece of metal imbedded at the base of the tree. Intrigued, he dropped to his knees for a closer look. Finding there were actually two separate pieces of metal firmly nailed in place; one a dog tag round in shape that read simply the current year, licensing county, name, license number, issuing state and the word "dog" impression stamped. The second piece of metal shaped like a tablet read from top to bottom:

Norse-
I belong to
The Springers
715 Roslyn Ave.
Highland Heights, OH
(216) 563-3532

"It is Mrs. Springer's memorial to her dog," Staves said reflectively. "She had that tree planted in his memory."

"We guessed that. We will not remove them," Mrs. Schindler said with commitment. "They will stay in place as long as we are here and as long as nature will allow. We both being gardeners will certainly keep up Mrs. Springer's good work and care."

George again wondered what their reaction would be if they knew Norse's ashes lay within their lawn and in reality the license and ownership tags were Norse's headstone. He found no reason to tell them.

The quiet observance around the tree was broken by the slamming of a car door, turning everyone's attention to the street.

"It's Mr. Mercer," Mr. Schindler announced, directing his comments to George Staves. "He's the lawyer I told you about. He represents Mrs. Springer's estate."

George nodded uncomfortably, not pleased with having to be in his company. He would have preferred avoiding him, so distasteful was the memory.

Mr. Mercer walked purposefully along the newly cut lawn, a man on a mission, joining them at the dogwood tree. He was dressed as George remembered him, typically lawyerly: a dark blue suit with a hint of a gray pencil stripe, a light metallic blue tie reflective as if polished, matching suspenders, all covering and defining a swelling five foot ten inch frame. His coat jacket was deliberately open to minimize a paunch that was straining his waistline. His slow-to-gray black hair, suspected of close maintenance by him and his sworn-to-secrecy barber, was carefully coiffed, every hair lacquered in place. An understated moustache, while partially framing, failed to subdue a rather large mouth. Always on display, never missing an opportunity to proclaim himself relevant, attached to his lapel was the familiar signature emblem of the Fraternal Order of Masons. Contacts his purpose rather than brotherhood, his suspicion. Seeing him again after all this time suggested little had changed in his style of living: best clothes, regular visits to a hair stylist, eating out often at the best of restaurants, credentials at the most exclusive of country clubs. Vainness walked with every step he took, moving quickly as if contemptuous of his shadow, unable to deceive when standing perpendicular, the sun casting truthfulness.

"Ah, there you are Mr. and Mrs. Schindler. I thought I might have missed you. I suppose I could have called but I decided to chance it," he said theatrically.

"You would have, but we had an unexpected visitor. This is Mr. George Staves," said Mr. Schindler politely introducing them.

Mr. Mercer disingenuous turned, showing pretending warmth held out his hand to George Staves "I know this man," he said to the Schindlers in his stare down. "He proved to be a worthy and respected adversary. We had a significant cause where we clashed. He representing the establishment, and I a devoted servant to the outcast and ignored," he pontificated, his ego being self-served

Shamelessly twisting the facts, George Staves said to himself. Normally tolerant, he was contemptuous of this man of contradictions, weakly clutched Mr. Mercer's extended hand, signally a response lacking warmth. Withdrawing his hand, silently nodding an acknowledgement

"Mr. Staves was a friend of Mrs. Springer," Mrs. Schindler offered. "You know in the letter that she had written?"

"Indeed," Mr. Mercer said. "I was in the process of trying to contact you, Mr. Staves. You know you are not listed in the phone book. Inaccessible to us common folk." His sarcasm implying privilege angered George Staves. "I was about to instruct my secretary to contact the police department for their help. This is indeed fortuitous meeting like this. I assume you know from the Schindler's that I'm handling the affairs of Mrs. Springer. The estate has been settled. I just have a few minor issues to conclude that involve you."

Warily, George Staves was on guard. "I was just someone who befriended her. I'm deeply saddened to hear of her death. Why would you need to contact me?"

"You're named in Mrs. Springer's confidential documents she instructed I write, which is what I'd like to talk to you about. As this obviously is not the right time, can I call so that we may meet? You know, she was very fond of you. And, oh yes of your terrorizing dog recognizing no boundaries, whom I and the police are familiar," he said with a feigned smile, confusing the Schindlers with his couching dialogue.

His last barb at Tasha, a misrepresentation, was not unexpected, knowing their history of meeting one another in conflict. What angered Staves further was his discovering Tasha's accidental incident as a puppy of biting Phyllis. The man was unscrupulous in what he would seek out to gain advantage. George Staves would parry his cutting thrust in due time.

While Staves would normally shun a relationship with this man, an obligation to Mrs. Springer existed. "Of course," he said reluctantly.

"May I have your unlisted home phone number?" Mr. Mercer asked.

"Keep it private," George Staves reminded, "I only give it out to close friends, never to anyone engaged in commerce. I know all about how telephone solicitation lists evolve." His insult as cutting as a surgeon.

Mr. Mercer's retort, "Mr. Staves my firm does not need to generate income or favors in that manner. We are a law firm that respects and is obligated to confidentiality."

The Schindlers were mystified, looked questioningly at one another, the dislike their two visitors had for one another was obvious.

"I live in the same house. You know the one you already visited," George Staves continued sarcastically, furthering the Schindlers confusion in the unraveling animus.

Mercer nodded contemptuously, his once forgotten recollection of his last visit to Staves home caused him to fidget at the Schindlers puzzled look. Trumped, he ended his parrying exchange, his score settling would be hatched at another day.

George Staves left wishing the Schindlers good luck with the house. They graciously invited him to visit, qualifying to any time during the summer months, noting that they and most of their neighbors spent the harsh winters in Florida. He thanked them.

"Counselor," Staves nodded in strained politeness as he left. Quickening his step as he walked back to his car.

On Staves' drive back to his home his thoughts were exclusively on Mrs. Springer and her death. His initial reaction of guilt, reined to a more appropriate, "taken aback and sympathetic" attitude. His mollifying distancing not diminishing the profound impact on him reading her letter. Each compelling word bringing him closer to the divide that a surging empathy would propel him to cross. His relationship, thought at arms length, now possessed him with self-criticism. It was burdening and emotionally draining, so impacting were the letter's pained words, opening his heart to her deep wounds.

Beyond the letters capturing words that transformed him, were the deeply touched relative strangers: the Schindlers. Conversely the words of notice from her obnoxious lawyer Robert Mercer disturbingly implied George Staves future involvement would be more relevant. Increasing his involvement and intimacy, certain to engage him from just being respectful of the deceased. His sympathy to obligate him, invalidating any thought of his preference to be peripheral. A fringe allegiance no longer appropriate, foregoing viewing his role as being in the back ground, a casual friend, fittingly not required to attend her wake, choosing to say his good bye's waiting in his car or as a pedestrian at curbside, paying his last respects at her passing funeral procession had there been one. He was convinced this would have been an appropriate response had he read her death notice, not being made privy to her impacting letter. But now things were different, his emotional landscape changed. To be altered further Staves suspected, from Mercer's implication, moving him in involvement to the forefront.

His mind built an image of himself one day at her burial site, saying a prayer, leaving blooming Dogwood flowers as his tribute. Now situated by virtue of reading her impassioned letter, and his brief conversation with Mercer implying a secret covenant involving him, making it impossible to avoid a greater intimacy after Mrs. Springer's death. He did not relish the thought of sharing in a secret with the distrustful Mercer. The consequences, he could only hope, if the covenant were made public would be minimal. His concerns he decided to table, not knowing what was being asked of him. He would be guarded, but refused to speculate further.

He then turned to his effort to alleviate her grief while alive, as he continued his drive home. Disappointingly unsuccessful, failing to draw her out of her despair; to share her grief with others equally destroyed. His troubling failure, initiated a mind search as to what he would do with her chronicle, that would be appropriate. Finally deciding on a course of action: seeking out a responsive Web site from the Internet, selecting one from the many listed support group's for grieving pet owners. Discoursing concurrence that Mrs. Springer's last words were their awakening, they consciously or unconsciously mired in a stunted recovery. Giving them pause to incentive redirection. A reason for correction from traveling the same ill fated path chosen by Mrs. Springer, tracking certain death. His thought's, inescapable from Mrs. Springer's tragedy, her words in retrospect a message, suggesting the ignored healing powers of reconciliation for others in the throes of bereaving pain for the loss of a pet – righting themselves – ending their punishment. An unintended but welcomed salvation for others, her final tribute.

No matter how he tried to think otherwise, George Staves kept coming back to Mrs. Springer's tragedy. He knew that this episode in his life, the turning of its page, would not happen until he found closure with Robert Mercer.

~

The transporter seeming to anticipate, its engine inhaling deeply readying its power for another part of the journey. This time he willed it not be chronological, but to travel in reverse, to find the past within the past. Its chronograph quickly shuddering it into a stall after almost imperceptible movement had it not been for the imagery which was new. He delivered himself to the time period on display; the source of his dislike of Robert Mercer.

Leaving the ranks of the parochial electorate, he was elected to a school board that represented three school districts; serving consecutively three four-year terms. The final term as president of the five-member board. All terms were served at the will of the people. He learned quickly that the darts and arrows of heated criticism he once unhesitatingly flung would be taken up by others and just as fervently directed toward him. His previous alignment with the voters proved of no consequence, their parochial interests dominating, at times contemptuous of his opposition, dismissing as dogmatic when acting in allegiances for the institution, to which he pledged to serve. He considered himself thick-skinned no matter how pointed the criticism. Almost all issues that came before the school board, were not usually contentious. The rules of parliamentary procedure diligently followed to permit governance. The usual issues; budgets, and allocation of funds, while encouraged for strong debate, were typically handled in relative calm at the mandated regularly scheduled weekly meetings.

The school board's mission was to ensure that most high school graduates were prepared for further academic or technical education or were able to enter and advance in the skilled workforce. The foundation of this commitment was through the shared responsibility of students, family, and community, to become productive members of society and lifelong learners.

Those controversial unavoidable special meetings, the issue's magnitude so fevered, they would deteriorate, the basic decency of people cast aside, overruled by emotions discharging the worst in people. Civility and respect ending up being victims, forsaken by the uncompromising, the blindly angered developing mob like vehemence: spewed venom coming from both sides of an issue. The school board – the arbitrator, on the receiving end of dislike and resentment; theirs a can't win situation – both sides feeling equally abandoned, prejudiced against.

"The greater good for the greater number." That basic tenet a protection of earlier courts formidable, heretofore an impediment, the words *a catch all* preventing state constitutional challenge – It's invincibility presumed if carried to final arbitration. Advocates of change disputing that "the greater good" policy was not inclusive enough.

Special meeting issues required a give and take exchange, a willingness to embrace modification. Extremism on either side of an issue sometimes turned hostile – attempting to intimidate.

It was on such an occasion, the first of many heated debates on the issue of admissions, that George Staves first encountered Mr. Robert Mercer. An activist lawyer who preened himself before reporters trying cause *celebré* issues portraying himself as a principled ideologue, a defender of the underdog and the downtrodden. His conscience to right a wrong a smoke screen, as he was driven by fees. He accepted no contingency cases and was usually conveniently unavailable for *pro bono work* unless, as was often rumored, they masked other lucrative retainers: his *quid pro quo*. Fitting his criteria, a public dividing issue, one resistant to change, presented itself for his challenge. Contending the admissions policy was not all inclusive, orphaning a minority. On opposite sides would be their introduction.

Before the school board came the matter of a Down Syndrome young girl of fifteen. All through her years of schooling, Lydia Santos had been educated at state supported schools for slow learners. The child's mother, Gloria Santos, deciding that at this point in her child's education the special state funded schools designed to handle and respond to her child's needs had become too burdensome and distant to travel. Presenting an unnecessary inconvenience that would readily be relieved if Lydia's educational needs were served by the local high school.

George Staves remembered Mrs. Santos saying that she would pursue this objective unrelentingly with no border uncrossable. Reminding all who would listen, or who she could corner, or write, that the local high school within her district could accommodate her daughter, having considerably greater access to state funds which she as a taxpayer contributed to and yet was unavailable to her child in her circumstance. Special schools available to her and her child's special needs, at best a poor solution in the overall – separation in this case lacking parity.

Contemptuous in her denouncement of school policy as unchallenging to her daughter, "Funding," she belittled scornfully, "crumbs left over from a bountiful table." Not to be deterred, reacting as a lioness protecting her cub from those who would do her harm, snarling warnings, ready to attack, regardless of institution or individual. She wore her impenetrable armor well, resisting catcalls and insults, hiding her dismay when friends joined strangers in one condemning voice. Not discouraged, she found supporters among her liberal bent neighbors who, without hesitation, signed her petition – funding, joined the fray.

Also offering moral and advisory support was a Mrs. Sylvia Price, a lawyer from a civil liberties group recognized as a grand defender of constitutional rights no matter how stretched it's interpretation, or the murkiness of previous law-making court precedents. Orchestrating and coordinating this growing alliance was Mr. Robert Mercer. This ensemble with the support of many petitioned signatures could not be denied, powering successfully for a special meeting to review the school board's position on admissions.

Word spread like wildfire, the issue quite fractious, stirring up emotions, pitting neighbors against neighbor. George Staves found himself unavoidably personally involved. Gloria Santos and her daughter Lydia lived on his street. While not close, they still knew one another, engaging in cordial talk whenever they would meet, particularly when walking Tasha who would greet a delighted Lydia with unrestrained affection. That cordiality would certainly change as he would immediately be branded unresponsive to individual rights if Mrs. Santos' petition was denied.

He remembered the many phone calls. At first they were from reasonable people from his district not reluctant to identify themselves. A slight majority was held by those who viewed with distrust the prospect of changing the admissions policy. Opponents and proponents expressing their views strongly, equally trying to draw out his uncommitted position. Highly influential in command, having the power, they suggested since he was board president, he could use his office to influence other board members particularly those who might be straddling the fence. Those phone calls ended in disappointment as he remained duty bound to be neutral, particularly until everyone was heard from.

With the scheduled board meeting drawing near, anonymous calls became more frequent, resisting their pleas for support, he would listen but not express his position publicly, rushing his judgment. The extremists pro and con interpreting his judiciousness as a sign that he was siding with the opposition.

In the final days before the meeting disturbing calls from what he thought were outside agitators were received, spewing hateful venom and threats, the message was always the same, "It would be in his and his family's best interests not to change the admissions policy." Going beyond reason, they predicted the demise of the school system, if not prevailing. Their time at home with little peace, he and his wife decided not to answer the phone unless screened. In constant contact with the other board members, George Staves learned that they too had received threatening phone calls, unhesitatingly reported to the police. Receiving the promise of increased patrol surveillance of their neighborhoods and a heavy police presence at the board meeting.

On the day of the meeting George Staves decided to have Tasha accompany him. A menacing visible guard, a dissuading formidable presence for those who might plan an alcohol influenced personal confrontation, she an augment to the police K-9 German Shepherds brought for crowd control. They arrived early. Tasha at his command sat down, her head between her front paws and watched with great curiosity as the school auditorium filled to standing room only. Tasha, not going unnoticed, lay at his feet as still as a concrete molded library lion, likened to the guardian; welcoming those seeking enlightenment, until aroused.

George Staves tried unsuccessfully to gavel the overflowing audience to order. The crowd noisy with shouts and epithets from both factions, took five attempts to quiet. Finally, forsaking the gavel, the public address system announced threats of ending the meeting prematurely, bringing it to order.

George Staves, again a witness to the event, relived his acknowledging Gloria Santos as the first person to address the board on this issue. As vivid today in real time as it was then; her pleading words seeking compassion and understanding, sometimes a confessional of doubt, sometimes a soliloquy of innermost thoughts and challenges, disarming everyone assembled. Her supporters respectfully silent and attentive; her opposition critics equally compliant, acquiescent with claws retracted, ready to pounce on their activist counterparts once their respecting period was over, the issue returning to dominate, Gloria Santos telling of psychological wounds history. While speaking, both groups hung on every word she spoke. No one could remain coldly indifferent. Even her detractors' were affected, so strong the instinct to empathize for the blow cruel fate bestowed upon her. Her opponents would give her that much, but not the cause she championed which was beyond appeal no matter the circumstances.

Mrs. Santos spoke of marrying later in life, of her burning desire for motherhood in spite of her age. Overruling the counseling of her doctors on the risks she took. She would beat the odds. Her child would be born normal. This would be her only gambled chance as future pregnancies would increase the odds against a normal child being born. "Risk enhances reward," she said. She would put her trust in God heeding her prayers and not denying her His precious gift. George remembered her saying her world shattered when her blood tests, confirmed by ultrasound and amniocentesis, showed her expected child, a girl, would have Down Syndrome.

"Embittered in self-pity, I turned within myself," she began, the isolation of the alone. "I was quick to strike out at everyone and anyone, hearing but not listening, self-sequestered, distraught, not to be reconciled by reason. For this short period I did decry God," Mrs. Santos continued, choking back a sob, "for what I believed was his abandonment. But my faith did not remain buried in self-pity. It was resilient enough to recover, clearing a path to understanding that all was not lost. I had not lost. I had not miscarried. What would emerge painfully from me was not a dead fetus but a precious being birthing, one I could uncompromisingly accept, a child of God, in one of His many variations- the only constant; one of mothering need. Knowing in time this special child, growing to know her meaning and importance to me; returning it just as freely. This is what I would live for, my declaration. Not wallowing in sorrow, or irreverently referring to my gift as a mistake of nature."

"And when that baby came, who among you could have identified my baby's shortcomings? She looked and acted every bit as normal as any newborn. During my short period of depression, in blind anger I forecast my baby's physical abnormalities: blindness, deafness, a horror of science fiction. With God's help, my resurgence made me resolute. I would take this baby whatever its shortcomings and nurture it with love and understanding. And when baby Lydia arrived and I held and fed her for the first time, I was joyous with tears. I did not sense the chromosomal inhibiting disorder hidden in her genetic makeup – only a beautiful child. Once again I cried, this time with joy believing that I had been spared, that the tests were fallible, that God had intervened at the eleventh hour."

"The doctors quickly reined in my exuberance that a miracle had taken place. The tests were conclusive; baby Lydia was a Down syndrome baby. The degree of affliction I learned varies from baby to baby. The doctors explained patiently, "With some children it's in the later years of the child's development that the Down syndrome characteristics become noticeable." "The finality of the doctors' review, while emotionally disappointing, did not scar me with defeat as it brought me back to my earlier reality and commitment. Requesting once again God's forgiveness, I would not deny his assignment to me by being my own false prophet.

"I had not beaten the odds. I had given birth to a chromosome affected baby, a one-in-thirty expectancy for mothers at the age of forty-five. My reawakened reality did not deter me from trying to discover the differences as I found myself studying her intensely during feeding." Gloria Santos paused and smiled reflectively as she relived those moments, drawing the embracing looks of understanding from all hanging on to every word.

Continuing, she said, "She had five fingers on each hand, her toes the same. A typically beautiful cherubic face with not the slightest hint of the Down syndrome characteristics that would later surface. Yes, as she grew, the differences in her development with other children her age became more apparent. The retardation was expected and I dealt with it, sharing in Lydia's delight in her every new discovery no matter how late in her development cycle. While I was prepared for it, I never anticipated Lydia's reaction when she finally realized she was different from other children, tearfully questioning why she did not have the skills and abilities of other children."

"'Why am I still learning to ride my bike?' she would ask tearfully. 'Why am I not able to jump rope quick enough like the other girls?' 'They don't like playing with me,' she would cry. Her playmates, joined in laughter, turned to ridicule when Lydia was unable to remember how to spell her name. 'Why can't I remember every time?' she would ask of me. And then came the cruel pranks that only bullying children would think were humorous, gleefully delighting in turning innocence to tears."

"My heart broke, succumbing to anger, I lashed out and denounced all that was holy to me, a reaction in motherly protection. Atypical, I distanced myself from my religiosity, once again the fissure of an earthquake venting from hell the irreligious question of why a loving God would create such a mistake in nature, leaving it in its innocence to suffer for the pleasure of those more in His image. My understanding was driven from me. My purposed test disavowed. I chose at that moment to descend into self-serving weakness forsaking my strength of commitment to curse my imprisonment. Cruelly declaring myself in servitude to abnormality, I screamed the question, 'Why? Why did the favored, unencumbered move freely, nothing more asked of them?' I did not need this experience which I judged to be punishment for unknown transgressions. To be damned was too heavy a payment for my faulted motherhood, I conveniently profaned.

"And then while holding my child in my arms trying to soothe her hurt, my blinding thoughts of condemnations were washed from my consciousness by Lydia's tears, reminding that I had turned my back on true motherhood. I had been charged by God to provide for her. She would be my ministry, I her parishioner in an extension of the church. Alterless, advancing the need for compassion and understanding needed by the handicapped or ill. The world to revolve equally for them; I pledged. Their lives would not be cheapened or disenfranchised. That would be my calling to which I would answer and defend. It became my cause, not only for Lydia, but for all children with manageable disabilities that societies ignorance treated as a inconvenience. It became my passion.

"I searched and studied every bit of information I could find on the subject and the care required of these children. I found in my research what I felt was significant and held out an opportunity to assist nature's shortcomings. Even though the tests were performed on lower animals, research suggested that mothers' nurturing stimulated neural connections in their babies' brains, enhanced learning; implicitly suggesting that it was broadly applicable to humans also. It's never nurture vs. nature, the influences are inseparable. Activity of the genes is always influenced by the environment. And the most important feature of an environment for an infant is its mother.

"Here was my answer. Here was my challenge. I had received God's message. Here within myself was the power to manipulate some of Lydia's disconnects, her discharges, stunted and falling short within her mental grid, influenced to closer proximity of connection, rewarded with improved skills. The evidence was there in the study: A direct relationship had been found between maternal care and Hippocampus development and spatial learning in adulthood. It is experience-dependent development. Use it and it grows. Don't and it disappears. My task became my full absorption and devotion.

"It cost me my marriage but that did not stop me. I was not distracted. Nothing would deter me. My daughter and I go beyond the bond of the same blood flowing through our veins. Figuratively, we are joined at the hip like Siamese twins, my intellect in part transferable, a teaching experience, showing increases to her level of understanding, she draws from it when needed; a nurturing contribution. I became obsessed with providing for my daughter, enthused that I could heighten her vision. To what extent, while limited I did not know, but change and improvement could be made as had been demonstrated. Armed with this knowledge, I'm determined to share this light.

"God had provided me a path to which I became dedicated. Lydia's response has been so rewarding. I have a loving daughter who is able to read and write beyond the basics, capable of making herself understood. Mischievous but not disruptive. Dependent upon others when needed, yes. An inconvenience, no. How could she? She's a child of God, a special child."

Mrs. Santos spoke tearfully of the pains of separation her daughter experienced as she and her playmates went their separate ways to school. "She found herself among strangers who, while resembling her physically, she could not comprehend." Mrs. Santos spoke of the great distances her daughter had to be bussed to get to her special school; the many times she had to drive her to school herself when her daughter deliberately missed the bus in the hope that she would go to the same school as her neighborhood playmates; hysterical with grief when she was forced into the car for the lengthy drive to school. "She knows that she is different from her playmates but as they grow older and more mature, they make accommodations for her. Her friends who once ridiculed her now openly demonstrate personal enrichment for their association. All she wants and needs is their nearness and touch. They don't feel threatened or burdened. She is not diseased. Her condition is not infectious."

"Why should she be separated?" she accused. The softness leaving her voice "She carries no contagion to pass on to others. Your children's being at risk, deprived or in harm's way is a hurtful misrepresentation. Her love for others radiates from her entire being."

"Don't stand in her way. Let her make this world a better place. Compassion was Jesus's countenance even as he was being put to death. Should we not in His spirit show the same in assisting a life in need?" she demanded of them.

Mrs. Santos finished her emotional plea with the admonition, "We are all equal under God. Do not violate His dictum. We are not separated; praying together, receiving His sacraments together. We are bound together for His teachings. Just as you, my daughter is part of His flock on earth, so will she be worthy in His kingdom. Thank you for hearing me," she concluded. Acknowledging the school board with a head nodding, her eyes fixed on George Staves, searching. She sat down wearily, smiling at her supporters, her spirit undiminished.

Sobs could be heard coming from the audience. Many handkerchiefs became visible within the hands of the unashamed. Ohers choked back tears, hoping to avoid attention when drawing deep breaths. The hardened of Mrs. Santos' opposing critics visage while conciliatory, beneath it's surface remained untempered, uncompromised in their fight to prevent change.

The next item to be offered up for board review was the signature petition of supporting neighbors and district residents, their number far and away exceeding the minimum.

"For further study and verification," George Staves motioned as the petition was made part of the record.

Next came the Civil Liberties lawyer, Mrs. Sylvia Price, who defended Lydia Santos' rights under the Equal Rights Amendment of the Constitution condescendingly extracting her interpretation: the law of the land was being violated. Dramatically fiery in proclaiming this issue of national significance and implication, weighty enough to continue a appeal to the courts if an unfavorable ruling were made by the school board was her scorching reproach.

Her highly incendiary threatening statement brought the opposing audience, entranced during Mrs. Santos' heart wrenching story, to seething hostility, shouting heated catcalls of "Pressure tactics" and "What about our rights? What about our protection under the Constitution?"

So elevated were the emotions that a deeply concerned George Staves heavily gaveled unsuccessfully, threatening the expulsion of the unruly. The threat finally restoring order. Again warning the audience against further outbursts as he acknowledged Mr. Mercer as the next speaker. Finding it necessary, he reached down to calm an aroused and growling Tasha.

Continuing the assault on the precedents of the admissions policy, it being no secret as Mr. Mercer, to raise the consciousness of the conscientious, forewarned his diatribe in the newspapers. Pursuing that tactic in this open forum, he brought the still buzzing crowd to its feet. In a worthy of an award performance of self-righteous indignation he accused the school board for not being responsible members, of ignoring the needs of the whole community, practicing favoritism, and being discriminatory. Ignoring the restrained hostility, confident in the phalanx of policemen and supporters around him, he flaunted his penchant for the theatrical, accusingly pointing his finger at the supporters of the status quo, he Samson they Goliath. His self-empowering importance inflated his ego, undeclared, *the under* study position of the school board on this matter he stated, "was a coded prejudice perpetuating inequality." Moralizing those opposed to change in the admissions policy are on the wrong side of the issue, their duty to be courageously proactive, safe and secure decisions are for cowards; he insulted. Raising his voice, challenging those on the dias with the opportunity to participate in history making. His remarks and belittling tone inflaming. He elicited screaming shouts of "no, no!" coming from the aroused.

He followed the lead of Mrs. Price, that the issue was growing in importance nation wide as reported in the media, the local school boards decision sure to interest lawmakers at both the state and federal level. Mercer promised his involvement to fruition no matter where it takes him, his plan's in place for the next step following an unfavorable school boards decision. In his finale he warned that he was aware of the board members' places of business, their church affiliations and locations, where they currently resided. Promising fervently that the signers of the petition would take to the streets as well as every shopping center – anywhere people met. "We will be there. We will slow down traffic, delay commerce, delay school classes, delay school bus arrivals and departures. Our cause is just." he bellowed, "It is important enough to risk jail. We will not be denied, we will persevere."

Following Mr. Mercer's vitriolic rhetoric, as if receiving a call to action by a Hollywood director, the divided crowd rose menacingly to its feet in a highly volatile state, screaming threats at one another from across the separating aisle. The crowd was out of control, posing distinct threats to one another, the police physically restraining the more combative from attacking one another.

The board, acted quickly to defuse the situation, passing a motion of cessation of further business. George Staves gaveled furiously to restore order, unsuccessful he was forced to shout above the bedlam as the public address system's wiring had been deliberately disconnected. "The meeting is now adjourned. A vote meeting is to be announced," George Staves shouted as he and the other board members availed themselves of their encircling police escort, attempting to leave the melee behind them.

Reaching the parking lot, George saw from the periphery of his vision that protagonist Robert Mercer, the attorney for the petitioner, had moved quickly to meet him, his directed police escort clearing the way. Trailing the Mercer entourage was a local news reporter frantically speaking into a voice recorder. Reaching Staves just as he was about to enter his car, to the concern of his police escort, allowing Mercer to resume his unrelenting tirade, demanding answers to questions he would have asked had the meeting continued.

Mercer shouted above the din, the pace of his pursuit of Staves amongst all the joustling, taxing his breath, "I heard you mention a vote meeting by the board. Will I be able to attend?" he wheezed.

"You will be invited to hear the tally," George Staves replied impatiently.

"How the individual board members voted?."

"No, only the tally," Staves repeated.

"It's illegal not to hold a public meeting. It's your duty and our right to attend," Mercer insinuated in criticism.

"Which we did. That meeting was held tonight with the public invited. You know, the one we just left. The one you helped end prematurely," Staves said sarcastically. Not pausing for a response that he was sure would be defensive, he continued, "We will take more testimony. We will have precedents to consider, judgments from our lawyers, all will be made part of the record, all to be reviewed at a private meeting by all members of the board without threat or intimidation. We are well within our authority under our By-Laws and Code of Regulations to conduct private meetings."

"If unfavorable, we will challenge that decision," Robert Mercer said repeating his threat.

"Do as you wish. We are in complete compliance as chartered. We will fulfill our obligations to our district members," George Staves answered dismissively.

Mr. Mercer's facial expression changed dramatically, his tactics failing, Staves would not be intimidated. It began with his eyes nervously blinking as if trying to clear an irritant, fanning them to tearfulness, a condition of his beginning anger and exasperation. His carefully attended face, his jaw typically set strongly, his self- assured defiance, all practiced, lost their effectiveness, his face reddened by his rising blood pressure. Heated to overcooked by anger, his thespian manner losing expression, leaving him vulnerable and reachable, egoless, and susceptible. Resourceful, as if he held a mirror before him presenting his image not to his specifications, regrouped quickly, he reascended to his lofty throne.

"And how will you vote?" Robert Mercer asked in a new strength of biting sarcasm, perceptive in recognizing Staves's internal conflict with the issue.

"The balloting will be secret," George Staves hastened, temporarily caught off guard by Mercer's quick turnaround and disturbing insightfulness. Disengaging, he moved quickly toward his car with Tasha in tow, moving past the reporter who had recorded the brief exchange. He was finished with his questions, and impatient with his arrogance. Robert Mercer, had more to say and moved to block his passage, going so far as to put his right hand to George Staves' chest in an attempt to stop him. A regrettable mistake as Tasha, reading his move as a threat, leaped, driving her front paws into Robert Mercer's chest so forcefully that it drove him backward, pinning him against the car completely immobilized, pitifully staring at the snarling jaws of Tasha. Desperate, he screamed for help.

"You ought to know better than to show a hostile act toward me in her presence," George Staves chastised as he pulled Tasha off of him, secretly pleased that an audience witnessed Tasha diminish Mercer's stature, making him cower.

Unhurt but pallid, Mercer, trembling, ceremoniously wiped himself clean of Tasha's paw prints. His ego the only injury, playing to the building onlookers his histrionics claiming an unwarranted attack. Finding no support he soon muted his verbal distortion of the event, his account challenged by the police and the newspaper reporter, confirming that he had provoked Tasha's reaction.

His moment compromised, a rebuked Robert Mercer surrounded by police and supporters, watched George Staves leave, his car and his path cleared of angered people by the police, who were continually commanding everyone return to their vehicles. While the pace was slow, people kept moving preventing gathering, lessoning a strength in numbers aggression.

During the weeks that followed while each board member studied the issue, often consulting with one another or seeking legal advice from counsel, they knew no peace. They were subjected to a never-ending harangue of condemning newspaper public opinions, receiving phone calls from both sides of the issue at all hours of the day and night. Because they, in most cases remained non-committal, they were cast adrift by neighbors who once were friends, prematurely drawing conclusions, interpreting the evasive responses as a counter position.

As the judgment day of the merits of the petition drew close, the dichotomy transformed, Confidence exuding, the opponents of the issue, buoyed by editorial comments and public opinions, citing the logic of precedents of record, anonymous sources politically connected, the impetus for the boards majority to vote against revision of the admissions policy, toned down their rhetoric. While proponents, enflamed by the same commentary, were spurred to even more aggressive demonstrations, their battle was just beginning. Fired up there would be no bounds, or restrictions in the final efforts to influence the vote in their favor.

The most disturbing tactic of the petitioners demonstrations George Staves was about to experience. At home the Staves accompanied by their daughter Phyllis, Rosanne at a sleep over, Edward at a movie with friends, occasioned discussions on the day's events including the exhausting countless phone calls. Tasha heard the commotion at the front of the house before they did. Alerted, she bolted from her comfortable reclining position at his feet, rushed to the living room bow window and as she was prone to do if alerted, leaped upon the ledge from which the bow window began it's distinct segmented curve away from the house Standing, Tasha displacing pillows, parted the drapes with her nose, beginning a low guttural growl of disapproving aggressiveness – her response to what had disturbed her. George and Rose quickly joined Tasha; Rose pulling the drapes further apart.

Startlingly, there stood a group of eight people, married couples recognized by the Staves's as belonging to the neighborhood – some from his own street. Within their midst stood Robert Mercer handing out signs to the would-be pickets. An incredulous George Staves ordered his wife and daughter to stay in the house with Tasha, preferring they not be involved in his confrontation with their neighbors. His patience exhausted charged through the front door, each step becoming increasingly agitated and confrontational. Ignoring his picketing neighbors, he went straight to the obvious instigator, the source of his anger; Robert Mercer.

"What do you think you're doing?" George asked irately.

"We are continuing our just cause. Taking to the streets and informing people of the correctness of our position," Mercer answered dismissively.

"By picketing my house?"

"You are a school board member, the president. You cast a giant shadow," he patronized.

George Staves responded angrily, "I told you at the school board meeting, this issue will be reviewed thoroughly and given full consideration. What you are doing is contemptible. You and your followers have had your say. What you are doing is no more than a pressure tactic. There's no end to your brazenness; influencing my neighbors, who I believe are sincere in their beliefs, to become your co-conspirators, denying the will and rights of others to disagree, corrupting the democratic process."

"A democratic process is the fair distribution of rights to be enjoyed by all," Mercer said pompously, pleased at the provided opening.

"Don't indulge me with your insincere declarations You are no more than a mercenary under the guise of championing a cause?" Staves anger increased. "You are a hypocrite. You'll not find justice by practicing pressure tactic."

George turned his attention to his neighbors – Pleading "You know me. Don't fall for the line of lies you are hearing from this contemptible man, a divisive stranger with an ax to grind. God knows, I know you're sincere in your beliefs in this issue, but this is not the way. You'll gain nothing by this action except lose a friend. Please leave now before this goes any further. This country was founded on the principles of democracy for the will of the people. Majority rules. Don't be party to an agent of divisiveness, agitating at someone's home, violating personal rights, to impose his will. Don't move in lock step with Mercer and his hidden agenda. Let the process work. It always has."

His plea drew the response of, "You're a member of a failed system." His neighbors turning away from him, insulted at his suggestion that they were being manipulated as puppets, given life only by the will and whim of their puppet master, Mercer; manipulated all their strings.

"We are as one," Mercer said. "There is no turning back. Our cause is just. We are united."

George Staves's neighbors, as if mesmerized, clinging to every word Mercer said, echoed, "We are as one."

"We are acting on your behalf to alert you that your supporting a prejudice, You and others like you, need enlightenment." Mercer pontificated.

Continuing their solidarity. Staves' a neighbor shouted, "See it our way." at their perceived enemy.

"I have my responsibility. Doing this is not right."

"We are acting lawfully. We have a right to express our views no matter where it takes us. This is democracy in action," Mercer continued, relishing his role.

Staves shaking his head in discouragement at his neighbors enmity retorted, "I'm duly elected. I took an oath. I won't be intimidated into surrendering my independence. As far as your right to picket, we'll soon see about that," cheered as he spotted two police cars pulling up to the curb. He learned later that his wife had called the police for assistance.

Police Chief Felice whom the Staves family knew very well approached them with his fellow officers, his demeanor uncertain.

"I'm glad you're here, Chief," Staves said, his anger and exasperation quieting somewhat, "They're here to picket my house, verbally attacking me personally."

Police Chief Felice, who was nearing retirement, George Staves knew was against changing the admissions policy having two sons in the challenged school, responded, "You're not going to like what I tell you… I'm sorry, George… They have a right to picket. The right of the Free Speech Amendment, as long as they don't walk on your property. The county sidewalk is public property and as a consequence, they have a right to use it, expressing their free speech. I must advise you not to interfere," he said almost apologetically.

George Staves had known this but still he had hoped that his personal relationship with some of the picketers and the presence of the police would dissuade them to pursue other means rather than personalizing it. Realizing that would not be the case, defeated he addressed Chief Felice while returning to the house, his tone still angry. "They can have it, even though you and I know, they are manipulating free speech to pressure me. I certainly don't want to be accused of violating their rights," he said sarcastically, adding threateningly, "If any of them violate my property, I want them arrested for trespassing."

"We have no choice," a flustered Staves said to his wife as he re-entered his home. "The law is on their side."

Rose, equally angered, blocked the front door with her body, preventing Tasha from visiting with the intruders.

"While you were outside arguing, all your board members called. It seems we are not alone. They all are experiencing Mercer's picketing tactics."

George Staves returned the board members calls, hearing first hand what they were experiencing, promising a second call after he talked to the school board's attorney, Sean Caffee, for direction.

"There is nothing we can do," Sean Caffee advised. "They are within the law. You'll just have to ride it out." Staves hung up resigned and disgusted, desperate to find a way to save the day.

Sitting at the kitchen table hearing the continuing shouts and insults from the pickets and their growing line of supporters, George hoped for rain to hasten their departure. Suddenly smiling, he devilishly hit upon a plan that would accomplish the same results. He called all of his fellow board members again, aroused by the opportunity, shared what he planned, hoping they would join the effort. Without hesitation they all agreed to participate. The plan was to be initiated at exactly 6 PM.

The collective agreement, "Coordinated at the appointed hour, was to turn on their lawn sprinkler systems," whose reach they concurred gleefully would cover the paraded sidewalk. At the appointed time, the result was immediate and satisfying. The picketers shocked as the day was cloudless, screamed at the sudden cold wetness, initially frozen in place, uncomprehending. When realization set in as to what had happened they were blocked by their slower picketers, stumbling over one another to reach the safety of the streets.

Women shrieked, the men shouted obscenities at their humiliation. Peering out from the glass window of the garage door, George Staves gleefully watched the rewards of his actions. Reacting too late to use the protection of their picket signs, the women's newly coifed hair was ruined, flat, wet and lifeless against their heads. The men who were equally inundated, their shirts sticking coldly to their bodies, rushed to the streets, some dropping their picket signs in their haste, the placards left to soak in their retreat.

Robert Mercer, who was leading the pickets, was the last to gain distance from the purging shower. Almost knocked down by the stampede, he finally escaped ringing wet, his hair heavy with water, slumped from its lacquered erect neatness, his handkerchief wet and useless, proving to be a symbolic surrender.

In the street safely beyond the reaches of the disabling water spray, they tried to regroup, spurred on by the urgings of a soaked but still combative Robert Mercer. Uplifted, George Staves raised his garage door, to expand his view while still within the garage's protection of the indiscriminate water. A torrent of insults and expletives greeted him which he ignored, too pleased with his success to be distracted, enjoying the moment of his tactical victory. He was comfortable with his action as well within his rights to water the lawn of his property, including the tree lawn owned by the township but required to be maintained by the homeowner. His a perfect response to their contemptable action, which tested their resolve in the presence of a watery greeting, a proper comeuppance the pickets outrageously using the ploy of public property to attack him personally – not considering that the sidewalk existed within the covering arc of the water spray. Mercer and his wet followers could only use the accommodating sidewalk which at the moment was inhospitable and would remain so, Staves vowed, as long as they continued to picket.

The watery outcome, George Staves was to learn was a total success among all the board members, and would be responded in kind if the pickets returned. The spirit dampened picketers, under the watchful eyes of Chief Felice and his officers, remained gathered in the streets plotting their next move impeded the flow of traffic. Unceremoniously they were told to move on as they were illegally blocking the street, preventing a line of cars, honking their displeasure, from moving.

"Traffic must move," Chief Felice demanded.

"But we have our rights," Robert Mercer protested.

"Not on a public street," the chief retorted, his patience waning. "If you want to continue to picket, then get back on the sidewalk," his eyes twinkling at the prospect, "or move. You and your people face arrest if you continue to block this thoroughfare." The picketers and Mercer grudgingly realized further discussion would be fruitless. Cold and wet, completely demoralized, they began leaving the area. Robert Mercer glared angrily at a smiling George Staves.

"You've not heard the end of this," he said bitterly as he turned to join the others.

"I water my lawn every day. Be my guest," a pleased George Staves replied as he nodded a message of silent approval to the police.

When he returned to his house he called the other board members, mutually they had shared the same joy, rejoicing in their victory laughingly, their spirits raised by their shared triumph, this battle was theirs.

With decision time drawing near, George remained undecided, ambivalent. His every waking hour was consumed by the divisive issue, tormenting him, casting doubt on his position of the hour. What should have been restful nights of sleep conjured up instead a symbolic repeating dream of dread. He found himself imprisoned in a concrete block room with no windows or doors. Fear engulfed him as one of the walls began to move, rumbling to overwhelm and crush him. Beyond the room he could hear the jumbled voices of proponents and opponents of the issue that occupied him, his neighbors and friends shouting demands that he embrace their position, of one intention showing no concern for the death dealing wall rumbling toward him. Looking upward, he found the room ceilingless. Without a savior, he knew this could be his only escape. But the motionless walls' ending height was beyond his reach. Nonetheless in desperation, his hormones flowing, tried to jump up and reach safety. Failing each time, rejected to the cold damp floor.

Fighting his panic he was suddenly beset upon by a torrential downpour. Voluminous water, the strength of which forced his eyes to squint, quickly flooded and out paced the contracting room, developing a narrowing pool. The rain providing salvation, allowing him to thread water, rising in it's volume until the top of the wall was a reachable perch, avoiding the walls closing jaw he jumped to safety, landing out of breath, coughing, and expelling water from his overtaxed lungs. The effects awakened him somewhat. Symbolically the walls were the sides of the tormenting issue, one wall the opponent of his present position, it's kinetic energy giving it life, moving towards the one fixed representing the alternative. Alternating his position proved fruitless in stopping the walls movement as the walls switched sides, he constantly in the path of the crushing danger. Fully awake, to join a concerned Rose, he sat upright in bed, finding his pajamas thoroughly soaked, the sweat of his anxiety added realism to his nightly nightmare, his mind in desperate need for the issue's conclusion.

While he wished for a diversion from the divisive school board issue, he would have preferred something more peaceful than his repeated nightmare. As the day of the vote approached, his ambivalence still plagued him when an unrelated event lifted his fogging confusion, solidifying his position from that moment on, never again to face his second guessing.

It was his daughter Phyllis' turn to provide the venue for her good friend Debbie Shahane; an opportunity away from tied-up phone lines, to discuss in secrecy the pluses and minuses of the personality make-up of the men in their lives. Evoking unrestrained girlish laughter at the mere mention of the quirks in their men's behavioral patterns. Spoken in confidence, accommodating pledges to each other's self-adopted sisterhood, not only for the afternoon but for as long as they remained friends. Needing privacy, as George and Rose suspected, a faculty they contributed to by going to an early Saturday movie, a needed respite from the continuing onslaught of unreasonable phone calls.

Debbie could best be described as newly flowered, a vulnerable offering in bloom. Bubbly, unusually responsive and accommodating, resorting to frozen immobility in Tasha's presence. Tasha sensing her fright saw her as a game, nearing Debbie deliberately, to evoke squeals of fear, rather than cry's of fear, suggestive that Debbie seemed to enjoy her own exaggerated outbursts. Disregarding Phyllis' repeated assurances that Tasha was friendly, noting Tasha's bi-eyed coloring, sinister and intimidating was contrarian. As Tasha would approach, Debbie sheltered herself behind Phyllis' shielding body, viewing Tasha obliquely advocating what she had read somewhere: "At all costs deliberately avoid making direct eye contact with unpredictable animals."

As hard as Debbie tried to give Tasha a wide berth, her cowering demeanor was instinctively recognized, as would her betraying body chemistry, taking measure of by the keenness of Tasha's senses. Tasha usually responded with heightened mischievousness, exploiting every instance as an opportunity for play. And play they did, which typically involved Debbie being intimidated and chased around the house with Tasha in close pursuit; Debbie shrieking for Phyllis' physical intervention, her shrieks of distress motivating Tasha further.

In clean fun, the moment relished laughingly in it's aftermath, except on this day's occasion. In a moment of panic, Debbie's histrionics chose to theatrically flee the house to escape. It would have been a hilariously successful tactic if not for Tasha, close on her heels escaping with her. Emancipated, the rules of the game changed as Tasha, enjoying untethered liberty, chose to ignore the pleadings of Phyllis and a now distraught Debbie. A new game began as Tasha playfully mounted charge after charge, speeding directly at them, crossing neighbors' lawns seeming to defy inertia by quickly changing direction at the last possible moment, mocking their futile grasp. Yelping in stimulated delight pulling up at the last moment short of their reach, dropping to the joints of her front legs, sticking her hind end up, tail at the battle readily curled position, barking defiantly to come and get her, enjoying every minute of her newfound freedom, ignoring the continuing pleas and entreaties of the girls.

Fear turned to apprehension as Tasha, tired and bored by the game, went looking for the other challenges followed by the pleading Phyllis and Debbie who were horrified as Tasha disappeared from view. Defeated for the moment, both girls rushed back to the house to arm themselves with treats. To cover more ground quickly, they jumped into their respective cars, driving off in opposite directions planning to encircle Tasha and lure her back, hopeful her like for being a car passenger would win out.

George and Rose returned from the movies approximately two hours later, finding an open garage door with neither girls' cars nowhere in sight – an ominous sign. Questioning the circumstances, they pulled into the driveway just as the girls, having completed another sweep of the search area, followed them into the driveway. As George and Rose were disembarking, they learned the unwelcomed news. Using their own cars, George and Rose joined in the search, four cars scouring an eight-block area for signs of the runaway Tasha. After an hour and a half effort with nary a sign of her, George signaled all to return to the house to plan the next move.

"She's done this before," George Staves said with frustrated resignation. "She'll either return on her own when she feels like it or we'll get a call from a neighbor to come pick her up, successfully coaxing her into capture. I'll call Police Chief Felice to notify him, to alert his patrol cars of Tasha's escape."

They waited anxiously for something to happen. After two hours, the doorbell rang. George was the first to reach the front door, anxiously followed by his wife, Phyllis, and Debbie. With the door opening, relief and amazement was experienced by all, the curtain to this episode not ready to fall. There was Tasha, mouth open, tongue hanging limply to the side, her thirst needing satisfaction, accompanied by Lydia Santos, the diminutive girl with Down Syndrome, the source of the contentious division amongst the voters pressuring the school board vote. George Staves recognized her immediately.

"Lydia, how did you get here?" he asked, relieving her of her grasp of Tasha's collar, profusely thanking her for bringing Tasha home safely. He looked past Lydia onto his driveway and then the street, fully expecting to see Mrs. Gloria Santos sitting in her car awaiting her daughter's return.

"I just walked here from the community park," she answered. "I wasn't sure it was Tasha at first. Then I read her license and name tag," taking great pride in her ability, smiling an engaging smile, beautifying her branded low intelligence features.

"Come on in, Honey," Rose cordially invited. Tasha, needing no invitation, rushed to her water bowl closely followed by a fawning Phyllis, Debbie cautiously behind her.

Taking Lydia by the hand, Rose escorted her into the house, saying, "You must be very thirsty. I have some lemonade in the fridge. Would you like some?"

"Yes," Lydia responded. "I'd also like to call my mother."

"Of course, dear," a grateful Rose acknowledged. George Staves was not over his surprise, the situation continued its confounding. "You mean you walked here and Tasha followed you without a leash?"

Lydia nodded affirmatively, pleased on one hand that an adult recognized her accomplishment yet disappointed that she could be doubted as having the understanding of what was required of her. The implication saddened her but did not diminish her victory, her brief emotional swing not going unnoticed by George and Rose Staves.

"But weren't you afraid, having to cross all those major intersections, all those cars?" Rose exclaimed, visualizing the scene.

"I know the meaning of the different colors in the lights. Red is to stop, green is to go and yellow is to get ready to stop," she said proudly. "My Mom taught me." Then as an afterthought she added quickly, "But you know? Tasha knew the difference. I didn't have to tell her. Her mommy must have taught her just like mine did," she said innocently.

Reserving for a later moment to ponder Tasha' insightfulness, George said, "That's wonderful, Lydia, but how did you manage to control Tasha without a leash?" A greater discovery would be revealed.

"Oh, it wasn't really that hard. She minded well. All I had to say was, 'I'm taking you home' and she stayed at my side. It was what she wanted, but you know what? She would step in front of me, blocking me from crossing the street while she looked at the moving cars until they passed."

George and Rose looked at one another, shaking theirs heads in disbelief, not just because Tasha recognized the danger of cars, and the position of the lights but she had found a reason to give up her romp, allowing a relative stranger to escort her home. Demonstrating a response never experienced before, they were amazed at the implications.

Rose interpreted George's thoughts, saying, "If you don't want any more lemonade, Lydia, I think you should call your Mom."

She nodded dutifully as Rose handed her the phone. Listening, they heard her say, "I'm sorry that you were looking for me, Mama, but I brought Tasha back home. She ran away. She came right up to me when those teasing boys at the park were playing a game with me. They had me in a circle, shoving me from one boy to the other, ignoring me when I asked them to stop, not listening to me when I told them what you had said about not being their plaything. They made me cry. And then they stopped and moved away from me when they heard Tasha growl and saw her teeth. Tasha came right up to me as if she knew me, wagging her tail, licking my face, giving me nudging signs with her head to take her home."

Pausing to listen, obviously receiving instructions from her mother, nodding repeatedly in the signaling language of children when listening, finally breaking the silence, saying as she handed Rose the phone, "I talked to my Mom on her car phone. She'll be here very soon."

Their perplexity was over. Tasha delivered a message, showing that this vulnerable girl in need of her protection, intellectually stymied by Down syndrome, defied its limitations. In her innocence she had the empathy for someone else's circumstances. A blessing characteristic, George thought, we who are sitting in her judgment this day, conveniently relying on unclear laws and precedents that are well short of today's circumstances to be relevant. Equally impacting him further; Tasha giving up her mischievousness and playtime when she sensed Lydia's greater need, as if empowered spiritually. Was that symbolic lesson provided by purpose, not to be ignored?

With Tasha under leash restraint, they decided to wait for Gloria Santos out in their driveway, not knowing what to expect from the fiery advocate. Subdued they hoped, in deference to her daughter's presence, reducing the awkwardness of the situation.

Lydia was petting Tasha lovingly, cooing to her how beautiful she was, shrieking in sheer delight as Tasha jumped up on her shoulders and licked her face moist.

Mrs. Santos' car pulled into the driveway moments later. With the driver's side window down, she said tentatively, "Good evening. I hope that Lydia was not bothersome to you."

"Bothersome? She's a joy, a lifesaver. She brought our runaway Tasha home. She's an absolute delight. I'm glad I had this opportunity to meet her in spite of the circumstances. She touched me. " George Staves said sincerely.

Her cause would not be diminished by this occurrence, far from being distracted she recognized an opportunity that could not to be missed. She interpreted his affectionate remarks about her daughter as possible movement towards her position, he now vulnerable. A key had been provided to her, opening a reasoning door she hoped to get him to pass through. Emboldened, she availed herself of the opportunity, subduing her advocates abrasiveness:

With Lydia preoccupied with Tasha she asked, "And what do you think of my daughter now, Mr. Staves?"

He knew she was misreading him, his empathy for her child programming. He chose his words carefully, keeping the fragile peace.

"Let's not spoil the beauty of the moment it deserves better from both of us, let's not pollute the cleansed of air with rhetoric. Ours is a difficult issue, one that neither you nor I can solve by ourselves. Let's remain civil to one another in each other's presence. What is a non-issue is that you have a beautiful caring daughter. Let's not diminish the sunshine she walks in by engaging in contentious debate. Let it be a beacon to guide us."

Mrs. Santos, disarmed further, studied him for signs of mendacity. None of it's signs appearing, "Of course, you're right, Mr. Staves. Thanks for caring for my daughter," she said hiding her tears. A moment to share prevailing, "Lydia honey, it's time to go. Say goodbye."

"Goodbye, Mr. and Mrs. Staves. Goodbye Phyllis, Goodbye Debbie Goodbye, Tasha," Lydia said proudly, easily remembering each name, as she climbed into the passenger seat of her mother's car, drawing down the window to engage Tasha with her loving wave, Tasha's tail wagging affectionately.

"Maybe you can come and visit Tasha again," Rose said. "You are welcome anytime."

"We can both play with her," Phyllis added

Mrs. Santos said nothing more, reminding herself of the battle to be waged. Her cordiality over, once again her determined position hardened her face with resilience, clearly saying compromise would have to come from others.

~

Within the last week of the four weeks he allotted for the decision, Sean Caffee the lawyer for the school board, having oversite responsibilities received sealed registered mail from the board members including George Staves detailing their reasoning and their position. On a need to know basis a file was established, To protect the individual Board Member, their position would remain as privileged communication between board members and their counsel.

George Staves called Mr. Caffee to confirm that all registered mail had been accounted for. Receiving confirmation, Staves then told him that a conference room would be reserved in his name at the local Travelers Motel at 3:00 PM As a precaution to protect the meeting's secrecy, no other board members would be invited. Staves extraordinary procedure, in the interests of maintaining privilege in this contentious matter, his phone resolution passed without exception, allowing that the vote be made by sealed registered mail addressed to counsel. The board's individual positions would be read by Sean Caffee as would the vote, witnessed by George Staves.

At 3:45 PM, Caffee called Robert Mercer, advising that the board had reached its decision. The results in a board statement would be read to him in person if he wished at the Travelers Motel conference room, prior to notifying the news media. Mercer accepted the invitation without comment for the present, creating suspicions of deviousness as in spite of the elaborate plans to maintain secrecy, proven as pickets appeared just prior to Robert Mercer's arrival. He was greeted with the cordiality scripted between the two lawyers, but from George Staves, avoiding the handshake, only a cold acknowledgment, signaling he was anxious to depart the chilled atmosphere- for a quick adjournment to the meeting. He hastened to read a prepared statement:

"It is the decision of this school board, acting within its purview that the best interests of all currently attending students, who by the grace of God are not physically and mentally handicapped, would suffer distractions and curriculum slowdown would the admissions policy be changed. While we are sympathetic toward Mrs. Santos, and the petitioners we cannot put at risk the achievements of past practices were we to accommodate her child by making an exception to the rules of admission. The board's decision also factored heavily that educational resources, albeit not local but reasonably available, were being funded by tax dollars. Mrs. Santos daughters situation pursuing an education has been properly responded to by local and state governments, and is not disenfranchisement. We reject outright the suggestion that the admissions policy is prejudicial. Therefore, it is the majority judgment of this board that the petition is inappropriate and without merit."

Mr. Mercer, having anticipated this decision displayed little emotion, except within his eyes that appeared to be smiling at the thought of continuing the reputation building cause and it's adjunct monetary rewards said, "That decision is regrettable and faulty, and will not stand."

Threatening to the end, Staves thought.

When questioned by Sean Caffee, Mr. Mercer who chose the word "regrettable" rather than "regrettably" to describe his feelings, continued his criticism, which without his clients presence lacked his usual fervor.

"I will not let this issue die." Then he added unleashing his dramatic flair, "The ashes of this petition would be stroked to produce a Phoenix that will consume the stubbornness and prejudice that caused the perpetuation of this grave injustice. We are just beginning our great battle. We gain supporters every day. Public sentiment is in our corner. You will be overruled."

Sean Caffee, smiling patiently, responded, "If the court system votes in your favor, we will abide by that decision. But as of this moment, Mr. Mercer, there is no legal justification that we have found in our search that is relevant."

"Ah, but it's coming. Would it not be better if you were history making proactive rather than safely precedent?" Mercer continued.

"We do not make the law. We only follow it. We leave that to the makers," Caffee replied pointedly.

"What was the tally?" he asked, needing a semblance of a victory.

"Three against, two for," Staves answered.

Robert Mercer's expression changed. He turned his full attention to George Staves. "And how did you vote?" he asked devilishly delighting in the anguish he sensed in Staves' demeanor.

"The individual ballets are secret," Staves answered, flustered that Mercer was reading him. Recovering, he said, "I see no reason for this meeting to continue. All issues have been addressed." He stood, its message clear, his dealings with Robert Mercer coming to an end.

~

Staves, temporarily on leave from his searching, smiled to himself, knowing the history that followed that day's events – how wrong he would have been had he maintained his original position, Staves conceded, in spite of his justifiable dislike for Mercer his tactics and motives, that he had concluded and so voted that Mercer for whatever reason was on the right side of justice.

⁓

Robert Mercer, living by his word, engaged as his first chair an experienced Appeals Court lawyer, cleverly appealed the school board's ruling through the courts, successfully arguing that Mrs. Santos' and her daughter Lydia's civil rights were being denied, as well as the violation of Public Law 94–142 called the *Education of All Handicapped Children Act*, whose center piece is the "least restrictive requirement." Mercers support among legislators, and advocacy groups grew and soon became an issue of statewide interest as well as a watershed of national implications. The Appeals Court ruling that the school board's decision was too restrictive. It's recommended remedies included that the location of the special schools be brought within the same reasonable distance as the other schools in the district, that funding by tax dollars be increased substantially. While not a complete victory for Mrs. Santos and her forces, subsequent history would prove the Appeal Court's partial accommodation as the forerunner of the more complete *Disabilities Education Act* and the *Americans with Disabilities Act*. Unfortunately, it was too late for Lydia Santos but not for the others who would follow.

Upon receiving notification of the court's decision, George Staves convened a special meeting of the board wherein the court's guidelines were unanimously approved for adoption.

The establishing foundation victory of this case that George Staves secretly cheered for was a double-edged sword. On one side, he was pleased and vindicated by the outcome; the other cutting him deeply: Robert Mercer's reputation gaining considerable acclaim in spite of his distasteful tactics and showmanship, Staves admitting Mercer was the shinning knight, albeit with chips in his armor, being honored by progressives as helping right a wrong could not be denied.

⁓

His excursion was interrupted by a sudden downpour typical of summer, it's suddenness startling, returned him to the shelter of the house. As expected it was of short duration, enabling him to resume his trip of recall outdoors, where the vast sky that he would travel invited him. He was back from his thoughts of his first involvement with Mercer, fast forwarding his transporter to more recent times; facing the death of Mrs. Springer and having to deal once again distastefully with Robert Mercer. Unexpectedly thrust upon one another, freshened the old wounds of a cutting Robert Mercer. The passing of time and it's psychological closure of healing scar tissue alluding him, not sealing unpleasant experiences.

Their recent encounter, surfacing his resentment of Mercer, with good cause he would be wary of his future involvements. What he thought was a finishing chapter in their history was suddenly incomplete. There was another page to be turned, earlier damaging experiences archived still influencing his tolerance for a new beginning, to enable from a forgiven and unencumbered past, metaphorically, as were the presentations of his turned on windshield wipers with each pass wiping away, he knew Mercer would expect as much, not his forgiveness. Adversarial, a venue for showmanship and competition his promotion, his sustenance.

He could only be judgmental for this man who was ruled by greed, embracing only paying clients no matter how disreputable, and controversial. The causes; and only if they enhanced his public persona, carefully crafting him as humanitarian, or socially conscious. Hiding his true colors, that of the mercenary and manipulative, duplicity never a restraint. While not easily manipulated, George Staves was uncomfortable, unsettled by what lay ahead, what was expected of him. He felt vulnerable to being exploited, whatever his role in resolving Mrs. Springer's situation.

Mercer's expected phone call came a few days later.

"Mr. Staves, how nice to talk to you again. Have you been well?" Robert Mercer asked.

"Yes, thank you for asking." he responded, knowing the inquiry was perfunctory and not sincere. "And you Mr. Mercer?"

"Fine," he answered, "but please call me Robert."

"That can't be that important to you, a lawyer of such high standing and praise deserves elevation, an equivalent to salutation." he responded sarcastically, rejecting the accommodation.

A faint smile of "*touché*" curled Robert Mercer's mouth, acknowledging that there would be no false pretensions from George Staves. He would be all business, expediting the discussion was a priority. Signaling that delaying pleasantries would not work, disarming should not be attempted. Knowing when they came face to face in the meeting Mercer was sure he could arrange with this phone call, confident the advantage would be his. He was in a win, win situation, his attitude of indifference his trumping card, emotionally unaffected. The feelings of guilt and obligation that he would exploit solely that of George Staves. Whatever counters or pleas Staves would make would be denied consideration. Not to be communal would be his position, fulfilling his obligation within a narrow margin of involvement, within which delivering as a conduit. He informing was what was contracted by Mrs. Springer- no other consideration or sympathy could be pressured by Staves in her behalf. Relishing victimizing Staves- in so doing, gaining the upper hand, securing a long awaited payback, achieving the exclusivity of Staves's burdening involvement portending risk. His maneuvered scenario; Staves in turmoil, guilt taking hold. Mercer's recompense: retribution. Pleased that his long denied victory over his rival was nearing fruition.

"As I stated in our earlier contact, I have a matter of great importance to discuss with you regarding a request of the late Mrs. Springer, that I'm duty bound to make known to those designated. It's delicate and confidential. A matter that cannot be discussed on the phone. I assure you it is most urgent," he said emphatically.

"And it involves me directly? I can't for the life of me figure why." Staves questioned, still looking for an opportunity to avoid the meeting.

"Yes," Mercer replied, sensing his continuing reluctance. You'll understand when we meet. I won't take too much of your time. Can we arrange for me to visit you at home this evening?"

That urgent, Staves thought. Now his curiosity was fully aroused, pondering what possible legal connection he could have with Mrs. Springer's affairs. Her Will had been settled. He could only think of her letter mentioning their friendship. That connection obligated him to assent to Robert Mercer's wishes.

He said, "Yes," hopeful he wouldn't live to regret it.

"Can I come within the hour?" Mercer asked.

"Please do. I've got other obligations for the evening," George invented.

"I'll be there within the hour," he affirmed.

Robert Mercer arrived within thirty-five minutes. His early showing acknowledging Staves' invented time constraints, was nothing more than a display of a feigned consideration, "one of his portrayals" when in need of something.

George greeted him at the door, bending over to hold back a barking Tasha, responding to the ring of the front doorbell. Staves, held Tasha tightly, sure she was still familiar with Mercer's adversarial scent. Confirmed as Mercer gained entrance into the house. Tasha, her neck hairs aroused, immediately glued her nose to his pants leg – hardly comforting to an anxious Robert Mercer who remembered her angered growling protection of Staves. Staves quieted Tasha with his commanding, "down girl. Everything is all right." His hold on her collar releasing as he felt Tasha's tension ease, for the moment she was pacified. Staves ignored Mercer's extended hand as he led him into the living room, Tasha close to Mercer's heels, sniffed, alert for changing signals.

Rose Staves was seated awaiting them, dutiful towards Mercer at her husband's introduction. Mercer remembering the last Tasha's nearness, was not placated by Staves's assurance's of Tasha accepting him as a visitor. Smiling to himself, Staves concluded that Mercer's anxiety was best, if the conversation turned heated, an aroused Tasha would hasten his leaving.

Staves typically dressed in after-work casual clothes, was surprised at Mercer's attire, guessed to be a ploy, a tactic of kinship, creating an impression to relax from formality; to defuse. He had abandoned his courtroom fashions. His somber dark blue suit replaced by a blue blazer, his button down shirt giving way to a turtle neck sweater that yielded to his neck folds when seated. His face showing signs of regrowth, was tanned by his country club membership. All for naught, as Staves looked beyond his presentation, a second examination more revealing. Mercer's portly physique, was accented as he had forgotten to unbutton his straining-at-the-seams blazer, suggesting the more subdued golf, not the more cardio tennis as his country club participation.

"I assume my wife can sit in on this conversation?" Stave asked.

"Please forgive me, Mrs. Staves, it is not my intent to offend you." Staring directly into her eyes, stating with his flair for the dramatic, "Because the nature of my call is confidential in nature, my professional commitment is to restrictive disclosure, I must request that we be alone."

"Certainly," Rose answered. Mercer looking to George Staves, said overbearingly, "you are not bound by any such obligation. When I leave, if you choose to discuss this matter with Mrs. Staves, that option is certainly yours."

Rose, excusing herself, went into the den to watch television. With the unexpected change in scenario, a torn Tasha raised nervously to her feet, looking at her Alpha for guidance, a plea to relieve her of her loyalty confusion. Tasha's questioning eyes locked onto Staves, he reading her uncomfortable "Is Tasha's presence needed?" Mercer asked, anticipating Staves's command to end her dilemma.

Tasha a guardian against this visitor with the familiar threatening scent, in conflict with her wishes to share in Rose Staves' company received his approval that she leave the room. Upon departing, Tasha again sniffed close to Mercer's presence. Scenting nothing hostile, departed, her scent lingering, reminding Mercer of her nearness.

With Tasha gone, Mercer's confidence was on the rise, no longer wary, breathing easier. With feigned thoughtfulness he said, "I hope I didn't offend Mrs. Staves."

"She'll handle it," Staves responded, his tone suggesting impatience with Mercer's feigned concern for Rose's feelings. George having noted that Mercers pretext of confidentiality, was purposeful in arranging there be no witnesses. Their conversation would be exclusive; it's consequence would be his word against Mercer's, invalidating each others testimony if ever needed in a official action.

"What's on your mind?" Staves asked. "What is it that involves me with Mrs. Springer?"

Seated in one of the living room club chairs, Mercer reached down and brought into his lap his attaché case. Ceremoniously unsnapping the fastener, removing a file jacket, thoroughly enjoying the drama he was directing. Opening it, he pulled out what appeared to be a bound legal document.

"I'm sure you know the distribution aspect of her Will?" he asked, waving the document in a hand beyond reach, relishing his center stage.

"I think I do. I was told by the Schindlers that the estate was evenly divided between her only relative and the Humane Society."

"You are correct," he said with exaggeration. "The Will, which you have no need to read, has cleared the Probate Court, surviving a brief challenge to the Humane Society's distribution brought by her relative. Found to be without legal merit."

Mercer paused for effect, knowing how anxious Staves was, enjoying the tease. "I have another document, a unofficial covenant to the Will, a declaration by Mrs. Springer, declared neither for publication or notice. It is a privileged communiqué bearing appropriate signatures. Obviously," he said smilingly, "my talking to you is indicative that you are named. This document contains the true wishes for handling the remains of Mrs. Springer. I don't know whether you knew this or not, but unlike her husband's remains interred in the neighboring consecrated grounds of Calvary Cemetery, Mrs. Springer, while a strong believer in God, for reasons of her own was not a fully subscribing member of the Catholic church. Officially she requested in her will the frowned-upon cremation of her remains, her ashes to be noted as housed in an appropriate facility a pretext. Not for public consumption she wished her ashes be dispersed. I, as her legally documented trustee, am fulfilling her final requests, making final arrangements."

George Staves felt his discomfort intensify. He didn't like what he was hearing. Angry with himself, he fidgeted while Mercer's demeanor remained business like; in charge. He was sure Mercer was mocking him, relishing that Staves was showing signs of angst; that he had the upper hand.

Robert Mercer's arrogance and matter-of-fact tone grated on Staves sensibilities. He knew that Mercer was feeding off his reactions, giving him sadistic delight in pursuing his flaunting ministry. He had no choice. He had to sit there while Mercer exhilarated in his sadism, this moment of needed explanation without options compelled him to bear. Uneasy George felt his heartbeat increase, the anticipation of what was developing, while not knowing specifically, feared the worst possible scenario for his involvement.

Impatient, he asked, "That's all well and good but how does that affect me?"

Mercer continued, it was his show, he would not be hurried, he had his adversary captive, "The will states I arrange for the disposal of her ashes, that I commit them to a burial plot or house them in either a mausoleum or church columbarium. Her unofficial addendum to the will expresses her true wishes, to spread her ashes on private property with or without the written permission of the property owner. I haven't, for the reason of our discussion, made a final decision as to what course of action I will take." Enjoying his building climax, he paused expecting a response from Staves, who choose to wait to hear what he already had guessed, words detailing his involvement.

Mercer continued, "In the addendum to the will, Mrs. Springer confides a fervent desire to have her ashes distributed on the property of her home. She also confides that you witnessed what she had done with the ashes of her," emphasizing his disapproval, he ridiculed, "her *dog, her passion, her life over, her will to live gone*. That women lost her perspective. She was fogged by dementia. Had she had caring relatives she would have spent her last days in a nursing home where they could have treated her with the rest of the enfeebled." his words cruel in tone

Staves listened angrily as Mercer disparaged Mrs. Springer, his client that had paid for a service, mocked after death, his fee in hand. His ire rising at Mercer's further disrespect, angry at his liberties, his demeaning reproachful commentary on Mrs. Springer's emotional and spiritual needs, scoffing; "Her passion an illnesses." While critical strong denunciation of Mrs. Springer, exorcized Staves to come to her defense, its momentum moving him closer towards fulfilling her wishes. Mercer exciting further George Staves's sympathies, pleased his personal attack had commanded his forthcoming score settling. Staves, his facial muscles occasioning twitching, managed with great difficulty to exercise self-control, believing in time this mercenary would eventually stand accountable for his irreverence.

Mercer, amused by the effects his words had on Staves, continued, "As I told Mrs. Springer, I doubted that the new owners of her property would give permission to allow an open grave burial site. Consequently, the disposal of her ashes on the property of her choice would have to be clandestine. As an officer of the court with legality an issue, I am bound by attorney/client privilege, I could not openly be an active participant to her confidential request. Stating that more than likely her ashes would be accommodated by a burial plot or mausoleum "

"Mrs. Springer, her health failing rapidly, incredulously assumed my full participation. Realizing waning time precluded the making of other arrangements, she became quite emotional at my refusal. Despairing to sobbing tears, her only concern, her ashes joining her dog Norse. Fragile and delicate, and yet insisting, and I equally adamant, refusing to directly participate in her secret plans. Finally, a compromise was worked out. After fulfilling my legal obligations, I would serve only as a messenger delivering her addendum request to whomever she wished. It was then that she mentioned your name as someone who, according to her, showed great understanding for her loss. I must admit I was greatly intrigued by the prospect of crossing swords with you again."

The mystery over, the ramifications many, tiring of his representations Staves agreed to consider it, the empathy for Mrs. Springer's words chronicling her tortured life a weighty factor. Thinking ahead he knew it would be a lot to ask of the Schindlers, relative strangers, sure to politely deny such a request as unreasonable, while privately viewing the request as morbid. This left only him, a surreptitious Samaritan if he acceded.

In finality Mercer said, "Mrs. Springer hoped you would respond favorably, granting her final request. That I plead her case when I located you."

At that moment Tasha returned to the living room, with her usual grunt lay down next to Staves. Her eyes peered expressively at him, then back to the stranger, anticipatory, on alert, as if in wait for the strained climate of the meeting to deteriorate further.

"You know what you're asking me to do, Mr. Mercer?" addressing him by name for the first time since the meeting started. "You want me to break the law? Showing sympathy for the spreading of the ashes of her dog is one thing. Spreading her remains on private property, as you well know without approvals is another matter and illegal," he said adamantly, his voice rising.

"Mr. Staves, I never asked you to break the law. This is a request of Mrs. Springer. I only agreed to be her messenger. What you do is your business." His cutting words trying to distance himself. "Are we clear on that point?"

"What's clear is that I was never made aware of this request until now. Further, I made no promises to Mrs. Springer. I was never asked," his voice continuing to rise, his anger increasing. "Nor would I have supported such a decision had I been asked. Why can't you choose the other options available to you rather than dropping this in my lap out of the blue, instead asking me to volunteer, putting myself and family in jeopardy?"

"I'm not asking you to do anything. I'm just relating to you a dead woman's wishes," he said defensively. "Just say 'no' and this conversation is over and I'll be on my way."

Tashas reaction to the elevated tone their conversation took; the animations of hand and arm waving, a disruption of tranquility- was to glower at the source. She rose to stand aggressively protective, her muscles taunt waiting to pounce if a hostile act was committed. Tashas reaction did not go unnoticed by Mercer. His self-assuredness gone, he nervously looked for Staves to calm her menacing presence.

Staves' anger management resurfaced, easing the tension that was his body language, placated an aroused Tasha nearing a highly agitated state. Coaxing her, soothing her, sadness now washing over him as he reflected on one of Tasha's breed, Norse's lifeless remains, lying unfulfilled, by virtue of his denial if he so chose.

His thoughts turned to Mrs. Springer's final days. Visualizing her weak, forced to be bedridden… no desire, except death and its promise of resurrection. Ignoring the need for delaying nourishment, she awaited death. Occasioned strength only to visit the bathroom, returning, clutching and holding onto the walls and furniture for support. Mis-stepping with weakness, slumping to the carpet. Unhurt, somehow finding the taxing mobility of slowly crawling along the floor to get back into bed where once again she joyously viewed arranged photographs of Norse, purposed to give her comfort as either sleep temporary or as she hoped permanently claimed her. Her faint pulse quickened as her fevered imagination answered her prayers to her divinity, her reunion with her beloved Norse in the hereafter closer to happen; spirit to spirit. Laying in bed, final fulfillment encouraged, suddenly the unknown brought doubts of a hereafter, that when life ended there was nothing. All that would remain bearing the footprint of one's life were their energy waves wandering aimlessly in the cosmos. What then, she must have thought, unable to bear the idea that in death Norse and she would remain forever apart. She had to have connection. She panicked, threatened by a world to come, vacant of spiritual coupling, an eternal abyss.

The only alternative left to her, George reasoned, her only guarantee, the only legacy that she would wish, was the bonding of their earthly remains. In death, planning that accomplishment before the eternity of nothingness would be satisfying in the absence of a heavenly hereafter. Their earthly remains connected as matter, symbolic of what was and would never be again. Their ashes would remain intermixed, together, forever touching almost in an embrace. This then would be the means of an enduring relationship, if her last minute concern for an afterlife of spiritual joining proved nonexistent.

It became clear to him that this was her motivation. He understood and would prevail upon himself to think the matter through. He Returned his attention to Mercer, benefiting from his discovery, believing his considering involvement had to be shared with his wife.

"Before I say yes I'll need more time to think about it. It will not be easy: lots of considerations, neighbors, police."

Robert Mercer was taken aback by the quickness of Staves' transformation from a vague, suspiciously weak "I'll consider it," to accommodating almost positive "before I say yes," all within a matter of minutes. What brought on this change he did not know. The only thing he witnessed, almost going unnoticed was Staves's sudden trance like facial expression, his eyes penetrating as if he were searching, envisioning beyond the room. Even Tasha recognized his departure, she frozen still, motionless. Staves dominated her vision, never taking her blinkless eyes from him, knowing her Alpha's mind had traveled.

"I'm sure it will not be easy," Mercer said cautious for the first time, in a hint of trepidation of what Staves' ground rules would be, almost certain any issue he could reconcile in his favor. Still he was pleased with his victory, the terms forthcoming manageable as long as not compromising, asking, "Can I hear back from you in two weeks?" Not an unreasonable amount of time he thought.

"I'll give you my decision in two weeks. That I can do. But if I do agree, it would not take place until later in the year or early next year when most of Schindlers' neighbors are in Florida for the winter. As I recall, they all go south."

"Fine," Mercer said gathering up his papers, trying hard not to show concern for Tasha who was following close on his heels. With feigned aplomb pausing at the door, he said, "My last official act for Mrs. Schindler, having the written authority to act upon, delayed of course until I get your response. I'll wait no longer than two weeks for the conclusion in this matter," he added smugly, savoring his victory, successfully involving George Staves, Mercer's ancillary payment to punish him with anguish. 'An uplifting compensation for me' Mercer thought, 'an overdue recompense for Staves's insults past and present.'

A burdened Staves muffled his anger while sensing Mercer's self-award, held Tasha by the collar, finding it necessary to restrain her, sensing his anxiety.

"In two weeks," Staves said looking up from his stooped over position.

Mercer pulled a card from his coat pocket and handed it to Staves who glanced at it briefly. It contained his home and office phone numbers under the bold type of "Mercer and Associates, Attorneys at Law." Staves quickly pocketed the card without comment, expediting his departure.

"Call me at any time," making a abbreviated extension of his hand, the offering of a handshake never materialized, his mind changed, thinking better of it. Being insincere facing rejection, "I feel for you. It's a difficult decision I'm sure," his words perfunctory carrying no weight on the scale of understanding. Mercer's audience lost, his final scene played said, "Thank you for your time. Give my goodnight to Mrs. Staves." He then walked out the door but not yet out of George's life.

In the days that followed, George's thoughts were still jumbled. It's travel choked with the weeds of rivaling correctness, no clear path yet envisioned. Contrary to his original thought, his judgment changed, at this time he would only tell his wife short of the full details of his involvement, not of the illegality of what was being asked of him. His meeting with Mercer he would tell her was to discuss an appropriate disposition of Mrs. Schindler's remains leaving out for the moment the crossing of the threshold option. Mistakenly judging his obligation he decided her protection in this illegal undertaking lay in not knowing, what he might decide. It would keep her from being charged as an accomplice and a co-conspirator if he decided to accept Mrs. Springer's proxy assignment and was caught in the act. Unfortunately his self-imposed isolation afforded him no sounding board, no debate, and no other perspectives. He truly was alone. Insulated, counsel was his and only his.

His daylight hours were relatively normal. Thankfully his thoughts were not exclusively his dilemma, other busied commitments: business, family and friends provided reprieving distractions. Night however, when darkness provides little escape, his thoughts would narrow, his body and his minds exhausted senses fatigued. He would welcome a restful sleep. Refreshed and determined to deal with the next day's challenges, and those still plaguing him. Instead, not finding peace, his need alluding him. Restless, he was envious of his loved one soundly asleep next to him. A troubled George Staves lay there awake in torment, no closer to a resolution than the night before.

Just say "no" he would berate himself. "It's no business of yours. You are not obligated to do anything more than hold her memory. Or am I?" he challenged himself. He knew one thing for certain, his must give a dedicated response. He would not subject himself to second-guessing, his answer would be completely committed, unalterably the right one no matter the consequences. He would restrict the risk of violating the law to himself only, would he judge himself morally bound to accede to a dead woman's wishes of cohabitating remains, a reward she would never have cognizance of; nor later generations discovery of their devotion. Motivating this compensating hedge, the existence of Gods Kingdom for worthy souls a fantasy- a damaging sacriledge to his beliefs. Should that be the overriding influence? Could he live with himself by turning from her cause? Excusing his rejection as mandated by civil law, and the pledge of his religion. Formulated or abstract answers never sound enough. His enigma: enlightment missing his discovery.

George's options limited, his mind assessing, tortured a parallel – making a strained analogy drawn from geometrics. He had remembered Materials Engineering courses in college on the properties of shapes, and curvatures– suggested a testing correlation. The highly polished convex shape, where image reflections appear correctly oriented, it's configuration having no holding power to accumulate depth. A consequence, encouraging, the superficial, making that which resides incomplete. Would that be his choice? The Convex shape, reflecting a truth not fully developed, absenting appreciation in value. Those that visit it's raised curvature that portends premature judgements as it's possible bi-product. Or the mirroring concave side where images are viewed skewered upside down, requiring a willing mental adjustment. It's substance retaining configuration, a rival to the physics of gravity and inertia, providing depth, worthy of value or consideration. Would this be where his analogy would take him: Concave? Figuratively capturing all of the dimensions of Mrs. Springer – those measurements in total, impossible to ignore. A consideration for the clandestine undertaking; his guilt vanquished. It served him well, his tortured reference, the physics of light and imagery on geometric shapes indeed a corollary to his conflict but not convincing enough.

His difficulty in sleeping, not going unnoticed kept his concerned wife awake Eliciting her endless questions, beseeching the reason for his restlessness. Not ready to take her into his confidence, prompted occasions of leaving their bed, his sudden insomnia his pretext, the truth of it's basis kept secret. A hostage to his burden, she couldn't possibly comprehend, nor should he ask it of her. He knew she would loyally support his decision, why then would he put her at risk as a co-conspirator, his pursuit of answers would be exclusive. Awaiting his arrival on the dens couch was the intuitive Tasha, her loyal presence a psychological comfort, the implications of her touch, putting his demons at bay, their sail not enough, as he navigated around them, searching.

With his time running out, a number of situations or events occurred during the last days of the two-week period, while abstract, helped shape his decision. The first began rather typically, then gaining value of note. After dinner, seated on the patio accompanied by Tasha, her tethered length allowed her full view of the street in front of the house, pleasing her. His meandering thoughts were interrupted, Tasha, leaving the cooling comfort of the Crabapple tree, yelping excitedly. Usually indifferent to the passing of other dogs, their passage short-lived as they moved quickly from her view. Except the occasions of the more aggressive dog, temporarily unaware of Tashas stealthy surveillance, marked his or her passage, flaunting and challenging any territorial claim.

This effrontery would evoke a long guttural growl from Tasha, the attention of the offending dog immediate. Seeing Tasha for the first time, no match to her cold unwavering stare. Capitulating, in symbolic retreat, ears back, tail between it's legs, intimidated, fearfully looking over it's shoulder, hurrying to gain distance. Tasha, still in a highly agitated state, strained her tether, George witnessed what had happened, meeting her demands, untethered her, while holding the leash fixed to her collar, tension relieved she hurriedly retraced the path of the violating stray. Her olfactory senses guiding her, spotting over the intruder's brashness, reclaiming her territory as her inviolate domain. Her spotting joust over, she willingly returned to her tree shaded oversight position, confident in her victory but remaining on guard.

A hurriedly passing dog not intent on colonizing, would virtually create little interest in Tasha. Excepting, the stray one of her breed–another Husky. Excited, releasing great joy, leaping and straining, the other husky was equally as excited. Clearly indicative this shared recognition special, products of the same ancestry, the unbroken genetic code, straight lined from one forbear to another. On the other hand, showing only token interest, easily distinguishing those representing a branching out, the cross-breed, diluted of their purity. The amazing kinship, Huskies in contact have for one another, crowning the occasion, with a zeal given no other, an acclamation, that they were not alone.

The intensity and need for this bonding on the final Wednesday, the torturing decision still not made. The hour when everyone in the house should be asleep, Tasha uncharacteristically howling, usually her outdoors response to screaming police cars or emergency vehicles alerting traffic ahead. Staves, sleepy-eyed and confused, awarded by the reticence of family members sought the reason for Tasha's disturbance, his position on the den couch nearer the commotion. As he approached, Tasha turned her attention from him, foregoing her howling to scratch at the patio door. Her purpose expressed, she reared back her head to howl, just as intensely. It was not a sorrowful or mournful howl but one of signal. Her howl, a two-way communication, an astonished Staves soon learned as there was a respondent outside the house shrilly matching Tasha's appeal.

Turning on the patio lights, drawing back the vertical blinds, George saw the reason for Tasha's excitement. Sighting Smokey, the gray-and-white husky who Tasha had recently discovered, began flinging himself against the thermal paned glass of the patio door. Together the din of their efforts, certain to disturb the usual tranquility of the neighborhood, the awakened residents sure to call the police if the disturbance continued. Restraining Tasha with one hand, he opened the patio door and let Smokey in, never as a suitor if Tasha were in heat, but to quite their tumult. Now inside the house, the howling ended, succeeded by yelps of excitement, affecting all of George's sleep disturbed family members. Led by his incredulous wife, followed by an enraptured Phyllis, and a visibly annoyed Edward, home from college.

"What do we do now?" Rose asked in disbelief.

Phyllis delighted in the dogs' antics; chasing one another, while Edward mumbled something about people not taking care of their pets.

"I couldn't just let them continue to howl, awaking the neighborhood," George said.

"You could have called 911. They would have arranged for the animal warden. Better yet, you know who Smokey's owners are. You could have called them," Rose said in exasperation.

"At this hour? Not a good idea. What if the situation were reversed? Would you like someone calling us at this hour of the morning, frightening everyone? I don't think so. They probably don't even know he's gone," George said reflectively. "I'll call in the morning at a reasonable hour. And besides, Tasha would never forgive me if I denied her this treat," Staves said trying to find humor in the circumstances.

They watched the dogs in fascination, who tiring of their reversing roles of chase, now were affectionately grooming one another, a serving tribute. With their playful antics, their grooming ministrations over they rested. The family watching, the dogs commune atmosphere, it's continuance to be tested as they approached Tasha's water bowl together, wondering what the ranking order would be at the drinking trough. In spite of the affection shown one another, not withstanding Smokey's larger male size, without hesitation he backed off to let Tasha drink first. Not in canine chivalry, but as the Alpha ranking demanded, the structured pack society prevailing. Their thirst satisfied they lay down together, close enough to feel each other's breathing. Phyllis, noticing the need, filled Tasha's food bowl with twice as much food. Anticipating their feeding pattern: the inviolate peacekeeping structured social order.

The dogs amusing presentations over, the hour of the day remindful Rose, hid her smile, her growing pleasure, feigned chastising her husband, "Since you encouraged their togetherness, they're all yours. As for me, I'm going back to bed." Turning serious, she said pityingly, "Judging from the way you look, I think you should do the same."

The hidden message of their mothers words registered with Phyllis and Edward, alerting them that their father had a deep conflict, one that he did not want to share. Suspecting it's onset had something to do with Mrs. Springers death Edward led the returning procession to bed, followed by his Mom and a assured Phyllis that Smokey would not be turned out, to remain with Tasha at least until morning which was nearing by the minute.

Staves waited until the sun was up, adding an hour before calling the Corso's, Smokey's owners. The Corso's having just determined that Smokey was missing, were about to call the police when George called. Expressing relief that Smokey had been found, a joyous Mr. Corso, anxious to return Smokey to his keep, said he would be at the Staves' home in fifteen minutes. He arrived with a leash in hand apologetic, Smokey somehow managed to unlatch the gate of his run, ignoring the painful electrical shock delivered through his receiver collar, the underground wiring system failing to restrain him.

"It's the first time that he has done this," Carl Corso said, continuing his apology. "His determination had to be compelling to knowingly submit to an electrical shock."

"I was frantic when you called," Corso continued. "Expecting notification of the worst of outcomes. Grateful to learn he was safe. Until then pessimistic, expecting doom. My wife, in denial, not willing to admit the possibility; chastised me as lacking faith visualizing Smokey dead or injured -accusing me of being a pagan sacrificing priest on the alter of pessimism. My pessimism actually a cushion to ease the circumstance of fatalism, countering as I secretly prayed for his safe recovery – avoiding the dangers during his escape. My wife, not conceiving a tragic outcome considered thoughts of that nature as good as making it happen continued her avoidance criticism As the moments passed, seeming like hours, with no sign of him she weakened to a tragic outcome. Faulting my open display of encouraging a unrealistic relationship of dependency with a canine species – her warning to me meant for both of us: "to get another life," it's truth; she was equally affected. Childless we will rejoice together. I will tease her when I return with Smokey, citing her charge that since I over indulge Smokey it will be my demand that if he passes on before me that I will have him cryogenically preserved until I die. Then we can be buried together just as they did in ancient civilizations."

"Your not serious," doubted Staves.

"Of course not. My wife would never allow me that exclusivity. It might have been a consideration if it were the culture of today allowing that we all be entombed. Notwithstanding I have an alternate plan. Not as controversial but still a salute to our bond that everyone can live with. I plan on having Smoky's picture framed in hermetically sealed ceramic, placed in both our caskets to be with us through the ages."

Staves was taken back, not expecting but recognizing immediately, a parallel without the befallen tragedy the connection with Mrs Springers fervor, being visited with again. "What about you and your families devotion to Tasha."

"We will pray to be with her throughout eternity in the Kingdom of God," Staves responded passionately.

"Amen to that if there is a heaven."

"I truly believe there is."

"But how would you memorialize her life when she passes," Carl Corso questioned.

George Staves paused to ponder then revealed a confidence, "I'll write a book about her," he hastened.

Staves changing the subject reminded him of their dogs first meeting, their excited recognition, reacting to one another. It's handwriting now clearer than ever to them.

"Yes, I do remember," Carl Corso quickly acknowledged. "It was quite a display, acknowledging one another as found treasure, an attachment that must be taken into account."

"You should have seen their reaction earlier, laying together on the carpet, close enough to each other for their breathing patterns to be almost one. Suggestive of their ancestry living with their peers in a secured den, where survival actions were taken as a team, before domesticity tamed them from their domiciled wilderness."

"I believe those instincts are inherent and remain despite centuries of genetic engineering and refinement, getting together undeterred by what appeared to be insurmountable challenges," Staves said, adding, "They're wonderful dog's, but as you know once there minds are made up they're quite determined."

Carl Corso, agreeing said, "This certainly is an example. I've decided to increase the voltage in our containing system to keep this from happening again, although judging from Smokey's determination, he might still tolerate it."

George Staves suggested, "Why don't we agree that they continue to see each other by making sure that our walk routes include passing each other's houses? Stopping when the other is outside for them to greet one another," both agreed it was a good idea.

Rose, Phyllis, and Edward strongly endorsed the plan.

Reacting to Mr. Corso's arrival, Smokey's body language changed; going to him reluctantly when called, showing dejection, sensing immediate forced separation. Tasha showed no such dejection, sensing the mutual commitment their owners made to promote future contact visits. Analytical of Tasha reaction, George Staves was not surprised the dogs were intellectually apart, the meaning of their words and tones she had understood while Smokey didn't. Also complicit in Tasha's understanding was the change in chemistry within humans, revealing scents that she responded to. Misunderstood by Smokey, his reaction separated them. Exemplifying Tasha's unique intellect, even amongst her breed was amazingly deviding. Happily, Tasha and Smokey would continued their relationship for years until death separated them.

~

Unexpectedly, Staves found linkage. A correlation, Carl Corso's expressions, and the wishes of Mrs. Springer from the grave. The principal connection: internment. The Corso's glorifying their respective event- their pet Smokey photograph denoting his importance in their lives and it's sharing- a relatively commonplace request amongst dog lovers. While Mrs. Springer's accommodation after death was extraordinary and shared with few, it's bizareness was not an exemption, as both expressions varying as they may be, were driven by expressing their Husky's meaning in their lives in perpetuity, making them inclusive.

Further spanning over the divide of connection. Tasha and the growing evidence of Norse, Mrs. Schindler's Husky, a possessor of special communicating assets. Separating; their extraordinary intelligence, their cognizant awareness in evidence: reactions beyond the pale of most canines. Emitting differing vocal sounds at differing decibel levels; emitting and recognizing telltale scents in the absence of sound, all components as their language of sensitivities.

Pursuing further, George Staves, he his own tribunal, searched diverse sources for greater understanding of the mystique that attracts humans to dogs, and dogs to humans – collating that information for significance, hopefully putting him on a path towards absolving his personal conflict.
The outgrowth of such devotion and commitment, Mrs. Springer, as was his register, learned not all their vocalizing is alike, that howling is a notice, equally bringing attention as the piercing sound emanating from an electromechanical alerting device, or the shouts of distress from humans.

Factually dogs hear sound frequencies that cannot be processed by the human ear. Could not this ability, Staves pondered, also suggest that they can vocalize just above the hearing range of humans, clearly expressing themselves, with humans none the wiser? Knowing that, could not the more intelligent of the canine species, their language for communicating at the human level, be hidden within their howling and barking? Wolves, from which all canines can trace their origin, communicate by varying decibel levels and pitch. Location at one decibel level to gather together, for pack strength. At another sound level which is more musical, expresses enjoyment and pleasure. At another level during mating season, a message for coupling to continue the species. At another level to would be intruders, the pack already having an Alpha, be it male or female, to be tested if the intent of the intruder was to challenge the present social order. Mrs. Springer had to have learned these signals were part of Norse's makeup, going beyond them, challenging his intellect, evolving a special magnetism to connect, it's mystique energizing their relationship, both lovingly embracing it, both always on the same page, servicing each others emotional needs.

What placed Tasha apart from Norse's gift Staves's was convinced was her gift of telepathic energies, receiving and sending, given credence by her actions and reactions. His thesis bolstered as members of the scientific community maintain the universe as having many energy fields- that forces exist that have not been identified or measured. Leading to his belief, beyond just simple awareness in varying levels, is a capability gifted animals can demonstrate. Believing Tasha was exceptionally gifted, her complex behavioral patterns, beyond the learning responses of trial and error, beyond nurturing.

Tasha was endowed with extra sensory perceptions, exhibitions beyond the "Nature Theory" which asserts that most animals in varying degrees know what to do instinctively. Staves's experience's justifying he discredit the myopic limitations of some quarters, a programmed prejudice, limiting truths, in some cases science minimizing animal behavioral patterns. Tasha an exemplar that animal consciousness was not limited to awareness only, as was, while not as profound as Tasha, Norse. He was convinced from their communications that Mrs. Springer lived her relationship with a Norse credentialed with extraordinary behavior, she becoming indifferent to species, Norse almost human in devotion.

Despite the denouncements of heresy from those that would dispute, the evidence was clear, albeit still primitive, that animals can think and reason. It should not be ignored but give pause to the loftiness of exclusively being engendered to humans only. George knew his conclusions went against the grain of doctoral wisdom. The noted social scientists, and the physiologists, who spent many hours of study would dismiss with very powerful arguments, his beliefs and those of comparable positions. Those of closed minds condemning as self-serving-when highly angered, insulting those enlightened as unrealistic. George Staves and his fellow believers having fallen, fell prey to folk psychology, given substantive meaning where rote reflexes were the only senses demonstrated.

His emotional attachment, they would say, had driven him to a murky philosophy, a fixation that barricaded him from the compelling sciences. Establishing a safe haven island for himself – of anthropomorphism where his sought-after answers comforted and did not deny. A manipulation, of reality, downplaying their sciences as too restrictive. Condemning his rationalization that all animal creatures were given birth by God communicating and feeling a need for one another. His and his ilk attempting to expand their necessarily secular science. Dismissing as unwarranted being more inclusive, to oblige strained truths. There community judicious not blind and prejudicial.

While he had no supporting "White Paper" written by notables, he found many subscribers whose positions were in acknowledged print. Biographer's examining and recording naturally occurring events among the animal species, unimpeded and unplanned, avoiding blemished conclusions of episodic nurturing. The threatened elitist scientist, his position cloaked in obstinacy, spun from aging threads into a ill-fitting fraying garment, failing to shelter from alternative findings or heart-felt conclusions. Still however a force arbitrarily holding as unproven, not credible, instances of alternative science. Planning an inconclusive grade in their studied findings, they remain condescendingly purist, banishing the controversial to a footnote in their journals, "Further study needed."

What is true without question is lived actual experiences, the experiences that laboratory conditions cannot duplicate or model, heralding a new threshold of understanding. Staves's evolved enlightenment on dogs did not stray him from accredited Darwinism, or the religiosity of creationism. That contentious subject better left to philosophical debate. His position while sometimes sur-real, was actually closer to St. Francis who believed spirituality was within all of God's creatures, saying to the non-believers who vent negativism, "Find God's blessings and the common chain of homeopathy that links many alternative philosophies. Bring together humans and perhaps all living beings that have energy bodies that underlie or form the means of communication for their physical form. Go find the energy fields that he has found and if you wish to become a believer, be at rest with expanded wisdom."

⁓

The two-week deciding time was rapidly coming to an end with his decision not any clearer. True he prepared himself for both options with his catalogist effort, needing a scale of measurement, to rate or to eliminate.
Delayed as he had premonitions that other factors not yet revealed to him will be weighty. Where he had earlier found it impossible to sleep, his sleep now was fractured, causing wide swings in his moods, his family not yet taking into his confidence bearing the burden. George had not slept continuously and restfully for the last few days. Blameless was the absence of dreams of disturbing consequences, at least none that he could recall. He concluded at a yawning punctuated breakfast that his deprived sleep had begun to take its toll. He welcomed his concerned wife's suggestion, agreeing to take the day off, hopefully to confuse his twelve-hour clock, attempting to sleep during his programmed waking hours.

Wearily, George climbed the stairs to his bedroom, his movement robotic whose power source was almost exhausted, Tasha as always close to his side, her eyes and face expressing approval for his decision to try to sleep. He slipped exhaustively into bed with Tasha, completely out of character, laying next to him. George was unwilling to remonstrate her for her transgression, noticing her countenance of sympathy for his sleep deprivation, curtailed him. What he did not notice in Tasha's visage was it's mysterious anticipation. He was not denied. Sleep came quickly as did the stress induced movement of his eyelids: the telltale sign of dreaming which did not escape Tasha's notice, as if expected.

⁓

George was in his shirt sleeves yet he knew the night should be cool enough for a jacket or sweater. "Not like me," he reproached himself, switching to being thankful that there was no chill, no discomfort, just confusion as he awaited the rising sun to start its daily journey.

"Where am I?" he questioned, in need of distinguishing light to illuminate this foreign place he inexplicably found himself visiting. He found his hands in his pockets, not for warmth but to immobilize them, to prevent movement as was the rest of the mysteriously forced immobility of his body. The lack of movement stiffened his back muscles, fully captive to this benign land. His eyes strained against the darkness for some recognition, perplexed as his intuitive mind's eye suggested a presence was missing bringing familiarity. His synapses struggled to comprehend, abbreviated and interrupted as if short-circuited by power surges.

Bewildered in his inanimation, fixed to one spot by some mysterious gravitational force, yet in defiance, he saw as wisps his body's image transport to investigate this strange land under siege. Nondimensional, the wisps moved as if his body's composition was frivolous smoke flowing through the gaps in the lifeless tree branches, permeating through oddly denuded hedges, searching, yet seeing nothing. His specter's exploring the land, fragmented to reassemble as one, stopping at the lands border, restrained from further travel, returning empty of message to be re-absorbed within his waiting body. His eyes gained assistance from a suddenly appearing moon finally shed of its cloud cover, moved by winds aloft. Given illumination, he adjusted to the darkness, bringing furtherance to the land's ambivalence.

In spite of his confusion, he knew it was summertime when trees should be bearing their beautiful coverings. Instead, they were barren of their leaves, having fallen to the ground beneath in premature death to remain an unmoving progeny in a common grave. The branches of the trees were ashen, the mournful color of death, bled lifeless from unseen wounds, made susceptible in their frailty, ready to be felled by the slightest of winds if not for inertness. Those sights were firmly imbedded in his mind, their message un-ciphered, his restraint vacating as he felt movement in his toes the beginning of his mobility.

While he had given up smoking years ago, George saw himself trying to light up, first unsuccessfully firing a cigarette lighter and then with matches that equally failed. There was no spark from the flint of his lighter and the matches crumbled after repeated strikes. It was as if there was no oxygen available for ignition yet he was breathing without difficulty.

He strained to hear sounds but heard nothing: no traffic, no rumbling of trains given greater range to their disquietude by conducting nighttime stillness, no sounds of commerce or emergency, nothing. It was as if he was in a vacuum with all atmospheric and sound producing bodies sucked out of this space he found himself involuntarily visiting. Absent also were the sounds of nature: no birds chirping or dogs barking, nothingness… only emptiness. But he was here, alive in this inanimate landscape.

He wasn't dead, at least he thought he was alive. His last memory was of laying down for a needed nap with Tasha, his guardian, at his side. Nothing traumatic had happened to him. He must still be alive. But why his separation from his family. He knew he couldn't call out to them as he was in a place without normal expectations of sound. Coincident, he felt a constricting in his throat effectively muting any calls he might attempt if possible. Confident it could not be an out-of-body experience as he was alive and not near death, his specter not hovering over him. He could feel his body intact, his soul's religiosity remaining unclaimed, his time as a human not at end. What had befallen him, alive visiting this barren place where time past and catatonic current time are one, a future unable to develop-at a standstill.

Concerned by his isolation, George again strained his hearing senses against the foreboding barrenness: nothing. This lack of environmental substance defied his comprehension. Anxiety began building within his body, making his breathing difficult as if the air, his oxygen supply was being exhausted, he gulped large amounts to compensate.

Suddenly as if time was fast forwarding, the sun was well advanced in its easterly rise, dawning an end to the darkness, his breathing difficulties easing. The advancing light was a valve to release the vacuum of nothingness, atmospheres that were kept away rushing back into the vacated chamber that was this place, bringing the consciousness of recognition and the sounds of the living. The clearing sky offered few clouds to prevent the advancing waves of light to vanquish the darkness revealing the vivid personalities of everything it illuminates. Could his understanding be far behind? When it was his turn to receive the approaching illumination, his expectations were denied. The land he stood on and it's immediate area, were rationed of light and warmth-tokenism, as if shielded by a giant canopy, refracting and bending the light's rays, denying passage, absenting shadows. An outcast as outside the enveloping shroud, color in all its magnificent shades appeared. Shadows were cast, life-size or distorted by the varying angles of light, infinitely changing with the sun's inexorable movement.

Life outside of his deprived sphere ongoing. Nature awakened, performing its functions, its passion for colors no longer hidden by lack of light, on proud display. But he and the land he visited prejudiced, still entombed in an inert environment. He questioned why was this land he stood on was excluded, imprisoning him initially with immobility? Why was this place orphaned and ignored by ongoing Mother Nature? What sins had it committed to be wounded so bloodlessly, to exist as scars on the landscape, this graveyard without a headstone? What would be the purge to cleans it of sin and dispatch its inertness? Flowers without scent; grass stunted in growth in mid-season hibernating beneath his feet. Unmoving fallen leaves denied the decay of their death cycle. Beyond his periphery, the adjacent bordering land absorbed full sunlight, proceeding unimpeded was nature's commerce.

Other questions arose as he watched the dichotomy. Was he the only thing alive, a courier of gloom? Was it he that cursed the land wherever he stood? No longer constrained, he found his answer, moving with trepidation he stepped beyond the demarcation line and was greeted instantly with warming sunlight, his presence casting welcomed shadows relieved that he was not the source of the affected lands plague, it was specific to this acre of land. Nature fruitful until stopped at the razor's edge of the begotten land of inertness.

His movement placed him in the continuum of life, amidst a new day: announced by the audible chirping of birds and the swishing of early morning sprinkler systems. Contrasting, the barren segregated land he left who or what was responsible for its plight, the land mysteriously blighted. A separation not in punishment, strangely communicating, it awaited it's decipher to restart it's life's clock. But what has the power to transform, to give rebirth to a nature being bared, being held back. Is that why he was there, a messiah having the power to transform, to bestow, needing only the key.

Suddenly distracted, he felt a heaviness on his chest making his breathing labored. He saw himself traveling in retreat, falling backward away from that place of mystery, returning to where he embarked. His face suddenly felt moistened as if being wiped with a coarse cloth. He awoke with a start, ready to cry out when he realized that the heaviness he was experiencing in his chest was Tasha atop of him peering down on him, deliberately returning him to an awakened state with her affectionate licking of his face. Fully awake, he remembered when he fell asleep, Tasha lay down on the bed with him. He pulled her off of him pondering his dream's implications, "Did she know and feel my anguish, giving me escape from my dilemma?"

His wife Rose came into the room, directing Tasha off the bed. "I heard you moaning. A bad dream?" she asked.

"Yes," he responded somewhat embarrassed, still shaking his head in disbelief. "The strangest dream I've ever had. It's still very vivid in my mind. How long have I been asleep?"

"About an hour. You can use more," she said with a concerned look in her eyes.

"You're right. I don't feel rested. I could use some more. I just don't feel like getting out of bed just now. I hope you don't mind " he replied.

Rose smiled and said, "of course." Turning to Tasha she added sternly, "Daddy can't sleep with you lying across his chest." Tasha hesitant looked forlornly at George. "You come downstairs with me," Rose insisted.

With her hand around her collar, Rose led a reluctant Tasha from the room, closing the door shut to prevent her from returning.

Again sleep came easily. As had happened earlier he began to dream, but this time the imagery was different.

He was inside the Springer home, ignored as if invisible amongst those gathered. Faith Springer ministering a wheelchaired Kenneth Springer. Having bathed him, had just finished shaving him, patting his face with his favorite after shave lotion, and playfully rubbing it on Norse's coat who stood nearby. After dressing her husband she began taking pictures, Kenneth Springer and Norse together as directed, never apart, partnering, never one without the other. Suddenly the scene changed as if he were viewing a revolving stage. Now the players were only Faith Springer and Norse. Again Mrs. Springer was taking pictures but only of a dressed up version of Norse, wearing Kenneth Springer's ties and baseball caps, admiring him as her creation, her lips moving soundlessly, lovingly talking to him. Another scene change; Mrs. Springer asleep, Norse laying in Kenneth Springer's twin bed. The scenes continually repeating themselves, as a disturbance awakened him.

Tasha whimpered and scratched at the door had awakened him after two hours, he remained in bed staring at the ceiling, as if his dreams answers would appear; their role appearing on a facsimile movie screen of whiteness, suddenly faced with a not to be denied Tasha's presence, having cleverly mastered the door knob with her teeth. Rose hearing the commotion commanded Tasha downstairs. In response George pet Tasha tenderly shouting down to her that he would be down shortly. He sat on the edge of the bed gathering himself, the strange and provocative dreams still vivid in his mind. Sensing a compelling need to decipher them, he reached over and pulled from the night table drawer a notepad and pencil. He remembered reading that to help in deciphering dreams, the first step was to write it all down, not in generalities, but to include all the details that can be remembered. With each word added, with each sentence completed, he relived in high magnification, his visits.

Augmenting his committed to writing description, that very day, he took his detailing to every website that dealt in dreams and their interpretations. Not satisfied, the following morning George visited the local high school library, spending hours absorbing articles and selected chapters of books that covered dream interpretations. There was plenty of reading matter, particularly with occult leanings and interpretations, which he perused for information gathering only as it that was not the path he wished to pursue, feeling his dream more pragmatic than supernatural. His dedication in being scientific in developing an understanding was found wanting. Science still debating the "what" and "why," with many theories being offered but few answers that would be pointed enough to accept, most in his judgment were unrealistic conjecture. A disappointing shortfall not meaningful enough to go beyond giving it cursory attention.

He turned his study from the secular to the scrupulously faithful. Interpreting dreams – a higher source was involved, the religious scholars would say, citing the strength for recruitment in parables and scriptures, evidenced in:

> "For God speaketh, yea twice, yet man perceiveth not. In a dream, in a vision of night, when deep sleep falleth upon men in slumberings upon the bed; then be openeth the ears of men and sealeth their instruction."[1]

As George was a religious man, he did not dismiss the biblical alert that a higher power might have been involved, orchestrating his visits of mystery. Finding more credibility, believing, as had been written, that dreams are important for many cultures spiritual belief systems. Dream visitations being usually individual, interpretations specifically dependent upon the individual's receptivity; whether dismissed as an incidental event, or belief and faith that something more exists beyond a physical life. Spectrally visible as conscious apparitions, or sleep induced dreams.

What had he learned from his study? Dreams, its characters and characteristics displayed in many disguises and varied roles, are really about you and your fears and suspicions. Understanding the distortions, presentations remain illusive without your recognition, it is you who is central in their determination. Acknowledging this, Staves's remaining task; identifying the meaningful event that manifested itself as compelling dreams where he was central. These dreams, a production of his subconscious providing a dreamscape cloaked in symbolism, in need of a cipher to break down the encoded message.

He left his reflective state and returned to his dream notes, penciling in the connections he needed to make:

Why him? Why was he the central object, its apex? Why in his first dream was the place visited familiar yet elusive? What was the reason for it's barrenness, the perpetual darkness and the ceasing of life and what were they symbolic of? And what of his second dream visiting the Schindlers home, the significance of the changing scenes he witnessed? He knew answering those key questions would lift the clouds of mystery. Still they alluded him, in consternation he starred off into space.

Once again he returned to his notes. Troubled and tired, repeatedly blinking, he stared at his written description and his post-mortem questions

1 Book of Job 33:14–16

he posed to himself. Drawing his tired eyes away from his notes, resting them while reflecting, George remonstrating he may be unconsciously thwarting his reasoning process to allow an escape. He circumventing the hidden truth engaged a two component internal battle–on one side delaying the only conclusion he could reach, the other, reasoning because of implications, wishful that another message was portrayed in his dreamscape scenario, continuing the inner conflict. Stymied, he repeated the process again, the answer escaping to deep inside his brain's command center, avoiding what was always available.

Again his notes drew his attention. As if given a life of their own, the words seemed to lift themselves from the paper, presenting themselves in such close proximity to his eyes they were all he could see. Dominating, effectively keeping his mind from other considerations, forcing forth answers of clarity and understanding.

Finding the symbols meaningless in any other scenario, he chastised himself for cowardly avoiding an earlier understanding, the answers now so obvious no longer repressed. Logic, rejecting meandering, his conflict easily fitting as meaningful to his dream puzzle. The picture developed as he connected the matching pieces, fore fronting; the issue of Mrs. Springer's cremated remains. A torment that manifested itself as dreams of pleading distortions and abstract symbolism. The place's of his dreams, sequentially Mrs. Springers guised property, stripped bare of personality, unrecognizable, existing only in desolation awaiting hope. The later a loving Mrs. Springer, corporeal within her property and family.

He didn't believe that Tasha's strange and unusual behavior was coincidental. She his first sight, as he awakened from his dreamscapes. Her presence purposeful, he was convinced, seeded by a higher authority encouraging him to draw her symbolic connecting role, establishing he held the key that he now recognized. He alone was empowered to deliver the land, bringing sun lighted re-growth, captivating scented flowering colors and the rebirth of cast shadows for contrast. Yet it was a incomplete enlightenment, complete only when he could reconcile the mystery of him needing to bear witness within the Springer's home, of the taking of photographs, their representations of the before and after of Kenneth Springer's death.

What had gained his cognizance, the message of the first dreamscape fulfilled, he was the surrogate to deliver that which would act as a catalyst bringing forth instant birthing from the loins of the awaiting land, reproductive once again, joining it's surroundings. Reconciliation that the life-giving substance he had access to was Mrs. Springer's empowered ashes. It was clear to him that fulfilling her wish of co-joining her ashes with those of her beloved Norse would return life to the land of figments, awakening it from a catatonic state should he visit it again in his dreams.

This was the message of this symbolic dream. The second dreams interpretation alluded him. On it's own it was not enough to convince him of it's rightfulness.

With full discovery still illusive, needing to clear his mind, he took leave of his pursuit. Returning from a walk, with Tasha at his side, George stopped at the mailbox to collect the mail. Annoyingly, some of the majority of mail was unsubscribed, directed to "Occupant." Turning toward the house as he continued to sort through the mail, Tasha suddenly balked, steadfast in her refusal to budge, unresponsive as he pulled on the leash. This was not typical of Tasha who was usually quite anxious after a long walk to quench her thirst. In bewildering consternation, he pulled harder on the leash urging her on. This time, her response was to jump up onto his chest forcing him backward, barking while staring up at him. He pushed her off him, chastising her with scolds of "Down, Tasha, down." She obviously wanted something which he failed to understand. In frustration, George looked back at the mailbox and spotted the reason for her unusual antics. There, lying on the ground next to the curbside mailbox was a piece of mail he had accidentally dropped. Critical of himself for his impatience and lack of understanding he was moved to smile proudly at her intelligence. Saying openly and rewardingly, "Smart dog."

Returning to the fallen mail, George retrieve it and placed it into her quickly grabbing mouth, suiting her playful fancy. Possessive, not giving it up until she received her blackmailing just reward. But not this time. Holding fast, not yielding her prize, not to be bargained away by her usual treat. Despite his pleas, she continued to ignore his expectation and the bribe offering. While surprised at her stubbornness, he attached no significance, busying himself going through the rest of the mail. Not forgotten he occasionally turned to look at Tasha still holding the letter captive, not ready to give it up.

When finished classifying the postal delivery, he once again called upon Tasha to release her guarded mail. Finally relenting, dutifully sitting next to him, holding her head up to allow the withdrawal of the letter from her mouth.

"Why now and not earlier?" George questioned, shaking his head. Only on her terms, he thought, his mind searching expansively. Was she being mischievous or was she telling him that this piece of mail deserved all of his attention? That its message would be missed if he was not in committed focus? He liked to believe that was the case, his pride hopeful to once again bestow upon her a unusual insight, akin to being a possessor of extrasensory perception.

The letter he learned was sent by the County Animal Warden advising him that Tasha's license renewal had come due. The county needed dual purposed confirmation: the coming year confirmed she existed in animated notice and life, and the Staves responsibility of her ownership. An official testament, to be issued that they belonged to one another; a license physically connecting them, serving at the pleasure of one another; renewable as demanded; priceless in metaphysical terms, notwithstanding the passionless bureaucratic fee.

Still wondering about Tasha's strange behavior, his mind was expansive, malleable to suggestion, a past success responsible for the deciphering of the first dream. His trusted intuition in play, George was convinced that Tasha's obstinacy display and the license renewal notice were connected, not a circumstantial happening ordained by the gods of chance.

The mail notice, for official recognition of Tasha's existence, taking on additional meaning in his present state of mind. It a sad reminder that Norse and Mrs. Springer's official connection would no longer need filing. Only the living need apply to the impassioned bureaucracies cataloguing. Death ending compliance to officialdom.

His word "connection" echoed in his mind. His puzzle pieces fitting, becoming a scenario less disjointed, and then suddenly it was continuous, he was no longer in a quest to decipher his second dream. Mrs. Springer's specter representation that haunted him was now reconciled, as was Tasha's amazingly purposeful behavior bringing him to proper focus. It was all about "transference." That Freudian meaning came to him as if runway lights of an airport, comforting in their sight, his plane vectored on instruments breaking through ground hugging fog. Transference was Mrs. Schindler's narrowing world, the conjured need of the photo's depiction, her beloved Kenneth Schindler and Norse as one. Dressing Norse in her husbands ties and caps, coaxing, inventing their duality of persona, becoming as one. Her fantasy precluding their differing physicality, discounting as meaningless in her state of mind. She would will Norse's image to include that of her husband. In life they were a triumvirate. In death they would be separated if in a heavenless afterlife. The bleakness of that as an occurrence unacceptable, her away from church religious belief she now compromised in that eventuality, a plan for the coupling of their remains answering a personal need, .it's satisfaction not to be known in a eternity without religions prevailing. A response fearing that God's kingdom was symbolic, that there might not be a heaven, that her place after death would be where she was reposed, until stirred from within the need to reestablish the priority of her religious beliefs. Purging herself of guilt her hands together in prayer – penance for introducing a doubt of an eternity without one another, praying to her maker to understand her weakness that led her to compromise its essence, and the certainty of repeating the hypocrisy while still alive.

Unable by law to include Norse in their common gravesite, she would direct the regrouping of her triumvirate, transference the key, creating after death togetherness with the co-mingling of their respective ashes. The possibility, to which she succumbed, that no afterlife existed just a hereafter abyss, justifying that she make additional provisions, their remains to lay in state connected, a retreat to a heavenless eternity more endurable. The location of her husbands remains were a deterrent to their grouping. The desperation of the circumstances demanding transference. Her husband and Norse becoming one, joined by her ashes bonding forever. Mrs. Springer's remains and the essence of her beloved husband communicated by Norses, merged in a secret afterworld of symbolism. This discovery, his role and it's message, joined the other tormenting episodes of symbolism were finally catalogued: Needing only his willingness.

Finally he brought Rose, into his confidence, no longer indecisive, but in need of a sounding board, and hopefully supportive once she shared his interpretations of his dreams. As expected Rose expressed great concern for the legal ramifications of his clandestine action. Resolutely he repeated the recent inescapable events, the significance he attached to his dreams; so specific the various methods of communiqué they were easily conceptualized as a message from the grave. While he was religious in faith, as she knew, a prospect of a non- existent spiritual afterlife was brought into question, coping with that void made her uncomfortable. Rose sat there transfixed, as he made connections to all the symbolic events to support his decision. Reluctantly, she acknowledged that these were not chance happenings that could be explained as circumstantial. Emotional, she clutched the crucifix that hung around her neck, admitting the strange events were unfolding; forces at work leading him. Silently praying they were the will of God, asking His forgiveness for her husbands responding to faithless meandering while remaining a believer. In his infinite mercy, forgiving his transgression: complicity in the only conclusion that would truly bring him peace of mind. She was comforted by Tasha's behavior during his period of torment, whose actions could only be interpreted as having prior knowledge, an extra sensory perception guiding her, directed by God.

The incidents giving him direction, enabling him to reach out and touch her, with this act of communication to where Mrs. Springer deceased, waits. He would respond favorably to Mrs. Springer's unorthodoxy; traversing laws, a kindness on this earth that could never be acknowledged, but rated in the afterlife of his beliefs.

The next day he made the phone call. "My name is George Staves," he replied when asked who was calling. "I'm calling for Mr. Mercer."

He smiled to himself, as he expected, the secretary's response was measured and efficient, implying only the pre-scheduled, those screened and accredited would be passed through to his eminence

With self-assurance she responded, "I'm sorry but Mr. Mercer is in conference with a client. May I take a message?"

"Of course," he responded. "Ask him to call George Staves at his home at his convenience. I'm sure he has the number but just in case, let me give it to you."

"What is it you wish to discuss with Mr. Mercer? Are you a client?" She asked cordial and formal, trying to establish his credentials as worthy of visiting with her employer.

"I'm afraid you won't find my name in the client file. It's a personal matter, one with which Mr. Mercer is familiar."

He sensed her hesitancy, undecided whether she should pursue the matter any further.

"I'm sure he'll want to talk to me. He's expecting my call That's really all Mr. Mercer would expect you to know," he said in assurance, interrupting her thought process.

"I'll give him the message," she said, her responsibility to screen served, elevating her callers resolve for confidentiality.

And so began one of the strangest episodes of his life. He was forced to enter into a bargain with a person of jaded character, compromised by an obligation to a briefly known decedent whose wishes he found so compelling in spite of the risk. George Staves knew he had no choice. Needing to get on with his life without being regretful, he had navigated through his ambivalence. He would be committed but guarded, devising a plan that would minimize the risks.

Robert Mercer called him back at lunchtime and judging from the background noise, he was not in his office.

"I'm calling you from a public phone so we can speak freely," Robert Mercer said in a tone suggesting he enjoyed acting clandestined.

Staves reluctantly acknowledged the need for caution but accepting Mercer's theatrics strained his patience.

"I hope you have been well," Mercer said with practiced solicitation as he checked his latest manicure.

Staves, despite being on the phone, could easily visualize Mercer's countenance: transparent in feigned concern and sincerity. Characteristically, Mercer did not wait for George's response.

His obligation over, abandoning his pretensions, "What decision have you reached?" Mercer expedited, returning to his self-indulgent lofty perch. The deliberate showiness of his attitude worsened Staves' demeanor toward Mercer.

"I've decided to do it," Staves responded with disdain, wanting to end the phone conversation and leave Mercer's theater. "But with certain conditions."

"And they are?" Mercer responded in arrogance, nonetheless remaining inquisitive, confident that he had achieved victory, Staves in agreement. The day was his he was certain, no matter what conditions Staves posed.

"In this community, in this state, as you know the spreading of cremated remains on private property without approval is illegal. Because of her unusual request the handling of Mrs. Springer's ashes dictates that it be done surreptitiously. That being the case, it presents a risk for discovery. To reduce my risk, I'm insisting that we create the following subterfuges:

"One, you purchase space at a mausoleum vault or cemetery plot, properly identified to accommodate what is to be believed are Mrs. Springer's ashes."

"Already arranged," Mercer interrupted.

"Let me finish," Staves injected.

"Two, arrange for a memorial service with prayers at the gravesite. Prior to those arrangements, you are to place a notice in the local newspapers announcing the service. In addition, you are to notify her only living relative."

"Three, have all legal documents showing that you personally witnessed the interment."

Mercer was quick to grasp Staves' plan, stimulated by it's audacity and the position he was being placed in. Again he interrupted, "What kind of substitutes for cremated remains are you planning?"

"Sand, stone, dirt, any substance of comparable density would do the job," Staves replied. The urn can be sealed so as not to be opened accidentally." Enjoying his moment of Mercer's expanded involvement, Staves added, "All you have to do is supply an exact duplicate of the original urn to avoid suspicions. Then call the funeral service you hire and tell them you have ashes that you wish interred. They will take care of all matters including the graveside service."

Mercer quickly returned to his orchestrating role, "That's an excellent cover plan, one I can secretly support but one I cannot directly participate in. What you're asking establishes greater public involvement than I wish. It positions me at risk for which I have no desire or obligation. This is your show. You will be responsible for all aspects in making the switch."

Preaching to Staves his rationale, Mercer continued, "My only obligation is to fulfill the requirements of the probated will. As far as I'm concerned, after this day, officially I know of no other request of Mrs. Springer. With all records to be destroyed, provable truth will be in absence. Until then you and I are the only ones privy to her final request held exclusively secret by our mutual cooperation.""One-sided you mean," Staves interrupted angrily.

Ignoring his anger, impervious to the insult, Mercer continued without hesitation:

"I can only act behind the scenes as an appointed messenger to relate her wishes to you. The final option of those wishes, I repeat, will have no paper trail to expose it's undertaking. I'm under no obligation to go beyond the on-file document signed for cremation and internment of her ashes. Serving a dead woman's secret wish with its moral implications, I leave that act of consciousness to you. If it is your exclusive wish to honor her, so be it. Beyond that, If I'm of mind I can unofficially show gratitude but that is all. The records will clearly show that my representations of her legal interests have been or will be concluded. My involvement ends in this matter when I turn over her ashes to you and as far as I know their lawful internment. My co-operation ends with the transfer. From that moment on I know of no other plans that you have in mind."

Much to Staves' regret, Mercer had successfully distanced himself from the issue. For that cold disassociation Staves was furious, but the reality of Mercer's personality said he was overly optimistic to conclude otherwise. He still could walk away and resume his life marked, living with the constant reminders of turning his back on Mrs. Springer, bordered on betrayal. He would not go through life punishing himself for not performing an act of kindness.

"All right," he said, bitter at Mercer's self-righteous sanitizing of himself. "You may think you can hide protectively, but in reality the truth of your involvement and manoeuvrings will imprison you. Maybe not now but in years to come when you face your maker. While my conscious will be clear."

Untouched by the assault on his character, Mercer proceeded undeterred.

"Your feelings and the success or failure of your endeavor is of no consequence to me. The file will be closed and archived. Without remorse I will move freely onto current matters." Equally calculating he continued, "Mrs. Springer's Will also provided for an escrow account to handle unexpected expenses. Your plan certainly meets those criteria," Mercer said in triumph, Stave's commentary forgotten. "Just send the bills to me marked confidential with no reference other than 'Mrs. Springer's funeral service and cremation.'

"For your information, I have rented storage space at a local storage facility where I currently store the urn. It's rented for six months which will certainly overlap the period of optimum opportunity that you alluded to. I will send you by messenger a legal document for you to sign, assigning you responsibility of Mrs. Springer's ashes. That document is to be returned to me by the same messenger. In addition, the messenger, after witnessing and receiving your signature, will turn over to you the address of the storage company and the key you'll need. You need not return the key to me. Dispose of it as you see fit."

"While you made your intentions quite clear from the beginning, mine weren't or at least I thought they weren't. But not to you. Am I so easy to read?" Staves said, annoyed with himself.

"That's what I get paid for," Mercer answered in a tone that did not hide his self-satisfaction his loftiness, said "I don't think we'll need each other's services again once this matter is concluded today. I'm sure you'll agree no further contact will be necessary. Again, I compliment you on your plan," he said in token offering, presuming that these would be the final words of the conversation.

"This matter is not quite done," Staves interjected.

On the other end of the phone line, Mercer paused to search his intellect, self-assured, unable to believe his preparation was faulted, that he had overlooked something. "And that is?" he scoffed, doubting the criticism impatiently.

Pleased that he had interrupted his march toward victory, Staves responded, "What you have overlooked, what you should insist on, having supplied the name of the manufacturer of the urn, its model number, to make arrangements with another source. It would not be good judgment on my part to buy a duplicate from the same source, one bearing your name is implicating. I also need, for possible reference, the name of the crematorium that handled Mrs. Springer's remains along with her only heir, Gloria Bowers' phone number and address so that I may contact her although from what I've learned, she won't be interested in attending the service."

Mercer paused, noticeably disturbed at his failings. Staves assumed this pause was a self-chastisement, ever demanding of himself, reproachful for his omissions, assailing his incompleteness in covering the details. His paranoia's wound was superficial as he quickly regained his balance. Beneath him to apologize, he said "You gave up an opportunity for my tie in. Why?"

"I expect to succeed not be in a position of naming co-conspirators. It is my greatest wish the future, with God's benevolence will provide no opportunity for our continuing involvement."

He paused as if taking Staves's measure. Then as if it hadn't happened he guiltless said:

"The messenger will also have all the information you need when you meet. Is that acceptable to you?"

"Yes," Staves replied.

"Then I see no reason for this phone conversation to continue and as agreed, to end further contact."

Hoping to further deflate his ego, Staves rejoined, "You've got all the answers but one," he said, enjoying his defiance.

"Which is?" Mercer retorted in breath expelling exasperation.

Again he sensed an opportune moment for further distressing Mercer, offering calculatingly, "I might just decide to actually commit Mrs. Springer's ashes to internment rather than a representation, and forego the spreading of her ashes."

Suggesting that he had anticipated such a move, Mercer was coldly dismissive, "That would be your decision that you need not share with me, one that you would have to live with."

"At peace," Staves moralized, "but somehow I don't think the uncertainty would satisfy you if I so decide. It will always be in the back of your mind as an unanswerable question. You could only guess. It's got to trouble you as proudly exacting as you like to present yourself. Unknowing is untidy for you. A loose end that portends unraveling vulnerability. Pleading ignorance does not sanitize your involvement. I don't have to tell you about being a co-conspirator after the fact. Claiming no knowledge, establish barriers to keep you safe from accusing complicity not only is perjury, paradoxically it separates you from the safe harbor of strength in numbers, of shared commitment with others equally vulnerable who act as guardians with honoring pledges to one another. I'm sure in your mind your detachment answering only to yourself fortresses you against exposure. Your criteria of hidden involvement giving you pleasure from afar will ultimately prove fleeting when in your final moments of life, facing the unknown, your departing agnosticism leaves you a confessor to your role as hardly that of a messenger or incidental."

"Spare me the moralistic psychoanalysis," Mercer angrily interrupted, his voice rising, "Are you now threatening me?"

"Not in the least," Staves answered, pleased with Mercer's reaction. "I'm not masochistic. To threaten you is to threaten myself. Have no fear. I accept the responsibility for what I'm about to undertake. Your role, at least from my lips, will never be revealed even to those who might stumble onto my involvement. Any unforeseen paper trail can only indict me, as you already know. A noble cause I undertake as a remedial act of kindness, an opportunity to make amends metaphysically. A cleansing of conscience for those of us who showed neglect or little understanding as she cried out when most in need."

George paused, hoping his admission, his self-berating would spurn Mercer to extend himself beyond his clandestine broker involvement, casting only a shadow, a specter lacking substance, missing Samaritan emotional fulfillment.

Continuing, Staves said, "I do this not because of your pressure, but for myself, given an opportunity not to fail Mrs. Springer again. My guilt, obliging me. My conscience not allowing me to short-circuit her dying wish."

Mercer interrupted sarcastically, "Mrs. Springers last provisional response, by the way my credo, her most sensible thoughts a confessional that there could be no after life, self servingly betraying her life's beliefs with the symbolic fantasy of the deranged."

Staves responded, "That's a cruel thing to say. Unlike you I'm not critical, it could still have meaning beyond symbolism. I believe there is an afterlife kingdom, death not being the finality, life's spiritual essence not stilled. If I'm wrong, what then is the harm if no injury arises by granting wishes that will never gain her cognizance? If that is the case which I doubt, the answer rests with the unknown, with the livings make up and spirituality, influenced by what one lives by. It's part of being honorable, my legacy to my progeny, to be seen as contributing to lift oneself by benefiting others, my image standing accountable, tall."

"Really," he interrupted, "How magnanimous of you but we'll never see it. Mrs. Springer's infirmed delusions: connecting with the loves of her life after death in a after life is pure superstition. That recognition became obvious to Mrs. Springer when she knew her death was imminent and the unknowns of eternity cast doubts. Resorting to hedging her beliefs, managing a physical connection in an empty eternity with at least one member of her family. Her fear seeking compromising Godless pagan practices, or subscribing to obscure folklore. While not embracing I can countenance her fall back option, using after death communications to gain sympathy, of what she, I'm thankful of, counted on- supporters like you. It is beyond my beliefs-superstitions, that I'm a participant in a underway spiritual event, it's currency, purchasing expansion of my role." Mercer responded dismissively.

"You're not fooling anyone, your preoccupation with agnostics is a subterfuge," Staves flaunted. "If you were so sure her beliefs were folly, why did you seek me out? Your privileged communiqué with Mrs. Springer and her easily destroyed letter would remain unknown if you so choose. Even in your peripheral involvement you are obliging her. Brokering the requests of, as you suggest, a frightened irrational woman, is indicative that you too are not absolutely sure that death is an empty infinity."

"Your correct. I am an agnostic, Mr. Staves. I only respond to what can be proven."

"But your action, limited as it may be, suggests you're hedging."

"Think what you want. That is all I'm going to say about my personal beliefs," Mercer said dismissively.

"I don't know if it's possible," Staves went on undeterred, "Within the last two weeks certain circumstances happened to me that without question gave support to the course of action I now take. One a dreamscape with coded scenarios, the others providential happenstance. Combined, their messages were certainly impacting."

"What does that mean?" he interrupted. "You're not telling me that you were being guided by mystical forces who communicated with you? That's laughable."

"Demean it all you want," Staves responded. "But think about it. Why would you, an officer of the court, forsake your basic tenet of self-protection, to involve me to bear witness against you. A hazard I would not expect of you. Circumventing not your usual judgment. You were steered to me. You could have turned it down as I would knowing our history, inviting risks you normally never take. Don't you see?" Staves impassioned. "You had no choice. You had to bring it to my attention. It was meant to happen."

"In this instance, we among many available, was the law firm solicited exclusively by Mrs. Springer for one reason only, being the best qualified to handle her affairs including what I privately regarded as her world of desperate invention. I wouldn't call culling through a phone book to select my firm an act of being preordained."

Staves interrupting said, "My research tells me you have twelve associates at your firm. Why did you decide to handle her issues yourself? Issues that are not high profile.Y our specialty. Why would you even involve yourself, beyond being updated by a subordinate more fitting? You interceding in a case relatively common had to have some unusual impetus. Think about it."

"The force your suggesting was nothing more than I needing a diversion, I will admit getting the upper hand after recalling being soundly defeated by you intrigued me. That's what's guiding me not some mysterious force arranging things."

"But you didn't know that until after you took the case, Staves spiritedly interjected. Continuing:

"Whether you admit it or not something else prompted your personal involvement at the outset, as if you knew special circumstances would evolve. Something beyond monetary, beyond your revenge, beyond your so called diversion influenced your direct participation albeit in narrow involvement. Why not go further, extending your participation as an equal partner? It might provide the answer."

"I won't comment further. I've gone as far as I will. Fantasies I leave to you and Mrs. Springer. I deal in facts, to do otherwise is to submit to beliefs foreign to me, " Mercer replied. Choosing not to mention the strange sudden flickering of lights set at low intensity, recovering to emit on it's own maximum luminescence highlighting her entrance into his office.

"Don't you see this circumstance offers an opportunity for a rewarding experience beyond your own scripted involvement. Life so narrowly focused misses the rewarding discovery of the peripheral, the abstract. A panorama not so one dimensioned, that includes all manner of beliefs. You can't always dismiss the unknown as unproven. There are issues, questions beyond black and white, where sympathy and knowledge, their density will make you more dimensional, enhancing your life," Stave persisted.

"I'm not a religious man. I provide for myself with my abilities," Mercer countered.

"Spoken as a true agnostic." Secular truths more convenient… easier to conclude.

"I am until formidable evidence becomes available, I will remain skeptical. You can continue to fanaticize, I deal in what I can see. Has substance."

"Mrs. Springer's wish asks that civil law and religious conviction be circumvented, its consequences I now accept. Your involvement if revealed would raise questions of ethics, endangering in the least your censure by the Bar Association, and still you do it- precariously testing your vulnerability. Dismissing with prejudice my feelings of a power beyond us, of great influence at work. Her death the medium that we travel a brief future, avoiding discovery together no accident. Why won't you admit your role and mine were already scripted. Nothing could change that, no matter the alternate choices we had." George said.

"Please spare me the supernatural, I know nothing about that. While you dismiss my position as denial, my actions are simply fulfilling an obligation that I take seriously: my professional promise to Mrs. Springer. There is nothing mysterious about that. I neither have found nor do I look for guiding symbolism as is your case. I deal in facts, not visions and hidden messages. My religiosity: is my clients contracted wishes- a business arrangement detailing obligations, for as long as it takes to achieve resolution, nothing more. I have protected myself in this matter. There will no evidence of specific or implied illegalities. That pursuit is the domain of others, you in this case choosing to undertake this task of stealth on your own – without my provable prior knowledge I can easily deny any accusations if it comes to that. These discussions taking place, our private unsubstantiated discourse does not identify both of us. Both of us I repeat. Remember this call I initiated is from a public phone," Mercer stated factually.

"What a pity. What a loss of opportunity for you to share in the good feeling of full involvement rather than that of an extra positioned in the wings of a stage with no recognizable role to play. Don't you see how unfulfilling that is. Always in the distance, a hideaway you visit frequently in exiled loneliness."

"It's my life," he responded, tiring of the subject.

"But don't you ever feel denied?" Staves questioned, persisting.

"Denied for what? I want for nothing."

"Who can you go to but yourself? Unable to escape yourself, imprisoned by a mirror that only shows your reflection. Unwilling to commit to look for answers beyond documents, beyond yourself, self-indulging in more of the same superficiality. Have a nice solitary life," Staves said in disgust as he hung up the phone.

His wife Rose, who had been seated in the living room, overheard his end of the phone conversation. Concerned but not distraught that her husband had essentially been abandoned by Mercer, she remained fully confident in her husband's judgment as she sat fully absorbed listening to her husband outline what had to be done. With the power of prayer she became fully supportive now that his mind had been made up.

Mercer's messenger arrived two days later just before suppertime. Staves working from a mental list of all unresolved items, checked them off as he went through the previously sealed envelope. Satisfied, he signed the document which transferred the ashes to his possession. The messenger, after witnessing the signing, also signed. Staves then removed a copy for himself, placed the original into the envelope provided, sealed it and sent the messenger on his return trip. Since it was now Friday, he welcomed the time provided by the weekend to think things through in final detail.

George awoke Monday morning to the usual sounds of Tasha sounding notice of her need for relief. He dressed quickly and soon he and Tasha were out the door for her usual walk along her well-spotted route. On the return trip a satisfied Tasha no longer anxiously tugged on her leash, allowing George's mind to wander in the cool and invigorating fall air for what he had to do.

While he was preparing to call the cremation facility, he realized with sudden clarity what he and Robert Mercer, while jousting for position, failed to recognize. He would not have to order an exact duplicate of the urn, the one currently housing the ashes was all that was needed to insure the illusion of an actual burial. Mrs. Mercer's ashes would be removed and placed in another container to await final disposition while the temporarily empty urn would be filled with comparable weighted material. As it was not sealed it could be opened, to complete its representation, the sounds of movement emanating from the urn must be discernible to avoid suspicion.

The urn as had been described to him by Robert Mercer was made of cast bronze, cylindrical in shape and engraved simply:

Elizabeth Springer
Born, 1920
Died, 2000
Rest in peace

He then called the funeral service and identified himself to a Mr. McMann, the managing owner. After explaining the reason for his call, George detailed his responsibilities and plans for the remains of Mrs. Springer and the services needed. Mr. McMann did not immediately recognize Mrs. Springer's name as he was heard to be turning pages of what was guessed to be his log.

"Ah yes, Mrs. Elizabeth Springer, her wishes carried out by her attorney, Mr. Robert Mercer. Bear with me a moment while I get the file."

Staves heard the file cabinet being opened. "Let's see," he continued. "I have the death certificate, medical examiner's cremation permit, a completed crematory authorization form, ownership certificate of a burial plot of three foot by three foot from the non-sectarian Knolls Cemetery Corporation. What we don't have is a headstone."

"Can you take care of that?" Staves asked.

"Of course. What would be the inscription?"

"The same as what is on the urn. I'll reimburse you for the costs."

"Of coarse," he repeated.

"Can you arrange for a graveside memorial service? We will be needing one. Again, the costs are to be added to the bill," Staves said.

"It's a service we offer. I assume it will be a non-denominational service?"

"Yes," Staves responded. "I will take care of the next-of-kin notification. She only had one living relative who resides in Florida."

"As you wish," Mr. McMann responded.

"I will also run a notice for two days in the obituary section of *The Tribune*. I'd like to read it to you for your commentary."

"Please do," Mr. McMann responded.

"It will read:

'Elizabeth Springer, eighty years of age; only living relative, Mrs. Gloria Bowers, residing in Florida. Graveside services at 10:00 AM Friends may meet at Knolls Cemetery in Elmont, Maple Road entrance gate, prior to the services. Arrangements by McManns Funeral Services. 450–4960.'

"Is that satisfactory?" Staves questioned.

"Perfectly satisfactory," McMann answered. "The only remaining issue is the date. When do you want it done?" With the business side of the arrangements completed, his tone became more solemn, more solicitous. "May I take the liberty of reminding you that the beginning of winter is only weeks away? Things get more difficult when the snow season begins."

"As of this moment, two weeks from today, Monday is the date. I'll call you within the next three days to confirm. I have a couple of minor issues that need attending. Is that date acceptable to you?"

"Yes, it is," Mr. McMann answered, obviously pleased. "I'll hear from you Wednesday to confirm the arrangements."

"Yes, Wednesday," Staves repeated. "Thank you for your help." He hung up the phone, satisfaction filling him.

He sat there thinking how relatively easy it was to make the burial arrangements. The only aspect of his plan with little threat, his only comfort to the coming difficult aspects of his endeavor, where things could go wrong, when he was most susceptible. Telling his wife of his immediate plans and avoiding the perceptive eye contact of Tasha, he left the house and got into his car. He could still hear Tasha scratching at the door leading to the garage as he pulled away.

George then drove to Mrs. Springer's old home now owned by the Schindlers. He parked in front, rolled down the passenger side window admiring the meticulous manicured lawn and landscaping, an eye-catcher in any neighborhood.

While he knew there would be no activity as the Schindlers were at their winter retreat in Florida, his real interest was the Schindler's neighbors on both sides of the street and whether they too were basking in warmer climates. This was not his first investigative visit. Others preceded and as planned, were conducted at different hours of the day. He needed confirmation that this very hour could be a consideration He didn't want caretakers or relatives assigned to house watching show up to complicate matters. The Schindler's neighbors directly across the street were a young couple who fortunately both worked. Nonetheless, as a precaution he confirmed their absence during this time and day. Taking their names off the curbside mailbox, he easily found their listed phone number which he proceeded to call by cell phone while in the car, anxiously receiving the activated recording message, establishing the time as fitting. He called many times at various hours to establish time constraints. While it was still daylight, he judged that discovery or suspicion would least likely occur at this time. While the police car patrols varied their routes and routine, he surmised and correctly so that most of their attention at those hours was given to school bus routes and major trafficked streets and thoroughfares.

That very evening after dinner and after Tasha's walk, George spoke of his final plans to his wife Rose. More so today than ever, he avoided Tasha's inquisitive eyes. He left the house through the garage and drove to the rented storage facility engaged by Mr. Mercer's law firm which temporarily housed Mrs. Springer's ashes. He used the key supplied to open the lock and raise the lift-up door. He then opened the trunk of his car, lifting out a partially filled fifty-pound bag of garden fertilizer along with an emptied one of matching size, carrying them both into the ten foot by ten foot storage space. After turning on the light switch on the wall, he pulled down the door to conceal his actions. Along the walls of the storage space were sealed filing cabinets tagged "Mercer and Associates" standing guard over a centrally located box approximately a foot square in size.

He gave pause momentarily to re-arm himself with resolve for what he believed was the compassionate rightfulness of his planned actions, setting aside the plan's faults: law breaking, violating laws for the treatment of human remains, as well as marginally at odds with ethical religious tenets. Any doubt

George had was short-lived as he remembered the words in Mrs. Springer's journal and its impact on him.

No longer pausing, he opened the box and withdrew the urn, opening it with some difficulty due to its testy locking mechanism. Removing the lid, he saw the remains of Mrs. Springer, crushed and pulverized to the smallest sieved particle size which he guessed to have been purposefully stipulated by Mr. Mercer to easily facilitate and hide their intended purpose. George commented emphatically to himself, "He did know. My response had been easily predicted."

Before he poured the ashes into the empty fertilizer bag, in reverence he dropped to one knee whispering the prayers: Hail Mary, and an Act of Contrition – Tears welling in his eyes.

"One step closer," he intoned, muffled by the protective surgical mask that covered his nose and mouth as he began emptying the urn of its contents of varying particle sizes.

When he was sure that all of the urn's contents had been transferred, he refilled the urn with the fertilizer. He then resealed the urn, lifting it to confirm the approximate weight so as to avoid suspicion or lead to questioning. He then carried the box which now held the urn, the fertilizer bag containing Mrs. Springer's ashes, the remainder of the bag of fertilizer, carefully placing them securely in the trunk of his car.

Under siege by his own imagination, he breathed a sigh of welcomed relief as he re-entered his garage, exhausted by the strain of the task, mentally uncomfortable with violating the law, imagining scenarios of discovery in his mind. Needing a stimulus for *reprieve and reinforcement,* his wife Rose, on edge driven by shared angst, greeted his return. Similarly relieved, at the initial success over a glass of Chardonnay, assuaging them both. Both reaching relaxation in the second glass. Thankful the first stage of his plan had been completed, he critiqued his demeanor as overly apprehensive, one certain to raise suspicion if confronted. Chastising himself to have greater control of his emotions to carry the task through to completion and avoid detection.

George was pleased that sleep came easily, his thankfulness short lived as he was immediately involved in accompanying nightmares in which the newspapers in his dreamscape identified him as a ghoulish grave robber, his perversions purpose holding cremated remains for ransom.

The next morning, not fully rested, the timing unusual he rose to the anxious whimpering of Tasha. Dressing quickly, he was soon on what he expected was Tasha's constitutional walk. Discounted as she strained unusually hard at her leash, making it difficult to keep pace with her. Continuing the unexpectedness she veered from the usual path, traveling a route that they hadn't traveled for months, directly toward Mrs. Springer's old house now owned by the Schindlers. Although it was not her usual time Tasha never paused to relieve herself or spot. When finally they were in front of the house she came to a decided stop peering penetratingly at him. He was perplexed, as her unusual behavior presented an unplanned opportunity to check out the neighborhood of his surreptitious undertaking. Her actions provocative, led him to imagine that Tasha was aware of what he had planned. Her expressive eyes supporting him, he put his fears aside, the timing was right, his cause a just one. As if on cue, suggesting she sensed that his panoramic overview had brought him confidence that no obvious threat existed, straining once again with equal vigor to return home and not lose a moment of opportunity.

Upon returning home, George went quickly to the garage and opened the trunk of his car removing the cardboard box, emptying it of its contents, replacing the space provided with his fertilizer spreader along with the bag containing Mrs. Springer's ashes and the bag of unused fertilizer. He then drove back to the house hopeful the opportunity still existed. He soon found himself traversing the property with the spreader, depositing a mixture of disguising fertilizer and the primary intended ashes to their final resting place. Grateful for completing the task without incident, he approached his car, opening the trunk to return the spreader and the empty bags.

At that very moment, he heard the low wail of a police siren gaining in intensity and decibel level as it turned down the very street he was parked on. Panic was instantly upon him. His immediate thought: that he had been reported by a neighbor as a unaccountable stranger. He assumed the worst; he had been discovered; he had been found out. He would have to have a reason for being there that would satisfy the police? Rationalizing, he reminded himself in desperation, they couldn't possible know or suspect, their was no evidence of his completed task. Their only possible suspicion was trespassing. He stood frozen, his hands above his head unnecessarily holding the trunk lid open, unable to move to turn to face his fastly approaching accosters. His mind racing, developed an explanation to account for his visit, a friendly favor from a not-so-distant neighbor, would satisfy as reasonable providing no confirmation would be sought if challenged by the police. Even in that worse case scenario, his confidence returning as he was sure he could convince the Schindlers that his purpose was friendly. However his mind reacted faster than his physicality, indicting stress-driven sweat coursed his face, his self-calming slow in arriving, apprehension prompting an increased heart rate. His stomach churned with sickening acid, forcing bile to rise up in his throat. The worst outcome had befallen him. He was portraying unknown guilt. He awaited his fate, renouncing poor judgment: putting himself in jeopardy. Doubtful he would be believed? He continued to show his back to the approaching police cruiser, fully expecting the nerve piercing squeal of brakes to announce his confrontation.

And then just as suddenly, it was gone, racing past him, sirens blaring in probable response to a 911 emergency call. He felt his taunt muscles beginning to relax as he lowered the trunk lid with his colorless hands, still drained by threat. His certainty of confrontation and arrest retreating, his benevolence influenced by his faith, protecting him from an untimely fate. His ability to move returned as he took a look around. No one was on the street. He had succeeded. He had gone undetected. He felt relieved. His doubts were gone as a sense of satisfaction filled him. "*Rest in peace*," he messaged in silence to Mrs. Springer. "*Find your Rainbow Bridge*."[2]

After lunch when he had fully recovered from the trauma of the morning's threat, he called Mr. McMann.

"Mr. McMann, this is George Staves. I'm calling to confirm the burial date."

"Of course," he intoned with the solemnity characterized by his profession.

"This coming Monday, the day we set aside, will be the day of the burial. I will make all the arrangements that I described to you right after this phone call. I'm prepared to deliver Mrs. Springer's remains today at 3:00 PM Is that hour convenient for you?"

"Yes," he responded.

"Then 3:00 PM it is," Staves reconfirmed.

After hanging up from Mr. McMann, Staves called the death notice department of *The Tribune* and dictated the notice. He then called Gloria Bowers. After the fifth ring, the answering machine came on. Identifying himself, he explained the arrangements that were in place. He did not feel any anguish inviting her to a faked burial service; he would rather enjoy it, her serving as an unsuspecting prop in his solemn theater, the "Knolls Cemetary." Rationalizing, a small payment due Mrs. Springer for what she had not done for her while alive. It was also an opportunity to re-identify herself as caring, to reclaim lost ground notwithstanding participating in a sham; her presence, a redemption from being an invisible relative all these years, publicly acknowledging Mrs. Springer's benevolence. Staves knew better but still held out hope that Mrs. Bowers might see the light and fulfill her obligations.

At 9:00 AM Monday morning, the day of the graveside services and the interment of ashes, as stipulated in the newspaper announcement, friends and relatives were to gather at the Maple Road entrance of Knolls Cemetery to proceed from that point to the burial site for services and final respects. As expected, few came, lack of response to the newspaper notice attesting to Mrs. Springers seclusion, serving the need of the public announcement objective of George Staves' plan for deception. The calloused cousin, Gloria

2 Rainbow Bridge; An imaginary crossing for reuniting grieving pet owners.

Bowers, of one mind did not attend, unwilling to disturb her lifestyle of self-indulgence.

George Staves and his wife Rose, whom he had hoped to keep from participating in the staged farewell, was unable to dissuade her determined insistence, reluctantly agreeing to have her accompany him. A Mr. James Downey, a retired former executive now a volunteer for the Humane Society, dignified and sincere in his appreciation of one of his organization's benefactors, stood waiting for the services to begin. Mr. McMann, doubling as the hearse's driver, was prepared to give the prearranged signal to begin. Reverend Hayes, the man of the wrinkled and threadbare cloth, pleased at the fee for his services, was pastor to the limited flock of the non-denominational Church of the Spirit, carrying from his pulpit the offerings of a religion purging sinful human frailties, benefiting not a specifically named deity but one's self, they their own sacred temple. Offering hope for the not-quite-fallen-from-grace. Searchers welcomed in his tabernacle, unpaced, seeking direction to religious uplifting.

The small group required little time for introductions or acknowledgments to one another. The passing of a reasonable amount of time produced no additional observers. As one, under the direction of Mr. McMann holding the urn containing Mrs. Springer's ashes, he directed the small group of mourners to the three foot square gravesite.

George and Rose prepared themselves, showing the expected dignity and somberness displayed by those at gravesites paying tribute. They could not escape the dichotomy and paradox, a fabrication that was about to be played out by real people. One, beholden to the services because of economic gain, a scripted tradition. Others unknowingly paying last respects to a facsimile, the knowing play acting props, portraying a sense of loss representation; the cemetery serving as the theater. Rose's countenance influenced by the many headstones of the resting diseased. George was guarding his thoughts as they approached the gravesite, suddenly amused, thinking within himself that the obituary could well have appeared in *Variety Magazine*, the bible of entertainers had this been an official theater, rather than the local newspaper; that playbills could have been handed out for reading this one day of comedic performance rather than serious scriptures read by a minister.

At the gravesite Mr. McMann relinquished the urn to one of the workers who carefully placed it on the bottom of the grave. On both sides of the burial plot, grass-like outdoor carpeting was positioned for the mourners to conveniently stand on during the services, separated from the disturbed Mother Earth. The gravesite protectively canopied, capturing the wind, it's canvas flapping above.

Reverend Hayes, following instructions for brevity, intoned his beginning solemn message of reminder: "*The body of the deceased returns to Earth as dust while the spirit lives forever in the House of the Lord.*"

Participants in the staged ceremony, while outwardly play acting somberness, the cemetery's surroundings and atmosphere stirring George's and Rose's inner piety, the words meaning as prayers taking them beyond the falseness of this scene to the deserving they were among.

Reverend Hayes's requiem message, was given cognizance sporadically in Staves's split consciousness. His intonations of "All God's children. Salvation in the believer. Put on Earth destiny" - Their power of religiosity finally registering the knowing turning from the hypocrisy perpetrated.

His subterfuge succeeding, he prayed silently, not for added effect at the unfolding charade, but for forgiveness from his God for his deceit and role in desecrating a religious ceremony, thankful that the ground was not consecrated furthering his transgressions.

Finally, the Reverend intoned, "*Ashes to ashes, dust to dust,*" signaling that Staves final ordeal was over. The curtain fell with the real life players none the wiser, compromised for the roles they unwittingly played at the feigned gravesite. Fitting the pretense of the scene was the artificial flowers left behind.

From that day forward, his wife and he never again spoke of that chapter in their lives. Reflecting in time to come as the dichotomy revisits him, embracing the role he played in the necessary charade, while simultaneously regrettable, it was a sacrilege despite his noble intentions.

Once again he freed the transporter to move effortlessly in time, mach speed backward, departing the chronology, reversing the sequence of events for perspective. His relatively new commanding Alpha relationship, an entrusting Tasha, on the brink of dissolution. Relived, a retelling of the fateful event; the evolving relationship facing challenge, bringing to question man's need to arbitrarily deny nature. Claiming the high ground of the greater good for all concerned while leaving as wreckage confused broken spirits. The carrying out of this act momentous in placing at risk, George Staves, his family, and Tasha's membership – the foundation bed rocking their relationship.

seven

Upon learning the news, Staves called for a somewhat contracted family conference. Missing was his son Edward who relocated to New York for business purposes, now only a phone call away for his input and support of his fathers wishes. Also relocated but nearby was his married daughter Rosanne. She and her husband Bill, for obvious reasons were requested to attend. Phyllis, still living at home, could be positioned as opposing, as well as the other women, their feelings for animals, their unusual bond with Tasha, a difficult sell. A meeting was to be held right after dinner. Other plans would have to be delayed; so important was their sharing in this issue, a worrisome George Staves treating it as a crisis.

As usually the case when discussing family matters of great importance the command center was the kitchen. The assemblage normally a welcomed advisory group in a democratic process stood no chance in countering George's militaristic posturing, be it their decision to challenge in matters of Tasha. Summoned by George, light heartedly referred to as the commanding General, after a measuring debate they all agreed that appropriate steps had to be taken, in this case becoming supportive of what George had planned. The reason for the consultation: Tasha, who was now seven months old, was beginning to spot, showing signs of the accompanying swelling of the vulva area, the telltale signs of the estrus period. She showed no signs of being traumatized by her maturing event but rather welcomed it, exhibiting a countenance of enhanced stature while quietly bearing the obvious accompanying pain and discomfort, particularly while walking. A willing price to pay for being blessed with a functioning reproductive system, setting the stage for her fruitful response of motherhood; fulfilling her destiny.

The veterinarian had advised George and Rose that Tasha was fertile and able and willing to submit to coupling. George Staves, frantically highly protective, had long before decided not to breed Tasha. The denial of her pregnancy paramount, her fulfillment in birthing a litter of no consequence to him, so concerned was he for the potential risk to Tasha. His position remained immutable, he was adamant in preventing Tasha's pregnancy at all costs. The ladies countering arguments of depriving her were not sustainable – setting aside their emotions, conceding to Tasha's best interests. Staves's a Centurion instituting rules of prevention, to be followed diligently for the three weeks of her estrus cycle, the "crisis period," the motivation

Expressing the need for the family's support he spelled out his plan. The ladies when alone spoofed it, likening it good naturedly as a plan rivaling the United States War College, repeatedly saluted the planner in innocent mockery. Tolerant of their frivolity at his expense, he smilingly accepting as a small price to pay as long as his command center instructions to his troops were followed:

"Always check the outdoors for amorous males before walking her."

"Never leave Tasha out alone no matter the circumstances. Always have her on a leash."

"Carry a stick when walking her to ward off potential suitors."

"Walks away from home are out of the questions. Her walks are to be limited to the backyard."

"To prevent her from responding to her own natural urgings do not answer solicitors at the front door if she is not secured. In that regard, wooden passageway gates are to be installed restricting her movements strictly to the kitchen, the downstairs bathroom that she isolates herself in, and the den area. Under no circumstances is she to be allowed outdoors without an escort, no matter how much she whimpers."

"Controlling her movements in the house during this time will restrict her blood spotting," George Staves pointed out to his family members in need of reminding. Continuing, "With dogs scenting senses twenty times superior to that of man, potential mates will surely come. We've all heard that males become so determined they will ignore the pain of electrically activated containment collars. Leash chains broken, attesting to their aroused hormonal strength dangling behind them, the advantage of stealth lost for the unsuspecting, the drive to mate compelling. Chain link fences which normally are a deterrent are easily scaled or burrowed beneath, failures in prevention, no match to the callings of the males in-season determination. Make no mistake," he emphasized, "they will come to strut their manhood," lightening his seriousness, bringing smiles to the faces of the girls, "to dazzle the female of the species with their ardor."

When it came to the subject of Tasha, it was recognized by the family council members, though undemocratic, his the final vote. Never more in evidence in this instance, overly dramatized or not, he was determined to save her from a life threatening experience, risking the consequences of preventing her wishes and ignoring her natural inclination. George, the sole judge and jury, dispensed arguably impassioned wisdom – he a self-appointed contrarian to extremist animal activists, who would damn as a dastardly act, perpetuating a crime, a sacrilege against nature, George Staves an elitist who would deny propagating of the species.

In his judgment it was the only response he could give at this time, not wanting to breed her reacting protectively and well-meaning. Stymieing natures coming-of-age maturation, a responding metamorphosis to Tasha's biological clock's natural cycle.

The reality, all were equally concerned with Tasha's well-being, treating it with the concern it deserved. The military tactics that George Staves had in place,, privately occasioned wishful thinking among the women who, if truth of wishes were to be known, secretly relished the idea of a house full of Tasha's yelping puppies, notwithstanding their attendant problems. George Staves actions, his uneasiness, occasioned tension lessening laughter to his girls, a humor he would not share in until his defenses could be dismantled, until a situation occurred that could not be critiqued as continuing the waged battle of his palace guard, but one of hilarity.

As expected, the first of Tasha's suitors came from their immediate neighborhood. Their close proximity brought them a first alert of Tasha's readiness. Her body chemistry producing a distinct scented message that wafted her readiness, an aphrodisiac titillating libido's, flaring nostrils held to the air, their discovery first. The advantage was theirs in the presentation of themselves at the beginning of her in-heat cycle, ending their search, lasciviously showing no discipline as Mother Nature's plans were evolving. Woe to the early arrivers during that first week of the three-week cycle. Still in wonderment for what had befallen them, the prohibiting pre-estrus period when the testy females will not allow males to breed. The males persistent, the females usually their equal.

Tasha, under tether gave a good accounting of this during George Staves's watch, a German shepherd from a nearby house escaped its usual close supervision, appearing without warning. Staves' shouts of alert hastily brought the family members to aid in resisting the threat. The presence of all excitedly shouting, waving their arms, brandishing sticks, did not deter the shepherd of its purpose, viewing the noisemakers as non-deterrents. It was Tasha, with her tail securely tucked between her legs, who stood her ground as the one-minded shepherd of equal size approached, responding to his first lust. With lips pulled back to reveal her menacing fangs, snarling with a ferociousness never seen before and unexpected for her age, precocious as her personality was still evolving. The tumult of her family's excitement, the anguish of their cries coupling, to the inappropriate moment, warding off a premature suitor.

She showed her displeasure to the intruder as demanded of her species by placing in dominance her enraged head over the head and neck of the shepherd while emitting small growls of disapproval. Fixed in this position riveted by the tether, she moved when the shepherd moved. Tasha within her arc constantly moving forward and backward, never allowing the shepherd a more opportune position. Stalemated, the shepherd backed off creating an opportunity to be driven off by the cold spray of water from the garden hose that Phyllis had turned on and handed to her anxious father. The shepherd, vexed, retreated quickly by going beyond the water's range, stopping to turn every few feet to face them in the hopes that the cold water torment had ended, thwarted he took temporary leave, slumping down on a nearby lawn to continue his watch. Regrouped, the wet onslaught repeated upon his return, Tasha being protectively brought inside the house, forced his retreat for the day.

Staves, breathing a sigh of relieve, remarked to his family, "I'm sure we'll be hearing from him again."

There were others that came, equally determined, not hiding surreptitiously for opportunity, advertising their intent with abandonment so brazenly driven were their urges, sitting and staring at the house, pausing occasionally to lift their snouts into the air to smell what was exciting them. Tasha's irresistible essence still tantalizing.

The second part of estrus brings a positive response toward males and their intent on breeding would usually be encouraged. It is the time during the heat cycle that females are most vulnerable and accommodating. This fact did not prove to be true in Tasha's case when late into her second week of estrus she had a second encounter.

Again it was the German shepherd instinctive of Tasha's willingness represented himself, re-offering himself for her fulfillment. Still the tethered Tasha resisted. Guarding herself with her tail between her legs, throating aggrieved growls, her disdain prominent as she again glued her clenched jaws over his head and neck, she moved everywhere he went, not relinquishing her position of dominance, augmenting her growls with an occasional flash of menacing fangs, thwarting his efforts not to be unrequited. This time the din of excitement brought the shepherd's alerted owner who immediately stymied any further advances by affixing a leash to the shepherd's collar. The owner, embarrassed and effusing many apologies, promised greater control of his charge as he left the unfenced by community requirement backyard. Staves hoped that it would be the last unwelcome visit by the shepherd but with one more week of the heat cycle to go, he was not too sure. Regardless, his troops were at the ready.

Within hours of the shepherd's denied efforts, the most unlikely of suitors came calling. Tasha, still under the watchful eyes of George Staves, was first to sense him, aroused she stood tautly confrontational, alerted undoubtedly of this suitors nearness by his smell well before he came into everyone's view. As they reflected later, Tasha had not dropped her protecting tail as her ever ready furry chastity belt, an omission sure to have brought concern until the threat presented itself amusingly as a fevered dachshund, he because of physicality an unthreatening suitor providing a needed respite from their fatiguing diligence – a escape in mirth for this miniature lothario exaggerating his opportunity. The panic raised by the suitor shepherd's ambitions were not part of this scene, the wonderment portending a theater of comedy about to be presented. The lack of alarm practical, their open amusement at the expense of an over-stimulated dachshund attempting the impossible the scene. The onlookers unfearingly inanimate, welcoming comic relief, the poor dachshund's overwrought hormones blinded him to his physical limitations.

It was then that Staves realized that Tasha's innate intelligence had already determined that no threat existed from the impossibility of the unfolding scene. A miracle wanting to happen: before everyone's eyes in displayed readiness stood a representation of the height of optimism, its difficulty scale comparable to climbing Mt. Everest without Sherpa guides. This ambitious dachshund, genetically bred with legs to support and propel a body built close to the ground so as to successfully find burrowed prey and annoying varmints that inhabited it, was resolute and would not be discouraged by Tasha's distanced, unshielded desirable anatomy. Still opportune, his adrenaline flowing freely, he tried valiantly to propel himself upward as if on a trampoline, springing repeatedly to mount Tasha, always falling short of his mission's task. The dog, stimulated by his sexually aroused wantonness, dismissed as irrelevant his physical limitations and continued to ignore those watching his efforts while the challenging opportunity stood before him.

The dachshund, still denying the impossible, continued to attempt a coupling with Tasha, who during earlier attempts, would move away from her seducer, her rebuke not more than a bark of annoyance. Determined to succeed, he continued unabated until his persistence leadened his legs to fatigue. His springless leaps became considerably short of the mark. Weakened, he stumbled onto a growling Tasha who demanded he cease and desist. Repeatedly unheeding Tasha's warnings, he paused only when he became overworked, panting for recovery, using the recovery time to sniff the nearby sites that Tasha had marked, permeating recharging his enthusiasm before re-embarking on his physically exhausting pursuit.

Tasha hearing the chorus of the Staves to shoo her suitor away, noting the dachshund reacting angrily to a broom brandished by Rose ended the amusement by suddenly turning on him, charging him bull-like with her head lowered, knocking the dachshund backward, sending him sprawling and yelping at the sudden turn of events as Tasha stood over him menacingly. Ignoring his hurts, his eyes still expressing lust, pleading for an accommodation that was not possible.

His daughter Phyllis, the comedic moment no longer important, laden with guilt finally intervened, grabbing the dachshund's collar with one hand, the other warding off a now highly agitated Tasha, speaking softly to the dachshund until magically it came under her command. It proceeded to lick Phyllis' hand in appreciation for her act of kindness. As if suddenly aware, the opportunity to express his sexuality gone, he faced danger with an aroused Tasha.

George and his wife Rose, to defuse the situation further, escorted Tasha back into the house while Phyllis continued to pet and soothe the disappointed suitor while reading its license tag attached to its collar.

The owner arrived within minutes of the call. His attitude of chastisement and apology voiced in his displeasure of his dog's escape and intrusion on a neighbors property suddenly changing when apprised of Tasha's condition, giving vent to amazed laughter at his dog's ambitions.

The departing owner with his amorous dachshund in tow, the Staves family, enjoyed moments of laughter as they recalled the day's events, wishful that Tasha's heat period was over and her normalcy returned. Victorious so far yet not to be deluded into believing that the worst was over. George Staves remained oppressed with vigilance, demanding no less from the other family members as they headed into the third part of the estrus cycle: the di-estrus phase where Tasha was going out of heat and less willing to breed.

It was a Saturday morning and Staves had decided to wash the cars. The time of day was perfect for Tasha, who lounged tethered beneath the shade of a backyard crab apple tree partaking of a cooling breeze while under the watchful eyes of his wife and two daughters; Phyllis and a visiting Rosanne all in comfort as the expected high for the day was hours ahead of them.

George was in the final rinse when he heard the hysterical cries of his daughters and wife coming from the back of the house. Responding quickly, dropping the still spraying garden hose, he ran right into a situation prepared for but not envisioned. There stood a magnificent male Siberian husky, it's black, gray and white colors glistening with brushed attention featured on a beautifully contoured and symmetrically proportioned body that was about to mount Tasha. A welcomed coupling was about to take place as she maneuvered her tail to the side to allow access. Frantic by the scene, George shouted commands to his daughters and wife to pull Tasha away by taking hold of her tail but not before he had simultaneously grabbed the tail of the intruding husky, pulling him backward to gain separation.

"Hold tightly to Tasha's tail," he shouted. "Under no circumstances are you to get in front of the male as he could bite when he realizes what we are attempting."

Strangely, the male husky never turned to face his obstructors. His mind on one course and one course only. His sexual appetite urging that he not be deterred, his opportunity thwarted.

Rose screaming at the top of her lungs that they not let up and hold fast to Tasha as George pulled back on the tail of the male, forcing him backward. Again the male didn't turn to face his protagonist to attack him. Still preoccupied with Tasha's nearness, pulling mightily against George holding his tail fast, ignoring the pain. As strong as the male was, he was no match for George Staves' strength and resolve. Tiring, the male husky's strength waned, showing signs of diminishing resistance.

Noteworthy Tasha, loudly barking her disapproval, alerting the choice was hers. She had chosen one of her breed to mate with her. Separating herself from her pack, in defiance, equally resistant, she tried desperately to rejoin the mate she had approved. Finally, after much effort including screams and tears, George's daughters and wife distraught over an unrecognizable Tasha were able to loop and tie Tasha's leash around a tree trunk holding her securely.

"Get me the spare leash from the garage," Staves shouted at the girls whose strained reddened hands were now free.

Immediately reacting, Rose bolted from a the scene, quickly returning with the spare leash. Still not recognizing what was about to befall him, the male husky whose tail was being held securely by George was fixated on a restrained Tasha, ignored a brave Rose, allowing her to affix the chain to the dogs collar ring matching Tasha's immobilization.

Stymied, their forced separation aggrieved as both dogs leaped and strained against their constraints, barking loudly in protest. Going over to Tasha, George Staves tried to soothe her with words he thought would comfort her. Instead, she looked bewildered in innocence, not understanding the cause of the intervention. She had made her choice she signaled. He was one of her breed. No hybrids would she bear. The makeup of her litter would match her ancestry, continuing the bloodline. Why had they interfered, her pleading eyes seemed to be saying? Finally, she slumped to the grass in weary resignation, her defeat only temporary as this male or his brethren would as she wished seed her. If not here and now then elsewhere, were her unspoken words, other opportunities would surely be created.

After fifteen minutes the standoff had passed, Tasha reconciled to the impossibility of her mission, for the first time made a movement away from the male husky toward the house, exhausted and in need of water. Thankful that the crisis was over, George welcomed the opportunity – the break in tension, led her back to the house. The police, responding to a neighbors alarm at the strange doings; the situation quickly accessed by the two patrolmen, who broadly smiled at the comedy of preventing dogs copulation, a welcomed departure from their serious duties, "This will be one for the station house," one of the patrolmen grinned humorously.

"I'd like to be in the courtroom when you try to explain the circumstances to a judge, said the other in amusement. Of course that won't happen as you have the situation under control and it's no longer a disturbance."
Together they approached the male husky. With Tasha safely in the house, defeated he no longer displayed aggressiveness, his true nature returning. He

allowed himself to be petted while his fitting name "Regal" was noted as well as the address on his ownership tag. Amazingly, he was from a township over three miles away.

"What senses and instincts," George said to himself when he heard, questioning, was it possible that selectivity was involved, the male driven all these miles and Tasha culling out the undesirables, for each other? While remaining completely committed to preventing a Tasha pregnancy, he was in absolute awe of their motivational forces, their activated hormones boundless.

The police called Regal's owner, a Mrs. Waters, who arrived in a van fifteen minutes later emotionally pleased at being reunited with her runaway. Showing great relief that her prized award winning husky, available and in much demand nationally for breeding purposes, had been recovered unharmed, copiously thanking the Staves family for their good citizenship.

George Staves, only for a moment did regret the lost opportunity of his Tasha, fortuitously being bred with a husky of such impressive lineage, returning to his position, and the coerced support of his family not to breed Tasha. Without a voice was Tasha, her guard willingly down, restrained from her consent.

In the passing days they awaited Tasha's return to her former self, watching attentively at her body's anatomical recovery, her recent in-heat cycle ending, this battle combativeness concluded in exhaustion, knowing another call to arms in seven months when the cycle would be revisited. Revisiting also, George Staves's hyperventilation.

At first Tasha showed no ill effects being prevented from becoming fruitful, seemingly unscarred by the ordeal of her metamorphosis. At least they all thought so but later circumstances and events spoke differently.

It was approximately six weeks after Tasha's enforced denial when she began exhibiting strange behavioral patterns. Changes in her temperament, completely unexpected, brought reasons for concern for her health. She became restless and excitable at the slightest provocation, resisting commands and panting incessantly. Incident to her change, during one of her walks, was her reaction to the sudden wail of a police cruiser's siren breaking the silence, previously responded to by howling. Now the shrill caused her to cower. Frightened, she would now drop her tail between her legs, pulling back her ears while whimpering. Her anguish extracting heavy salivation from her mouth- to pull anxiously on her leash to return home. Tasha casting nervous glances over her shoulder as the siren's shrill faded in the distancing background, as if expecting its unwelcomed return.

They collectively: his wife Rose, his daughters Phyllis and Rosanne and son Edward when contacted by phone… became anxious over Tasha's hypernervousness. After much soul searching, they surmised what was being witnessed were the readjustments of her internal organs at work to rebalance her body chemistry, to hibernate her estrus induced reproductive system. Concurring patience and understanding, its loving expression a key rehabilitation therapy while evolving Mother Nature completed the dynamics of change within her body, hoped to be a matter of days.

Their assumed nonprofessional assessment partially accurate. Tasha in transition changed outwardly. abandoning her apprehensive nervous behavior, while physically she become bloated as if retaining water, yet her frequency for urination relief remained unchanged. Now her demeanor lacked enthusiasm for play, turning away from thrown balls she normally would have eagerly fetched. Her appetite in decline, reaching a point where she practically stopped eating altogether.

Frantic and despondent. This was not their Tasha. This was the behavior of a dog they were not familiar with: unresponsive when called as if her name were alien, a stranger in their midst. Concluding it time to seek the professional help of Dr. Kerrigan, Tasha's veterinarian.

After Dr. Kerrigan completed his examination, while Tasha watched lethargically without her usual apprehension for veterinarians, elevated everyone's worry, astonishingly declaring that Tasha was undergoing a false pregnancy.

"I can't believe that," George Staves said at the shocking revelation, unaware that dogs may experience this phenomenon, shaking his head in a "no" fashion, not in rejection, but in affirmation of over looked understanding.
"Tasha's body was manifesting her desires, said Dr. Kerrigan.

"Just about every living creature is capable," Dr. Kerrigan counseled. "This is particularly true when they go through their first estrus period and do not become impregnated."

Rose and George looked at one another, their visage immediate guilt as the words of Dr. Kerrigan resonated in their troubled minds; the implication was quite clear.

"We did the right thing?" George Staves questioned. "Didn't we?" his rationale coming into question, doubt and misgivings in his mind. Continuing he said, "We did forcibly prevent her from getting pregnant, something she wanted, with the mate of her own choosing. One of her own breed, as if she waited for him, literally fighting off other male suitors with a determined aggressiveness," shaking his head in remembrance, "Strangely, in their greeting of one another, the ritual dance to establish dominance before copulation was not played out. Tasha submitting herself as if fulfilling a calling, her genetic code urging her to continue the propagation of her species; undiluted. They weren't quick enough as we literally, physically restrained them within nanoseconds of becoming co-joined."

"It would be my judgment: the actions taken were a factor," Dr. Kerrigan commented.

"What are we to expect? What are we to do? Have we forever damaged her emotionally?" Rose Staves asked, biting the corner of her trembling mouth. Her eyes blinked uncontrollably trying to hold back her tears.

Dr. Kerrigan, sensing the burden they were imposing on themselves, interjected quickly. "Your actions should not cause long lasting psychological problems with Tasha. They are resilient animals. Time will bring healing both chemically and physically. What's needed more than ever is patience and understanding. Recognize that this denial was a traumatic experience for her, from which she will recover," he emphasized sympathetically.

Continuing, as counsel he said, "Her current lethargic state will vanish once she recognizes being biologically inert is cyclical and that she can once again become fruitful at her next estrus period. Until then, she will be unable to become pregnant. Biologically inert," he repeated, his liking for the phrase obvious.

"And then what?" George Staves interjected.

"She is either encouraged to become pregnant or you run the risk of Tasha repeating her false pregnancy behavior," he answered, then adding, "If it happens again, it will be a repeat of what is being experienced now. But then you'll know the effects and how to deal with it."

Straightening to stand erect, as if to gain credibility, in full stature to emphasize his deeply felt convictions. "I, as a professional veterinarian, am committed to extending the lives of animals, and are aghast at those who allow actions leading to mass death sentences as solutions. I'm in full agreement that if you do not intend to breed her, then preventing her pregnancy is the right answer. I'm sure you are aware of what happens to unwanted animals. The yearly statistics are horrifying."

To measure their reaction he waited, about to cover new ground, testing that he held their attention. Assured, he continued, "There is another alternative and that is spaying. Not only does it greatly reduce the incidence of false pregnancies, it also reduces the likelihood of developing life-ending diseases. You should consider it. It's a merciful solution. You shouldn't wait too much longer."

Suddenly mindful to check his wristwatch, realizing his time constraints, he proceeded to politely walk them out of his office toward the exit, with a disengaged Tasha in tow.

Looking down at Tasha, he said, "Medically, we would prefer it be done within the first four to six weeks before the estrus period." Appropriately, he handed George a booklet on the subject for reading. Leaving, they nodded affirmatively, thanking him for his help.

And so they waited out the false pregnancy period, searching for signs that recovery was beginning. Instead, two days after the visit to the veterinarian and during the eighth week after estrus, their expectations were jolted further. They noticed that Tasha had repositioned the throw rug in the downstairs bathroom to an area to the side of the commode and the wall. The informational booklet's words and description the veterinarian had given them were recalled, she was preparing herself for delivery of her litter. She had built her nest in preparation–the second action in a sequence of acting out–Tasha, evading reality, escaping to give life to her fantasy.

That evening the family heard the cries of anguish and pain coming from the downstairs bathroom – her transformed new nest. George led Rose and Phyllis as they rushed to tend to a distressed Tasha. Proffering words of comfort, they tenderly pet her on the neck, hopeful to soothe her of her anguish and display their support. Nothing George tried helped as neither did the efforts of Rose and Phyllis.

"Her food tray is full; so is her water dish," Rose acknowledged, hoping for the simple answers and yet the markers of full food and water dishes were foretelling; another step in the sequence, the booklet advised: Tasha, in preparation had purposefully stopped eating and drinking. Bringing agreement from all that she was well into enacting the pangs of labor: lack of thirst and appetite, a further announcement that she was ready to give birth to her litter.

Suspecting their presence was attention diverting, and with nothing more they could do but wait out the completion of this episode, disconsolate the Staves's returned to their rooms. Not intentional they remained fully awake, anguishing throughout the night with each of her cries and yelps. Finally exhausted, the individual battles of fighting sleep ended, their allegiance to remain awake experienced failure. Sometime during the night, the yelping stopped, the exact time unknown, exhausted, they succumbed to a troubled sleep.

The next morning, rising later than usual, robotically rigid in movement from reduced sleep, George, as was his practice was the first to descend the stairs to make the awakening first pot of coffee.

Passing the entrance to Tasha's "nest," he was astounded to see that in spite of being forewarned, Tasha had at some time during the night when her enacting contractions were unyielding, an obvious notice that her womb was empty, in stealth she fantasized further. Continuing the delusion, she stole from each of his daughter's rooms. Taken were childhood collections of stuffed inanimate toys which she then positioned carefully within her nest in close proximity where she could easily gather them to her bosom to enact feeding them lactate, maternal eagerly awaiting the response of satisfying feeding. Or to engulf them protectively, almost hidden from sight within her bosom when dangers were perceived, the four facsimile puppies lavished over, Tasha acting out her motherly role, quickly changing to guardian, issuing occasional warning growls between pulled back lips, revealing intimidating canine teeth, in her confusion only sighting threats. Tasha, in her self-hypnotic state, forewarning her displeasure to anyone who got too near to her "litter."

A quick call to Dr. Kerrigan to discuss this latest complication ensued, he counseling that the end of Tasha's fantasy was near. He reminded them once again that, "Time and patience is still needed."

Staves' determined search of the Internet on the subject of false pregnancies with huskies turned out to be a double-edged sword, enlightening him on the one hand but also furthering his concern.

False pregnancies, he was to learn, is a remnant from the ancestors of pack dogs. Huskies trace their ancestry to that of wolves who are followers of the pack society. In the pack, the leader, the Alpha is often the most important in the hunt for food. When a female is the Alpha, the pack cannot have her on depriving maternity leave for up to two months. Mother Nature in her infinite wisdom will have all females in the pack have their estrus at about the same time. Yet, only the Alpha female will be mated, much to the displeasure of the other females. If violated, the Alpha female will openly show her disdain and will summarily outlaw the offending female from the rest of the pack, who in capitulation will almost always absorb the fetuses rather than run the risk of isolated starvation. Choosing instead from a position of weakness within the pack to go through the hormonal changes and produce milk, essentially offering themselves as surrogate mothers at the time the pups are born to the Alpha female. The result is a lot of willing nannies with milk and maternal instincts who are ready to take care of the newborn, freeing the mother Alpha to lead the hunt for prey, their contribution preventing themselves and the pack from starving.

Each day of the final week of false pregnancy, everyone had expectations: "Will this be the day of breakthrough? Will we see the hungered signs of her return to the pack-the social order, or must we again be pained by her aberrant behavior for another day?" Hope shared by all had peaked, the days remaining hours concluding the anticipated change to soon, disappointing as Tasha remained captive to her fantasy. Tomorrow would be their wait.

The optimism of the fourth week which began with high expectations lost enthusiasm, her mothering figments still real and prevailing Their disappointment heightened further by the not surprising discovery that Tasha was now providing whole food from her bowl to her imaginary pups, placing before them the small briquettes of meat enhanced and bound together by cereals, paralleling the regurgitation of wolves feeding their young after the kill. Weaned from mother's milk, announcing the pups ready to grow into a more mature state, coincident with the mother's lactate drying up. That circumstance confirmed by this furthering fantasy, she forceful in lessoning her reluctant pups to no longer be dependent on mother's exhausted glandular nourishment,, needing that they take the next step in survival.

It was supposed to mark the end of the Staves family's ordeal, so said veterinarian Kerrigan. "Praise that day," George lauded, and prayerfully echoed by his family members. Unfortunately the fourth week, so anxiously awaited, was disappointing as it continued without resolution of Tasha's affixation. His wife Rose, depressed with the slow pace of Mother Nature relieving Tasha of her demon, decided in frustration to take matters into her own hands. She would try to assist Tasha's late-in-arriving recovery. While sympathetic she wearied of this stranger that inhabited Tasha's body, resisting her fervent entreaties as if sealed off, her only obligation was fulfilling the fantasy, oblivious to the toll it weighed upon others, her a shadow of herself, in an emotionally derived metamorphosis.

The prospect of that scenario continuing at its present pace was unacceptable to Rose. Out of desperation and her wish to return to longed-for normalcy, she chose to seek out the principal cause of Tasha's state of despondency and who could possible Pied Piper Tasha back to reality. Hopeful of the prospect, she called Mrs. Waters, the owner of Regal, the personifying husky… the willing mate Tasha had emotionally bonded to for coupling only to be denied her right of selection by being physically restrained. Rose pleaded while Mrs. Waters listened to her emotionally explain the present circumstances and the reason for her call.

"An invisible wall separated them from one another," she explained passionately. "Tasha's catatonic escape prevented communication and expression. Her demeanor was confused and bewildered," her appeal to Mrs. Waters, "in a self-imposed exile, living a fantasy that we helped create."

The conversation was not going well as Mrs. Walters was reluctant and hesitant, protective she exaggerated the risk to her prized husky. Still Rose persisted, pleading that a relationship renewal, even a fleeting one might be the final therapy to break the spell.

"Please help us. The passing of each additional day without her returning to us is deeply concerning. Her condition, if not reversed, could have lasting psychological effects. She needs an awakening," she sputtered. "Regal could provide that. His presence might force her to regain normalcy," Rose pressuring, "Forgive me, Mrs. Waters, but Regal's runaway encounter with my Tasha is part of the cause as well as our family's decision. the connection can't be denied. Hopefully with your concurrence, Regal will be part of the cure. Please," she begged, "please help."

Mrs. Waters' position to deny weakened, responsive to Rose's impassioned plea, mindful of Regal's share of responsibility and thus hers. Her penchant, bordering on the ostentatious, motivated her further. The opportunity to proudly declare Regal, the magnificent heir of a well-conceived breeding program rescuing another of his bred, would enhance the next influencing press coverage during the next rating of his prize winning conformation.

Regal by declaration was now sitting on a throne of distinguishing awards among his breed, a source to continue further refinement. Those dedicated breeders pursuing the ultimate, eager to factor his credential genetic profile in the never-ending pursuit of breed perfection.

This time the Staves family would see Regal in his magnificent well-groomed beauty, not with matted and smelly fur, wet and dirty paws, attesting to the great distances he traveled while randy, his nose directing his of one-mind-aroused libido. The Staves's waited anxiously for the doorbell to ring announcing Mrs. Waters and Regal.

While they waited, the distinctly extra sensitive senses of dogs, was never more evident, easily outdistancing humans. Long before the doorbell rang, Tasha, as if given sudden unexpected buoyancy, surfaced from her sea of gloom and despair. Tasha was possibly returning, they rejoiced, abandoning her solitude to become active concluding she was receiving motivation. She stirred within the protection of her bathroom den. A stirring that was noticeably different than the movement of the lethargic, it was typified by the occasional twitch of leg muscles or a subdued almost inaudible yelp to bring her to the verge of consciousness from a dreamscape she wished to escape from. Her long surpressed stirring, it was hoped forecast a revitalization, a more responsive being they longed for. Now in actual movement, she arose to all fours to stand at the doorway, no longer guarding her imagined litter but in anticipation and expectance.

George, hearing her arousal, rose from his seat at the kitchen table and approached the entrance to Tasha's den at about the same time she was rising to her feet, a definite sign that something was motivating her from her moroseness. She walked slowly at first, her back bent as if burdened; straightening as muscles relaxed and circulation again flowed freely. Her tail raised from her downcast retreat was now aggressively displayed in its curled position over the center of her back; her alert ears straight and rigid; her nose sniffing in all directions seeking her reawakening.

Signals of mysterious origin were being transmitted, well beyond the range of human senses. Tasha, on alert, screened out the static from the meaningful.

As a car door slammed, its sound jolted the final awakening in all. The family having been waiting bringing the unimaginable to the fore, while Tasha response: yelping excitedly, her eyes alive, brightening from melancholy, her down trodden face showing a perceptible smile. Under no restraint she rushed for the door, her paws with unworn nails moving too quickly, scratching for traction on the highly polished tile floor, challenging her balance. Adjusting, she regained registry, a formidable moving mass propelling herself against the front door with such force that it tested the strength of the fasteners holding the hinges. Her excited yelping joining the front doorbell ringing its announcement.

Rose, and Phyllis their mouths open in amazement at Tasha's sudden revival, filled with wonder knowing the mysterious signal that had motivated Tasha, powerful enough to pass through the restricting mass of the house. A power that knew no boundaries had been unleashed to energize Tasha. Improbable as it seemed, there was only one answer, now so obvious. Tasha displaying extraordinary reasoning powers debunking animals had limitations and could not possibly have fathomed the phone call arrangements made with Mrs. Waters. Yet how could her strange behavior be explained without drawing incredulous conclusions, they asked silently of themselves. Their minds freely traveled the only path that would make sense despite it being surreal: "An unidentifiable energy field with its own language had been received by Tasha's gifted paranormal senses."

They reached Tasha just as she was readying another assault on the front door, prevented by the intervention of George who quickly reached down to grab her collar and restrain her.

Having lived disconsolately these many weeks while physically and spiritually Tasha took her leave, they marveled at the emergence of her unrestrained long dormant aggressiveness. They were elated to be witnessing the dynamics of her transformation from an almost catatonic state to a boiling-over cauldron of passion, flamed by the release of pent-up emotion. Coincident with Tasha reaction to her restraint, she switched from yelping to barking, her signature that she wanted something of them.

Suddenly the din that assailed them seemed to overlap which at first sounded like a rebounding echo until it was apparent the sounds were not spaced enough, that no bounce back was possible to be an echo. Not an echo, they realized but almost an overlaying. Not one dog but two; an exchange, a communication; language sending and receiving. Two dogs they concluded, a duet of one mind and purpose orchestrating the din against the door. Physically under great pressure, George had to ask his wife Rose to open the door as it now took both hands on Tasha's collar and all his strength to restrain her.

What followed would have to have been witnessed to be believed. A new order of believers would have been pledged. Believers that animals have human characteristics, have emotions, are constantly aware of themselves and the role others play in their lives. How else could one explain the greeting Tasha and Regal gave one another? Both dogs stiffened, muscles taut and rippling, a tremendous energy flowing between them as George Staves backed Tasha into the house, followed by a charging Regal literally dragging Mrs. Waters into the foyer. Both dogs, nose-to-nose as if fused, allowed fields of charged energy to pass through their connected bodies, electrifying their fur to the touch. Their mutual yelps now sounded as chirps of lost lovebirds expressing the joy of having found one another. They began a display of affection that would be difficult to capture in words of prose or poetry no matter how gifted the author. Attempted, it would pale, a one-dimensional passion whereas what was transpiring was three-dimensional, boundless, with no size, scope or intensity limitations. It began with the smothering of dog kisses; licking each other's snouts, lips, eyes and ears, each delighting one another. It could not be foreplay for coupling sex and its satisfying conclusion as Tasha could no longer bear it's fruit. It was truly, freely, openly expressed affection for one another. Satiated by their initial greeting, they began the inspection of each other's gender, a tease of days gone by for what might have been, surfacing longing stares from one another. A two thousand year-old history of evolving the breed in their coupling's promise-enhancing further the genetic code of their ancestry no longer their opportunity at the moment.

Mrs. Waters, George and Rose, joined by Phyllis, watched the touching scene. The dogs took turns to show respect for one another. They displayed commitment to one another assuming the submissive posture of lying on their backs, stomachs exposed, front paws bent signifying supplication, making each other vulnerable. An ancient expression of conceding, unexpected of each other, each at present a non-combative Alpha, setting aside their code of social order for this moment of rejoicing in one another.

The ensuing conversation of the in awe owners, while cordial, was distant, their dominating thoughts and observations on their pets. The Staves' preoccupation on the continuing recovery of Tasha, while Mrs. Water's countenance was watchful of her Regal, always wary of possible threats and injury that could fault him forever, ending his showing.

Tasha and Regal put all minds at ease, their excited panting having subsided, refreshed from drinking water from Tasha's bowl. Tasha her social status as the Alpha of this den never relinquished, drank from the water bowl first, then Regal. Despite this distinction, there still was parity in their relationship.

Again, as dogs will do at the slightest whim, they re-inspected themselves, and one another. Developing the question: is the passing of time indistinguishable in dogs… one continuous day from birth to death as some believe. Were they again inspecting or sniffing for natures metamorphous moments earlier found absent? Or for confirmation in their physical differences and the absence of her estrus period, a willing respondent when nature was ready?

As if by a mysterious signal audible only to the dogs, they abruptly stopped their inspection. Renewing their game of chasing one another around the first level of the house, repeatedly switched their leadership roles in the chase to exhaustion, finally lying down in their tracks; contorting their bodies to be sure they were able to see one another for reassurance.

The Staves family members, viewing Tasha's excitement were of one thought, "Was Tasha's emotional disturbance of false pregnancy now over?" The answer they would learn was imminent.

Watching shockingly at first Tasha, then Regal enter Tasha's den, almost immediately they set upon and ate the briquettes of dog food that Tasha quartered. Their purpose was obvious: to render as history the weaning nourishment for her facsimile puppies. Their true identity ground between eager teeth for nutritional value, no longer the food in Tasha's illusions.

They paused almost imperceptibly as if to further fathom their next therapeutic step in Tasha's recovery. No cautioning growling from Tasha was heard. Acting quickly, simultaneously they dismissed the furry playthings for what they were: in despair icons of substitutions, representative creations of another life, another time. Each dog with purposeful mouths grabbed the objects of their attention, as their ancestors did to small prey, shook them violently from side to side. In this case symbolic, eliminating the facsimiles remaining spark of life. Tasha in particular was even more zealous. As if in need to demonstrate to herself, "I'm free of my demons."

The Staves's were now convinced, this act showing Tasha's final reality, her dark period of false images and worshipping of surrogates for motherly expression over, her *fait accompli.* Returned to their original intent, instinctive play toys, no longer surrogates of her litter.

The dogs repeated their purposeful ritual until all playthings were dislodged and ceremoniously discarded. Returning to play time, raced from room to room with breathtaking speed, claws aggressively scraping for traction, confident in their youthful abilities to handle any challenge; unheeding, taking license on this special occasion; a respite to break house rules. Tasha led Regal in a coordinating leap, a *Grande Jeté* performed magnificently in tandem on and off the couch in the den. It was the highlight in their path, never hesitating, their athleticism – a frenetic ballet. A further announcing that the real Tasha had emerged.

Countering their earlier first meeting, this chapter in their lives ended happily, memorable as complete exhaustion was reached. Their vigorous aerobic celebration, as the curtain fell, brought closure and a new baptism.

Once again physically spent, they collapsed to the carpeted den floor to lay panting together, back to back, their chests falling and rising as one. Phyllis joining them, watching them adoringly. A symbol of today's commitment to togetherness knowing the separation of tomorrows was about to beckon, a resumption of the lives chosen for them. Each was pleased that out of the ashes of their first encounter had come a revival.

Regal's pride had been restored. Claiming a double bounty. He, the beneficiary of prearranged love trysts, had never been repelled. Always successful, faced slow-to-heal mental scarring for failing a willing partner, now reunited – discounting and remedying.

Tasha was deeply wounded by the same circumstances, in its wake left as a devastated partner, in need of his visual presence to compass her misguided psyche;. Responded. She had been renewed. Their reacquainting an act of exorcism, purging the grip of demons and pulseless idols.

"All the elements of a Shakespearian play for animal lovers. Emotional conflicts, unaccountable mystical expressions. More questions asked than answered except the expression of love and affection clearly primitive: sounds and intonations as poignant as his cultural writings," Mrs. Waters stated.

"A Greek tragedy in the animal kingdom where one life is saved at the symbolic death of faux others. Self-imagined motherhood failing to be reflected in the mirror of life placed before yearning eyes, the denial in the hands of other's, releasing a reawakening reflection of light saving a darkening life fulfilling it's enlightment," Rose sadly commented.

"Isn't it beautiful the way they love one another?" an emotional Phyllis asked

"It was beautiful." George offered smiling at his daughter. "But something beyond that took place today. Think about how it was possible for Tasha to filter for the signature of Regal, from all the vast scents, the noise, the energies that assault her senses; the distance they had to travel, interfered with its flow by topography and man made structures. Prevailing, heralding his approach and visit well before you arrived, Mrs. Waters? Amazing, just amazing," he added voicing his astonishment.

Mrs. Waters hung on every word he spoke as if mesmerized. She nodded as a believer, "I saw similar strange behavior from Regal as we neared your house but nothing as spectacular as Tasha's reaction."

Continuing, he said, "Those forces that travel over great distances, were they sound waves undetectable by man that we just experienced? This has been proven scientifically as factual among elephants," he said with authority. "What strikes me," nodding his head unconsciously, "is that those energy fields, either sound or scent or whatever, had to be sensed by other dogs in its moving path who unhappily turn away as the unintended."

Rose Staves commented, "The sounds of their barking through closed doors announcing one another, in a language only for each other's ears. All others are shunned by its censorship. They were vocalizing to one another as the front door was opened, as in a musical score, an aria, the final act, the drama of deliverance."

"It was an absolutely glorious experience, one I will never forget. I'm glad you prevailed upon me to come," Mrs. Waters said, nodding appreciatively toward Rose while speaking to all of them. Continuing, "It adds to the growing evidence that animals are conscious, have feelings, can communicate and display affection beyond belief. I knew that something unusual was happening when I answered your phone call. Regal, who had been asleep, leaped to my chest with his forepaws as if he understood the conversation, panting nervously until I accepted your invitation. I'm sure his actions had some influence on me."

"It also says that they have telepathic powers, that they can develop an energy field that can travel many miles," George Staves added supportively.

In awe of what had happened they all wondered about the composite picture their thoughts had crafted. Over coffee and cake, and treats for the dogs, they departed from the days mind captivating mysteries of the unknown. Their search for the more pragmatic, undertaken in earnest, succeeding only in adding to their bewilderment. Trying to force more practical conclusions, an inevitable failure, as a reasonable answer to dogs communicating over long distances, remained elusive. The "to account for all" explanation falling short, unable to reasonably explain the dogs' actions before actual physical contact was made. There would be no reasonable explanation, they reasoned. What had happened, what had been witnessed was indeed illuminating if not mystical, proudly important enough for them to counter, narrowly focused demeaning of the depth of the dogs intellect. To cite, standing tall to disbelievers no matter their credentials."

When it became time for Mrs. Waters and Regal to leave, they all expected reluctance and difficulty from the dogs. Once again the dogs proved to be the masters of the circumstance, their individual plagues displaying no residual frailties, acknowledging that the curtain must come down on their real life drama. They would go on without one another as they must. They would forever miss one another, so impacting was their presence. But their lives must continue apart, each having a special place in each other's hearts and minds.

The dogs,' recovering from exhaustion,. obligations fulfilled, no longer beholden to one another, demagnetized, prepared to go their separate ways. Establishing priorities they endearingly lay their heads in the laps of their masters.

Mrs. Waters leashed Regal, anticipated her action turned to face Tasha, fully recovered and satiated. Their body language at the moment passive. Their co-dependency at an end. Their Alpha ranking elevating a visage of independence foretelling that the time had come. Mrs. Waters with Regal in tow receiving fervent thanks of appreciation from the Staves,' the two principles turning toward one another, their eyes independent, expressing acknowledgement of having marked each other indelibly as co-saviors, participants in a phenomenon.

Tasha joined George and Rose in the den, lying down at their feet as she had done hundreds of times before, normally not noteworthy, but after weeks of self-seclusion; remarkable. Confident and comfortable in her surroundings, ready to script a new day, a new cycle. While looking down at her affectionately, George Staves was mindful of an abstract philosophy he once read, "No matter what happens, the world would continue to spin on its axis around the centerpiece of this universe's incendiary sun, both revolving stages,, a final act awaiting them both. The message in that inevitability: tomorrow is impossible for you physically, a never occurrence, as your tomorrow is your today. Eternity, the future, the tomorrows belonging to the spiritual." The message of those words he found appropriate, Tasha returning this day to pursue a time to come without end metaphorically but literally a sequential clock whose personal unwinding of the coil an act of the creator. Demonstrating further her reawakening; Tasha responding to Phyllis call from her upstairs bedroom to join her, a first since seized by her melancholy, George Staves his abstraction applied was being visited by another torment that if undertaken would once again test her over lapping chronology.

George needed to expand his previous readings, so important would be his decision. Tasha's denied pregnancy and it's complications a considerable factor weighing heavily on his mind. Challenged he sought rationale: for and against hanging in the balance. The study while presenting new insight, while cogent mandated he extend his own thoughts and conclusions beyond the writings. Inescapable in gaining a further intimacy of the pack animal's social structure and socialization, was his inevitability for comparison: were Tasha not an Alpha would she have been less traumatized by her denial to mate? A question he soon answered from his readings, Tasha's extreme reaction bore all the signs of being influenced by her ranked elevation. Nature's call to animals to proliferate the species inherited, usually oblivious to social structure. Their arousal seasonal, solely to propagate, absent of resistance, curtailed only by the influence of man or lack of opportunity. On a strata intellectually lower, for reasons of survival itself in a commune setting, pack animal societies, are autocratic by humans standards, as only the strong of deed lead, providing for the subservient within their territorial domain," Staves absorbed.

The words of study kept burnishing what was branded in his mind from earlier readings. The message constant; building a relationship between man and dog must be persuasive and reassuring. It had taken on added emphasis when dealing with an Alpha already in status becoming an adoptee under another's cognizance. Man's elevation to Alpha conceded and ascribed to as the provider and protector of the family pack, must be constantly earned and perpetuated. Any weakness or indecision displayed in its presence will surely embolden aggressive behavior and challenge a demonstrable loss of affection.

George Staves recognized this as a factual dread and was guided accordingly, hopeful his judgments and decisions would avoid eroding ensuring gratifying affection and protection, a *quid pro quo* would always be his while he maintained his command and control as the human Alpha. As a consequence he must always be aware of the delicately balanced social order and the importance that it be maintained. He committed himself to a doctrine of informed decision making; studied and conferenced as needed. This philosophy proved reasonably successful in Tasha's development until now, at the figurative precipice-delicately in balance, the relationship of trust. Now he wasn't so sure a shared decision could be possible at his roundtable. The emotions too fevered to be a consideration. Not willing to submit his family to vexing anguished problems. His imagery, threatening to leave its well-intended wake, being toppled from the peak of love and affection, followed by an avalanche of snow slipping from its sameness anchor The figurative snow melting before being reached by man or bird, leaving no trace of moisture for seeding. His disastrous potential would be his exclusively as he would be the only one to decide.

A troubled George Staves stood fast to a social consciousness borne of disgust. He had read all the horrible statistics; ten to twelve million dogs, cats, kittens and puppies worldwide euthanized annually as reported by the Humane Society. The conservative ten million estimate of life-bearing beings, now just an arguable statistic, equating to 192,308 every life ending week; 27,473 every day, 365 days per year.

"An absolute national disgrace," a disgusted George Staves lamented. The shocking voltage increases when you learn they are not all feral or mongrels forced to survive in the streets by their wile and tenacity until captured. Included in those statistics are those that were once wanted because it was fashionable...or the capricious whim of a child... or are found to be out of favor representing an inconvenience... or are too time consuming to be cared for.

Twenty-five percent of the total euthanized annually involve abandoned purebreds who, if they avoid the fate of road kill, mercifully wind up in shelters, conspiratorially stripped of their identity collars by owners who irresponsibly turned their backs on an avowed protection alliance. The smell of death is around them as they in fright await sentencing, a life-ending consequence.

Guided accordingly, he had successfully and painfully avoided being labeled as a caretaker of a purebred, remiss in their responsibilities, allowing unplanned pregnancies to doom the unadopted offspring of their pets. Staves came to grips with this dilemma.

Reading further, he learned of a start to a more humane outcome. While a minimally contributing beginning, a spark of hope was achieved by responding animal shelters, personally or with donations financed spaying and neutering, housing their charges until adoption. This noble life maintaining alternative under attack by those serving no master but their own narrowly focused purest ideology, life,propagation, and deaths evolution. Well intentioned in preventing the indiscriminate use of Euthanasia. However in Staves' view misguided overall, ignoring the positive role of spaying and neutering, as a reasonable alternative to over breeding. employing picketing and public awareness to achieve their aims, damming the procedures as mutilations. When successful, they turn away from their foisted burden put on the public as they glorify their achievement as the animals' right to live or exist as intentioned.

Spaying and neutering, these activist claim, lacks sensitivity and understanding for all living creatures. "Another ploy favoring man's social order of superiority to dominate," they would editorialize. "Sacrificed at his discretion all other forms of life. Where he and he alone decides who shall live or die or be mutilated. Equanimity not Nietzscheism is the Creator's path and our choice," they loudly proclaim to whoever will listen. Resistant, heatedly arguing as incidental, a non-issue, ignoring as propaganda the fact those that they saved without the cycle reducing benefits of spaying or neutering are eventually abandoned and become road kill; equally of no relevance to their position- the staggering number of drivers and vehicles increases yearly. Or die from diseases. Or are recaptured by the local warden and eventually euthanized. But not before bearing litters with the same needs facing the same consequences.

Inertia driven, the horrendous euthanized figures grow, the cycle continuing essentially unabated, almost relentless. Astounding as it may seem, one male and one female if left to their instincts to reproduce when nature prepares them can produce after seven years of cohabitation 4,372 puppies. Equating to every person that is born, there are fifteen dogs born. A staggering figure. George Staves didn't have to be a mathematician to conclude that there are not enough homes for all.

It is no small wonder that some backward nations across the world still maintain the practice of ancient foraging man to eat dogs as part of their food supply. Did this barbaric practice evolve out of necessity for food or the paring back of the numbers? His suspicion both played a role. Cutting him deeply he repeated the author's conclusion. "We are an advanced nation and have the ready assets capable of establishing a food supply without resorting to pseudo cannibalism. Hypocritically we also practice a form of genocide by condoning euthanasia to pare back the numbers, equally as barbaric as those cultures that eat dogs."

His decision lay just beneath the surface of his cognitive thoughts; the answer obviously lay with prevention before the fact as in spaying and neutering, setting an example to be replicated by other nations of the world not yet giving it the priority it deserved. In time, this approach and commitment by pet owners to spay or neuter house pets as a condition of ownership would leave intact the reproductive organs only for the breeders. This approach over generations could bring the euthanasia number to practically zero. It should be all animal lovers' dedication.

He came to believe it was the humane thing to do as he had no intention of breeding Tasha. He wanted only her best interests. His research brought to the forefront other benefits of spaying that are hardly ever mentioned and should be. It prevents pyometra, an infection of the uterus that is potentially fatal. It reduces the chances of cancer developing in the breasts and uterus. Spaying or ovariohysterectomy, the surgical removal of the ovaries and uterus, in most cases, reduces physical stress that accompanies pregnancies. The ever searching male finding her free of spotting heat, canceling the need for a stressful twenty-four hour watch.

Staves also learned the humane operation can usually be performed on an in-and-out basis. While not painless during the twelve-hour post-operative period, soothing medications are thankfully available, not only to reduce operation recovery symptoms but to lessen one's guilt.

Armed with that information, it reinforced his commitment to do what he knew he should do. With all factors considered, it became clear the right thing to do was to have Tasha spayed. His children, concerned for the post-operative trauma, reluctantly supported the decision after a brief holdout; arguing for delaying the procedure, wishful of seeing Tasha achieve gratifying motherhood nursing her pedigree puppies at least once in her lifetime. They did not know how prophetic their concerns were – a distressing outcome on their shoulders.

What was not factored in the decision was Tasha's age of fourteen months. Capable of being impregnated, underestimating her capablity of motherly expression. Denied motherhood through two estrus periods, her age well beyond that recommended by veterinarians of six to fourteen weeks.

As no reasonable alternative existed, with trepidation they brought an unsuspecting and trusting Tasha to face the birth denying procedure that flew in the face of that trust. It was nine in the morning when they arrived at the veterinarian with plans calling to pick her up six hours after the procedure.

Staves remembered that fateful day as if it were yesterday, so burdensome was the decision. Tasha, her usual trusting self, jumped into the back seat of the car on his command. Soon the excitement of a ride with the window down, facial hair and hackles wind-blown faded as she realized they were not going for a pleasurable ride. They tried hard to conceal their emotions, temporarily transferring their thoughts to distance themselves, unable to keep from returning in angst. Their worrisome demeanor prevailed, initially perplexing Tasha until she recognized the scent of their anxiety effusing from their stressed sweat glands. Her answer came quickly as she recognized the route taken would deliver her to her veterinarian. Her reactions in the past were strong and distrustful but never as animated. It was unfathomable to think she was aware of what was in store for her and yet, her reaction gave pause and worrisome notice. Upon arrival she dragged her hindquarter paws in resistance, giving way finally to his pleading, her eyes doleful as if begging for reconsideration. Instead they, unable to bear the sight, rushed to leave her, least they change their minds.

With no reprieve, deserted to face her ordeal alone, she howled as a baby would cry for the comforting presence of her mother. Unable to escape her howls, the cries reverberating in their minds and hearts, constricted their throats. Weakening their claim as visionaries committed to a better society, to correct the injustice of pairing back euthanasia, self-serving implications rose to their consciousness. Emotions ruled, their convictions no longer bolstered.

The six hours moved tortuously slow, creating tormenting images. Finally the allotted time was reached, solemnly they returned. While expecting the subdued demeanor of a recovering patient, they were still unprepared for what greeted them, finding a shaken and wobbly Tasha, the effects of the bewildering anesthesia slowly leaving her. She brandished an antiseptic scented bandage hiding the wound of the deprived. Without assistance, she gingerly entered the car for the trip home. Upon arrival, she immediately sought refuge in the downstairs bathroom, curling around the cool commode, attempting to hide. This repeat response so early revisited isolated her, resorted to as her only protection, as if to secret herself from them, making herself invisible to those who failed her.

In the days that followed, a disturbing pattern and routine emerged, arising only to quench her thirst or to scratch the door in need of relieving herself in the backyard. She no longer walked proudly enhancing her size- withdrawing within herself, appearing smaller and fragile, her body language, a signature of her withdrawal. The signs disturbed the Staves,' preferring that she live as if vanished. When approached within her sanctuary, when it was impossible to deny their existence, she became aggressive as if she was vulnerable from within; no longer confident of protection from the pack, defecting from her human social order. Finding it a failure, she detached herself, departing from her unifying pack, so inbred into her species these thousands of years, growling to insist she be left alone.

Their worst fears had befallen them; recriminating their actions as acting in cooperative consort presenting her for mutilation. The cost was heavy; she was no longer able to experience the wonders of nature. Aghast at the turn of events, they sought the wisdom of the veterinarian.

"Physically, she's fine. Her lack of appetite does concern me but it hasn't reached the point that would endanger her. Psychologically and emotionally is another matter. She is in a state of depression that in some cases happens after the spaying procedure. You'll have to show patience and wait it out. She'll eventually come back to her normal self. Of course, if you wish, I could prescribe an anti-depressant but I wouldn't recommend it at this time. She might become chemically dependent if this treatment is protracted. Her prognosis is good," he concluded.

"I agree, no anti-depressants," George said.

Returning home, Tasha continued her separation, deliberately avoiding eye contact with her betraying Alpha foremost, resisting all of his overtures. She returned to her world inside the house slinking into the downstairs bathroom sanctuary, again in a hidden retreat.

Following Doctor Kerrigan's advice of patience. They continued unsuccessfully to encourage her to rejoin the family. Burdened and disconsolate, they would retire for the night, praying the next day Tasha would be herself. Her psychological damage so catastrophic that she ignored Phyllis' call to her bed rejecting their special bond.

Finding difficulty in sleeping, they heard her whimpering anguished cries of despair. Their meaning was painfully clear, they were not cries of pain from the healing process, but a soulful language, vocalizing against the act that made her vacant, forever denying her adding to her species, ending her role in contributing to the lineage of over 2,000 years.

Her whimpering bemoaned the lost-forever privilege status of a female Alpha bearing offspring carrying her genetic code. Her minimized situation was now no different than the other females in the pack denied pregnancy. It was a painful parallel to a once proud female Alpha, reducing her role to secondary surrogate duties.

The burden of guilt visited heavily with Rose and Phyllis. Rosanne circumstanced as an adjunct. George Staves had been the voice that directed the decision, all had agreed, chorusing his orchestration. Now they had a troubled aftermath, mentally wringing their hands at the wisdom of having Tasha spayed. "We had to," Staves said hiding his distraught emotions, "It was our obligation and duty. It was more humane." The family, hearing his repeated rationale, were not freed to escape what they had wrought. Guilt-ridden, they tried to reach out to Tasha for forgiveness. Denied a conciliatory reception, Tasha cowered and refused to be summoned. They would sit for hours in the den, the television set on with no one captured by the programming, hopeful that Tasha would join them. Finally retreating to their own bedrooms at her rerjection, staring blankly into space, kept awake by guilt and from hearing Tasha's anguished cries.

Determined to reconcile, George held out hope that his special relationship with her would help cross their divide. George would not wait for the next mornings announcement of her recovery, he decided to approach Tasha in the middle of the night. The full moonlight escaping scattered low lying clouds provided enough light to descend the stairs, those awake heard him, prayerful for the success of his journey.

Another disturbing aspect of Tasha's demeanor presented itself to the visiting George Staves. This time she stood up rigidly facing him, seemingly transfixed, as if mesmerized by the unseen flickering of the hypnotist candle. Her eyes seemed to be clouded over with mist, on the verge of tears if she were physically able to. Her cries reaching a higher pitch in his presence, carrying a special meaning, pausing intermittently to search his visage for understanding as to why he had abandoned her. Sorrow filled his face at her presentation.She left him as her ears went taut, her auditory senses beyond his words frequency, traveling afar, listening to the voices of her ancestors. Suddenly, she was on her back, her twitching legs giving rise to violent movement as if running from a torment, stopping just as suddenly to sit upright, grunting to find movement in the restricted space. Eyes still glazed over with unreleased tears, while her nostrils flared to receive the environmental change taking place within her surroundings: the hormonal change that those that injured waft. Her panorama still did not include him, looking but not seeing him, he was invisible. Her escaping trip exhausting, her scent influenced by the heat that didn't escape from her panting mouth. Her coat, particularly her upright hackles, eerily glowing as if electrified.

It was not Tasha in a dream of disturbance that he first supposed, as there was not the telltale rapid eye movement of a nightmare. Instead her eyes held fast, not blinking, its lenses clouded but staring blankly straight ahead right past him. Catatonic, he recognized the signs, ciphering meaning, he was convinced it was Tasha's encoding an out-of-body experience. Her purpose… searching for the reason for her sacrifice… seeking a spiritual understanding, he witnessed how her devastation affected her psyche.

The personification of her soul bared, was apparent as she whimpered not because she was physically hurting, she cried because of lives never lived: the lives of her future offspring denied existence. Barren forever she would be. No progeny of differing color patterns or gender. No personality differences to recognize and deal with. No past to reflect on as they matured. Only the sorrow of what might have been. What a shock it must have been to her, he thought with great emotion, sacrificed by those whom she embraced, acting dictatorially, creating a wasteland when Mother Nature's reproductive powers were voided.

Motivated to a higher allegiance on behalf of arguably a greater good, now under internal turmoil he faced his accuser, himself. Had he been wrong, he asked himself? Was his guilt in controlling the inventories of God's creatures without merit? She of no consequence she had been denied her natural function to replicate… her lost motherly instincts, to be found only when responding as a longing surrogate. She whimpered because she was shamed, no longer could she be part of that vast network that brings productive partners together, coupling for the power to resist extinction. She whimpered because of the loss of innocence that only pregnancy could bring. She whimpered because she would never know what her offspring would look like. Who would be the Alpha? Who would be the Beta? Lost forever would be the fulfilling process of bonding; the unique attachment between mother and offspring that begins well before birth.

Bordering on irreverence, almost as a prayer of contrition, he asked forgiveness avowing, "To start anew, to reconstruct. I will have the patience of Job while we are rebuilding, and rebuild we will," he pledged. She returned to him not intact, not of prior personality, messaging she was handicapped; her heart bleeding internally, the wounds of damage to be slow in healing if ever, "Share in my loss," beaconed her soulful eyes, "as it is your loss too."

In silent acknowledgment he pledged, "We are bound together, you a victim and I a collaborator of fault, both needing to heal the wounds that will forever scar us."

In retrospect, critical of himself, he questioned how he could not have concluded animal awareness of being denied forever the status and fruits of the estrus period, anxiously awaiting its seed bearing opportunities. A future once bright with the electricity of expectant motherhood now reduced to a surrogate.

He couldn't reverse history to make amends, but he could go forward building a foundation that would ensure them revitalized tomorrows as they provided for one another. Yesterdays not to be forgotten but relegated to the past, by lives that had more to live.

A fortuitous event was about to take place, one completely unexpected, one directly responsible, Staves would be certain, in completing Tasha's rebirth. The common occurrence of pregnancy was psychologically inspiring as a blessing from God. Events and happenings that occur during pregnancy are usually coincidences or exaggerations of this world, not mystical or paranormal. That conviction in this instance to be refuted by the occurrence of something extraordinary.

Tasha well into her recovery from the effects of the spaying procedure still experienced occasional bouts of depression. The family and the veterinarian agreed she was still in need of the passing of time, as no miracle could be summoned to expedite it's passage before recovery would be complete.

Tasha afar from healthy and vibrant, a mutant scarred forever, seedless, unable to accept the gift of the fruited all in the name of a greater good, defined by man's elitist intellect. The incident would jettison Tasha's final melancholy, enforcing his belief that animals are more than automatons.

As if it was preordained, the final breakthrough presented itself. It happened quite innocently with no expectation other than a pleasant dinner invitation at their married daughter Rosanne's house. It was a usual occurrence with no special significance attached; an opportunity for the family to gather enjoying the company of each other and play with their granddaughters, Samantha and Dianna. The atmosphere was pleasant and enjoyable. Idle conversation set the tone and pace, occasionally overshadowed by the attention seeking mischievousness of their granddaughters, remonstrated into quieter tones by their parents.

They all, including the excited grandchildren, waited their turns to speak by phone to Phyllis, in California on a job interview.

Phyllis and their daughter Rosanne, outgrowing their sibling rivalry, were extremely close, manifesting in the grandchildren's complete adoration of "Aunty Phyllis," who mesmerized them with stories of their mother's youth. Squealing in delight at the hidden expected surprise gifts, captivating them with her mimicry playing up to their innocence. The children where never satiated, there was never enough story telling, favorite repeats never tiring them in the retelling – persistent in asking they be part of the agenda.

Their son Edward, who had relocated to New Jersey, was also very close to his sisters Phyllis and Rosanne. It was not just a loving relationship but a protective one he perceived to be demanded of him, recalling incidents as opportunities, Phyllis mimicking his chauvinism and premature manliness to the laughter of the children.

While George was searching the TV channels for a program of interest for the grandchildren in the den away from the others in the dining room, his two granddaughters, out of the hearing range of their parents, found the perfect opportunity to reveal their burning secret, anticipating and receiving his pledge of secrecy.

"Grandpa," they whispered in a hurried unplanned chorus not wishing to be upstaged by the other, "We have a secret to tell you." His quizzical pause of reaction gave Samantha the opportunity to seize the moment for leadership saying, "You can't tell anyone what we tell you." The eyes of both children sparkled with delight, their visage displaying the power of their surprise holding his attention.

"You must promise, Grandpa," Dianna whispered, interrupting her sister's dominance, pleased that she held his attention.

Both children, wide eyed nodding an guiding affirmative in emphatic unison, excitedly needing his commitment, the final persuasion before breaking a confidence.

"I promise," Staves whispered back theatrically, happily a participant, guessing he was playing childish games. His imaginative juices, while stirred, remained cautiously cursory as he expected trickery, children putting a high value of glee in getting adults to believe in fantasies during the playing of games His reaction as planned to bring laughter to all. "You can tell me," he proclaimed in exaggerated excitement.

"Mommy has a baby in her stomach," Samantha, the older of the two happily proclaimed while Dianna listened, in emphasis both vigorously nodding their heads, as only excited children can do.

"Yes, Mommy has a baby in her stomach," Dianna joined bravely, now that her sister had broken the pledge, continuing to nod her head many times over eyes widening by the excitement that the secret was out.

"A baby," he whispered incredulously, genuinely surprised, to the delight of the grandchildren. "When will Mommy and Daddy tell us?" Staves asked, smiling broadly, enjoying every moment of the grandchildren's intrigue.

"Tonight after dinner," Dianna said rushing to be heard ahead of her sister.

"Remember," Samantha said, finger to her lips, "It's a secret. You promised. Don't forget to act surprised."

Dianna's symbolic finger mirroring her sisters, positioned across her lips as George responded, "Not a word. It's our secret." With assurances received, they squealed their way back to their aroused parents animatedly awaiting the unfolding of the evening.

All through dinner as the opportunity presented itself, first Samantha then Dianna reversing roles, would caution him with their eyes, narrowly avoiding being observed. "It's a secret," their eyes flashed reminders "Don't tell anyone," they would smile knowingly as the hour approached.

After dinner while coffee was being served, Rosanne broke the news that she was expecting, that she was three weeks pregnant. The grandchildren jumping up and down in excitement.

Rose was ecstatic, hugging and kissing her daughter and son-in-law, then the grandchildren, joyfully exclaiming, "Another baby."

George kissed his daughter warmly at the same time playfully winking behind her back at the delighted grandchildren, continuing their secret alliance. He then followed by shaking the hand of his son-in-law, maneuvering him in front of the grandchildren, repeating his game of fulfilling winks.

"When will you see the doctor?" Rose asked of her daughter.

"I have an appointment Tuesday at 10:00 AM I'll call you when I get back," Rosanne replied.

The rest of the evening was spent at the kitchen table discussing possible names, both male and female. Believers of the advanced school of parenting, the early education in the symptoms of pregnancy experienced by Rosanne were openly discussed and absorbed in wonderment by the in attendance precocious grandchildren.

The girls, no longer allied by a secret, openly and lovingly vied, as siblings do, for their mother's attention and reassurances. First one, then the other sitting on their mother's lap, slipping off, their heads against their mothers stomach in wonderment of any sound, they prematurely wished to be the baby moving.

On the following Tuesday, Rosanne called her mother as promised.

"Everything is fine," Rose said, nodding in George's direction emphatically, attracting his notice as he sat at the kitchen table pausing from drinking his cup of coffee. Her voice raised for his benefit, echoing Rosanne's encouraging words.

"The fetus and placenta are implanted on the lining of the uterine wall," Rose heard her daughter say, continuing to nod in his direction, momentarily wordless, indicative of the privacy the text of their conversation had taken. Breaking that silence to share the excitement once again, she shouted happily, "It has a heartbeat. It's less than half an inch long and growing."

"Tell her I'm pleased to hear that everything went well during the ultrasound examination," George said. "Tell her I love her."

Messaging, which his wife Rose clearly understood, it was no longer necessary to repeat Rosanne's words for his benefit. He was relieved with what he had already learned from his wife, releasing her to hold a more liberated conversation with Rosanne as only two women can do. Turning his thoughts to his newspaper did not capture his full attention. His concentration was challenged as he heard Rose say anecdotally, her tone incidental: "morning sickness"..."food cravings"... "rise in body temperature."... "granddaughters Samantha and Dianna's reaction." His interest remained temporarily in the background, not reading but scaning his newspaper,ready at a moments notice knowing the details of those unprivileged fragmented statements would be furnished by his wife, not missing a beat, exchanging conversation to one of reporting with the conclusion of the phone call.

Tasha, who lay splayed at his side, muzzle on the floor between her paws, ears would stiffened erect when familiar words and names were spoken. Knowing this would be her reaction, indebted he automatically reached down to pet her reassuringly. While hopeful for demonstrably more, he gladly accepted her passive response, her tail wagged, showing scant exuberance. Tasha's return expression, while token, was promising, a light growing within her, guiding her away from her darkened despair. A sign she was undergoing a transformation.

He would share his thoughts, as he had done in the past, on an Internet

Web Sight welcoming the telling of experiences with animals. Shaking his head, pitying those in the scientific community who would automatically refute his beliefs, preaching parochially from elitist pulpits repudiating his example of a dogs consciousness. Their minds antiseptic; protective against contrarian contaminating beliefs. Declaring Tasha not possible in fathoming his involvement.

"It's beyond their intelligence," would be their counsel. "An unscientific bestowing of human instincts and comprehension to an animal. He accuses himself of abuse, humanizing her reaction to him. His misguided guilt responsible for misreading her post operative response as deep desolation and depression rather than the anguish of recovery typically affecting behavior patterns, the foundation of his rationale," they would say clinically.

"His perception of her revived demeanor," the critics continuing their refute, "rote response and not a wishful forgiving display." Adamant, Staves counter continued the cyberspace exchange, "Tasha still finds herself eyes glazed, staring hypnotically at the recovering area of the forced invasive surgery, moaning under no duress, a sorrowing of what had befallen her the only explanation, her cognitive abilities at work."

Continuing his supporting rationale, he would argue, "What is it then that she manifested, if not her loss, her devastation. Her eyes watered, short of releasing tears, a mirror never to reflect motherhood?" In his mind's eye, her understanding was not perceived but a saddened matter of fact in the hearts of believers. Ceding this belief to no one, willing to face challenge and ridicule, he remained steadfast. Resisting the dilution of his belief no matter how credentialed.

It had snowed… the first significant snowfall of the season. Early morning accumulation coated the landscape and situated homes and buildings. The stark beauty worthy of depiction on a holiday greeting card when unblemished. Artistic appreciation fleeting, as the beginnings of the demise of its unadulterated whiteness was announced by the rumblings and mechanized sounds of smoke belching snowplows. Unfired carbon pollutants darkening the snow beyond the blade's reach. Vehicles of all types, for the most part quartered during the night time hours from the elements, were active again. Stymied drivers preparing to travel the plowed streets, their passage assured as snow of corrupted color was displaced.

Tasha was a link to finely tailored genetics, customized by need during 2,000 years of selective cultivation. It would be her inbred credentials first exposure to snowfall. He envisioned Tasha as initially confused by the falling flakes of wetting coolness until her hereditary signals brought acknowledgment. He anticipated Tasha matching the magnificence of Zuni, his first husky, standing erect searching the originating sky, joyful as the snow sprinkled her, glistening her coat, shaking it free as the light dusting gave way to greater volume. He hoped to see Tasha equally exhilarated, leap high into the descending snowflakes, mouth snapping shut to catch them in flight, delighting in her cooling success.

His eyes clouded over as he fondly remembered Zuni burying her head in the snow, a crystallized nose and muzzle used as her digging shovel to expose the ground, searching or sensing for some hidden movement, scenting the leftover tracks of squirrels digging up their buried bounties sequestered for such a day. She would also be in search of the burrowed network of tunnels chipmunks planned and dug beneath the ground to gain access to their hideaway, away from the danger Zuni posed. Welcomed challenges brought her the joy she wanted without the prize of prey.

George saw Tasha, curious about the accumulating snow, watching his every move, standing upright on her hind legs her front paws parting the living room sheers and peering out at him. His exhaling breath blended with the falling whiteness, he hoped it a positive sign, an interest that would occupy her, crowding out her melancholy. When George had finished snowplowing the driveway, his final task was to clear the backyard patio, giving Tasha a command position to lord over her spotted territory now covered with snow, to forewarn four-legged transgressors that they would face challenge.

George Staves, delighting in her first exposure, brought Tasha under leash out into the gray skied day shedding its crystalline beauty. Only to be disappointed, Tasha's interest had waned, not birthing his hoped-for excitement. Her limited response; holding her head high into the blowing snow, sniffing for scents, blinking as the snow feathered her eyes. He realized she remained unenthused and detached; her display what she was bred for not included in her response. Removed, she quickly relieved herself, her mind preoccupied with no interest to the day's significance, wasting no time in leaving, what should be delighting her, to reenter the house. Ignoring the protective bathroom commode, she chose to lay down on the carpeted floor of the den, a reassurance that she had not regressed, fragmented yes, but on her way of becoming whole again.

"She still has a way to go," Staves anguished disappointingly. "She'll get there with my help," he vowed passionately.

~

The snow had stopped falling around 3:00 PM after eight hours of snowfall. Drifts and accumulation were everywhere. He made ready for his second snow plow bout against the elements.

"I wish Rosanne would call," Rose worried. "Today was her doctor's appointment. Another ultrasound."

"The weather probably backed up all appointments. Besides, you know doctors are always over-scheduled," George said in an attempt to ease Rose's concern.

As if on cue, the phone rang. It was Rosanne, Rose announced, "The snowfall did back up all appointments. The doctor didn't get to see you until way past your scheduled appointment. Almost two hours late," Rose echoed for his benefit.

For the next few moments George did little more than watch Rose nodding approvingly, undoubtedly woman's talk, her visage showing delight. "That's wonderful, Honey," he heard her say. "I'll let Dad know. Bye," smiling with pleasure as she hung up the phone.

A blissful look framed Rose's face at the thought of being a grandmother again. "The doctor confirmed that she is in her third week. The fetus is about the size of a grain of rice. The, mouth, liver and intestines are beginning to take shape. They can see a primitive heartbeat. It's absolutely amazing what today's science can do. Amazing."

"Science willed by God," George added reflectively beholden.

"Of course," Rose acknowledged.

Noticed by George was Tasha, who during the phone call had come out of her seclusion to quench her thirst, was moved to listen, alert in recognition. A stimulating interest now in her forefront, searching from one to the other as the conversation continued, suggesting an understanding, if not for deciphering the words, certainly cognizant of the change in their demeanor and the emotional telling scents that came from their excited body chemistry – as if she was gathering intelligence.

Every day after the first significant snowfall, they would look out the kitchen window and watch the diminishing of the snow's unspoiled beauty, giving up some of its pure whiteness to serve as a background for the last vestiges of dying leaves fallen from the trees standing nearby. Gnarled serpentine aqueduct branches starkly unappointed and naked – inviting limbs, encouraging new birth. Driven by hunger, the snow also showed despoiling commerce, tracks of squirrels, rabbits and haughty blackbirds. Their footfalls interspersed deep enough captured shadows, adding to the disturbed pastoral setting, despoiling it's virgin color. Even the rooftops were bearing a price to melting temperatures and airborne contaminants.

The phone rang breaking their concentration, Rose answered, "Hi, Honey," It was Rosanne. George quickly sensed something was wrong as the conversation turned silent, immediately noting his wife's face drain with muted concern.

"Something wrong?" Staves asked worriedly.

Rose didn't answer him immediately, choosing to raise her index finger to delay his additional queries, remaining exclusively committed to listening. Alarmed, he was about to rise from his chair to approach her when he heard her break the silence, "Your appointment with your doctor is at 1:00 tomorrow afternoon," Rose related as a statement for his benefit.

Unable to piece together Rose's clipped conversation increased his anxiety, his concern; as he considered the implication of his daughter seeing her doctor again within the same week. He sat there trying to rein in his angst, faltering as he found nothing comforting in his wife's words… only the pain displayed in her features. Managing to hold his thoughts in check, he awaited Rose's words to bring him understanding. Finally she hung up the phone solemnly joining him and Tasha who had just come into the room not to drink but to sniff the air about her, sensing their heavy-of-heart mood, trying to decipher the reason for the sudden gloom.

"She's showing signs of bleeding," a distraught Rose said. She has to have another ultrasound to find the reason. The bleeding has me very worried," her eyes filling with tears. "It could be a sign of losing the baby. It's not the best of conditions." She strengthened, "We must be optimistic. Her doctor did say that a lot of women bleed during pregnancy and go on to have healthy babies. The doctor also told her that since she has no history of her immune system rejecting the embryo to cause a miscarriage, everything was in her favor. I'll pray for her and the baby."

"Rosanne is stalworth as you know. She'll handle it," George said quietly trying to build on the positive, masking his equal concern.

Tasha had joined them, noticing immediately the weighted air shrouding them, the dejected slumping of their shoulders, Rose biting her lower lip, her voice tremulous, all in witness to their quick makeover to dark foreboding, affecting her own mood, bringing new heights of melancholy. Powerless to comfort them, confused, she retreated to her den away from the specter of the unknown threat.

"Why don't you go visit your daughter, spend some time with her, cheer her up?" he suggested to Rose.

"I plan to," she acknowledged arising from the table. "She'll need me. I'll go get dressed."

Their greatest fears were confirmed. They learned after Rosanne's searching ultrasound examination, the doctor reporting her placenta's implantation to her uterine wall showed a slight separation known medically as placenta abruption. Unusual in Rosanne's case the doctor commented, "her condition more apt to occur in the last five to six weeks of pregnancy." While it was of great concern to the doctor, he did not conclude miscarriage was inevitable. However, he was concerned enough to advise that precautions be taken. He prescribed complete bed rest for Rosanne- essentially off her feet for at least the next eight to ten weeks. The doctor emphatic in his cautioning: "avoid all strain or a miscarriage is a certainty."

The council of family members quickly responded from near and far.

The plan: Rosanne's husband Bill on his way to work would deliver her daily to her parents' home at 8:00 AM Her old room, essentially as she left it when she married, was in readiness. She would get all the rest she needed to assist the healing powers of nature. The doctor agreed, granting Rosanne's only provision: that she be returned home in the evenings at a six o'clock pickup to tend to her young daughters, Samantha and Dianna, assuring their needs, requiring nothing more than verbal communiqués from her bed of rest. The weekends were another matter, with Bill home from work there would no need for her parentaol care, however Rose and George would be available on an as-needed basis. It was to start the very next day without delay, so compelling was the urgency.

George didn't know it then but would soon learn that Tasha would not only be a comfort to Rosanne by her therapeutic presence, but surprisingly a recipient of therapy. Collaborative healing, kinetic energies radiating from the physically damaged, sharing the experience of self repairing themselves. One ambulatory the other consigned to immobility becoming co-dependent upon each other in curing reciprocity. One psychologically in need to be a maternal self-appointed guardian, sensing an opportunity to share… to see… to hear… to witness… the sounds and sights of pregnancy that were no longer available to her. The other, while physically being tested, was also under psychological strain, at risk of losing her long-awaited pregnancy, her biological opportunities nearing the age of not recommended restriction. Unfolding events, completely unexpected presented themselves, holding promise's that ministrations from one another could avoid tragedy on one hand, and the gift of surrogate motherhood on the other. Two females, divided only as differing species, of common interest, fate bringing them together to serve one another. Their current positions, equally stressful, their polarity different, attracting one another in a magnetism of potential healing.

This fortuitous tend-and-mend response in both humans and animals, particularly amongst females, is recognized in scientific studies as the curative workings of hormones and chemical responses. Science makes a strong argument that animals, including the human species, respond to stress by preparing to do battle or flee, a psychological syndrome commonly known as "fight or flight." In Rosanne's and Tasha's cases, the consequences of acceptance as a preordained misfortune of fate were never a consideration, they were determined, victory was their only pursuit.

The hormone Oxytocin is one of the many hormones that appears to play a role in the female response to stress, contributing to the determined strength necessary in a figurative circling of the wagons response.

Their only ordinance would be the will to succeed. Their battlefield, while not cratered and shrouded with the smoke of spent munitions, was nonetheless just as dangerous. Psychological maiming over remaining lifetimes.

Rosanne arrived the next day, her face's features showing considerable strain. Carrying in her hand a small suitcase, included were items to tend to her everyday needs. Her cell phone at the ready to stay in touch with her workplace employment agency – to contact her husband Bill as well as the nanny Traci, who watched over Samantha and Dianna to directly reassure the children themselves, conditioned on avoiding doctor warned stressful situations.

As George and Rose escorted Rosanne up the steps to her old bedroom, they were pleased to see Tasha following, entering the bedroom on their heels, sniffing Rosanne with an intensity and fervor that bordered on a worship she had never displayed before. Her senses were fixed to Rosanne, imploring eyes exclusively on her, deliberately excluding peripheral vision from her focus, nostrils quivered as she tracked her body scents, distinctly different… certainly not for Rosanne's identification, as her scent was known to her. While they were taken aback with Tasha's unusual conduct, deciding Tasha's motivation was more than the lure of Rosanne's dog Carry's foreign scent carried in her clothes. Tasha's profound abilities were given more credibility, the more probable scenario: incapable of being detected by humans; the telling scent of amniotic fluid that joined the slight physical changes taking place in Rosanne's body. Of no challenge as it was easily detected by Tasha's innateness.

Tasha quickly confirmed their conclusions. As Rosanne lay down on the bed, Tasha reacting jumped up onto the bed to join her, moving gently to nestle close enough for her head to make soft controlled contact with Rosanne's stomach. Tasha's countenance changed quickly; her eyes half shut relaxing, mouth parted, panting softly, her lips curled. Almost imperceptive, her display of a knowing smile, a banner announcing to the world the longed for role she was to play in Rosanne's recovery. Unbeknownst to her, her role resonating her own recovery.

Shaking his head in amazement at Tasha's recognition of Rosanne's situation, declaring herself guardian. Solicitous, George Staves posited, "She won't bother you, Rosanne," asked not as a question but as registering his approval that Tasha would be good company for her.

"She won't bother me, Dad," she confirmed. "She'll keep me company."

Under close watch by all, they began their therapies. Corresponding, to extract healing and recovery. Each at the same time a self and collective intervention, to render their harms spent of any further consequences, spiritually or physically. A shared recovery, communal, willing participants at a crossroads. Rose Staves believed it was providential, as an encouraged religious experience. Not a direct divine intervention but a release of the power of the aura of each, the more likely scenario. To radiate, granted by God, ancillary powers to do His good work. Rose convinced it was God's response,his way to entreaties and prayers. His divinity they finding their curative powers of nature responding in each others aura, contributing to each others needs. No church, no cathedral, no house of worship was needed for supplication His oversight everywhere, there being a feeling of a "presence" abounding both natural and mystical-supervising the aura's swirling around them, its vortex funneling them toward recovery, a missioned navigator.

When Rosanne would awake from a short sleep, she would find Tasha in physical contact with her, attentively listening in on the unfolding miracle, the baby's heart pumping blood being heard by Tasha' extraordinary auditory senses resting lightly on her abdomen.

Rosanne's old room, her shared bed, became an extension of a pack den, where safety and protection was readily provided by Tasha, her a surrogate and guardian. Tasha never moved from being watchful, alerted to all sounds close in proximity. Tasha, Rosanne's Centurion guard, never left her side save for drinking from her water bowl, feeding time or to relieve herself in the backyard, always returning quickly to resume her vigil. She even accompanied Rosanne to the bathroom, sitting outside the door and emitting anguished cries, anxiously awaiting her return to escort her back to the bedroom, continuing her oversight.

Still gripped by anxiety as she continued to spot, Rosanne was still under threat, being frightened she would awake suddenly sweating profusely, reaching out to find Tasha's reassuring presence. Calmed by Tasha's comforting kisses of her hand, she would return to sleep to fight her fight.

When Rosanne communicated by cell phone to her office, Tasha would come to attention and sit upright, alerted to the disturbance of the guarded tranquility. She repeatedly nudged a smiling Rosanne to tell her that she was exceeding her time limits on the phone until Rosanne accommodated her wishes.'

Tasha had little tolerance for the break and separation during that first night and weekend. Anxious, she brooded continuously. Seeing daylight advancing close to the hour of Rosannes expectation, responding excitedly to the sounds of a car door being slammed, yelping in anticipated delight she would rush to the living room bow window to peer out, hopeful it was her treasured Rosanne. The light in her eyes dimming when it failed to be her. The experience of separation prompting mood swings repeated time and time again, particularly over that first night and first weekend of false alarms until Rosanne's arrival, the time registering in Tasha's mind modulating further vigils.

Finally fruitful, sighting Rosanne emerging from Bill's car in the same troubled state she left with. Immediately Tasha's mood changed, her lips curled back revealing the typical pleased smile of a husky. Her hindquarters and tail moving emphatically in obvious excitement, the separation at night and during the weekend- period not an impairment to her mission's success.

Still, when the time came, Tasha would resort to protective trickery... hiding the small suitcase under the bed to prevent Rosanne from leaving, creating a small panic until Tasha's actions were guessed by an endeared Rose Staves. Thwarted in her attempts to hide the suitcase, she would lay across it refusing to move until cajoled and gently nudged by George Staves. Her delaying tactics would also include the hiding of Rosanne's cell phone until the rings revealed its hiding place.

Rosanne's spotting stopped, a clear sign that her condition was strengthening. It was her seventh week of pregnancy, the embryo was only one inch long, the miracle of growth progressing with features forming. The developing heart beat at one hundred fifty beats per minute, detectable by humans with the assistance of ultrasound imagery. But not to Tasha, with her head fixed to a sleeping Rosanne's stomach, her sensitive hearing matched man's enhanced sonic wizardry.

And so it went, each succeeding week, with the nights and weekend separation reluctantly accepted by Tasha. Significantly, Tasha's demeanor elevated, she relished her role as a self-authorized Centurion guard in waiting with the power of ministrations. Her self-appointed charge, her developing progeny protected and being enhanced. At the same time, the mortar that held Tasha captive in dejected seclusion, her self-imposed monastic exile, began to crumble and disintegrate.

The beginning of Rosanne's thirteenth week of pregnancy, the final week of the doctor ordered bed rest, the day for the much anticipated ultrasound examination and imagery comparison drew near. Tasha's reaction that final week was completely out of recent character. Instead of waiting for Rosanne to fall asleep to place her head surreptitiously on Rosanne's stomach, this time she did so openly without hesitancy or stealth, listening to the now of legal age fetus swimming within the protection of the amniotic fluid.

The baby's vocal cords sounding cries inaudible to humans but heard by Tasha's gifted senses.

Unlike the earlier weeks where silence prevailed and set the tone, Tasha, began emitting the strangest of sounds: a low octave constant murmur, a cooing soulful siren, luring, distinct in it's voiceprint. The wonders of nature providing at this stage of development the opportunity for the rapidly growing fetus to recognize and relate to her, joining the true mother whose voice was already recognized, the communicated sounds of the surrogate who watched over both of them.

Rosanne's response to Tasha's "voicing" was to pat Tasha on her neck, confirming what Tasha already knew... an affection that, "all will be well with my baby,"... not knowing her voice in chorus with Tasha was what the baby needed to hear repeatedly in the darkness of the womb, assurances to soothe it's cries.

Her spirits rising, her crestfallen periods no longer dominating, a radiating glow in Tasha's eyes increased in intensity that last week, a meaningful sign; her assurances the danger to Rosanne's pregnancy had passed.

Being a believer in interspecies communication, ever faithful the Staves's accepted Tasha's message, waiting only for confirmation from the doctor.

Rosanne called later that Friday. While they were ecstatic, they were not surprised at the doctor's findings, supportive of Tasha's message; indeed the placenta had reattached itself and implantation was secure. Her pregnancy no longer in need of extreme protective measures

What intuitive unidentified sense beyond what humans possess did Tasha call upon, enabling her to go beyond the sounds of the baby's movements and its cycle of growth? What made her *"see"* the miscarriage had been avoided? The magic of an unnamed power source within her called upon?

Rote was inconceivable; there had to be a consciousness that brought Tasha's response. It had no language as humans understand yet messages and pictures were being sent. Communication was being conducted, an understanding traveling the abyss, by those sensitized or empowered. The brain as a storage house for electrical energy, a varying power amongst all specie's. When compelled a generator to print electronic imagery. Or could it be, undetectable to human ears, a high pitched sound wave emitted by Tasha, bouncing off the fetus, a sonogram in Tasha's mind's eye? The developing brain of the fetus releasing energies describing it's plight? Mysterious, possibly mystical, that Tasha was availing

Tasha, whose metamorphosis was begotten by shared therapy radiating from each other, was now complete. With growing confidence, she displayed her old self; anxious for new challenges, once again playful until bored. She was no longer morose or isolated. Her countenance was a statement that she had overcome her obstacles. She had emerged from the darkest reaches of her mind, distancing as light years her troubling experience, coincident to Rosanne's baby's development with each passing day.

She had now come full circle regaining her persona, understanding the love they continued to bestow upon her. History her previously turning away, feeling betrayed by her pack; retreating. She now accepted her fate of sacrifice for other callings and focus. She had shed her demons, returning into the social order of her pack, bedrocked with greater devotion. She now walked liberated from her shame, sharing in the knowledge of a birth in progress, albeit a sacrificed mother proxy who had contributed to it's survival. No longer would she feel completely cheated.

The evidence: the results, clearly establishing that Tasha had participated in preventing Rosanne's miscarriage. Her bonding, her own need for finding herself, created conditions for the production of higher beneficial levels of the chemical Oxytocin, delivering a restful state conducive to speeding their own recoveries.

In the weeks preceding the baby's delivery; to be named George William, pleasing both families, whenever Rosanne would visit, as soon as she was seated, Tasha would cozy up to her, tail wagging, ears at attention, lips curled to reveal a knowing smile. She would place her head on Rosanne's lap, an ear in contact with her stomach listening and cooing affectionately until satisfied that all continued well, bringing smiles to the Staves family at Tasha's doctoring, her bedside manner reassuring.

Tasha's response to the threat of Rosanne's miscarriage once again demonstrated her intelligence was something special. While he never openly bragged of her abilities, George was comforted that his bias was deserved. Supportive of his readings. Studies dealing with the b*iology of emotions*, which noted many similarities between the brains of humans and animals. Emotions rising from ancient parts of the brain, away from the heavy traffic of neurons that frequent the cortex regions. Conserving themselves, resisting when unused from becoming snuffed out embers or dysfunctional across many species, the degree of which is circumstanced. Suggestive that these ancient areas of the brain are not always equally active and sensitive, dormancy and expressing varing from person to person, or animal to animal, particularly within the same animal species, needing inherent stimulated senses to express.

Elitists, he would once again disdain, animal behavioral scientists were obstinately narrowly focused, content to troll shallow waters where only humans can be cognizant. Animal responses only taught to provide reactions, instructing acts, the combination of repetitiveness and predictability, providing a feedback course of action for the animal. Branded as nurture developed.

Undeniably, George Staves admitted, sensed imagery was true even in Tasha's case. Her everyday reactions boosted incrementally by nurturing, mirroring in repetition what she was environmentally exposed to. This was the only acceptable rationale usually promoted as unimpeachable by the dissenting animal behavioral scientists. But not a finding in Rosanne's situation; Staves reasoned, that Tasha's recognition of her circumstances went well beyond a summoned limited intelligence.

The transporter enabling George Staves to revisit questions he had posed at a earlier time. "What if animals, dogs in particular, were left to their own dependency, separated immediately after being weaned, would they react when threatened or tempted, not being able to borrow life's lessons from others? Of course they would," he had reasoned, "Necessity being the mother of invention would intervene. Instinct for survival would prevail. Without that consciousness, the current switch thrown in moments of need would short circuit. They would join the world of robots, power deprived, silenced and motionless, unconsciously awaiting a merciful conclusion or the unlikely to happen slavish dependency on others."

George vividly relived his stunning observations, Tasha had revealing, almost human-like characteristics by interacting intelligently, recognizing the pain and fear of others. Her reactions reflected thinking, planning and empathy, not as complex and profound patterns of humans, yet relatively clearly powerful, persistent and determined. Tasha's biology of emotions: influencing a countenance and body language exemplifying the varying intellectual chasm that divides all God's creatures.

He remembered questioning: When had the consciousness that Tasha displayed first appear in her ancestral lineage that was passed along to heirs that followed? Had it developed from her direct descendent – ancestral wolves?

Finding the answer a resounding "Yes" as he read, "Molecular genetic tools were used to establish the relationship between dogs and dog-like carnivores, and the inter-relationship of species within the family of canidae clearly establishes the lineage and the starting time period."

George Staves read eagerly, taking notes, occasionally pausing for complete absorption, then continuing his search for the only truth that would satisfy him.

His notes his captivation:

Committing to memory, "The results of allozyme and chromosome analysis suggests several phylogenetic divisions within the wolf-like canidae; began seven to ten million years ago supported by fossil records, revealing close kinship between gray wolves, dogs, coyotes and hyenas – all canidae of high intelligence and cunning."

"The first canidae domestication to come through the evolutionary process remains shrouded in mystery as is the exact nature of the relationship between man and the evolving dog in the early days. He could easily visualize somewhere in early history, a young wolf was brought into the family circle of man and became the source of a co-dependent dog, man's most successful and useful experiment in domestication.

Dogs primeval he absorbed "Approximately 12,000 years ago, the native tribes migrating from the cradle of civilization having a major impact on the evolution of dogs. Given the ensuing millenniums, they selectively bred mutants that cropped up in dog colonies. Humans to the present manipulating an almost incredible diversity in the canadae species, growing to more than 800 true breeding types worldwide."

Further connecting the relationship of dogs to wolves he read: "Recent findings of ancient dog remains dated from ten thousand to fifteen thousand years ago; DNA analysis revealing either identical, or within 0.2% of the DNA sequence of gray wolves, despite dog's diversity in size and proportion. A range in adult morphology is probably the result of simple changes in development rate and timing.

"Repeated genetic changes between dog and wolf continue today with resultant mutants. Paradoxically, the gray wolf and coyote also experienced a high rate of genetic exchange during copulation but in their case, hybridization was suppressed: science continued to ponder why.

A task for future anthropologists as George Staves armed himself with intelligence,having digested: "Dog's exact evolutionary process is shrouded in mystery as is the exact nature of the relationship between man and dog in the early days of domestication. Remains 12,000 years old demonstrating the closeness between man had existed; fossils found in Israel sharing a common grave are evidence of this fact. The Saluki (Persian greyhound) holds the privilege of being one of the first selectively bred and meticulously lineaged canines."

"Early man's selectivity unknowingly ran parallel and was part of Darwin's evolutionary theory, tailored for their specific needs and wants as influenced geographically and environmentally. Instinctively, man contributed unknowingly to the science of evolution, which was accomplished by selective breeding; exacting mutations, ranging in size and proportion from squat daschund like bush dogs to the long-legged manned wolf dog."

Adding to his knowledge "It generally accepted that the wolf provided the seedlings for the birth of the Husky 2,000 years ago. This scientifically accepted as originating in southern Siberia. Before, they were raised by plains-dwelling Chukchi people."

The time traveling George Staves remembered being engrossed by what he had read, with the answer he sought still evading him, it licensed him to extrapolate from his readings a rationale to foundation his own theory on the still remaining mysteries.

Engrossed by the theory of ancient man, captive to ignorance and superstition, prayed to his pagan deities for his canidae evolutionary development to accommodate his needs. Risking being smitten, angering his wary gods as he pursued faster responding selectivity, hopeful that he had placated their anger by attributing his reacting intelligence as their purposeful gift to him. Judging him as cooperative in their grand design, he could imagine early man's presentation as a contribution, helping engineer evolution by his selectivity. Those thought to be cursed by genetic short comings fit his earliest of needs, at the very beginning and subsequent periods of engineering a dog."

Continuing his arguable logic, George theorized, adding another brick to his foundation theory with supportive mortar:

"Within the circle of member wolves, strong assertive Alphas were conceded dominant, providing leadership to the other productive members of the pack. While the Betas were the weaker, limited by size, or arthritic-ridden, diminished of speed, it's coloring inhibiting its stealth were invariably menacingly ostracized, disdained by others in the pack as inefficient hunters of poor ranking, forced to live on the outer periphery of the pack, retreating from snarling viscous attacks greeting their every attempt to rejoin the inner circle. Defeated, dejected in indignity, they were left to feed on the remnants of the kill only after the glutinous satisfaction of the ranked pack members-sometimes having to fight off scavengers for what was left.

"Those mutants held in disfavor by those not faulted genetically, gravitated to one another from other packs as they too were driven off. On the verge of starvation, escaping threats of becoming well-scarred prey, they banded for protection. Together they interbred, establishing the first mutated departure link of wolves evolving toward dogs. Each succeeding generation of mutants carried the genetic seed of the originally discredited forebear continued to seek out each other, adding a further link to what was to evolve as the first newly-bred Siberian husky. Each succeeding generation increasing the gap between themselves and their original wild ancestors.

"During the beginning years, in their apartheid environment,some of those first progeny produced physical characteristics that reverted back to their ancestral wolves, returning to the wild of their original calling, escaping man's efforts at engineering while the other mutants continued to fractionally dilute their genetic makeup to further affect size, temperament and lust for prey. It was these mutants that became camp followers, it's food source- rewarded for contributing protection as an outer periphery warning system… howling or barking of impending danger; until that moment in time when man brought the new breed into camp for assimilation and the beginnings of domestication of the Husky."

Convinced from his readings, George believed it highly likely that it was the Chukchi people who lived in more or less settled family groups, finally judging no threat in the purchase of this new breed A step up in ranking; friendship,hurled bones and scraps of their meals to the hungry, once outcasts. Encouraged mutants, no longer ostracized and banished, bearing the scaring of forced exclusion for their inability to contribute to the pack.A new venue, no longer to succumb to their size and strength limitations, disadvantaged as a killer of prey, banished.Before assimilation, of necessity to prowl and scavenge around the periphery of the village, awaiting man's generosity. Distinctly limited and marked wolves gradually and fortunately realizing that man was a superior hunter. Acknowledging this superiority, they cowered toward man as their adopted leader, their Alpha. No longer following him for great distances during the hunt, stripping carcasses clean often fighting off scavengers. Now, recognized as shields gratefully sharing in the allocated meat. Extensive interbreeding within the mutant colonies, those temperament modified characteristics not affecting hunting skills were encouraged by man. to not only be observers but helpers, successful in flushing and isolating the kill.

It was not unusual for the puppies of the appreciated and valued mutants who had lost their birth mother to be nursed by lactating women of these plains people who lost their child at birth.

Such practices, Staves extrapolated, may have occurred even at the beginning of the man/dog relationship and may have played a major role in cementing the closeness between man and animal, suggesting the beginnings of domestication of the Husky Canis Familiaris. At the beginning he envisioned holdouts born with the physical size and the naked wildness of their wolf ancestry had forsaken this new identity and formed their own wolf packs or back-crossed to satisfy their wanton needs.

Standing there watching himself, the revisiting George Staves nodding in acknowledgment, that he had seen Tasha retrace her labored footsteps in the deep snow to conserve her energy, an action remindful of her ancestors in the pursuit of prey. Paced in a disciplined line, following one another, the strongest, nose to the air, leading the way with its footfall impressions in the snow, taken up by those that followed. In tandem as an energy conserving alignment, the last of the procession, usually the youngest with still developing strength, brought up the rear with relative ease. In the replaying this scenario he saw how repelled and horrified he was at his conjured vignette of the killing of prey, questioning Tasha of the future. Now reading as shockingly threatening the slight magnitude of difference in her genetic code insignificant in separating her from wolves, his imaginative mind troubled, suggesting Tasha's breed precariously on the edge of reverting to nature's brutal side, given the right circumstance. Tasha recycled to a ferocious predator of the wild, abandoning centuries of her species evolution.His imagery's consequence:the loss of Tasha's innocence George Staves of yesteryear,his emotions in a state of upheaval, overheard by his visiting self, "are we vulnerable to a Tasha on the edge circumstances to a return to the feral.

He on the other hand, as a visitor, equally as horrified of Tasha as primeval- benefiting from Tasha's ended lifetime. Still he was plagued by the viciousness of the conjured hunting scene, he needed the reacquainting of lived instances crediting distancing evolution as a final purge of Tasha's imagined connection to the horrors of killing prey for sustenance. He would distance Tasha further from that imagery, proving in her case she capable of keeping her ancestral instincts latent, her aggressiveness redirected. Traveling again seeking out signs, events and instances of her superior intelligence, to counter her visualized wildness. Intellectual prowess foremost, setting her apart from her marauding ancient forebear's savagery.

The transporter summoned, responding to his will to depart this time period, its silent engine became activated. The only sound heard was his breathing, as the events of other periods in time rushed by, their time for revisiting not yet on his agenda. His purposeful priority; to visit those events demonstrating Tasha's true being, revisiting happenings that demonstrated her superior intelligence,for events forefronting her ancestral resourcefulness-dealing with problems until solved by cognizant intelligence,that which also separated her from her peers. Almost as quickly as it had started, the kaleidoscope came to a halt.

Selective witness to times passing onto history, albeit known, the results and quickness in her responses were still surprising in this re-imaging, a reaffirmation of Tasha's reasoning ability his needed antidote. Remindful of Tasha's performances at odds with the scientific community's conclusion; more manufactured then instinctive. Experiences that were superficial happenstance.

He smiled in recollection as he watched himself plan the test. Before its essence, the challenge established in fundamental groundwork. Simply taking a dog biscuit favored by Tasha, placing it unseen within one of his hands held behind his back and then presenting both hands to Tasha, who with moistened nose, touched the rewarding hand. Realistically he would be the first to acknowledge that it was hardly an elevating test of intelligence as all dogs with their astonishing olfactory senses would come away successful. His smile broadened as a more worthy test was introduced, planned as a precursor to a task even more formidable.

Tasha, enjoying the game, continued to participate. Anticipating her losing interest, as described in his readings of noted anthropologist, Elizabeth Marshal Thomas, he placed a biscuit on the floor, concealing it with a towel, drawing curious stares from Tasha aroused to the new challenge, sniffing the location of her reward. Absent hesitation or confusion, she grabbed one end of the towel and quickly pulled it aside, exposing and devouring her prize. She repeated her problem solving acumen no matter where he positioned the biscuit beneath the blanket.

Excitedly, he called his wife Rose to witness the next attempt. Not in the least distracted by the increased audience, she repeated her successes, swelling his chest with pride.

"Do it again," Rose demanded, not sure of the significance.

Close to her limit of interest, he again tested her. Her zeal for this game waning, she was decidedly slower of pace, indicative of diminished challenge. Creatively, she changed her method of recovery. She now used her front paws to move the biscuit from under the blanket until it saw the short-lived light of day.

Pausing with heads shaking disbelievingly at her ingenuity, her accomplishments increased their respect, both wondered, he silent and his wife out loud, “How many dogs could do that?”

Rose Staves answering, “Not many.”

“She actually was playing games with us with that last effort,” George exclaimed. “Not the other way around. She was on stage enjoying every moment of her performance, delighting in our expressions of amazement as her captive audience, and then taking the time to tell us she was tiring of our silly game. Introducing a change in pattern, a variation to counter boredom.”

“She can be mischievous when she wants to,” Rose interjected. “Drawing great pleasure in our underestimating her intelligence with our simplistic games.”

Tasha, no longer in need of treats, her last performance given for the night, retired to her bathroom den, leaving them to ponder the imponderables.

What did it all mean, this simple unscientific test? There were no carefully measured rise and fall of heartbeats, no synapses or neuron measurements, and yet it whispered her reactions, when taken as a whole, were not just instinctive. Unaware save the time traveler, were circumstances yet to present themselves that would add to her mystique. He knew of the coming recognition of her perceptive powers and extraordinary senses, elevating her, an internal guidance system capable of finding the proverbial needle in the haystack. A capability first recognized by Tundra tribes, with today’s man all the more grateful for their selectivity in driving hybridization. George of the past not yet experiencing this, while George, in the present, acknowledged circumstance after circumstance, time and time again during their lifetime together, making it an irrefutable fact; Tasha was a possessor of high intelligence and awareness.

He sat there watching Tasha’s usual reaction upon awakening after a night’s sleep: boundless with energy, impatient with his slow response to her need for relieving herself and overseeing the day’s presentation of her world as seen at the end of a tether. She responded with point making rushing and slamming against the front door. Continuing that impatience when his pace outdoors was still not fast enough, she responded by forcing the pace, disregarding the discomfort of her choke collar, leading, instead of heeling, in her tethered adventure. She would search the skies, the rooftops and trees in search of those pesky blackbirds that were quick to alert others of Tasha’s approach. With the blackbirds out of reach, she was still hopeful. Unsuspecting foraging squirrels would freeze her motionless in place, her eyes in protracted stares, Tasha stilled, not for invisibility, but to be unnoticed at the periphery of her antagonists vision, disappointed this day as neither the blackbirds nor squirrels, well beyond the length of the leash, would venture close enough to promote a chase. Her ritual half-finished, having relieved herself just short of completely emptying her kidneys, she set about leaving her mark, overlaying previously visited sites, regaining her territory that recent rains had washed away her scent. A warning, crowning of scents left by intruders.

Returning home, her pace was moderate until she burst through the opened front door, a forcefully relinquished leash trailing noisily along the tiled kitchen floor. Quickly lapping at her water bowl, thirst satisfied at her trough, satiated she turned and ran wildly, tail trailing behind her, a battle flag in a charge, sprinting from room to room. Achieving needed physical exhaustion, her heightened electrolytes having energized her body were now spent. Exhausted she slumped to the floor with a contented groan, leaving George, Rose and daughter Rosanne, son-in-law Bill, and grandchildren Samantha and Dianna who were invited for breakfast, delighting in Tasha's antics, newly arrived baby George sleeping through the din.

Tasha's respite lasted as long as breakfast where her baleful stares and demanding barks did not bring table food. With breakfast ending, her attempts at coercing food futile, she left the room for a short period, playfully returning with an old sock in her mouth, swinging it wildly from side to side.

"She's awfully hyper today," Rose commented.

"Been that way all morning, right from her return from her morning walk," George said.

"I know Tasha," George said as he playfully grabbed the end of the sock being offered to play tug-of-war. Growling enjoyment in her counter-response, Tasha dug in her back haunches, resisting his attempts to dislodge the sock, strenuously resisting herself from being pulled forward. "She wants to play," George added as he continued to play tug-of-war with a competitive Tasha.

The presence of the sock and George's quick imagination provided the basis for his designing a new game, one that would be intellectually testing, raising Tasha to new heights, or risk failure and a weakening intellectual accreditation. The more he thought about it, the better he liked the idea. When completed, there could be no doubt of the extent of Tasha's intelligence and superior senses or her limitations.

He carefully explained his cleverly designed game. Not everyone agreed that she would be able to solve all aspects of the test they were about to expose her to, expressing concern that increasing difficulty might cause her to become frustrated at being stymied. Reflective of her sensitivity of bearing the burden of failure and disappointing those she knew held her in high expectations, they all promised to downplay her failure if and when it came, acknowledging the risk of psychological damage.

He held a box of treats. Tasha quickly noticed.

"Mom, will be the first test," he announced.

Before leaving, Rose gave him her handkerchief, handled repeatedly to carry her particular scent. He then called Tasha to his side, stroking her pleasingly on her forehead and under her muzzle while she stared hopefully at the treats. He then placed Rose's handkerchief to her nostrils, which she quickly turned away from, the treats dominating her interest. Again he stroked her chin and forehead. Again he placed the handkerchief to her nostrils.

This time George spoke to her, "Let's find Mommy and you'll get your treat."

When she was convinced that no treats were in the offering, they all rose as a group, including Rosanne holding baby George in her arms, not wishing to miss out on the fun of Tasha's reaction.

His granddaughters squealed in delight, "Grandma, Grandma, where are you?"

As planned, they went searching from room to room on the first level of the house with expected failure. Tasha, her nose to the luring box of treats, still distant to her task, not knowing what to make of their strange antics. Again turning from the handkerchief thrust at her, the grandchildren continually broke the silence by repeatedly shouting excitedly, "Grandma, where are you?"

Clustered together as one, the pace quickening, they all rushed upstairs searching all the bedrooms,Tasha among them. When they got outside the master bedroom, the grandchildren could hardly control themselves, their decibel levels rising as they shrieked, "Grandma, where are you?"

Tasha, caught up in the swirling activity, confused, barked at the children's excitement. Upon his command, they all became quiet. Tasha looked from one to the other searching for understanding.

"Tasha, find Mommy," George pleaded as he once again placed the handkerchief to her nose. Suddenly, it became clear to Tasha what all this strange behavior was about. She quickly matched the scent from the handkerchief to the giver of the scent, Rose hiding within the master bedrooms closed clothes closet. Pushing her snout against the unyielding door as if pointing, the grandchildren were wide-eyed and hysterical with glee, " Tasha found you," they screamed as Rose finally opened the door amidst the cheers and praises for Tasha's success.

"Good girl, good girl, you found Mommy," they all shouted. Staves completed the complimenting by rewarding her for her discovery.

They all rushed back downstairs, again with Tasha in hot pursuit barking an excited understanding of this new game, anxious and encouraging another attempt. This time it was Rosanne who was selected along with his now-awake grandson in her arms smiling up at his mother not knowing he was about to become part of a test. As her mother had done previously when the center of attention remained fixed upon Tasha, Rosanne moved unnoticed from the gathering in the den to her hiding place, leaving behind her burp diaper scented with mother's milk.

Tasha, in immediate recognition of what was being asked of her as George brought the diaper to her nose, identifying the latent signatures of the two contributors. Armed with this knowledge, she rushed back upstairs to what was Rosanne's closed bedroom door. The trailers reaching the top of the stairs just as Rosanne opened the door to let a scratching Tasha into the room. The grandchildren cheered at Tasha' success, pleased at their appointment of handing Tasha her just reward.

All of them participated in testing Tasha's bloodhound capabilities; all of them happy willing participants in her credential building… whether hidden in the bathroom after turning on the shower to coat the mirror with moisture, steam hanging as a still fog… to the basement cedar closet, whose distinctive forestry scent influenced stored, freshly dry cleaned out of season clothing of family members… or the garage and its multitude of smells and noxious fumes, all unable to mask the presence of the hidden from Tasha's discovery.

The game continued as Tasha's interest remained high, bringing Rosanne back for a second try at disappearing, this time without baby George. Tasha's task was made appreciably more difficult as this time personal articles of clothing that housed the distinct scent characteristics of the missing were not provided, testing Tasha to relate the name called to her memorized signature scents catalogued in her memory bank. To compound the difficulty, a hurriedly applied in secret deodorant spray now wafted from her hiding place in the upstairs bathroom. The added difficulty proved of no consequence as she was easily able to separate Rosanne's memorized scent, quickly filtering out the superfluous.

The final search and the full extent of Tasha's finding ability, decided in advance, involved Rose. This scenario would represent the most difficult cognitive test yet to be presented to Tasha. Rose would dress in George's clothing, including a golf hat stained with sweat, it's inside band deliberately heavily coated with hair pomade, shoes washed and shined, their interior dusted with anti-fungal powder. In crowning difficulty, Rose would get into his garaged car and with Tasha's attention diverted, drive the car and park it one hundred yards away from the house to wait hopefully within a reasonable time period, before discontinuing, averting the curiosity of neighbors or the police.

When George gave Tasha the command to go find Mommy, the cheers of exhortation quieted, in stillness all attention remained focused on Tasha. Skepticism began to erode confidences as Tasha immediately sensed a difference. She became hesitant, switching directions repeatedly for bearings. She sniffed at the head of the stairs, climbing to the upstairs rooms, inspected one by one, turning away still searching. Returning, moving toward the door leading to the basement steps, sniffing for recognition; ears stiffening, all her resources in play, again to be denied. She turned toward the garage door which sealed the bountiful odors of spilled gasoline, motor oil and traces of carbon monoxide along with bagged unused fertilizer, proven earlier as of no consequence as Bill's hidden presence was uncovered. Disappointingly nothing excited her. Her sniffing of the air fruitless as she repeated her earlier search. Was she about to be defeated by a task beyond her capabilities? Suddenly she stopped all movement, her attention intensifying.

"What is it," George asked. "Where is Mommy?"

They all waited anxiously, holding their breaths. Tasha, suddenly turning toward the front door, shocked all of them as they watched in silent disbelief as she unfurled her tail from the center of her back to stand straight out at a ninety degree angle, a reaction usually reserved for aggressive behavior, a forerunner to the baring of teeth, ready to fight, or as a bird dog would do in pointing to a hidden pheasant. Her tail and head a frozen compass needle, directing but not intimidating.

Amazed, this the first sign restored hope that she would succeed, defeating their creeping pessimism, recovering the lofty expectations for this exceptional dog, George, his confidence restored, announced, "I'm taking her outside. All of you follow."

Tasha, tethered from running free, the air heavy with humidity, the sidewalk puddled with falling rain,normally an effect on olfactory senses, her tail once again curled over her back, with other senses in play quickly covered the distance to where the testing car was parked. Arriving with no alert given, leaped happily up against the cars window, startling a disguised Rose Staves, her mouth wide open in amazement, shouting disbelievingly "Tasha." her thoughts of an impossible task for Tasha in flight.

What had they experienced he asked of his family, still awash in awe for what they had all witnessed, excitedly lauding Tasha's uncanny demonstration. Trying for perspective, George said to his family:

"The hide-and-seek portion of the game demonstrated senses: thought processes, developing task understanding," shaking his head in disbelief, "pale in comparison to her climatic finding of Mommy. Her keen senses of sight, hearing, and smell, proved practically useless in overcoming what were impossible conditions in finding her. While she called upon these senses for the hunt, they ultimately proved limited.

"We all saw how troubled she became until she called upon a higher order, her special gift. What is left I ask you?" Answering his own question, "it had to have been mind-to-mind contact," pausing in reflection. "I must confess to not ruling out that possibility when I planned this challenge,"

"To open that potential network, I instructed Mom to clear her mind of everything and think only of Tasha while she waited to be found. Creating opportunity to find her empowered with what I suspected was her suspected gift when her natural extraordinary senses were not enough; finding Mom through the energies of her thought waves, Tasha hopefully in possession of extrasensory perception powers of sending and receiving… mind-to-mind telepathy at work. In this case the sender prearranged," he concluded, exalting in the presumption.

"I still can't believe it. I did concentrate on her while I waited just as you suggested. If she could read my mind from where I was, could your thoughts have provided a tip-off just as well?" Rose said.

"I hadn't thought of that," George pondered. "that certainly was a possibility… Reading our minds, our thoughts, it's energies, but only that you were outside the house. It had to be your telepathic signals that vectored her. Remember you did not reveal what direction you would take." The thought elevating further his awe and amazement.

"No ordinary dog could have done what she did. Finding me under those circumstances. She is something special," Rose said, her tone confidently a matter of fact.

"Do you think she knows magic?" granddaughter Samantha asked, her eyes wide in wonderment as she listened. Her sister Dianna equally in awe, nodding in agreement.

"No my dear angels it's no trick," George Staves said smiling adoringly at their enrapture. Turning to the adults he offered his explanation, "It's true magic not deception. She demonstrated she's capable of powers that she can call upon when she needs to. A power that is God-given that we don't fully understand. Shamans and Animist according to believers understand. It has been written through the ages that it was possible for humans to accomplish mystical communications with animals. St. Francis in his writings and beliefs suggested as much." He paused his mind journeying afar, pondering the moment, confounding his audience he presented other possibilities that would only add to her mystique. "Tasha could have called upon senses not yet identified by science: impulses that travel unfathomed frequencies, bouncing back as comparable sonar echoes locating and producing identifying imagery in her mind's screen… A possible answer," he offered… "Another challenge to science." George pleased at the prospect added another consideration, "Mom as instructed upon reaching her secret site, her thoughts energies picturing her position, joining other's aloft for Tasha to cull from. Captured returned by Tasha's powers to the originator, emitting microwaves from her surrounding aura directing her discovery. Another possibility – triangulation: Tasha's ability to measure distances between two points, establishing zeroing in latitudinal and longitudinal coordinates. Putting those phenomenon's in play, as it was obvious after her initial frustration she unleashed those powers, relentless in finding the scenario that would work."

"But what does that all mean Grandpa," a bewildered Dianna asked.

Smiling at his grand daughters innocence "It means that Tasha is gifted, and we shouldn't be surprised by what she does," George Staves answered, then adding proudly "Grandma was discovered by the mysteries of Tasha's abilities."

Looking back, the time traveling George Staves, remained as convinced as he was then.

Their would be no reason at this moment to journey further in his transporter, a second incident demonstrating Tasha's special abilities immediately presented itself in his unscrambling kaleidoscope. Paradoxically a countervailing duality: serving to further distance Tasha from the savagery of her ancestors, while in fact using the special abilities of her ancestral heritage.

Husky owners somehow gravitate to each other. The attraction is an almost cult-like admiration for the significance of the breed and the mystery surrounding its historical beginning. Initiated when in joining a local Internet Web Site of Husky owners dedicated to the breed and their rescue.Through the vehicle of chat rooms he had made contact with other owners in his area. Leading to informally getting together, forums for anecdotal storytelling of their most recent experiences with their pets that left them impressed; the event worthy of sharing, all unhesitatingly with prejudice proudly agreeing the Husky breed the most beautiful dog ever created. While some, in spite of joined acclaim for their attractiveness and conformation, high lighted the negative traits of the breed. Frustrating comments such as "difficult to train"... "not responsive"... "blows their coat"... "easily bored" were always part of the meeting exchanges or phone calls, a transparent attempt at excuses.

In truth, they were envious, discounting as a fortuitous luck of the draw by the others victorious in meeting the challenges of the breed's nuances. Wallowing in cursed fate, defeated without corrective effort by the breed's unfavorable trademarks would, with some eventually, lead to ownership abandonment. Their defeatist commentary was, unfortunately, indicative of their inability to communicate and not recognize the importance of replicating the den mentality, its organization and enforcement. After being summarily uprooted, those absences turned into barriers preventing an absolutely necessary accommodation for this breed with the human social order they were placed in. Tasha assimilated as a member of his family held them in envious awe. Almost in every case, those wishful were first time owners of Huskies.

When the new comers were asked the reason for their selection for the

Husky breed, they invariably answered they were enamored with their celebrity and good looks, faulted as serving an ego that needed to share the inevitable attention given them. Not having done their homework, it was easy for George to understand their disappointment and discouragement. Hearing claims that Huskies were impossible and undisciplined, blinded them from recognizing the importance of training. Lost to their failure was the interdependency, the lifeblood of man/dog relationships. Impatient with their apparent laxity, feeling an obligation, he nonetheless advised them to keep trying and consider the assistance of expert training sessions. In support, they were told that in those moments when the dogs were under leash restrain, presented the best opportunity for conducting training sessions as long as they made it interesting. They were reminded that under no circumstances when outside the home should they ever give up leash control as they would surely loose their Husky to the adventures of a runaway preferring freedom, relegating as unimportant their new world, preferring to satisfy instincts to roam at will, abandoning domesticity and its benefits, favoring the intrigue of stirred-up independence, returning only when exhausted of the adventure and hungry. With allegiances not formed, they were likely to repeat their voyaging at the next opportunity. Running away would be an absolute certainty, so strong would be the urge. Particularly at a capricious young age, they would roam without hesitation as did their ancestors, so strong was the wanderlust.

He didn't realize how prophetic his comments were until he received a phone call from Jim Kennedy, a dedicated responsible owner of a Husky and a member of the it's tale telling admiration and rescue group. His deeply troubled voice lamenting that his Bridey, who, with a history of escaping, had once more found an opportunity to run away, defeating not only leash restraints, but the restraints of what should have been a deterring electrical shock delivered by an underground fence system. Bridey continually successful in avoiding the alerted authorities and neighborhood watch groups, virtually disappearing without a trace.

It was now one week since her disappearance he told Staves, and not a word; describing Bridey to the authorities as "my gray-and-white beauty" wearing a collar fitted with a transducer, license and ownership tags and the remainder of her broken chain." Recalling that early during Bridey's disappearance, with good reason remained confident in her returning, history showing recovery or return in every previous instance. Stating, as he had done in the past, he visited all the dog pounds within a five-mile radius… called or visited veterinarians, inquiring if they were aware of or treated any strange Husky within the last few days. His inquiries fruitless.

"I started to get real worried," he said. Resorting to getting additional coverage of his plight, ran notices in the newspapers offering a reward for her recovery. He received many calls, his voice now angry from the recollection, "from all kinds of people, including the vicious low life dog haters," investigating those calls that seemed probable, only to find continued disappointment.

"Desperate, I increased my coverage to a ten-mile radius. The police remaining very cooperative," giving assurances their patrols were alerted and on the lookout for Bridey. I even called the local radio stations expanded the search even further, paying a fee to cover a lost dog announcement during the news broadcasts."

Kennedy, his voice cracking with emotion said, "After one full week of relentless, fruitless searching, as painful as it was I had to face the prospect that my Bridey, had either been killed or kidnapped. I wanted her to be alive even if it meant being with robbers. After cursing the thief, I prayed, 'Dear Lord, please let it be someone who loves the breed, and not a despicable supplier of animals to testing labs performing inhumane experiments.'"

His voice hardly audible, a sad whisper, continued, "Before I admit Bridey as history, I had to satisfy myself I had exhausted all possibilities… the reason for my call, I would like to mobilize a search party… leaving within the hour," he paused perceptively dreading the fatalistic implication of his words. Staves sensing his incipient resignation, the fight going out of his voice, the signature that Kennedy had conceded that it would take a miracle to find Bridey alive; all he could ever hope for was to bring back her remains for closure and burial, a final resting place among those that she followed, all beloved predecessors.

Kennedy told George he had enlisted other Husky owners: Jack Mayo and Ben Shupc, to join in searching a bordering township creek bed that was within his search range, ready and awaiting his call.

"The creek bed, running north for miles, has an entrance close to my house," Jim Kennedy related, "that we could access from public property. I originally ignored it as Bridey's previous runaway patterns suggested it not be included. But now with hope diminishing, my re-examination suggests it is highly suspect as a possible route taken by Bridey. She'd be easily ignored or invisible as she accessed the creek bed having kept within the tree-lined neighboring backyards, unrestrained by fences.

"Bridey could have been lured there by a stray cat or other small animal that inhabited its difficult terrain," he conjectured, "to become a victim, possibly of nature or accident for her adventure. It would be better than not knowing," he said his voice tremulous.

George said he would be glad to help, offering to bring Tasha along, reminding Jim of Tasha's finding ability successes under difficult conditions,that he had shared. "It will improve our chances," he counseled.

Kennedy, understanding it was not a boast, was momentarily silent, responding, "I hadn't thought of that. By all means bring Tasha."

On the phone unseen, Jim Kennedy was going through a transformation, his countenance showing signs of strain at his experience, a recent gray facial color framing his darkly circled eyes; his nights had been sleepless. Facial muscles twitched nervously in objection.

Kennedy saying, "If we find her, while I wish differently, more than likely she will be dead." Stunning himself at the fatalistic meaning of his words, his surrender created the feeling of guilt, at war with himself, denouncing his blurted out concession as seeking pity for the desperation closing in on him.

In retaliation for his resignation, hope reasserted itself, quickly adding factually, "Although I have read that dogs are very resolute, staying alive for weeks under extreme conditions. In that recent earthquake in Turkey, rescuers found the master dead, but miraculously the faithful dog was alive, guarding his master's remains, surviving on scurrying rats and water from broken pipes seeping through the ruins."

His was only a momentary visit to optimism, a quickly fading respite. He must be realistic, anguishing Bridey not being found after all this time, hearing nothing held little promise. He set aside his wishes, forcing an unavoidable confrontation with reality, realizing an intervention was his only chance.

His throat tightening, gulping his speech, he added, "If we find her dead after all this time, badly decomposed and ravaged, we'll bury her where we find her. I must put her underground and bring closure," he said, his voice cracking. "I'm having nightmares of rats and crows eating away at her lifeless body. I see torturing images of sockets without eyes, insects moving swiftly along her once beautiful coat, swarms of flies buzzing, searching for flesh openings to deposit their eggs, birthing maggots with their voracious appetites. When I awaken, my pajamas are disheveled and wet from perspiration. Reflectively, I reach out searching in the hope of finding Bridey," his voice unsteady, mournful.

Sympathetic over Kennedy's agony, physically unable to reach out and touch him, a gesture that would possibly soothe Kennedy's phone voiced anguish, Staves, offered escape from his torment, "You did your best, Jim. It's in the hands of God." In response, Jim Kennedy's end of the phone line went silent, allowing Staves the opportunity to seize the moment to take charge of what had to be said, "I'll call the others. Give us a half hour. We'll leave our cars in the driveway. Don't forget to bring Bridey's sleeping blanket."

Reminded of the urgency, Kennedy, back on track said, "I'll be waiting. I won't forget the blanket." Dejectedly he added, "I'll also bring a shovel, a plastic sheet and rope, everything we need," his speech hardly audible.

George and Tasha arrived at the Kennedy's house, husky owner Jack Mayo, a burly standout ex-college football player now a Doctor of Oncology,and a Urban Spelunker on weekends and Ben Shupe, a bespectacled, slightly-built partner in an accounting firm and a skiing enthusiast developing skills, were already there. Their personalities light years apart. Acknowledging one another, welcoming Tasha in the search, anxious for experiencing firsthand her extraordinary senses.

They would gain access to the creek through a long ignored hole in the bordering chain link wire fence. Carved out by mischievous bored neighborhood kids, creating a virtual open invitation for anyone wishing to enter.

Forcefully angled contemptuously downward, almost pulled from its moorings going almost unnoticed was the battered, barely readable warning sign of "No dumping allowed heavy fine penalty warnings for violators," they would soon find out, was not ever a deterrent as it had been largely ignored.

Not mindful of Jim Kennedy's and Jack Mayo's caution for the slope's slippery condition, Ben Shupe, properly shoed, exaggerating his trail skills, attempted to descend the twenty five feet of thirty degreed slope without the belaying rope Jack Mayo rope had provided. Quickly proving no match to the challenge, falling to his backside within the first few steps of his descent, continuing his unintended slide downward, stopping within feet of the creek itself, stunned and embarrassed, brushed himself clean. His fall brought muffled comic relief to an otherwise somber moment. Jim Kennedy, and Jack Mayo using the rope as intended wrapped around a tree for support successfully negotiated the difficult terrain without incident. All three looked up from the bottom of the slope in wonderment at Tasha and George Staves. Tasha, having watched the descent of the others, after her Alpha tied the ends of the rope together to create a pulley around the support tree, with his urging fixed one leg of the pulley within her mouth. The mechanical assist her tether to be manipulated by an awaiting Jim Kennedy. With one line of the rope held between her vise-like jaws, using her legs to rappel, she descended the slope backwards as Kennedy below, holding both ends of the pulley taut helped move Tasha along as if she were attached to a tenement clothesline. Her trip complete, she was claimed by the hands of astonished Shupe and Mayo.

"Outstanding. What a smart dog," Ben Shupe and Jack Mayo, eyes widened in amazement, were quick to proclaim, still doubtful of what they had seen.

"Unbelievable " Kennedy said, traces of a smile briefly showing on a sadly set face. "She sure is a winner," he added reminiscing his happier days.

"Amen, amen," supported Shupe and Mayo as Staves completed his descent, leaving the makeshift pulley around the tree for their return and smiling appreciatively of their compliments of Tasha resourcefulness.

"Look at this place," Shupe commented as he scanned his surroundings, shocked at the man made dumping grounds. The signs of stealth visits were everywhere. Among the bushes and the undergrowth rested treadless tires,serving as their own cemetery headstone marking this junkyard landscape.

"Just look at all this junk, wanton disregard" Shupe repeated his disgusted assessment as he swept his hand across the landscape at the evidence of the self-indulgent whose mission to surreptitious escape or entertain for deceptive purposes, leaving empty beer cans, crushed to achieve greater flight, considerably outnumbering the same purposed broken whiskey bottles barely visible among the dumped fermenting grass cuttings. His anger rising at the despoiling.

"Commerce also had a role in the devastation," Jack Mayo said as he and the others looked at the discarded tree trunks cut and sized for convenience in handling, torn from the ground by land developer's bulldozers. The best were taken as fireplace wood while the rejected or surplus lay rotting where they were secretly dumped, home to hornets and inedible mushrooms.

With no need to comment, adding to the scene was the inevitability of nature contributed to the corruption: uprooted trees in slow death after being ripped violently from the ground by passing thunderstorms. Leaves from previous seasons, blackened as if diseased, lay rotting on the banks and surrounding area, creating a forest floor that was slippery and slowing passage; forming a disgraceful eyesore, hopefully hidden, continuing the appreciating values of the affluent neighborhoods.

Tasha culled Bridey's scent from her sleeping blanket knew her purpose, leading George and the others from her tether with determination. Commanded to be of single mindedness in finding Bridey, pausing occasionally to purge the rotting smells of contaminated vegetation from her nostrils by what appeared to be a deliberate act of sneezing, not as a response to an irritant but to prevent interference with her captured essence of Bridey.

While they were a search party of five, they all knew that until Bridey became visible, this being Tasha's show they followed her lead.

The scent of vegetative death was everywhere as they continued in tandem to follow Tasha, remindful to both of the George Staves identities of the similarities to the wolf hunt that once plagued memories.

The flooding of the creek bed earlier in the week left its purged residue. Small fish long dead at the bottom of the creek were now part of the putrescence that they stepped amongst. Dead by poisons deposited upstream by uncaring environmentally insensitive members of industry,on the verge of being cited. The fish were separated from their watery entombment by the turbulent rising waters of the creek which reached heights exceeding the creek banks which in the aftermath, when the waters finally receded, abandoned where the rising waters had deposited them, the motionless fish would continue their matter deterioration unless eaten by unsuspecting hungry animals whose indiscriminate satiation would bring the pain of poisoned intestines, the corruption finally expelled during a bloody painful bowel movement, the coming of death welcomed as merciful relief. Skeletal remains of cats, small and large dogs and what remained of large blackbirds almost laid bare of feathers occasioned both sides of the creek bed, the executed fish remains laying besides them.

"A killing field Ben Shupe said gloomily.Is this where we'll find Bridey?

All watched Tasha for signs of slowing down, the end of Bridey's adventure,she amongst the carcasses of the more recent to succumb.

"Not here George Staves assured Tasha only sniffing in the direction of the remains continuing the pace of the search.

Relieved, all imagining animals more fortuitous chokingly surviving by vomiting the poisons of decay rejected before digestion took place. Would a hungered Bridey be among them, not part of the collection of decay purposed for future vegetation in natures cycle?

The ground beneath their feet, softened by the recent storm, gave way easily under their weight. Unavoidable puddles slowed their pace as they grimly and cautiously walked through them, each mindful of their earlier days at another time, another place. The yielding mud determinedly grabbed hold of their shoes to be held until extracted with the exertion of a force greater than that which held them. In their departure, a moist reluctant sucking farewell sounded. Tasha leading, her wading legs and underbelly wet and dripping, minimizing the backwash of splashed water to those that followed. She too was slowed by the grasping mud underfoot.

When they were an hour into the search, the pace slowed even more as the wet difficult terrain took its toll. The puddles that still occasioned their path soaking through their hiking boots, not quite as waterproof as expected. Their blue jeans below the knees also soaked through, clinging to their legs as they proceeded through the rain-laden underbrush, the splashing waters of the puddles. Saturated they experienced shivers.

They moved in tandem, arms raised and positioned as a shield attempting to ward off yielding bushes and branches springing back to their original position, not always successful as all of them had scratches somewhere on their faces, encouraging flies and mosquitoes who were no longer dissuaded by insect repellent. Yet no one complained so dedicated were they to complete their mission. Their voices grew hoarse from shouting Bridey's name but they still continued to follow Tasha's sniffing lead. The clang of Jim Kennedy's shovel, used as a staff, would find an occasional rock beneath the ground surfaces and in concert with their searching shouts, resonated sounds of question to the animals that inhabited the land… noises of intruders.

After considerable passage, Tasha's nose, scanning in all directions at the start, her path meandering with uncertainty, became steady and lineal, convincing Staves that she had picked up the scent as they continued to trek north alongside a deepening and widening creek bed. He did not reveal his conclusions to the others until he, as expected, was proven right by Bridey's sighting.

The water moved more rapidly at this section of the creek suggesting other feeds, rather than just rain runoff. Its level receded, exposing previously submerged rocks serving as baffles to the fast moving waters, creating turbulence and scenic miniature waterfalls, under the circumstances a display they reacted to minimally.

The vegetation within sight of the creek bed was heavy with wild growth, regaling in the innocence of the undisciplined, forming a quilt patterned beauty. The wildflowers such as violets, lamium and lily-of-the-valley comingled with the ground cover or as isolated patches cultivated by the free-to-create wilds of nature.

Surviving trees from a once heavily populated asembly, suggested a frivolous force of nature sporadically paring back their light filtering canopy, those laid waste to disease and lightening succumbing lay where they fell. Sacrificed by nature to allow the sun its role in the cycle of regeneration, bees and wasps now inhabited their rotting carcasses, cellulose fibers dieing since their fall from grace.

Although passage became more difficult, it was ruggedly beautiful as they distanced themselves from commercialization. Following Tasha along the serpentine creek presenting changing conditions as they moved quickly in and out of the tree's canopy, finding shadows of coolness, then warming light. The quickly changing scenarios bringing a tolerance to the smells of natural decay, freed to nurture beauty among the designated areas of rebirth. Change also taking place within the flowing water, which at times disappeared as an underground stream and then reappearing in the creek bed, no longer carring the odor of foulness, in all probability purged by filtering soil and porous underground rocks.

Trees, majestic in their display of the splendor of their seasonal greenery, leaves abounding its branches peering down on their fallen kin lying at the base of the parenting tree, lives spent, glistening with the recent rain reflecting their alive successors; their life cycle complete, shed of what they had been a part of.

Edible colorful berries, the sustenance of birds and the vehicle for nature's reseeding, were offered without the protection of thorns. Flowering trees were part of the forestry collage, breaking the dominance of the color green, as did in full view hanging just beyond reach, mistletoe, romanticized as a symbolic rewarding interlude for those of mind to stand beneath it… a stimulus… a prelude aphrodisiac.

Frightened animal tracks scarred the sodden soil in fear of their approach, scurrying to locate a vantage point, watching unseen, satisfying their inquisitiveness, as the intruders trod through their domain.

The comparison of this part of the creek bed became inevitable, the difference decidedly noteworthy, quietly lauded by all as a more natural untouched setting than the passed-through corruptions at the beginning of their search. Those recent revulsions were welcomingly dismissed by the pastoral setting they were viewing, knowing the pervasive foulness of the corrupted land awaited their return.

Tasha seemed more resolute, given a replenishing whiff of Bridey's blanket, responding she raised her nose high into the afternoon air to locate the scent ahead of their immediate area. On a path of dead reckoning, George thought to himself.

The giant culvert passing directly under the highway, their agreed upon termination point, appeared in the distance. Without saying as much, the signature of disappointing failure on the minds of some, however relieved the search was about to end. They had traveled approximately three miles. The pace had slowed considerably, the exhausting wet conditions of the terrain taking its toll.

Without warning a ten-point buck crashed noisily from the bushes, stopping them in their tracks. The buck in his season of sexual arousal also stopped to consider if these intruders were threatening. His mood highly charged, his flared nostrils exhausted snorts of challenge as his muscles quivered nervously. Under normal conditions when not pursuing mating, the buck was non-confrontational. However, this time he dropped his head menacingly, about to mount a damaging charge.

"Oh, oh, we're in trouble," an alarmed Ben Shupe cautioned. "He's about to charge."

Jack Mayo's muscular bulk stiffened as he searched and found a broken branch of sufficient heft, preparing to defend himself from this overwrought antlered threat. Jim Kennedy's defense was the shovel which he now raised in readiness. All were shouting at the top of their lungs in the hopes of driving off the buck.

Tasha was initially curious at her first sighting of a deer until aroused by its apparent hostility. Sensing imminent danger, she snarled viciously, showing her sizable canine fangs. Her genetic code at work aggressively raised the hairs on the back of her neck in readiness to defend without quarter. Her aroused strength gave George all he could handle as she strained at the leash to attack the attacker. The rutting buck's fear of wolves and their direct descendents handed down over the centuries gave it pause. Thinking better of it, the buck trotted away. In an act of confidence in its escape skills, stopped to drink the creek's water; indicating the creek's underground passage through sandy soils effectively filtered it of contaminants making it potable for animals. Its thirst quenched, it leaped off, graceful in flight as a ballet dancer, to continue its search. A sigh of relief expelling from their mouths, all thankful for Tasha's presence. Tasha's growls lessened as she watched the deer disappear into the woods on the other side of the creek bed.

"That was close," a calmed Ben Shupe said. "Thank God that Tasha was with us. The buck became suddenly mindful that she was in for a fight."

"That's for certain," a wondrous Jack Mayo offered. "I for one being a husky owner never would have expected such aggressiveness from Tasha."

"It's what I've been telling you guys. If you did your homework in learning more about your dogs, you wouldn't consider them as unresponsive," George Staves said, proudly lecturing as Jim Kennedy listened silently.

Their attention back in full focus, they resumed their search. They were within one hundred yards of the culvert.

"She's not here," Jim Kennedy said, then adding forlornly, "I'll never know what happened to her. For awhile I thought that Tasha had picked up the scent earlier and it would only be a matter of time till we would find her. It must have been that buck she scented."

No one spoke, nodding regrettably, yet relieved that they weren't part of a sad ending. Except George Staves, while sympathetic, his confidence in Tasha was unshakable, silently disagreed with Kennedy's assessment.

Suddenly Tasha stopped in her tracks, threw her head back and howled mournfully. Its pitch unsteady, cracking and wavering, expressed a roller coaster of grief. Her monotone, low and reverent, was likened to a chant at a funeral mass symbolic of parishioners intoning. One could easily have imagined the scent of burning incense at a funeral site so compelling was Tasha's emotional release.

Staves went to her immediately. "What is it, Tasha girl?" he asked sympathetically, the others frozen in apprehension, awaiting the confirmation of Bridey's discovery.

Again Tasha howled, again reminiscent of a bereaved expression for the deceased, a prayerful mourning loss and at the same time an entreaty for resurrection elsewhere.

But where is Bridey Staves asked himself, slowly studying the terrain before them without success. The others, doing the same, quickly deciphered Tasha's actions, putting aside their conclusions of doubt.

"I don't see her, George," Jim said, voicing bewildered frustration. "Tasha must have picked up another scent. It must have been that buck," he insisted.

The air was brisk with clouds moving quickly across the sky, intermittently blocking the sun's path of warmth and lighting of the serpentine creek, frustrating their sighting with teasing expectations.

Staves was cautiously expectant yet apprehensive. The others were exasperated with the absence of her sighting, verged on returning to being doubtful. Led by Staves' insistence, they again searched the landscape ahead of them. Still darkened with deep shadows, a large cloud persisting. Frustrated, they waited for it to be moved by the winds aloft, the sun illuminating another scenario.

They all moved cautiously forward, eyes fixed, Tasha still leading but closer to Staves' side, whimpering having replaced her howling.

Staves looked down at what appeared to be tears welling up in Tasha's eyes, her message unmistakable.

"But where?" Staves asked again just as the sun's rays were given passage by the morning clouds movement.

A flash appeared, disappearing just as quickly, surely missed if you weren't looking in the right direction. Zeroing in on the spot, Staves saw her before the others, pointing and gesturing at his sighting, shouting, "Over there. Follow me."

With Tasha whimpering, he leading the way, they approached the bloated motionless animal, learning as they got close enough for confirmation that it was Bridey, obviously dead.

She lay half in and half out of the creek's receding water, the current bringing waves to lap at her lifeless body, slightly animating her hydraulically. Her leash which she had broken bringing her joyful escape proved to be her death sentence as it was wedged forcefully between two large rocks, imprisoning her. She would be captive but safe as long as she could sit on the rocks above the water line and await rescue. In pity, their throats constricting in sorrow, they saw what remained of the nails on her front paws ground almost to non-existence, exposing cut and bloodied pads. Her captive rocks showing discernible scratch marks on its hard surfaces, giving witness to her frantic futile battle. Equally visible not washed away were her paws above her foot pads showing blood streaks of desperation staining at her imprisoning keeper. The pain wrought would be of no consequence, anesthetized by her determined and exhausting effort to escape. Her apprehensive wait for help had to seem interminable, victimized and befallen by an unintended paradox. Her life compromised by the failure of the same implement that provided the opportunity for escape turning against her, the very freedom it provided earlier recalled, she was a fatality among the creatures of the wild, living their emancipation, she joining them in her journey before returning. The very essence of her motivation expressed in these surroundings being visited, until the forces of another capture ended this and future escapades.

Were the animals that watched her desperation sympathetic? Did they try to comfort her while awaiting the growing inevitably? Had sympathy evolved from animals normally her prey, twitching nervously at the scene they were viewing; the hunter becoming the hunted by the forces of nature? Even if empathy did not exist among her prey animals, their presence meant she would not die alone. She was captive in the wild of her forebears with escape deemed impossible. Would she then call upon her genetics to relive the storied past of her ancestors and challenge death until the very end? Could she be so courageous?

She knew she couldn't be saved as the ozone smelled of the beginnings of a violent rainstorm, clouds moving rapidly to join energies, leading the developing trailing thunder and lightning. Once distant rumbling she knew would soon begin to crash around her. This secluded place discouraging visits by humans; a fulfilling treasure trove of nature would no longer be peaceful. A powerful gust of wind carrying whipped-up dirt stung Bridey, a prelude as a relentless torrent of rain, dense and driven enough to be a wave of water, began to fill the creek. She exerted great force,absorbing great pain against her captive chain,the rocks that restrained her, they remaining immutable.

Now she was truly alone as the inhabiting animals sought shelter from the wet onslaught. Bridey could hear the water rushing toward her driven by severe winds moving north, forcefully increasing the creek current, creating a powerful deluge, rushing, surging, sweeping away anything in its path, rapidly overwhelming the creek and its banks. Bridey, under restraint, panicking could only attempt to swim as the sheer volume of water engulfed her and her precarious perch. It's burdening force quickly wearied her aching body as a frantic Bridey succumbed to drowning.

Her last act to save herself from the rising water, they were to learn, was to bite down on her imprisoning chain, unleashing a force that broke off her teeth at the gum line on both sides of her mouth. Her muzzle still stained with the blood of that last determined effort.

The creek's killing waters overflowing the banks would eventually pass through the culvert, entering a planned basin to catch its turbulent overflow. The rain continued to fall, a torrential downpour, its sheer volume overmatching the speed of the creek's current to the catch basin, keeping the bed's water level well beyond its limits.

A mournful Tasha, her leash tied to a tree, watched as Kennedy and Staves unsuccessfully attempted to move one of the rocks that held Bridey's chain. It took all four of them, knee deep in the creek water to finally move the rock to free the chain. They could have, as Shupe suggested, unfasten the collar to free her. The suggestion was quickly rejected by a somber Jim Kennedy saying, "I want all of her free. That leash and her collar were part of her life and now in death it belongs with her."

Staves could well imagine the self-inflicting torture Kennedy was going through as he heard him condemn himself.

"If only I had looked for her here that first day before the storm, I would have saved her," he lamented, his eyes brimming with tears, disbelieving the remains before him, quieted in death the once playful and inquisitive Bridey. A companion always there for him. A partner who shared this period in his life.

After a few minutes of quiet reflection, Kennedy returned to the inescapability of the situation: "She's bloated and stiff from rigor mortis but she is intact. The scavengers hadn't gotten to her for which I'm grateful. With the water continuing to recede, another day with her body fully exposed, it would have been different."

He then reached down and picked her up, bringing her head to his mouth and shamelessly and quietly kissed her forehead as he had undoubtedly done many times through the years. With Bridey in his arms, he climbed out of the creek bed, laying her gently on her own scented blanket, pausing to clasp his hands together, lips quivering, offering a private prayer. They all joined in silence. When finished, Kennedy wrapped her in the blanket, tied it down with rope leaving a loop at both ends to create a sling into which he ran his long handled shovel for one man on each side to lift and carry.

Emotionally overcome, Kennedy choked back sobs, said, "I'm going to have her cremated. I've changed my mind about burying her here where she died. The scavengers would surely get to her. I'll bury her ashes in my backyard along with her four predecessors."

They all empathized with Jim battling his emotions, taking turns to demonstrate sympathy with an understanding grasp of his shoulder. Solicitous of his agony, telling him he did his very best under the circumstances; to be at rest as he has found her, and was bringing her home where she belonged.

They all were involved in carrying Bridey, stopping periodically to change hands. Her weight and bulk combined with the difficult terrain was exhausting in spite of the mechanical assist provided by the sling, forcing the dirge to take welcomed rest periods to recover.

Jim and George had the last leg of the return journey, their procession quiet as smells of deterioration filled their nostrils, masking the faint odor of Bridey's decomposition, retarded somewhat by the refrigeration effect the cold waters of her grave imparted.

Wearied and saddened by the success in finding Bridey, all but Jim Kennedy climbed back up the slope using the clothesline configured rope to their starting point.He to follow after fixing the remains of Bridey to the pulley for ascending

Tasha, in reverse of her descent, with one strand of the rope firmly between her teeth,again tethered was pulled up the embankment, clawing the bank to give her climb upward an assist to an awaiting George Staves. This time because of the somberness of the moment, respectful, silently shaking disbelieving heads greeted her accomplishment.

Tasha hadn't relieved herself the entire trip. It was her way of showing respect for Bridey's markings during her fateful journey. The more Staves thought about it the more he became convinced that her willed restraint was symbolic of her respect for the dead and to extend the presence of Bridey's scent beyond death until nullified by nature's elements or another animal staking out his territorial claim. Once outside the chain link fence of the creek bed, the scents of others abounded, Tasha responding by not squatting in the typical female position but to raise her hind leg emulating the males of her species, to purposefully raise her spotting beyond the height of her forerunners. The notice of an Alpha passing through.

Jim Kennedy, upon reaching his driveway, Bridey's remains over his shoulder, said, "thank you... George... Ben... Jack, for your help, I really appreciate it," turning to face Tasha, a forlorn look of sadness in his eyes, he said, "We would never have found Bridey without her. She knew of Bridey's fate when she started howling, didn't she?" he asked of George who nodded a silent yes. They all watched sympathetically as he tenderly reached down to stroke Tasha's willing head, his hand and heart reminiscing in the luxury of her coat's texture.

As if she understood his words, Tasha, her tail hanging symbolically limp, her eyes fixed on the blanket bearing Bridey's remains slumped over Jim's shoulder.

"Yes, she knew," Staves acknowledged. "She also knew well before we found her that Bridey had taken this route. Initially it was Bridey's alive scent of markings that she traced until sadly the scent of death predominated."

"She truly is a remarkable dog, one who anyone would be proud to own," Jim Kennedy said.

"I know what I've got," George acknowledged. "She truly is unbelievable, almost human-like in many respects and magical in other ways, authoring new chapters of her mystique when called upon."

The sky which earlier held a capricious brightening sun turned disconsolately gray, as if to acknowledge the occasion as sad, it's restrained tears of rain, moments away as they left Jim Kennedy to his somber task. Driving their cars away, going their separate ways, promising to stay in touch. All of them, while sharing in the loss of Bridey, also experienced a gain beyond their expectations.

~

The visitor of history, George Staves backtracked, while saddened at the memories of the day Tasha found Bridey, the kaleidoscope presentation as he had hoped diminished his blemishing of Tasha with her ancestors predatory predisposition, her more compassionate side dominating. Revitalized he readied himself for the picture components of his next stop. His internal kaleidoscope sourcing and fitting the pieces together.

eight

When injured or hurt, most animals, particularly feral, react self-protectively. Out of fear, retreating to be alone to bear their great hurt, reacting instinctively to distance themselves from the pain... only to find the pain never left its side, its shadow cast wherever the poor animal cowered... Physically at a disadvantage, fear of what was in store for them, feeling cornered in the open expanse of the woods, pain and vulnerability driving it's growling ferociously baring teeth, suspecting of all as the origin of the pain they are experiencing. Conversely, in domesticated animals the ultimate expression of confidence in humans is to seek out those trusted to provide ministrations from pain in times of needed relief.

The injured countenance pleading for help, symptomatic: dilated pupils, the fast beating of their hearts, the frightened panting, and constant movement to find a restful position. Seeking only their anointed to deliver them from this painful experience with their words and action, magically soothing... willing to endure a peaking of the pain during the very ministrations. An outgrowth of having learned to interact with humans; dogs, intellectually able, develop communicative skills, placing their vulnerability in the hands of others, sensing deliverance.

The Alpha ranking, manifesting social order within the pack, is bestowed only after a test of wills; all others become followers, expecting provided protection. The rare exception in moments of pain when they entrust the healer whether an Alpha or not.

This extraordinary trust to minister or heal pain with animals, usually the result of cohabitation of animals within the human pack. An expression beyond the mutual foundation of love and tenderness. A special affinity,bringing forth a silent declaration of connecting,something magical- finding during an occurrence that rises beyond the reach of all other relationships no matter how passionate. Issuing warnings, "those not having the gift need not apply." The deliverer having an alarm system proven credible as beyond a command for discipline, in time given special significance by responding to without curiosity or weighting. The recipient avoiding a later recognized threat of injury before the fact, their savior granted a possesser of power to foretell. Their benefactors aura special, bestowing they their healer subsequent to taking root in a complimenting extraordinary occurrence.The elevation conveyed by a means of communication exclusive to the two of them, *foundation in past indebtedness, credentialed only to the specific human interceding in her behalf, turning from all others as vacant of the power to make well.*

His daughter Phyllis, involved in an accidental biting incident with Tasha held those credentials. Flowering since childhood naturally and freely expressing love and affection for all manner of animals, unconsciously a disciple of St. Francis of Assisi, a source of relief, be it physical or spiritual.

Tasha, in recognition, singled out Phyllis as her guardian and now healer, being blessed by a attentive disposition, having demonstrated this duality; to be carried forward time and time again during their lifetime together. Staves confirmed this when he revisited the origin of Tasha's trust of Phyllis.:

"It had to be then, that time… it gave birth to Phyllis' worthiness as Tasha's protector even when injured by Tasha, accepting the blame. Her devotion, almost spiritual, never wavering or faltering, a figurative martyr earned Tasha's endorsement."

That event, remembered clearly, Tasha inadvertently biting Phyllis when aroused from a deep sleep. Phyllis' nuzzling close to her eyes, perceived awaking from sleep as a threat. Hurting, her voice emotional, words of exoneration passionately delivered, brought Tasha this extraordinary devotion, he reasoned.

In an extraordinary bond she would present herself to Phyllis in her moments of pain. Phyllis' credited with healing powers, perhaps spiritual, perhaps ordained by a higher power-her anointed healer

Having made the connection, Staves was at a loss as to how Phyllis would minister to a pained Tasha with little more than petting and comforting words. The times he watched in amazement as Tasha hobbled after returning from a walk or backyard romp would approach Phyllis, extend her affected limb and watch attentively as Phyllis picked, with the aid of tweezers, bits of glass or stones wedged between her paw pads. Tasha whimpered but never in doubt that she would be delivered from her pain, sitting attentively, ears erect listening to Phyllis' comforting words. Most dogs, he realized, would have to be held down under those circumstances, some muzzled for assurance. But not Tasha, as long as Phyllis was doing the ministering. Staves himself never tried to doctor Tasha as Phyllis was always present when those situations occurred. Rose, Edward and Rosanne, in spite of deep affection from a devoted Tasha, were not encouraged. If persistent in intent to doctor, were turned away by a growling Tasha. She wanted and sought no one but Phyllis to treat her pain. And if the pain producing incident occurred when Phyllis was not home, Tasha would bear the obvious pain, awaiting Phyllis' return to be healed.

It was absolutely amazing the way they had connected, how comforted she was by Phyllis' almost mystical words, mesmerizing her, easing the task of treatment. He remembered the defining moment, an obvious telling experience.

It was a battle that never should have taken place. Two animals of different species knowing only enmity towards one another, provided specific strengths by nature both physically and mentally in defending themselves. One whose offensive prowess held few equals when cornered and defensively giving ground; the other intelligently cautious, at bay looking for a weakness to exploit, aggressive, ready to attack, waiting only opportunity. When confrontations took place, fortuitous interventions ended the standoff, one fleeing to avoid physical contact, the other restrained left to ponder if the opponent was as formidable as it appeared, nonetheless pleased that its marked territorial rights were purged of an intruder.

The neighborhood had recently become a hunting ground for a band of searching raccoons that left in their wake torn garbage bags, its contents spread asunder, bird feeders destroyed with the intended chirping in nearby trees denied a food source. Marauding Raccoons, being nocturnal it's most opportune and least dangerous time to hunt for food unseen, thus avoiding confrontation, leaving as calling cards extensive clean-up while most people were asleep.

They would avoid contact unless cornered or protecting their newborn kits- instinctively becoming vicious, chirping anxiously looking to escape while ready to rake anything that came within striking distance of their powerful talon-like claws, causing considerable damage to unwary challengers bloodied and defeated in their bravado. The raccoon's harmless,taken with appearance deceiving, ones approach guarded, the species reputed to have the highest incidence of rabies, dictating avoidance.

Reacting to the raccoon invasion, George took all the necessary and recommended steps to discourage their nocturnal foraging, apprehensive of Tasha's nightly aroused growling. The evidence of torn up lawns telling his treatment of his lawn was not deterring the raccoons from seeking nourishment. Still Tasha's life had to be lived. Always careful he would turn on the patio lights before releasing a tethered Tasha to the backyard. The sudden illumination was usually enough to drive the raccoons to the safety of the surrounding darkness. As an added precaution, he physically checked and reconnoitered the area while armed with a golf club to support his bravado, not as an offensive weapon but for defense if cornering a raccoon. With trepidation, he released a very aggressive Tasha to the backyard, hopeful the noise and the lights had driven off the reclusive and non-confrontational invaders, usually, but not this night.

A very anxious Tasha smarting to do her own inspection leaped into the night, exiting with such power and speed, to force open the collar ring, producing a gap from which the leash's link easily passed through, allowing

Tasha to begin her untethered search. Shocked he followed quickly, trailing Tasha whose nose was to the ground, sniffing and searching for distinguishing scents. So intent was she to screen for intruders that she blocked out his voice commands.

Suddenly she caught a foreign scent, charging directly at the line of bushes that framed the side of the house-evicting and cornering a rather large male raccoon of forty pounds. Menacingly standing upright on its hindquarters to just over two feet, appearing larger with its twelve inch tail in the typical aggressive position of a bear to fend off or attempt to discourage an attack by a growling Tasha. Not discouraged by the size of her opponent and menacing stance, Tasha showed her teeth, eyes fixed without blinking, snarling a challenge to fight. The raccoon, taken by surprise, had unfortunately positioned itself between two large bountiful hedges which seemed too high to scale its density providing no passage. It seemed trapped from escape, the preferred choice.

George chastising himself for not seeing the raccoon during his check of the property, shouted anxiously "heel" for Tasha's return. Tasha, her protective instincts dominating ignored his command, unafraid but cautious, choosing not to attack at this time but rather move from side to side of the hedges in a containing maneuver just beyond the reaches of the upright raccoon flailing away with its flesh-tearing claws. The raccoon vocalized mounting panic at his trapped predicament, escape being his only salvation as Tasha played a waiting game knowing time was on her side. George reached down and grabbed Tasha's collar in an attempt to pull her back far enough for the raccoon to escape. Responding she dug her claws into the grass becoming unmovable. Her adrenalin flowing freely transferring heightened strength to her muscles presenting a weight force seemingly three-fold above her formidable eighty pounds anchoring herself as a monolith. The raccoon chanced this moment of Staves' interference as an opportunity to escape, chosing to attempt to scale the hedges in a lightning fast movement, unfortunately failing, its weight beyond what the hedge could bear, without foundation he lost his offensive weaponry, unable to retreat the raccoon became hopelessly ensnarled, shackled within the branches, wildly chattering at its worsened position. Its mobility slowed dramatically, paws and formidable claws handcuffed uselessly in the hedges.

Tasha recognized the opportunity to attack. Snarling and spitting breaking loose from Staves's hold as he shouted in desperation, "No Tasha No" again he was ignored, as Tasha leaped upon the vulnerable and frantic raccoon, slamming shut her powerful jaws around the back of the neck of the screaming raccoon unable to defend itself as Tasha cleverly held the raccoon away from her, it's damaging claws too distanced rendered useless, the flailing slowing until the raccoon was choked to stillness. The din of their battle ending dramatically, the only sound the rustling of Tasha dragging her combatant off of the executioner hedge. With the lifeless body in her mouth calmly walked just beyond the Staves property line, unceremoniously dropping the motionless raccoon having defended her territory, standing victor above her vanquished intruding enemy. It was not a battle for sustenance as the victim was not a source for food but the satiating of instincts.

It was then that George learned that Tasha did not come out of this battle unscathed. The raccoon somehow in the throes of death had managed to rake Tasha's nose before death shorted all it's electrical impulses, slicing it open, a profusion of blood gushing at an alarming rate. This time she came when he called her, her body language subdued, her inherent aggressive unrepentant behavior in storage. With his handkerchief he cleared the oozing blood from her nose, temporarily revealing a ragged cut of approximately six inches long before the blood flow covered it again. She would need a veterinarian's doctoring.

At that moment, his wife Rose, awakened by the sounds of the feral combat, and her husband's shouting attempts to control Tasha, arrived, quickly assessing the aftermath, aghast as her husband pointed in the direction the dead raccoon, explaining what had happened.

"Oh my God," she pitied.

Tasha, shaking her head, dislodged blood everywhere. Turning her attention to Tasha, she anguished, "She's hurt."

"I know. I couldn't hold her. She was so determined. Forcefully separating her leash from her fatigued collar ring. I couldn't get her under control," he lamented. "She needs help. Call the twenty-four hour emergency veterinarian hot line, explain what happened and that we'll be there shortly," he commanded of Rose. "Then wake up Phyllis. Tell her to meet us at the vet. She would be a comfort to Tasha," he reasoned. No sooner had those words left his lips the impossible happened, the raccoon thought lifeless, choked to unconsciousness within Tasha's strong jaws had slowly risen to it's feet, George reacting immediately grabbed Tasha by the collar finding her subdued and complacent, not in the least interested as the raccoon unsteadily distanced himself from the Staves's property.

His emotions ranging: amazed that Tasha did not kill the raccoon which she could have easily done with her powerful jaws. Relieved as he would no longer doubt the genetic difference from her ancestor wolves as significant for domesticity of the breed. He realized that in those final moments of combat that she had the intelligence to serve his will and not the deeply buried instincts of the feral for the sheer pleasure of killing. He had preferred that realization coming to him without the drama of this experience. Anxiously he sat on the bottom of the patio steps trying to stem the flow of blood from an uncooperative Tasha. Rose recovering, literally ran back into the house. Staves heard her talking to someone on the phone.

"Yes, we'll be there in twenty minutes." She then rushed back upstairs to change clothes, returning in three minutes with bandages and Phyllis right behind her, who somehow had slept through the entire event but now comprehending fully what had happened, her eyes filled with tears.

"Hold Tasha while I change, and get the car" he instructed Phyllis. "She'll let you put pressure on the wound to slow the blood flow. Mom will help you," he said as they both nodded in agreement.

George had the car out of the garage within minutes, his clothes haphazardly selected, his facial expression one of guilt.

With Phyllis to follow in her car, Rose drove while George, seated in the back seat, ministered to Tasha who he held in his lap. Her muscles twitching nervously responding to their raised voices of concern and apprehension. They arrived at the veterinarian in ten minutes, traveling in excess of the posted speed limits. They were quickly ushered by one of the assistants into one of the examining rooms. Knowing the routine, George Staves strained to pick Tasha up onto the examining table. Tasha, also knowing the routine, resisted his attempts.

Doctor Marks soon entered the room as Staves held Tasha's mouth shut, muffling her growls. Commenting after examining the wound, "She'll need sutures both inside and outside, the wound is that deep. She'll need sedating. While you've told me her shots are up to date, I still plan on giving her boosters for extra protection."

At that moment Phyllis arrived to hear Dr. Marks' plan for treatment. Tasha's eyes brightened when she saw Phyllis, her wagging tail messaging approval. Her reaction did not go unnoticed by Dr. Marks.

"Let me get her ready before you do anything," Phyllis pleaded as she watched teary-eyed at the bleeding and apprehensive Tasha. "It will make things a lot easier."

George and Rose voiced agreement, confirming to Doctor Marks what he had already guessed… that a special relationship existed between the two of them. All their attention captured they would marvel at what they were about to witness.

"All right," Dr. Marks said patiently as a matter of courtesy.

Phyllis quickly sat up on the examining table.

Responding to the coagulant, Tasha's bleeding had subsided. As if on cue, she laid her head onto Phyllis' lap preparing herself for words of comfort, eyes fixed toward Phyllis' mouth so as not to miss the shaping of her words, co-joining with the sounds of her voice… a libretto of emotion and passion coaxing, then directing that Tasha's pain and apprehension surrender to her subconscious where real and substantive change can occur, where stress and anxiety can be reduced… the foundation for alleviating palpitation; pain and discomfort.

Phyllis' voice was a steady and relaxing monotone. The change in Tasha's demeanor could be seen immediately as she responded to Phyllis' message. Her tautness left her. Her eyelids moved rapidly as if dreaming, one more eye closure away from somnolence.

Under Phyllis' guidance, Tasha induced to deep relaxation, gained access to her subconscious, drawing upon her natural anesthesia – endorphins – to replace stress hormones that constrict and cause pain.

Under pain earlier, Tasha's focus could only be narrow and outward, preventing the subconscious to function, resulting in stress chemicals being produced at high levels causing mounting muscle tensions, the brain not well oxygenated. Phyllis sensing she had the gift of hypnosis, effectively brought to her willing subject a special kind of intoxicating sleep, resultant of sustained attention, effort and will, paramount in stress chemical reduction, leading the way to diminishing physical pain and body sensation… absolute keys that open the subconscious mind for all kinds of programming and reprogramming. Tasha's subconscious, responding to Phyllis's guidance, ordered her muscle groups to release stored tension coincident to diminishing pain experienced or anticipated. Her hypnosis was complete and enduring as long as Phyllis kept her in a dream-like state.

"She's ready for you now, Dr. Marks." Phyllis advised He responded with syringe in hand, ready to anesthetize Tasha. Phyllis stopped him by raising her hand, warding him off, giving him pause.

Incredulous, "You mean you want me to stitch her up without anesthesia?" he asked in astonishment.

"Yes," Phyllis responded confidently.

Dr. Marks skeptical looked toward Rose and George for intervention.

Overcome by what he had just witnessed, George Staves did not descent; stating a confirming, "Yes," becoming a willing participant to the unfolding magic. "She's right, Doctor Marks. Go ahead. If she comes out of her sleep, take other action."

Apprehensively uncertain, he repeated as a test of Phyllis' hypnotic efficacy and duration, an unnecessary second cleansing of the wound, fully expecting to awaken her suddenly. Instead it brought no reaction. Tasha remained distant and motionless, her head still in Phyllis' lap, her eyes mirroring, her very being, her psyche under command, her synapses short circuited incapable of sending any message while under attention, desensitized, fulfilling Phyllis's words of encouragement; remarkable the superiority of her subconscious. A still wary Doctor Marks cautiously shaved the surrounding area of the wound.

"Here goes," Doctor Marks said as he guardedly began the first of six internal sutures, Tasha remained in her trance-like state, reaching full relaxation as he gingerly completed the remaining ten outside stitches to close the wound.

Stepping back to assess his work while removing his latex gloves, he said, "I wouldn't have believed it was possible with animals. I know hypnosis is used and is recognized by the AMA. in performing certain procedures, but to hypnotize and not anesthetize a dog for surgery flies in the face of what some animal behavioral scientists say are 'intellectually limited in responding to mind manipulations by humans.'"

"She's a special kind of dog in many ways," Staves offered.

"She must be. This was a first for me. I'll have to write a paper on it," he said smilingly, his shock wearing off, "Another benefit of avoiding the use of anesthesia is the absence of post-operative lethargy. Her recovery from surgery will begin immediately after awakening. Her entire system will respond and function."

Tasha, under Phyllis' coaxing words, returned from her subconscious journey, immediately standing steadily, eyes alert showing no effects except for her shaven appearance, her stitches lined up like the lacing on a football.

Phyllis advising, "Tasha won't need an Elizabethan collar to keep her from scratching the healing wound. I'll see to it," she promised.

"The stitches will dissolve on their own," Dr. Marks commented. "She should see her own veterinarian. Tell him to call me when you arrange it," receiving a nod of confirmation from George.

Then it was over, leaving all to their thoughts. What had happened from beginning to end strained credulity, defying the best of vivid descriptions as you would have had to experience it to believe it, requiring an act of blind faith to conjure up belief by those being told. The sincere listener, in a captive atmosphere is politely attentive but emotionally distant, tailoring and downsizing what he hears incrementally. Inwardly negative, an agnostic effectively reducing the power of the event unless it subscribes to his measure of probability.

George recalled other instances that foretold the special bond between Phyllis and Tasha further making the case that Phyllis was Tasha's healer; she being the only one who Tasha would allow to trim her nails, the only one who could remove painful ticks from the inside of her ears, voluntarily presenting herself at the urging of Phyllis' words. He recalled Tasha as a puppy, with the special bond still evolving, developed a serious ear infection, one that leaked from odorous pustules that required a sedated scraping by the veterinarian to remove the infection. George remembered a mothering Phyllis insisting on staying in the recovery cage so Tasha, after two hours, would find a friendly face among the strangeness. All of those events were seeds in developing the special relationship, adding to Phyllis' mystique, to alleviate or outright dismiss the monster of pain.

~

He of the past wondered about the future in silence: what form or shape of things to come would add to Tasha's amazing and surreal accomplishments; her capability for accomplishing deeds never imaginable for her species; the haunting mystical responses that would keep her extraordinary. What she demonstrated was in the history yesterday, he wondered what the future held, for their lives together.

nine

It was after the winter solstice, temperatures visiting only the lower scale of the thermometer, the forces of nature's seasonal change awakening from the sleep of the vernal equinox. There certainly was enough advance warning from the National Weather Service as reported on the television weather channel. Classified the first day as a troubling disturbance of far-reaching implications, spawned at latitude and longitude coordinates, of the frozen tundra of Siberia. On the second day it had matured to a stationary heavy mass of worrisome frigid air awaiting its meteorological command for movement. The third day it began it's passage, elevated to an alarming "severe weather warning," cautioning everyone in its path as the front began to move easterly, crossing over parts of Alaska and moving toward Canada and then to the United States. Alerting history had shown the storm's direction was expected to be altered somewhat by the immutable Canadian Rockies, forcing its howling path in a more easterly direction.

The evening of the sixth day, as it entered the United States, its location now over the plains, the power of the storm increasing. The Canadian media describing in graphic detail its impact during its path through Canada reporting, "A major storm of vast proportions with record-setting low temperatures and heavy snowfall has ravaged Western Canada," leaving in its wake impassable snowbound roads and streets in the effected cities, towns and countryside, foretelling of the monumental removable task awaiting the citizenry. The majority of citizens snowbound and confined to their homes. The only visible activity was the heavily taxed snowplows and other snow removal equipment in service, their trailing exhaust as well as the smoke from the chimneys of the snowbound dissipating before they reach high altitudes. Only the residue of pollutants reached the upper atmospheres, temporarily offering the only break in the starkness of color as government helicopters made low flying passes to assess the storm's impact, awaiting commerce to regain its motion, having been inanimate during the storms siege.

In the aftermath the Canadian air was stilled with extreme cold, ice crystallizing the exhaled breaths of those who ventured out into its severity. Its consequences deceptively masked by a brightly shining winter sun in a cloudless sky glorifying the landscape. It's brightness tracking passage toward's the western horizon. Its magnificence a memory as clouds of stealth, laden with the coming night's snowfall moved to cover the moonlit sky.

Aerial surveillance reported seeing thousands of dead deer and caribou littering the landscape. Their stilled bodies marked their Armageddon in the battle lost to the elements. Their carcasses were now the source of food for the more resourceful bears and wolves that waited out the storm in the safety of their dens, a bounty awaiting their denied appetites.

Royal Canadian Mounted Police in snowmobiles reported thousands of birds dead from the cold still attached to the interior branches of trees where they perched for protection. Overmatched the brittle branches snapped from the trunk by howling winds, its occupants frozen in tandem as if skewered.

The Canadian government reported a record number of homeless people reluctantly acceding to offered refuge, reconciled that their clothing was meager at best. Conceding the cardboard shelters they called home, would not offer enough protection, putting their lives at risk. By the hundreds, many in their first year as street people, turned to shelters, soup kitchens, town halls and school gymnasiums opened specifically to accommodate them. Others whose intellect had long been mummified by drugs or habitually altered by alcohol, failed to comprehend the storm's threat to their well-being, becoming fatalities whose numbers began to mount at the local morgues and hospitals, requiring a thawing out before the official cause of death could be stipulated.

They became, in death, a *cause celebré* by the same well-meaning officials who fought for their release from treatment hospitals and institutions… turned loose with their problems of drugs, alcohol and delusions, escaping to their own isolation; a wandering existence unable to comprehend the seriousness of the storm.

Following the lead of local television, the radio stations interrupted their regularly scheduled programming to read bulletins from the National Weather Service alerting listeners of "a severe weather advisory in effect until further notice."

"A seasonal Alberta Clipper," the meteorologists warned. "A massive, seemingly endless front of sub-zero air emanating from the Siberian Tundra has left a freezing snowbound Canada in its wake."

Its relentless path moving east, reported to be dropping in its passage up to three inches of snow an hour immobilizing affected areas, forcing closure of airports and highways as inoperable and snowbound. Snow removal equipment, inoperable on roads they normally conquer, where no match to the magnitude of the arctic elements. Wind gusts of up to fifty miles per hour as well as patches of black ice hidden beneath the snow made driving hazardous for road service maintenance and police, if not impossible. The suggested alternate street routes were littered with abandoned cars, causing considerable accidents as motorists caught by the storm tried desperately to reach the safety of their homes. The death toll rose to eighteen from traffic related whiteout conditions. The fatality count was expected to rise before the storm, in its early rampaging hours, showing signs of abatement.

The massive front was well into the Plains States. Ranchers and farmers reported isolated cattle and other farm animals huddled together, the calves or the youngest surrounded for protection in their midst, the elders willingly sacrificing themselves literally within feet of the safety of their barns in obvious disorientation. Others, separated and blinded by the storm's unrelenting intensity, accepted their fate, laying down in a fetal position, their last act of desperation and delusion of safety, hoping to ride out the storm. Their lives were taken from them in a frozen pre-birthing position.

The major cities of International Falls, Pierre, Bismarck, Minneapolis, Superior and Chicago that were in the storm's wide coverage had fallen victim announced school cancellations and hundreds of miles of highway closures. Electrical power lines, heavy with ice, lay spitting out its energy aimlessly in the snow. Gas and water lines ruptured; unable to be demanded of. Industry was at a standstill. The populace was instructed to remain indoors subsisting on their stores and if affected by the loss of electricity were heated-by-wood burning fireplaces.

The storm system was significant enough to justify repeated weather advisories as it advanced into other sections of the country. To compound matters nature had unleashed an equally dense low pressure system, heavily laden with moisture over the warm waters of the Gulf of Mexico its capriciousness directed its turbulence toward the United States. During it's route, it dropped two to three inches of rain per hour, swelling rivers and overflowing creeks. The second day inundated the southern states moving in a direct course to meet the frigid front. Like its counterpart it forced closure of schools and home evacuations as it made its flood damaging way north. The two systems were expected to collide over the Ohio Valley, setting off thunderstorms and lightning as the leading edges of both systems met, bringing a disastrous six inches an hour of snowfall along with freezing temperatures and swirling winds. The conditions were sure to further the standstill of commerce, the fronts combined as one continuous white curtain dropped from the sky, concealing shapes, configurations and colors of the spectrum.

George clicked on the kitchen radio. Hearing of the weather advisory, his face showed concern, he asked his wife, "Do you have anything planned today?"

"Just the fashion show at the club. It's been sold out for months." Reminding him coyly as she exaggerated a model's strut down a reviewing stage. Speaking with a dramatic flair she said, "As you know, I've been asked to model the new mink coat that you recently bought from the show's presenter, Allen Fox, at a conditional discount: modeling my purchase and his other latest furry presentations. My friends are anxious to see me wear it. Judging from the weather forecast, it will be of good use today."

Watching her pretentious antics and feigning a smile George Staves, tried to hide his concern and said, "What time will you be home?" His countenance turning serious as he quickly added, "Make sure you have a full tank of gas. And don't forget to bring your cell phone."

"Don't worry, Hon," she said confidently. "I'll be home in plenty of time, well before the storm gets serious. Light the fireplace. We'll watch the storm together."

Her confidence and self-assurance didn't assuage his concerns. "Make sure that someone checks the weather forecast periodically. Storm movements and characteristics can turn on a dime," he said cautioning.

"Good idea," she said as they both rose from the kitchen table. She kissed him goodbye as he left for work. In deference to the weather advisory, he planned it to be a short day, not knowing the many hours of worrisome vigil that were in store for him.

As George drove away, the caretaker sky, a somber gray, began to give up what had been spawned in the atmosphere. Sprinkles of snow began to fall, heralding what was to come, dotting the cold ground, and immediately fusing. The snow crystals in a freefall broke the monotony of the sky.

~

The visitor of time past: George Staves paused in self-reflection these many years later, preparing to watch the recalled events unfold, nodding that they remained clear and recallable as if it were yesterday. Today he called it an memorable adventure he shared in, yesterday it had all the implications of an unfolding tragedy coming to pass. Again contemporary, it was excitement that would visit him knowing the outcome – expedited the kaleidoscope presentation.

~

Within two hours of George's departure Rose was fully dressed, carrying the mink coat in her arms. In her hands were the cookies she had baked the day before. Her entry in an unofficial friendly competition with the offerings of her friends, the winner awarded a one hundred dollar gift certificate at the clubs pro shop; planned as added stimulus for the success of the fashion show. She raised the garage door with her radio wave opener, noticing as she waited that on the floor of the back seat was George's Driving Club, needing a new grip, alongside a bottle of filtered water. Holdovers of the last days of the golf season. Rose smiled and shook her head good-naturedly, promising to tease him about his mental lapse.

She too would be faulted for having forgotten to replace the weakened battery of her cell phone that she now removed from her purse in anticipation of receiving phone calls. Her attention turned to the building snow in the driveway crunching beneath the wheels of the car, reflecting that the snowfall would exceed two inches, triggering the snowplowing response from her contractor before she returned home.

Rose was aware as she gained higher elevation that she was bordering the Snow Belt… land hugging portions of the Great Lakes stretching from Cleveland to Buffalo, New York… known to have its weather greatly influenced by the movement of air over these great bodies of water. "Lake effect" the meteorologists called it. When she arrived at the club, the snow was falling steadily. She noticed the snowplows were busy clearing the parking lot as others of the club's maintenance crews salted the sidewalks.

The weather had caused related travel difficulties for some of the members and their invited guests, experiencing delays of up to one hour. Outright cancellations had reached eight when the program finally got started. With lunch completed, everyone's talk and attention turned away from the developing storm to the models and the fur fashions on display. The heavy drapes of the formal dining room prevented witnessing the rate of snowfall increasing significantly. Management assured those attending they would keep them informed with the status of automobile traffic. Reports were that it slowed significantly, continuing in a steady flow, therefore not cause to consider cutting the program short at this time. The fashion show ran to completion, the center of attention returning to the weather and its ominous forecast ahead. Sparking precautions, including an urgent return to their respective homes in advance of its full impact, particularly those with greater distances to drive, to avoid testing their driving skills.

There would be none of the usual friendly time consuming exchanges between the women, no procrastination, all were anxious to leave crowding the parking lot attendant's desk awaiting their car's delivery; dutifully cleared of snow and ice. Rose was fifth in line when one of the attendants, cold and snow covered from the exposure, gasped to Evelyn Hughes, Rose's good friend, that her car would not start, the likelihood, she surmised regrettably was the battery's already weak electrical charge sapped completely by the quickly falling temperatures.

Evelyn, frantic with her predicament, was distraught to tears as local gas stations, swamped with requests for road service, said it would be hours before they could assist her. Rose, while the others were solicitous of Evelyn Hughes predicament, were preoccupied with their own concerns, came to Evelyn's rescue, acknowledging she would take her home. Rose tried to use her cell phone to alert George as to what had occurred. A lack of dial tone attributed to the cold weather and blustery winds stymied her, she would try again after a charge from the cigarette lighter.

Evelyn Hughes lived an additional fifteen miles southwest of the club. Rose reasoned that the highway was her best choice to travel. She was concerned but not alarmed, confident in her car's front wheel drive snow handling capabilities.

Rose, while driving, repeated her attempt to call her husband. Again, no dial tone. Her battery's failing life had been snuffed out completely, critical of her forgetfulness in leaving the phone in the car as temperatures dropped steadily.

Cedar Road, the main thoroughfare to the highway, was bumper to bumper with vehicles, the result of plant, office and school closings. It took forty minutes to drive to the highway entrance when under normal circumstances it took ten minutes. It took another ten minutes for her position in line to enter the traffic flow of the highway. While passage was slow, traffic was in motion. Rose settled behind the wheel, comfortable in her ability to handle the conditions she faced, bolstered by her experiences of having previously driven in snowstorm conditions. She chose the middle lane, giving wide berth to the car in front of her, anticipating emergency stops. Losing the safety margin as foolishly impatient motorists seized it as an opportunity to pick up ground for mere milli-seconds, ignoring the risk their maneuver presented to them and the more safety conscious drivers. Their aggressiveness becoming contributors to the dangers they were trying to escape. Rose was thankful her car was equipped with traction adjusting wheel RPM's and an anti-skidding brake system that could handle most challenges in evolving road and weather conditions.

On edge in the rapidly worsening conditions nervous tension dominated both as Evelyn remarking repeatedly on how appreciative she was of Rose driving her home under these awful conditions. Rose, stressed by concentration, her mouth dry in intrepidation hoarsed a "Don't be silly. What are friends for?" response. "It's no problem," she said in an obvious understatement, guardedly keeping her eyes fixed on the road ahead of her. They sighed a collective relief as they arrived at Evelyn's highway exit, a normal drive of thirty minutes stretched to one hour. During the difficult drive, the snow continued at its unrelenting pace, reclaiming recently plowed and salted road surfaces.

Evelyn lived within a mile of the highway exit in a community she affectionately called "country" where snow plowing services were not given a high priority in community needs. This low rating showed in the building snow on the roads, tracked occasionally by light traffic.

While exhausted from the tiring trip, Rose's confidence remained high, her front wheel drive successfully handling the ever worsening conditions. Upon arrival at Evelyn's home, Rose left the car's engine running, her planned stay obviously short. She waited anxiously for Evelyn's return from using her home phone, troubled when told the phone lines were down, furthering her apprehension as Evelyn was unable to reach her husband. Waving their nervous goodbye's Rose reminded Evelyn that if phone service was restored within the next hour and a half, to call George and tell him of her route and expected arrival time. Rose, backing from the driveway, received an ominous sign; for the first time her wheels spun and labored to gain traction.

On her return trip, the lightly traveled road leading to the highway entrance was finally being tended by the late arriving snow plows attempting to keep the road open. She felt the good Lord was providing for her as the snowplows entered the highway before her, making their return run. Sensibly deciding her best chances were to stay behind them for as long as they worked this stretch of the highway, prayerful that other plow crews were also working the highway. On alert for the plows to concede if it became impossible to keep up pace with the heavy snowfall, abandoning their efforts would persuade her to find a sanctuary from the storm. She wanted desperately to succeed in reaching her home to avoid being alone in a motel that night or nights to follow.

Following the snow plows she entered the highway cautiously allowing plenty of distance for cars and trucks before proceeding. Only two lanes were open and being maintained by the plows. She chose the outside lane close to the roads shoulder and median giving her some margin for safety. The shoulder and median included in the plows efforts to clear the snow, purposed to allow passage of emergency vehicles. Her confidence in her driving abilities was continually tested as the cars tires struggled with the icy conditions. She repeatedly adjusted her speed and direction forestalling the beginnings of a skid. The effort fatigued her, resulting in perspiration building on her forehead, anxiously wiped away before blurring her vision. The snow plows tires outfitted with chains traction was unfailing, enabling the operators to travel at speeds that kept increasing the distance between them. Under siege her confidence in handling the situation remained, in spite of anxieties. Demonstrably affected, she tightened her grip on the steering wheel in renewed determination as she faced the confronting conditions, prayerful it would not appreciably worsen.

Rose clicked on the radio she had silenced during her attempts to contact her husband by cell phone, hearing for the first time: "accounting for the ever-increasing snowfall was the arrival of a warm water air mass spawned in the Golf of Mexico combining with the arctic front producing a storm of major proportions, setting records for low temperatures and snowfall. The lake effect also contributing, snow falling at a rate of eight inches an hour in the Snow Belt," the meteorologists reported, of concern to Rose but not an intimidating fear for surrender. Rose's car location at the time of the report was at the buckle of the belt. She became aware of freezing snow beginning to accumulate at the end of the arc of her overworked windshield wiper blades, progressively reducing the blades' travel and her peripheral vision. Narrowing her focus and line of sight to a restricted straight ahead view. The ice build-up was directly related to the car's heater functioning as the defroster, being taxed beyond its engineered effectiveness.

The snow crunched beneath the wheels of cars and trucks, spewing a backwash. Passing cars created trailing clouds of snow that splashed onto her windshield. The wiper blades, slowed by the additional burden, were rendered momentarily useless, eliminating for frantic seconds her line of sight, making her vulnerable, threatening a life-ending in her abyss. Panicking, she moved to press on the brake to come to a stop. Thankfully recovering her composure she brought her foot to within a whisper of full use, her slight touch activating the brake lights, slowing her perceptively. Blinded, without a choice she lived through a greater danger, waiting for the windshield to clear, driving with a dead reckoning, remembering her last view before it disappeared.

She experienced disorientation, yet somehow summoned a never believed latent courage as she waited for the struggling wiper blades to function again, albeit with limiting visibility. Determined to get more visibility she opened the driver's side window, and was immediately greeted by the cold biting wind, her face blasted by snow and ice that attached to her eyebrows and lashes as well as the interior of her car. Being a tall willowy woman of athletic ability, she leaned and stretched out the open window, reaching with her gloved left hand, the steering wheel in her right, to wipe the accumulating snow on the drivers side windshield, accumulating from the blade's narrowing clearing arc. She was also able to grab hold of the ice encrusted windshield wiper blade itself, holding it against the will of its purposeful motor; releasing it with it's stored up energy to crash down onto the windshield, freeing the captive ice.

One more vital necessity she told herself, assisting her chances substantially, using her gloved hand brushed the ice and snow from her side view mirror. Moments after closing the window, she was brought close to tears as she saw how short-lived her efforts were, the snow and ice began to form again. Nonetheless it was her only counter, no matter how temporary her success. Although her contribution was small, she took solace that she was helping, making a contribution toward her safety; repeating the process.

She had no choice, the onset of skids increased substantially endangering her, responding by slowing the car even further, threatening the loss of her umbilical cord attachment with the brake lights of the car ahead of her, her "beacon" replacement for the snow plows and salt trucks. Judging correctly that cutting her present speed would reduce her risk of not enough time to recover from a passing car or a truck's backwash. Conditions were worsening but safe passage adjustments were still available to her, it was the prudent thing to do in the event of having to change lanes or suddenly stop. She hoped that the cars following her would read her signs of caution and duplicate her driving tactics. Most did while others didn't. Impatient and throwing caution to the wind left her wondering how long before they skidded off the road.

The wind had picked up considerably, grabbing the snow about to land, including that which had fallen earlier still having its own life, not frozen with its predecessors. Also clutched within the blasting wind was the snow stirred up from passing motorists, all combining to create a swirling dense white cloud that swept unchallenged in the open countryside, unleashing its strength as it clashed head-on with the cars and trucks knifing through the whiteness. Its demise temporary as it became airborne again resurrected by the howling winds to again pummel and buffet the slow-moving vehicles, engulfing them in cold, wet whiteness.

Her tire treads maximum traction pattern for all weather conditions was practically useless, its creviced and serpentine molded design was caked with ice and snow, lessening its holding power. Rose experienced this as well as the cars that passed her, reacting as a sail in the wind temporarily unable to avoid drifting from her course.

Her efforts during exposure to the raging frigid storm had not only reddened and chaffed her face but the extreme temperature differentials had layered the interior surface of the windshield with moisture worsening her visibility, requiring her to quickly clear the window with the wiping of her gloved hand, increasing her physical efforts in highly stressed circumstances. Her mouth dried, her lips parched. She was thankful her husband's forgetfulness enabled her to quench her thirst, drinking from the bottled mineral water she remembered to bring to the front seat of the car while stopped at Evelyn Hughes' home.

Rose's determination to reach home remained unwavering in spite of the interminably slow pace. Although stressed physically and mentally she was handling the difficult road conditions the storm had wrought to that moment. It was inconceivable to her that her labored driving would worsen as she was about to find out.

She kept the radio on, keeping abreast of the storm's path and road conditions. Switching to a music only station hoping the music to be soothing and calming, she played it loud enough to break the hypnotic spell cast by the monotonous thump thumping of the windshield wiper blades. Her purpose strengthened when she heard that all highways were being kept open to those currently driving them while discouraging their use by those starting out with the rejoinder, "Don't drive unless you have to as driving conditions will only worsen." And so they did.

She continued to drive in the left lane chosen strategically for the closeness of the median. Rose noticed as she slowly moved past the exits off the highway, many abandoned cars, whose drivers, unable to cope with the road conditions, braved the elements trudging through the snow, ice and biting low temperatures to reach a nearby sanctuary. Some of the cars were abandoned in the exit ramp itself blocking anyone attempting to exit, had that been Rose's wish.

Rose was not prepared to surrender, not while the roads remained open and not while she had come this far. Her driving skills were continually tested. In the rearview mirror she saw the trucks in a building caravan gaining on her. She decided to leave the left lane to allow passage of one of the road behemoths rapidly closing the distance that separated them. The renegade driver, deluding himself with the invincibility of his eighteen wheels beneath him was determined to complete his earnings producing run. The expected passing truck's backwash covered her windshield. This time it included propelled salt and ashes that splattered noisily, cutting off her vision. Rose knew the time for the windshield to clear would be dangerously longer.

Needing to find perspective, she hurriedly rolled down the driver's side window while continuing to drive, thrusting her head into the elements to gain sight, reference and guidance. The cold blast of air numbed her senses. Her beading forehead tingled with perspiration, the early signs of freezing. Finally, when it seemed she could no longer take her exposure to the cold, the windshield wipers prevailed after a labored struggle. Her view remained limited, dispatched snow joined by grime collecting at the end of the wiper blades' arc.

This last dangerous incident demanded that she question for the first time whether it was prudent to continue in the face of the ever-increasing density of the snowfall, the winds rising to gusts of sixty miles per hour, her sight restricted to mere yards, further waning her determination. The radio reporting that miles of the highway were determined impassable and would be shut down within the hour.

Her thoughts were interrupted as a trailer truck suddenly loomed behind her, its headlights as it approached appearing and disappearing, curtained by the white out conditions. Before she realized, the truck was upon her, appearing within feet of her, dangerously tailgating, angrily flashing his lights, blaring his horn for her to move from the left lane she returned to. Thoroughly intimidated, she thought of moving right but with her sight restricted or practically non-existent, facing an unknown judged a greater threat, delaying her moving over until she could be certain. Losing his patience, the truck driver pulled out into the center lane to pass on her right, misjudging the distance of another car traveling just ahead in the same lane, forced him to turn quickly back into the left lane, the truck's back end fishtailed, barely clearing her car.

Rose had no choice. She reactively pressed down on the brakes, sending the car into a groaning pull to the left, the car's anti-skidding mechanism responding, straining to regain control. Then the truck's backwash hit. Blinded and disoriented, all reference to the highway lost, she panicked and hit the brakes even harder at the same time sharply turning the steering wheel left, putting the car in a full-scale forty-five degree angle skid, before a correction could take place she had moved off the highway surface.

Inertia driven, out of control, the car plowed through the mounds of snow deposited on the median. While safely contained by her seat belt, she felt her shoulders press against the back of her car seat as she plunged downward, the roads grade too steep and slippery, her car was without traction. Her plowing fall abruptly ending as the built up snow in her path was too voluminous to allow passage to her wayward vehicle, absorbing it with a crunching sound. The rough descent and the sudden stop banged her upper legs violently against the dashboard, her right foot distorted was injured. While her injuries were painful they were not serious beyond perhaps, hobbling. Searching for a reference point, she was unable to penetrate the engulfing clouds of snow, surmising she had settled after her hazardous descent at the bottom of a deep gully, it happening so quickly she didn't cry out until all movement ceased, screaming at the top of her lungs, "Oh my God. I'm off the highway, God help me."

Stunned and shaken by the suddenness of events, thankful to God she had not overturned during her uncontrolled descent. She was basically uninjured save nothing more than a minor injury to her right foot. She sat there in the front seat recovering from shock, on the verge of tears, fearfully cognizant she was separated and alone in a howling snowstorm, blaming herself as irresponsible for not having a cell phone in working order. Bemoaning that her cautious effort would have succeeded if not for the maliciousness of an irresponsible truck driver cruelly defeating her. Her moment of self pity spent, she assessed her current situation as dangerous only if she lost her composure. She was convinced she would be located, fear and apprehension management her only test until recovery, not considering any other fate in store for her. Strong willed, helplessness to be guarded against, banishing submitting to the dangers that had befallen her. Raising the white flag of defeat and not helping herself was out of the question.

Confronting her situation, she rationally judged that her downward plunge, coming to a halt quickly, assured her that she couldn't be too far off the roadway and should be visible when the prohibitive conditions of the blowing sight reducing conditions eased. She searched straight ahead for a break in the starkness and saw none. Nervously questioning she turned from the front windows to the rear window where her vision had more travel, seeing the fallen snow propelled by the winds swirling around, hearing the icy pellets crash against the rear window and roof of the car, she finally realized her plunge ended in a snow bank completely absorbing the front end of the car including the windshield, at rest in a cold monolith. A duality presentation: the front end of the car in a shielded scenario within it's mass, belying the surrounding dynamics of the storm seen rearward continuing unabated around her; the monolith a gathering threat. The thought of it growing, becoming her frightening consciousness.

She confirmed that the car up to the driver's side door as well as the front passenger side door was blocked from opening as an escape route. For now the relatively unencumbered rear doors would open, she reasoned. Giving her access to a backup escape venue would be the sunroof, making it imperative she keep it clear of the snows buildup. Relieved she was not trapped and could free herself anytime she wished; Rose currently judged her best chances for survival lay with staying where she was, out of the storm's elements. She laid out her plan; she had plenty of gasoline to burn to keep warm if she conserved it. Mindful of another consideration in her survival: the dangers of carbon monoxide poisoning, she shut down her still running engine.

The security and company of an active life saving engine ending, suddenly deathly cold, doubt occasioning her plan for conserving, it's sudden attendant dramatic change un-nerving her. A hostage to time, she began to feel caged in isolation, feeling threatened by claustrophobia. Her breath labored and difficult, she was on the verge of panic. Anguishing over the loss of freedom in movement, she sought references to the outside worlds expansiveness, finding she was captive to limiting horizons. The product of the snow and ice that covered the car, while her sanctuary, it also portended to be her tomb.

Her rationing period of fifty minutes over, for now her period of allocated catnap sleep not needed, her work began. She turned the cars engine and its electrical system back on. Wincing at the pain of her injuries, she climbed into the back seat. Ignoring the frigid air, and the stinging ice and snow that hurled against her exposed face as she lowered the back windows, reaffirming that both doors were moveable and would remain so with her repeated attention. Using the doors themselves as plows, Rose forced a curved path away from the car. The confirmation of one escape route confidence building, feeling less desperate with the reassurance. Buoyed, literally shoveling and pushing aside the buildup with her gloved hands, ignoring her frigid exposure she cleared the sunroof, it operational as her alternate escape route. She would continue her maintenance, challenging the daunting storm through the night and beyond as necessary.

Rose then tried her cell phone, checking to see if it had responded to being charged, chancing unrealistically that it had risen from the dead. Its lack of a dial tone confirming it's demise, leaving her downtrodden but not desperate.

Reacting again, by sheer will she reclaimed her emotions, reining in any negative thoughts. She took stock of her situation. Although currently isolated, when reported missing, people and the police would be looking for her and others who might be trapped, but not until the storm had passed and the closed roads reopened, she would expect. She also knew that her husband would physically and independently join the search for her as well, while maintaining phone contact with police and the highway department officials, sharing news in their search to find her.

She took inventory: a full tank of gas at idle speed, although not anticipated, rationed would last for days, she extrapolated, her warm mink coat and matching hat, a driving golf club, a bottle of mineral water and the box of remnant cookies. She was not without resources. She was in a position to wait out the storm which was her only option. Her injury and the worsening outside conditions made it impossible to attempt to climb back up the embankment and in all probability to a closed highway, increasing the threat to her life.

"I will be noticed," she said aloud, tearfully strengthening her conviction. "They'll find me," adding in empathy, "as well as all the others who are marooned."

Her words gave her a confidence emboldened with belief, not an entreaty without hope. That conviction would seek an assist before the night was over, an appealing prayer for her Gods intervention.

George Staves arrived home at three in the afternoon with the roads still relatively passable. His initial reaction was one of surprise, not alarm, that Rose was not home. He expected the activities at the club would be over. At 3:30 PM he called the club and learned the fashion show was long over, learning management had decided to close the club for the day with all employees sent home. At 4:00 PM he began to worry. Why hadn't she called? Was she experiencing trouble? Even under the present weather conditions, she should have been home by now. At 4:30 PM, hiding his deep concern he called his daughter Rosanne to find out if her mother had called her. When he was told that she hadn't, feigning detachment to placate his daughter's concern, he assured her that she needn't worry, "there would be a logical explanation," he said trying to sound confident.

"I'll call you when she arrives," he promised.

At 5:00 PM deeply concerned he called the police, learning there were no reported accidents involving his wife. He was also told that the entrances as well as miles of the highway had been closed, citing hazardous conditions. Only the well-plowed and salted-off ramps were to remain open for the few remaining cars and trucks exiting traffic.

"Maybe she used the streets instead of the highway," he said to himself, momentarily hopeful until the reality of the trip's time discouraged that consideration.

With the police and highway officials alerted, both assured him that the message would get out to the patrol cars and the snowplow crews still working the highway, told to be on the lookout for a 1993 black Cadillac sedan with Rose's license plate number. Both agencies had assured him they had received reports of traffic still on the highways traveling in single file following snowplow operators with driving conditions at best extremely difficult and at a snail's pace. More than likely, they offered, "she was in one of those processions of cars and it was only a matter of time before she would reach home." or they offered, "she was joining others who decided to leave the car on the median close to an exit and walk off the highway for help as some travelers had already done. Consideration must also be given that she might have decided she had had enough and pulled off the road to wait for improved driving conditions."

Having made the same conclusions earlier, George knew that any of the offered scenarios would have brought a phone call, angrily it was obvious to him that she had not replaced the battery of her cell phone and at the moment did not have access to one. He had no alternative with the highways about to close, the police and highway road crews alerted, but to wait by the phone for someone to call.

Disturbingly, the snowfall at the last weather report was still falling at the rate of six inches an hour, reporting streets and roads impassable.

After another forty-five minutes and two calls from a worried Rosanne, he still had no word. The turned on radio announcing that the Highway Department had closed down miles of the highway as well as the entrances and exits. All vehicles that were reported moving were now off the highway. In addition, all city streets and roads were now closed to vehicular traffic until further notice. The decision resulted from the storm's intensity as being too much for the snowplow crews to keep pace with. Their objective would be better served when the storm ended.

Disconsolate and fearful but not without hope, George moved to the last of considerations as the more probable: Rose had been forced to pull off the road, in all probability too far to walk to an exit, staying in the car waiting for the storm to move out of the area enabling the road crews to clear the highway. He trusted her judgment as a wise one. She knew what to do under these severe conditions. She was well versed in survival techniques and the need to conserve fuel for heat.

In spite of his confidence in her, he anguished over her solitary position. The absence of phone contact enabling scenarios of dread to weigh heavily in his mind, punishing him with guilt for not insisting that she cancel her participation in the fashion show. He felt helpless, wracking his brain to contribute more in her search, more than sitting and standing sentry over a silent telephone. His mind frantically at work, reasoning that stymied truck drivers staying with their fully loaded rigs, not abandoning them at either weigh stations, truck stops, or at the side of the road, awaited relief, still in open contact with their dispatchers. A no better source for finding Rose if mustered, known for their special kinship for their brothers of the road, sharing a common dilemma, bringing camaraderie. If called upon their network would strengthen the search, increasing prospects dramatically. He called every trucking company in the yellow pages offering a five hundred dollar reward to the truck driver who found her. He was given a needed confidence boost when he learned that three of the companies had drivers on the same highway who, rather than continue risking life and limb as well as their load, elected to pull their rigs over and wait for improved travel conditions. All three dispatchers gladly welcomed the opportunity to help.

The sudden ringing of the phone gained his attention. Its disquieting shrill announcing the phone lines survived the ever-increasing ravages of the violent storm. It was his daughter Rosanne who needed to hear his repeated assurances to placate her fears. Hearing his own words of optimism, resurrected his fading belief.

The still functioning phone rang again. This time it was his daughter Phyllis who lived in California. Her concerns were not assuaged by his confident words. She would continue to call all through the night. The only words that would relieve her were those spoken by her mother reliving her experience in what surely would be a lengthy phone call.

Another phone call came in over the remarkably resilient overhead phone lines. This time it was his son Edward, living in New Jersey with his wife Francine and daughter Miranda. Innately protective of his mother as most sons are, he was judgmental of his father, critical for not insisting that she cancel her participation in the fashion show. Bemused that his father had been concessionary when he should have been more adamant as he now wished, anguished him to lash out. Staves listened to his son's emotional release, tolerant that impatience and frustration dominated his nature when stymied and feeling helpless; bemoaning the fact he was so far away in an hour of family need. George's assurance that all that could be done was being done was not enough to dissuade him from flying out to them for his own assessment. Only when his father's revelation that he would find all roads leading to and from the airport closed left him with no choice but to cancel his plans, disrupting his wishes for what he felt was his obligation to be there.

During the initial hours that passed, Rose continued her life saving regimen: turned the ignition on every hour, to run the engine for ten-minute intervals monitored by her closely observed watch. Her expectations not only to generate welcomed heat and charge the battery, but to blow clear any snow that might be blocking the tail pipes, preventing expelling noxious carbon monoxide fumes harmlessly into the atmosphere and not deathly silent into the car.

It was now 9:00 PM She knew the two fronts had clashed when she heard the unusual out of season thunder as the cold front quickly vanquished the heavy-with-moisture warm front, released upon conversion as cascades of snow and ice, continuing as one strengthened system.

As Rose planned each time she turned on the engine, she pulled back the cover of the sunroof, confronted again with appreciable amounts of snow that had accumulated since her last effort. Responding, she activated its rollback system, effectively clearing the roof of snow as it retracted to nest in its housing. Disturbing the snow with nowhere to go, it fell freely into the car, mixing with the night's continuing snow that descended through the opened sunroof. It chilled her face and stuck to her fur coat, a tolerated consequence under the circumstances. Her assignment complete, she quickly returned the roof to its closed position.

Keeping her gloves on for protection she cleared her face and coat of the crystallized attachment of the cold invader. The unrelenting snow, as planned mandated she opened the leeward door, thrusting it forward to move the building drifts of snow, this time it was tight of clearance, marginally establishing an escape route. Her job half done, she quickly moved to the other side of the car, gasping at what confronted her: the windward passenger side door was unmovable, the packed snow proving too formidable. The prospect of being completely surrounded by cocooning snow was unnerving. Fearful, she felt her throat tighten, worrisome of her diminishing prospects. Her options reduced, she regrouped, finding new courage. Keeping her wits, she returned to the somewhat cooperating leeward door, determined she lay on her back, placing both feet to create additional leverage. Exerting adrenalin rush pressure, she managed to clear enough snow to now allow the door to open fully extended, no longer marginal, guaranteeing enough room for her to escape, subduing her fear that her car would be her coffin, subliming the terrifying claustrophobia that lurked within her from prominence. To protect her regained passage for escape, pledging to increase the frequency of her snow clearing duty to every thirty minutes, cutting her sleep period in half as a precaution, a necessary action, to combat a change in the directions of the fierce winds.

The passing of time put her plan in full exercise, her driven awake period prompted by her effective enigmatic internal clocks brain connection, so effectively used during the feeding of her infants now relied upon, shutting the engine down she engaged herself in a mind occupying game of counting to one hundred with no visual conformation until completing the count, trying to match her pace with that of her wristwatch and the car's clock, purposed to keep her occupied, challenging her mind for productivity to avoid the consequence of drifting off and it's subsequent death by exposure. In preparation of her attention focusing game, her face was surrounded by her coat's collar, her hat pulled down to cover her ears, her legs curled beneath her body and inside her fortuitous heat containing mink coat as she verbalized her count. She would stare through her sunroof's escape hatch at the frenzied snow, her alternate escape opportunity into the snow filled storming sky, it's venue hopefully remembered during her agonizing cat napping, curtailing nightmares of entombment.

To stay where she was and await help, she again judged was the right choice. With protection maximized, her mental diversion game of play steeled her, warding off unplanned sleep when she was most vulnerable to freezing temperature.

Snarling and growling, the storm, a vicious animal of prey having bullied the present land with its contemptuous display of power, killing and immobilizing. Its pervasion finally satiated continued it's route leaving a white blanket devoid of any activity, motionless with the rigor mortis of the dead. The jugulars of the cities and towns free flowing commerce having been choked by the bite of the storms icy fangs, its devastating quieting aftermath to be tested by man's countering determination for recovery.

It was after 9:00 AM the next morning the storm moved into Pennsylvania where neither the upper reaches of the Alleghany nor the Pocono Mountains could reduce the storm's intensity. The ski resorts initial elation fading as they became immobilized and impossible to access as snow fell far beyond benefiting expectations. Only after leaving upper New York State, heading out into the Atlantic did its intensity and mass reduce. Abandoned by the propelling force of a capricious jet stream, its vortex divided into pockets of weather fronts, icy squalls engaged by unsuspecting ships briefly in their path. No longer marshaled together as one, they discharged moisture inconsequentially into the sea. The separated multitude of the disturbances size and locations depicted on the radar screen of the more alert vessels were easily circumvented; the most to be expected was sleet and choppy seas, no longer considered of significant importance, citing it's eventual death knell by downgrading meteorologists.

~

His sleepless night's vigil left its mark. His ignored stomach groaned for attention. Caffeine inflamed his nervousness. An unrelenting headache throbbed at his temples. His physiology, in spite of the stimuli, in a losing battle. Somehow mustered from exhaustion; optimism at the news of the overwhelming storm beginning to withdraw, succeeded by a peaceful serenity, beginning the recovery from being overwhelmed. The snow was still falling within the area of the Snow Belt, the lake effect at work but not as endless swarms of wild fireflies but at a softly floating rate, layering the snow already on the ground, in sharp departure from the previous day's howling harshness of snow and ice building monoliths.

The snow would continue, the forecasters predicted until 11:00 AM, dropping an additional two to four inches, adding to the thirty inches already on the ground and drifts of over six feet, forcing isolated lifestyles until communities and cities could begin digging themselves free to intermingle.

South beyond the Snow Belt the sun had already broken through the layered remaining clouds, glaring the sheer whiteness, discouraging direct viewing.

From above, commercial aircraft originating from spared cities flew with its pilots assessing the storm's effects on the barely detectable arterial network of highways. Missing from their view were the feeding crisscrossing roads completely under the cover of snow with hardly a hint of their location, spotting briefly plumes of smoke coming from indistinguishable chimneys, dissipating as they reached skyward.

Looking directly downward, the tall trees, their uppermost reaches visible, appeared as flailing arms of overboard victims in a sea of whiteness, as one of the pilots called them. A closer view from ground level would have presented another picture; the tree branches drooping with the burden of snow, its branches and leaves cryogenically caked in ice, the trunks glazed stalagmites waiting passage of the revisiting ice age.

At 11:30 AM, the snow finally ended with the sun glaring, the atmospheric disturbance of vast proportions soon to be noted in history by the survivors mourning the unfortunate who became part of it's statistics and folklore.

George called the police and highway departments, receiving assurances that the highway crews and patrol cars were on the lookout for his wife's car. As planned, he then called the local helicopter service, learning that while the airport runways would remain closed for another forty-eight hours, the helicopter pads would be cleared by 3:00 PM that very day. Helicopter flight and ground crews to be available for all contracted services. Welcoming the news, he engaged the service with the condition that unless they heard from him otherwise, he would be under contract starting at 3:00 PM for two helicopters and their respective crews. This proviso a prudent last minute hope that Rose would have been recovered before their engagement time.

Not to be entrapped, in preparation of his participation in the search, his driveway was snow plowed every three hours during his exhausting night. Frustrating at times, the snow plow balking when used under extreme conditions, stalling repeatedly, the heaviness of the snow taxing its design limits. He also would extend the perimeter of cleared snow three feet beyond the patio, deep enough to see patches of the ice glazed lawn, to allow Tasha access to relieve herself.

Tasha also kept vigil, knowing her mistress was missing; she sat expectantly at her usual perch, the shelf of the living room bow window, staring out, anxiously waiting as she had done numerous times in the past for a family member's return, one whose absence continued.

During the stressful night, Tasha would leave her surveillance position to lay at the side of her Alpha, occasionally whimpering to break the agonizing silence, waiting hopefully for the phone to ring. She instinctively knew this wasn't a typical waiting period, showing immediate startling cognizance of his despair and anxiousness. Tasha displayed an unusual fidgeting and sensitivity to his sudden movements, rising quickly, eyes alert, awaiting his command, demonstrating an uncanny understanding of the situation when she unexpectedly brought down from Rose's bedroom closet one of her slippers… a master at an early age in the mechanics of turning a closet door knob. Laying it before George, her eyes inquiring of Rose's whereabouts. Staves patted her head solemnly in subdued amazement of her powers of perception, speaking directly to her as if she were human, "Mom will be home soon. We'll soon be together again."

~

Circumstances dealt she bear her burden alone, yet her family was with her in spirit, her life as wife and mother, if it be Gods will not fulfilled, she considering it His test encouraged she bear her burden until either He came to claim her personally or His help arrived. The aftermath dangers of her exposure time to the overwhelming elements would visit her with little notice, diabolically subtle it would penetrate her protection over time. With the engine running she began the necessary maintenance of the escape routes, time spent her criteria for exposure sounding the alarm, dictating interruption, it's observation forcing her repeatedly to seek protection within the car, short-circuiting the developing damaging effects of frost bite. Within the car during fuel conservation, as she curled up within her protective mink coat, a time at exposure limit would also be in order. Her sanctuary and her imprisonment becoming deathly chilled over time, subject to the effects of outside freezing temperatures penetrating, overwhelming the dissipating heat. The timing of such coincident with activating the cars engine was her plan until the threat changed or modulated. Compounding her difficult situation: ceding to the demands of nature… it's consequence: the ever-raging snow and below-zero temperatures stealing heat from her body, her feet inappropriately shoed, her eyebrows and lashes brushed free of the freezing snow, her lungs allowing only limited amounts of frigid air, her nostrils almost sealing themselves frozen, her difficulty in breathing leaving her gasping. She hurried her task, departing the wicked weather, shivering as she closed the car door, her breath stolen. She hurried to get back to her curled up position, cocooned in her mink coat, fighting off life ending demands for sleep; the passage of time imagined to be slow in cooperation, her watches frequently referred to… appearing not fast enough, each passing hour an eternity. Finally her time allotted was completed, quickly turning on the engine, she and the cars interior atmosphere made potentially death dealing, responding to its warming life saving comfort, knowing it short lived, for how long would other episodes test her mettle?

Rose thought of her husband and children, tears welling in her eyes as she thought of what they were going through, sorrowful what circumstance had wrought upon them, visualizing their angst and concern for her well-being in not finding her. She wiped away her tears not wanting to become wallowed in self-pity distorting her plight as impossible, her attempts at self-preservation useless – a concession she would continue to resist for death was a sure consequence, be it her Gods will. Resolved to think otherwise, Rose was certain that Evelyn Hughes' telephone line had been repaired and the call to her husband made. She again wiped her eyes of tears with her gloved hand, watching her vaporous breath that engendered the reality of her surroundings, confirming she was not asleep and dreaming.

The storm continued it's path towards subsiding, its swirling howling mass not going quietly its power moving aggressively eastward, it's treacherous rein over at 11:30 AM

Rose awakened prematurely, sensitive to the suddenly quieting surroundings, elated and uplifted by the help the new silence portended. Seeking visual confirmation to match what she wasn't hearing. She turned on the engine and activated the sunroof, shocked when there was no response. Remaining stubbornly closed, its growling engine straining to open. Her immediate reaction was disbelief, trying a second time, a third and fourth time. Each time met with little response in movement, the whirling motor still trying. Stricken with anxiety, she tried her primary designation for escape: the back leeward door, moving it slightly ajar but not enough for passage to escape when called upon. Sweating profusely, her plight desperate, she positioned her feet against the door exerting greater force with her legs, finally succeeding in moving the door to trace its earlier path.

Relieved of dreaded entrapment, she ventured out into what was still frigid air, the effects of the change still to early to dispatch the residue cold. Standing on the flooring of the door frame, her gloved hands on the roof, she saw the reason for her inoperable sunroof. Between the time of her last exerting response, thick ice had formed, effectively welding it's opening with ice. Her determined effort to chip away at the ice weld with the golf club's head proved fruitless, as a thaw was needed. At present her only escape lay with the opened car door. Acting protectively, using her gloved hands as shovels, the golf cub as a hammer she aggressively opened the path further. When she was finished, she stared upward at the sky's slate gray thinning clouds, no longer voluminous with free falling moisture, victim to being spent.

"It can't be long now," Rose said with anxiety, authoring an appealing prayer, "Dear God make the worst of it over." Expressing a belief of her religion asking of her God to intervene and not let the universe reign by it's own devices, a form of Protestantism. This religious concept not the teaching of her Catholicism, as God's involvement in the Universe's happenings is complete in all things and matters. As the new day slowly arrived, the sun cast shadows of the clouds in flight on the welcoming land, heralding that recovery of the storm had begun. Rose was wishful for sounds previously stilled or muted by the howling winds. She heard none at that moment; lives of the fortunate remained secluded, the storms departing affects being measured by those it dominated.

"It's only a matter of time," she assured herself as in the brightening south- western horizon surviving Canadian Geese were seen in flight having descended from altitudes that shared commercial aircraft – no longer necessary as the storms full furry had abated. Cheering her to say, "It won't be long."

With her escape door open, in pain and stiffness, she stood on her toes on the car's flooring, the pileup of snow cleared from the roof of the car, enabled viewing the desolate surroundings in temperatures undergoing change thankfully increasing her tolerance to exposure. What she saw completely overwhelmed her. Her breath stolen, she returned to the attention of her car which was completely covered with snow. Drifts had built up against the windward side of the car, the path on the leeward side cleared during Rose's vigil during the night. Unless closely inspected, the buried car could not be separated from it's capturing snowdrift. The only possible way she could be spotted was by air or if accidentally stumbled upon. She prayed for continuing warming temperatures staring incredulously at the white sea that surrounded and isolated her. Disoriented and confused by lack of reference, she searched for the engulfed highway that would seem almost invisible if she did not know of it's presence, she knew where it had to be: the sculptured higher elevation from which she plunged bringing cognizance. Engineered movement of tons of dirt in the highways construction, all in the name of progress and commerce were still a separate topography not withstanding it's overwhelming winter blanket. Now it was massive snow that had to be moved, a formidable task on it's own, not exclusively for commerce but for recovery of the surviving.

Her vision panned three hundred sixty degrees. What wind remained produced whiffs of cyclonic white powder as it traveled the land freeing the least resisting of the snowfall. The voluminous whiteness continuing for as far as she could see. Returning to the obscured highway, it's commerce now housed inoperable trailer trucks, a tenant snow glazed with ice. Looking upward, only their top half was visible from where she stood; the lower half hidden by the forty inches of snow that bound their eighteen wheels. Also barely visible were the tops of many cars, they too immobilized and sharing the same circumstances, some of the truck drivers she would learn had made their way to shelters when it was still an option.

She noticed plumes of smoke rising from some of the trucks, cheered that other drivers had stayed with their vehicles to wait out the storm. Not knowing it's uselessness, the range of her voice shortened by the lands openness, she began shouting in the direction of the occupied trucks no more than one hundred feet away. She yelled repeatedly until her voice became hoarse, her waving arms unsuccessful in alerting the drivers sitting in the cabs of their trucks. Unheard and overlooked the opportunity of a responding rescue was remote under present conditions as highway cleanup crews tended to the vehicles that blocked the highway. Disappointed and frustrated to tears she knew that if recovery were to happen today she would have to be spotted by aircraft.

Emotionally down, the stilling air still dangerous to over exposure necessitated she return to the warmth of the car where she once again took stock of her situation. She offered up prayers for Gods providence to direct her search, and prepare that she endure as long as necessary.

The storm thankfully had ended; temperatures were sure to rise; her gas reserve not threatening; the remaining bottled water still plentiful, the continuing nourishment from the cookies still plentiful, her predicament not without resources. Rose decided, during the daylight hours to abbreviate her schedule to run the car's engine every fifteen minutes, reasoning that the car's exhaust could be spotted. All she needed was to keep her senses and her recovery would be inevitable.

It was after 3:15 PM in the afternoon when George heard the helicopters fly over his house to start their search. At 4:00 PM he received a call from the owner of the helicopter service who, at that very moment, was in radio contact with the helicopters. They reported seeing many vehicles abandoned on the highway and the median, that a massive cleanup was underway by the Highway Department and outside contractors, acknowledging participation in information with the police and the Highway Department to fix exact locations. Also spotted were many people mulling around their vehicles, having spent the night. George Staves was buoyed by the reports anticipating his wife was among them, her recovery imminent. Unfortunately he would come to learn that was not the case, her car was not among them. The helicopter crews in their fly by pass, would identify her car's roof as partially covered sheet metal debris, apparently torn from a nearby metal roofed warehouse, He called the trucking company whose drivers were still on the highway. The dispatcher reported that all of his drivers were in contact with him and none had reported seeing Rose or her car at either the truck stops or weigh stations. The dispatcher, sensing his disappointment, offered up a buoy of encouragement.

"The drivers were busy with their own needs during the storm's ferocity. With the storm over and highway clearing underway," he rationalized, "they will have more time to intensify their search." Staves responded by increasing his offer to 1,000 dollars.

It was now nightfall with Rose still unaccounted for. The Highway Department reported making progress, expecting to clear at least one lane in each direction within the next eight hours. Streets accessing the highway had been cleared as well as all highway exit and entrance ramps. In addition, an army of tow trucks from gas stations, auto wreckers and repair shops were hired by the local townships along the highway's path began the task of removing the abandoned cars and trucks. Radio reports advised those involved call the township's police departments after the next forty-eight hours and prepare to make plans to recover their vehicles.

All three of the Staves children, consumed with apprehension, called their father in spite of receiving assurances that he would call as soon as he had word. Purposefully sounding upbeat for their benefit, he bared his torture alone. Advised of his contact with the trucking company and the hiring of two helicopters, brought them renewed optimism and hope. Nonetheless, Phyllis from California and Edward from New Jersey advised their father of their flight plans for the following day when, as announced, one runway would be open for renewed traffic.

During the second night, George slept tortuously, the phone within easy reach, ever present Tasha at his side with Rose's slipper next to her. He awoke suddenly, his pajamas soaking with perspiration chilling him, his dream anguishing doom no longer tolerated. Tasha whimpered, reading his body language, moving close enough to receive his awakened touch, comforting both.

~

The last radio updating forecast troubled Rose, hearing as the sun faded in the west, the forecasters reporting the cold air mass movement had slowed, to expect below-freezing night temperatures to prevail for another night and morning after which a complete thaw would begin. The report while gladdening, offered little consolation, remindful for what she faced for another night. With limbs stiffening from confinement and lack of movement, resisting being gathered together to contain her body heat, her tiring discomfort hardly welcomed the coming nightfall. Shunning the images that darkness and loneliness bring, she lifted herself spiritually with images of her own creation; flourishing in pleasant memories, she closed her eyes for their fulfillment, beginning the second night of her survival.

The frigid air, a minus five, continued it's assault on her exposed car taking its toll, the engine's lubricated moving parts sluggish, its weakened battery causing difficulty in starting. Frantic for the battery's life and its effect on her own, she prayed openly for Gods intervention. The engine was finally powered after her third attempt. Sitting apprehensively as it idled roughly on the verge of stalling, finally warming up to operate. Rose exhaled a sigh of relief, her prayers answered.

Sitting there waiting for the engine to complete its one hour run tired her. While it was this period that she planned to sleep, her tension-filled worry never waned, awakening prematurely to battle physically inadequate cat naps, leaving her stressful and exhausted. Causing concern her sleep deprivation affected her ability to stay awake during the conserving engine shutdown sequence as all would be lost.

Conquered by her deprived physical state, she slipped into a sound sleep after engine shutdown, her guard given leave put herself at risk to exceed the time constraints, the threat of freezing at longer exposure becoming very real. The disciplined regimen of her physically demanding survival program departed from, her situation threatening to become critical.

~

At daybreak George heard the helicopter pass over his house announcing another day in the search. Soon they would be reporting considerable progress in removing abandoned cars and trucks, recovery gaining the upper hand as patches of the concrete and macadam highway reappeared, promising an end of commerce's forced sabbatical.

With Rosanne and Bill present, George Staves called the police department for any late news. They reported nothing new in Rose's search, however announcing that the Highway Department would completely open two lanes to traffic in both directions late that afternoon. Until then, only vehicles equipped with snowplows would be permitted. The third lane – that which was closest to the median – would remain closed as abandoned trucks and cars needed the availability of the passing lane to be removed. Solicitous of Staves' anxiety, they tried very hard not to paint the bleak picture the circumstances were presenting, offering "the search is ongoing, finding her our greatest priority. Other mounting business presently taking a back seat." Staves immediately recognized the words and language of "police speak" the second days tone more officious, the degree of optimism waned. Sympathetic but deliberately evasive they avoided the phase "found alive," implying a higher priority could draw their attention elsewhere. Staves' conclusions he kept muted, not challenging them with his concerns for the degree of their participation, recognizing he could not expect the police departments of all the communities that the highway cut through to be at his complete disposal. However, it did disturb him that they were subtly implying Rose was another fatality, going missing this length of time in a storm of such consequences. He and his family, in the absence of the car being located, endorsed enough reason to remain optimistic, and strongly resistant to the thoughts of a worst case scenario. They stayed convinced she was somehow prevented from seeking shelter beyond her car which now trapped her, keeping her from a telephone. She might be still in her car somewhere surviving freezing exposure, fending for herself, fighting despair and waiting for help.

Staves called his local gas station, one that he had patronized for twenty years, explaining what had happened. Responding with understanding that Rose's prospects for survival diminished with each passing hour they agreed to supply, for as long as needed, the use of one of their tow trucks, fully equipped with a snowplow blade, a winch, a two-way radio and a driver at his disposal already alerted to pick George up within the half hour. Fred Nieland, the gas station owner, deeply solicitous, would need to adjust other calls for service, giving notice of "unexpected circumstances would affect their waiting period," all safely at home or safely marooned at work, sharing in Rose's increasing dire straits.

He knew of no other way to ask Rosanne without her tearful emotional outburst but it had to be done. He assigned her and Bill, the implicit task of calling all the hospitals and clinics in the vicinity of the highway, seeking information relating to any recovered Jane Doe victim of the storm, whom in the unlikely absence of a purse, prevented identification. While the consideration of that scenario was disturbing, their strong disbelief in Rose's resilience and police reports to date consigned it as remote, thwarting defeat yet its slightest possibility had to be explored and ruled out. He deliberately avoided mentioning fatalities, not wishing to introduce a hint of negative fatalism, knowing Rosanne's and Bill's inquiry would draw that information.

The tow truck arrived on schedule; the plowed driveway's most recent snow showing its first tire tracks.

He planned to bring Tasha with him to use her hunting skills and to lavish affection in welcoming Rose when found, hastening her recovery from her ordeal. Tasha seemed to sense this, rushing to the front door with Rose's slipper in her mouth, looking back at him with anxious eyes, awaiting him to answer the driver's ring and be on their way.

His attention was temporarily diverted by Tasha's reaction, questions abounding "Could she have read my mind?" he asked himself, or interpreted his body language, his scenting chemicals of anxiety effusing from his pores. However learned, he was asking her to use her abilities for discovery. Her enthusiasm told him she would not fail, so certain was she of her role in finding Rose, emphatically welcoming his plans to include her.

Their vehicle qualified, they entered the frozen highway as planned, against what would be the normal flow of traffic, carefully entering through the exit ramp, going the wrong way assuming that Rose had taken the highway for the return trip home. Safely driving for the most part in the cleared center lane, as were the other snow clearing trucks, seeing immediately the snow plows effects, forcing the white sea to yield its snow and icy garrote. They all sat in the front seat of the tow truck with Tasha's head out the window, the wind brushing her fur, sniffing the chilling air for scents. Staves was hopeful, anticipating signs turned from watching her, on edge and alert compelled to stare unblinking at the abandoned cars freed from the shackles of icy nature, none proving to be his missing treasures vehicle, their search continuing.

Fully involved they participated in the snow clearing effort, weaving in and out of the abandoned vehicles, the blade engaged moving snow, when it was opportune, they created occasional purposeful clearings to look beyond the median, participating in the cleanup while searching.

The going was painstakingly slow; his driver frequently yielding to the larger workhorse highway plows, their tow truck tracking as a "trailer" participating in the final clearing once the abandoned vehicles had been removed. The end of their run completed they changed direction upon reaching the Cedar Road ramp, turning full circle to cover the same ground from the other direction this time in the right direction.

As needed, all through the daylight hours while searching, they participated in helping dig out and clear other trapped vehicles to access the purposed tow trucks. While anxious with anticipation, his heart pounding, none uncovered proved to be Rose's. The removed snow adding to the continuous wall of snow bordering the highways, restricting the line of sight beyond the medians unless climbed, a condition inhibiting Rose's rescue if her car was not on the roadway. Fortuitously the expected reopening of the highway at 4:00 PM proved optimistic, resulting in having the crews held over until all three lanes were cleared and ready for traffic. The delay extending unimpeded access in continuing the search

Tasha on a roller coaster of emotions. At times, during their drive-by search, she kept her head out the open window, her senses alerted while she searched through wind swept eyes, enthusiastic and eager. At other times stirring restlessly, her attention redirected: elsewhere. Just as he was about to conclude the prevailing conditions to much to ask of her, she became aggressively enthused. Until again an off point passenger, despairing as if the search were senseless, repeating this inconsistency all through the search. He couldn't understand why her pronounced change took place during their drive by search when retracing in the direction of home. Was it suggestive that she had given up. Her strange behavior so unlike her.

Staves called the helicopter service just as dusk approached as they were about to complete their last run, learning they had found a number of cars that had skidded off the highway. All were recovered after drivers, with functioning cell phones called in their location to the police who in turn notified the Highway Department. None were found to have passengers with them, for the moment ending speculation that Rose had joined with another of similar fate. In spite of his disappointment, he remained optimistic that she would be found waiting to be discovered in a situation illusive to those searching, including himself.

With daylight a consideration, it's fading given notice. The normally well-lit highway darkening, the storm having severed power lines strung from the utility poles that lined the highway, the effects that of a domino. Knowing a night search would be impossible, he painfully ended his search, leaving the highway emotionally spent.

"Continue holding on" he silently begged of her. "I'll find you," challenging himself and the increasing odds. During the drive home, harboring befuddlement by Tasha's unusual behavior, George hoped sleep would provide a better focus when they returned the following daybreak. The driver who shared in the emotional swings of the day would be available and agreed to update his sympathetic boss with their lack of success and of his continuing need.

All Rose had done through the sun brightened day, ignoring freezing temperatures, was to awaken and respond repeatedly to low flying helicopters. Gritting her teeth in pain, she would move limply to stand in her clearing, accomplished by her snow plowing exit door. Ankle deep in snow, shouting at the top of her lungs, waving her arms frantically at the helicopters, begging for their notice before veering off. Teary eyed as once again she remained unseen. Slumping dejectedly in her car, knowing her chances would be greater if the sunroof were open. In a reflex reaction, notwithstanding her last discouraging attempt she again tried to start the mechanism it's reaction repeating the last failure, refused to open, mechanically inoperable by the elements, stubbornly frozen. After resting and tending to her duties, her confinement getting to her, she braved the cold nightfall, ignoring her pain, she again stood outside the open door whipped by the wind carrying clouds of loosened snow, shifting from one foot to the other in the snow: easing the pain of her swollen foot, dissipating the cold momentarily with movement. Wiping her face of the cold moisture, she watched for the second night, the sun declining in the west ushering in an earthly night of darkness. A disappointing ending of her wishes for recovery, remaining hopeful, the light of tomorrow a beacon in finding her.

Her attention was now drawn to the use of artificial light, the haphazard movement of vehicles headlights moving to and fro. Windshield wiper blades electronically raising and dropping, their resonance temporarily dominating the sound of their propelling or idling engines, the din muting the shouted instructions and voice commands of workers communicating with one another in a cacophony of an orchestrated recovery. Witnessing as she had all day the cars and trucks victimized by the storm being driven or towed away, she was wishful that hers was one of them. The next morning recovery continued all around her, yet her life threatening predicament ironically had not been noticed, straining her belief of recovery. She could see and hear the helicopters swooping down onto the highway but only briefly in her location if at all. No knowing why, she prayed they would find a reason to expand and intensify their search into her area. Missing the times when they finally did sweep over, she awakened from sleep with a start, dejectedly too late to try for their attention, unaware that the visible portion of her car remained identified as insignificant metal debris left over from the storm, too far off the highway to be anything else.

Depressed and frustrated, angrily she again resorted to shouting, her throat not fully recovered from her last effort, completely raw. Angrily she held her hand to the car's horn, an irrational action its elevated pitch muted by the snow that encased the front end of her car. What did consequence was a battery drain, futile to her use, it's signal obviously out of range in this nullifying environment, increasing her frustration. Frantic, she turned on the engine. After one unresponsive click of failure, it engaged in cold spasms.

"Thank God," she said weakly, being heard by no one but her creator.

Clutching her raw throat, she slumped dejectedly onto the back seat, the stark reality and irony of help so close yet so far away manifested a smothering helplessness, choking off confidence in her imminent recovery. Her will yielding, raising the specter of a shortened life, its paradox; her dying unnoticed while rebirth and life was going on around her. Her salvation unreachable brought agonized tears at being denied. She was frightened that she would die alone, found when the snow melted, in all irony by the same Highway Department workers who were now so close to reaching her. With her death a certainty with the loss of her will, resisting she again fought surrender, rekindling the will to survive the ordeal of another night, cold and alone, awaiting daybreak and it's promise of warmth and opportunity for recovery reclaiming her. She wiped her tear-filled eyes, a new resolve committed to survive to be tested. In her darkness, her only light the voicing of beseeching prayers to God, helping her live through the night.

The night became silent as the snowplows completed their work. Migrant clouds, in advance of the next weather system deposited another two inches of snow and sleet to greet her as she awoke to the rumblings of returning snowplows. At that moment, Rose, her mind dulled by her ordeal, failed to recognize the scenarios significance and importance.

~

Having gone to bed early, the need for rest pressing, the ringing of the phone woke George with suddenness, ending his recouping prematurely. It was 11:30 PM by his night stand clock, well before his alarm was scheduled to go off. It could only be an official calling, insisted at any hour with news of his wife. Apprehensive under the circumstances, he picked up his wireless extension during the second ring.

"Hello," George said with early morning hoarseness.

"It's me, George, Evelyn Hughes."

"Evelyn Hughes," he said, suddenly awake. Exasperated that she would call at this hour, not the time for a supportive call he thought testily, forcing himself to remain cordial in advance of what he expected would be her inquiry regarding Rose's well being. Impatient to abbreviate her call, curtailing his eruption he volunteered, "I have no further word on Rose's situation. I'm helping in the search… Resuming again at daylight… We'll find her," the tone of his words confident – defiant, not submitting to lessening possibilities as the days of her missing accumulated.

"Oh, George, I'm so sorry… I feel so responsible."

"Responsible?" he interjected, confused at first then subdued, her words assumed to be an attempt in sharing his grief. Yet he questioned, "How could it be your fault?"

"You don't under… drove me… the storm…" her wording garbled, fragmented as she sobbed on the verge of hysteria.

Aroused by her inference his tone now cathartic, "Calm down. I don't understand what you're saying," recognizing his patience needed tolerance he deliberately withheld his exasperation, to coax what appeared to be vital information, unable to be expressed meaningfully in her highly emotional state. Bringing him to full attention, his muscles tense as he waiting for her to gain control, giving a clearer meaning to her words.

She choked back a sob, struggling for control. "My cars battery went dead in the clubs parking lot… Rose volunteered to drive me home," she hastened breathing heavily, in need of pausing for his admonition to take hold, steadying her, "Both of us thinking there was plenty of time before the strength of the storm hit." Effective, the essence of her words he no longer misunderstood. "We were wrong. It came sooner than expected, making the drive slow and difficult." she reflected.

Staves interrupting "Your home?" his voice incredulous.

"Yes, my home. I couldn't call you sooner as I was snowbound with the phone lines down and no electricity. My phone service and electricity has just been restored- shockingly learning from the local television news that a Rose Staves was among the missing, " she said tearfully remorseful.

It hit like a thunderbolt, exciting his heart rate, critiquing within himself. No wonder my Tasha behaved so erratically. We've been searching in the wrong area. Tasha knew it, I wasn't getting the message. How could I have missed what she was telling me? No wonder she hasn't been found, all that time I using Tasha in the wrong area, he criticized.

"Your call is a tremendous help," he practically shouted. "I've got to go now, Evelyn. We'll explain it to you later, " he said hurriedly "I've got some work to do."

Tasha, hearing the excitement in his voice, left her sentry post at the living room bow window, barking excitedly, leaped up upon his chest, her tail wagging non-stop, ears back, smiling as only Huskies can do. Her body language acknowledging he wasn't disappointed in her, happily accepting his words of praise.

It would prove impossible to return to sleep, laying in bed weighing the implications of what had transpired. He knew from reports that the section of highway from Cedar Road to Evelyn Hughes exit had been cleared of trucks and cars, matching the section he worked on, leaving little doubt that his wife had skidded off the road beyond the median. But where? Evelyn Hughes' phone call and Tasha's mysterious behavior pointing, unbeknownst until today, her route home that stormy night was diverted and extended. Somewhere during her return claimed her, overwhelmed and invisible. But where? There just was no way of knowing just how far she had driven that night. His new information and concerns he shared with the police and highway department, collectively deciding that the search would continue north of Cedar Road while he Tasha and her extraordinary senses participate in the ongoing search south of Cedar, ending at Evelyn Hughes exit. He expressed faith and trust in Tasha's abilities, certain she was right but not strong enough to dissuade continuing the search north of Cedar, if other possibilities existed, his zealousness guarded against costing his wife's life.

The tow truck driver arrived as scheduled at 6:00 AM The weight of the situation for potential tragedy overwhelmed George Staves, his normal steeled and guarded countenance overcome by the effects of lack of sleep and torment. His voice hoarse straining his listeners, continually expressing confidence to Tasha and the driver an outcome of his wife's recovery, notwithstanding the ravages of time under extreme conditions taking a physically damaging toll, if not death itself. Prevailing: his faith in God, his wife, and Gods instrument: Tasha. As was his nature, even under duress, asked of the drivers and his family's well being, surprising and unexpected under the strain of the moment – receiving an emotional affirmative "Thank you for your interest and consideration," in support mentioning his family's prayers for Rose being uninjured and safe when they found her.

After entering the reopened highway still abounding with all types of snow removal equipment at work, including salt spreading trucks, they drove south to Evelyn Hughes' exit, crossing over the highway overpass to re-enter the northbound lanes: the starting point of Rose's return home. Confirming immediately that the inside lane and its berm was cleared for as far as he could see, freeing his search exclusively to the median and it's adjoining ground.

The median this far south claimed significant acreage in separating the highway, before narrowing further north, contouring to the available land designated for highway construction. Reducing the depth of the median to where the driving lanes in both directions were minimally separated. It's boundaries east and west were commercial and residential developments

The highway functionally operational, a reluctant incision amid the frozen landscape, it's healing conditions allowing safe passage for the travel of vehicles in building numbers, in sharp contrast to the inundated frozen nearby landscape feet away turned into a tundra, threatening death to those that traveled it's surface exposed, confused, and desperate. His depiction temporary, dispatching those thoughts quickly, assuring himself his wife would recognize the danger… never considering the disorientation of injury. She must be here he impassioned. But where? He questioned. He trusted Tasha to supply the answer.

As planned, Tasha and Staves would walk the median while the truck followed close behind, determined to inspect every inch of roadbed close up, including the adjoining ground. The median, cleared earlier, now contained the additional snow of the early hours before dawn, further layering it's bordering created foothills of snow and ice. As they pulled onto the median, a car bearing the official seal of the Highway Department pulled to a stop in front of them, blocking their path.

"Why are you driving on the median? It's only to be used for emergency repairs and emergencies. It's dangerous and against the law. You could cause an accident," the official said testily as traffic drove by underscoring his concerns.

"It is an emergency," Staves said interrupting, introducing himself while explaining the circumstances.

The inspector immediately showed recognition, remembering that his marching orders for the day included an alert for a missing woman reported to have driven the highway during the height of the storm.

"My understanding was that the search area was further north around the Cedar Road exit."

"That's right," Staves responded, "but my latest information is that she started further south than first believed, having dropped off a friend."

Hearing this, the inspector went back to his car and returned with a slip of paper which he handed to Staves.

"Here," he said. "It's a special authorization permit. Show this if you get stopped again. I've also included my cell phone number in case you need help," he said expanding his cooperation. Then adding as an afterthought, "I'll also alert the varying township police along your route. Good luck. My people are alerted. I certainly will keep a lookout."

Staves shook his hand warmly, acknowledging his help and well wishes. Before returning to the tow truck to his awaiting driver and a very anxious Tasha- in parting gave the inspector his cell phone number, expanding the network.

Starting out with Tasha under leash restraint, his mind building rationale: since the median nor the berm had not given up Rose's car, she must be off the highway itself. Believing, he followed an agreeable Tasha and climbed the man made foothills of snow that lined the highway. The snow crusting further from the nightly freeze, made it easier for Tasha to traverse, while Staves, his weight a factor, occasionally broke through, forced with difficulty and strain to regain his footing on firmer snow, pausing every one hundred yards or so for needed rest, his arduous efforts free flowing his perspiration. His minimally protected face required his constant attention to prevent the sweat beads from entering his eyes, blurring his vision or freezing upon his face.

The helicopter company had been alerted by a call from Staves's cell phone. A helicopter, expanding the area of search appeared, hovering and moving slowly along the terrain earlier given token search, inhibited by blinding moving clouds of snow vortexed by the blades.

~

Before daybreak Rose awoke with a start, bringing an end to the most difficult night of her ordeal. The quieting stillness alerted her that the car's engine had stalled. She tried to bring the engine back to life. The battery doing its job failed in its attempt to ignite the fuel. Looking at the gauge, terror stricken, she realized she had run out of gas, a death dealing circumstance. Her weakening condition could not tolerate spending another night under worsened exposure.

"It has to be today," she cried openly, wrapping herself tightly within her mink coat. Her mind in turmoil, an imagination projecting fatalistic scenarios of impending doom, creating doubts that she was witnessing helicopters, and Highway Department snowplows, all hallucinations she cried in self-pity. Her fatality a certainty if not found this day – death would claim her, to be found in the spring when the snows had melted for her sighting, preserved in death by the very elements that participated in killing her. Calling attention and significance were her nose and ears, deprived of heat for God knows how long, first numb, were beginning to tingle, she knew as the first signs that her circulation was given way to frostbite.

Tired mentally, no longer physically able to keep awake, the next three hours she slipped in and out of a nightmare filled sleep. Spent rather than rested, she awoke with a start. Admonishing herself for overlooking the significance of the passing night not being as dark as her first night; the highway lights, with electricity restored, were operational. Its full meaning now understood, she sat up suddenly, leaving her gloom where she lay, realizing that her location could not have been known as phone lines had to be down, preventing Evelyn Hughes from calling her husband. Rose guessed that Evelyn had to be snowbound these past two days. Guided by optimism, she was sure her husband now had to know, leading the charge to find her.

Turning on the radio brought her confirmation, reporting that new information had come to light, expanding the search area for her. All municipalities services reacting, as well as the helicopters hired by Mr. Staves, the husband of the missing Rose Staves.

She was resting after assuring herself that the rear door still opened when she heard the loud thump thumping signature of helicopters flying overhead, this time louder than ever as their search included her area at altitudes as close to the ground as the highway wiring would allow. Once again, the pilots saw no reason to alter their opinions: the partially obscured sunroof remained confidently judged as sheet metal debris. Rose, standing in her escape path with arms flailing, arrived too late to say otherwise.

Before returning to the car, she saw one of her prayers had been answered; the caked ice on the car's roof responding to her repeated blows from the golf club given assist by slowly rising temperatures began to splinter- melting had begun. Rather than wait for the water to trickle off freely, she anxiously hurried back into the car, knowing the engine need not be turned on for the sunroof to operate. With only the briefest of pauses, the sunroof opened with a lurch, freeing the remaining ice fragmented into her lap.

"Thank God," she exalted, elevated, anxious for the next helicopter pass.

~

George Staves, Tasha and the tow truck driver first heard, then saw the rotating wings of the helicopters banking and hovering for closer looks, sending swirling clouds of snow in their direction.

Having covered miles of highway, George was exhausted, Tasha pulling at her leash aggressively, unsuccessful they had traveled within a mile of the Cedar Road interchange, he facing creeping doubt, questioning his judgment in over rating Tasha's abilities: finding Rose a certainty. How could he have been so confident in her special gift, the conditions overwhelming- diminishing her extraordinary faculties – abandoning her in disappointment. He, while limited to eyesight, participating in the search-recovery failure about to be a reality, strained for optimism. He having the presence of mind to agree the recovery effort be carried out as two pronged, with communications by cell phone flowing between the two groups. Desperate, gave them more credence in finding Rose to their greater numbers. Communicating this conclusion, if their efforts remain thwarted they planned to make one more pass collectively after meeting up at the Cedar Road ramp. With each passing moment,, the effects of failure insidious, time at exposure prolonged, deleteriously acting upon her being.

Nothing more could be planned or arranged- now retrospective of his abandonment, understand his desperation. In pain he looked pleadingly at Tasha for restoration of his confidence in her abilities, just as capable under conditions well beyond her previous scope of measurement. Still wanting to believe her screening of the highways parallel landscape and beyond were within her mystique. Demonstrated as they neared the completion of her task, her success imminent. Her test of discovering still before her. Rose would be found, Tasha having played a defining role.

Tasha, covered with powdered snow, clear of the engulfing white spray would not move, standing still muscles taut, her nostrils flexing, indicative of finding a familiar scent carried in the swirling whiteness. Her tail perpendicular as a bird dog pointing at the prey, remindful of an other event of her discovering. He had been premature. He looked in the direction she was pointing and saw nothing but snow given a free ride in the winds of the helicopter blades. Staves moved closer, venturing into deeper snow only to sink to his waist while Tasha continued to move cautiously but freely. Intelligently close to the ground, Tasha's legs splayed as far apart as she could place them, as her ancestors had done, purposefully creating the weight distribution advantage of a snowshoe across the crusted surfaces of the snow – leaving only slight impressions.

It would be extremely difficult for him to go any further, literally having to wade waist high in the exhausting snow. Tasha demonstrated she could continue, the snows crust deep enough to support her weight. With trepidation, the essence of time influencing, Staves decided not to wait until Tasha's discovery became visible to him, he committed a course of action. Prayerful he was right, he released a straining Tasha, leaving her leash still attached to her collar, a lifeline if she sunk below the surface of the snow.

Rose's survival instincts were recharged. Her chances vastly improved, her yoke of circumstances lifted, no longer fearful, her breathing expansive and easier, quieting her, her heart rate accelerated in the excitement of being spotted by the searching helicopters, who at the moment were over the most northern part of her search route. Thankful to God her confidence increased, verbalizing it would be a matter of time before she would be with her family again. With the sunroof remaining open, exhausted from her sleepless ordeal, not daring to move from her seated position, bearing the numbing cold she awaited the return of the helicopters. What happened next would be impossible to forget as witnessed, remaining forever indelible in one's mind as long as one would live… an incredible incident bordering on the impossible, savored and fitting for world wide publication, emotionally overwhelming her. A curious scratching sound on the roof of the car was what she heard first. Rising up wearily to find its source, was immediately set upon by a howling snow covered Tasha leaping through the opened sunroof, lavishing kiss after wet kiss of excited joy upon her. Rose, in a state of shock with her quickly turning fortunes, tearfully returned her affection at the reunion, freeing her cries of "Tasha, my beauty, you've found me."

Moments earlier George Staves watched with deep concern as Tasha negotiated the crusted snow on her downward then upward traverse of the built-up drifts. All going well until she, in reaching the peak of the furthermost mound, disappeared. Horrified, he screamed instructions for the driver to start releasing the winch cable that he had wrapped around his waist as his safety line, preparing to wade after the disappearing Tasha. Her sudden visual loss panicked him. He assumed the worst had befallen her shouting, "Tasha, Tasha."

Having descended ten feet down the hill, he saw a golf club periscope through the top of the mound that had claimed Tasha. At first completely incomprehensible then ecstatic, realizing it was Rose signaling with his remembered golf club her hidden location. Not in need, he struggled with the help of the winch line, he retraced his footsteps to the median. Being out of breath did not delay him in pulling out his cell phone, gasping excitedly to the helicopter pilots that Rose had been located by Tasha, ordering their immediate return to where his tow truck was parked, using it as a marker for their low level search, the car still hidden. He also notified the police and highway departments for their needed assistance.

Rose's words of lavishing praise finally stilled Tasha's excitement, heard the approaching helicopters. This time she was ready, with Tasha at her side, standing painfully on the front seat, head and arms through the sunroof waving enthusiastically. She was easily spotted, shockingly her sunroof no longer mistaken as storm debris.

While Staves watched the helicopters hovering over the site whipping up clouds of snow, his cell phone rang. It was the incredulous lead pilot relating what appeared to be a healthy Rose with Tasha in the car with her. His disbelief aside, the pilot instructed Rose through various hand signals what they were prepared to do in order to free her.

Rose, complying, closed the sunroof and her escape door, sealing off the clouds of snow from entering the car, given new life by the vortex. The noise anticipated, surrounding Tasha with her fur coat she then placed her gloved hands over her ears muffling the decibel level of a full throttled engine increasing the revolutions per minute of the accelerated blade wings cutting through the air with it's whining ear deafening voiceprint. Its purpose: the downdraft easily blowing off the crusting snow, revealing when the snow clouds settled elsewhere. The missing car, its place of consequence exposed. Expanding their mission, proceeding to create a path, widening it as much as necessary to assure passage of the car when extracted by the tow trucks wench, taking a half hour to complete the operation as anxious onlookers waited. Staves now joined by the newly arrived police, their parked cars flashing notice, in a psychedelic collage. With a sense of urgency, the Highway Department supervisor shouted out instructions to the tractor operators now manning shovels to put the finishing touches on the path to the tethered car, allowing greater ease hauling it back onto the highway.

As all four wheels of the car rolled safely on the highway, Staves hardly restrained himself almost tearing the car door open, to assist an unsteady Rose from the car, led by Tasha. Her ordeal over, she collapsed teary-eyed into his arms. Equally exhausted, they slipped to their knees, Tasha in their midst, part of the celebration, watching protectively their open fervor for one another. She lovingly included in the reunion, expressions of emotion running full circle. From their kneeling position Rose acknowledged tearful thanks to God for His blessings and intervention. Arising from their exhaustion, having gifted their love for one another, they had used their fatigued position as one of supplication in acknowledging the benevolent power of God.

George supported her within his strong arms, positioned at arms' length; eyes fixed searching for her ordeals effects. The initial joy of the reunion over, seeing her drawn and nervously twitching, deciding she was in need of professional assessment and treatment, particularly after she mentioned the warm tingling sensation in her feet and hands.

Watching and cheering happily at their reunion were the Highway Department supervisor, his workers and police officers from the highway township and city police departments. Within minutes the highway was sealed off accommodating the landing of one of the helicopters. Filming the event were the crews of covering local television- arms of the major networks for national exposure. With highway travel temporarily at a standstill; three hundred feet back, out of breath members of the print media rushed for interviews, as the helicopter, bearing passengers Rose, George and Tasha whirled away by it's rotating wings for the short flight to University Hospital. Grumbling they might miss their deadlines the print media reporters, joined with their photographers, struggled to get back to their cars to resume the chase.

From the helicopter, heading for the hospital, George called his tearfully relieved daughter Rosanne to give her the good news, telling her to call her out of state sister and brother, asking her to meet them at University Hospital.

Concluding the rescue, the tow truck driver engaged by George, after hooking up Rose's car, towed it back to Fred Nieland's Gas Station for servicing, certain to be the center of attraction for days to come.

The University Hospital's emergency room doctor in his follow up examination, concluded the prescribed intravenous treatments bringing her temperature back to normal, replacing lacking electrolytes. Her recovery was so rapid she could leave the hospital that very evening provided she had plenty of bed rest for the next forty-eight hours, followed by a visit to her doctor.

They were home, the threat over, resuming their lives together. Critiquing the incident, invariably led to Tasha's amazing demonstration, inconceivable that other dogs to come would stand taller. "To think I doubted her he admitted. She's a legend in the making," unashamedly prideful to anyone listening. With her remarkable accomplishments building, no elitist theory would suffice or resist challenge, she's arguably a possessor of consciousness beyond intuitiveness, joining the ranks of man.

~

George Staves,' of today, his eyes tearing after reliving the emotionally draining experience with Tasha playing such a key role. Never more pronounced was her extraordinary instincts on display in finding his wife, her success preventing devastation of his family, insuring it remain intact for years to come. He knew he would again revisit this event, it highly charged and stressful it melded them as one mind and heart.

George Staves of the past would learn in the aftermath, the event would bolster him for what was yet to come in Tasha's lifetime… a strength needed when challenged by the tragedy of her life ending.

Under command the transporter revved up its engine, readying the time traveler further journey, moving amongst the building blocks that established Tasha's true essence, a memorable remarkable totality within her life's calendar.

ten

The presence of Tasha overseeing the school bus stop in her view, made immediate by cleverly manipulating between her teeth the draw strings that parted the drapes – an easy task for the precocious Tasha. Positioned on the shelf of the living room bow window, staged her over seeing, her head resting between her paws watching the children intently was a guaranteed occurrence. Responding; the children waved at morning pickup time and when disembarking upon return. Tasha, self-appointed guardian of the children's well being; amazingly, known to react troubled if those greeting her in the morning did not match those retuning, whimpering anxiously until they were accounted for. Her guardianship was well known amongst the children of the Staves's neighborhood who bragged to school mates of their champion, increasing Tasha's celebrity. In inquiring of their parents and school supervision, Tasha's charges came to understand how extraordinary she was, demonstrating an uncanny ability to recognize the school buses diesel fumes in advance of its arrival, stemmed from an elevated sense of smell together with, her measuring the passage of time. Her appearance in wait, always an anticipated delight during the children's bus ride home. Tasha's instincts in play she "saw" the bus from her seated windowed position before it turned down the street to become visible. Her presence looked to as an expected foreteller giving assurance to awaiting parents. On those occasions the bus was delayed by traffic, anxiety prevented her seated position of oversight, to pace frantically back and forth on her drape parted stage panting nervously. Her reassuring demeanor returning when the bus was within her sensing range, telling to those waiting: seeing her at rest in her reassuring pose… a bellwether for the parents.

Somehow she knew, perceptive in differentiating an active school day, spring breaks, summer vacation, weekends and holidays. George Staves attributed her keen senses to cleverly discerning the scent of new exclusively worn school clothing, the assembling of greater numbers waiting for the school bus. With the beginning of a new term the word "school" created a dichotomy; pitting the children excited for the new term and those moaning resentment for the loss of summer friends.

When a second bus was added to accommodate preschool age children, excitedly beginning their adventures in school learning, Tasha was quick to include them as part of her surveillance, her watch now twice a day. Typically disturbing the average canine: glaring sun rays and searing lightning flashes preceding crashing thunder, never dissuading her from her first priority – watching for the neighborhood children.

Tasha's waiting at the picture section of the bow window, a continuation of the deceased Zuni's practice of shepherding, had become *cause celebré*. Casual, cordial chit chat between parents, included Tasha's commonplace appearance, not to the children, exploding when spotting her, screaming, "there she is!"

As the children got awkwardly older, advancing in maturity mattered not to Tasha, her display of love just as openly intense. The past practice of an equal response a casualty with some of the more senior children, their maturation bringing with it an eagerness to demonstrate a sophistication among their peers, of no longer fixating on animals. Others showing a feigned aloofness, copycats of herding lobbyist's, secretly enjoying the pleasures of yesterday's innocence, their excitement hidden and private. Programmed to be distant in public to Tasha's demonstrative welcome. Secretly pained internally by their held back public display, recovering its reinforcement in private, freed to embrace Tasha lovingly, avoiding exposure. Their response to the confluence, matching their precocious peers, protecting their conditioned emergence from a status of adolescence.

The abbreviated Staves family, Phyllis, Rose and George did not escape Tasha's positioned vigil until all were accounted for, akin to the always watchful library lion, its molded expression anticipating the return of her truth seeking charges. When Rosanne and Edward were married and Phyllis nearing acceptance of an out-of-state job, Tasha knew immediately- George and Rose's body language and lack of angst, a signature of peace and acceptance reigning within the den. The condition to adapt quickly to the change in the number of charges left for her watchful eyes. Not that she didn't miss any of them, or wouldn't, as instinctively she knew that a change in lifestyle was inevitable with the approach of adulthood. First Rosanne and then Edward moving out, with Phyllis' independence nearing, to become visitors when no longer in the den.

Could she have likened the human maturing process to that of her breed? Her brethren? Equally compelled and expected, leaving the pack to test their own courage and resourcefulness in establishing their own den and social order, continuing the cycle. Could she sense the obvious parallel? George Staves, her advocate, would be the first in shouting resounding yes's, so strong was his belief in the intelligence of this amazing dog gifted to them by God. So clear was the message she embodied: "Conscious life and awareness were not limited to the human species exclusively."

The school year over, trees fully in display acknowledging nature's seasonal resurrection, ambient temperatures preceding days of taxing summer heat, it's oppression eventually responded to by pitying spontaneous cooling storms. The summer, part of a continuum, a connection, as were three occurrences effecting and shaping the lives of many of Tasha's watchers. Each event interconnected, a seed yielding another seed, rooting a sequenced blossoming of phenomenal implications. The beginning incident; children of the area, in need of an outlet, perhaps starting out as a game to evoke excitement in the others, repeatedly declaring Tasha at the bow window whether she was there or not. Gaining pleasure from the reaction successful among those easily manipulated, followers not wanting to be left out in a show of solidarity, regardless of how many times they were fooled, the bullying continuing to intimidate, fabricating Tasha's presence. Snowballing into a second manifestation occurring after days of tiring repetitiveness, suddenly the game turned on it's own accord, eyes being manipulated distinguishing a true facsimile, a sighting presenting itself contingent on the time of day, the sighting dependent upon shadows cast by the westward moving sun through trees taking on differing shapes as it yielded to the wind. Very real in their eyes, this found imagery enfolding the former purveyors of practical jokes, the tables turned, joining their influenced followers as equal partners.

The inertia of this shadowy discovery in the bow window, a status symbol for those sharing the experience, led to an outgrowth of invention and exaggeration. Distanced children being driven by their parents, with their panorama undergoing rapid changes, living the experience of those initiated, imagined Tasha in the window, so dependent, so indelibly fixed and expectant was Tasha's image in their minds eye even though the conditions in many instances were not conducive.

If that wasn't excitement enough, the third marrying incident, the strangest of them all, occurred within weeks of the children returning to school, mysteriously, the positioned sun casting shadows was no longer necessary in creating Tasha's silhouette. A phenomenon had occurred, Tasha's image could be seen by the children in the glass itself. Ecstatic with their importance, they shared the impossibility of their discovery in self-aggrandizement, all listening were captivated by the occurrence, the tellers spreading their privileged word, suggesting those who shared in the experience were visiting another world, frenzying those being addressed to visit and experience. Effectively using their tools of networking – excitable words of mouth – as only children can exhibit, word spread beyond the immediate neighborhood, to other schools bringing the curious from miles around, hopefully to bear witness.

Tasha's silhouette in the bow window took on a life of it's own. Parents responded to the proclamations of their children, skeptical at first, then inquisitive, the sophistication of adulthood bringing misgivings. Seeing this as an opportunity for a closer bond in discovering their children's not-to-be-denied vision, they witnessed Tasha's imagery, even when the sighting was an invention for some.

There were others, adding to the growing numbers; welcoming zealots for the surreal heralding Tasha's amazing silhouette as a glorifying paranormal event; the product of dimensions that today's science can only hypnotized. A still life portrait etched in glass by mysterious means, devoid of color and tone but rich in unmistakable form and geometry. Revisiting adults sharing the event were scoffed at by cynics succumbed to doubts of what they had seen. In need of a reality check, they revisited the site. Again finding Tasha's extraordinary display. All turning to Tasha's cellular being penetratingly, her reality, while compelling, became secondary, her shadowy manifestation the rage. A marriage of heart beating substance with a one-dimensional silhouette of unknown origin becoming a singular entity.

As more and more viewings took place, not all were sightings. Those satisfied scoffing the denied as astigmatic, energizing into its own gravitational force. A building multitude, feeding upon itself, considered themselves privileged. Newspapers, aroused by the sensational aspects of the story quoted a noted physicist, sensationalizing, advancing two hypothetical possibilities: the image that of static electrical energy and compound forming chemical reactions, released by the mysterious mystical workings of nature intervening to create a life form, equally possible electrical energies attracting when the conditions were right, mostly invisible residue vapors from many sources, drifting in the still air, blanketing moistened particle matter having foiled the windows sealing gaskets, laying trapped between the double panes of glass, combining to present a stereogram to those highly focused to extract the vision. Concluding their report with the rejoinder, "regardless of source potential all you have to do is to stare at that window and the silhouette will appear."

With Tasha's celebrity status increasing, a bewildered George and Rose Staves, still not witnessing Tasha's image were not persuaded of its phenomenon, continuing attempts at confirmation proved disappointing. To each other in privacy, their guarded conclusion was to dismiss those who bore witness, their analysis: a Pied Piper syndrome persuading followers with an overly active imagination. Not easily dismissed however were those highly regarded in the community: doctors, lawyers and teachers coming forward with their unsolicited acknowledgments, forcing them to other considerations, in search of reasons that kept them unfulfilled.

The respected religious leaders opportune, declaring the image as a message from the Creator: to live a miracle, birthing prayers in reinforcement of their religious commitment. Cajoling those fallen: a religious lifeline encouraged to reach for a manifestation by God.

Frustrated and questioning, the Staves were still among the missing. Resolving nonetheless never to openly express any of their doubts to the children gushing with excitement. Rather than damper their uplifting experience and risk alienation, they decided to follow their lead feigning their sightings, notwithstanding continuing to come away denied, still in pursuit of answers for their isolation.

Hoping to bring closure to their internal dilemma, they rationalized the imagery of Tasha had escaped them because they had the real thing living among them, it's heart beating, it's blood pulsing, her life real, her genetic code functioning; absent in the inanimate specter. They had lived through her amazing exploits first hand. They need not become the adoptive parents of a shadow or image to be a part of her life. Tasha was them and they were her, celebrating together in life, not imagery. Their rational forced by convenience, a shortcoming, unable to bridge to Tasha's total experience by spanning the void. Awaiting them a incident, finally bringing initiation, their eyes finding the additional focus for the specter to appear.

The squeal of the brakes of two busses intermingled with the excited voices of children interrupted their watchfulness of the early morning walkers in curiosity pausing in front of their bow window, repeating yesterdays scrutiny. Fully expectant, the ring of their doorbell announced the phenomenon was about to entertain another visiting school, they being asked to be hosts.

Tasha, who usually barked and rushed reactively to the front door at perceived intruders, strangely reacted quietly differently, flaring her nostrils to take and exhale greater volumes of informative air. Satisfied, the visiting represented no threat she dutifully joined his pace as he walked to answer the doorbell. "Good morning," was his cordial words to his visitor before his attention was preempted by the disembarking of a fully occupied bus with children of special needs: legs braced on crutches that moved by dragging feet side to side, atrophied legs moved by straining arms and hands to give motion to wheelchairs, their only means of movement. Others of the assembling group, their affliction the result of sustained soaring body temperatures, somehow escaped death but were forever scarred by an underdeveloped brain and dysfunctional vocal chords. Completing the group were those children arriving at birth deprived, who when recognized would speak in familiar surroundings, freed from intimidating newness cowering them to guttural sounds more consistent with prehistoric man, still evolving meaning.

This was the assembly of fate, wounded children gathered on the sidewalk in front of the Staves home, their supervision presenting opportunity to share or stir the sweeping excitement of Tasha's silhouette, holding out hope of at least a glimmer of recognition amongst some of the mentally challenged, a moment in time for satisfaction and strained gratifications, responding in their own manner. Sadly anticipating there would be among the group, those fogged to incomprehension apart and bewildered, the best their teachers and escorts could hope for in their isolation was mirroring the display of excitement of the other children without an understanding of why. That outcome, hoped to happen, a welcomed step in broadening the narrow focus of their infirmities.

"Mr. Staves," the lead teacher asked after waiting patiently for his return from his sweeping study, "I'm Mrs. Selkirk from the Holyoke School for Disadvantaged Children."

With the door open, a visible Tasha at his side prompted squeals of delight from those empowered. With his history of serving on the school board, he immediately knew of the Holyoke School as being run by dedicated professionals and volunteers teaching and training handicapped children from five to thirteen years of age.

"What can I do for you, Mrs. Selkirk?" he asked cordially, already knowing the reason for the visit.

"We are on a field trip, Mr. Staves. Please forgive me for not asking you sooner but late developing circumstances forced our originally scheduled site to be cancelled. With your permission, I'd like the children to share in the excitement that is sweeping all the schools – seeing firsthand your Tasha's image in the bow window. That's all these challenged children able to express themselves have talked about, ever since word got around. It would be a terrible blow to them if denied, particularly after the disappointing cancellation. May I have your permission?"

"Of course, be our guests." Rose Staves her smile sincere and understanding as she looked at the children of a thousand faces.

"We intended to restrict them to the sidewalk but their excitement could carry them onto your lawn for a closer look," she said apologetically.

"It wouldn't be the first time. I wouldn't want to interfere with their excitement." George Staves answered reassuring her.

Smiling at his understanding, she added, "I promise we will be very careful of your flower beds."

She avoided saying anything about the foot tracking and the paths of the wheelchairs marking a lawn still saturated by recent rain. Mrs. Selkirk read people well, recognizing the Staves's countenance empathetic, a display of "a small price to pay" for these children of misfortune for the joy this experience would bring them. Looking past a dedicated Mrs. Selkirk, the Staves's could see the physically handicapped children wide-eyed in anticipation, looked to for example, those shied by their retardation following their lead, not quite understanding why. The others being coaxed to leave their confusion, the escorts establishing a game appealing to their instincts for play, rather than questionable levels of intelligence. It was opportunity to test their reactions.

With Tasha, the warmth of the day prompting, choosing to remain independent, children at the site nothing new, unless stimulated would remain indoors. Rose and George moved freely among the staring children awaiting fulfillment, marveling at the dedication of the teachers, and assisting parents.

With the children's energy levels raised, it became more difficult to contain them as they pushed amongst themselves on the fronting sidewalk. Excitement, curiosity, and rote reaction from the confused. Their caution, "to be careful" forgotten, George and Rose actively encouraging, "Don't worry about the lawn. Go ahead get up close. Have the children move freely Mrs. Selkirk. Mrs. Staves and I will enjoy their reaction."

Mrs. Selkirk nodded appreciatively and produced from her hand a folder containing the cutout silhouettes of a dog, a horse and a rabbit; visual aids that she would use as confirmation for the children rendered mute and auditory challenged and those who believed in their invisibility, returning from vacating their world. The physically handicapped, being intellectually cognizant, were purposefully selected to go first along with the Down Syndrome children of limited maturity. Of those, children on crutches who refused assistance, their feet splayed wide for better balance in the difficult to maneuver grass, fearlessly approaching the bow window, an assistant hovering close by.

"Concentrate," shouted Mrs. Selkirk. "Focus steadily. It will come together within seconds." Her encouragement brought the excited exclamation, "There she is. I can see her. It's Tasha," they screamed to one another, some later than others. They relished the moment longer than the others wished, provoking angry complaints from those waiting their turn. Finally giving way, they returned to the sidewalk as ordered, pleased with themselves as being able to share this defining moment on an equal basis with those not handicapped.

The mentally challenged went next, one by one, their escorts trying to defeat their wandering by resorting to holding their heads to view only straight ahead, hopefully for enough time for them to experience the sighting. One by one, they were shown the cutouts. Four out of the first five, when realizing what was being asked of them, selected the dog's silhouette. The fifth child, not in the least curious having spent the least amount of time concentrating, pointed to the rabbit, sure that he had matched what the other children had done.

Then came the children whose voices and hearing had been lost to the ravages of burning meningitis or encephalitis fever. They approached unescorted, fully mobile, brimming with confidence in their abilities, their faces quick to acknowledge their success, quickly pointing to the cutout of the dog.

Finally, it was the children of varying degrees of autism who were quick to attempt matching the other's successes, their brethren whose intelligence would continue to grow, unlike them, their intelligence was at it's peak.

The last, a holdout traveling other worlds was the recalcitrant severely autistic boy confined to a wheelchair, guided by an assisting mother, unaccountably finding interest and recall of the world before creation, where the earth's molten center core spewed to the surface, was beginning to crust. Formed were inanimate monoliths whose emitting gases of various chemical compounds would, when properly sequenced, combine to produce life in its most primitive and insignificant form that this bedeviled child, millenniums later found kindred. Not the complex world of today, multitudinous and bewildering, nothing simplified except when of mind, and not deliberately mute, his abilities to recall days of the week no matter how distanced in the past. His present thoughts veering far and distant straying not conducive to what was asked of him: the need for concentration. He approached the bow window unhappy with this strange environment, wishing to return to more familiar surroundings, to the safety of his own time warp. Rejecting his movement he moaned and shrieked, deliberately lolling his head from side to side, allowing lingering spittle to hang from his mouth, flinging his arms wildly, and screaming unapproachably. Not comprehending, he was a danger to himself exciting a concession, to be returned when one of the earlier children approached, one whom Staves now recognized as Lydia Santos, the Down Syndrome child of divorced neighbors, unaware that the future would bring them in contentious contact with one another in a controversy of far reaching implications. She, being all of five years old yet carrying the bearing of a protective mother, approached the disturbed child.

"Calm down," she ordered softly. "No one is going to hurt you, Scotty," referring to the boy by a derivative of his first name. Within seconds of Lydia's quiet admonishment, the boy's sobbing and head lolling stopped as he responded to her presence. It was immediately obvious that these two held a special bond for one another, nature's mistakes of differing levels providing the impetus for sharing a common bond. In her presence he knew safety, the imagined threats vaporizing. His face took on softness, his eyes without fear, brightened, his vision no longer threatening.

"I think, Mrs. Selkirk, it would help if Scotty were raised out of his wheelchair," Lydia offered.

"Here, let me help," George Staves volunteered unthinking, bending down to pick up the boy. The boy recoiled immediately, fear of the unexpected returning, venting his anxiety, he resumed his wailing.

Lydia Santos intervened again. "Scotty," she spoke forcefully, "he's a friend. He won't hurt you. He'll help you see. You know – what I talked about."

His moaning once again stopped, limpness came over him as he allowed George Staves to pick him up and approach the window, his head moving from right to left searching. Lydia encouraged him to focus. His body stiffened not out of fear of the unknown but a registering experience.

Mrs. Selkirk also guessed the telltale body language, rushing with confirmation silhouettes in hand, provoking another outburst. Scotty, flinging his arms wildly, put great strain on Staves' ability to hold him. This time his hysterics were not assuaged by Lydia's ministrations. His hands flaying out fending off his imaginary threat, suddenly he turned them upon himself pulling large clumps of hair from his head, indifferent to the pain, anesthetized by his compulsion.

Staves had clearly misunderstood, attributing his masochistic antics as symbolic of his affliction until he realized that his arms were not only flailing but pointing to the image of Tasha in the window.

Rose Staves also reading Scotty correctly, offered, "Perhaps he would be soothed by Tasha's presence – the real thing, not a cutout," moving quickly to bring Tasha from the house whereupon she, to everyone' astonishment, proceeded to assume the position of the image, amazingly to guide his confirmation, suggesting that she was aware of the window's silhouette.

Scotty, upon seeing Tasha, shocked the adults as he pointed to her and then back to the window, clearly establishing that he had seen the image. What misguided circuitry had temporarily righted itself for Scotty to make that connection? What bonded Tasha to this child of nature gone awry as she shared in the understanding that he was crying out for her, that he needed the respite of her reality before returning to his world of bleakness?

It was at that very moment of heart wrenching empathy the shielding curtain parted for the Staves'; finally sighting Tasha's image, their barriers of intellectual reasoning giving way to these children lost amongst themselves but not to God. Their penance served in the delay of experiencing what these unfortunate children had and now relished.

"Applaud the children," Rose Staves said recognizing the signs in her husband. Seeing Tasha's image was contagious. "We have them to thank."

Mrs. Selkirk hearing Rose's remarks smiled, she to a believer remarked as they gathered at the bus door before entering, the moment de-escalating "We haven't tracked up the lawn too badly. Foot marks and wheelchair tracks will disappear," she said apologetically. The children remained transfixed at the bow window and then back to a reposing Tasha under the Crabapple tree.

Under the guidance of Mrs. Selkirk and her assistants, the children were about to re-enter the bus for the return trip, when Tasha, for no apparent reason, began barking at Scotty, not in a threatening manner, but one of anxiousness getting everyones attention.

George tried to quiet Tasha, not understanding her sudden outburst. Turning his attention to Scotty, he immediately saw change taking place. He had stopped his head lolling as if in a vice while sweating profusely, his face contorting, drained of color. Suddenly, he stiffened as if an errant electrical charge had entered his body, flinging his head backward violently. All witnessing were aroused yet subdued, by his disturbing reaction, affliction related and expected. Quickly changing to alarm as an even greater surge propelled him forward convulsing onto the lawn. His entire body shaking. His legs kicking out at an unseen menace. The stain of released kidneys darkened the crotch area of his pants. Rushing to his assistance was Mrs. Selkirk and staff members, each assisting Scotty in his dreaded epileptic seizure.

In the days that followed, George and Rose reasoned that a suddenly alerted Tasha knew by whatever mysterious means, forewarning Scotty was about to have a seizure. They had heard of this phenomenon as being possible with some animals, gifted to foretell upcoming physical events, not only within a ravaged living body but within nature itself, secretly planning a cataclysmic event. Tasha, they were convinced, offered living testament of having this gift.

The time visiting contemporary George Staves, approximately ten years senior to himself at this time period, brightened as he knew this chapter in their lives was only part of what would be told, much more would be added to Tasha's mystique during her productive years. Those unfolding events to be relived as his memory rebirthing kaleidoscope, presented the original presentations. A scenario of sights and sounds that he was part of.

eleven

Prompted by newspapers, local radio and television accounts, Tasha's celebrity continued to grow. Her fame was like a wildfire, spreading beyond the local neighborhoods to surrounding communities represented in the parade of vehicles that visited the site. An ongoing invasion to which there was little defense. Paradoxically this type of organized inspection by the matured in contrast, brought relative peace during the school hours that kept the children occupied, the Staves family and their under-siege neighbors welcomed this brief respite. It was hoped that the passage of time would bring diminished interest.

It was under those circumstances that he and Rose welcomed the news that their daughter-in-law Francine, their son Edward's wife, had given birth to a baby girl, a new granddaughter named Victoria. It would be a timely visit, an opportunity for all of them to escape, including Tasha, leaving behind her silhouette to continue to acknowledge her mystique. They planned on driving, as the trip to New Jersey was relatively short – approximately eight hours. It would cover the coming Friday and the weekend, returning the following Monday. As had been his practice on previous trips when the house was left unoccupied, he notified the police of his plans and what lights would be left on in the house. Their next-door neighbors agreed to pick up the mail. Forgotten in their rush to leave, the rescheduling of newspaper delivery, judging of minimal impact as it only involved three days delivery; they rationalized. Perhaps in noticing, his neighbor would graciously pick them up along with the mail. Judged as probable, downplayed his omission, newspapers with old news taken of no real consequence – his second mistake as he would soon learn…

What followed was derived from police and newspaper accounts:

It was Saturday, approximately 9:00 o'clock in the evening. Heavily hanging dark clouds had moved into the area unleashing wind-blown sheets of rain, defeating pedestrians umbrella counter. During those moments the weather conditions so severe it limited surveillance, creating opportunities for stealth.

Amidst the heavy downpour they left the highway to search the nearby residential area practically empty of cars and pedestrians, the car circling the block deliberately chosen for it's proximity to the highway three times, each trip slower than the previous one. On the third pass-by, the rain intensity relentless.

To the few onlookers, the slowing of the car a expected reaction as they passed the front of the house, the occupants slyly searching for signs.

They were dressed alike, joined in purpose and philosophy, arrogantly members of a blameless societal deprived fraternity, getting what was owed them, no conscience if the gain was illegal. Travelling within the car, displayers of greasy shoulder length hair, untrimmed goatees surrounded by unshaven stubble. Their attire, weathered jeans, black T-shirts and baseball caps turned around as if proclaiming, "I'm watching my back." – shoes with no socks. All signatures of the non-conforming including the impressionable, breaking from convention taken with the independence of: "I answer only to myself, the malefactors among them not discerable to the inexperienced."

"You notice that there are newspapers on the lawn; at least a couple of days worth?" the older man riding as passenger said, "A dead giveaway, in spite of lights on in parts of the house."

"Yeah, I noticed," the driver said, his voice cracking as he tried to remain calm in spite of his nervousness.

"Another go situation," the passenger, the obvious leader judged. The neighbors houses on both sides have their lights on in their dens obviously watching television. I'd be in and out before the next commercial break with no one the wiser," he said in growing confidence. "Let me out," he commanded.

"You have your cell phone with you?" the apprehensive driver reminded.

"Yes," the other replied, impatient and exasperated by the question. "It's in my pocket where it always is. Get hold of yourself and be alert.," he admonished. "If anything suspicious happens, buzz me and I'll be out of there."

"Right, make it quick," the driver said uneasily, his partner's confidence not assuaging him.

The leader and passenger, Jake Bowert, the Staves' would subsequently learn, was out of the car in seconds, quickly and quietly moving to the back of the house.

The on edge driver, Stan Fuller, pulled further into the driveway away from the street, turned off the engine and waited nervously, his body and it's system under attack by his drug dependency.

The patio door, Bowert's first choice to gain entrance, not unexpectedly had double pane glass and was locked tight, making breaking in at this location of the house too difficult and time consuming. He chose instead to climb up on the air conditioner unit just beneath a less formidable kitchen window. Hearing the neighbors surrounding sounds – their television audio raised to counter the continuing heavy fallen rain, bolstered his confidence. The occupied neighbors posing no threat of discovery.

The driver, Fuller, having developed a nervous twitch over his left eye, unable to pull himself together lost his confidence. A consequence, he began to perspire, the clock for his drug dependency well past its servicing hour, cursing his partner as responsible for losing his manageable control by insisting he delay getting his fix until this break in was completed. His nerves, raw and sensitive, pained at being deprived, on the verge of hyperventilating. His counter; inhaling then exhaling large amounts of air, bringing relief; momentarily subduing being wildly imaginative, his next attack of nerves building His courage without drugs was non-existent, deprived his persona now seeking to take flight, as he felt his chest tighten, his sweat becoming more profuse, trickling into his eyes and blurring his already limited vision.

The weather, without a reprieve, had worsened. The voluminous ceiling of clouds had dropped, worsening already poor visibility, the wind, not just surface, reached high into the sky to move layered clouds, relentlessly churning hot and cold air masses across the darkened sky, spawning a line of high energy cells releasing bolts of lightning, the light of extreme heat piercing the darkness to reveal briefly the configurations being assaulted by the elements. Fuller looked up at the house just as a bolt of lightning exploded with a deafening crash just above him. It's white hot energy reflected in the bow window. He saw for the first time a very large dog capable of inflicting serious harm staring back at him, a formidable danger greeting any intruder. Without delay, certain that his partner would be thankful for his alertness, he buzzed a warning to Bowert.

Jake Bowert standing on the air conditioner wet and chilled by the fast dropping temperatures, had just broken the glass of the kitchen window, paused to check the neighboring houses for 'signs that they had been alerted before entering the house when the buzzer went off in his pocket, freezing him in place apprehensively. The warning ominous, he jumped from his perch slipping to his knees in the wet grass, quickly recovering he sloshed his way through the drenching rain, the booming thunder rolling across the sky expediting his returning steps to enter the waiting car.

"What's wrong?" he said breathlessly, his clothes so wet they clung to his body, quickly closing the door behind him as the violence of the storm increased.

"There's a large dog in the house, one you don't want any part of," Stan Fuller said. "I saw him in the bow window… there are easier marks," relieved that they would be on the move again.

"A large dog?" he questioned. "I didn't hear any barking. Did you?"

"No. No barking," Stan Fuller admitted, "but he's there in the house. I saw him," he repeated defensively.

"Damn, I was just getting ready to go in," an exasperated Jake Bowert berated, as if Fuller was at fault. "I know you're strung out and need a fix badly. Could you have imagined the dog?" he said reluctant to give up on the break-in.

"I know what I saw. I couldn't let you walk into that risky situation," he said offended and uncomfortable at the challenge.

The electrical storm was directly overhead. The smell of burnt ozone pronounced in the wake of the jigsaw path the searing lightning traversed through the clouds.

"Look," Stan Fuller said in astonishment. "The hairs on the back of my arms are standing straight out."

"Mine too," Bowert joined, his attention diverted from what he perceived as a lost opportunity. He reached back and slid the face of his hand across the back of his neck, finding those unbarbered hairs were also charged, tingling to the touch. They were in the middle of a lightning field sparking static electricity. They needed no further warning.

"Let's get out of here," Bowert shouted in realization, safety now his only thought.

Their angst turned to terror as they realized the intervals between actual lightning strikes and the vacuum produced booming thunder almost overlapped, the area they occupied being a lightning rod.

They slowly backed out of the driveway, Jake Bower wiping away the windows interior of coating moisture. Through streaming water that ran down the outside of the window he viewed the house, the panoply of lightning framing the house.

"I see him," he shouted. "I see the dog. He's in the bow window, just sitting there unaffected by the thunder and lightning. Incredible; let's move."

No sooner had he sounded the final retreat than the entire sky lit up with a series of rapid discharges of lightning. Frightening Fuller to a crawl, overwhelmed by nature's awesome display, he considered waiting for the worst to pass; comforted they were grounded and safe within the car.

"Get this car moving," Bowert screamed. "We're in danger."

No sooner had those prophetic words left his fearing mouth than twin-legged lightning tendrils, its selection process a mystery, struck within milliseconds of one another the magnificent maple tree planted on the county strip that bordered the side walk for years shading the front of the house. The first leg stripped the bark from it's trunk as it sizzled into the ground following the tree roots, exploding a shower of splinters and bark to pelt the car with hailstorm fury. The second leg struck directly midway up the now denuded trunk of this very tree suspected as the source of Tasha's short lived shadow, sending it crashing onto the car just short of exiting the driveway. In its fall, it sheared through the overhead electrical power lines. Released from tension,, the power lines coiled around the fallen tree, spitting defiantly white hot venom, inflicting additional pain to the dying tree, burning where it touched, its severed end hissing a defiant notice of its kinship to the unbridled power roaming freely in the stormy night sky. The smoking and splintered tree and its deadly coil in its final resting place: the crushed car's roof midpoint, making escape impossible, rendering the doors inoperable, sealing off the snared occupants as Tasha's silhouette continued to watch, unaffected.

~

They were all sitting around the television set in his son Edward's home in New Jersey when the phone rang. It was Bill, Rosanne's husband. The call was unexpected, portending circumstances that could not wait for their return to be revealed. Taking the phone that was handed to him, George after voicing a concerned greeting, found himself listening intently, sitting quietly incredulous, as he heard what had happened, all the while shaking his head in disbelief, finding his voice somberly interjecting abbreviated inquiries of "When?"… "How?"… "Police."… "Damage?"… "How bad?"

When he heard the reaction of his father, Edward hushed his children, while quickly turning down the volume of the television set, the others of furrowed brows, faces drawn, on tenterhooks, awaiting words of explanation. Unable to bear the suspense a moment longer, Rose, fulfilling the role of spokesperson's pleaded "What happened?" her words ignored except for George's raised staying right hand as they heard him say cryptically:

"Call your tree service friend and have him remove the tree and the stump… We're leaving first thing tomorrow, Monday morning… I see no reason to leave immediately unless you feel it is vital?… You agree… We'll see you then."

Hanging up the phone, Staves faced his family. "You're not going to believe what has happened."

"What? What?" they chorused anxiously.

"It seems that a violent thunderstorm passed through our community, downing power lines and trees, literally pulling off roof shingles… a real mess. There's also flooding being reported in some areas."

"You mean our property and house got damaged?" a distraught Rose asked, her face ashen, anticipating the worst.

"No," Staves responded, "we were lucky," "We were fortunate, our only damage occurred to the county supplied maple tree that fronted our property just off the head of our driveway. We lost it… struck by lightning… felled right across the driveway entrance."

Still she questioned, needing more assurances "The house?… The garage?"

"No, no other damage," he repeated being more specific. "We were lucky compared to other streets, other neighborhoods."

An audible sigh of relief parted Rose's lips. Readying to relax proved premature as she heard her husband add, "That's not the end of it." Apprehension surging back into her mind, as it did the others. "It seems we had visitors."

"Not children!" Rose gasped.

"No, no, not children," he interjected quickly. "Two men. The maple tree on its way down sheared the overhead power lines, the tree entangled in hot wires spitting electricity fell onto the roof of the car these two men were driving, causing enough damage to trap them inside of the car right in our driveway."

"Oh, my God, were they hurt?" Rose cried alarmingly.

"No, they weren't. A little shook up from their experience when the police, repair crews from the power company and the fire department finally freed them."

"Why were they in our driveway?" his son Edward asked perplexed.

"Good question," his father answered. "Their first explanation to the police was that they pulled into the driveway because they had become concerned over the severity of the storm – to wait it out. The police, already aware that the house was vacant, in a routine check found the kitchen window broken, suspicious, decided circumstances warranted that they be taken to the police station to file a report."

Staves continued, "As is routine under suspicious circumstances, their names, Stan Fuller and Jake Bowert, were run through the police computer files and guess what? They both had criminal records ranging from possession to burglary. With a warrant granting search of their car, the police found all sorts of multi purposed tools a possible violation of the terms of their parole; as the tools could be used beyond carpentry as they weakly claimed. Those circumstances prompting they continue their denial of attempting to break into the house when confronted by the police. They knew the law and its over-taxed system, particularly under today's liberal interpretation, the evidence circumstantial, no conviction would be possible without witnesses or being caught in the act. In this instance the worst charge they could face was parole violation and dubious trespassing."

Staves, holding everyone in awe, continued, "Earlier, the police while awaiting the computer background checks, had already determined that they were drug dependent from the drug paraphernalia found in the car – the parole violation. Being held as parole violators, the police decided to test their linked defenses by deciding to question them separately. Hoping to weaken their resolve and break them down, they let them sweat out two hours alone before resuming questioning. Concentrating on Stan Fuller, whose resilience was fading in the midst of paining withdrawal. He proving to be the weakest link during his interrogation, conceding a signed confession to the attempted break-in, encouraged by the promise of a methadone injection to quiet his raging bodily functions at the county treatment rehabilitation center. When confronted that his partner had confessed, Jake Bowert, in the hopes of a lighter sentence also confessed."

"That's unbelievable," Edward interjected. "I can't believe that happened."

"Wait, there's more," George resumed, receiving incredulous looks from all. "It seems that as the break in was about to happen, Stan Fuller, the driver acting as a lookout ended the attempt. As prearranged, buzzed a warning to his partner that danger was imminent. Scared out of his wits when a lightning bolt lit up the front of the house, revealing, a menacing dog staring down on him."

They all looked at one another in disbelief, not sure of what they heard. Rose finally exclaimed, "Tasha's silhouette!"

George nodded "yes. A housebreaking foiled by an image… Incredible." He voiced, a smile creasing his face, "A spectral vigilante assisted by Mother Nature; that's one for the books."

"Oh, my God," Rose said suddenly. "What will the media do with that story?" her mind anticipatory for the days to follow and the attention sure to come by an aroused public as the media sensationalizes the event.

Tasha, who lay in the center of the den, home to the television set occasionally dozing. Aroused, watched and listened to what was transpiring, perplexed by the angst in everyone demeanor interrupting the peaceful setting – raised her head and stiffened her ears at the mention of her name.

Monday morning couldn't come soon enough. On edge to return home, their departure was understandably earlier than planned. Having driven through the heavily trafficked feed highway they entered the interstate, leaving six more hours of driving before reaching home. During the first few hours, they talked sporadically about the thwarted burglary and its impact. Other times, they talked exclusively about their new granddaughter. When they were within the kilowatt coverage of their regional radio stations, they learned firsthand the amount of attention the story was getting, in particular Tasha and her spectral surrogate enhancing her celebrity nation wide. Her legend now taking on the implications of not only being an exceptional dog but one capable of supernatural powers to create images.

It was well after 7:00 PM when they arrived home. While expecting notoriety, they could never in their wildest imagination have expected what greeted them. Almost one hundred people were all over the front lawn, including neighbors. A local TV mini-cam crew who was filming the multitude approached the car as they attempted to enter the driveway still littered with leaves, small branches and fragmented bark. Rolling down the window on the driver's side while restraining an excited barking Tasha challenging the intruders, Staves shouted, "Please clear the driveway." His neighbors, with a waive of the hand, complied. The majority of others completely ignored his request attracted by the mini-cam crew who arrogantly continued to approach the car, their reporter attempted to shove a microphone in George Staves's face, prompting Tasha to bare her fangs unapprovingly.

"Mr. Staves," the reporter shouted above the din, "would you like to share your thoughts on this newsworthy event with our viewers?"

"Look," he said testily of no concern he was on camera, not hiding his consternation, "we're just returning from a trip and we're tired. We're just catching up on things. Perhaps tomorrow. Now please get out of the way."

"Can we at least tape the dog?" he persisted, undeterred.

"No, you can't," was his angry response. "She's confused and anxious. No pictures, no interviews. Now, please move."

Two patrolmen whom he recognized approached his situational dilemma, arms spread steering the spectators and the TV crew away from the driveway, allowing an opening for him to pull into the garage. George responding with a relieved "thanks," the grumbling of the dispossessed continuing.

In the comfort of their home, unwinding from the drive and the confrontation, George's periodic checks at the bow window showing that the number of curious and inquisitive were still plentiful.

"We'll be late getting to sleep tonight," George said. "People keep coming and coming."

Staves awoke the next morning at 6:30 nudged by an anxious Tasha, the excitement of the previous day throwing her off schedule. Rubbing his eyes to improve their focus, he scanned through the bow window for any early morning visitors. Finding none, he proceeded to walk Tasha. He immediately noticed more than the usual vehicular traffic of trucks and cars of various age, their passage adding to the morning sounds, theirs a disharmony of muffled combustion. Most of the vehicles, pooled with sharing workers, drivers and passengers purposefully altering their route to their daily commerce for a spectator's opportunity of sharing in the sensationalized event. Their attention captured, they would slow their vehicles to get an examining acknowledging look at Tasha in the flesh. Open mouthed awe at her magnificence, however, her in substance, alive, in spite of her mystique, not their main purpose. Of greater impact to them at the moment, their priority, witnessing the famed spectral, inanimate silhouette.

The gawking of Tashs in the flesh while arousing, not satisfying their passion of the moment. It was the surreal surrogate they enthused to see. An image from another world – a rare opportunity to witness something that has the tracings of being paranormal before disappearing as suddenly as it appeared.

In disappointment, Staves conceded the images celebrity was beyond anything he anticipated or wished for. Prejudicing the silhouette as akin to a photo's negative before the personality of development. It's attraction, it's mysterious origin, held in awe because of its sensationalized wide ranging implications of the paranormal. Suddenly feeling resentment that an intangible, had reduced the weight and impact of the exceptional qualities of the pulse beating creature living with them: Tasha, to which the specter is connected and owes it's pseudo amorphous life.

Creating a completely unanticipated irony: a smoke colored silhouette of Tasha's replication received cult observance pre-empting it's maker deserving of hero worship. Stirring within him mixed feelings for Tasha's silica procreation – her lifeless image, now in the forefront, culling from deserved attention. Troubled he shared his feelings with his agreeing wife, their pride injured by Tasha lessening significance, fermenting resentment of the publics capricious priorities.

On the walk back home, Staves anticipated other ramifications, his thoughts the pinnacle of Tasha's silhouette celebrity would soon be reached; the majority of the curious satiated, other developments, local or on a national scale getting the center ring of attention. Yet when that happened, he questioned, how long should he be expected to host the occasional curious, the uninitiated? If it were up to him he would end the dominance of the specters attraction immediately. Mitigating influence he sought would soon be directing him.

Finding the property still vacant of visitors upon their return, he became optimistic, the absence, indicative of interest waning, things getting back to normal within sight. His wishful thinking faded at lunchtime with the arrival of the half-day school children and their parents, their excitement ruling, his hopes deferred for another day.

Completely unexpected, never imaginable, an opportunistic purveyor of fad memorabilia arrived to set up shop at curbside, not in the least deterred by George's presence. Shocked at the audacity, Staves witnessed an attempt to create a cottage business startup as the purveyor hawked from boxes taken from his car stenciled and painted T-shirts bearing a replica of Tasha's silhouette, captioned with various phrases such as "Neighborhood Watch In Action."... "The Long Bark Of The Law."... "Burglars And Thieves Not Welcome."... "The Enemy From Without, Meet Your Enemy From Within."... to name a few.

Flabbergasted at the street vendor's audaciousness, he was equally stunned as sales were brisk. The parents, intimidated by their children,, purchased and donned their T-shirts proclaiming their witness... being a part of the historical scene. A crowd of onlookers and customers quickly developed moving beyond the wooden horse restraints protecting the property. The vendor selling the T-shirts was eventually dispatched by the police, citing him for conducting business without a license. Undeterred he would set up elsewhere.

A commercial enterprise offering a silk screened cartooned sham depiction cheapening the occurrence, the impetus needed to decide his path for him. His willingness to share the phenomenon would end. Now more than ever he knew what had to be done. He had no alternative. His family, disturbed, no longer enjoying privacy, their lives intruded upon agreed to his action to end the spectacle. His wife Rose, no longer willing to cope was not hesitant in her support, her feelings, "We can't continue to live like this."

Around 10:00 PM with the onlookers reduced to adults, and a mini cam crew Staves moved quickly to hammer in place a canvas tarpaulin, shielding the bow window and its spectral occupant from the view of the outside world.

He heard the catcalls of disappointment when the visitors realized what was happening, acted out their displeasure in front of the TV crews quick to respond, filming the Staves act of censure for the next presentation of the news.

The police without admission were pleased that this step would eventually relieve them of an unpopular duty, motivated by it's promise, kept the visitors moving at a faster pace with the advisory, "There is nothing more to see. Keep moving."

All though the early morning hours, with the canvassed curtain remaining drawn, shielded the image from its only audience – the bored occupant of the patrol car parked outside the house. His presence preventing temptations for unveiling.

At the beginning hour of industry George called a local window replacement company, his earlier plans hastened. The owner, quick in name recognition, was sympathetic to his situation and promised to have one of his technicians out to the house that very afternoon to write up the specifications. The company official was relatively sure, knowing the neighborhood and the home builder that they would be able to handle the job from stock with an upgrade to welcomed paint free vinyl covering the outside wood of the two new casements and picture window combined configuration. On a expedited basis, priced accordingly given one week notice, he could assign enough men to finish the job in one day. With visitors expected to be minimal, he agreed to start at 7:00 AM, the hour Staves had been granted as special permission from city officials.

He was up early that start-up day, anxious not only for the window replacement crew to get started, but accommodating the representatives of the local newspaper. He had decided to grant an interview that centered around how Tasha's image happened in the first place, taking this opportunity to make his case for its removal, their hostility to the plan expected, nonetheless hoping to gain from their openness at least an understanding expressed in their reporting to their subscribers. He also capitulated to allow photographs of the family as a unit in an effort to limit exploitation. The reporters valuing the impact on sales – the opportunity to report on the closure of this amazing event would bring, in their mind already planning the stimulating newspaper's headline: "Specter's Demise."

Rose joined him at the kitchen table while he drank his freshly brewed coffee, talking out their replies for the interview. Relieved that it would contribute to ending the circus-like atmosphere, the normalcy of their lives returning as this episode became part of history. Equally as compelling; the return of the children's adoration, encouraging Tasha in the flesh would be more satisfying and stabilizing.

The workers were on time, arriving within minutes of one another. Their setting aside the tarpaulin evoking excitement in what they saw:

"I would never have believed it if I hadn't seen it with my own eyes," said one.

"The most amazing thing I've ever seen," said another.

"No question of whom and what it is," said another, turning his attention toward a curious Tasha tethered at George's side on the front lawn.

"What could have brought it about?" the foreman questioned. "A quirk of nature, a phenomenon?"

The photographers took pictures as a group. Tasha under restraint sat in the same pose as her famed image with George and Rose to the side of her. They were carefully positioned to show the background bow window capturing the difficult to delineate silhouette. Tasha responded by blinking nervously at the intrusion of the high intensity flashbulbs.

With the photo session over, the reporters and the Staveses sat in the living room watching the workers disassembling the bow window, showing the extra care in handling the picture window section showing the image. Tasha at Rose's side, always watchful and attentive when strangers were about, ready for situational changes that suggested hostility in the making.

The interview began immediately. More calculating than friendly having a tone of disapproval from the questioners.

"Mr. Staves, can you tell us why you're removing the bow window?" the lead reporter said beginning the challenge.

Knowing that the newspapers always support the underdog, he replied openly patient:

"There are many reasons, but my primary reason is that it was turning into a circus. A distraction from what this neighborhood is about. Originally, we were tolerant and accommodating when the children were our main visitors, delighting in their excitement." Smiling at the recollection, "The truth be known, it was the children who were responsible for my wife and me, long denied, to finally see the image." Turning serious, "But now, it's mostly adults showing no respect for property or privacy with their bad behavior, taking advantage, exploiting."

"But the image is celebrity," the second reporter countered, the moment his to be shared, the public adopted it as it's own. Excitingly mysterious, a visit by the paranormal to which they can bond. A needed hero worship... An opportunity to take temporary leave from a predictable mundane life... To figuratively touch another existence... another dimension... To share in what they believe is a once in a lifetime experience."

George Staves not interrupting could hardly wait for the overly dramatized dissertation to be over, pained by the implication that the Staves's were uncaring, bond shattering ogres.

"Excuse me," he said sarcastically, "you're suggesting that we were not sympathetic or encouraging is not true. We were as long as we could be, until, as you had to witness, image seekers gave way to the indiscriminate. Behavior unruly and inconsiderate, infringing on other people's rights. A fore fronting factor in our conclusion to remove – hearing from some of the parents of the children, complaining their children were mesmerized, exhibiting disturbing behavior modification both at home and at school – disdainful of unwittingly surrendering control and discipline to their children's fantasy preoccupation."

Continuing, "A major factor is the building diversion, making the image an idol, fantasizing as supernatural. A paradox, Tasha in real life, lives, no fantasizing needed, Her well known amazing powers of perception and understanding are being overlooked by the absorption in the specter. " His pride in Tasha bringing the criticism of the worshiping. "If anyone is to be celebrated, it should be Tasha who is the magic spawning her shadowy image, not minimizing or ignoring her. Those of higher intelligence have yet to figure out how she did it,"

George paused to see if his words had any effect, sensing the reporters were missing their intent and not being persuaded

Speaking with belief Rose entered the exchange. "Your newspaper provides the perfect opportunity for those whom you feel will be deprived, to bring closure to this happening. "

"What do you mean?" the lead reporter questioned.

George interceded. "The photographs that you took today, I assume will be published in tomorrow's edition – will allow your denied readers the experience. Fanaticizing, your words prompting, attaching themselves as a magnet, becoming part of the experience. So much so that in a few years, they will be part of the actual throngs, inventing their presence, participating freely in the common bond with the actual witnesses. Their transference coming from exposure to newspaper accounts dramatically written. Their numbers to grow literally to thousands beyond those of opportuneness, superimposing their beings, glorying in the event – their place in the sun."

Staves depiction, known to have happened, showed influence. The reporters visage suggesting recognition of a story line of more potential to sell. Concluding depicting them in print as uncaring in the finalizing story, a presentation of lesser impact. Conceding the Staves's action was, possibly motivated by judgments of a greater good, bringing equitable closure. That story line they envisioned would sell newspapers at a fevered pace.

"We don't ask that you completely agree with us," Rose interjected, "only that you present the facts without prejudice and let your readers decide."

"Tell us your thoughts as to how Tasha's image came into being," the lead reporter asked, his tone without an edge, more solicitous.

George answered, "I wish I knew the absolute answer to that… I can only hypothesize… guesswork that won't hold up under scientific scrutiny."

"It's all we can ask for. We're dealing in abstractions, not absolutes," the lead reporter stated.

"We know one thing for certain as you do. The image exists, it's real; some power that can't be fully explained caused it," Rose responded.

"On that point, we have parity with the scientific community," George stated. I can't prove my theory but neither can they disprove it, creating conditions for debate and convincing thought."

Continuing, "We first heard about it from the children, having evolved from one of their games of inventive imagination, playing the game repeatedly with growing numbers. Mysteriously it became fixed, it was there for most to see, no longer could it be dismissed as a game with imaginations running wild. We as the one's denied assumed the power of suggestion at work, a willed apparition of Tasha's known practice of sitting and waiting on the shelf of the bow window whenever someone was out of the house. That theory fell apart as the image did not resist being photographed, or mirrored." Counseling, "apparitions can't be photographed or reflected in a mirror in most cases, according to the followers of the occult. Remember, initially Mrs. Staves and I were not believers; the image remaining invisible to us."

"We then thought it was again shadows cast from the trees when the wind moved them a certain way. That conclusion lost its merit after we had the trees pared back significantly with no effect. It thwarted our discovery until the time when my wife and I had a shared emotional experience with a group of physically and mentally challenged children who came to witness while on a school field trip. That day it happened Tasha's behavior flabbergasted us, displaying self-recognition, self-awareness. Assuming without coaching the very posture of the silhouette, without a doubt an encouraging assist for a faculty impaired young boy to demonstrate his sighting and bonding with the image."

"We to this day are still in awe of what we saw as Tasha displayed an understanding of that impaired young man we hadn't expected but should have. His short-circuiting mind limited to his troubled dark world. Finding as most of the other children had, something real while remaining lifeless, emerging from swirling overlapping limited colors of a stereogram to form an eye-strained complete figure, as if cut from black paper and glued to the window. But it wasn't paper glued to the window. It was the window itself. A touch established texture anomalies within the image itself, differing from the surrounding glass."

"What did those surface anomalies tell you?" the lead reported interrupted, his interest increasing.

"I zeroed in on that discovery, as offering a possible explanation."

"And what might that be? Do they differ from the hypothesis of some scientists quoted in my paper earlier." the other reporter questioned, his interest heightened.

"I have a position as a lay person, certainly not as credentialed as your experts, particularly since what I'm about to suggest can't be duplicated in a laboratory, at least not at this time. Still I think I would have some supporters in the scientific community, my theory being founded upon engineering practices based on the law of physics."

There were no interruptions for edification, just acknowledging nods of understanding. Staves continued:

"I believe it is entirely possible that Tasha secreted onto the bow window body chemicals that were reacted upon by either the sun's ultraviolet rays, causing the treated glass surface to be etched, or was bombarded with a source similar to x-rays, the glass acting as a film exposed. Both processes in wide use throughout industry, continues to evolve from its current state of practice. I offer my theory with one weakness: while the processes are viable in industry today with chemicals of known composition, Tasha's actual chemicals can only be guessed, leaving to mystery what is the medium that activated the process."

"You think it's possible?" the junior reporter questioned.

"I do. What greater proof that it is possible, without being sacrilegious or irreverent than the *Shroud of Turin*? After all these years, it still remains a mystery." He smiled, his point made also his closing words to end the interview.

"Just one more question, Mr. Staves," the lead reporter rushed. Receiving an approving nod, "What will you do with the removed glass that contains the silhouette? You're not thinking of destroying it?"

"It has too much meaning in our lives to be destroyed," Staves response genuine. "I plan to keep it safe and out of harm's way," he answered, abruptly standing. "Gentlemen, I know you have deadlines to meet so I won't detain you any further. I think we are finished here. All I ask is that you quote me accurately," he said as he walked them to the door. "One other comment on the humorous side worth mentioning: unsuspecting salesmen making cold calls, when spotting Tasha and her image as they were about to ring the bell become faint hearted, leaving in a hasty retreat." Staves smile broadened, "can you think of a better way to discourage door to door solicitation?"

The reporters smiling at his humor, agreeing it would add to the story. As they left they could not help noticing the reduced number of people gathered outside the house. No image, no interest were their thoughts, sure to please the Staves.

~

The time traveling George Staves acknowledged that, indeed, within a few weeks all that transpired was no longer central to the world of issues, casually reduced to a happenstance as time passed, people resuming their lives without the images distraction. Safely removed and secure, the image on the glass framed, would hang in the den where Tasha, George, his wife Rose and their children and grandchildren could watch the image watching them, no longer a distraction but a motivator to bring the family unit closer together.

Fast forwarding his thoughts to the present: "Now that Tasha's physical presence is gone, the image impact is never greater, a legacy to this wondrous animal who provided so much joy as she touched you in so many ways, asking so little in return." With sadness he took leave of this capsule of Tasha's life, continuing his transporter travel, revisiting events sure to diminish his melancholy.

He would revisit beyond the mundane contact with his bordering neighbors, during the times of their respective families association, highly charged and emotional instances bearing the imprint of Tasha's extraordinary range of persona to their outcome.

~

The Staves, constructively outgoing, easily managed trusting relationships with their neighbors on both sides of their home, one north, the other south, witnessing continually over the years their bordering neighbors ignoring dislike for one another.

The Staves home, a territorial buffer zone, divided the differences in years and culture. George and Rose Staves were medians to the recluse elders of the north and the contemporary yearlings to the south. The Tunius's disdained the neighbors to the south as counter culture nomads with little promise of neighborhood sinking roots, prejudiced as transients unworthy of their recognition regardless of legitimacy. While sympathetic to each, the Staves exercised the wisdom of neutrality at the first signs of a developing conflict. The product of their efforts, maintaining good relationships with both for the future ahead whatever it might be.

Their northern neighbors, the Tuniuses of Lithuanian birth, were the original owners, their southerly neighbors: the eighth in twenty years, to the chagrin of themselves and the neighborhood association. Unlike the original owner, the majority of successors that followed were not buyers but rather lease holders. Without the pride of ownership, the house was a merry-go-round, minimally cared for. The average occupancy of two and a half years rarely brought a pride beyond minimal lawn cutting-weed killer application to prevent blossoming and the distribution of the wind-blown seeds was never a thought, a blame quickly assigned by the Tunius's to the newcomers. To his chagrin, the mailman had difficulty keeping track of the latest inhabitants, often intermingling mail for those already gone failing to fill out a change-of-address notification, grumbling the next day for the previous delivery remaining unclaimed.

There was nothing wrong with the house, built by reputable builders of sound design and construction, easily satisfying strict building codes. Its only blemish was its turnover, pleasing no one but the real estate agents as a very active fee source. Serving the criticism of the Tunius's who viewed each new lease holder with the contempt reserved for gypsies; property values their issue, the house plagued by lack of permanence. Showing disdain for the transients awaiting additional move instructions from their transferring multi-national companies, following the bait of promotional opportunities.

The history of the original owner's was the family's dismay with the severe winter weather of the Midwest. Both husband and wife college professors born, raised, and educated in Iran. One winter's stay being enough to provide the impetus to move to the more compatible environs of Arizona. Some of the leaser successors; newlyweds without enough pooled resources lost the buy option on the house, victims to the challenges to their stability as couples, disenchanted in business or marriage, becoming part of the growing statistic.

The Staves concerns were minimally at rest with the homes revolving door; trouble a certainty if the new leaser openly disliked house dogs. Luckily never the case, all were animal tolerant, if not lovers of varying scale in accepting the two generations of dogs that the Staves's raised. Quick to recognize the warning posed by the restraining tether; a caution meant to discourage uninvited contact in the name of showing affection.

The old world Tunius's were "different," having lived in their house for over ten years when the Staveses moved in; entitled them respect for ownership seniority, their age also having a bearing. Openly self-proclaimed sage advisors regardless of the situation or undertaking but only to the befriended. Conversations, disciplined polite in its one-sidedness, required attentive listening, trying to fathom their labored ethnic mixed syntax. Always a test, but with patience, coming away with the general idea of what they were attempting to communicate.

Felix and Julia Tunius were Lithuanian émigrés. Their only child, a boy, was born late into their family arranged marriage, escaping the odds at being born normal despite their advanced years. Fervent in their belief of God's providence, proud of the gift he had bestowed upon them in answer to their prayers, their miracle lost in his early manhood, victim to a senseless murder. Overwhelmed with grief, sealed in an isolationist cocoon, they shed tears of sorrow in their loneliness; their grief irreconcilable yet never losing their devotion to their God when answers remained unfathomable.

Secluding themselves in his room to mourn, it was now their primary place for prayer. Sanctifying its memorabilia and furnishings as he tragically left them, abandoning their church but not their God. The passing of time not healing their bleeding wounds, in need of ministering beyond themselves, they responded to the pleas of their church, returning to the house of their creator for prayer. Finding therapeutic; their increased visibility and contact with fellow parishioners.

In the months that followed their son's untimely death, a shared sorrow relationship developed, an outgrowth of Edward having befriended their son Alex while alive. Collateral from that relationship was a growing bond between Alex and Tasha that Julia and Felix now reached out for.

The Tuniuses could always be seen together in their garden, legs straight as reeds bent from the waist frozen for what seemed like hours, weeding and grooming, their garden giving them occasional leave, a temporary solace from their sorrow. Historically they only waved or nodded a polite acknowledgment to the Staves's, but now still beset by the tragedy easily leaving their gardening diversion when spotting Tasha, crossing the Staves property line, their eyes forlorn and tear-filled, feasting on her, anxious to pet an accommodating Tasha, displaying a dream-like reverence that suggested their affectionate display retracing, connecting spiritually with their demonstrative son.

Tasha, whose body language showed understanding, never moved beyond their petting reach, presenting the past, a recipient of their dead son's affections, communicating, "Touch and caress me, travel his same path, find his energy and together share. Put aside your grief, be brightened by the memories you cling to – his endless light."

Rose and George Staves welcomed the expanding relationship as therapeutic for the Tunius's who normally were strict and demanding in observance of their property line, dropping their military guard demeanor when seeing Tasha. Although Felix and his wife Julia would never have a house pet to despoil their carefully and meticulously arranged and cared for property, they would emotionally raise to a higher priority the sight of a resting Tasha. Usually it was during the care of their garden, rising from their stooped over positions, calling her name to encourage that she could cross property lines if not for her tether. In redefinition of priorities, they showed no concern if she expanded her territorial boundaries to include the tree's fronting their house when out for a walk by depositing the distinct scent carried in her spotting. They're recovering usually included repeatedly boast's to all who would listen that Tasha's breed originated in their native part of the world, supporting folklore that the early Siberian husky lived amongst their respective primitive ancestors, co-mingled, dependent on one another.

Before the death of the Tunius's son the Staves's collaborated in a relationship only when their signals of encouragement were apparent; if not they deferred to each other's privacy. That was the criteria that governed their relationship until the tragedy. Now the Staves's reached out to the Tunius's, especially Julia Tunius, who cried herself to sleep every night sobbing inconsolably, beseeching to be taken, that she was ready to join her son. Unbearable the thought that her son lay in the ground alone, his only connection to the outside world; the cold chiseled marble tombstone announcing that his life was stolen from him all too early. She was sickened by depression, overwhelmed she was unable to recover. While absolute connections have not been made between depression and dementia, it is difficult to disassociate a connecting relationship; particularly in this case, so severe was her depression, straining her mental health.

The signs were there, more obvious to those who knew Julia, recognizing the subtle changes taking place. In growing evidence was her forgetting Tasha's name… her difficulty at times to read her watch… not being able to complete her thoughts in the middle of a sentence… to put the right words together to express herself. Staring blankly until rescued by temporary cognizance, embarrassed at her dwindling communicative skills, she would withdraw further.

The bleakness of her situation never more in evidence when George Staves, arriving home for the evening, found the street being blocked off by fire trucks and police patrol cars. He soon discovered that Mrs. Tunius, while preparing dinner for her showering husband, had forgotten that she had a roast in the oven. The roast, burnt to a crisp with flames leaping from the shattered glass window of the oven, clouds of billowing black smoke setting off the smoke detectors, while she, impassive to the danger, remained seated at the kitchen table choking, unable to comprehend and unable to call 911. If not for a hysterically barking Tasha summoning Rose Staves, the discovery might have come too late to save an incoherent Julia Tunius and her unknowing husband Felix.

The harsh reality upon him Felix Tunius, no longer felt secure for her and his safety, his pained admission forcing him to take additional steps to assist and care for his wife. Contacting relatives still in Lithuania, he arranged passage for a distant relative's spinster daughter to come and live with them.

The proximity of their houses to one another kept the Staves's informed of Julia's condition. Since there were no cures for her deteriorating condition, only marginally affective treatment with drugs to quiet her, the increasing pace of the inevitable awaited her.

Occasionally they would hear raised voices in undecipherable Lithuanian coming from the Tunius's home; Julia shouting and screaming while Felix attempted to quell her imaginings. Usually their skirmishes ended without further incident while at other times, the police had to be called to restore order, assisted with a hastily called doctor administering Julia a sedative.

Her mental condition, while occasionally showing recognition at times, her husband while joyous was not deluded, he and her live in assist the giver of constant surveillance to correct or avoid misdeeds. Lucidity becoming rare, mostly in bewilderment, her blank stare, showing no recognition, passed through George and Rose as if invisible or transparent, recovering to exhibit delighting cognizance when Tasha came into view, frustratingly berating herself in Lithuanian when she failed to name her. Requiring an escort to lead her to where she could pet Tasha. Lovingly, tears welling in her eyes in flashes of memory of other times of happiness, before the foreboding world of confusion and fuzziness returned.

Recognizing that it pleased her to be in Tasha's company, the Staves's sympathetic, quickly agreed to Felix's request that he and Julia take Tasha on short walks limited to their own back yards, purposefully to keep Julia from the stares of the curious searching to define her condition. Julia, leash in hand and with each step taken, a smile across her face brightened, cooing words that her husband later explained were from her mothering days when nursing her son Alex. The therapeutic walk finished, none witnessing her joy had a dry eye. Her look of happiness, while only temporary, would be remembered forever, prompting the walks be repeated.

Her periods of instability became more frequent until seized totally, her mental acumen stolen from her as she struggled in the spinning vortex of bewilderment that was her a world, making cognizance rare, moored in a harbor perpetually fogged. A reaching out George Staves arriving home found Felix, Julia and Rose seated on the patio in a setting seriously somber; soon to learn he would be a participant in discussing Julia's reasoning abilities that were no longer a rational faculty exampled in an event this very day of endangering behavior.

"What's wrong?" he asked.

Rose hesitated, looking sorrowfully at a now silent Julia, at peace in temporary armistice from her dividing forces, staring off in the distance. Rose turned respectfully to Felix for his leadership in responding but found only muted dejection, finally answering, "Julia had an exceptionally bad day," returning her view to Felix hoping he had found his voice.

"Go on," George encouraged recognizing a continuing muted Felix the reason for Roses hesitancy.

"Somehow Julia sneaked out of the house while Felix was busy shopping, undertaken secure in the knowledge that she and her companion were both napping. Her immediate direction was our house, our backyard, looking for Tasha." Again she paused, hoping to steer Felix to vocal involvement.

"Yes," George urged anxiously.

"It seems all she was wearing was a nightgown," reacting, Felix's face reddened from embarrassment although he still did not speak.

Rose continued, "Tasha had to be completely devoted for her to do what she did next."

"What do you mean what she did next?" he interrupted excitedly. "Where is Tasha?"

"She's all right," she assured him, "she's in the house in spite of her protestations. I thought it better because of the circumstances."

Thoroughly confused, George demanded, "What happened?"

"You know how we attach Tasha's leash directly to her tether? I learned later that somehow Julia managed to separate them leading an accommodating Tasha on a walk. All of this going on while I was out of sight, busy doing the wash. Once I realized she was gone, not knowing what had happened, I called the police. What's absolutely amazing, I subsequently learned, is that they got so far strolling the streets, with no one finding their walk bizarre enough to call the police. Suggesting initially people refrained from involvement, prioritizing their own problems or to blasé to react, until the dangers of a not so common occurrence -a vulnerable half-naked woman muttering to herself, leading a dog on a journey with no idea where she was going prevailed. Imagine my shock after opening the door to find Tasha in the company of the police, who were taken back by my screaming a deafening relief, turning their hold of the leash to me. Tasha after energetically accepting my embrace her adventure over, released, rushed through the open door, leash trailing noisily behind her, lapping eagerly at her water bowl."

"I didn't know what I was about to hear from the policeman," Rose told her husband. "My imagination was running wild… expecting a complaint had been filed against Tasha. My concerns were relieved as the policemen explained what had happened."

"'We finally caught up with them on Cedar Road,' the younger of the two officers said with a trace of humor glinting in his eyes. With difficulty controlling himself from being flippant, mindful and exercising restraint said, 'We started getting 911 phone calls at 1:05 PM and every few minutes thereafter. Serious minded and concerned pedestrians openly angered by the do nothings told us a nearly naked woman with a dog on a leash was walking the streets of the neighborhood. At the same time, motorists began reporting what they guessed was a High School initiation prank. Other motorists, not believing their eyes, were guilty of rubber-necking, their inquisitiveness influencing traffic.'"

"His tone unmistakably serious as he related, 'An elderly lady reported that when she approached the flimsily clad, wild-eyed woman to offer help, reaching out to comfort her, the woman responding angrily, wildly swinging her arm free of Tasha's leash at her perceived enemy. In point of fact, she actually struck the intended Good Samaritan in the face, surely an assault had the woman, after being apprised of the circumstances, sympathetically refused to press charges."

"It's amazing,' the lead policeman interjected, "that they crossed major streets without being struck by a car. Witnesses reporting that while the woman appeared out of it, the dog was aware of the danger, backing away from oncoming traffic before stepping off the curb, protectively resisting, immutable to the frail women, moving only to force a change in her direction, crossing instead at the connecting side streets running perpendicular to the major thoroughfare. Witnesses claiming the dog clearly made the judgment when automobile traffic was light to cross the selected shorten distance.'"

"'What happened next would have been dismissed as an exaggeration if not for the confirmation of many others, including parents. A school crossing guard reported seeing them at her crossing. The dog resisting all efforts by the scantily clad woman to cross against traffic as a school bus for children of special needs stopped at the very intersection, lights flashing alerting traffic in both directions of disembarking children. Amazingly the dog alerted to the unexpected opportunity to cross, led the woman flanked by the children on both sides, delighting at the dog in their midst, providing a happy faced escort."

"The younger policeman interrupted, "we learned what we were dealing with from her distraught husband having earlier filed a missing person report at the station house just as the 911 calls started coming in. The woman who fit his wife's description we were told, was incapable of making judgment. It had to have been the dog, who recognized safe passage was associated with a stopped school bus. Absolutely amazing to the people who witnessed it. Marvelling, how intelligent of the dog,"

"Not surprising," George said proudly. "Tasha recognizes traffic. She senses danger. Won't cross a street until it is clear of traffic. She has a sixth sense."

Felix Tunius finally found a voice with little hint of composure, embarrassed for his wife Julia's state of mind and actions.

"I'm sorry… the trouble," he said in fragmented English. "She very bad…

can't control her anymore," flustered, searching for words, sputtering, "Hard to hold her back. This morning she attacked me and my cousin with knife… no know us… strangers. Eats all kinds of things, then vomits… danger to herself." His face, bearing the agony of his experiences, his words emotional said, "Needs help. I can do no more. Doctor come in half an hour, she screaming all the time. I sorry." Rising consumed with devastation, he escorted a passive Julia back to his house. The Staves's, not knowing what more they could do or say, remained seated, sharing his sorrow in silent pity.

Breaking the heavy silence to move beyond the troubling event, George solemnly praised, "Tasha's actions, rather her reactions. Under most circumstances she would have resisted being led away by someone other than family. She must feel a special affinity toward Julia, accommodating her as she did."

Around noon the next day, the doorbell rang, setting off an alerted Tasha's barking. It was Felix Tunius, his car in the driveway. In the back seat sandwiched between his cousin and who they were to learn was the doctor, sat Julia subdued by sedation. While they waited, Felix, not entering, stood at the entrance to the front door, his face bearing the strain of a sleepless night.

"I'm taking Julia to home; doctor wants," he said, choking back a sob.

"You mean a nursing home?" Rose questioned.

"Yes, yes," he said with tearful resignation, "Nursing home. They take care of her… no more me, cannot do anymore," appealing for understanding.

"Perhaps it's best," George said compassionately.

"Yes, best," Felix said. "Please I have favor," his voice cracking.

"Of course, just ask."

"Need for you… wife… me and Tasha to visit Julia once in awhile, she like. O.K.?" he pleaded.

"Of course," Rose acknowledged sympathetically and without hesitation.

It was weeks before hearing from Felix Tunius, who spent most of his time either visiting his wife or in the garden.

"Can we make visit this Wednesday morning?" he asked, spotting George on his patio.

"Of course," George replied mentally canceling his plans. Not sharing his concerns, not knowing how Tasha would react in a nursing home environment. As confident in her intelligence as he was, she had no training as a therapy pet yet she was essentially being called upon for that very capacity. Would she socially interact? Would she enjoy visiting with Julia Tunius? Would she be comfortable amidst unfamiliar sights and sounds? Answers to those questions he would soon learn.

After parking the car in the area reserved for visitors, the path to the administration office took them by a group of uniformed nurses and orderlies tending to patients, declaring, when in their sight, admiration and pleasure for Tasha who did not resist the attention – a positive sign. The walk under normal conditions should have taken no longer than a few minutes but because of all the attention and praise given Tasha, it took closer to half an hour. This provided an opportunity for George to measure Tasha's demeanor and willingness at being socially active among strangers with special needs. Her reaction surprised him as her breed could display obstinate independence. Her availability suggested that she judged the surroundings as non-threatening, peopled by the infirm and the terminally ill in need of her comforting diversion.

After clearing admissions, they quickly moved to the day room where they found Julia Tunius strapped to her wheelchair along with others not under restraint, awaiting their visitors. While Julia Tunius stared blankly ahead, her husband Felix devotedly administered to her needs, all the while speaking encouragingly to her in her native tongue; his hope for a sign of awareness was elusive as she remained impassive, the divide to recognition not crossed.

Encouraged to do so by grateful responding attending nurses, Tasha was monopolized, the wide eyed recognition and interest of the patients replacing their melancholy. Making the Staves proud that she hadn't rejected their fondling, for to have done so could have had a psychological impact on those in need of distraction from their pain and infirmity. As George noted in his readings on the subject of animals effect, "highly depressed patients becoming more responsive during and after visits of therapy pets, self-imposed muteness and passivity giving way to imaginative conversations." Resulting in equally noteworthy dropping of blood pressure readings; so therapeutic would be their visit.

The slamming of doors, patients shrieking from imagined threats, the dropping of bedpans producing a sudden unexpected din did not tense Tasha to nervousness, evoking nothing more than alerted curiosity, a testament to Tasha's controlled demeanor. The only discernible change, noticed by George, was her pace of movement. Usually purposeful and accelerated, it had slowed, a deliberate response to match the movement of the patient, downplaying her vitality and the lack of theirs: an illusion of stretching time suggesting enjoying a longer presence to one another, slowing the passage of their lives, a figment expression extending her visit and periods of their satisfaction.

While Tasha was being shared with the other patients in the day room, Felix Tunius continued to lovingly administer to his wife's needs, his hands brushing back her moist, now unkempt hair from falling into her eyes, wiping the beads of perspiration from her brow, assisting the nurse in feeding her food, it's consistency for newly weaned babies. Her appetite lacking she moved to avoid taking the food into her mouth causing most of it to dribble down her once proud chin before being wiped off by a saddened Felix.

Tasha, released finally by the other patients arrived at Julia's side – seeking recognition, laid her head down in her lap within reach of her hands outside the restraints, whereupon she immediately began licking them in a show of affection. Felix, sensing an opportunity for a communication breakthrough, became increasingly animated pleading for his wife to respond to Tasha's stimulus. Suddenly her world took on meaning. Her fog lifting. Recognition showing, Julia Tunius no longer staring blankly ahead at that which she could not shape into being meaningful. Dropping her head to fix her eyes on Tasha, her hands coming to life, began stroking Tasha's wet nose, across her eyes, and erect ears. Words could now be heard coming from Julia's mouth in her native Lithuanian, engaging in a dialogue with her excited husband, questioning they were to learn later, where she was and why she was strapped down. Julia, sitting quietly, listened to her husband's explanation, hearing assurances that all would be well after treatment. Lucidity, while expected to be only temporary, momentarily allowed her to avoid jumbled thoughts, view her surroundings, finding other patients in similar circumstances. Listening patiently as her husband attempted to uplift her with optimism, on leave from her disabling mental stupor. The far away look returning, slipping back to her world of confusion, learned later, putting aside her husbands optimism said in Lithuanian as her debilitating fog rose from the swamp of her minds deteriation to reclaim her – her illness terminal, her longed for reuniting with her son nearing.

Her last of this world act sobbing softly, tears welling in her eyes, her crying, a mixture of her native Lithuanian, occasioned with quivering accented English "my baby, my baby, together we be," her moment of lucidity over, her curtain of disorientation dropping again, the unstoppable degenerative disease continuing.

They made many more visits in the months to come, her condition worsened, her periods of awareness, brought about by Tasha's presence, became shorter and shorter. Still, they felt they were successful, doing some good, their's a diminishing light, a dying ember temporarily illuminating her darkening world.

Almost six months to the day of their first joint visit to the nursing home, Julia Tunius passed away peacefully in her sleep. She was eighty-three suffering from Alzheimer's disease, its debilitation bringing on death-dealing pneumonia, the result of food being swallowed into the lungs.

In the months and years that followed, Felix Tunius retreated further into his gardening seclusion. The pain of his losses dominating, his advancing age suddenly more in evidence. Most recently, reluctantly, his failing heart necessitated a life sustaining pacemaker. His legs, while still strong, could no longer be held ramrod straight as he bent from the waist, stooping, taking longer rest periods as he tended to his blossoming garden.

George and Rose could still evoke a friendly wave from him when his clouding vision allowed recognition, but now he limited his ranging, no longer venturing across property lines to engage in idle conversation unless spotting Tasha who still commanded his attention and motivated his visits. Smiling and petting, speaking in Lithuanian while his eyes messaged volumes; recalling times past when his loving son constantly spoke of his fondness for Tasha. Felix regretting that he and Julia were at first aloof towards Tasha, to subsequently seek their sons connection after his death. And now sadly with the memory of Julia radiating during his lessening visits with Tasha, grateful for her role easing the final days of his beloved wife and his transformation during whatever time was left in his life cycle.

The Staves neighbors to the south, the Monteleone's, Ken and Laura, ended the parade of transients and the acrimony of the Tuniuses. They were in their early thirties, parents of an only child, a boy Steven, who was two years of age. Boundless with plans and an open checkbook, the result of his recent inheritance; restored, reclaimed and renovated the severely ignored and scarred house, abandoned by the last occupants as well as their mutually abusive marriage.

Much to the pleasure of the community association, the Monteleones dove into their house pleading for attention with excitement and zeal, tradesmen of carpenters, painters, tile men, exterminators and landscapers in an endless procession crawled all over the house and property. It soon showed the effects of their campaign, bringing the house back to life, blending easily with the rest of the well-kept community. The amount of cleanup and renovation work expended was measured by the amount of trash filled plastic bags awaiting pickup covering their tree lawn, along with discarded furnishings and fixtures. The Monteleone's efforts went on for months, judged finished when the tree lawn's amount of pickup matched those of the inquisitive, confirmed when invitations were extended to visit.

Never escaping notice was their devotion to their son, out of necessity importing playmates into a mature neighborhood undergoing demographic change. Play toys from after each visit lay strewn about, attesting to the children's quickly changing interests, never discarded long enough on the lawn to be called an eyesore.

Their preoccupation with the house did not lead them to ignore their son and his playmates,' headstrong and fearlessness, cautioning the children not to venture onto their neighbors Staves's property, at the time unsure of Tasha's reaction as she lay there in curiosity watching them; imposing restrictions their only confidence. The Monteleones interpreted aggressiveness to be concerned about when Tasha, attached to her leash leaped at the children when they went streaking by, believing it an act of hostility and not play. Lost in their initial fear, until learning different, was the significance of her delighted yelping in the new game she hoped to be part of.

A toy house and a playground swing set were added in the early spring increasing the delights for Steven and his playmates. These new interests and diversions reduced their usual running about, an activity pleasurable to Tasha now minimized, leaving her to bark for their attention.

In the early summer, a recreational above-ground swimming pool was added to complement an existing wading pool. The new pool, twenty feet in diameter and plastic lined was designed to hold five feet of chemically treated recirculating water but cautiously kept to three feet for concern of the children. It had a removable ground-to-water "A" frame ladder to provide access and egress. When the pool was not in use, it was mandatory that the ladder be removed and stored in the tool shed. Only adult supervision was authorized to position the ladder at the next swim session. This edict was intended to prevent unsupervised children from secretly accessing the pool. On order, but not in place, was the state law required a four-sided four foot high isolation fence positioned around the entire periphery of the pool, designed to include a self-closing and self-latching gate, an added safeguard to prevent children's direct access.

It was Steven's third birthday, the colorful banner proclaimed from its anchored position on the front lawn, joined by colorful balloons dancing in the slight breeze as if stimulated by soft music.

The children, six to be exact, accompanied by their mothers would be arriving soon, to be treated to a show of magic and puppeteers sure to hold their approving attention, the thankful mothers helping in the preparation of the fare: the food to be served before the birthday cake and the opening of presents. Tasha's appetite limits would be tested before the day was over by the over-indulging children ridding themselves of their plates excesses. The children apart from their parents, brazened by their collective strength, their disciplined behavior closeted, the more aggressive sought center stage, directed their bullying at a tethered Tasha. Starting as taunting and deteriorating to throwing pebbles and twigs. Tasha not cowering when hit, still sought a rewarding involvement, not their sudden hostility. Witnessing all of this was a chagrined George Staves who reacted quickly to the cruelty of the children and brought her into the house. Her separation bringing dissatisfaction at having to listen and sniff at the sounds and smells of the children, whimpering at the loss of playtime and treats.

All went well during the pool time as the life jacketed children, supervised and assisted by mothers, showcased their swimming abilities of varying levels. The excitement ended when an unexpected thunderstorm cloudburst stopped the play, releasing a shower of rain down on them, bringing commands from the reacting parents for the children to be out of the pool, expressing concern for a torrential lighting laced downpour. Watching in disappointment were the children crowded in the Monteleone's finished den, shivering within the towels theirs mothers had provided.

The rain that all had hoped would be short-lived continued unabated for most of the afternoon. The children, waiting patiently for the rain to end, became increasingly restless, showing little interest in the backup games suggested by their mothers, necessitating the early presentation of the puppeteers and magician, advancing the birthday cake and opening of the presents.

With the rain still a consideration, the advanced birthday agenda having been completed, the invited children and their mothers began leaving under protective umbrellas. When the last of the invited children left, the sun was given passage by the finally retreating clouds.

As Tasha had been forced to be quarantined, first by the cruelty of the children and then by the incessant heavy rainfall, it didn't take much encouragement on George's part to get her to leave the house. With her collar and leash affixed to her tether, she scampered down the steps to the patio to find, after doing her business, a rain cooled spot in the grass on which to lie down.

George remarked to himself what a major cleanup of the backyard lay in store for Ken Monteleone when he returned from work. What Staves didn't notice in hindsight was the pools removable ladder was still in place, undoubtedly forgotten during the eager flight to evacuate when the rains came. By an oversight Laura Monteleone was now party to her precaution being violated- forever scaring her. The positioned ladder remained unnoticed as she acceded to Steven's pestering wishes, sitting him in the wading pool after removing the overflowing rainwater to a level she was comfortable with. Looking around she spotted Tasha, and knowing her presence would excite her son, quickly said, "Look, Steven, there's Tasha watching you."

Steven, a smile of delight occupying his face, pointed with his index finger offering his word sounds for Tasha as "Sha, Sha."

Tasha, hearing the semblance of her name, wagged her tail in acknowledgment.

Judging everything safe, comforted that she had done this before, Laura left Steven, not knowing how significant her words of Tasha watching would be, fortuitously blessed by her vital presence and timing, the threat of the uncontained danger only feet away – lurking.

Steven busied himself in the wading pool squealing in delight, throwing water up with his hands splashing himself, filling and emptying his pail, excitedly talking gibberish as Tasha watched lazily. Tiring of his games, he looked for new challenges. While glancing about, he spotted a butterfly that fluttered into view. Following it with his eyes, he saw it drop down into the pool only to rise almost immediately as the pool's water was not potable. His attention captured, eager for a new adventure, Steven climbed out of the wading pool, heading for the attraction of the big pool, remembering all the fun it had brought him in the past.

Tasha rose quickly, recognizing the danger posed by the still-in-place ladder and barked a warning. Steven waved gleefully at Tasha, fulfilling his part of the game he thought they were playing, continuing undeterred toward his objective.

George Staves was out front of his house rinsing off his car which had been parked in the driveway during the sudden downpour. Preoccupied, he assumed that Tasha's barking was to chase off a searching squirrel.

Laura Monteleone also heard Tasha's barking but missed its significance, having minutes earlier checked to find Steven still busy with his water games, never noticing the forgotten ladder.

Tasha continued her barking, now frantic as Steven neared the pool, flinging herself violently against her restraining tether and collar.

Steven in innocence continued his unrestrained freedom, smiling and turning mischievously away from Tasha, focusing on the movable ladder left in place. Not of concern, he being carried into the pool, having observed the older children and adults, confident and unafraid that he could also climb the ladder as he was now successfully doing, pulling himself up one step at a time.

George Staves, hearing Tasha's barking, smiled at the brazenness of Tasha tormenting squirrels, knowing that being tethered assured no consequences; unconcerned he continued his rinsing. Equally at ease was Laura Monteleone busy with her cleaning, confident that her son was preoccupied in the wading pool away from any threats, unaware that statistically seventy-five percent of all child drownings occur within five minutes after last seen.

Steven reached the top step of the movable ladder just as Tasha, mustering a tremendous surge of strength sheared the pin of her collar, free she raced toward Steven, intent on snaring within her mouth his swimming shorts, leaping too late as he went over the side of the pool, shocked at his inability to stand above the water that engulfed him having risen to heights he had never experienced before.

Tasha quickly reversing herself raced toward the Monteleone's back storm door, flinging herself against the screen panel forcing it free of it's restraining clips with such force that she shattered some of the panels of glass of the French Door, the shards of glass cutting her front legs.

Laura startled when hearing the tumult, dropped the whining vacuum cleaner. Leaving its motor still running, her brow furrowed, questioning as she opened the inner door, finding broken glass at her feet, her pace increasing she flung open the partially denuded storm door, crying out when not seeing Steven in the wading pool, a sickening feeling of understanding coming to her as she saw a bleeding Tasha turn from her to move towards the pool. Laura was ashen faced, panic about to overwhelm her as a frantic Tasha repeatedly looked back to her to be sure that she understood and was being followed. Reaching the pool Tasha leaped upon it barking furiously.

Laura, her heart pounding, a cold sweat of panic building on her forehead, dreading the worst, flew out of the shattered door, unconcerned for the shards of glass beneath her tennis shoed feet, with her eyes fixed on Tasha, in a reflex response hoped against hope, her peripheral vision not locating Steven, the wading pools, adjacent area empty. Grief-stricken, she now screamed at the top of her lungs, "Oh, my God… No! No! Please help me."

Laura's screams brought George running to see Laura climbing the ladder, her face distorted in a mask of agony as she saw her son Steven motionless at the bottom of the pool. She immediately jumped into the water and with a purposeful swoop retrieved her son limp as a rag doll into her arms, hysterically screaming, "Steven, Steven," prayerful that he would revive.

Steven remained motionless and unresponsive. Laura, fitfully in tears, unable to cope with uncertainty, relinquished her son to George, beseeching that he help her. Her moaning, wounded and animalistic turned to screams of, "Oh, my God, what have I done?" her face pale, drained of blood, her eyes dilated by shock, her wringing hands in prayer at her chest. All the while Tasha, bleeding from her cuts, was at George's side panting heavily, eyes flashing anxiously, searching each of them, finding the language of their bodies desperate.

George, with Steven in his arms, dropped quickly to the ground. Not knowing how long Steven was under water, he knew he was fighting time. Acting quickly, he put his ear to Steven's chest, anxious when he did not hear any breathing – worried that no oxygen was getting into his bloodstream. Frantically, he searched for a pulse beat, finding a very faint one. "Circulation poor but there's hope," was his assessment to a wailing Laura to whom he shouted commandingly to call 911, breaking her out of her paralyzing hysteria. With time of the essence, he knew it would be up to him to keep a life from slipping away. He began CPR, quickly compressing the chest cavity, then mouth-to-mouth as he breathed air directly into Steven's non-functioning lungs. He repeated the procedure again and again. Sweat trickled down his forehead into his eyes, blurring his vision, but still he didn't stop, determined to continue his attempt at resuscitation. In the background he could hear the wailing of the emergency vehicle's siren announcing its mission just as Steven finally began to respond. Coughing up pool water and bile, he finally opened his eyes, crying tearfully for his mother who had returned prayerfully to George's side. Praising God for His mercy, she moved beyond George

Staves quickly gathering Steven in her arms, smothering his face with kisses, her tears now joyfully mixing with those of fright shed by Steven.

The emergency crew arrived, rushing to the back of the house with a defibrillator in hand, finding Steven conscious in his mother's arms. They quickly took charge, throwing a blanket around little Steven to ward off shock while checking blood pressure and pulse rate, declaring Steven out of danger but in need of precautionary examination by a doctor.

Laura, still visibly shaken, received comfort from a solicitous Rose who had returned home from shopping as the potentially disastrous incident was still unfolding, Laura thankfully accepted her offer to accompany her to the hospital.

Staves in turn would bring Tasha to the vet to check her wounds which appeared to require stitching, the bleeding not responding to pressure bandaging.

They were home within three hours. The doctor, after checking him thoroughly, found Steven clear to be released with the proviso that he be watched closely over the next twenty-four hours. Ken Monteleone, rushing to the hospital from work after Laura's heart stopping phone call, joined her in time to hear the emergency room doctors findings, extracting a gasp of dread from them both for what might have been an outcome if Steven had not been pulled from the water before the critical four-minute time period had expired, after which full recovery would drop off dramatically, if at all.

Tasha, with her front legs shaven, her wound sutured, did not take to her bandages, a medal representation in helping to save a life, more than once George had to chastise her for attempting to bite them off.

Later that evening George and Rose paid a supportive visit to the Monteleones at an hour they expected Steven would be asleep, only to find him protectively in his mother's arms where she would keep him for the next twenty-four hours.

"How is he?" Rose asked.

Laura would only nod, not daring to divert her attention from Steven in answering, as if a mysterious force would see it as an opportunity to take him away from her.

"Outside of his fright, which according to the doctors he should outgrow, he shows no physical effects from his ordeal, for which Laura and I are extremely indebted to you and Tasha," Ken Monteleone said somberly.

"Thank God," Rose said sincerely, warmly placing her arms around Laura and Steven.

"We were blessed to have Tasha and you as our good neighbors. We owe you our thanks for the life of our son," Ken said, his voice cracking with emotion.

With Rose and George still unsettled by the experience, sincere modesty made them uncomfortable with the profuse praise, dismissed their contribution as one that any neighbor would do for one another.

"In the name of God, I pray thanks to that truth," Ken responded passionately, then added reflectively, "But how many have a Tasha? All efforts would have come too late if not for her alertness and sacrifice. An amazing dog. I'm going to get her the biggest porterhouse steak money can buy."

"No need for that," Rose said smiling. "Seeing that Steven is fine would be enough payment for her."

Laura, overwhelmed by the compassion and giving nature of the Staves's, started to cry. Steven asleep in her arms, disturbed, began to moan, distressed by a dream.

On the verge of being awakened, his mother coaxed his composure, continuing his sleep, her eyes never leaving him she said, "Tasha's actions were almost human… she tried to warn me. I just wasn't listening, confident in Steven's safety. She is a very special dog," her speech now difficult, stammering, "she saw it about to happen right in front of her. Knew the danger to my Steven. Knew she must do something when I didn't respond. To break her collar pin with such a display of strength is almost impossible to believe. My son's life the motivator. I'm forever indebted to her," she said choking back a sob.

"She is special," George concurred. "I'm thankful that she was here to help. She never ceases to amaze us."

Rose nodded proudly, "She never ceases to amaze all who come in contact with her. Dependable, she is always there, recognizing developing danger, rising to the occasion."

When they returned home from their visit, they found Tasha expectedly in her usual perch sitting in the bow window waiting for them. By the time the automatic garage door closed and they entered the house, she was upon them sniffing and searching. Finally satisfied with her reading of their telling demeanor, she lay down in a heap, expelling her breath. Dissuaded by a foul tasting repellent, her bandages showed no signs of gnawing. She would have to wait until the sutures were dissolved before the benefits of her medicinal saliva.

~

Tasha's latest celebrity, it's event sparking debate amongst the divided, cheered by the anthropomorphist, while running counter to those who view the overwhelming certainty: animals being essentially automatons, programmed to mimic, reflective of nurturing, incapable of cognizance.

"If the naysayer view were an absolute, Tasha's role in saving little Steven from drowning would never have happened," scoffed the time traveling

George Staves, advantaged over his younger self, knowing what the future held while his counterpart at that moment could only anticipate. Ending this time period's heart wrenching stay, commanded infinitesimal movement from his transporter knowing this time period held tandem events, continuous of Tasha's unusual intelligence confounding all that knew or heard of her.

~

At 1:30 AM George Staves awoke to flashing lights. His first thoughts: he was experiencing a migraine headache. Bracing himself for the tortuous experience, anxiety dampened his whole body. Anticipating the worst, his only hope before the excruciating pain was upon him was in the medicine cabinet of his bathroom, his prescription for migraines, specific analgesics and antidepressants to reduce the dilation and constriction of blood vessels in the brain stem. Sleep left him as he entered the bathroom fully awake, relieved yet apprehensive to learn the flashing lights were not throbs behind his eyes but reflections off the ceiling. He joined an earlier awakened Rose at the south side window to find the source of the flashing lights were two police cars parked in the driveway of the Monteleones, their band radio's squawking clipped messages.

They dressed quickly, assisting the Monteleones their purpose. With Tasha in tow Rose opened the front door, they were immediately halted by a unidentified firm voice of one of the policemen cautioning them back into the house. "A crime investigation is taking place," he warned.

Shocked at the revelation, they quickly closed the door returning to the window facing the Monteleone driveway. The Staves's as well as all surrounding neighbors had turned on their house lights completing a welcomed illumination for the investigating police. The Staves, as expected, received phone calls from inquisitive neighbors: repeated the policeman's advisory. While troubled that they had not heard from the Monteleone's directly, cautioned by the police deciding to stand by until more information became available.

"We'll just have to wait for answers," they offered politely, hanging up the phone.

It wasn't long; a resounding commanding knock at their front door by a flashlight holding police sergeant and a young officer, a declaration of an update anticipated, "Good evening, sorry to trouble you " the young officer said courteously as they greeted him. "I'm officer Dallas and this is sergeant Blanchard. We're just about finished investigating a reported crime scene. Have you noticed anything unusual? Any odd occurrences? Any strangers sighted?"

"No," George Staves said finding the question worrisome. "What's going on?"

Sergeant Blanchard responded, "It seems that Mrs. Monteleone, while visiting friends, believes she had an attempted break-in, the patio screened paneled storm and back door windows were broken. The dispersion of glass indicates the force that broke the glass came from the outside, certainly a suspicion of a break-in. Convinced, she was afraid to enter her home. We arrived within minutes of her 911 cell phone call. Escorting her, we searched the house from top to bottom finding nothing stolen or the house ransacked. Concluding that if it were a break in, our audible sirens scared the perpetrators off, or most likely they were non existent, the broken glass attributable to a baseball from children's earlier play not her sons discovered by the police in the room. For added assurance, this inquiry our final phase of our investigation – asking neighbors like yourselves if they saw or suspected something was wrong."

"I'm afraid not, Sergeant. Neither of us noticed or heard anything that would have aroused our suspicions. Our dog Tasha never showed alarm."

Sergeant Blanchard and officer Dallas, their questions over, ended their brief meeting. "Thanks for your time. Sorry to disturb you," Blanchard said apologetically, we'll be on our way. We have other neighbors to talk to," turning to descend the entrance steps, looking over their shoulders to say, "Good night."

"Good night," Rose and George said to the backs of the preoccupied officers. Rose closing the door when they were sufficiently distant.

Rose immediately went to the phone and called Laura Monteleone finding her relatively calm, quick to relate what had happened. Frightened initially by the circumstances, her husband out of town on business, apprehensive to enter the house alone. But not now, Laura assured Rose, admitting she might have over reacted to the broken window pane, particularly after finding the baseball, the police easing her concerns with their escort and thoroughness in checking the house. They were also kind enough to nail a sheet of wood from my garage to cover the broken panels of glass on the interior door. Still, Rose being a good neighbor offered Laura a room to spend the night. Laura graciously declined as unnecessary having conferred by phone with her husband. She would manage "thank you," finding courage and resolve in knowing police patrol cars would keep the house under close surveillance.

It was 3:15 in the morning when the Staves finally returned to sleep. At 5:00 AM, two hours before dawn, they were again aroused by flashing lights, the repeating circumstances coming so close to the earlier event it was thought by them to be a dream state revisited, until the voice of the police radio dispatcher confirmed the reality. Quickly dressing, they rushed to open the front door, again halted by an admonishment to "stay indoors" as a police investigation was underway. They recognized the youthful voice as the same officer Dallas who with Sergeant Blanchard had contacted them earlier. His tone authoritative, more impatient and curt. George deciding this time not to be dismissed so easily, pressed him further:

"Officer, we are more than just neighbors to the Monteleones, more like family. Their very important to us."

The impatience of youth surfacing within the young officer, exasperated, took liberty from protocol, confident that no one was at risk he shared his perceptions and what he suspected would be the police findings and position.

"As you know, this is the second time she's called, this time claiming there was an intruder in the house. We responded and conducted a second thorough search, again finding nothing. Still, she insisted that someone was in the house watching her, relying not on a sighting but her sense of danger. Again with her closely following for the third time we searched the house from top to bottom, again coming up empty. We can't convince her that no one is in the house. She's being paranoid, staying in her son's room armed with a kitchen knife. Can you imagine that?" he said in frustration. "I don't know what more we can do to convince her. We can't stand guard around the house. There's no justification for it. She's unwilling to understand we've got a responsibility for the whole community. We can't be catering to her run amok imagination and still serve the rest of the people in our area."

Not liking what he was hearing, Laura's concerns being brushed off as irrational, hysteria driven, George boldly interjected:

"Officer, I'd like to help and offer to put this situation to bed once and for all."

"I'm sorry. It's police business. You're a civilian," he said dismissively.

Staves ignored his haughtiness. "It's not me. I would never make that presumption. It's my dog. I'm sure you're right – amateurs have no place in police business," Staves said, attempting to placate and win him over. "If the house is clear of any intruders, my dog will confirm it. Surely you can't object to that. She's got unbelievable senses. It can't hurt. After all, the police use dogs in their work. It won't be discrediting."

The policeman was not persuaded. However, he did agree to take his suggestion to his sergeant for approval. Responding to the young officers call, the sergeant and the other investigating patrolmen soon appeared at the front door of the Monteleones. Staves was motioned over by Sergeant Blanchard.

"Do you think that your dog could do more than we have in searching the house?" he asked.

"Nothing more than augment your search," Staves responded quickly. "Tasha, that's her name, has done similar acts of discovery before. If for no other reason but Mrs. Monteleone's peace of mind, it's worth the assurance."

"We can't allow you to be an official part of this investigation," the sergeant countered. "We can't risk your safety. If I agree it would have to be your dog alone."

“She’ll do it without me if I tell her. Just let me escort her to the back door where the break-in is suspected.”

Sergeant Blanchard reluctantly agreed, not happy with George Staves’s interference.

Laura terror gripped, her son awake in her arms wrapped in a blanket, joined the Staves. Grasping what was being suggested, immediately welcomed the plan resisting being led away by Rose until she had her say with George Staves. Distraught grabbing his arm with her free hand, momentarily restraining him, her face frightened and concerned, her other arm tightly clutching Steven, she stammered:

“They won’t accept it. Finding that baseball a clever diversion. I know that someone’s in the house. I can feel and sense him. I’m sure I even heard him.”

“Did you tell that to the police? That you actually heard him?”

Finding composure, her demeanor quieting, said for all to hear, “They listened but didn’t believe me. They’re convinced that the first search was quite thorough and no one could have escaped their detection. I believed them then but not now. When I insisted they check the house a third time, they reluctantly agreed and then only to appease me, again finding nothing, practically accusing me of seeking attention.”

Sergeant Blanchard quickly interjected.

“I’m sorry we gave you that impression, Mrs. Monteleone,” he said solicitously. “We tried. He would have had to be invisible for us to have missed him. Just think about it.”

“But I just know someone’s in the house,” Laura insisted, no longer feeling alone and deserted.

Sergeant Blanchard said dubiously, “If he is or was, he left no traces, outside of the back door’s broken glass. We found no other evidence other than the baseball. We have to consider it an act of children. Remember, the back door lock was still engaged.”

“Yes, but it has to be a ploy.” a frustrated Laura said

Coming to her defenses, George interjected, “Tell us what you heard.”

“Sir, we’ve heard it all before. It’s time for us to move on” the sergeant said, becoming impatient.

“It won’t take but a moment,” Staves insisted, drawing an exasperated nod.

Laura gathered herself for the telling, relating that she had had difficulty falling asleep. In the darkness of the bedroom, she could hear her son breathing peacefully, drawing her to join him.

As she began to fall asleep, on the edge, she could hear her own breathing distinct and separate from her son’s. While not coordinated, she found they did follow a repeating pattern, one that can be anticipated and listened for while struggling to find sleep. She was just short of that final longed for step, on the verge of sleep with only a few grams of consciousness remaining, her submitting brain in a final conscious act told her that something was not right. Her son's breathing and her own breathing predictable, suddenly she realized another breath, once overlaying her own or her son's, was no longer deliberately synchronized, mimicking. Someone else's breathing, deliberately heavy, intending to be heard, a degenerate's titillation being derived from the danger of discovery. She screamed with comprehension, eyes wide with fright. Reflectively, she reached for her son bringing him to her bosom with her surrounding protective arms, expecting to see the face she intuited emerging from the darkened room, leering at them, the sociopath's breath fouled with encouraging alcohol. Startling her son awake nightmarishly, his arms flailed wildly in defense, striking nothing. His sudden movement caused his legs to become entangled within the bed sheets creating a feeling of being shackled by unknown forces worsening Steven's frenzy.

She searched the darkness for movement and saw nothing. Unsure of what she would find, having no choice she turned on the reading lamp, revealing only her frantic appearance in the bureau mirror as she clutched Steven protectively. The reality of light holding no discovery of the intruder, concluding that he was forced to retreat to his hiding place, he misjudging her deep sleep, her cries destroying his stealth, his moment of eroticism. Laura paused, searching the faces of her listeners.

Repeated, it still wasn't resonating with the police as an actual experience but rather her imagination. Her continuing emotional fright while difficult to ignore was politely summarily dismissed, so certain were the police, their search complete and thorough. Their reticence suggesting that Laura being alone and vulnerable, her reactions were highly emotional; her imagination overreacting, her stealth house visitor the bi-product of anxiety.

George wanted to be a believer but being a rational man made it difficult for him to ignore the police findings.

"If we, with Tasha's help, fail to find something this time, Laura, I insist you and Steven spend the night with us. Ken will be home tomorrow and together we can sort things out."

"I think that's an excellent suggestion Mrs. Monteleone, in your present state it's one I would strongly urge," said the sergeant, compassionate for her distress yet official, recognizing the benefits of Laura relocating for the night.

"I fully intend on accepting that invitation. I wouldn't think of spending the night in the house," Laura shuddered.

The police, sensing closure was near, while adamant in their position, were reluctantly ready for their participation in what they believed would be an exercise, their final act in this matter.

In preparation, upon command, George exposed a sniffing Tasha having added to her storage the scents of the policemen, counseled Tasha to ignore. Clearly, she understood her task was to search and screen to differentiate the known from the strange. He turned over a leashed Tasha to the control of Sergeant Blanchard, confident in her abilities to distinguish as foreign traces of perspiration or hopefully blood from superficial cuts during the suspected break-in or, for that matter, anything forensic.

Tasha energized and aware of what was expected of her, eager to please, started with a jolt, her powerful muscles almost dragging the bulky large framed Sergeant Blanchard with her. As directed, the other policemen followed closely behind them with Staves trailing reasonably out of harm's way. Rose took it upon herself to escort Laura and Steven to the safety of her home to await the outcome. Laura hopeful with buoyed expectations, certain that Tasha would find the intruder.

The house was a split level. Tasha paused at the steps leading to the bedrooms, her sniffing search turning her away, finding pieces of what appeared to be aluminum foil. Dismissed during the search as inconsequential, apparently missed during housecleaning. Instead of climbing the stairs, she selected the lower level to start, the obvious path for an intruder's break in and escape, hopeful for a scent in confirmation.

Tasha gave the door leading to the garage only a perfunctory sniff… not here she signaled. Nonetheless, the garage was to be part of the search. The sergeant directed a reluctant Tasha to Laura's car which she investigated from stem to stern including the trunk. Her pace not surprisingly rapid, Staves thought, knowing her interests were elsewhere, leading she camped herself panting by the closed basement door.

Alert to Tasha's stronger interest, George asked one of the accompanying policemen, "What did you find down there?"

Responding, an aggressive investigative rookie officer said, "The typical, furnace and water tank, with available space for storage. There's some drywall and wood paneling standing upright against one wall. Against another wall is a large couch covered with bed sheets. On top of the couch are boxes that contain Christmas decoration including an artificial Christmas tree." Anticipating questions, he added confidently, "All those boxes were probed searched with our night sticks."

The sergeant impatiently interjected, "We've searched the basement thoroughly. There is no one hiding, I assure you. We're wasting our time." Exasperated that Staves was not convinced of his assurance, exhaling in frustration he ordered, "Let's get on with it."

The basement door had a simple hardware store bought locking mechanism that was set in the lock position. If the intruder was down there hiding he was trapped unless he had the skills and tools of a locksmith he theorized, coming and going as he pleased, Staves's pulse rate increasing expectedly.

Blanchard, watching Staves check the locking mechanism, his sixth sense aroused alerting him said, "Mrs. Monteleone told us that she engaged the basement lock and garage lock right after she called 911, following the directions of the police."

"You mean she said that she had left those doors unlocked?" George Staves questioned astonished.

"That's what I was told… that she and her husband sometimes forgot."

"Sergeant, after your first inspection of the house, did you lock the basement door before leaving?" An aroused Staves anxiously queried.

"Yes, I did," he replied.

"You know what that suggests?" about to voice his opinion that the intruder is somewhat of a Houdini. "He could have been there all along, playing everyone as fools, making his second visit to Mrs. Monteleone's bedroom not the figment of her overwrought imagination."

"Are you suggesting that he does exist and is still down there, not escaping when he had the chance? Why would he do that knowing the police would be arriving shortly?"

"Unfinished business with Mrs. Monteleone. If you believe her that there is such a person, he must get his kicks out of flaunting his presence in the face of discovery," George said.

"Not possible. He's not down there," a testy Sergeant Blanchard interrupted. Annoyed and defensive realizing being adamant broke with his experience not to be too committed, always have a safety net, offered the caveat, "I must admit I've seen better locks picked in break-ins."

"Let's finish it," Staves insisted, "and put this to bed once and for all."

The basement door was opened, greeting them with the typical dank smell of below ground, held in check by an overlaying odor.

"Mothballs," one of the policemen volunteered in answer to Staves' questioning frown. "It's in the couch, its pillows and the covering sheet to keep out the mildew."

"It's certainly strong," Staves commented, wondering what effect it would have on Tasha's olfactory senses.

With the basement lights turned on, Tasha leading the troupe, descended the steps in short order. Her head bowed to the task, her nose to the damp floor of the unfinished basement, sweeping from side to side in the pattern of a vacuum cleaner, stopping on occasion to dwell and paw at her interest. She completed her circuitous route, stopping once again by the couch, nothing unfamiliar registering; she moved to return upstairs.

The two policemen and their sergeant were quick to voice their vindication."We told you all along that we would be wasting our time," cockily adding, "We know our job. We were very thorough. We missed nothing."

Rose and Laura, seeing some of the searching police exit the house, anxious for word, re-entered the Monteleone's home, Laura, with one arm holding Steven, her other hand up to her mouth in shock receiving the news.

"Oh my God, it can't be. I was so sure. I feel so foolish for what I've put everyone through."

With Tasha sitting, Staves reached down to pet her, rewarding her with words of encouragement, confident in her abilities. His hand accepted a deposit from her mouth. It was another piece of what appeared to be aluminum foil.

Missing its connection, looking up he said, "Laura, you can rest assured if Tasha couldn't find anyone, then there isn't anyone."

Yet his attention was still drawn to the open basement door and the basement smell. His sense of smell detected a hint of another odor resisting the domination of mothballs in the mix wafting into the den where they all had assembled. Suddenly he was cognizant, making a connection to the aluminum foil in the basement. It pleasant when used sparingly but overwhelming the senses when used excessively. Needing confirmation, he asked Laura as he knelt close to the floor to validate the lingering higher density fragrance, his hand fingering the aluminum foil.

At first Laura showed no hint of recognition, but his insistence prompt another more determined effort.

"Why, it's after shave lotion. Ken's favorite, Aqua Velva."

The policemen looked on, perplexed by Staves' actions, curious as to where it might lead.

"Why would it be in the basement?" he asked of Laura, his excitement growing.

"Ken set up an alternate shaving station including Aluminum foiled packets of the fragrance Aqua Velva by the basement sink to free up the upstairs bathrooms in the event of overnight guests and time in short supply. Why do you ask?"

"In a minute." Staves said, delaying his response "That means he has some in the master bathroom?"

"Yes," Laura replied, not clear of his meaning. The police were becoming impatient with their exclusion.

"Get it for me. I'll explain everything when you return."

The policemen's patience strained, Sergeant Blanchard bellowed, "We've had enough of this circus. Play your games on your own time," he scoffed disapprovingly, assembling his remaining men to leave.

"Please," Staves implored. "We've gone this far, a few more minutes of your time couldn't possibly hurt. I intend to do it with or without your presence. I can assure you if you leave now and I'm proven right, it will prove very embarrassing for the police department."

Backing off, troubled by Staves confidence, the prospect of placing his judgment in question, Sergeant Blanchard capitulated protectively. Having lost his moment, attempting to save some face in front of his men, said pointedly, "It's your last nickel. Spend it wisely," just as Laura returned with a bottle of Aqua Velva.

Emboldened with confidence, Staves said, "I supplied Tasha with the wrong cues. We have a very clever person we are dealing with. His personal scent was masked by the mothballs to further confuse Tasha, who had been told to only search for foreign scents and ignore the scents of those she's familiar with. Unless I miss my guess, our perpetrator cleverly camouflaged himself further with Ken's after shave lotion, having overheard me tell Tasha to accept and ignore all familiar scents. But he's outsmarted himself. We'll beat him at his own game. Bear with me."

Laura's eyes were glued to him, brightened by the recognition of what he was saying. A restoration of hope in her vindication.

"Tasha," Staves commanded. Immediately she rose to his authority and moved to his side. He doused a handkerchief with the lotion, holding it to her nose until it dominated her olfactory senses. He removed the leash directing her to "Go find." She literally flew down the basement steps to the couch, knocking off the sheet covered boxes with the piston-like strokes of her front paws, zeroing in on the largest that contained the artificial Christmas tree, she savagely pulled out the branches still hanging with traces of tinsel. Exposing a diminutive man sent sprawling to the floor in fear of his life. His Body in the fetal position his arms and hands brought up to his face in protection, intimidated to motionless as he was confronted by a snarling threatening Tasha only inches away from doing damage. Screaming, "Get her away from me."

The two red-faced patrolmen, mouths agape looked from one to the other and then to their equally embarrassed astonished sergeant. The embarrassing scenario toppled them from their high ground of aloofness, thankful for an opportunity to reestablish superiority, drew their guns, moving quickly to apprehend the perpetrator; Sergeant Blanchard backing Tasha off as the perpetrator was handcuffed and arrested.

The slightly built captive was dressed entirely in black including his woven cap, the uniform of those finding opportunity and passage while hidden among the shadows. Unshaven, his dark bristles meant to reject facial glare, grown with little care or prideful contouring covered his craggy hawk-like features. His dominating feature was his nose, showing signs of being repeatedly broken telling of a violent background. A loosely tied ponytail, unkempt and greasy, further characterized this social outcast. His police data sheet would show a progression of law breaking ranging from petty theft early in his career to lusting voyeurism, a aberrant sexual outlet that continued rejection forced him despicably to gravitate to. In his pockets were the tools of his trade: wires of varying diameters and plastic strips undoubtedly used to open the basement door.

Returning from the patrol car after calling in the arrest, Sergeant Blanchard, in need to regain respect and dampen criticism, attempting to placate, spoke directly to Laura Monteleone.

"I don't know how I can apologize enough for doubting you. Regrettably, we just made a bad search. I dread to think of what might have happened," turning his attention to Staves, "had it not been for your dog." Nodding toward Tasha he said, "She is one smart dog. She could be my patrol partner anytime."

"Thanks for the compliment, Sergeant Blanchard. Let me assure you, we hold no ill feelings toward the police. It was the final outcome that was important. I, like you, dread the thought of what might have happened if Mrs. Monteleone had not remained steadfast. I must admit there was a period of time when I too doubted her."

"I appreciate your honesty, Sergeant Blanchard," Laura interjected. "The police action taken under normal circumstances would have been sufficient." "It was his unexpected deviousness and contempt for all, his appetite for danger escaping our understanding." said Sergeant Blanchard.

"I'm grateful to the police coming to my assistance," said Laura. "I shudder to think what might have happened. Your fast response stopped him. I don't diminish that."

An appreciative Sergeant Blanchard said, "We needed the intervention of another species, one with special gifts to keep the police from making a dreadful mistake. We're deeply indebted to Tasha."

"Dear Tasha," Laura said adoringly. Upon hearing her name, Tasha responded by wagging her tail, always on automatic for friendly voices.

"Where would we be without your having been an important part of my life and the lives of my family," Laura continued, her feelings strong, unconsciously clutching Steven protectively until she realized he was safe, and the threat to his well-being history, written by Tasha. Tears flowed freely wetting her face as she adoringly petted Tasha. Without understanding his mothers tears Steven reached out to Tasha, attempting to emulate his mother.

A period of supportive reflective silence fell upon them as they watched and shared in the marvel of Tasha. Laura, her experiences vividly imprinted, held a passion for Tasha as if she were a deity, a guardian angel materialized outside of a house of worship, devoid of the prayerful smoke of lighted candles.

The respectful silence was broken by Sergeant Blanchard. "I have a favor to ask of you and your wife, Mr. Staves."

"Which is?"

"If a situation develops… a police situation where Tasha's special talents could help… can I call on you?"

"As long as the threat to her well-being is minimal, I'll consider it."

"Let's at least talk about it," Sergeant Blanchard asked, pleased that his request was not outright rejected, receiving a polite affirming nod from George Staves.

In the days that followed, the local TV stations and newspapers carried the story. With politics prevailing, only the smallest amount of credit was given to Tasha's role-preferred by Staves to prevent reawakening the public's adoration frenzy.

Paul Dever was identified as the break-in perpetrator, his name finally surfacing. His record, in police jargon, his rap sheet not matching his stature was lengthy. At the age of thirteen, he was convicted of petty theft and shoplifting. An expert practitioner of stealth, he found success in auto theft, matriculating to housebreaking. Apprehended and sentenced to a juvenile facility where his time spent included mandatory education and the "righting therapy of psychologists" were patently ignored or rejected. He would bide his time knowing the crowded conditions of his incarceration and his coming of age would bring him release.

Duplicity his nature, during imprisonment he portrayed a more compliant personality, lacking substance, fooling no one. Having paid society for his past misdeeds, at the time of his release he was judged as a borderline sociopath. The conditions of his release under the enforcement of his parole officer were to continue participating in programs to bring him to social awareness. His promises were token as his drug dependency became his main focus, ultimately being caught and convicted of possession of trace amounts of marijuana, a minor offense. Undeterred and addicted, he graduated to distributing, a much more serious offense. A crowded court system allowed him to plead down to possession with the admonition that he enroll in clinical rehabilitation at a state hospital for his addiction, receiving a suspended sentence in the agreement.

During his treatment stay, he learned his physiological impotency was not his only abnormality, cursed further by gynecomastia – male breast development, an imbalance of estrogen and androgen. Coupling those conditions with his diminutiveness made him an easy mark for the degenerates. His low intellect, his desperate need for fulfillment, his chromosomal imbalance, intimidated he identified with bi-sexual missions for his sexual pleasure, becoming a male prostitute to pay for his growing drug habit, expanding his deviancy to include the libido stimulant of voyeurism.

The introduction of added danger to himself became his trigger mechanism for his deviancy but only after careful selection: breaking into homes of women, either widowed, or alone while their husbands were out of town on a work assignment. Reducing his field of possible victims further, he selected younger women with a single child still in a crib. After successfully breaking in undetected, he would wait until all were asleep, then creep softly from his hiding place, leering and smiling down on the intruded. Titillated to a Mount Everest high, the danger of being caught stimulated his blood flow; engouraging being as close to the unsuspecting victim as he dared, quieting his groans by forcefully biting into his arm, drawing blood, maniacal in his pursuit of deviant intimacies while precipitously close to discovery, the victim unknowingly providing the passion to complete the act. Sexually satisfied, he then went about stealing whatever he could carry away in his stash bag in one trip.

Interrogation of Paul Dever at police headquarters revealed that he did in fact use the plastic strips to leave and return to his hiding place. The ineptness of the searches was never a criticism in the media and yet questions remained – the perceptive troubled that he was missed in every search.

Paul Dever was judged as criminally insane and committed to a state institution where he could receive mind altering drugs and therapy. Removed from his perversions, his brain irreversibly damaged, a threat to himself put under close watch until his dying day

The just concluded, purposed to elevate episodes given kinship with the occurrence that preceded it and one that would follow. Their individual characteristics, their coloring, intersecting one another, blurring the lines of separation. The lapsing time period milliseconds, traveling at warp speeds. By the power of his will the occurrences with their energies of images and sound were married for this visit only. In the future the separate events place in history were returned, the events giving way to be visited chronologically. This accommodation obviating the need to full empowerment of his transporter. His distinguishing, his separating easily performed by his kaleidoscope.

He moved with confidence among the pipes and ductwork over the hastily built cinder block auxiliary girls shower room. Tight-fisted school authorities and limited funding left the eight foot high by forty foot square structure without windows and ceiling. The room was a temporary response by this school and others to the federal law Title IX requiring parity between men's and women's athletics at educational institutions receiving federal funding The controversial law forcing some educational institutions to drop other boys/mens subsidized sport activities to fulfill the law's requirement of matching gender registration. The structure location and rough bare bones design highlighting its afterthought adopted status. One end of the gymnasium that paralleled the Olympic size swimming pool used for conference basketball games had its viewing stands relocated to make room for the minimally cost impacting new structure.

The existing concrete floor, with no plans for tiling, showed a path of freshly poured concrete covering recently laid drain pipes beneath shower heads. Bathroom stalls and wash basins, installed on the wall that housed the lockers and their attendant metal folding chairs. The supplied heat and air conditioning were diverted from already overtaxed operational ductwork above the room, aided and abetted the surreptitious voyeur, pleased to no end by the provided opportunity.

His movement practiced stealth, quiet and confident, disturbing settled dust particles to seek other resting places. Out of unsuspecting sight, he moved among the shadows that would envelop him in their cast. Reaching his vantage point and mindful of his weight distribution, his slim upper body hugged the ductwork while carefully wrapping his strong lithe legs around heavy gauge pipe, his movement more primate than human. He would wait with anticipation, knowing the shower room's usage was imminent.

His eyes wide eyed, fixed with anticipation, awaiting the kindling for his lewdness. His facial characteristics concealed beneath a stocking mask wet with perspiration not from his physical exertion but of his libidos arousal. Arriving with their chatter and shouts, his hunger was satiated, feasting on unsuspecting girls stripping to their naked athleticism, hearing their shrieks of delight as the water rained down on their soap lathered bodies. The thrill, while exclusively his, would reach new heights of delight as he and others of his genre of perversions, shared in his voyeuristic photographs their primary venue.

As hard as he tried not to leave telltale signs of violating the girls' privacy, he could not prevent marks of dust disturbance – accidentally providing intelligence when he cut his hand on one of the hanging pipe straps, leaving blood residue in spite of his effort to wipe it clean, a DNA fingerprint a certainty if discovered. Clever in his protection, he purposefully set up his automatic camera one hundred eighty degrees from his actual vantage perch to take the photos, when studied, easily discernible shooting angles could be established, but misleadingly away from potential forensic evidence.

When the last girl was gone, titillated he removed himself from his hiding place. Moving quietly, his agility matched that of prehensile tail-bearing species. Maintaining his distance, a quick pull of the clear plastic wire that held and tethered the automatic picture taking camera in place released it from its anchored position, allowing the voyeur to reel in his catch of the day.

As there would be other instances, photography would suffice their lust, this being the only occasion of opportunity for he and the other voyeurs physical presence, minimizing suspicion.

~

Having distinguished himself on the job, his meritorious service rapidly advancing him, Police Captain Blanchard now sat in the office of Hillside High School Principal Schmidt's office searching through photographs, visibly showing disgust and disdain, he a father of three teenage girls.

"You say that you received them today?" he said curtly to Principal Schmidt.

"Yes, they arrived in the early morning mail," uncertain of Captain Blanchard's meaning.

"Ever receive pictures like these before, Mr. Schmidt?" Usually there is a pattern, a prior history, his tone accusatory and faulting.

Taken back by the question, Schmidt responded, "Actually, we have, I'm troubled to admit. We received others before; as a matter of fact… twice before."

The Captain clearly showing hostility spoke coldly, "Why weren't the police notified earlier?"

"I apologize for that, Captain. We thought it was an outrageous prank from one of the male students… thought we could handle it on our own and not involve the police," he said weakly: reaching with trembling hands into the middle drawer of his desk to pull two set's of photographs of young women slipping in and out of gym clothes and bathing suits, showering before dressing into their street clothes. The photos shown were taken from above, the angle the same in all of them."

"It's the same newly constructed shower room in all of the photos," offered Principal Schmidt.

"I can see that," Captain Blanchard said dismissively, still harboring resentment. "If you had been more open with us, perhaps we might have apprehended the voyeur after the first two mailings. You are right it is a male we are after, the wiping out of the faces in the earlier photos inclines it is not a discrediting female "

"We can say that now, Captain, but our thoughts were to protect the children and prevent the turmoil that usually occurs with public knowledge."

His confidence returning, he continued, "And we did just that. As you can see, the girls' earlier photos were not recognizable except to themselves. All the faces the voyeur blanked out. It was reasonable for us to think we could keep the matter confidential – we were protecting the school. Lacking facial identity, if other copies showed up, the children's identification would be dubious, remaining anonymous. We've been successful until today's latest photos – we now know that it was a mistake in not reporting the earlier instances in spite of the discrediting and embarrassing implications to the school. Now he is no longer blanking out the faces. They no longer can be spared from identification… from feeling violated. I can't imagine a parent's greater outrage than finding out from sources other than ourselves that their daughters were compromised under our watch. Those prospects would be a certainty if we did not go public at this time. Sorrowfully, a needed sacrifice from all involved. We hope the notoriety he is looking for would satisfy this chapter in his degenerate pursuit and end his despicable acts."

Captain Blanchard, understanding his motives as honorable, deciding it senseless furthering a debate. He would not concede his objectives and priorities were misguided, accepted Principal Schmidt's conceding… as close to an apology that would be given – returned to civility.

"The comparison of the photographs tells us something about him. It tells us that he has access to his own photo developing equipment as no commercial operation would process this film." Gaining a nod of agreement from Schmidt and anxious to start his investigation, he asked, "Can you take me to the site?"

"Of course, Captain. You'll see it's a temporary site, newly constructed as auxiliary girls' showers and lockers while the regular locker room undergoes changes and renovation."

As they left Principal Schmidt's office, they were joined by two uniformed policemen. A third man in civilian clothes, his searching alert eyes never at rest, his closely cropped hair fulfilling the regimental bearing of a discharged military man choosing a career in law enforcement. Stripped of either uniform would not give him anonymity in a crowd of civilians.

"Meet Patrolmen Hughes and Valente," Captain Blanchard introduced, "and this is Detective Zampino, our forensic expert," all shaking hands with Principal Schmidt.

Principal Schmidt, walking the school corridors on his own, a reminder of his authoritative presence among them was greeted with the hushed warning tones of students attention. This time flanked with two uniformed patrolmen, a police captain equally resplendent, and an obvious detective froze the students in their tracks, in raised tones abuzz with conjecture, some risking being late in the hopes of picking up information to impress their fellow students.

The contract workers, automatically suspects, also paused from their tasks to take note of the display of law enforcement before being shouted back to work.

Detective Zampino, having viewed the photos, quickly took charge, obvious to the camera's position and angle being overhead. Calling for a requested

Tow Motor with a boom from school maintenance, maneuvering until he located himself as the perpetrator had baited the camera's exact position one hundred eighty degrees from his actual location. After expending an appreciable amount of time scouring the area's network of pipes and ducts, he told Captain Blanchard that he found nothing of consequence except scratched paint marks and disturbed dust, but no fingerprints or other forensic evidence supporting his mistaken judgment that this was where the voyeur had positioned himself taking the pictures.

The boom retracted, climbing down, Detective Zampino reiterated disappointingly, "There's nothing more that I can see that might prove useful. My dusting for prints proved negative. My portable battery powered vacuuming of the area got nothing but dust. There was nothing unusual about the paint scrape marks. Our perpetrator was very careful. A tall male to be sure from what he had to accomplish There is no evidence that he climbed to his perch from inside the room by using the lockers. I dismiss that as his venue as that approach would have decidedly increased his risk. I believe he used the relative safety of the outside walls. To do that, he has to be at least six feet tall and have a vertical leap of three feet to successfully scale the wall and position him to ascend further." Captain Blanchard did not challenge Zampino's assessment.

The group then reconvened in Principal Schmidt's office.

"We're going to have to depend on an informer or catch him in the act, I'm afraid," Detective Zampino commented. He and Captain Blanchard were by ranking the only ones to speak in mixed company while the other patrolmen looked on and listened.

"While I suspect it's an insider, either student or worker, nonetheless I'll bring in all the known sex offenders registered in the area for questioning and see what that brings us. The perpetrator strikes me as being an unknown arousal freak safely closeted," commented Captain Blanchard.

"I will have to notify the parents of the girls involved," a concerned Schmidt said. "The media will have a field day sensationalizing this story. It won't be good for the school," he added knowingly.

"As well as for the police. It goes with the territory. Our job is just beginning; the heat will be on until we make an arrest. Keep us posted on any developments, Mr. Schmidt. We need your full cooperation. Let's not repeat past mistakes," Captain Blanchard reminded pointedly.

Flustered but not at a loss of decorum, Mr. Schmidt, attempting to patronize said, "You will have our full cooperation. We've taken additional steps. A drop ceiling will be added to the room this very day."

"That should help satisfy some of the critics. Smart move. That's something the commissioner and mayor should know."

Principal Schmidt, opening his desk's middle drawer a second time, pulled out an envelope and said, "In anticipation, I've prepared a list of names given to me by the contractor of its employees on the school grounds involved in the project."

"Thank you," a more cordial Captain Blanchard replied as he took the list. "We'll run a check."

The meeting ended.

Back at the police station Captain Blanchard perused the list supplied by Schmidt, none of the workers' names matched the names with his list of known sexual offenders. Undeterred, his suspicion strong the perpetrator was among the workers. Toward that end, he called the contractor's project manager, deceptively assuring him that his call was a routine inquiry "for security purposes" to become more knowledgeable regarding the Hillside High School project. Mr. Frank Jefferies, son and heir to Jefferies Construction Company, duty bound, cooperated readily.

"The project will be completed in three months, working one shift only from 8:00 AM to 3:00 PM except for overtime. The project involves construction workers, carpenters, electricians, plumbers and others – the usual trades on a project this size. We have in fact three other schools under contract in this county."

Blanchard startled, sat upright, calming himself to control, muttering a profanity beneath his breath for Principal Smith's finding this important fact insignificant and not relative. Recovering "Did you submit your bid on an individual basis or did you tie them all together?"

"The requests for bids come from the individual school boards from within the district it serves. All four schools, while in other cities, cross-reference one another on their bid requests. Since all the work is essentially the same, I chose to price on the basis of getting all four jobs at the same time yet the individual job costs will be different for many reasons."

"What are the other schools?" Captain Blanchard asked pointedly, his interest intensifying.

"Crestmont, Lincoln and Franklin," the names quickly made note of by Blanchard, retaining the deceptive calm in his voice difficult.

"Are the workers used interchangeably among all four projects?"

"If the need arises, yes," replied Mr. Jefferies, unaware of the path he was being led down and the potential of consequences of liability to his company if the manipulative Blanchard's building suspicions proved correct. He was expert in extracting information and concealing his purpose under the pretext of innocuous questions.

"I see," said Captain Blanchard, remaining in feigned aloofness of a stenographer.

His naiveté abandoned yet again he erred in judgment, a suddenly defensive Jefferies interjected, "I now know why you asked the question of worker interchangeability. We run a tight accountability ship. All our workers must have signed-off time cards properly punched by the time clock at the project superintendent's trailer. He attests to hours worked and the project worked on for allocation of costs. The transfer of men and accountability is the responsibility of the authorizing foreman."

His eyes brightening further at the possible significance and lead that information would provide, Blanchard asking for more foundation, "If there is transfer from one site to the other, how is their time accounted for?"

Jefferies responded, "The next day the foreman receiving the transferees calls his counterpart from the transferring unit to square accounts."

Captain Blanchard listened attentively, secretly concluding that hard evidence could exist that might provide a corollary between the worker and the voyeuristic incidents, particularly after getting all the details of the four schools' work schedules. His appetite whetted, his instinct sensors working, he now had an investigative path to follow, hopeful it would lead to discovery if he found the connection.

"I appreciate your time, Mr. Jefferies. I'll see to it that the information you graciously supplied is given to my men so that no surprise situation develops. Thanks for your cooperation. If I have further needs, I will call on you personally."

"Of course," a still amenable Jefferies invited. "Just give me a call."

Hanging up the phone, Captain Blanchard was pleased that the outcome of his call provided what he hoped was a promising lead to follow.

All three of the other schools, while in Captain Blanchard's county, were under other city jurisdictions. He knew all three of his counterparts policing Crestmont, Lincoln and Franklin schools. Prevailing upon the county police commissioner to have his precinct designated as primary, he contacted his fellow captains by phone to brief them. As suspected they immediately reacted as if their authority had been lessened, hesitant in discussing the issue, purposefully brief until he emphasized the commissioner's involvement would not be token, turf ownership preventing resolution would not be condoned, so political were the implications. Though uncomfortable with the commissioners edict of inter district cooperation with them playing a secondary role, they acceded to full cooperation. The ensuing open discussion revealed they too had experienced the same circumstances of voyeurism. The same pattern… the other schools choosing a go it alone in secrecy… repeating the misguided failing of contacting the police on two earlier incidents… deciding it best to handle the situation themselves. That position changed dramatically threefold, the police summoned by each of the schools Principal's having received the latest identifying photos of nude female students. Captain Blanchard's willingness to share, while remaining primary in the investigation, would credit as a combined cooperative resource investigation if an arrest was made, satisfied all political agendas. Hanging up the phone, he mused angrily that the perpetrator, encouraged by success, was quite busy sending his trademark photos to the other schools who had students intruded upon, their privacy violated, flauntingly victim exposure to his lust, his perverseness needing the additional stimuli of publicity from the admission of school officials.

Captain Blanchard called Detective Zampino into his office, telling him of his findings and suspicions. He assigned him the task of visiting the schools, and meeting the students in the photos to establish time lines. Additionally he was to get with the construction companies individual paymasters on each site. His assignment; to get copies of all the time cards, suggesting he use the pretext that a detailed analysis of assigned or transferred worker time cards on the school project was a necessity, as he was investigating a series of unusual house break-ins in normally placid neighborhoods, all after the projects were started. His hope was to find a connection with the contractors workers, and their interchangeability at the other schools within one or two days of the dates shown on the photographs. His charge, to work with his three district counterparts in the other schools in the investigation.

Detective Zampino returned to his captain's office the next day, both were holding copies of newspapers whose headline would shock readers: "Voyeurs At Work In The Schools, Children At Risk" the accompanying article damaging to school officials, condemning as lax and uncooperative with the police, asking the mayor what he intends to do about it, suggesting strong action be taken.

"The newspapers are having a field day. TV and radio continually broadcasting the story." Detective Zampino remarked unhappily

"It's impacting. It seems every parent of school age children is aroused… Calling the mayor… Demanding action. We've been spared temporarily since we were late being informed. Now that we're involved that's history. We've got to move fast before the public redirects it's criticism towards the police," responded Captain Blanchard.

Returning to their focus; "What have you learned Detective?"

"Not very much," he responded, obvious disappointment in his tone. "During our first look, we found cause for suspicion with two plumbers, but not in all instances. After examining their employee folders, we quickly dropped them as suspects."

"How so?" Captain Blanchard asked.

"First off, they were well past fifty and overweight, with histories of back injuries causing them to move like rusting robots. Hardly fitting the profile of a sexually fixated athletic voyeur. Their physical limitations, and only a corollary in two instances steered me away from them as suspects. What began as a promising lead turned into a blind alley, I'm afraid. It was to easy to be true that we had found our man or men. What we need to do is lay out all the data on a spreadsheet: names, dates assigned to the school, matched to the dates and times of the incidents to find a pattern. We could have overlooked something."

"I share in your disappointment, Detective. I think your spreadsheet is the best approach in searching for a corollary. While it's only a theory and suspicion, I think we're on the right track. Certainly the opportunity exists for our man to come from one of the workers."

A heavy work schedule prompted Captain Blanchard to check his watch, noting the time he walked from behind his desk, politely escorting Zampino to the door of his office saying, "I'm pressed for time… along with your report, I would appreciate a copy of your spreadsheet."

"I'll make sure you have it before Friday's meeting."

Captain Blanchard nodded approvingly, "At Friday's meeting, I want your reasoned conclusions. Your findings will be used in my report to the commissioner and mayor, who will issue a joint public statement to the media. I don't believe that public awareness will drive the perpetrator or perpetrators underground. The profile says he enjoys the notoriety; it's a game which he believes he can't lose – part of his disturbed psyche."

Principal Schmidt as promised met with all the female students and their parents. One on one he fared better than when he reassembled them as a group for counseling with the school psychologist. Their strength in numbers changed reasonable attitudes. An attacking pack mentality ruled. Hunger for blood brought on heated condemnations of "Not enough security… failure to provide for the children's safety and welfare… mismanagement," and finally the charge of "wasting public funds." Nonetheless, his bearing remained steadfast, welcoming discussion, remaining professionally non-confrontational. Listening patiently to the critical until all their venom was spewed, proved to defuse. Reasonableness returned as they conceded that the police investigation and the school officials, while not blameless, had responded and taken appropriate steps.

The student girls, all in their senior year, ranged in their reactions. The naïve in deep shock at being spied on. The shy suffering humiliation.The adventuresome boldly flaunted among themselves their maturing sexuality; laughing mischievously as only young girls can; acting the gyrating temptress able to stir men to risk; dismissing the voyeur's perversion and hormonal arousal too distant to be a danger. Enjoying their new role as discovered *femme fatales*, they planned to test their best boyfriends' reactions, continuing to act out risqué behavior.

Friday morning found Detective Zampino in Captain Blanchard's office. Easily reading his countenance as being stymied, Blanchard surmised: "Still no tie-ins?"

Shaking his head negatively, Zampino in obvious disappointment said,

"Only insignificant isolated ones. No matching patterns including subtle ones. If there's a correlation we haven't found one. I'm afraid we're drawing blanks."

"Keep trying. In the meantime, we'll have to expand our investigation to avoid criticism in case we're wrong; increase our contacts, our interviews. We'll open it up.See what that brings us, " commented Captain Blanchard.

"Like where?"

"With the students and teachers themselves. I'm going to ask Principal Schmidt to call a general assembly and ask for help. Encouraging that they search their memories on those dates for any occurrence that might provide us with a lead. It will work if it involves an outsider or a teacher. I'm not so optimistic if our voyeur is a student, experience tells us that if he is known to a few, they will protect their own with a loyalty that rivals a street gang's code of silence. Nonetheless, we can't discount any possibility."

Detective Zampino, concurring with his captain's judgment said, "You already have a copy of my spreadsheet. With your permission, I'd like to delay my final report and conclusion until Monday. I want to go over all the data one more time to make sure I haven't missed anything."

"By all means, Detective. I have until midweek to get my report to the commissioner. I intend to do the same thing. I might call you if I need clarification or find something."

"Anytime," Zampino acknowledged.

Evelyn Blanchard, upon seeing her husband come through the door of thc attached garage carrying what she knew all to well as an ongoing casework file in his hands, her plans for the evening to separate him from police work, keeping him distant from a carefully arranged house party in trouble. Flustered she foresaw his turning every freed-up minute to the file, in essence making him a missing co-host for the evening. She knew, knowing his disdain for the perpetrators, the file's primacy would dominate, his involvement with the invitees secondary, if available at all.While politely present, his thoughts would be on the high school voyeur case No where in his memory were other instances that inflamed him more than the voyeur's sickness His brashness, adding another condemned dimension – his titillation accomplished, blatantly allowing identification of his compromised victims for the entire world to see.

Being the father of three girls, who, had he not chosen parochial schools for their education, might but for the grace of God be the subject in those photos. The angering thought that his daughters, who should feel secure in assuming privacy, could lose those moments to a sexual deviant drove him.

His preoccupation would limit his interest for the night to tokenism, monosyllable responses, distant even to her.

All through the labored night right up to their guests' saying their "Good nights," Evelyn Blanchard's concerns proved accurate. Only his unenthused body presented itself to the guests, his mind elsewhere; within his file.

As soon as the last of the guests departed, her anger flared.

"You could have been more involved with the guests," she complained. "Your performance was pitiful: unenthused listening when cornered, an obvious feigned smile your only expression, plotting one of your many escapes to your study. Otherwise, you were comatose," she added sarcastically.

Now she had his attention as he attempted to defend himself.

"You know how I feel about degenerates who prey on children, how involved I am in this case. I tried my best under the circumstances."

Her anger not appeased, she continued berating, "Those were your friends from college – your fraternity brothers. You lived together for four years. How could you treat them so poorly?" she said disgustedly.

His response, an unexpected glint of recognition in his eyes framed by his raised eyebrows, her words registering for his poor behavior during the evening, delivering another message. "That's it," he shouted barely able to contain himself. "That's the bell ringer I've been looking for – the addresses. That's what we've been overlooking; the mail drops." Unexpectedly, he reached out lovingly to hold her shoulders momentarily, bewildering her and cryptically thanking her for her help, far from the contrition she hoped to hear to placate her feelings of disappointment in him.

His sudden affection surprised her to silence, her mouth agape, leaving her words of further condemnation over his behavior unsaid. Possessed he quickly departed for his study. She heard him moving papers around, then pounding his desk demonstrably before returning with the Hillside High School file in hand, furthering her bewilderment as he continued to wave the incriminating file in his hand in an unusual demonstration.

A ray of light bringing him from darkness, elated as he was, as a professional he tempered his excitement at this lead's promise. He shared his thoughts with her: "They tried to remain nondescript… limiting personal information. They are about to find out it is no guarantee of remaining inconspicuous, particularly during a criminal investigation. Delayed yes, but not unearthed." Captain Blanchard continued in his promising theory, "Seven names with seven different mail drops with no out-of-town addresses or current address listings. Highly suspicious, particularly when they can have their mail addressed to the company office for their pickup."

Interrupting him she regained her voice. "You haven't heard a word. You're impossible," she said, resigned to the hopelessness of trying to make her point. Finally frustrated, she said, "I'm going to bed." Not completely abandoning him, she suggested that he do the same, shaking her head in dismay as she moved to leave the room.

Having finally heard her, he said, “I will, Hon. I need just a few minutes more to sort things out. Thanks for providing me with the insight I was lacking,” he said smiling in appreciation.

His gratitude, while not understood, diminished her anger. “Don’t be too long,” she said, her concern sincere for him overworking himself.

He moved to the den which also served as his study. Turning on the desk light, he laid out the spreadsheet before him, his mind busily building his case.

Reflecting, he thought it is common knowledge in law enforcement that the use of a mail drop address offers concealment of a true address and identity; held anonymous unless prevailed upon by the law to release such information as it is pertinent in an ongoing case.

He knew his conclusion only a building block towards finding hard evidence yet undeniably a strong lead. He remembered the counseling of the psychologist during his police academy days, “People of similar views and obsessions gravitate to one another.” He hoped that insight would be proven right in this case. However, he was doubtful that there were seven co-conspirators. It certainly had to be investigated further, but not compelling enough for a judge to sign off on a wide ranging circumstantial search warrant. Again he reviewed the employee files of the seven who now stood out as prime suspects hoping to find more incriminating evidence. Finding none, he returned to the spreadsheet and found none of the newly considered seven suspects were working at the school on the confirmed date the photography took place. How is that possible he thought? Someone had to be there to take the pictures. It then hit him they didn’t have to be there if a camera with a programmable time release was set up beforehand. This conclusion was supported when he found that one of the seven was at the violated school a day before and a day after the event took place.

Captain Blanchard knew it was late but his discovery important enough that he take liberties, his critique, his suspicions needed the sounding board of another professional. He called Detective Zampino, apologizing for the hour. After hearing the captain’s theory, Zampino soon shared in the captain’s enthusiasm. Convinced, he recognized the need to investigate the captain’s findings further, necessitating a rescheduling of Monday’s meeting to Tuesday. Captain Blanchard agreeing said he would notify the others of the change.

After hanging up the phone, Captain Blanchard was alone again with his thoughts and trusted instincts. Continuing to follow his hypothesis, he reasoned it was the suspects plan to cleverly influence their work schedules to be innocently at one of the other sites the day the school was hosting a girls’ basketball game or swimming event, planning and fulfilling their lust by the opportunity of their work; filming unsuspecting participants equally arousing, the shy freeing their inhibitions, other unknowingly feeding the flames of their passion by acting out as emerging sirens, his *nudes dé jour on film*.

Continuing his thoughts, he saw through their devious plan to avoid suspicion; one of the men not involved in the camera's positioning would work at the school the day after to recover the camera. A deliberately planned scheduling maze to confuse and minimize suspicion. The co-conspirator who recovered the camera along with the others would develop the film, date stamp the photographs to coincide with the scheduled sporting event validated by the girls identified in the photos. Continuing his reasoning, Captain Blanchard was sure that the girls' team schedules of events published in advance by all the participating schools were known to the voyeurs, reminded by the school's heralding rally. Knowledge of those schedules was the key in scheduling their clandestine photo sessions and their viewable feast.

He wondered how often they had used this *modus operandi* to satisfy their lust. Certainly it would not surprise him that further investigation would show other unsolved instances. How clever they thought they were Captain Blanchard repeated to himself… attempting to avoid suspicion by not working at the hosting school on the evidenced date… setting up the camera the day before the event and conveniently working at one of the other schools during the event, their time accounted for, further complicating an investigation based on physical presence.

Additionally, he found the stamped date of mailing by the post office as one week after the dated photos. Postmarked on a Monday from the Pittsburgh area, a clever attempt to avoid detection but when added to the other evidence, albeit circumstantial, made them highly suspect.

Captain Blanchard, crediting the perpetrators as he was discovering, with deception and clever subterfuges, but not hidden or deceptive enough to escape the eventuality of persistent police work prevailing, finding patterns of behavior or unusual inconsistencies that would identify suspects worthy of further investigation. Equally significant, detective work finding patterns that don't exist when they should, suggesting manipulation in the contradiction. The absenting of seven tradesmen at any of the schools during the event met the second criteria, violating the laws of probability, presenting odds high enough to consider that paradox as deliberately misleading, demanding closer scrutiny.

In this case, their efforts to avoid connection were their undoing as indeed they had established a pattern by their very absences. Four schools, three incidents at each school, forty men of various trade groups all having worked at least one of the incident days, sans the seven, equated to a highly improbable circumstance, signaling a search beyond, to underlying surfaces for mitigating evidence, albeit circumstantial, the connecting lines drawn were undeniable.

He finally went to bed around 3:00 AM with little sleep available to get before the 6:30 AM alarm. While asleep, his eyes blinked rapidly, indicative of dreaming. The dreamscape he painted for himself was troublesome, colors and tones with no distinguishing borders. Madras bleeding… no ending, no beginning. Hinted at but not distinguishable… a whisper; describing his thought process in his dream state. A connection of circumstantial evidence providing a field day for a drooling defense lawyer, cockily requesting dismissal for lack of evidence of substance, in his sleep moaning an objection as the judge dismissed summarily. Blanchard, showing the signs of his tormenting dreams when arriving at work the next day, was relieved somewhat when meeting privately with Detective Zampino before their scheduled meeting. What he learned gave greater credibility to his continually strengthening case, moving it from theory.

All were seated around Captain Blanchard's desk for Tuesday's 10:00 AM rescheduled meeting. Detective Zampino, Captain Storey of the Crestmont precinct, Captain Secula of the Lincoln precinct and Captain Murphy of the Franklin precinct, all veterans in law enforcement, rising up through the ranks and all showing the effects of essentially a sedentary desk job attested to by broadening waists. While they were cordial to one another, all were on the defensive, uncomfortable being away from their precinct headquarters where they ruled. Promoted to leadership positions commensurate with achievements in performance displayed proudly on chests full of acclaiming medals. Cooperation not rivalry was the edict from the police chief and mayor's office, the fire heavy from angered parents and the media, left them no room for pride of ownership. Politically, and procedurally mandating the call for synergy, very much in order.

"I know we all have full schedules so let's get started. Detective Zampino, will you bring us up to date?" Captain Blanchard ordered.

"Captain Blanchard," Zampino began, "discovered late Saturday night the connection we all have been searching for. Before I get into the specifics, let me review what we know."

"The out-of-state awarded construction company, because of the similarity of work exercised its option and put out one bid rather than individual bids which proved to be the most cost effective. Most of the key workers were assigned from the company's home base: union affiliated craftsmen enjoying journeyman status, living the three months for job completion in motels and rooming houses. Nothing unusual; quite ordinary.

"Captain Blanchard's discovered; distinguished from the majority assigned, was a group of seven men who were hired from the union local, a requirement to satisfy the national organization's insistence that a local be included in the worker makeup. Again not unusual by itself; however, separating these seven is that they are journeymen members of a local, all having separate mail drops. Four of the seven we subsequently learned have the same boarding house residence address. A closer check of the spreadsheet showed that none of these seven men worked at the school on the incident days, seeming to clear them as suspects, until you factor the suspected use of an automatically timed camera set up the day before the incident, under that scenario at least one of the seven worked at the subject school. Digging the circumstantial hole deeper, one always worked the day after; he in theory presumably the camera retriever.

"As I see it, even without a slide rule or calculator, the law of averages makes that highly improbable, arousing Captain Blanchard's suspicions. Mind you, all are hypotheses but worthy of continued investigation. I agreed with Captain Blanchard to zero in on those seven suspects.

"In that pursuit, I met with the postal authorities, cooperating fully after being reminded that they were required by law to release all information in an ongoing police investigation. Take a look at this listing:

Name	*Job*	*Age*	*Mail Drop*	*Residence*
Steve Skorich	HVAC	26	1165 Hillcrest Branch	25 Fulton Rd.
Len O'Neil	Roofer	46	515 Cleveland Branch	YMCA Cleveland
Ralph Rossi	Roofer	48	590 Cleveland Branch	YMCA Cleveland
Jim Callahan	HVAC	26	1016 Crestmont Branch	25 Fulton Road
Bill Yanesh	HVAC	27	1270 Merrill Hill Branch	25 Fulton Road
Bob Gutrill	Roofer	46	612 Cleveland Branch	YMCA Cleveland
John Shumaker	HVAC	26	1505 River Mills Branch	25 Fulton Road

Everyone at the meeting agreeing the connections were worthy and should have been investigated further.

Detective Zampino continued quieting the commentary "The three roofers choosing to reside at the YMCA during the contract period proved not to be suspects during my investigation. Their YMCA accommodations were bare with minimal privacy, without room for photographic development equipment. Factoring in their ages, married, overweight and not being athletic, countered the profile, ending suspicions they were the voyeurs. I suspect they chose the YMCA for no other reason than being the most economical for transients.

"That rationale moved us to concentrate on the other four, all journeymen rooming together in a rented house having the latitude of privacy that venue brings, all four meeting the profile, using mail drops as added subterfuge. Another incriminating factor: while currently located in our area, their roots trace back to the Pittsburgh area, establishing the connection and affiliation we were looking for."

Pausing to emphasize his point, he said, "here's the kicker: we found they all had worked for our contractor Jefferies Construction before, and could reasonably have learned of the awarded contract. Having left the company for the contract site earlier registering with the union, they reestablished ties, notifying the contractor of their journeyman status made them available for the school project through the union local – all that was needed to guarantee hiring. Further background checks uncovered typical minor traffic violations and a guilty plea of disturbing the peace, with all four suspects involved in the same incident. After receiving the details of the charges, I learned that the overcrowded court system allowed them to plead down to the misdemeanor of disturbing the peace. The details showed they were inebriated and arrested for public lewdness as participants in a nudist colony, our four voyeurs masquerading as nudists, certainly an incriminating factor in furthering our nomination as suspects."

As if orchestrated, all of the visiting captains raised their eyebrows at this revelation. On the edge of their seats smelling victory, they circled the wagons, becoming more comfortable with the building incriminating evidence, voicing compliments for Captain Blanchard and Detective Zampino, pleased that they would be benefactors of the political spoils of credit.

"There's more… it gets better," Detective Zampino said quieting the room. "It seems our four were also arrested at a lover's lane for peering into the cars of parked teenagers with flashlights, claiming at the time of their arrest that they were searching for the car of four girls who had agreed to meet with them. The charges were later dropped as none of the witnesses chose to come forward."

His thunderbolt dropped, Zampino returned the meeting to Captain Blanchard. All captains were energized by Zampino's findings.

Captain Secula of the Lincoln School District spoke first, "It seems that we have enough probable cause to have an arrest warrants issued."

Captain Blanchard responded, "I invited Sidney Marks from the prosecutor's office to hear what we have put together. He should be here momentarily. While we are waiting, I'm going to call Mr. Jefferies, the projects honcho, I will have to bring him into our confidence as to our investigation and be more forthright, in order to get his full cooperation."

As the phone conversation ensued, it became obvious to all that Captain Blanchard was under attack for his deviousness during their first phone conversation. Deliberately restrained and apologetic Captain Blanchard waited for Frank Jefferies anger to subside. Eventually the conversation was no longer a one-sided chastisement, continued as strained but cooperative dialog, Mr. Jefferies responding to his social obligations having salved his damaged ego with his lecture.

"All four projects are on schedule and will be completed by this weekend," Captain Blanchard repeated for the benefit of his listeners, requesting of Mr. Jefferies; I would appreciate if you kept me informed of the going's and coming's of the four men I've identified." Receiving assurances that he would, Captain Blanchard gave promise that he would inform the mayor and the press of Mr. Jefferies cooperation, protecting his firms good standing. He hung up the phone just as Sidney Marks walked in.

"What have you got, Captain?" Listening intently as he received a detailed account of where the police stood in their investigation. The others, silent, unsuccessfully tried to read Sidney Marks' nonplused reaction, his words anxiously awaited:

"Certainly their actions and history make them highly suspect, but the evidence is circumstantial. Judge Whiting, a strong rights advocate known to liberally interpret the law, might not be persuaded to issue a search warrant that is all-encompassing: covering their workplace, lockers, cars, mail drop boxes, and residences. Whatever the judge gives us in the warrant, we'll only have one chance to strengthen our case, which remains at the moment essentially founded on circumstantial evidence. We must be thorough and hopefully come up with evidence of substance, more incriminating."

"Like what?" Captain Storey asked.

"The camera for one. Negatives of photos for another. Since they are transient journeymen with the job ending this weekend, their future plans not known, we'll miss a chance to put these degenerates away if we can't produce stronger evidence for an indictment. I can't promise but I'll do my best under the circumstances, I can only hope Judge Whiting sees the merit of our probable cause." Sidney Marks commented.

"That's all we can ask for, counselor. Call us when you get an answer," said Captain Blanchard as Marks left the room.

"Hand me the file, Detective Zampino," Blanchard requested, commenting, "Just as I remembered." As he studied the file, those in attendance were puzzled at his meaning.

"The name Whiting. I was sure I had seen it before with regard to this case. I just confirmed it. The name Whiting shows up as one of the girls photographed at the Hillside School. She could be a relative of Judge Whiting." He quickly called Sidney Marks' office.

"Sidney, Captain Blanchard. I wanted to get to you before you left to see Judge Whiting. On Page Six of the file copy you have you'll see one of the girls named is a Catherine Whiting, a possible relative of Judge Whiting that could help our cause."

"If that's true, I don't dare use it to influence the judge," Marks said, shaken by what he thought was Captain Blanchard's suggestion.

"No, you can't. I'm not asking that you bring it up. As detailed as the judge is, I'm sure he'll find it himself. There's a good chance they are related and he already knows about the situation. An advantage of a family tie could give you the edge you need in broadening the judge's latitude. I wanted you to know this beforehand. Based on his reputation, it would be insulting and indelicate of you to mention this to the judge. You can only plead on the merits of the warrant. However psychologically, it has to have a bearing. Giving more weight in our request for a broad search warrant."

"I'll see what I can do," was Marks' reply. "I'll call you as soon as I have his answer."

Within milliseconds of returning the phone to its cradle, it rang. It was Frank Jefferies of Jefferies Construction. After exchanging rote cordialities, Blanchard listened and took notes during the abbreviated conversation,his jaw bone muscles rippling. After hanging up the phone, without explanation he called Principal Schmidt of the Hillside School, receiving the information he was seeking.

Turning to his group, Captain Blanchard, his face drawn tight said, "It seems our four Peeping Toms are working at Hillside High School today. What's also scheduled tomorrow at Hillside, I just learned, is a cheerleader competition with our four schools involved. The event starts at seven in the evening tomorrow, long after the construction crew calls it a day. Today, gentlemen, is the day before the event. If our voyeurs follow their suspected practice, they will be planning to position the camera sometime today, safe in their belief that they have outwitted the police.

"We need those search warrants more now than ever," Blanchard said pointedly, then added, "Captains, I know your relieved as I would be in your circumstance that the Hillside School is the front stage attraction, and in my precinct – I still suggest you be there at the time of their apprehension. First hand observation by the police commissioner, the mayor and you as part of the investigation team in this matter will duly be noted by the media."

All nodded in agreement, relieved that the voyeurs' closing finale did not involve their schools, enthused by the opportunity of visibility in the capture of the perpetrators, highlighting the mayors promise, all good politics. It was noon when Captain Blanchard received the call:

"Captain," a pleased Sidney Marks said, "Judge Whiting, after expressing some doubt, mindful of the excellent relationship of trust we shared, signed off on the warrant as it was written. You can pick it up in my office immediately."

"Immediately won't be soon enough. Tell me, counselor, what was Judge Whiting's attitude? Did he need a lot of persuasion?"

"He went through the paperwork, asked a lot of questions, asked to see my file. I noticed he perceptively paused at page six."

Digressing for a moment, his self-pleasure fading, the implication of losing his future credibility with Judge Whiting troubling him, Marks said, "Lets hope we find the evidence we need. This is a marginal situation. I know other judges who would not sign off on it. Too circumstantial for their liking and in their judgment, lacking probable cause. I wouldn't want to be a party to discrediting Judge Whiting's judgment if there are any repercussions."

At 3:00 in the afternoon Captain Blanchard's men returned after exercising the search warrants, reporting:

"At each of the four mail drops we found letters along with checks and money orders purchasing nude photos of young girls from their individual Web sites they had set up. Each of the four was authorized to open each other's mail drop," Sergeant Davis said, "all mail confiscated, taken as evidence. None of the nude photos matched up with ours."

"Certainly a business enterprise that titillates both buyer and supplier. Another reason for the four mail drops," Captain Blanchard said,"beyond being pornographic, the pictures not of our girls is circumstantial, it doesn't make our case. I hope you discovered something more incriminating?"

Sergeant Davis continued, a smile creasing his face, "We did as a matter of fact. At their residence, after we gained access through a very cooperative rental agent, an ex-policeman who swore to secrecy, we found camera equipment, photo development chemicals, basins and a timer. A large walk-in closet being used as a dark room with string spanning the room to process the photos. We also found shipping envelopes in one of the file cabinets, along with unfilled orders to their Web sites. Bank statements showing a brisk business were also found. In another file we found our most damning evidence – photos and negatives of our unsuspecting high school girls."

"Great job, well done," a pleased Captain Blanchard exclaimed.

"Thank you, sir. I hope you also approve of my decision not to search their workplace lockers and their car at this time," the sergeant said. "I decided not to risk exposure since we had more than enough evidence. Holding off, conducting those searches immediately after their arrest."

"Good judgment on your part," the captain agreed. "All four of our perpetrators are at Hillside High School as we speak which is where we are heading as soon as I call the police commissioner."

It was 3:15 in the afternoon when they arrived at the school parking lot. Detective Zampino, who had arrived earlier with other police officers, anticipating the warrants' approval, greeted Captain Blanchard, showing signs of anxious frustration as perspiration beaded on his forehead in spite of the coolness of the afternoon.

"I'm afraid we've lost them, Captain," Zampino said, unconsciously bringing his hand to his forehead to wipe away the sweat of anxiety

"How is that possible, a disturbed Captain Blanchard responded? "A11 of the other workers are accounted for, having punched out on their time cards and have been off the school premises since 3:00 PM

"Our infamous four had their time cards punched but their car is still in the parking lot. I'm afraid they knew their goose was cooked when they saw us find the camera during our search of the locker room ceiling. They probably guessed that search warrants were issued and we now had direct evidence that they were the perpetrators. They purposely avoided their car, preferring to hide in the school until they could figure out an escape or outwait the police guards posted at every entrance and stairwell."

At that moment Principal Schmidt, who had been alerted earlier, approached with the police commissioner and the mayor, all sharing a countenance of being pleased, anticipatory. When told what had happened, they were aghast in disbelief, having prepared themselves for credit contributing photo's by the media for providing leadership in the capture of the voyeurs. Disappointment and vulnerability showing now party to potential failure, a change in headlines to be feasted upon by the gathering reporters and photographers.

"The rehearsal starts at 8:00 PM. There within our grasp.We should find them well before that time," Captain Blanchard said bolstering everyone's confidence. "We have the school completely surrounded. There is no place for them to go. It's inevitable that we will capture them."

It was now 4:30 PM and all members of the various search parties radioed back disappointing failure.

"Go back and repeat your search," an exasperated Captain Blanchard criticized into his two-way radio. "You're overlooking something. I want those perverts captured."

Forty-five minutes later the two-way radio communiqué again reported lack of success. Captain Blanchard, his superiors having oversight felt trapped and betrayed as each moment passed without success, threatening the loss of a reputation building photo-op, turning into a vulnerability for charges of incompetence by critics increased his anger, his patience lessening, his tone elevated said, "They have to be somewhere. They could not have slipped by us. Repeat the search," he demanded.

After another hour passed with the search teams dejectedly reported no trace of the voyeurs' whereabouts in spite of the intensity of their search. The captain modulating his feelings over his men's failings, knowing they were good men facing a formidable adversary, in need of his direction to un-stymie them. 'Where can they be hiding he thought? How can they keep avoiding capture? It was sure to embarrass him and his precinct if they escaped under his very nose. For the first time he expressed doubt that the perpetrators were still on the premises.

With the stealth of cats, they moved noiselessly concealed and in darkness undetected, outwitting the search parties' every effort. Their muffled movement occasioning the resident insects and pests who avoid light for the dangers of being revealed, to flee in wonder of the intruders who sought their same safety. Hidden as if in a black hole, remaining still, secure of foot and structure, their path memorized to remain one step ahead of the searchers.

'Do I dare?' Captain Blanchard challenged himself. 'She certainly displayed the characteristics of a hunter extraordinaire.' His rationale building as he reflected on those memorable previous experiences, her remarkable astuteness filtering out the myriad of superfluous scents, conditions foiling lesser hunters. A sixth sense that would ignore the scents frequenting the school building and its inhabitants, to find secreting chemical prints of fear of the perpetrators, leading to their capture. Her majestic beauty coaxing a smile out of his dejection, his twinkling eyes joining as he envisioned her. Scene stealing from politicians, relegating them to the background, in their photo op. A promise made is a promise kept; he recalled conveniently, his decision reached, after all his job was to use all means at his command or volunteered.

Tasha and George Staves arrived within minutes of Captain Blanchard's phone call. Without delay Tasha sniffed through the impounded car. Burying her head among the dirty work clothes, filtering the residue odors of grease, dirt and grime to the very being of the individual's olfactory fingerprints.

Given his marching orders, Detective Zampino, Tasha's leash in hand entered the school through the gymnasium entrance. Immediately her nose dropped to the floor searching for incriminating odors. Her path was a meandering one yet always moving ahead, stopping on occasion to raise her head to sniff for airborne particles that would tell the tale. Her pace quickened as if no longer in need to cull and separate the smells. She was locked in. She moved toward the newly erected temporary girls' locker and shower room. Pausing at the perpetually dampened cinderblocks; her olfactory nemesis. Finally ignoring what could be misguiding iron oxide stained wetness to stand on her hind legs, her front paws reaching and scratching up the cinderblock wall, her smelling senses striving for greater heights, forced to drop back down to all fours she threw her head back howling chillingly. Its meaning and piercing tone announcing as her ancestors had once done, she was a predator, this located prey was hers, the kill imminent.

"What is the howling all about?" a questioning Detective Zampino asked of George Staves.

"She just announced the location of those you're looking for," Staves answered proudly.

Captain Blanchard, reflective of the past became ecstatic at Tasha's alerting signal, while the others at first taken aback and curious, joined in the excitement with Staves's announcement that the voyeurs had been found.

"Are you positive?" a skeptical Zampino questioned.

"You can bet on it; up there above the ceiling," Staves responded confidently.

Captain Blanchard acting quickly commandeered from the school maintenance department two ladders. Ordering Detective Zampino to position the details policemen one hundred eighty degrees apart, the many others of the detail to surround the locker room. Briefing the mayor and his entourage along with the police commissioner and Principal Schmidt of what had been discovered and what was planned. The selected younger recent graduates from the police academy began to climb the "A" frame ladders, caution ruling as they climbed the strategically placed ladders setting aside the installed drop ceiling.

"Nothing here, Captain, but pipes and duct work" reported the lead policeman of the two groups, his tone of disappointment.

"I don't believe it," George Staves interjected incredulously, unwilling to concede failure. Not deterred he boldly asked:

"Captain, may I have your permission to let Tasha climb the ladder with me?"

Captain Blanchard, who was still undaunted and confident in Tasha's abilities, quickly responded, "By all means," ordering one of the climbing crews to descend.

Reaching the platform of the "A" frame ladder Staves found himself reluctantly agreeing with the search teams' findings: nothing was amongst the crowded highway of conduit and pipes. Still Tasha persisted, doubters concluding she appeared to be barking aimlessly into the air as she strained against her leash, her language of reaffirming telling in her exertion.

Motivating George Staves eyes to again trace the network of pipes and conduit that were hung from the beams and steel joists. The recently added rectangular shaped welded-at-the-seams aluminum ductwork caught his attention. Installed to facilitate the temporary locker room, directing seasonally accommodating air to blow through the registers, spilling out into the room. Having a mechanical leaning, he noticed what had escaped him earlier; the added ductwork had more frequent and heavier steel strapping supporting its length than its counterparts.

Certainty ruling again, Staves shouted down, defying the season and it's moderate temperature, "Captain, tell Principal Schmidt to have the heat turned on to full blast."

Incredulous words began forming on Captain Blanchard's lips, suppressed as he gained understanding of Staves meaning; he ordered the request be filled. Within minutes the sounds of expanding ductwork reacting to the heated air were joined by sounds of foreign movements. The perpetrators losing their resolve to remain hidden as the heated air moved through the network of ductwork. Forced to finally remove one of the air registers to escape the building heat, sweating profusely they climbed from their concealment, the four voyeurs extracting themselves into view, hanging precariously from the water pipes. Immediately,with no where to go, the scene burlesque as the the shouts of "Keep your hands in sight-You're under arrest" were heard coming from the lips of the younger searching police officers, inexperienced they unnecessarily drew their guns, the four voyeurs,the confrontation, being fimed for the world to see.

Like scurrying cockroaches exposed to the light, their desperate act to escape was thwarted. They had been found after stymieing and mystifying the police, so well did they conceal themselves, their sanctuary ignored as a possibility until exposed by Tasha. The searching policemen frustrated and defeated up to now, ordered the voyeurs toward the ladder closest for descent. On the ground the apprehending complete with their handcuffing – surrendering limply like rag dolls, easily maneuvered and manipulated, their minds resigned to the realities of capture, acknowledging their Miranda Rights.

With flashbulbs lighting up the room with soundless explosions was the frenzied response of the reporting media to the opportunity. Disappointed, they had to contend without full face exposure and silence from the prisoners. The voyeurs bowed their heads, not in contriteness but in an attempt to conceal their faces, an absence of reference by jurors ploy, exploited by inventive defense lawyers, learned from previous experiences. Their mouths frozen shut, remaining so despite the coaxing and belligerence of the press. Mercifully, prosecutor Sidney Marks stepped forward ending the atmosphere of a three-ring circus, returning decorum to the arresting process. Authoritatively shouting above the din, insisting the four arrested had individual rights that would not be circumvented by those reporting the event, declining any request for more time with the perpetrators. Judging the spent opportunity sufficient, he hurriedly escorted them to the police van, ending the intimidation.

Moving away from the melee, Captain Blanchard approached George Staves and Tasha, who had grown skittish at the flashing lights, repeatedly swiveling her head quickly toward the outbursts.

"I would like to take her home, Captain Blanchard. It's too unsettling for her with all the confusion," Staves said.

"As you wish, Mr. Staves, but first allow me to say this in deep gratitude," his face beaming with appreciation. "Once again the day was saved by you and that wonderful-beyond-belief Tasha. The mayor, the police chief, the community and I are forever thankful and in your debt." Enjoying his lead role he said, "Further, the Mayor has come up with an excellent idea of how we can show our appreciation. He is going to recommend to City Council that concluding this year's Home Day Celebration will be the presentation of awards to outstanding contributors to the community. He will be honoring firemen, emergency medical technicians and policemen, all who have served the city with performance over and beyond their calling. Equally worthy of that recognition is Tasha. It is our wish that Tasha's accomplishments also be honored. Will you allow a grateful community to show its appreciation?" Captain Blanchard said deeply beholden – unguarded, his grizzled crustiness of officialdom chipped, revealing a humane grateful persona, taken by Tasha's mystique.

"I'd be most proud of a tribute like that," said an emotionally overwhelmed George Staves.

Within days of the capture, George Staves received a confirming phone call from a pleased Captain Blanchard. "Council has approved the Mayor's recommendation to honor Tasha. In addition I'm happy to report, she will be the Grand Marshal at this year's Home Day Celebration."

Before Staves could offer an opinion on the appointment of Tasha as this year's Grand Marshal, Captain Blanchard, anticipating his reluctance, eased the situation by quickly adding, "A poll was taken of all the honorees and none offered any objection. In fact, they were all very supportive of the choice,they do not feel minimized."

Nonetheless, Staves found himself speechless after hearing of the endorsement and was humbled to silence, giving Captain Blanchard the opportunity to end the discussion, "Then it's settled," adding before hanging up, "Someone from the Home Day Committee will be in touch with you by the end of the month."

Staves discussed Tasha's appointment with his family members. All were thrilled with the idea; distanced Phyllis and Edward requesting they be included in copies of the proceedings taped by Rosanne and Bill.

Discussions with the program manager established the times that Tasha be available with enough break periods intersperced to get away from the excitement when needed.

With the Home Day Celebration approaching, work crews were busy positioning banners whose both sides announced the event, to span the heavily trafficked Green Road parade passage, affixing them to utility poles perpendicular to one another on each side of the parade route leading to the community park's entrance. Other equally announcing banner's spanning the parks entrance welcoming visitors. In addition flags in sets of two, angled at forty-five degrees from vertical, adorned the two miles of the parade route's utility poles, paired stars and stripes flapping in mild breezes leading vehicles and pedestrians through the entrance. The decorations complete, the park was prepared and in readiness for the opening day ceremonies, notice mailings having been sent out to the hosting community residents inviting them to bring friends to the festivities.

Police on idling motorcycles prepared to flank either side of the assembling parade components, giving escort along the route. Policemen stood on foot next to wooden barriers blocking the side streets, detouring cars from entering the parade route.

Drivers not so fortunate, having little excuse for their stymied predicament were guilty of ignoring the forewarning announcements. Dismayed and angry when reaching the end of the street finding barriers ending their journey. Their inability to turn around non existent, blocked by following motorists, either unknowing or gambling now faced a shared impasse, reacting by blaring their car horns in frustration. The police admonishing authoritatively to quite the din – of no use. They along with the others would have to wait until the parade passed. To accept the predicament of their own doing.

It was a cacophony of car horns, strident and demanding that greeted the spectators now lining the parade route, almost muffling the intended message of the baton tapping musical conductor, a forerunner to his startup whistle, heralding the parade's start, putting into motion the marching bands.

The delayed motorists captured, abandoned their cause and joined the gathering crowds curbside, transformed immediately from a hostage to a reluctant viewer, the parade on its way.

Some of the children, wanting a closer view left the comfort of parent supplied canvas backed beach chairs, preferring to sit on the curb eating popcorn. Anxious in their wait for the startup distant drumbeat to draw closer, as expected and countenanced the sounds both discordant and in unison, that of the initial marching band and its in-tandem successors.

In the open convertible bannered as the Grand Marshals, sat George and Rose Staves, with Tasha occasionally between them in the back seat. Her keen inquisitive eyes searching, her instincts while not alerted to a threat, were nonetheless wary of the gathering crowd, nervously fidgeting from one side of the car to the other, not knowing what to make of the strange voices calling her name as they moved past. The open convertible a moving time machine, viewing a presentation of all aspects of time: the people curbside sharing in it's dynamics, accelerated with the cars motion, the present, past and future presented; time spent, time already spent and time about to be spent. Tasha had turned her focusing head excitedly in every direction – now rearward, her second viewing of the fleeting present joining the past. Her attention switching to the future in store for her moments ahead of the procession as the distance shortened, harvesting from a indistinguishable distant background, an emerging foreground of vivid color. Sharply defining features, distinguishing adults from the children, the movement forward bringing the clarity,when parallel – the present. Tasha liked the effects of the breeze from the cars movement, linking times spectrum. A remarkable gift for a remarkable dog, so ordained the three dimensions of time would not be beyond her conceptualizing.

Rosanne, accepting an invitation, sat next to the volunteer driver enjoying the attention, searching the line of watchers for familiar faces to wave acknowledgement.

The Staves son-in-law Bill with his children had positioned themselves along the parade route near the entrance to the park. Anxiously sitting in beach chairs, their prideful close association with Tasha obvious, stirring excitement: cheering, applauding each float and band that went by, Tasha's name on their lips, anticipating the appearance of the Grand Marshal's car, the children abandoning the comfort of the chairs to follow the lead of the other children seated on the curb.

As one band passed distancing its sound, followed were floats and marchers of the parade sponsors. The next approaching drumbeat heralded another blaring band of brass and woodwind instruments to which to react. When signaled to musical silence, their step remained in cadence, in sync with the lead drumbeat. The band upon command periodically broke from the timing staccato to add their musical score just as their predecessors music faded in the distance. The costumed band a marching recital, gaining in crescendo as it approached. Their treble and brassiness increasing to eventually dominate – kind applause greeting their abbreviated notes and off tune efforts.

The parade provided escape to all. The children were ecstatic and in awe of the visual pleasures of the floats, led by a marching bands' music. The babies in strollers hypnotically captivated, were guarded by reminiscing parents reflecting on earlier days when they were children of innocence, when it was their memory that they too were demonstrable stimulated by the excitement of parades.

The captivated children reflecting the joy of being entertained, mesmerized faces comically bearing traces of candied apples and chocolate ice cream among the first to cheer the Grand Marshal's convertible, undeterred by the bands' decibel level with shouts of "Tasha, Tasha." Tasha reacting, standing inquisitively to their calls. Parents in awe of the idolatry their offspring held for Tasha, elevating her from mere animal status.

Accustomed to being the headliners in any parade, they became underachievers, forced to subdued animation were the normally attention driven clowns. Even their balloon figurines, cleverly crafted, lost center stage to Tasha, a secondary role obliged to be accepted, another day awaiting their dominance.

The honoree portion of the program was scheduled for 8:00 PM as it was hours away, the Home Day officials agreeing that Tasha would not have to be seen again until the awards ceremony. Hurriedly, Tasha was transferred to Staves's car and spirited away during the attention diverting commotion of other attractions, fortunately encountering during departure only a few of the late arriving children, their disappointment placated with the promise that she would be back for all who came to honor her.

Tasha, rested and fully alert, returned to the community park and resumed her highly visible presence along with the other nominees. Word spread quickly of Tasha's arrival, children and adolescents of all ages of both gender spilled from the other area's of park activities.

The children moved excitedly, the moppets leading their parents toward Tasha's last reported sighting. Some of the children were skipping trying to outdo one another in height and length athleticism. Adolescents having missed the parade, their wait to see Tasha about to be over, anxious, they started out by walking briskly until the thought of being at the forefront urged them to run, propelling themselves faster closing in on their target, screaming wildly in expectation. The surge created a wave of the wide eyed, a disjointed force quick to be harnessed by monitoring volunteers directing to a section of seats facing the viewing stands. Once individuals now a group within the rope restraints shouted Tasha's name, whose ears stiffened with attention. Diverting the throngs attention momentarily, sudden chilling temperature and gusting winds blowing newspapers, candy wrappers and other wind sailing debris in all directions, all looked skyward, hoping it was not a precursor of event shortening rain.

The dais platform was assembled on the lighted main baseball diamond's outfield grass. A configured semi-circle of chairs to accommodate the event officials and honored guests conveniently position to be seen by all. A second semi circle fifty feet deep of grass and soil in front of the dais was set aside for positioned folding chairs, added to the diamond's viewing stands presented plentiful seating opportunity for early arrivals. Those with time constraints, arriving late, planning ahead brought their own folding chairs to be placed as they wished when finding a vantage point, the even later arrivals, a unprepared overflow, content with standing or sitting on a grassy knoll beyond the outfield grass. In most cases, the view was unobstructed, binoculars assisting those distanced, enabling a closer look.

The stands quickly filled with spectators as the hour of eight approached. Staves was grateful to the city fathers' and the event organizers, allowing the public to bring their disciplined dogs. On a first come basis the first row of the assembled seats was set aside for this purpose. Staves counted ten well-trained dogs, disciplined to the commands of an occasional leash pull or voice control by family members. Tasha alerted by the first arrivals lay quietly at Staves' feet, her head between her front paws, her senses determining that the assembled canines were not threatening, her aroused body language having sent an easily recognized message, she an Alpha of special privilege, being apart from them, not to be challenged.

A scattering of token applause almost unnoticed ended as quickly as it began as the park commissioner introduced the Home Day President and members of City Council. The mayor, having the advantage of a captive audience, politicize the event; reviewing home owners service increases during his term in office but avoiding mention of the highly controversial property tax increase. The applause became more sustainable and serious as the honorees were introduced by the highest elective officer- the mayor to bask in their limelight as he handed out the awards.

First came the grammar school Student of the Year, his Tom Sawyer look compelling: a wind blown wave of red tumbling from his head, repeatedly brushed aside, embarrassment swamping his freckled face of innocence. His gaze no longer seeking his parents in the multitude, staring straight ahead least he make eye contact with some of his friends bent on embarrassing him.

Second was the high school Senior of the Year, whose style of dress was shared by legions of his counterparts; hip-hugging longer-than-necessary blue jeans whose fraying cuffs were dragged underfoot. Their copied symbolic garb identified as a "in your face" attitude of the convict serving time, straining his credulity of reaching the threshold of maturity. His a show of disdain for societal codes, perceived for it's injustices, imprisoning life's unfortunate, those without privilege.Their distasteful attire,it's prompting countering their individuality of freedom of expression, succumbing to a herd mentality. Thankfully reprieved by his scholastic accomplishments highly distinguishable as was his irritating,in some cases inflammatory causes. Contrasting his attire and attitude, that of the third honoree, a grammar school student, whose dress code and mannerisms had not been corrupted, offering a rationale of the more conventional hopeful for his generation. Bound by intellectual achievement, they both received scrolls for academic excellence.

Next came the Fireman of the Year receiving a medal for heroism in saving latchkey children trapped in their burning home. While accepting the medal he smiled broadly to the cheers of his uniformed battalion sharing in the glory of one of their own, doing so with the aplomb and humility of a professional. An experienced well-decorated veteran, in modesty would not speak publicly of his achievements, he would however share his latest award as he had with the others he received over his noteworthy career with peer firemen, those privileged as close friends and family in private, reliving the moments.

A new wave of applause greeted the policeman's turn to be recognized and acknowledged as Policeman of the Year, voted by his peers, receiving written commendation for his personnel file as well as a medal to adorn his convex shaped chest. Received in recognition for thwarting a bank hold up while off duty, coming upon a robbery in progress, an example of his commitment to twenty-four hour police enforcement, never a removed civilian.

Next in line was the EMS technician, a work in progress in becoming a doctor, delivering in the course of one year five baby boys while their mothers were en route to the hospital, one of which was a breach birth. The parents in appreciation gave their newborn boys his name as a middle name, acknowledging his birthing contribution.

Saved for last was Tasha. When her name was announced, the children cheered long and wildly, clearly whom they came to see recognized. Not that they minimized the accomplishments of the others honored, but her mystique held special meaning for the children. Captain Blanchard and Detective Zampino talking briefly to the crowd extolled her considerable accomplishments in serving the community: saving the life of a small child, apprehending criminals and degenerates. Those in the local audience included the attending Felix Tunius with his nurse, Ken and Laura Monteleone, their son Steven seated at their side, nodding approvingly at the retelling of events. Others from other environs gasping, finding voice in whispers of disbelief and acclaim.

While the Staves family and all who had shared in her extraordinary accomplishments beamed in pride, the invited canines, under restraint by their owners watched in bewilderment, Tasha, one of them continued to sit remarkably on the dais, leading one to wonder if they sensed the reasoning for her isolation: worthy of such recognition from humans.

Tasha's accomplishments, having been cited and shared with the audience by Captain Blanchard and Detective Zampino, elevating the level of her deeds to that worthy of humans received an honorary detective designation, the mayor soliciting benefit from the photo op hung a medal of bravery from her neck. Continuing his reputation enhancement, promoting his re-election, posed for the cameras as he presented Tasha the key to the city, to be held in stewardship by George Staves. The ceremony neared completion as handshakes, petting and accolades abounded as both professional and amateur photographers alike took a multitude of pictures, recording this special day in Tasha's life.

It was drawing close to 9:30 in the evening, the time for the fireworks display to begin, the event that George Staves hoped to avoid, not needing additional proof of Tasha's resiliency. George with Tasha in tow left the dais and approached the seats where they, the relishing audience and her invited counterparts heard the first outburst of the fireworks. The dogs no longer seated, were aroused to nervousness, panting in the cooling night air, becoming acrid with the smell of explosives.

Completely unexpected, as if he and Tasha were conducting a military review, a response took place that will remain forever in the minds of those who witnessed it. Without coaching, yet individually subscribed to, each dog stirred by Tasha's approaching nearness rolled onto its back, front paws tucked tightly to their chests, the soft vulnerable flesh of their underbellies exposed, the typical posture of the white flag surrender of canines, a salute conceding the strength of Tasha's leadership. It's implication, "I lay here vulnerable, no match, submissive, inviting death if you so choose." Tasha's figurative return salute was to sniff each dog as she passed. Only once did she withdraw to tense readiness, a young precocious Irish setter, curious, rose irreverently from his subservient position momentarily, until realizing he was mismatched.

An extraordinary spontaneous event to the many witnessing the happenstance, raising the question, "How was the expression of acknowledged superiority communicated amongst the dogs." Surely there were Alphas in the group, he or she capitulating, influenced by some understanding of the gathered humans paying tribute. Was it the visualization of her sponsors countenance? Words spoken with fervor that tolled Tasha's elevated status?

Animals among themselves recognize superiority, bringing immediately to mind thoroughbred race horses. For example: a record breaking time set among horses of dubious lineage, the winners next race moving up in class of opponents. Over the same racetrack, the same horse carrying the same weight now finishes among the trailers with a time significantly slower than his earlier winning time. Not a surprise to experienced knowing horsemen. Thoroughbred horses instinctively know their lineage limitations, genetics always ruling. Thoroughbred associations and breeders recognize a lineage connection for success, established a formula, calculating a standard for the likelihood to win index, the lowly rated winning a high stakes race highly doubtful, if not unlikely, particularly true in the prestigious Triple Crown events, where breeding is a most significant factor.

It wouldn't be a stretch that this same cognitive mechanism is already in force amongst dogs of varying mixture or pedigree bred classifications, within which an internal calculation, a weighing takes place at every meeting instance that must be acknowledged… their code of alignment within every grouping.

As they departed, the darkened sky was being challenged by artfully engineered explosions of colorful short-lived brightness, temporarily revealing shadowy shapes of billowing clouds screening distant stars. Falling from grace in extinguishing sparkles, its aftermath life of spent explosives blanketed the air, its smell lingering. As the Staves family left the community park, they were hopeful, that becoming less accessible over time would quite the demand for Tasha's celebrity.

twelve

It was unavoidable; he knew it would come, the bounty of her fruitful episodes of the past essentially exhausted, depressed as he had reached the point in Tasha's life that he dreaded most. Not enough time had passed, those reflections not released from, their dilution, absence dependent – awaiting it's onset. Revisiting the desperation in finding Tasha's savior. A pursuit that eventually separates allegiances, an unexpected devastating division. An irony of consequence, as a remedy seems imminent, an inprobable redirection, a greater calling for Tasha, dividing them, his conceding to reconciliation with her loss. Visiting George Staves would have to endure recalling those final fateful days. He thought of dodging to avoid his painful conflict – screening, selecting and dwelling only on those few gratifying moments when it appeared that her treatments would prevail.

He would not escape, giving him no other recourse but to include re-experiencing his missions failure, steeling himself for the punishing struggle of right or wrong. In finality he understood, it would be a theft of her memory, how she coped, her motivations, if he were to edit out that drama, reliving only the hope of their allegiance. Now still despairing of failure, he remembered seeded from that disappointing efforts darkest moments – amongst his overgrowth of melancholy, grew understanding that would recover their relationship. Two different species elevated to new heights, while tears of a great loss continued to flow. Those final thoughts were the ignition to propel his transporter through an awaiting emotional roller coaster.

He had halted his time traveling transporter, its propellant ceasing, this days disbelief just as inhibiting, Once again he and Rose heard the veterinarian's heart stopping prognosis that fateful day. Those echoing words a rising tide of emotions hardly ebbing in the waters of the past, symptomatic that recovering from her loss was still in process. Today's reliving enabled introspection: judging himself guilty of a selfishness evolving from his close now judged overly dependent relationship with Tasha, one occupying the irrational at times. His new truth an admission, holding himself responsible for discouraging any thought of her vulnerability. His perception, a sense of her invincibility to debilitating aging, forestalling death itself proven a fantasy – the fatalism of physical change.

Today's somber assessment would never have visited the George Staves persona before Tasha's decision, selectively ignoring recognition of the preconditions to life; animals, all animals having a biological clock that unwinds, the aging process part of the ticks as systems and function wear. A sunrise to sunset phenomenon genetically coded and predestined to its natural conclusion. A process sometimes interrupted by premature death, an intervention that short circuit what began at birth to the inevitable end of the normal life cycle. Life, while a continuum starting with birth proceeding through sexual activity and aging, culminated in death, is not linear. At differing rates, the aging process a variable, strongly influenced by factors of size, medical history, trauma and genetics, those factors opportuned the credo of the earlier George Staves, building upon those criteria, attempting misguidedly, God-like control.

George Staves believed, his beloved Tasha, now thirteen man years of age, religiously receiving all her shots to ward off disease – following a closely monitored diet, cautiously protected from trauma from any external direction, her role as a family member guarded against internal emotional problems, management in his favor or so he thought. These preparations and her extraordinary senses and intelligence misguiding him into believing those absences as short comings to the lesser of canines. Tasha was extraordinary. He ignored the passage of days, months and years and what the unrelenting aging process was fermenting in darkness and secret, a pathology continuing unabated; relentless nature at work. Not expecting parity with his own species, yet awakening each day planned to live it, until this sobering awakening.

The transporter still motionless his kaleidoscope's presentation on hold while he attempted to rein in his emotions, having trepidations for what he was about to see: his earlier self's inner conflict reawakened, the final desperation crossing the border into occultism, all other remedies having been tried and failed. Leading to the unexpected separation of wills, an inner peace of acceptance found by the very one who would leave his world, leaving the other in painful transition: accepting her rejection of seeking an extension to her life cycle, a probability never thought possible. Her metamorphic enlightenment was her line in the sand. Tasha's remaining burden, how he would accede. Could she void his mindset of deterring a common enemy, no longer principle in her wishes?.

The first sign that something was wrong occurred during the routine return from her daily walk. Without the slightest hint of her experiencing difficulty, literally within yards of the house an unknown force struck Tasha causing her balance to leave her suddenly. Within milliseconds she went from standing upright to listing, her weight precariously to one side, the nails of her paws clawing the ground to stay upright. Her legs showing no signs of strength collapsing her body toward her listing side, completing her mysterious uprooting. Unaware where she was, eyes rolled back as if in a faint or fit. Her legs convulsively searching for register. No cries of her in pain were heard; the moment soundless until Staveses emotional entreaties. Confusion reigning, he fell to his knees bewildered by the cause.

"Tasha," an alarmed George Staves responded, his throat tightening, choking back a sob as he reached out tenderly to comfort her. Crestfallen, he pleaded, "Dear God, what's wrong with her? Bring her back to me."

As if responding to his prayers, her collapse and disorientation proved temporary as Tasha's recognition returned. Staves still shaken, seeing her struggle to raise herself, moved quickly to assist her, not understanding the cause of her loss of consciousness episode. Her eyes showed the recovering focus of affection. The strength in her legs returned accepting her weight's distribution, her balance now intact. Without hesitation, as if just a happenstance, she resumed her walk home while Staves's eyes remained glued to her every movement, the shock of the occurrence dominating his every thought. Apprehensive, he tightened the tether in an unconscious act of shortening their lifeline connection, his nearness a protection of her.

Upon reaching home, Rose and George quickly arranged for a visit to Dr. Kerrigan, their veterinarian. Agonizing during two anxious hours of testing and examining of Tasha, Rose and George were finally escorted from the waiting room into Dr. Kerrigan's office just as an assistant returnd her to them. Tasha lying at their feet panting, uncomfortable with her surroundings. The heart rates of the Staves's increasing rapidly, awaiting the findings. Dr. Kerrigan his tone considerate, yet his solemnity forewarning: the results hurtful to them.

"Her fainting episode, while usually heart related, was not borne out by the tests. Her monitored heart rate and her circulation rate show no abnormalities for a dog her age. However decreased blood flow reducing the amount of oxygen to the brain causing her to faint can't be ruled out in spite of the tests good readings. Additionally we checked the possibility of seizures, the brain wave examination for epilepsy proved inconclusive. While not completely ruled out, seizures are not a consideration at this time. Neither is hypoglycemia, known to cause fainting as her levels of sugar and calcium were normal. My hypothesis in spite of lack of corroboration is that decreased blood flow accounted for a disproportionate distribution of blood to the legs instead of the brain, depriving the brain of oxygen at the time of the incident. My experience strongly suggests that probability. Had you been able to discern that the color of her gums turned distinctively blue, there would be no question that at the time of the incident the brain was starved of oxygen."

"But you're not sure?" George Staves interrupted, "What then?"

"True I'm not absolutely certain."

"Then where are we," George Staves asked in exasperation, "what else could have caused it?"

" What I can't rule out is that it was an incident attributable to food poisoning, however I don't rate that possibility highly."

"Why is that," George Staves queried, quickly accepting… obviously in favor of the least painful determination.

"You reported none of the obvious signs; diarrhea, vomiting. No high blood pressure, no temperature readings of concern. Yet we can't rule it out completely."

Acknowledging the strong feelings held for Tasha, Dr. Kerrigan paused momentarily to gather himself, wishing he had more favorable news, not comfortable with his duty.

"She has another condition that is indisputable that you should be made aware of, a possible contributor to her fainting. She has arthritis in her hip joints., not unusual for her age," the veterinarian said as he pointed to the X-ray films on the viewing screen. She also has spondylosis, a form of arthritis in her neck which has been known to be caused by food poisoning, my reason for not ruling that out as a cause."

Time traveling Staves seeing himself relive those devastating moments in real time felt empathy for himself in anguish, transferable, immediately mirroring on his own person.

"It's part of the aging process, diseasing the nerves and the skeletal systems," he said softly watchful of the Staves fretting over his diagnosis. Dr. Kerrigan spoke gently, delicately, yet authoritatively, the trauma of his words inflicting wounds.

"Age is catching up with her," he repeated. "She is in her twilight years. Thirteen man years equates to ninety-one dog years of age. We must accept the fact that she is getting older and will have to be treated under that criteria."

Dr. Kerrigan continued his clinical diagnosis, internal tremors shaking the Staves's foundation. Incredulous George questioned, "Does that mean this situation is not curable?" his voice unsteady? Rose was stunned to silence, following the dialogue with trepidation.

"I'm afraid so, Mr. Staves." His head moving from side to side negatively. "The best today's medicine can offer is to make her as comfortable as we can to relieve the pain."

"Your telling us there is no hope?" Staves repeated, his heart aching, the pain glazing his eyes unashamedly.

"I'm afraid her age is catching up with her," the veterinarian repeated.

"What can we expect?" a downcast Rose Staves asked, the stupor of her shock ending.

"Her arthritic condition will only worsen. She'll become completely debilitated… unable to move pain free… her disease progressing to a point where the medication will no longer work for her. She'll be in extreme pain. You will face making a difficult decision… doing the humane thing."

"But she shows none of the signs. Are you telling us that the fainting episode is the first sign?"

"In my judgment, yes, but there are other factors I suspect" Dr. Kerrigan replied.

"Such as?"

"The diseases impact on her heart. Which we can treat But I can't prescribe for that until I'm sure."

~

Those words were a biting reminder to the on looking time traveling George Staves, his denial of age's impact an unreality. He projecting her uniqueness, her good health continuing beyond normal expectations initially, his creation. It's substance, he had rationalized: her separating superior intellect voiding the calendar of her breed – a projection ignoring the support of scientific findings. A belief offered without clinical confirmation,in his mind Tasha's longevity to be a bellwether.

Dr. Kerrigan's maintaining the reality of Tasha's age was the most significant criteria in her overall health's decline. His findings strongly resisted by George Staves. Self serving, comforting himself rated as most probable: food poisoning as the cause of her fainting episode,with prejudice denying as fateful the physiological change Tasha was undergoing Their split precipitating challenge, their impasse ameliorated with an agreement that she be watched closely for further incidents.

They left Dr. Kerrigan's office armed with uncertain tortured logic, George's persistence influencing Rose with it's offer of their world remaining intact, however agreeing to consider the administration of the prescription of a anti-inflammatory drug if her mobility showed pained decline. Planning to primarily treat Tasha's fainting as episodic, judging as sufficient, a bland diet until her system was purged of the food poison – taken as fact, not a possibility.

It happened again three weeks later, the circumstances and conditions repeated, except this time it was preceded by a slight limp. a still in denial George Staves attributing to an accidental strain. Dr. Kerrigan, having justification, would not trumpet his first call as her testing again proved negative.

However, with this second episode within a month, the lack of clinical confirmation would do little to support George Staves continuing his resistance arbitrarily. His position weakened considerably: a second incident repeating food poisoning while under close watch was improbable. Continued denial in the face of that fact an indefensible distortion. Aggrieved, disillusioned and subdued, their resistance crumbled, tortured as no other options were available to them. Their secure world damaged, ceding as they must to Dr. Kerrigan's conclusions The visualization of Tasha hurting, experiencing pain, contributed to by their resistance an untenable position

Dr. Kerrigan, while still uncertain, the tests of the hearts involvement again negative,did not preclude his recommendation of a herbal cardio strengthener,not ready to prescribe a canine dosage of the more aggressive pharmaceutical Atenalol. Supplementally supportive, cautioning against long walks, her heart not to be taxed, her joints avoiding further inflammation. The anti-inflammatory medication to her diet along with the food supplements, Glucosamine and Chondroitin no longer debatable, easing her arthritic pain while promoting joint tissue growth.

The success of the shorter walks proved temporary, the progressing debilitating disease claiming control of her body, bringing her once again to helpless unconsciousness. While again frantic with worry, this time having the presence of mind to push back her lips, George seeing the bluish discoloration of her gums, left no room for doubt,her disease taxing her heart. After consultation with Dr. Kerrigan, Atenalol was prescribed and the stopping of walks altogether, her exercise limited to the backyard brief jaunts. Accepting this change in regimen which under healthier circumstances would have encouraged Tasha to make independent adventuresome journey's, her passivity acknowledging the need – her language for concurring.

Over time other disturbing signs began to appear. Her zeal and quickness in climbing steps slackened considerably. No longer did she jump up and off beds and couches with abandon. Now she would whimper, unable to join George and Rose in bed until George carefully assisted her; lying at their feet exclusively on her right side, her tested choice. No longer going from room to room as she saw fit in independence. Nor was she able to descend the stairs with impunity, standing at the top of the landing willing yet hesitant, the task warning of a pained outcome. Tentatively placing one paw out in reaching for the bottom of the step, painfully retracting it halfway, the limit of her extension. Switching cautiously to the other foot, the result repeated, her restrictions forcing her to lay down in defeat at the top of the stairs whimpering at her predicament, waiting for help. Too big and heavy to carry down the stairs, George slinged her hindquarters with a towel that passed beneath her stomach – Rose preceding them one step ahead at a time, her words giving encouragement, her hand holding Tasha's collar to control the pace of descent while George took most of the weight off her hip joints with his hastily rigged sling.

Disheartened, with the fainting syncopy's seemingly under control – they proven wrong in their judgment, the evidence so undeniable, Tasha indeed had crippling arthritis invading her joints as forewarned by Dr. Kerrigan, they were still however openly shocked by how quickly and widespread this insidious disease had traveled in a relatively short period of time.

To learn a deeper understanding, education was essential, arranging an after-hour's meeting with Dr. Kerrigan at his office. Tasha at their feet, the background noise only that of cleanup from a heavy appointment schedule.

"The central concept to body functioning," Dr. Kerrigan began, "is homeostasis, a dynamic process whereby the various body systems function to maintain internal stability, keeping the body operational, repaired and protected."

Carefully selecting words to avoid sounding like a lecturer reading from prepared text risking pedantry, his voice was modulated:

"Normal cells are excitable," he said informing them, "they can pass on electric charges when properly stimulated. They can't, however, divide or replicate as is Tasha's case, therefore the ones born with are the same ones at death, less the ones lost through trauma and the normal aging process. The system performs three generic functions; muscle activation, glandular secretion and sensory functions; conscious and unconscious thought associated with neuron activity within the brain guiding the response."

Continuing, Dr. Kerrigan said, "Aging is the net effect of negative changes in the system's physiology, it's homeostasis. Interconnected, some overlapping, a grouping of systems, each in its own role the key to maintaining optimal functions. Typically, as in Tasha's case, her situation clinically involves the musculoskeletal system affected by relentless aging, bringing with it the wearing out of weight bearing surfaces such as joints, muscle and bone: dysplasia is the medical term potentially crippling and exceedingly painful." he paused, in sympathy for the anguish on their faces. His unpleasant task, his professional duty, report regardless of consequences. "Not unexpected, Tasha shows the onset of joint dysplasia and the intervertebral disease – spondylosis a degenerative disease most commonly affecting the lumbar vertebrae as evidenced by her loss of muscle mass and sensitivity to touch. There are no cures," he said in subdued authority. "It's the inevitability of aging we're dealing with. We can only hope to reduce her pain and try to make her comfortable during her final days."

In spite of deliberate care while being clinical, Dr. Kerrigan's pronouncements were devastating, Rose brought her trembling hand to her mouth to stifle a cry. George willed himself, steeled to the circumstances, unable to prevent a noticeable despairing slumping of his shoulders. The unprepared fateful sentencing burdening them. To think of Tasha's bountiful energies as a thing of the past, her mobility reduced to only painfully slow reflex actions, swamped them in a tidal wave of melancholy, inundating them in sorrow. Floundering in silence, anguish frozen on their faces, they nodded understanding, robotically.

"Her remaining quality of life cannot be much," Rose Staves finally stammered, desperately morose.

Dr. Kerrigan, schooled in understanding owners' emotional involvement with the animal member of a family, remained resolute and steadfast, sympathy avoiding the torturing prolongation false hope brings, "We can only provide to ease her pain."

"You mean how much she can live with?" George Staves, his anguish suddenly converted to angers flashing point.

"Yes, I'm sorry, Mr. Staves, it's all we can do, all medicine has to offer at this stage of her disease is to make her comfortable."

George Staves tensed in his seat feeling guilt, misunderstanding: "What are you saying? That we could have eased her present situation had it been diagnosed earlier?" needing to lash out, relieving his pain, aggression in his tone.

Recognizing George's words as guilt association and a building hostility, the doctor became defensive, attempting to ease the situation and its implications, "She was always given the best of care and attention. Our records of previous examinations show no clue of her disease as sometimes happens. Not until symptoms manifest themselves, when the disease is deeply rooted are we able to make the right diagnosis."

Continuing on, knowing he needed to say it all in spite of George Staves' anger: "There will come a point in time when she will tell you that she has endured enough; that it's time to let go."

Those fateful words spoken crashed their world, bringing tears to Rose's eyes. Dr. Kerrigan moved from his professional perch, his evolved emotional involvement moving him to the receiving line, no longer able to steal away, finding refuge in the dispassionate safety of his profession. There it was out on the table, a loss in the family unit; the pack, to be forever affected, her fateful tombstone being chiseled while alive and under siege, enduring painful awakenings, growing resistant to relieving medication. Sentenced in her remaining days to figuratively live in a narrow path tunnel, unable to turn around, a reduced mobility, made more difficult as the only light was at the entrance behind her, fading with each advancing painful step into endless darkness. Her life's diminishing light disappearing in the distance.

George Staves was angered and frustrated at conventional veterinary medicine, unable to do nothing more than make her comfortable. That failing in his present state of mind amounting to cohabitating with the disease, robbing the Staves's of her precious life... her fate fixed. Visualizing her wasting away, crying out for help; scarring his heart and conscience. George Staves faulting veterinary science,it's lack of discovery limiting the practices of veterinary medicine. Treatments awaiting expansion, still the foundation for today's veterinary doctoring, openly decried by those facing a loss for the lack of advancement. Irrational to a point of damming inadequate stock treatments too quickly referenced in veterinary medical books, it's pages worn by convenient repeated reference. Its limitations, in his judgment, voiced to Dr. Kerrigan, "in desperate need of supplementation or replacement, by a proactive science discovering or developing advanced treatments." In bitterness going so far to say, "in my search for knowledge preparatory to today's session – elsewhere in this world, or beyond to occult mysticism, or recluse religious beliefs held in secret, treatments could be found for her condition far and away more promising than what you're offering."

Attempting to defend the good name of his profession, Dr. Kerrigan denounced his reference as rumored or isolated instances of success needing, confirmation after considerable study. He cautioned unproven treatments that preyed on the desperate. Of no consequence as Staves pledged he would seek them out and test them no matter the cost and sacrifice. He would leave no stone unturned. He would continue to search the Internet. He would explore alternative medicines. He would seek out the knowledge of ancient cultures. He would supplicate to God to lead him on his mission, strengthening him along his journey to maintain his resolve, until fulfillment or exhaustion would be His will.

This he owed Tasha for all the years of love and devotion, always giving, whether subtle or exuberant. He would fight the inevitable, the impossible odds to gain her seconds, minutes, hours, days, and possibly years in her life. To maintain as long as possible their gratifying earthly bond truly intertwined as one.

Family conferencing was called; a figurative circling of the Staves wagons was conducted by phone. The mood of everyone was somber, their tears having already been shed at the shock of the devastating news. Committed and resolute, all were completely supportive of what he had outlined as his plan to assist Tasha in her hour of need. Prayerful, they hung onto every word of hope he spoke to keep her insidious monster at bay, agreeing with the active pursuit of non-conventional treatments, anxious to be part of the reported claims of success, no matter how sporadic. While the atmosphere remained somber, potential hope for Tasha loomed over the horizon of failing conventional medicine, diffused somewhat when asked:

"What if none of these newly accredited treatments work," what then, the repeated question?

Answering, "There is the last hope of surreal treatments, the mystical that I'm holding in reserve, our last lifeline. Beyond that, it's between us, God and Tasha," George Staves said solemnly, creating a period of silent reflection at that prospect.

Trusting his belief, rather than Dr. Kerrigan's situational description, dismissed as a premature epitaph, reignited the spirit of hope and optimism for all who would live the search along side of him, adding, "we haven't reached that crossroads. Help exists, pray that we are successful."

The expense would be of no consequence while hope still existed, Tasha was a family member now threatened with loss of life, a insatiable disease internally eating away, laying waste a debilitated skeletal system. It's corrosiveness on its own timetable. Its onset surreptitiously seeded, accelerating as age became an unwilling co-conspirator, shed of its anonymity, named and dammed within the same breath. Its resistance to conventional countermeasures proving to be overmatched, a medically ineffective "Marginot Line" allowing continuing passage to the invader. Claiming another victory as crippling pain and deterioration forced the notice of succumbing, comforting, petting and embracing evoking growls; a victim forced to deny herself, longing for painless expressions of sincere caring.

"Why aren't you helping me?" would be her communication, he was helpless as she laid her head in his lap staring hopefully up at him. "Help me as you have in the past… my leader… my Alpha."

The language of her pained filled eyes making focusing difficult, yet she would not tell him that it was time for her to go, for him to accept her death and life without her, that all was lost. Not while there was still fight left in her body and he was championing her cause.

The final motivation came a few days later when Staves noticed blood intermixed with her stools, forewarning blood gushing diarrhea, quickly and correctly attributed to the medication Rimadyl, her principal anti-inflammatory medicine. Immediate contact with the veterinarian, Dr. Kerrigan, confirmed his judgment as he withdrew the Rimadyl, replacing it with a mild form of aspirin, increasing the dosage of Glucosamine and Chondroiton, mainstays of the remaining treatment. Staves questioned why he had not been alerted to Rimadyl damaging effects. The answer, not to his liking, Staves desperation for Tasha precluded any restrictions.

He later learned, when searching the Internet, that the manufacturer, Pfizer, had issued an alert letter, warning all veterinarians of the potential danger of Rimadyl to some dogs, particularly ones of larger size. Notwithstanding, he remained unwaivering, it was an effective treatment. George Staves relented, her treatment would have to be aggressive, he would not discourage the proactive medicines approach, nor developing treatments still anecdotal. The potentially promising not too premature to be of value. He would continue this pursuit in treating Tasha's condition. George more than ever committed to finding alternative medicines and treatments, his zeal making him vulnerable to the preying unscrupulous, a price he would be willing to pay if his judgment proved faulty.

The day, nine in the morning, moments of rain were within the threatening clouds, grayness crowding out the blue sky. Ladened it lowered the sky's ceiling, a mist no longer airborne. A separating interface impossible to detect. The dismal weather conditions did not set the tone or subdue the enthusiasm for the day's event. The prospect of Tasha's first visit to a veterinary acupuncturist, a new source of hope, countering the day without shadows, prayerfully offering the first challenge to the limitations of conventional treatment.

Rose as always accompanied George and Tasha to the veterinarian; Tasha standing, the more painless position, in the back seat of the car, peering out an open window, hopefully distracted from her pain, her face awash in the rushing air. George Staves selected Dr. Angeli, a doctor of veterinary medicine; because he was state certified and had more than three years of bona fide accredited acupuncture training. He had once been a board certified acupuncturist on humans before becoming a veterinarian offering acupuncture in his treatment arsenal for over five years. The connotation of his name did not go unnoticed in Staves' selection process, implying a server of a greater good, an emissary empowered by God, whose name leaped from the page listing the members of the Acupuncture Association, giving him an additional reason for his choice.

Staves had, along with Tasha's medical records and X-rays, a letter of introduction provided by a very skeptical Dr. Kerrigan, who proved no match to George Staves' unrelenting insistence, not heeding his warning that the treatment of acupuncture would prove fruitless in Tasha's case. Rose and George, arrived with a reverence reserved for a deity, solicitous of Dr. Angeli and what the potential for his ministrations held – a potential life restorer.

Dr. Angeli, seated after their introduction, wrote notes in an abbreviated language that only he could decipher; all the information on Tasha's health history, to be placed in a newly created file, repeatedly bringing up the question of trauma in her lifetime and their knowledge of Tasha's ancestry. Dr. Angeli picked up the X-ray film and excusing himself entered his viewing room. He returned after minutes, his face showing no reaction.

"These X-rays are quite complete. Coverage is extensive and definitive, clearly showing the extent of Tasha's arthritis. It is very apparent that it is severe but not without hope." The Staves's finding expectation in his initial assessment.

"Let me explain the treatment I have planned for Tasha but let me first explain the science of acupuncture, for reassurances that it is a bona fide treatment. China or the Far East is credited with the discovery of acupuncture, having been discovered by war lords. Lame battle horses were found to recover after being hit by arrows at distinct points in their bodies. With its development and refinement over the years, it is now recognized by the American Veterinary Medical Association, approving the stimulation of specific body points by use of acupuncture needles.

"There are many explanations as to why this system of stimuli works, the most widely accepted being the Neural Opiate Theory where pain control is achieved by the release of endogenous opiates called endorphins which are released upon needle or pressure stimulation of specific points of the body interacting at different levels in the central nervous system by inhibiting pain transmission. In addition, endorphins control pain by causing blood vessels to dilate, thus increasing blood flow around joints and muscle, thereby increasing nutrient and oxygen delivery in the desired area. It is sometimes referred to as the "gate theory," closing the gate of pain, hypothesized within the spinal cord.

"I must tell you that this procedure is still undergoing challenge and skepticism in western cultures that claim viewing internal medicine as treating the imbalance of energy called "Chin" by the use of acupuncture, is metaphysical and not medicine. Its opposition," Dr. Angeli smiled, "it is not without paradox, as western medicine recognizes irrefutably that disturbances to the flow of energy are indicative of illness within the body. Examples: recording electrical activity of the heart by electrocardiograph: ECC, electrical activity of the brain by electroencephalography: EEG, muscle activity by electromyography: EMG." Pausing, Dr. Angeli said, "Someday medicine of western culture will co-join out of necessity for the good of the patient."

"You mentioned points. What does that mean?" Rose asked.

Dr. Angeli answered, "Points exist along fourteen meridians… channels if you will… selected among hundreds of points by the acupuncturist."

"Will it cause pain to Tasha?" Rose asked with rising concern.

"No," Dr. Angeli answered without hesitation. "The procedure is well tolerated. There is no risk to her well-being."

They were both comfortable with his answer, George Staves asked, "What are Tasha's prospects?"

Recognizing their growing optimism from a countenance of desperation, he returned them to reality.

"In Tasha's case acupuncture will not cure her condition, I'm sorry to say," sympathetically joining them in their obvious disappointment. "On the positive side, we do have a good chance of making her feel better without the use of strongly reacting drugs. It has the potential of improving her lifestyle, making her happier, improving her movement if only for short periods. You'll see the gratification in her eyes."

Tasha lay at their feet, moving occasionally to change her stiffening position for one temporarily pain free. Moving freely were the perking of her ears at the mention of her name. A response of forthcoming help countering her baleful stare, her countenance and eyes now brightening with excitement already scripting words approving the procedure to treat her condition.

Her cooperation communicated, George Staves asked anxiously, "What treatment program were you planning for Tasha?"

"First of all, we are going to change her diet to one more appropriate to her condition. Secondly, I'm prescribing four treatments over four days; a half hour each time over the next four to six weeks. If she progresses as anticipated we could reduce the treatment time considerably, possibly down to ten seconds." He paused, needing assurances of their continuing interest, asking, "Are you prepared to make such a commitment?"

Comfortable there was minimum risk, hope beckoning, George and Rose answered almost in whispered unison, quietly resolute, "Yes."

"Good, now for today's session: What I plan to do is shave the contact points." Pulling from his top desk drawer he showed a drawing of a Labrador with sixteen needles that they both counted protruding from her rear spine and hindquarters.

"This drawing depicts almost the same alignment I have planned for Tasha. I will manipulate and massage the sixteen shaven points to detect the area's sensitivity and the depth of penetration of the needles. You might see her reflectively shudder or shake the area as I hand maneuver the needles of flexible hair thin wire, which are two to four inches in length. Her muscles will seem to sense the needles' presence until relief in energy balance occurs and is sensed by me before withdrawing." Rising from behind his desk, he asked, "Are we clear of what the procedure calls for?"

"Yes," George Staves responded, adding, "Both my wife and I want to be with her during the procedure, if you don't mind, to reduce the possibility of her becoming aggressive, forcing you to sedate her."

"Agreed, that's not a problem as long as you don't interfere out of exaggerated concern for her welfare. She must be under my control during the procedure. For that reason I must insist you not be a distraction."

"We're indebted to your trust," George Staves voiced somberly as they were led to one of the treatment rooms.

Tasha's pace was slow but not from fear, her tail curled proudly over her back. They both addressed Tasha, finding it necessary to relieve their building tension by speaking soothing reassuring terms to her as Dr. Angeli shaved the selected contact points with an occasional curious movement from Tasha, indicative of her trust. Nonetheless, she did whimper as he massaged her bare skin, raising her head, to the chagrin of Dr. Angeli, to eye George. Her attention, unbeknownst to Dr. Angeli, was drawn by his tensed body effusing telling chemical scents distinguishing love not a danger alert for her well-being. Reassurances received, with a reconciling exhale she dropped her panting head back onto the examining table satisfying Dr. Angeli, allowing the procedure to continue while Rose continued to coo encouragement.

Attentive and apprehensive, Rose and George watched as Dr. Angeli began to insert the fine needles. Finding themselves captive and instinctively guiding the needles penetration, seeking the enemy scourge within Tasha, ravaging her towards physical separation, joining in silent prayer for the good Lords personal intervention.

Tasha's every movement in the aftermath of the first two sessions was under close observation. Rose and George were both encouraged by signs that she was responding favorably; showing a greater mobility, confidence replacing fear in her maneuverings, particularly on the slippery challenge offered by the tile floor of the Staves' kitchen, indicative that a return to health was approaching as her infirmities were responding. Unfortunately, as they had been forewarned, the improvements proved to be token, the promising signs never appreciating.

They were into the sixth week of treatment with Tasha in and out of improvements, all proving to be short term. The duration of the acupuncture, still at half an hour, was foretelling, diminishing prospects and hopes. After the completion of the sixth week, the twenty-fourth treatment, they met in Dr. Angeli's office expectant of a worrisome assessment.

"I'm afraid the treatments are not bringing about the desired results. Of course, you didn't need to hear that from me – noticing unfortunately that success was limited."

Their response was to stare blankly while nodding dejectedly, muted by their disappointment and fading optimism.

"The latest X-rays show her condition not optimistic. Her slight improvement was not sustained; proving temporary. While we could continue this treatment, I must advise against it."

"You mean that's it?" George said crushed and disconsolate.

"Not quite," Dr. Angeli quickly answered. "We still have other treatments in our arsenal of acupuncture available before I would be willing to concede hopelessness."

A renewed spark of hope ignited in the Staveses darkening melancholy, brightening them.

"What are they?" an aroused George Staves asked.

"With your permission, I'd like to proceed with electro stimulation: hooking up conducting wires to four of the acupuncture needles, using voltage to assist stimulation."

"What are the risks?" a concerned Rose Staves quickly found need to ask.

"None, really. The only problem is that the electrical charge is not well tolerated. She will inevitably twitch, forcing out the acupuncture wires. If she is too resistant and sheds the wires faster than we can reinsert them, the process will be ineffectual. Under those circumstances we either discontinue the treatment or it becomes necessary that she be sedated."

"No sedation," George stated flatly, interrupting, "She'll handle it." Continuing, he asked, "And if this fails, there are treatments beyond it?"

"Yes," Dr. Angeli informed. "Let's take them one at a time, as you agree."

Staves turned to face Tasha whose eyes glistened with suppressed pain, nonetheless expressing her answer to him, the often repeated message that bound them, "I'm in your hands. You are my trusted Alpha. It is your leadership I follow without question."

"Yes," George responded freely confident of Tasha's endorsement, "we'll continue."

Again a concerned Rose Staves asked, "How many treatments this time and for how long?"

"Treatments will last fifteen minutes at a time. We should know the effectiveness in two weeks."

Hope restored, the second phase of acupuncture treatment began, watched over with tensing anxiety, occasioning their tender words of encouragement: "You'll get well, Tasha girl… That's a good girl… We're right here with you." Encouraged, she licked trustingly the reassuring hand of George Staves; willingly submitting, giving of herself, abiding the foreignness passing through her aching body.

After two weeks, the results were disappointing, almost negligible, not the building block of portending success that all had hoped for, the shortfall advancing inevitable doubts. Have we reached our precipice? Must we descend? Are we exploring heights too lofty and rarified, accommodating only experimentation? Rose and George Staves' downcast thoughts were easily recognized in their visage.

Dr. Angeli, a kind and considerate man, clinically assessed Tasha who laid at their feet, animals his passion saying, "I know you're as disappointed in the results as I am but we aren't through yet. As you have told me your concern is Tasha's well being, committed to leave no stone unturned; to go as far as medicine, all medicines will take you."

While Staves nodded affirmatively, his enthusiasm was minimal, shackled by disappointment.

Knowing a bolstering recommitment was needed, Dr. Angeli again sparked their falling darkness of despair. "There is still hope for acupuncture. A relatively new treatment… bringing remarkable results in some cases that we must consider in Tasha's case,"

"What is it?" Rose asked, buoyed once again, pushing aside her dejection.

"It involves the use of laser – for which we are state board certified. In this procedure, instead of needles we use the laser beam to stimulate the points by emitting varying frequencies of infrared light, displayed as a red beam at the instrument's focus point. The patient feels nothing whatsoever. As Tasha is not a hyperactive dog, the beeping sound of alert when the equipment is in use should not be bothersome."

"I know my dog, she'll tolerate it, putting her welfare in my trust. You're a good man Dr. Angeli, I have confidence in you and your medicine."

Tasha's demeanor, always reflective, mirrored their rejuvenated confidence, reaffirming her willingness to continue the treatments. Her disease was being pursued, while tiring was not yet exhausting her or her tolerance.

"We'll extend the treatments another three weeks – half hour sessions twice a week," Dr. Angeli outlined.

Since the beginning of treatments over the past weeks, beyond Tasha's guarded tolerance for Dr. Angeli, an unexpected outgrowth of affection had developed between the two. Dr. Angeli was in awe of Tasha's abilities, having remembered the newspaper articles detailing her unusual skills and the human-like characteristics attributed to her, his eager eyes hoping to experience a firsthand account. His wishes fanciful, filing away her credentials, absorbed in the unfolding drama of Tasha's reaction to treatment. He openly complemented Tasha's high tolerance level for the pain he hoped to relieve, the responsiveness to those she loved – traits of character he recognized as special, a separating aura.

Tasha had responded to Dr. Angeli, departing her usual arousal of angst for veterinarians. This unknown person, effusing a disarming scent, coupled with her beloved family's expressions of confidence, credited in bringing a guarded tolerance to his ministrations. His sensitive fingers massaging, aiding, preparing her well for the acupuncture. Dr. Angeli, an Animal Rescue League staff veterinarian, volunteered his services and treatment in support of keeping abandoned charges emotionally happy and physically attractive after neutering, increasing their chances for adoption… enhancing their lives, the motivation of animal rescue. Recognizing the role of stress affecting treatment, he arranged for Tasha to meet a recovering devoted rescued male Siberian husky placed under his care, cleverly intending to promote confidence in his care and eliminate lingering wariness. The abandoned husky had suffered physically and psychologically, lice and parasite infestation and a severe intimidating case of mange, all personality damaging, all diminishing prospective adoption. Dr. Angeli doctoring him from near death to a blossoming vibrant husky. His thinking Tasha meeting one of her own breed under his successful care and treatment, would result in a positive influence in their own relationship, easing their circumstances further.

Tasha's reaction, unexpected, was immediately impacting. She stood proudly before the recovering male Husky her tail waving at an abnormally slow pace – cautious. Amazingly, Tasha, in her weakened condition projected the dominant Alpha, staring down the male Husky coldly, posturing, and growing before everyone's eyes as her shackles were fully extended.

Ignoring her pain, stretching, she magnified herself, growing from the minimizing vulnerable effects of arthritis. The male husky ended the stare down with voluntarily reposing before Tasha on his back, legs tucked in, exposing his vulnerable underbelly, the final act of subordination. With the act of respect completed, they began circling one another, Tasha's body language expressing domination, using their eyes, ears, mouths, tails and fur to share information as well as feelings. The male Husky, occasionally breaking from the ritual to seek Dr. Angeli's approval, conveyed his recovery was in the best of hands, worthy of Tasha's trust.

Dr. Angeli watched in disbelief at what had unfolded, although planned to relieve Tasha of any remaining angst, the totality of events was completely unexpected. Tasha asserted herself in spite of her pain wracked body; his role filling male husky supplicating before his superior, his status below Tasha in the hierachy ranking of a pack animal. Dr. Angeli's ministrations of Tasha from that day forward proceeding with a greater freedom.

Again after three weeks, the results of the treatments were disappointing. However Tasha's strength and will showed little tiring, not conceding, not rejecting; remaining stalwart, a challenging victim attempting to thwart the relentlessness of the diseasing invader in her body.

The Staves and Tasha shared each other's strength. To find an effective treatment: putting the disease in remission for her remaining years.

This time Dr. Angeli advised the procedure would include Adequin injections at the points, as a precursor to laser, known for helping thicken joint fluid and decrease inflammation pain in the joints. A ratio of one c.c. for every thirty pounds of body weight was recommended. Since Tasha's body weight was seventy pounds, a total of 2.3 c.c.'s would be used, distributed over the four points. The combined system of laser and Adequin injections to continue twice a week over the next four weeks.

After the second week of treatment, the Staves saw a noticeable improvement. The daily supplemental massages that George administered to her meridian points were now accepted with only the slightest whimper; indicative of diminishing pain, a welcomed beginning: the new therapy bringing the gift of soothing blood flow and its disease fighting white corpuscles. Flexibility of the joints became more evident as her pace quickened. Her ability to rise from her position of somnolence was no longer labored, more mechanical than fluid but unquestionably an improvement. Her ability to rise steadily, lessened her tentativeness with each inch gained, testing her new bearing on hind legs that previously yielded under the pain. Confident in her surging strength she leaped up on him, her joints tested as she forcefully positioned herself on his chest. Fully extended, once again standing tall, delighted in herself, nuzzling and licking George copiously. He was emotionally overcome at her restored ability as he choked back a sob, no longer in need of recalling memories, this event current, a restored range of motion and flexibility on display.

Equally revealing in the days that followed was her confidently summoned ancestral role as a predator, proudly acted out in responding to the lure of the hunt, nose sniffing close to the ground, each exhale designed to part ground cover as her ancestors had done in the tundra, uncovering a prey's scent, finding it, leaping excitedly, both front paws together as coordinated ramrods, repeatedly landing with enough force to seal the entrance or exit of the borrowed tunnel of either a chipmunk or rabbit who had advantaged Tasha's infirmed absence. Now having to deal with the rebirth of a challenging Tasha, a danger to their commerce.

A sun as if summoned to celebrate this eventful day burst through a week of tiring gloomily painted skies of gray. Its bright rays welcomed by the Staves, illuminating through the breaking clouds, hopefully symbolic, it's brightness a parallel with the emerging promise of ending the search for Tasha's treatment, offering up hope that continuing on this prescribed path would subdue the common enemy. All had cause to now believe, the signs so positive.

Dr. Angeli after confirming their judgments as not imagined, contained his rejoicing as his experienced warned: cautioning it was premature, needing the completion of the remaining treatments and a reasonable period of time thereafter to declare a victory. Tasha's crisis over.

The sounds of hysteria and footfalls running away from the waiting room filled the hallway outside the closed door of the examining room. The door was suddenly pushed open by one of Dr. Angeli's aides. Visibly shaken, her face ashen, unable to regain normal breathing, prematurely exhaling in anxiety, breathlessly blurting:

"Dr. Angeli, Casey, Mr. Stewart's Malamute is completely out of control," she screamed with the little breath she could muster.

"Calm down," Dr. Angeli ordered.

Nodding "yes," the circumstances of her fright inhibiting her from making a stronger effort to regain her composure, nonetheless decelerated her labored breathing, stammering a clipped account: "Can't touch him…" "Snarling…" "Frightening us to stay away…" "Cowering in a corner…" Each of her comments winded her as if racing against time, the pace of her words bordering on being incomprehensible. Dr. Angeli, anxious not sure of understanding, raised his hand to signal that she take a calming breath to regain her composure. After her instructed pause, her words were more deliberately spoken:

"Casey's heart rate when last allowed to measure was beating like a trip hammer ready to explode, nervously drooling from an open mouth. While I fear for myself, I fear for him too. Now we can't get close enough to either muzzle or sedate him. The situation is a calamity. All of your waiting patients are in cowering fear, their owners,with their pets in tow scrambling from Casey's ominous threatening behavior, scattering in all directions; some exiting the building congregating outside the front door, out of harm's way," the assistant said.

His understanding no longer escaping him, Dr. Angeli recalling one hour earlier Mr. Stewart had called expressing deep concern at the strange behavior Casey was exhibiting since their return from a two-week camping trip.

"He seems disoriented," a worried Mr. Stewart had stated, "undergoing wild swings in mood. One moment seemingly himself; confident and responsive, the next disoriented and confused."

"What is he doing right now?" Dr. Angeli asked urgently of Mr. Stewart.

"Nothing," he replied. "As a matter of fact, listless, lying down. His only movement unusual heaving and exhaling of his lungs."

"During your camping trip," Dr. Angeli asked, "did he have any contact with other animals?"

Too quick to have given much thought he replied, "None that I'm aware of."

Impatient Dr. Angeli scoffed, "You mean he showed no curiosity for his new surroundings, never exploring beyond your site?"

"No, your right, " he conceded after reflection. "The area is loaded with caves. He would disappear for hours exploring them."

Deep lines of concern now coursed Dr. Angeli's face, "We must examine him immediately – bring him right in – I'll alert my assistants."

A piercing howl, the urgency of a terrorized scream came from the waiting room. An agonizing cry for help from Casey's failing throat, not for his master who was standing nearby, but by its primitiveness to the instincts of his saviors, his brethren, his pack. His a chilling call of the wild proclaiming his danger, "Bring me your collective strength. I fight this monster alone. He steals my patience. Explodes normal sounds in my ears. Turns me against my beloved, confusing and bewildering me. My fevered infection causes me to tremble, to seek isolation, hopefully distancing myself from the demons that appear in my vision no matter where I look."

Equally as sudden was Tasha's howling response. Its tone penetrating and directing, as a fog horns piercing alert signaling the Malamute he was not alone, not deserted in his raging sea of madness. Suddenly Tasha surged unexpectedly forward easily breaking free of George's relaxed grip of the leash;

rushing past, leading Rose, George, Dr. Angeli and his still frightened assistant to the waiting room.

The waiting rooms drama was unfolding as the rushing group came into full view, threatened with fear, the pet owners indeed had scrambled for refuge outside the facility, others, not so fortunate slow to react, stood on chairs and couch's holding their frightened pets to their bosoms screaming in fright, expecting Casey manifesting irrational behavior to rise up and harm them, panicky they dared not move for fear of provocation.

Mr. Stewart, confused, prepared to intervene and had to be restrained from moving to quiet Casey's by an attendant, not understanding Casey's snarling response to his admonitions. Ignored, Mr. Stewart tried tender entreaties to no avail. He was dealing with a stranger in an evolving hell.

Dr. Angeli, armed with a forty-eight inch animal snare, who planned to capture and immobilize the strangely behaving Casey, at the last moment was held back by George Staves. George Staves alerting him of Tasha's response, her muscles taut, her leash chain a kite's tail noisily behind her, taking prominence. Tasha's pace slowed when Casey's cowering form took her notice, her movement now a testing stalk.

Barking assertively as she moved unhesitatingly right up to the demonized Casey, whose slack jaw hung stalactites of drool, falling of their own weight and volume to a gathering pool beneath him, permeating: her distinct odor of fright. Without fear, not intimidated by Casey's crazed demeanor, defiant in her leadership qualities and ignoring the portent of drool from Casey's mouth, Tasha moved almost nose to nose, her hackles showing attack readiness, not at Casey, but in support of dealing with the monster only visible to Casey. That was what she was conveying, that help was her offering.

Growls coming from each dog began to fade until silence trumpeted an understanding. Tasha, from experience, recognized this as a sign of being welcomed moved quickly to stand over the bigger Malamute, placing her muzzle on the back of Casey's yielding shoulders. The ancient rite of canines establishing dominance over a rival on display, urging him further with increased downward pressure, he responded to the reality of Tasha, his demons for the moment having been dismissed, no longer threatening him, to lurk in the shadows awaiting the progression of a deteriorating brain for resurgence.

Casey's demeanor calmed, finding Tasha's nearness and touch therapeutic. His mind temporarily clear of fog, acknowledging his brethren had responded to his call for help; a kin of evolved genetics heeding his summons.

Tasha continued to exert downward pressure with her muzzle. Casey's irrational fear vacated, dropping suddenly to the floor, rolling over on his back capitulating. Reacting thankfully for the momentary opportunity, Dr. Angeli moved quickly to sedate Casey. With his mobility ebbing quickly as the drug took effect, sleep about to overtake him, the relieved assistants still somewhat cautious, latex gloved their hands, their breathing respiratory masked, muzzled a limp Casey in his final movements of spasms before unconsciousness overtook him.

In the confusion that followed, the Staveses priority was to quickly regain control of Tasha, did hear above the din, Dr. Angeli's comments to Mr. Stewart.

"It doesn't look good for Casey," Dr. Angeli saddened to an overwhelmed and physically exhausted owner wiping the perspiration from his forehead, his comments not surprising continued.

"It appears that Casey is showing the early symptoms of rabies, displaying all the warning signs of the so-called "dumb phase"; usually lasting up to seven days. What we saw today is typical of the disease's complete reversal of Casey's usual sociability. He went from his usual docile and affectionate behavior to mean and attacking, acting out as wildly aggressive and non-responsive. The opposite would be true if he were normally aggressive. He's probably at the mid-point of this stage. His mouth open grotesquely to allow drool to escape as he is unable to swallow. The closing of his jaw becoming more difficult – remaining open, the face muscles in the early stages of paralysis, telltale signs – adding the personality reversal to wildly aggressive, leaving little doubt at what we are faced with."

"But he has had his booster shots," countered a dismayed Mr. Stewart.

"I know," Dr. Angeli responded. "I'm hard pressed to explain, except there are no cases of vaccine failure – a misnomer, as in most cases it is usually the failure of the immune system."

They shook their heads in disbelief, silently condemning the quirk of preventative medicine. A mystery to be held accountable. Modern medicine bearing the burden of not sought infallibility reverence.

The attendants, having received the word from Dr. Angeli, still cautious and still wearing surgical gloves and masks removed an unconscious Casey to the room housing the cages as the onlookers who had not left or were dispersed relaxed, the situation under control.

Dr. Angeli, fulfilling his obligations, ordered the closing of the facility for twenty-four hours in order to thoroughly clean all the walls, floors and furniture that Casey could have come in contact with.

"I want the reception area completely sanitized with the strongest viral and bacteria fighting cleaning solutions available," he announced.

Returning his attention to Mr. Stewart, he said sympathetically, "We will keep Casey under observation for the next few days while the blood work is being done. We should have all our confirming answers in a few days. There's nothing more you can do here. I would urge you to go home and await my call with the results."

"You're already convinced Casey's got rabies so why prolong the agony?" a distraught Mr. Stewart agonized.

"I've seen enough cases to be relatively sure," he said patiently. "Still, you would want me to be positive for what has to follow."

Mr. Stewart, his composure obviously shaken reluctantly left for his home, his world unexpectedly in a state of upheaval.

Dr. Angeli had earlier asked the Staves's to take Tasha back to the treatment room while he confided with Mr. Stewart. Having fulfilled his clinical assessment, freed to reflect on events, shook his head disbelievingly at what had transpired. In all his years of practice, the event never an equal or anything near seen before, amazed him. Bordering on the impossible, paranormal had he personally not borne witness.His a description not an explanation, far and away devoid of being commonplace.

Addressing the Staves's, he said, I'm absolutely amazed at Tasha's reactions. Domestication not stealing her of her genetic obligations, howling her message; bringing help to a fallen brethren unbalanced by uncomprehending forces pleading to be beholden, a diseased creature frightening all foreigners.

Dr. Angeli addressing George Staves said "I was restrained by you, from intervening, as Tasha approached a cowering Casey, disregarding and modulating the threat, Casey becoming more manageable. Amazingly, most dogs would have fled in extreme fear of a diseased canine, growing more menacing by the moment; inbred self-preservation their only reaction. But not Tasha," Dr. Angeli smiling, paused in overflowing admiration, savoring the memory before continuing.

"Is it possible she recognized the symptoms of the disease? Its devastating effects on mind and body?Spoken in the language of Casey's piercing howl,her quaking body effusing odors? Could shc know that thc combating antibodies surging through her bloodstream protected her, or did she recognize beforehand that the maddening Casey would have moments of cognizance and lucidity? To recognize Tasha's Alpha qualities, seeking refuge and relief within her leadership?" Again Dr. Angeli paused looking fondly at a reposing Tasha.

"A truly amazing dog displaying heroics and wisdom not to be expected of animals under stressful testing, placing the welfare of others before herself, ranking her own physical problems secondary; instinctively Samatarian and sacrificial," he concluded reverently.

Rose and George said nothing as they watched Dr. Angeli administer Tasha's scheduled treatment, their eyes prayerful that the success of the treatments continue, Casey's outcome weighing heavily in their minds; nonetheless, prideful to count their blessings at being selected by God's lottery, now calling for His intervention in Tasha's behalf. Tasha's extraordinary past, painfully looked upon as time consumed, never to be reclaimed, her spent history of remarkable events adding age to her winding down clock; time consumed in her lifetime, passing into history.

Within days after the Casey incident, just as they were beginning to take for granted Tasha moving toward a semblance of earlier health recovery, its dynamics peaked and was now in a descending mode, giving back hard fought agonizing ground to her persistent tormentor. Her slow motion pace returning as she labored to rise from reposing positions, tentative, forced to test beforehand the willingness of her joints, and its painful inflammation. Dejectedly they saw other unwelcomed signs of reversal: her willingness to freely move from room to room following a family member. Her underfoot nearness so dear to all was now absenting, instead choosing a resting place at the center of activities, commanded by her difficulty in moving on smooth and slippery surfaces such as tile and polished wooden floors. The Staves in response, returning to the patchwork of strategically placed non-skid rugs.

A distraught George Staves called Dr. Angeli, receiving wordless silence relating the news of Tasha's reversal. His muteness a response to his pain internally, the silence, a means of recovery, to revert to arms length, the emotions of a professional guarded, observing his professions creed. Professionalism preventing him from venting a highly emotional disappointment at the reported failure of his ministrations… his only emotion: exhaling a breath of frustration, thinly veiling deeper feelings.

"When can you bring her in?" Dr, Angeli asked, his voice sounding strained, his distancing professional bearing under siege.

"Immediately," George Staves painfully responded.

The mood was dark as they sat around Dr. Angeli's desk. "This has been a bad few weeks for me. First it was Casey and now Tasha's reversal," he said solemnly.

A new fear rose within them at his association, his coupling made it analogous with lost causes. It's direness overwhelming any remaining optimism, obviating any last minute reprieve of alternative medicine providing a silver bullet.

Tasha lay at George Staves' feet, stirring at the mention of Casey's name, watching her Alpha, ready to read his body language, weigh his vocal intonations, sniff the scent of his changing body chemistry, combining, collectively speaking of Casey's fate.

His reprieve,his inquiry, while honest and sincere, providing opportunity to delay hearing confirmation of Tasha's failing response – the inevitable diagnosis… resulting in a brief moment of diversion: Staves asking, "What happened to Casey?"

"It was rabies as I suspected. While I was awaiting the test results of his blood and saliva workups, his condition worsened. He became more disoriented and lethargic, deteriorating from ataxia to progressive paralysis, ultimately to flaccid terminal paralysis if we hadn't intervened. The tests came back positive, confirming my original diagnosis. He had the insidious virus for which there is no cure, bringing an agonizingly painful slow death. I called Mr. Stewart who agreed that the most merciful course of action was euthanasia, putting Casey out of his misery. A direct fluorescent test on his autopsied brain tissue and microscopic examination removed any doubt that our decision was the right one."

"He was a beautiful animal," Rose sympathized. "A no choice ending, but still a tragedy."

"Yes, it was," Dr. Angeli agreed, "But life continues. Mr. Stewart, while still grieving over his loss, being an animal lover is checking with breeders for the right litter."

His words had very little tolerance and were crushing to George Staves, abbreviating the grieving process would never be his contemplation, it would just be beginning, were he faced with the same situation, the duration of which commensurate with the value of the relationship. He could not dismiss death of a canine family member so incidentally and inconsequently,the bereavement spent, a time to move on. No recess for coveted memories. He was more pitying than angry with Mr. Stewart for not having the special feeling he held for his Tasha. In the least, in replacing Casey, he should have had a reasonable period of mourning; a sincere representation of his love before his tragic death, not exclusive for humans. George Staves, not in the least, considered it irreverent. He knew that Dr. Angeli, while well intended, had underestimated their devotion, obvious in his lightly veiled message of what Mr. Stewart had planned: a motivation to replace Tasha within day's of her death. That would never be a consideration nor would he concide her death nearing, giving up in his fight to save his Tasha. Inconceivable, as her heart was still beating, and they still able to reach out and touch her and receive the blessing of her loving reaction

Dr. Angeli, his intervening, philosophically well intended but short of reality, having not given enough weight to their special relationship.There mourning period a continuence, their developing acceptance not predicated on a scheduled tally of time,just the evolving of the freedom. Pre-released, prejudicing a replacement, it's own personality and traits, falling far short of the monument in construction.

The avoidance over, a temporary diversion, the purpose of their hastily arranged meeting upon them, Dr. Angeli downcast asked, "Tell me again what has happened since Tasha's last treatment."

Dr. Angeli sat and listened quietly as George Staves essentially repeated the words of his earlier phone conversation; finally voicing, "Those events are disheartening. It's unusual for complete reversals in veterinary medicine, when it appears that stabilization is within reach and remission is possible, her illness over riding successful treatments with such suddenness is painful and baffling."I suspect the tests and X-rays will not give us hope.

Dr. Angeli burdened in fulfilling his responsibility as the treating veterinarian his emotional attachment to Tasha too deep seated to keep from feeling a personal loss, he was captive to this extraordinary dog whose active life he essentially had declared as over.

Rose Staves choked back a sob, raising a trembling hand clutching tissue to dab her tear filled eyes, turned adoringly in Tasha's direction for another absorbing look, sorrowfully painting that very moment indelibly on her canvas of memories.

Tasha, who was repeatedly changing resting positions, once again seemed finally settled, her ears moving firmly upright at the mention of her name. Usually rejecting when not hungry accepting a treat offered by Dr. Angeli, not as a prelude to another treatment, seemingly aware that there would be none, accepting as an act of appreciation of his efforts on her behalf. A respecting toast to a non-sharing future, saluting each other.

George Staves' immediate reaction was that of a fallen tree. A crashing fall from ambitious heights, uprooting the roots of hope and trust in the promise of alternative medicine holding the answer to Tasha's condition. Reeling, he accepted her vulnerability; her deeds, a special gift, had not elevated her, just as vulnerable as the rest of her species, in spite of being extraordinary, shared a common mortality. Sentenced as no different in susceptibilities; nature not differentiating, calling death to overtake her, only her uncommon accomplishments separating her, assured to be remembered forever by all who came in contact with her. In that sense, achieving immortality, living forever. Misguided hopes lay where they had fallen. Before it's final ember was extinguished, he asked pleadingly, "Is there anything more we can do for her?"
"I'm afraid not. No further opportunities from my medicines practice exists. Dr. Angeli responded His words an assembling dirge.

Continuing, attempting to placate: "You've done more for her than anyone could imagine. You have not failed her. You have not turned your back on her. Tasha knows you haven't abandoned her. You'll be by her side continuing to build that special relationship. She knows you've tried. In time it will be for her expectation of peace that you will serve." Pausing,his words weight accessed. "I can tell from your expression that you'll not concede, but I must tell you, dismiss from your mind continuing the battle; finding another battlefield without charlatans and opportunists is not possible. The best of available medical procedures have been spent; unfortunately technically lacking. I wish I could offer more hope. I'm afraid we've reached the end of the line."

Dr. Angeli, the battlefield commander's somber pronouncement: lowering the colors of his exhausted medicine, raising the white flag in surrender of his American Veterinary Association Code. The battle having been lost, the symbolic handing over of his battlefield sword: his combating doctoring ending, the final act of his surrender taking place.

" This approach is over" George Staves acknowledged, nodding understanding: this roads travel fruitless.

"What remains for us to do is ease her pain. until she tells you it's time for her to go. Time for her to find the peace that you must release her to, bringing closure to this period in your lives." Anticipating Staves's further pursuit, to cease future endeavors said, "Do not bring criticism of self-serving by stretching her dying days beyond what is reasonable. Share in her peace as you mourn her passing. The bounty of beautiful memories will be found searching her kaleidoscope, free to wander and recreate what had been. This will sustain you." Dr. Angeli said.

Both maudlin and melancholy, they reviewed the meridian pressure points that George Staves would massage daily or as needed. "Massaging will give her some help," he assured Staves. The moment becoming weighty and awkward, Dr. Angeli advisory, return to his veterinarian, Dr. Kerrigan, for follow up consoltation. "I'll send him all the files," he said, defeat in his eyes.

The Staves's with tightness in their throats, sadly acknowledging and recognizing an emotionally effected Dr. Angeli, couldn't bear treating her in her final days, let alone perform her emotionally scarring eventual euthanasia. The dreaded time had come, with their visage forlorn they turned to face each other, their eyes disconsolate, repeatedly blinking. Parting was awkward for all of them. Dr. Angeli, his usual proudly erect shoulders slackened as he fought his moistening eyes, his voice unsteady.

Shaking his head sympathetically sharing their heartbreak, he rose from behind his desk, finding the opportunity to excuse himself, "Please excuse me while I review her latest blood work and other tests."

"Whats the point, we already know what they'll say," said a somber George Staves.

"There to be sent to Dr. Kerrigan along with my report.An update on her condition will be useful to him."

After a few minutes Dr. Angeli returned, his face strained and colorless.

"Her white cell count, as I suspected, is up," his voice somber and grave. "She is currently running a low grade fever, her weight is down ten percent. The X-rays show the arthritis is spreading. Density differentials show greater incursions into areas previously negative."

"My poor Tasha?" We have not helped you," Rose cried.

To late for professional aplomb, he said in the subdued voice of the deeply affected: "Your right, all our efforts on Tasha's behalf, over these many months, developing a treatment have failed. Alternative medicine, my life's work, was not sustainable,the challenge victorious" his tone now one of disgust. "all that can be done for her is diet and anti-inflammatory medicines to try and make her as comfortable as possible."

Rose Staves gasped: Where once existed hope, now existed unbearable images, watching hopelessly as she fades, losing her mobility, her dignity? Struggling to find moments pain free?

Dr. Angeli, his voice tremulous, control of his frayed emotions lost, his professionalism abandoned, "We were not seeking a miracle or complete recovery but to gain some control. But no, not to be, not in Tasha's case. Her disease continues in defiance of signs of earlier success," he bemoaned.

And then there was silence, nothing more to be said or heard, a vacuum moment where silence held greater meaning in it's nothingness.

Tasha pityingly struggled to raise herself, knowing it was time to leave. Rose Staves, in her melancholic state, responded to the urging of her hand holding husband.

All eyes were tearful. Unashamed, given freely, their alliance committed to a common cause about to end, its conclusion inescapably painful – acceptance a path they must travel.

A somber Dr. Angeli reached for them one at a time. First it was Rose, taking her hands into his, priest-like in expressing his sorrow. Unable to contain himself, tenderly he reached out to hug her sobbing shaking body, quieting her with his commiseration. He and George Staves bear hugged each other in silent communion, their chests heaving as they choked back their sobs.

George and Rose saddened, watched as he reached and patted Tasha lovingly, then a lingering embrace of her head and the mane framing her ever-expressive bi-eyes, readily positioning himself for her returning kisses. Finally excusing himself for his "other patients," his tone was tremulous as he approached the door, gulping, "God speed" and walked out of their lives forever, seeking refuge for his drained emotions.

"You, too," Rose and George murmured to the departing Dr. Angeli as the door was closing behind him. Left alone to communicate with God and each other, they both reached for one another in conciliation for each others loss, embracing, tearfully commiserating the difficult times that lay ahead. A signatory was a panting Tasha, now standing, moving lovingly from one to the other anxious to depart, unmistakable with her body language and communicating eye language she was master of, suggesting "We leave one, then cross another threshold, saddened by the outcome yet thankful, no matter how remote for the opportunity for success. We face the future together in interlocking strength," as she led them to the door.

The inevitability of a future world without Tasha faced them, the sorrow weighed heavily, finding relief in reviewing their relationships. Celebrating Tasha's trivial, unimportant and incidental instances of their witness, elevated with reverence as joyful and as important as her amazing accomplishments. Inescapable reminders of yesteryear, recollections of any time period of any presentation of equal value comforting them, easing the burden of each passing day becoming history. Tasha's life calendar unrelelenting shortening, approaching her last day when at that very stealing moment death ended her future, the past claiming her totally.

Rose disconsolate in her acceptance, she reconciled with Tasha's impending death. George still harboring a miraculous occurrence, still hopeful of an intervention, their divided minds paralleling one another, finding needed solace in personal reflections of their lives with Tasha.

They found this in periods of accommodating silence, the occasion not in need of the many words that would pass between their lips, tearful condolences to one another, scripting Tasha's circumstance. In separation each awarding the self-imposed mental isolation by respecting the other's silence, free to transfer mind and spirit. A personal, needed emancipation for visiting time spent, making present time stand still. A respite, recalling personal pleasures; remembering and cherishing those countering moments, brief and short-lived as they may be, as returning sadness would again rule.

There was everything exclusive about Tasha: large for her gender, weighing at times as much as one hundred pounds; standing taller at the shoulder than her counterparts. Her ancestry was never in doubt; one hundred percent husky evident in her strength and countenance. Her forebears traced to wolves. Her genetic code so similar, the slight separating distinction amazingly evolving to a species not as feral. Her coloring, predominately black, gray and white, fastidiously and artistically distributed along her well-sculpted torso. Blemished slightly by a trace of red on her rear flanks attesting to her mother's red-and-white coloring, evidence that she had participated in mating with a large, black, grey and white male husky, credentialed by the American Kennel Club. Tasha, one of a litter of six and the only one who bore a red blemish, did not need a quirk of nature to set her apart from the rest of the litter, never failing to show dominance, her ranking order at the feeding trough of her mother's teats always first.

An Alpha personality from the very start of her life, she quickly turned away all challengers. Still, a determined Alpha after joining the adopting Staves new pack, capitulating that ranking to George Staves only after considerable testing and resisting. However, never failing to let all know she was easily bored and needed to be challenged to bring satisfaction to her high intelligence and comprehension.

Her personal reflections in solitude, sitting alone at the dining room table, Tasha at her feet, Rose Staves found it difficult to escape her thoughts, her consciousness: predominately Tasha. The daily newspaper pages were turned and rumpled, glanced through but not read. Local and world news not registering as if the pages were blank or transparent. Her vision, absent of purpose, staring blankly as she looked past the raised sheer blinds of the dining room window, nothing registering.

A sudden awakened focus, the rain delayed about to be mowed back lawn solemnly awaiting its fate. It's extra growth stirred to a waving motion by a temperature dropping wind – the shafts of grass in flow. Rose's attention captured by their aided movement, the lengthened moving grass hypnotic, drawing her as it grew towards the nourishing sun.Extracting, relating to, she to be nourished- moments in time with Tasha she wished to recall alone at this moment, feeling special and privileged, growing her love.

A smile creased the grief housed in her face, it's natural softness returning; her transport tracking through heart and mind,, joyously recalling with great clarity the testing of Tasha's skills, the very moment when she easily found her: not secreted, nor distanced, nor disguised enough to avoid Tasha's sensing skills, ending that game of hide-and-seek; treated to her vectoring abilities. Building upon that dimension Rose taught her to find personal items that she had misplaced: purses whose last location was forgotten, eyeglasses left behind in the basement utility room, all quickly located upon command. Even the smallness of earrings was no match to her "finding skills."

Only her cigarettes and lighter would be ignored, Tasha stubbornly refusing to obey her command. Not surprising, showing little enthusiasm, thought Rose, attributing Tasha's refusal to having understood her husband's repeated admonitions and warnings of the health hazards associated with smoking. Amazingly, her protector she thought, her way of protecting her against an enemy. The concern of her Alpha also lovingly hers.

Continuing to penetrate the grayness of despair, Rose's face brightened further remembering the treasured incident of her weekly card game.
It was her turn to accommodate her all woman's card group. Her husband George, as always on those nights, conveniently arranged to visit friends, delaying his return until he was reasonably sure the game was winding down limiting him to a cordial acknowledgement, the women's attention and time primary for recovering losses limited exchanges particularly during the evening news broadcast.

It happened earlier, during the coffee and pastry pause. While clearing the dining room table for this short break, somehow some of the cards accidentally fell scattering to the floor, notice was immediate and they were quickly recovered,so everyone thought. With the coffee break over, the poker game was anxiously resumed, starting with the latest women's fad: a derivative of poker, "Black Queens Wild."

Normally, Tasha would either lay next to Rose or one of the other dog friendly players, delighting in feeding her dog treats made available by their host. As always, her demeanor after sniffing "fingerprinting" the visitors, was friendly and quietly subdued. When tired of the treats, she would return to her reclining guardianship of Rose. Unaccountably sudden, and seemimgly without provocation, she began to bark alarmingly. Non responsive, not even Rose's command, to her chagrin, would quiet her, bringing diverting annoyance to the players. Undaunted Tasha began to move around the table in never-ending circles, barking as if she had cornered a prey.

Rose, knowing Tasha's behavior strange, guessed that she was messaging a need for a walk. Placing her cards face down indicating her play for the hand was over, Rose asked to be excused while pushing herself away from the table holding Tasha's collar heading for the patio door.

Not to be denied Tasha pulled from Rose's grasp to rush to the vacated opening at the table, entering the space created by Rose's departure, moving quickly and purposefully among the shrieks of surprise by the seated players trying to avoid the probes of her snout.

Rose, admonishing Tasha's surprising unruliness, returned quickly to the table, arriving as the shrieks ended, Tasha emerging from beneath the table with two playing cards in her mouth which she presented to her, Rose discovering they were the two black queens. Astonished she peered down lovingly at Tasha, whose tail was waving joyously, proudly giving back the game the players thought they were playing.

The girls, wide eyed in amazement, shocked to be a contributing party to Tasha displaying extraordinary intellect, known from Rose's storied occurrences but never witnessed. A few deliberately tempering, it being too much of a stretch to believe that Tasha knew the significance of the two black queens. Prefering the not as controversial attribution to happenstance, notwithstanding the heavy odds. Yet in spite of their conclusion of convenience, it remained undeniable that Tasha had interrupted their game purposefully to draw their attention and hold up play. A strong case could be made that she did know that all cards were needed – recognizing that the game could not be played without the complete deck. Force fitting happenstance could only be argued weakly by those narrowly focused while the strength of a phenomenon of nature – gifting a dog with incredible insight – would find believers among advocates.

Rose reflected on that day remembering clearly the consensus of those present – included with those tempering were:

"That's what she was barking about," said one.

"She was trying to tell us that two of the cards had fallen and had not been picked up – that the game couldn't proceed without them," said another.

"Wasn't it amazing that the two missing cards were the Black Queens?" said the third.

"She couldn't possibly recognize their significance to the game," another questioned, "or could she?" she quickly added, uncertain, her assurance weakening, her mind open for a more radical belief.

Rose in retrospect, eyes sparkled at the girls' difficulty in explaining what had happened and still remain credibly earthbound, her smile broadening as she remembered her words of explanation:

"I have no doubt in Tasha's perception. You've seen just one example of it today. I've seen her perform other examples – I couldn't even attempt to explain them away. I do know, as you know that something incredible happened here today. I have learned not to underestimate her. She truly is a remarkable dog, displaying uncanny insights." Repeatedly shaking her head in an affirming motion for emphasis she said, "She no longer astounds me with her intelligence."

~

The wind aided movement of the grass subsided, its length and reach about to be shortened by the cutting mower's blade. Rose's reverie was broken by the sputtering sounds of the lawn mower; reawakening her melancholy, ending her ranging of the past.

Rose and George Staves transporting was not coordinated nor in consort, individually visiting with their own thoughts, once given accommodating silence by each other to travel.

Not ready to concede Tasha's loss, at that crossroads, George Staves in desperation challenged reality for its absoluteness. He, a tide of human emotion, crossed the line, emotionally fevered with Tasha's loss, his mind ever in search, seeking other worlds that offered him hope, guiding that he dismiss events as fatalistic, challenging preordination's natural order, set in motion millenniums ago.

Confident in his deep rooted beliefs in his own church armed him well from becoming irreligious, sustaining him from blasphemy when offering up an entreaty to mysterious occult entities to intervene. He sensed he had been guided by the hand of God himself in finding hope, submitting him and his religiosity to test.

Can one, while alive, separate himself from his earthly being to become spiritually two… one real, the other surreal? A duality of purpose; outgrowths of the other. One a specter traveling in mystery hoping to harness mysterious gifts of energies and power. The other, corporeal with the strength to reverse the separation when called for, his body to remain the foundation for his spirits return to it's humanistic base. Living and dying cells of flesh and blood welcoming the return of its spectral other, dispatched to find the gift of his new calling: Tasha's desperate need.

Having found God, accepting all His teachings, he would not risk His wrath, if by chance successful in his search, by turning his back on his savior after being guided by his benevolence: the granting of his prayers for another opportunity, in so doing confident that he would tap into his inner strength and avoid temptations. Still, the question plagued him: can he do His bidding as a committed advocate while attempting to change events, or are these very events in motion unalterable, already written, the outcome predestined, impossible to change? God assigning inertia to bring birth and demise, an eternal clock set aside, its purpose its own, ticking away as life's spectrum was traveled. Horizons bringing darkness for the fallen while ushering in the brightening of the new, beginning another cycle.

Tasha's eternal clock's unwinding pace was steady, her life's door closing to the metronome ticks of her mortality. Dr. Angeli's alternative medicine was not opportuned. Staves discounting: Homeopathy as to soon in it's evolving, Herbology's toxic effects too life threatening. Desperation drove him, reaching for what he knew to be the remotest of hope, a puzzling ancient rite of attaining out-of-body experiences; energized *Shamans* performing acts of healing. *Shamanism*; a creative process to explore an ancient art, to experience a connection to your faith and nature's spirits: the making of the inner *Shaman* with its attendant use of nature; prospective.

For twenty millennium, beating drums and rattles have guided those auditory connected to seek the sacred space between creation and the formless, so moved they would learn to make their own drums, form a creative community and engage the power of solitary contemplation; treading paths of experimental learning, creativity and healing. Practitioners believed to be able to diagnose, cure and if aroused, cause illness, imparted by a specific relationship with the spirits. Ancient medicine men and witch doctors: Shaman adjuncts.

The Shamans basic tenet and belief: the visible world is pervaded by invisible forces or spirits that affect the lives of the living. Central also is the ability for out-of-body experiences; to move consciously beyond the physical body to higher levels of existence or to parallel worlds or other regions of the world.

Shamanism, not having to be central to religious life, buoyed George Staves, existing right alongside, or even in cooperation with religious practices. In contemporary lore, the Shaman at times fills the role of priest, magician, metaphysician or healer. Classified by anthropologists as an archaic magical phenomenon in which the Shaman is the master of ecstasy, exhibiting control over fire, wind, or magical flight. It's specialization: healing.

While exploring the possibilities of ad hoc medical treatment, catalogued as holistic medicine, his last resort, resisting Dr. Angeli's admonition, he was desperately hopeful of the mystical world of Shamanism coming to Tasha's rescue. Intrigued by the very name, Shamanism, coming into the English language via Siberian Tunglusi language traceable to Russia, the birthplace of Huskies.

The powers of Shaman healing, George Staves' last held-out hope, his enthusiasm, tempered somewhat by its special exclusiveness, raised challenging questions:

"Can I qualify? Can I alter my state of being to travel the land of beaten drums and rattles?

"Am I force fitting and exaggerating my pseudo ESP abilities? Does my penchant for consistently picking three to five cards correctly out of a deck of fifty-two qualify as gifted? Duke University taking notice and extending an invitation to participate in their study of ESP? Was that personal ability a determinative for Shamanism?

"Would my amateur meteorologist prognostications, rivaling and sometimes surpassing the accuracy of professional weather forecasters, identify as having greater insight and judgment when reviewing the same weather charts, front patterns and wind conditions?" George Staves hoping it was another display of unconscious budding Shamanism.

His building rationale eagerly adding the dubious credential of being personally banned at the Las Vegas gambling casino's for his abilities at Black Jack, counting cards played, increasing his odds at winning, hopeful a distinguishing quality for Shamanism. Dismissing the possibility of self-deluding embellishments, the law of averages, or luck as possible rational explanations.

His assessment, not the workings of wishful desperation, additionally, hoping that lurking beneath his consciousness were other dormant powers of special abilities: a supernatural calling released with the assistance of the Shaman.

A determined passion to find a connection, linking his being with a mysterious ancient rite, an acknowledgment yet to be established. Harboring within him fifth dimensional mystical powers, the principal of which was healing, his goal and commitment. Needing the lacking ignition to power from within. Clearly in his mind he had separation from his peers. But were they unique enough? The questions remained. Did they meet the criteria, the potential of being welcomed into Shamanism?

"I'll present myself, a supplicant in waiting," he said humbling himself, "responding when guided to focus on the ecstatic state – seek a communion with the spirits through vision quests; magically becoming a spectral being to ascend the heavens or descend to the earth's underworld."

He knew that this opportunity would be his last, a final hope before the fading light of Tasha would be extinguished forever. While the situation was desperate, he was intrigued by his opportunity as a Shaman to travel worlds unknown as one of it's denizens, propelled by its mysterious currents and gravities to explore the secrecy of the metaphysical. He was a candidate displaying powers of the paranormal, the alchemists of sorcery, he was a discovered designate, not as a god but as his disciple who could border on sin, purged on contrition to his maker. A chance he could not retreat from, paying almost any price; to turn the tide against Tasha's insidious ravaging invader fulfilling his commitment to the painful pleas expressed in her eyes to help her, to cure her, to extend her future.

He was apprehensive, all previous opportunities exhausted, reprieves unknown, if denial was the outcome, it would be the end. Time was running out, great odds were stacked against them. Each earlier disappointment now viewed as a temporary setback, this opportunity bordering on blasphemy a formidable challenge he could navigate, compassed by his religious beliefs.

With time an ever-relentless enemy, moving inexorably forward, absenting any hope, would return them into a world of despair where all things are bleached colorless, stunting growth. A wasteland of stark white, depriving the development of interests, it's buried roots unproductive, its bloom kept from the light of day by their suppressing melancholia. Making it no wonder that this spectral possibility portended a life preserver, opportunity in a sea of desperation would be eagerly clung to.

Upon being told, Rose Staves was profoundly worried that her husband's latest pursuit was irreligious. Her deep religious commitment, uncomfortable with the threat of committing blasphemy, kept her from being an enthusiastic supporter, remaining troubled in spite of her husband's assurances that Shamanism was an adjunct to God, existing only with God's purview, not independent of God, not an agency of the underworld of Satan; conspiratorially evil. Figuratively with prayer beads in hand, she reluctantly acquiesced, silently prayerful, presupposing God's forgiveness was needed for seeking out the occult.

George Staves had made peace with God; his strength of devotion would keep him safe from godless temptations. No unholy alliances would he attempt to forge. A spectral accommodation is what he sought, finding either fantasy or fortuitous salvation; or else live a remorseful life forever.

He considered it faithful that he may be the source of mystical powers should he qualify as a medium. If rejected, his hope was with back up Tasha, who after considerable thought in his judgment had the attributes to be a Shaman, having demonstrated uncanny insightfulness in a world they shared. Performing unbelievable feats on the edge of disbelief, demonstrating travel in worlds of dimensions he knew so little about. Rationalized as proof that she had the personal experience, the prime determinate of the potential

Shaman. Once granted with the spectral powers of the Shaman, it was taken as fact that she would treat herself.

"Why not animals? Why not Tasha?" George thought. Animals have always been identified as the bridge between man and nature. Displaying an instinctive link with past realms and cultures including their own. A capacity downgraded among elitist humans by the conditioning and the dulling of the senses earthly pleasures can bring. Animals transcend time and space to complete the connection.

George Staves reflected on his own merits, deserving of being the presentation to the Shaman elders, significant enough and not marginal… placated that Tasha would not only accompany him but be part of a collective offering; hopefully one or the other to be chosen to release themselves. Separating, seeking out their spectral images – fifth dimensional beings: they a delivery conduit of mystical powers.

Tasha lay there whimpering at his massaging touch, her mirroring eyes reflecting pains intensity before being soothed to tolerate. His prayer was that he would be chosen to receive the Shaman's sacred incantations; passing its mystical powers through his massaging fingertips, curing or putting Tasha's disease into remission, his payback for her fortuitously being his.

The spirit of the ancients, the guardians and dispensers of primitive states of elevation, traveling worlds privileged only to them, commanded to screen out the frivolous and adventuresome as unworthy, allowing only the true advocates and believers to enter their world. Clearly delineated as the criteria: recognition as hereditary – forebears practitioners. Blossoming displays not of this world. Spontaneous and personal choice, were the only credentials considered, in seeking the tranquility of connecting with Mother Earth. Passive normally, yet when called upon by the chanting, bead rattling and drum beating, capable of entering an aggressive state to defeat its psyche war enemies.

George Staves judging he would best qualify under the criteria of personal choice, failing in his study of his family tree of not producing any ancestor reputed to have magical powers to claim the criteria of preferential consideration.

Tasha, to be taken measure of having demonstrated during the course of her life incomprehensible insight bordering on magical prowess, qualify as meeting either the criteria of hereditary guided or blessed, following his lead responding and volunteering herself as a candidate in offering.

As he loaded up the station wagon, he checked off from the list he and Rose had prepared the night before, those items he would need on the trip: maps, tent, sleeping bag, mats to lie on, bottled water, a heavy duty flashlight, insect repellent, a notebook, fountain pens, charcoal briquettes and enough food and clothing for five days; concealing at the last minute, a twelve-gauge shotgun for the unexpected and a compass, which he doubted he would use, knowing of Tasha's extraordinary senses.

His study of the written word of the rite of invitation; found no reason to eliminate his religions prayers. Finding them fitting and protective chant's preparatory to acceptance into Shamanism, providing a conducive and attracting environment. Another key element of the rite, that Staves welcomed as additional encouragement that Shamanism was an adjunct to religion and not a insidious ploy, he encouraged to bring a special item that he held sacred; choosing unhesitatingly the bible, his choice significant in guidance and comfort it would provide, it's religious passages a strength if found to be in irreligious setting. Additionally, a requirement that he bring a crystal or a talisman to help ground himself to Mother Earth; easily picking his defrocked St. Christopher medal, its significance fitting for the jouney he was about to undertake.

His selection's for Tasha: holy water from his parish church, paired with rosary beads that he would hang around Tasha's neck, his prayer chants hers, their readiness apparent… a site to be selected.

They drove for six hours before they reached their destination, heralded by a noteworthy sign proudly proclaiming that the magnificent panoramic view greeting them was attributable to the highest point east of the Mississippi. Exiting the highway, Staves descended into a valley surrounded by the Appalachian Mountains, its trees in full greenery, the casting sun positioning shadows across the valley and its foothills bringing shaded coolness, while the upper reaches of mountains basked in the sun trekking its way west.

Having been here before during fishing season, he was familiar with this site known for its deer and wild turkey, who with anxieties temporary abated, moved freely enjoying the reprieve of a hunting season one month away.

"My dog Tasha and I came here to relax and enjoy the solitude, wanting to camp out in the fields for four days. Although not the right time, to occasionally fish the streams and lakes," Staves said to the approving nodding owner of this vast acreage, "but primarily to clear our lungs of the city's pollution, restoring our sensitivity to smell the wonders of nature."

"That's why I don't live in the cities," the owner proudly proclaimed. "I can appreciate your wanting to camp out and enjoy the outdoors but my advice to you is to rent one of my bungalows and use it as your base or place of retreat if the weather turns bad. It can't hurt," he suggested not wishing to lose additional monetary opportunity.

Anxious to proceed George Staves accommodated him, taking the keys after paying in advance for the four day stay, knowing full well he was committed against the use of the bungalow. Following the owner's directions, he drove his station wagon as far as he could over a rain sculpted torturous road, he and Tasha being jostled along the rutted route until they reached the clearing used as a parking lot equally gouged, the bungalows ringing the area empty of vehicles attesting his fishing catch would not be bountiful had that been the truth of his mission.

He parked the car as close to his bungalow as possible. While available for safety, he did not intend to use it and introduce a comfort inconsistent with the rite of contact he expected to take place, the importance of an outdoor venue not lost to him. He and a laboring Tasha proceeded slowly, making their way through the fields until a purposeful campsite had been found, fitting the needs of the ceremony.

They walked along the tree line, he picking up broken twigs and branches for the required perpetual fire, Tasha sniffed the air for scents while occasionally marking this new territory. He paused scanning the landscape, while not the preferred prairie, he hoped provided the vista of expansiveness where the Shamans of antiquity could be called upon to demonstrate their influences on nature. As if an omen of confirmation; summer heat lightning flashed in the cloudless sky, sudden winds danced the overgrown grass momentarily – Shamans using the powers of nature, encouraging his presumption they would accommodate, a preamble to connecting inhabitants of an adjunct to heaven with earthly beings, fostering a sense he and his searching belonged. The campsite was a ground covered elevated knoll sighting down upon a lake whose waters were dependent upon a fast moving stream; the replenishing gurgling feeding connection disappearing beyond eyesight, in the rolling northern hills in the near distance.

The stream banks as well as its bed, continually being unearthed by the forces of nature, displaying rocks, stones and their remnants of differing mineral enhanced colors. A three-dimensional mosaic continually evolving by the cutting and shaping aggressiveness of flowing waters and eroding winds, commissioned millenniums ago.

The clover growth beneath their feet was a patchwork of nature; the knolls controlling draft rushed the fallen rain in a downward path carrying with it populating seeds; the knolls, a hit or miss growth in envy of the valley's counterparts growing in flourishing density.

George Staves planned to build the perpetual fire within a surrounding firewall of rocks yielded by the stream bed, their final resting place. The forces of nature over the years having loosened their grip from the stream and its bed; while the next generation of imbedded rock and stone would soon be forcefully exposed to light.

Staves finished positioning the starter charcoal briquettes, the ignited fire ravenously consuming the feed of dry twigs and branches, building quickly into heightened dancing flames. The rising plumes of smoke, visible above the tree line for surrounding miles and what he hoped, the attention of the spectral sensing an offering, an invitation to visit aspirants – the ritual beginning.

His first act; starting a fire that had to be maintained without interruption throughout the four-day duration of trial and judgment moved him to be captivated. Mesmerized to picture the fire's atoms running wild, giving impermanent shape to its hypnotic power. Attracting, its draft a magnet, drawing into its fiery flicking tentacles that which got to close by curiousity of inertia – a Pied Piper invitation to become consumed. If ignored, subdued by starvation, insidiously it's grey ashes portending being extinguished, laying in wait, bursting forth a roaring insatiable inferno when fed. The fire capable of captivating the unprepared and unguarded – extracting deeply hidden pleasures from the disturbingly titillated. Truly a force of duality: its destructive powers cleansing before a rebirth could begin, a power among powers.A shaman tool.

The spectral honored its powers in a circle of tribal dance seeking connection. Imaging giants of all that stood or danced before it. A birthing atmosphere for seekers of the hypnotic state of spectral beliefs, adding its potency to the rite of offering.

The chosen site unspoiled and natural, as near primitive as he could reasonably hope for, was purposed to draw the spirits; the specially gifted, helping him access alternative states of consciousness at will… mediators for the sacred over the profane, a recourse for the unfortunate: ill or injured.

It is here at this chosen site that he would be judged. Desperate after experiencing earlier failure for Tasha, again resisting her fate as inalterable, its reality too harsh and premature. Was he reaching for the impossible dream, grasping for straws in the swirling winds of the inevitable? Messaging: let life's cycle continue, as every entity known must eventually become part of the archived. Or would his prayerful entreaty be realized, successful in transporting, joining others so gifted, anointing him as one of their own.

At this time of year, the site was secure. Cautioned against trespassing as private property, the difficult terrain challenged only by the experienced during hunting or fishing season. Chosen for it's isolation providing uninhibiting freedom to seek communion with the illusive spirits through a vision quest; the unlocking key to entering into altered states of consciousness. He would try to induce a trance-like state by autohypnosis, enhanced by fasting and self-mortification: his material values stripped away to spectral nakedness, his unencumbered psyche engaging the surrounding spirits with telepathy. Together in consort, energizing a new spirit… a new Shaman in his birthing indoctrination.

With his refuge tent positioned, the fire spitting embers into the air as fireflies. Their threat and attraction brief, falling to the ground extinguished. Comfortably distanced from the fire, Tasha at his side, they staked out a periphery, a encircling of the campsite; Tasha spotting her claim to the outer boundaries. The terrain's first seasonal evidence of man's visit, he and his dog molding footprints in the moisture laden ground cover.

Beyond the periphery, disturbed nesting birds took leave from the concealing higher grasses of alfalfa to seek the protected safety of flight until their perceived danger had passed.

Their movement disturbing ravenous grasshoppers, whirling suddenly from every direction. In panic their temporary flight ending in the lake greeted by searching government stocked fish, rising from their seasonal bottom dwelling hungrily devouring the sudden amphibians.

Their first trip around the periphery of the campsite purposed for survey and to leave their scent, Staves hoping to discourage most prey animals from stumbling upon the out-of-season intruders, sure to be confused as a breakdown of their internal instinctive calendar.

On the second trip and all the others that followed, Tasha would accompany George as he traced the five points of the mystical pentagram encased within his circle. The top of the knoll, the point of the pentagram's upwardness, signified the spirit. The other four points in conjunction with one another connecting the elements of earth: air, fire, wind and water; held sacred by the Shamans. The pentagram configuration traversed repeatedly while he developed his personalized chants exhausted Tasha. Returning, she would slump down in the wet grass, head between her paws to rest her painfully stiffening joints, needing his loving massaging recovery before resuming.

The repeated trips, tracing the pentagram, brought him as planned eventual weariness and the developed words of petition he would draw upon. Delivered as chants to fuel his trance-like state, to stand outside of himself or transcend himself; the Shaman ecstasy. A vision quest, a planned passage of withdrawal. Entreaties encouraging contact from the mystics: composed not to forsake his God, dismiss His omnipotence, or blaspheme His kingdom and His teachings with irreligious supplication, but in words of chant recognized and tolerated as a tribute to his God.

His developed chant hoping to draw the sympathies of the spectral to counter nature's life cycle rulings as preemptively shortening Tasha's. A miscarriage, premature – equating it with a forced evolutionary event. Rationalization found from the annals of animals world's history, in this case canines. Diseased past inhabitants sacrificed, their affliction largely ignored as transient. The culture of the day, emphasis on a more adaptable species, the progeny of enhanced genetic codes, driven by human science failing in developing cures to extend lives. Today's need; spectral beings exercising their reprieving gift. George Staves chanting for that intervention.

He had chosen fasting and autohypnosis to facilitate separating himself during his conscious meditation; concurrent seeding his unconsciousness for continuity during his eventual sleep, essentially alone to focus on a word, a phrase, a mental picture. Placing yourself apart in this world and other worlds, resistant to distraction. You are the focal point, pandering to yourself, your needs; harming no one.

Tasha, her head resting on his chest, her gaze fixed upon her Alpha, was instinctively sensitized to the unusual actions, his unusual pattern of behavior since their arrival alerting but never waning her trust. Her eyes of devotion were clearly visible from the crackling flames as Staves searched for signs while gently massaging her meridian points.

George and Tasha would sleep outdoors as planned: he in his sleeping bag with Tasha tethered to his wrist within comforting range of the recently fed fire continuing aggressively throughout the night. The erected tent standing in readiness, offering a hasty retreat from unexpected rain were that the eventuality, also prepared to carry into the safety of the tent, contained within a empty coffee can glowing embers preserving his perpetual Shaman fire.

Heaven gazing, it's immensity and depth forever. Within it's infinity he watched a retreating sunset, the first signs of stars to reveal themselves in the slowly darkening skies. The maturing night sky spewing occasional speeding meteorites ending its brief sparkling life as charred ash, consumed by the very atmosphere that it once shared,Unless of size enough to outlast it's friction consuming hurtling through the sky destined as self-burying debris as it pockmarked or cratered other celestial bodies in its path. He was reminded of his childhood: "Make a wish," his mother sharing the attraction in the heavens would say. "Falling stars make them happen." Connecting his present situation: were they still fanatasies of childhood or today; signs that someone was listening?

A feeling of insignificance; of being alone overtook him, as the last vestiges of light disappeared, beginning it's visit elsewhere in the world, the horizon's curtain falling, ending the daylight, night creatures to stealth the darkness. The vastness of the sky housing numbers of stars beyond imagination, at best estimated by astronomers. Dwarfing them, mere mortals. The endless space insignificant to time and distance; an uncompromised master of the universe; manipulating and dictating the dimensions of measurement. At once creating a past, present and future, it's dimensions presented simultaneously.

He lay there in his sleeping bag staring intently at the star-filled heavens; drawing imaginary lines connecting the stars forming the symbolic pentagram to match his earth bound version, a harmony encouraging the setting to elevate him trance-like... the ecstasy of an out of body experience. The Shaman's sacred markings established in his world and the world beyond. He willed himself to physically relax, starting with his toes; deliberately sequencing his anatomy to more manageable parts washed over by a wave of releasing tension bringing sleep. Progressing he moved upward, his mind willing his body to feel spent with exhaustion. His physical body verging on ceasing to be awake, quiescent as he approached the borders of his conscious world and the world of trance, the gateway for his spectral being to travel. His breathing pattern was purposefully slower and deeper. His pulse rate calmed, for the final step: going beyond ordinary consciousness to the different planes of the Shaman.

All through the night Tasha, herself sleepless with pain, heard his determined whispering chants, her ears attentive as she heard her name in the singsong monotone, now encouraging nothing more than the chirps of crickets in response. Her Alpha pleading to the disciples of the afterworld to find him worthy to separate from his mortal body. Embracing him to do the good work. Arrousing unto him what he seeks; the power to heal with God's blessing.

Tasha nuzzled her face into his ribs whimpering, awakening him to a fire and bodily functions needing tending.

His efforts in seeking a trance-like state were physically taxing, slowing his understanding of his circumstances until the cool morning air brought organization to his thoughts, his insufficient sleep had left him exhausted, worsening to deflated dejection as his clouded mind cleared and he realized his failing: Tasha's unimproved condition evidence that he had not been anointed. During the night never experiencing his spirit escaping his body's gravity to visit other worlds. Disappointingly, he had not transcended himself. He had not been favored, remaining a mere mortal throughout his uneventful abbreviated sleep, not one given the gift he wished; to cure Tasha.

Furthering his disappointment was the realization that he had not even been visited while asleep. Remembering his researched lore of Shaman's presence, eagerly he searched for redemption. George scanned his panorama for visual signs: the skies for the lone eagle majestically soaring, its spread wings riding unusual early morning thermal currents. Denied, he then strained his auditory senses for the sign of a normally nocturnal coyote baying at a moonless sky – it's silence greeting him. Hearing only the faint rustling of the wind passing through the branches of the trees, not the surging flaunting power to bend them close to breaking – another calling card. His searching sight returned skyward to the cloud formations given motion by the winds, their shapes offering no clues or messages for interpretation. No swarming bees regarded as wise and the holy possessor of many secrets, the divine messenger of antiquity not seen searching the flowerless terrain. His panorama only of his earthly world's sights and sounds, absent of evidence of being joined by the surreal; he bringing no seekers to investigate him.

In spite of the disappointing first day, Staves' resolve was unwavering, judging his purposed chants not self-purging enough, his Shaman awakening to be more fervent, aiding his efforts at self-hypnosis. To be more intense during his next attempt at the journey. Fasting another day, this time offering complete sustenance denial as additional penance, the pangs of hunger, servicing his devotion to his cause.

Today, the second day, he would prove himself more worthy beginning with he and Tasha retracing the territorial altar; the points of his pentagram. Carrying the bible in his right hand and the holy water in his left which he symbolically sprinkled on the five points in homage. Around his neck he wore his talisman; the denied St. Christopher medal. Tasha's neck bearing the swaying rosary beads as his repeated chant broke the silence of his mass-like setting:

"I walk the pentagrams path in sight of the Shaman. I implore; accept me as one of you. Allow my inner source the power to heal my beloved Tasha – to continue her extraordinary life."

He would include expanded self-mortification in his second days purging, forgiving all who had given him cause to hold in low esteem. Writing letters to them, shoring up fractured relationships, holding them harmless for the aggrieving incident that wounded him, accepting the humiliation of his petition willingly. A letter of contrition, extending his hand benevolently forgiving the perpetrators of self-indulgence and the harm inflicted. He was the author grown spirituality. Magnanimous in his forgiveness.

He wrote six letters, all individual, all different, all tailored to the damaging issues. Reflective in the conciliatory writings; no deed whether intentional or accidental be allowed to grow to issues unworthy of reasonable men. Even as he wrote he paused as if expecting to hear the telling approvals of the inhabitants of the other worlds. He would welcome the muffled drumbeats, the hypnotic chants as a beginning privilege.

He would intensify his focus on his words, becoming mesmerized by the curved lines of his handwriting; creating letters grouped to form words; their very essence, their purpose beyond their stand-alone definition, gaining significant power when in legion: the dynamic of co-dependency.

His concentration was intense. He succeeded in placing all other issues in the periphery of his thought processes. He had focus; he felt an elevating energy level building. Would it be kinetic enough to allow his spirits release from the gravitational pull of his body? He lay there by the fire sweating profusely Tasha at his side. He strained to escape, bringing trickles of blood to his nostrils. While his physical body was programmed at rest, the spending exertion internal, where his spirit resided, fighting exhaustively for exiting into a dream state.

Unaccustomed to sleep at this hour of early afternoon, he remained awake, unable to sleep sighting the flames of the heightened fire, the waving branches of the near distant trees commanded by increasing winds. Their thick branches bending and flailing one another, battered leaves freed, falling to the ground distanced from their harvested tree. Suddenly the wind subsided, increasing his audibility range; he began hearing faint drumbeats and coordinated muted voices as he watched birds take flight in the stilled air, gliding from one tree to the other. His confidence rising that he was in a dream state, he too would take flight. He willed himself aloft. Viewing from above, he was presented with objects in miniaturization while the panorama was laterally vast in every direction. Flocked in flight with the naturally airborne noisily chirping in wonderment at the featherless intruder of their skies.

But none of that happened, again turned away from directing his spiritual awakening; the Shaman out-of-body experience. The suddenly stilled air, the drumbeats, the chants, airborne in wingless flight, all hallucinations transcending his wishes to access another world; an imagined mystical traveler.

Forlorn and disappointed at this second failure, bringing with it the suggestion of doubt: his self-identifying credentials forced and exaggerated. In reality undeserving and unworthy of the high expectations of Shamanism, more common than extraordinary. Stealing himself not quite ready to admit defeat, he reviewed his preparations, recharging his confidence that he possessed the criteria, sure his arranged ceremonial environment was conducive and not alien. Not quite ready to accept the absence of contact as rejection, but a need for more time for the Shamans to evaluate him. Only evidence that they had visited and ignored him as unacceptable would persuade him of his inadequacy. He watched the fire cast distorted shadows of Tasha and himself, their weight bearing footsteps still leaving temporary impressions on the moist ground as they walked the pentagram, his thoughts, *why do we remain inescapably fixed to the world of corporeal matter and all its derivations, our efforts denied?*

Before climbing into his sleeping bag, he watched his discarded letters, sacrificed to the fire, reduced to ashes. Their composition, tendrils of smoke eagerly reaching skyward before dissipating. His message of conciliation this night telepathically, the venue of the mystical, testing his belief that he is a fledgling candidate for Shaman acceptance.

The first and second nights, Tasha heard his chant as passionate and determined as if a whispered confessional, that only those reasonably close could hear. This time the tone was desperately loud, in dual purpose: searching the skies before heaven, and penetrating the depths of the nether world, in both cases summoning the attention of the inhabiting spirits. Repeated often enough to bring hoarseness to his words, "Hear my plea. Let me join you. I am worthy to share and deliver your magic," the strength of his voice falling off… weakened, his words now muffled by exhaustion, failing to be repeated as stirring echoes.

He awoke with a start, not the result of the teasing awakening of the brightening sun alighting on him as it moved past the towering trees westward heralding a new day. Instead, a premonition, a warning that all was not right, that his cause for concern forced his wakeful consciousness for real time comprehension.

His self-induced awakening preceded by his fully involved dreamscape, traveling distressed among message bearing symbolism, bringing him awake with a start. Escaping a cryptic world with urgency, having solved the range of ciphers: current, past and surreal. Symbols melding for relevance, picturing a dreamscape not to his liking but under the circumstances he dare not ignore, suggesting an ominous occurrence.

Troubled, his mind dulled by his sudden awakening, reacting automatically reached out for the assurance of Tasha's presence. Not expecting to come away unfulfilled, sitting up immediately shouting, "Tasha." Receiving no response, he hurried from his sleeping bag as if electrified, anxiously scanning the campsite, repeatedly shouting Tasha's name. Frantic and in a cold sweat, he knew he had to gather himself if he were to find her.

The roaring fire and the heat it generated caught his attention as his perception returned. Expecting the fire smoldering after all this time as it usually is, not the roaring dance, he saw. He knew he had not awakened earlier to tend the fire bringing into question, "Then who if not me?"

Confused and unsure of the circumstances, his eyes returned to where Tasha had lain, this time seeing immediately Tasha's collar positioned on top of a neatly folded blanket surrounding her offerings of rosary beads and holy water, purposeful in messaging that she had not been forcefully taken, an effort he was sure she would never allow. Clearly, she had been released, that message a certainty, precipitating regrets and suspicions. He had heard no commotion, no barking alert. Could she have been bribed by food; vulnerable as she too fasted was his first thought? That hypothesis didn't last long. He knew his Tasha. She would never submit to a bribe under any circumstances, trained never to accept food from a stranger. She had to have gone willingly, disarmed and trusting as if charmed. Her abductors special talent.

His certainty becoming more credible, his indictment building as the most plausible. Factors influencing his building case: the care taken in placing Tasha's collar, the holy water, the rosary beads on the carefully folded blanket, the unattended raging fire, all telltale signs, signatures that they had visited his pilgrimage. He having been rejected as a Shaman, Tasha now among them, the purpose finding confirmation moments away. An outcome harbored all along in his mind now having to be dealt with. His anxiety dictating he not wait for her to return. It was to big a risk if he were wrong.

Carefully Staves searched the immediate area for tracks of matted down grass leading to and from the campsite. He found only his and Tasha's earlier foot impressions at and around the campsite's perimeter holding early morning moisture, nothing more recent, as well as the surrounding area's coating wetness showing no disturbance.Another calling card? No sooner had he made his obsevation, without warning a wind of hurricane force invaded the tops of the tall trees overwhelming their branches, hurtling those torn free to the ground, stressing roots just short of being uprooted. Then just as suddenly, the wind subsided to stillness as if choreographed for the moment – a second expression of unleashed Shaman power. Intimidated, "what was he being prepared for," he asked of himself? "Were Tasha and he in danger in any way?"

Automatically reacting to his survival instincts, he moved quickly towards the storage and refuge tent to retrieve his twelve-gauge shotgun, stopping after only a few steps, recognizing its futility in dealing with the Shaman, dissuaded he resumed his search within the campsite unarmed.

Immediately in his notice was a brightly colored blue feather not more than five feet from Tasha's blanket that he was sure had not been there until now. Its color remarkable, an underwater coral blue never seen by him before in feathery plumage. He picked it up in quizzical admiration and immediately felt radiating heat of such intensity that he was forced to drop it before it burned his hand. Repositioning itself as it lay on the ground, turning forty five degrees to assume its original position.

As he was trying to sort out it's meaning, a second feather in the same remarkable color suddenly appeared, aligning with the first. He realized a plane was being established… a feathery directional formed for his behalf. Remembering the heat of the first feather, he poked at the second one with his foot, not daring to pick it up. Disturbed temporarily, responding as if powered by magnetism, returned to its position; on path.

The alignment continuing, directing he follow the trail of feathers. In reaching the periphery of the campsite they ended, the feathers replaced by rocks sculpted by talented hands. Carvings of animal effigies in flight, detailed enough not to be imagined or credited to nature's eroding tools over time. Braving the expected heat, he picked one up, gingerly moving it from one hand to the other to minimize the inevitable. Discovering it was primitive aboriginal workmanship, the radiant heat finally forcing him to release it. His awe no less, the artifact after freefall duplicating the feathers maneuvers regained it's pointing alignment, continuing the path laid out for him by unseen forces. Not understood beyond the wishful implication at the moment was where would it take him.What would be asked of him. He would confront those issue's hopefully when reunited with Tasha.

Now the trail's beacons were strands of gorgets – faultless, beautifully polished copper ornaments crescent shaped, designed to adorn the throats of the pleased of all ages, beauty worshipers drawing attention to themselves.

Captivated by their beauty, the phenomenon of heat continued as he moved one of them with his foot, immediately feeling the heat through his shoe. The copper gorget, returning to position in a matter of seconds, its directing mandate resumed.

He was amazed at the surreal energies. Power over matter moving tangibles by an unseen force. In spite of his determination and studied assurances of the Shaman culture he developed a concern for his personal safety amongst such power, yet retreating without Tasha was never a thought. He was in their trust; the artifacts part of an invitation to him exclusively. Theirs a purposeful action, it's unfolding while serene and beautiful displayed weighty forces at work, the implications of their sudden appearance accenting his vulnerability.

The directional chain of various Shaman artifacts stretched for over two miles along semblances of old trails. Traffic sculpted, leading to once bountiful hunting and fishing sites, now discarded as deer population thinned and the failure in restocking the streams and lakes, the vegetation well into reclaiming the land.

Strange sounds quickened his heart rate compelling him to pause, hearing what he thought were drumbeats leading what appeared to be voices droning prayer-like vespers. He stood alone, when he realized the sounds were the product of conspiring winds given imaginative meaning in his highly emotional state.

When he took his last steps out of the trail laid out for him, he came upon a line of heavily populated elephant grass miles in length in hues of yellow and purple reaching well beyond their expected ten feet height, their lower profile so close to the ground extremely dense, it's blades razor sharp making passage through them almost impossible. Directing all but the smallest of animals to an interrupting canopy of Pin Oaks: a natural tunnel through the populating density of elephant grass, the only passage for as far as his eyes could see.

His vision through and beyond the canopy; sighting hills and meadows bearing foliage in various colors, ranging from bright yellow to creamy white, sweet flags, silvery blue fescues, russet red and copper bronzes, centered by various shades of green. All grasses of breathtaking beauty; it's differing colors in quilt alignment, exclusive up to their borders in individual color expression. It's profound beauty: the contrast taken as a whole of the individual unblemished segments.

As he viewed the panorama searching for a name for this place of soft blending hills coming to rest in the lushness of meadows, he heard the soft yelps of dogs barking in frolicking joy. Where were they he asked of himself as he searched the terrain fruitlessly, until the happy sounds were gone.

He again dismissed the sounds as imagination, his attention freed to ponder the beauty of the intruded land, wondering how it was possible that this magnificent site existed in all its manicured and well-tended glory without a human in sight meticulously caring for what had to be landscaped gardens.

The absence of being renown he knew was improbable. It was a wonder, easily drawing crowds, acclaiming it's magnificence. But yet its anonymity was true, for he was alone causing him to doubt the beauty he was beholding existed. In reaction, he closed and reopened his eyes not with the brevity of a blink but sightless enough to assure his returning vision was true and not an illusion or a mirage, the product of his fasting and anxiety. His awe remained, the sight still real to his visual senses, an abundant magnificence of harnessed Mother Nature's magic remaining in focus.

If not for the scent and his touch, the color splendor if viewed as a photograph, easily attributable,the magnificence beyond mans ability to cultivate, as a artificial creation. The viewer persuaded it a horticultural impossibility, or the expectations at an art museum: the surreal expression of the artist having mastered the mixing and blending of pigments, committing his mastery to canvas for the entire world to acclaim. Why had he been so honored, he asked of himself? Allowing only those invited to see their compelling horticultural magic, suggesting exorcizing after the fact when deemed fitting, the ultimate in guarding their secret, overwhelmed claimants unable to substantiate, in time believing it an illusion.

Appearing out of nowhere as if standing guard at the canopied meadows entrance was Tasha, her tail wagging furiously showing no signs of her crippling arthritis as she stood up excitedly on her hind legs, letting him hug her expressive head to his chest. Clinging together in joyous reunion, the moment apropos. Plagued by the thought of her being physically stolen unsettled him, he remained frantic at the possibility, highly defensive of Tasha physically belonging to him, acting protectively he secured her collar, rosary beads and her leash, all purposely brought with him, her physical presence secured in her tether. Tasha was happy, her eyes trusting… his tearing. Suddenly he backed off, uncertain, caring reminded of the pain she should be experiencing. His mind questioning and answering when he spotted lying on its side a crudely fashioned tambourine-type drum, its stretched leather almost worn through.

He carefully picked up the primitive drum, unexpectedly cool to the touch. Was it left for him to find? To give credibility and meaning to the sounds he heard on his magical trip of recovering Tasha? Evidence of one of the sounds he had heard earlier and dismissed?

Tasha watched him attentively. Torn between loyalties, nervous, muscles tense on the verge of issuing a warning growl as he examined the drum, anxious as a recent mother concerned for her newborn puppies vulnerabilty, finally sensing that no harm or sacrilege would befall this ancient artifact in his hands. Her loyalty to him to remain untested, absenting a careless or purposeful act.

Noticing her apprehension he returned the drum to it's resting place, as he accepted her adopted devotion,it's taking seed, it's influence on her reaction to him as he handled the ancient artifact. Responding, Staves reached down and patted her head in affection and assurance. Tasha responded happily to his understanding, panting and yelping excitably; relieved that her aggressive, protective on edge stance had not divided them. Again she jumped up to his chest, her forelegs planted firmly. He hugging her tightly, calling out lovingly, "Good girl. Good girl, Tasha."

Reassurance's over, Tasha abruptly dropping off of him, anxiously sitting down, barking an invitation for him to do the same. She looked up at him adoringly as she lay her head on his lap, her eyes commanding, not suggesting that she was in need of his soothing massage but to offer up her face, more specifically to present her impassioned expressive eyes, inviting him to search within them. Immediately he felt pressure surrounding his head. A feeling of arrested concentration, his eyes seeing no diversions, no peripheral views to distract him. The intensity took its toll. His eyes growing heavy, he felt willed not to blink lest he lose discovery. He felt commanded, controlled, a conscious sleep fast approaching, his resistance once as formidable as a seawall to the incoming tide; negated. His wartime experience prepared him well for hostage interrogation, was of no match for Tasha's hypnotic will, overpowering him.

Tasha, sensing his resistance ebbing, compelled he search deeper into the very essence of her eyes, penetrating beyond the bi-eyed coloring of her iris to where what she had seen and experienced might still be reflecting on her eyes' crystalline lenses – to see previous events within her eyes. The hope; to visit the eyes camera, picturing those pertinent events not timely; the internal process of coding for storage within the brain's electronic network having already taken place. Offering instead a more recent occurrence. Staves amazed, seeing himself emerging from the directing trail to find Tasha waiting for him many moments after the occurence.

He was dazed by the experience of witness a reflecting feedback. While not timely enough, Tasha sensed him beginning to show understanding. He was conveying to her that he knew she had taken that final step: energizing spectrally outside of her body, transposing as she willed; in the suspended state. His understanding clear: Tasha had been anointed a Shaman. Her accomplishments as an earthly being judged extraordinary, a wonderment for her species bannered her as a possessor of surreal powers that can only be visited upon the mystical.

With the hypnotic spell spent, questions persisted. With Tasha looking on approvingly, encouraging as a director, he engaged in the process of discovery: connecting all the relevant dots, producing a picture. Pausing to notice the eagerness in Tasha's demeanor as he spoke aloud of his conclusions, Tasha his sounding board confirming with excited yelping, always a step ahead of him, encouraging, and guiding his thought processes.

They lay there together, Staves holding her in heightened reverence for her added gift. He openly speaking to her new remaining hidden brethren, as he was not one of them, acknowledging that he was pleased with their selection of Tasha.

He could easily visualize Tasha in a trance-like state, transporting herself, standing apart from her earthly being, celebrating her new dimension by mischievously cavorting with other disciples displaying powers of the ancients: controlling fire, wind and unlocking the mysterious power of internal energies, a Shaman trilogy. Equally envisioning Tasha as fully empowered to express the use of kinetic energy, to move and heat those trail pointing artifacts while awaiting him at the entrance of these completely unexpected beautiful meadows. All magical appearances.

At present only one unfathomable question remained in Staves's mind:

"Why here?" "Why this place?" "Is it significant in our lives?"

Looking down at Tasha who stared back knowingly at him, gave him comfort that the mysteries would not last, certain that she would somehow provide the answer.

A quacking gaggle of Canadian geese diverted his attention surprising him, glaringly the only other life forms seen since their reunion, creating an interlude for diversion as they watched the geese in an aerodynamic complimenting "V" formation designed for minimum air resistance begin its descent. The point position occupied by the biggest and strongest leading the lowering height of the flock's aerodynamic formation. Centrally located within the tight angled descent of geese, flying within the accommodatingly slowed phalanx, struggled a member appearing to be injured and weakened. Its flying abilities benefited by the lifting air inherent with such configurations easing it's distress.

With powerful wings no longer violently moving air, it's glide path taking the formation beyond the sloping hills, beyond their line of vision, but not beyond their signaling sounds. They tightened their formation around their escorted member close enough for their extended powerful wings to amazingly support during descent the stricken member, struggling with his lessening lift as they landed.

Tasha moved a few steps in the direction of their landing, pausing to see if George was following. Satisfied, she continued to move through fields of beauty and hypnotic fragrances, her purposes elsewhere. He, on the other hand, not concluding any special significance remained committed to self-indulging allowing his eyes and other senses to become captured and held spellbound, bringing pause to further journeying. His breath taking respite momentary, Tasha quickly nudging him from his reverie.

They were still some distance away when they heard the familiar squawk of geese taking flight, becoming visible almost immediately as they became airborne in their traditional "V" shape flight formation.

They both watched as the geese gained altitude flying at a faster rate. Searching, Staves did not see the protected member in the center of the formation, left behind to recover and then follow was his immediate thought. With the geese airborne, rapidly distancing themselves from view, Tasha once again commanded his attention.

When they reached the last hilltop, looking down they were greeted by a landscape completely different from the one they were about to exit, bringing into wonder why there was not a transition zone rather than this shocking suddenness. Here the landscape bore pockmarks of various sizes; the open wounds of being rained upon by celestial meteorite storms his only thought. Where they once stood as proud trees, they lay uprooted by the violence of earthly forces. Rotting and decaying within feet of its once sustaining ground, a speckled mix of earth, silica sand and limestone, occasioned with shale and slate as was the surrounding land. The loose mixture of particles, churned up by frequent winds settling into the surface voids. This forsaken part of the valley was surrounded by rocky hills, it's carved caves and fissures formed by nature's forces millenniums ago when upheaval of the land came from within, pressured relief for the earth's slipping strata, deepened further by erosion.

"What is this place," he thought, as he swept the panorama. "Why did you bring me here Tasha," he asked?

She stood quietly for a few moments. The only movement was her magnificent coat rippling in a sudden breeze. Then she purposefully moved to his left, his vision following her. It was then that he spotted movement, distanced, beyond his identification. Tasha moving in its direction, showed no fear for this unknown. Her demonstrated lack of concern, contagious, relieving his angst, dispelling any safety concerns he might have.

Following her closely, they got near enough for Staves to realize what Tasha already knew; the movement was being made by a mouth-frothing Canadian goose, sadly in the final throes of death, frantic that its strength was ebbing, her wings flapping feebly trying to maneuver itself into a freshly dug hole among the meteorite pockmarks. The land mix soft and easily moved lay strewn in piles surrounding what was obviously the goose's final resting place. Staves stood there not interfering and saddened, knowing the final throes of a life's final moments were upon her. A kinship of humane sympathy upon him, knowing this dying goose was seeking repose, was the same one he witnessed being escorted, her gaggle bringing her to her gravesite.

Caught in the scene's pathos, sorrow in his eyes he turned his attention skyward for diversion from the heart wrenching scene, unexpectedly seeing a familiar "V" formation circling overhead. In truth the stricken goose had not been left alone. Its guardian family was circling the chosen site, squawking a mournful flying dirge for their fallen member, an observance equaling a human's wake.

When Staves looked down again at the stricken goose, it had succeeded in dragging itself into its burial plot. The exertion brought labored breathing as she lay at the bottom of the grave. Her gasping rattling breathing sporadic, delaying her demise it achieved a moments recovery just when her life seemed over. Forlornly she again looked skyward, sighting her brethren continuing their salute, the inevitable conceded, closed her eyes for the last time expiring peacefully.

Staves again gazed skyward, the geese as if they knew, completing its final pass, it's point leader redirecting to fly elsewhere. Their dedicated inherent obligation fulfilled: accompanying one of their own to the threshold of awaiting death, to take it's final step unafraid; her gaggle having respectfully saluted, her final comfort.

Still not sure why Tasha had led him here; he looked beyond Tasha, who left his side straining against the tether to move further into this bleak land, yelping eagerly that he understand: not restrict, but to follow her. A comprehension developing as he spotted a magnificent twelve-point buck's skeletal remains bleached white by the sun, its crowning rack lying separated by the forces of nature. Testimony of having failed to dig a burial site before death overtook it. In it's death it was surrounded by fallen trees, the flowers of its funeral, decomposing at a much slower rate.

He continued his searching scan of the land, finding at the base of the rock strewn hills the dusted skeletal remains of other deer, death again had not waited for them to reach it's final resting place. Urged by Tasha to investigate further, they moved closer towards cave entrances, pausing momentarily as his sense of smell should have been attacked by putrefaction but was not, his intellect under siege as inside the caves were the remains of bears, coyotes, deer, dogs and other vertebrae animals in various stages of odorless decomposition,, this final evidence that they were in the middle of animal burial grounds and chambers… suspected but not under these conditions, the ongoing mysterious. The animals having come to die when it was their time; sometimes succumbing together, no longer enemies or prey. Most times alone yet among the fallen species remains of all who could manage. The common bond, not bloodlines but impending death.

What was Tasha's purpose for what he had seen and the implications? The bewildering aspects to be interpreted required they be linked – not possible until all his questions were answered.

Remaining unanswered in Staves' mind: Tasha leading him here to this land of extremes? What was the purpose of it's paradox: seeing life ending in depressing bareness after seeing life in its simplest form beautifully flourishing? Foremost: would she continue her new powers to extend her life, now that she was a Shaman and could self-cure, remaining joined, of one mind. What was beyond her allegiance change, as showed in her dramatic strained demeanor display as he was examining the ancient drum? Her unique and uncharacteristic communiqués intent swirling in waters at present he could not fathom.

Perplexed he presumed it was time to leave, he called to Tasha to begin their return to the campsite where the setting was not distracting. His thoughts freed to ponder what he had seen and experienced within this land of mysteries. Tasha's purpose was stubbornly otherwise, sitting, not moving, suggestively yelping that he join her. Amazed by the strength of resistance, in fear of her hurting herself he moved to her side to encourage they return, manipulated she again presented her eyes to him; capturing him, directing that he search.

Immediately he felt the intensity of her stare, it's pressure imaging a vision of a whirling pinwheel building momentum amongst bursting colors of the spectrum. The pitch of the pinwheel's blade creating a vortex drawing him to follow.

In a trance like state he felt his body lightening, his spiritual being separating from his body, concurrent Tasha's will a purging magnet force, drawing from his physical being, his prejudices and denials. His spiritual body transport affected by Tasha, he in an out-of-body experience, enabling him to be more visionary, more perspective, more philosophical. Distinguishing the difficult answers he sought were not continuously forward but hidden in the abstract. Until that moment Staves remained adversarial to any other considerations or judgments – the weight of his dedicated pledge he would bear as Atlas bore the world, until his commitment was reformulated. It began to happen, seeing Tasha, no longer in league. Influenced he moved from being so rigid, to be more responsive to an alternative outcome – a greater cause. A peripheral not given dimension earlier as an over riding factor; her role in their cause annulled, notwithstanding the painful emotional scarring to both.

Full understanding verging, his gate of protection serving his and what he thought were her unalterable interests, forced open by Tasha's insistence of new priorities,he learning when her actions were fully understood, not hinted at. She elevating new cause, abrogating her sharing pledge – thought never to be at risk- immutable.They partner's in a life extending cause, was no longer sustainable. Staves in reverence, likening inception of their relationship to the magical moment of conception where a two fold need was rewarded. Spawned from a common womb a twinned birth, to stand singularly in independence of one another, yet advantageously co-depending when needed. Each never far away, the thought of being apart never a factor until now; her compromising a trust, sadly a mystery unfolding.

Tasha defaulting, realigned, messaging he be philosophical expansivene to close his wound. With Tasha guiding hypnotically, responding introspectively his examination developing a metaphor to solace "ultimately humans, all animals, all living beings are out of necessity social animals for all or part of their lives, except when obliging fated for death for the hereafter, crossing the border of life, making that passage alone."

Expanding the other end of that spectrum, the thought of being alone after death influenced the Egyptians of privilege, reacting by entombing wives to continue the companionship. A social order in the afterlife, countermanding the alienation of death, believing it physically possible, preferable over spiritual communications.

With her message solidifying, no longer in a state of flux, his vision cleared; not a pinwheel in sight; he returned to real time. His philosophical acumen liberalized, the extraordinary hypnotic means of Tasha communicating had ended, her eyes now an entreaty searching his countenance. Had he learned the meaning of her unspoken words and wishes: telling she had now booked solitary passage and would not defer her death?

Tasha's heart raced, her movements whenever in great anticipation were abbreviated steps in place, quick and exaggerated. The strain of focusing her eyes on him was forced to relief by repeated blinking. Her pained yelps voicing questions:

"Had my Alpha accepted that my time has come? Was he reconciled with the imminence of the final chapter to my life being written: passing into history, not prematurely but as preordained? Would he respond to his out-of-body search, my telepathic message: that I was prepared for an interim after life. I not abandoning him as it will be my new freedom, traveling as a Shaman spirit. Gaining existence: to visit, to console, to comfort, to influence all manner of living things troubled. I chose mortality as my fateful path, to submit, not exercise my newly endowed Shaman self-healing powers. Supportive of my decision; stirring within my inner self, the imagery of my wizened ancestral forebear – the wolf. The father of my species echoing past wisdoms: Do not deny one's self, face the end of one's earthly presence with dignity and courage."

Tasha knew her species would continue after her death. Her only regret was that it would not include her progeny, wishful for what might have been: her litter at her trough, hungrily suckling her teats, she watching motherly wondering which of them would have her abilities and skills. It would have been too much to suppose they all have her gift, her fantasizing, knowing her reproductive system was cut from her body, losing forever her God-given genetics, longing for the pleasure of being a mother. Even at this moment standing tall, accepting her second sacrifice, her life, when she had the power to extend it. Additional gratification with her chosen fate, incidental and immeasurable, easing canine overpopulation.

Her concerns about him directed that she search his eyes for answers. Would he resist, stay the course, attempt to coerce her to use her power. Finding her resistant, immutable, her enlightenment her passion. There could be no alternative. She had chosen another path, one that she would travel without him.

While it was painful he acceded to her wishes while his understanding was still fragmented, his self-ascribed roadblock, once impenetrable, was no longer a factor. The mortar of his dogmatism yielding, creating fissures, seeded with previously unthinkable outcomes; Tasha's persistence, not to be denied, had reconstituted him.

Tasha not yet aware of the beginning of his yielding to her pleas both of this earth and beyond, continued her anxious movements, seeking as complete his sign that he would abide by her decision. When he called upon her to begin their return to the campsite, she resisted, forcing him to return to her side where she continued her dance-like abbreviating steps of anxiety. He aggressively pulled on her leash, not in anger but to command. Incredibly he was unable to move her, she offering the resistance of a deeply rooted tree stump, belying the weakness of her illness. She would not be moved, not as long as this division existed between them; not here in this place of burial for animals. Leaving here without reconciliation was unthinkable. An opportunity of understanding lost, her guidance for naught.

Suddenly she was digging in the sandy soil, uncovering a spear tip of the ancient Shamans, assuming it was for his keeping as memorabilia, her discovery a gift offering easily removed from her mouth. Presumptive, after examination he put it in his pocket for safe keeping. Immediately bringing an alarming unexpected response of sustained barking, prompting his realization it was not for his keeping- a sacred Shaman property to return to it's resting place. Her message impacting, a Shaman telling him that this is where her physical body should repose after death: among the spirits, among the artifacts – in the surrounding land of the Shaman. He would do as she asked when the time came, but it would not be her resting here but her ashes. The thought of decomposing here alone in these confines not an outcome he would support, he knew she would agree as her ashes were still representative and would have evolved in time.

Their common cause agreement broken, the reality of separation upon them, previous commitments relegated to another time. Tasha sharing in the original pursuit relegated to a lesser value when weighed against her newly found spiritual one – inescapably more meaningful. They both knew pledges painfully cancelled would not affect the special bond that joined them, resistant with emotional ties that would continue to connect them no matter this failing.

While deeply saddened by Tasha's choice, he presently intensioned to accept her wishes that her mortality not deferred; leaving this world she shared with him for a spiritual interim. Ever giving, she the product of a deteriorating body, its intense pain rallied against by her Shaman powers for this moment of receiving his blessing. Accomplished she returned to the pain of their earth bound relationship for whatever time she had left, supportive of her selected worthiness-a preparation for the final journey that would bring it to it's end.

Tears clouded his eyes as he knelt before her extending both hands, drawing her face close to his, the electricity of affection sparking between them. Tenderly petting her, speaking the soft words she longed to hear, assurance that all was reconciled. Brightened, she showered him with kisses of comprehension.

Side by side they started their return walk leaving this place, his pace deferred to hers of pain, he was patient knowing this lands secret as a final resting place for animals who had come to die amongst the Shaman spirits. Their bodies losing their physical structure: it's materials decomposition aided by the limestone rich earth, leaving only skeletal remains for the ages, in time eroded by the forces of nature, disappearing entirely as non-entity dust, or to exist forever fossilized, birthed from another time.

"But where does the spirit of the dead not Shaman go, having limited movement?" George thought meditatively as his eyes scanned the panorama of their return. "All creatures of God have a spiritual being," sounding the words of St. Francis of Assisi.

Beyond the melancholy of finality this scarred place posses, beyond the death for those instinctively drawn, seeding the grounds with their bodies, impregnating the soil with their nutrients, denied meaningful contribution in assisting natures land enrichment… flowering an impossibility. Guided by the patron saint of animals dead before him and his master, their spirits in an incorporeal world provided for them, shared with other spectral beings selected to do Gods work. He looked behind him just as he was about to step into the contrasting visually rewarding magical greenery, seeing wind driven clouds of blowing sand and granulated limestone moving across the barren landscape, noticeably pausing in its forward movement, it's velocity almost zero, to dwell and deposit its transport, then continuing in resurgence, moving across the pockmarked terrain until its task was completed – ceasing at the razor-edged border of the extremes where they stood. The accelerating and decelerating wind the mechanism for covering and filling freshly dug graves. The limestone shroud providing an assist for decomposition combining with rainwater; later the electrolyte for the bleaching process of skeletal remains. The power of wind and water, two of natures forces relentless working at internment and disposal.

He remained bewildered by the sudden contrast of the land bordering one another, mystified by the abruptness in their separateness. Not a trace, not a clue offered in the adjacent land coming from either direction, exampled in foothills rising from the flat land leading to mountain ranges. Not a hint. A suddenness. Going from one world to another so opposite in their characteristics, that it was inconceivable that there was a relationship. Yet here it existed side by side suggestive of a grand design in the cohabitation. To dramatize the immediacy of the demarcation, straddling the surgically defined border, his body halved, his mind split, each feeling and noting the differences; barren and cold on one side, fertile and warm on the other, yet he developed a sense there had to be inter-relationships, perhaps even a marriage.

As they moved into the meadows, his mind searching for the meaning of this out of nowhere beauty, his thoughts were suddenly interrupted by the rustling wings of a bird in flight. Searching skyward he did not see what he expected but a sight that astounded him. With not a cloud in sight; the sky was hosting a full colored vibrant rainbow, arched over the magnificent greenery, a meteorological impossibility. His disbelief furthered when he realized he and Tasha's labored movements through the tall border grasses remained soundless. The rustling of wings repeating were now joined by the distant barking of dogs while there own movements remained soundless. He was hearing telling sounds, arranged as in a musical score – a full composition. Suddenly he knew; his abyss finally capturing light. He had all his answers. Tasha intently studying his signals excitedly, as his complete understanding began to register, his frowning countenance disappearing. It was final, the telltale key unlocking the remaining mystery, hearing the squawks of a goose he knew to be the very spirit of the one that he had witnessed expiring, announcing its presence, not a providential happenstance. Tasha's full purpose was now revealed.

His mind, arranging, "Of course this meadow is where the dispatched spirits of the deceased animals, freed from illness, gather and frolic, just a short distance from where their remains repose side by side, having departed the world's dangers and threats. Their physical bodies; the matter of corporeal beings taken leave of – to inhabit a spectral world; animal spirits interacting in a memorial home. The fabled Rainbow Bridge crossed."[3]

With those conclusions in his mind, its electricity energizing a message to all animal spirits held heretofore to watch mutely, to signal their presence. Freed, there came a celebratory outburst; the multiple sounds of happy

3 Rainbow Bridge, a place where animals live in spirit from this side of heaven. (Author unknown)

animals havened in the mysteriously enchanting meadows chorusing. A cacophony of chirping, barking and mewing joined in brotherhood with the non-menacing deep throated growls of predatory animals, in harmony with their once earthly prey. A chorused expression acknowledging the latest to join them: the spirit of the goose.

The din of the animal spirit accompanying them as they moved through the captivating beauty of the meadows. Just prior to leaving leaving the invisible chorus ceased abruptly,the fallen goose's spirit now in membership,awaiting the next so welcomed- the dividing curtain had fallen. A time warp separation ending. Concurrent the sounds and sights of the life they left were now reestablished, expressed freely without hidden meaning. The scents of familiar surroundings were also an olfactory recapture welcomed in their breathing. Dusk rapidly approached, light was still available, defining that which is not deeply shadowed keeping their individual countenance visible to one another their reconcillation: one defeated and dejected but resigned, the other accomplishing her purpose… her emotional conflict settled.

Still missing from reality, the rising and falling of their feet that left no footprints, their absence Shaman purposeful as they were still too close from whence they came, creating no witness to their passing.

Exiting at the entrance of the meadow where Staves had last seen it, sat the ancient ceremonial drum, the final artifact in the trail marking. This time he didn't pick it up, its purpose achieved, no longer a curiosity but guessed to still cause an anxiety within Tasha that he wished to avoid; carefully he stepped over it.

The way back to the campsite still bore the mysterious trail markers. Buoys in the wind-blown sea of the tall waving grass. The winds force against their backs urging them forward, there was no turning back. For a moment he swore he heard a whispering farewell, marking a culmination of a visited world forever indelible in his mind.

The sun was to their backs and rapidly descending, altering it's casting length of shadows in its fall to the horizon. All objects birthing shadows when intercepting the fading sunlight. All but Tasha, whose coat sparkled with reflecting sunlight, her mouth agape panting, her only relief from the heating sun, yet casting no shadow. Hers a free spirit display of a Shaman at play, circumventing the display of light when interfered with.

He sought relief from the paranormal expression of Tasha's absenting footprints, his reality manifestation: watching the retreating sun of his world. His vision shielded protectively by his hand, proved a farewell salute. Astonishingly the artifacts they passed had disappeared as if vaporized or plucked by unseen hands. Anonymity protected, leaving the uninvited to remain unknowing.

Tasha and her brethrens, whom he believed were around them, magic continued. Her painful footfalls continuing to leave no prints, yet had ended for him. His footprints clearly visible; his sharing gift had been withdrawn; he was returned to his world of the mere mortal while Tasha continued expressing the fun loving aspects of her mystical powers.

It was almost dark when they reached the campsite, mentally and physically exhausted. The night was clear and non-threatening. Knowing it would please Tasha, he decided against the cabin, ceding to continue to sleep outdoors where she could be closer to nature, visiting with the spirits at will.

Disciplined to do so, her presentation still among the corporeal he continued the use of the leash to prevent her wanderlust,he still protective and accountable as her Alpha for her welfare- pointless; release certainly a power she could call on. Defenseless if she transported herself spititually during the night-her spectral being returning after a sessional with her new bretheren, her physical being he sensed remained committed to him and her pack: living the balance of her earthly life. Nonetheless apprehensive, awakening several times during the night to reach out reflectively and touch her; for reassurance. Fulfilled once again, he returned to sleep until another dream episode awoke him.

When he awoke to the new day, he was sleep deprived; his sporadic sleep insufficient and telling on his physical reactions. An unsharpened feeling occupied his senses, intellectually dulled of perspicacity Tasha helped his awakening and readiness by licking and nuzzling his face.

He needed the invigoration of the morning chilled waters of the lake, Tasha dutifully escorted him. On his hands and knees, he immersed his head completely in the cool waters. While his skin tightened with invigorating cold, his mind slow in reacting, remained dulled and unsharpened. Repeating the process but submerged longer to chase the effects of sleeplessness until his senses responded. His third effort, he withdrew his head permanently, letting the cold water run off.

It was then that he noticed Tasha, who was alongside of him, was not reflected in the lake as if she wasn't there. Thought to be his imagination, he reached down to touch and pet her, smiling at the reassurance. The strange occurrence continued as he again looked down into the lake's calm waters to see nothing of Tasha, only himself and his hand stroking space. Tasha was non-reflective by powers not of this world.

He rose to his feet shaking his head in awe at what the Shaman spirit was capable of. Turning toward Tasha, he detected a faint smile curling her lips; an expression of satisfaction with the test of her newfound powers. On the way back to the campsite, Tasha suddenly stopped to sniff the air anxiously. No sooner than his words, "What is it, girl?" escaped his mouth, a deep throated growl came from within her. "What is it, girl?" he repeated, Tasha responded with aggressive barking, alerting him that danger was near.

It was then that Staves saw her; a black bear sow with her two cubs emerging from the tree line heading for the lake. The sow reacted, after picking up their scent, by standing upright to forewarn them, their presence a perceived threat to her cubs. Staves, initially frozen in place, responded nervously to the warning by backing away, aware that a mother bear accompanying cubs still vulnerable would respond viciously, protective of them if confronted. Reacting to the very serious threat, Tasha, who was free of her tether, growled and barked aggressively not intimidated, yet followed obediently. His objective was to get back to the campsite without arousing the sow any further, both repeatedly turning their heads warily to be sure the bear was still posturing – undecided, not moving towards them in hostility. Tasha, ignoring her pain and weakened condition, continued her arousal, alerting the bear that she should not be taken lightly.

He and Tasha, nervously cautious, looked over their shoulders wary of a surprise charge. George was hopeful they could reach the campsite convincing the sow they were too distanced to be considered a danger to the cubs. The mothering bear, in a highly agitated state showed uncertainty, moving with her cubs towards the waters edge, stopping every few feet in precaution. Staves' uncertainness of the sows intent moved him to walk backward, unexpectedly stumbling over Tasha underfoot, the sudden movement interpreted by the sow as a hostile sign responded aggressively, standing mightily, in an aggrieved challenge, her mouth revealing tearing teeth in her crushing jaws, their threat having increased appreciably, her protective instincts the call of the wild.

Hurriedly Staves and Tasha reached the campsites outer perimeter just as the sow considered moving toward them, his twelve-gauge shotgun in the tent, the distance too far to reach in time if the sow decided to make a charge, not that his first inclination was to shoot the sow, but to fire a warning shot frightening her off. His only recourse was to do nothing, to stay put, avoiding any sudden movement that could be interpreted as a further aggressive act, their passivity calming the sow. Tasha, as if reading his mind, reduced her aggressive barking to guttural growling. He still had hopes that their distancing, their act of conceding, would dissuade the sow of any hostile action to protect her newborn cubs.

Instead, the 250-pound sow chose the moment to lesson her cubs, standing tall on her rear legs, contemptuously confident in her five-foot elevation, snarling viciously from tearing jaws, flailing her raking claws at the empty air in a show of strength that could be exercised at the slightest provocation. The responding cubs learned their lesson well standing on their hind legs in mimicking miniature fury. The sow ignored the wide latitude given her and her cubs, her combativeness dominating, judging their proximity a danger, she drooped down to all fours, her perceived danger triggering her slow testing movement in their direction.

Remaining motionless as the angered bear spotted over Tasha's marking of the camp periphery, urging her cubs to do the same, Staves was hopeful it would be the sow's last aggressive act. A hope wishful as the unpredictable bear exploded into a snarling furry mass of combativeness, prepared to give her life for her cubs who trailed their mother; curious of Staves and Tasha's presence, unsure of the lesson of survival being taught by their mother who moved relentlessly forward. The hairs on the back of Tasha's neck stiffened, reaching upward, her electrolytes signaling danger was imminent.

Staves had read somewhere as he watched the danger closing in on them that waving and standing tall usually dissuaded black bears from attacking. These tactics proved fruitless as the sow picked up her pace.

Tasha responded by baring her teeth – her only formidable weapon, not backing down or turning to run in spite of being no match against a 250-pound bear even if completely healthy. Nonetheless, her instincts, her commitment was to protect him and that she would do. The risk of losing her own life was never a factor. Her growls and barking were now more vociferous, steeling herself as the bear closed the gap.

Staves had no choice but to look for a weapon. Nothing sturdy enough could be found in the immediate area, with his time reduced to seconds. All the branches of significant heft were in the burning fire. Instinctively, his options limited, he began flinging stones in the forward moving bear's direction. The sow, close enough to be struck, was infuriated even further. Seething that she was inflicted with the first pain of her confrontation, no longer testing, she increased her menacing pace. Without another choice, Staves, the heat on his handkerchief wrapped hand intense, reached into the fire pulling out a partially consumed branch, one end still aglow with fire, proceeded to wave it frantically in the bear's direction, hoping the animal's inherent fear of fire would discourage her. Still the sow came, determined and fearless.

The sow was now within twenty feet; making visible the crusting cuts and slashes to her nose and eyes, eyes that were almost swollen closed, limiting her vision; the resulting experience with her mate while protecting her cubs from certain death at the jaws of a father hungry for copulation. Once again the sow paused, issuing her final warning, rising up again on her hind legs; the fierce stand of intimidation. Her huge head nodded up and down, snarling and spitting threats. Her claws extended viciously, her fangs dripping saliva, ready to rake and bite in combat. The only challenge she faced was Staves brandishing his firebrand and a dog sensed weakened with illness, hardly formidable.

Suddenly Staves heard Tasha's barking and growling reach decibel levels he had never heard before; levels that were foreign and disproportionate.

Arroused he momentarily took his eyes off the constantly moving bear to look down at Tasha. To his amazement she had grown in size, befitting her new voice. Tasha was double her normal size, her growth easily breaking her collar in the process, positioning herself in front of Staves, defiantly protective. Her body taut, rippling with massive muscle. Her enlarged head with lips curled back revealed equally imposing fangs.

The bear was not deterred by Tasha's size, and moved to within ten feet, the smell of her hot breath upon them. The pungent foul scent of her excrement covered coat filled the air.

Looking down again, he saw that Tasha had not stopped growing. She was now of a height and weight comparable to the oncoming sow. her growls and barking proportionately increasing to a deafening crescendo suddenly stopping the bear in its tracks. No longer could Tasha be dismissed as a physically unchallenging opponent. The pausing bear was no longer belligerent, conceded a possible loss in combat to a gargantuan Tasha, forced a reassessement of her chances. Ambivalent, the sow looked back at her disinterested cubs for assurances of their safety, spotting them about to test their unproven swimming skills in the lake without their mother's supervision. Intent on play, they ignored their mother's bellowing warning as Staves and Tasha remained guarded and apprehensive… the conflict at a standstill.

This new threat to her cubs gave the bear an opportunity to stand down without being physically vanquished. Turning quickly, bellowing additional warnings all the way, she returned to her cubs. Amazingly she now considered the distance to be sufficient, ignoring Staves and Tasha as non-challenging to her motherhood as she put her cubs, under her close supervision, through the learning experience of swimming.

Well after they were gone from sight, Staves, exhausted from the ordeal sat dumbfounded and in awe at the power Tasha had called upon to save their lives, again the metamorphous in evidence as she returned to her normal size and her pain-wracked body.

At first he thought he dreamed the entire experience until he saw Tasha's torn collar and scattered prayer beads lying tellingly on the trampled grass. Their condition in silent testimony that the event actually happened and was not imagined. He became teary eyed, their near-death experience, prevented from that fate by Tasha standing her ground, calling upon magical skills to excite her growth hormones at a frenzied and desperate pace.

With the campfire carefully extinguished, the firewall of carefully arranged rocks left intact, sure to be appreciated by the next camper, Staves loaded up his station wagon with his camping equipment and the unused supplies. The station wagon with only its windows cleared, was caked with the mud and dirt of the country road, in readiness for the return trip. Turning, George Staves stared saddened at the abandoned campsite reflecting what might have been had he been chosen by the Shaman. Instead, it served Tasha as her ceremonial stage. To him in defeat a sacrificing alter – Tasha repudiating the search for longevity.

Scanning the waters of the lake watching its stillness end with an occasional fish breaking the surface, hunting to snare an insect that ventured too close. The time inopportune, the bounty of well-stocked fish had not been tested by George's considerable fishing skills, one of his pretext's for his visit. The outcome not anticipated, it's success not deterring his grief,contrarily bringing a sorrow to manage. He had crossed the fabled Rainbow Bridge to the strange hypnotic lands; purposed by Tasha during her escort,to call him back under mourning circumstances.

They drove back in silence, Tasha curled and furry on the front seat, her magnificent tail- her plumage covering her wet nose. He tired and weary,his strength in need of a reawakening.His conscious thoughts slowed by what he suspected was a pre-existing condition: sinus membranes flaring during the recent events.He warning himself to be alert to the demands of the long drive home

They had fought a noble fight. The last battle had been waged. Its outcome not as he envisioned or hoped for: an alliance victory they would not have, yet they were not vanquished. The objective had been changed; their meld of wishes that had separated were rejoined by a reluctant concession. One that secretly remained conditional if another intervention were possible. Devotion to Tasha; Staves's persuader to concede at this time,in the back of his mind the opportunity to reestablish not forsaken under another venue. A new plan, their original pledge a casualty to pursuits anew with one of the two a signatory

He was tortured by what he still regarded as her premature death, if he could not find further appeal. He prayed secretly for it's coming opportunity. His broken heart overwhelming, annulling his recent declaration. His only consideration – its opportunity faithful, not a matter of duplicity.

During the drive home the passing scenery became increasingly sculpted by man, following the highway construction with housing developments and suburban shopping centers. Their return direction, facing the rising sun, its brightness shielded as he dropped the sun visor, the flared sinus pain across his eyes no longer besetting him, accomplished without his medication,his weariness still a visitor.Without further thought, attributing it the strain of spending energies in seeking he be conferred upon.Conditioned, connecting to his reach for the hyonotic state, his out of body experience. But his selection did not happen he reconsidered, prompting it's manifestation as imagined. Removed, advancing his inevitable doubts of what had transpired entirely. His ambiguousness of short duration as he looked at Tasha's broken collar and the remaining prayer beads, the truth was undeniable – his mind retuning to certainty.

It was clear to him, if allowed to happen Tasha, empowered as a Shaman had chosen God's continuing creationism, forgoing self-healing. Acceding sacrificially to her spectral being, wherein healing and renewal would be better served – forgoing extending her mortality. Creating space by giving up her space, departing from her corporeal inner world reborn and gifted, gaining new energies translating to unique powers, used from the outer world of spirituality.

In physiological terms, he knew he would have to go through a physical healing after her passing. The inevitable time the issue, as hope for a deferment still remained within him.

∽

His commanded transporter had given him travel, his kaleidoscope sorting the meaningful moments of the actual events, re-witnessing circumstances that cycled most of his emotions. Now as the end drew closer, Tasha's life a consuming candle, her light fading, darkness and despair to visit those who would relive the most scarring of emotions as she was let go: delivering her to the humane choice of euthanasia. A traumatic undertaking; the crossing of the bridge with one less returning.

∽

Rose Staves ended her brief phone conversation with her husband, her prayers answered by their early return; living regretfully within hours of their departure, self-critical for ceding, in desperation, to her suspicion of questionable surrogates of her religious beliefs. Burdened, her conscience was that of a Judas; her thirty pieces of silver: Tasha's salvation. Following her husband's request, she invited their daughter Rosanne, son-in-law Bill and grandchildren, Samantha, Dianna, and George William for dinner; the adults to hear firsthand his experience and the expectations of the future.

By Rose's order while the children were present, the subject of the search was to be censured and casually talked about. Unaware of the censorship, Samantha and Dianna repeatedly asked detailed questions about their grandfather's trip. His responses were abbreviated and guarded leaving them perplexed, politeness kept them from insisting for more information. The children developing disinterst at deliberately clipped dialogue amongst the adults. Excused after dinner they moved to watch television. Freed, a solemn George Staves held family court, to discuss the events needing a complete airing. His daughter and son-in-law hung on every word, captive to his telling, spellbound as he related the extraordinary events. Relishing his experience, wishing that they had been part of the Shaman adventure in spite of the saddened outcome.

Rosanne and Bill were philosophical in attempting to assuage Rose's voiced concern of participating in a sacrilege. Liberally expansive, believing God's work has many faces, many expressions, supportive of ever-broadening ecumenicalism. Strong of belief, his goodness was equally impacting though delivered by his surrogates. Rose on the other hand, thought quite differently; drawing a parallel: the credentials of Latin to the mass... the language of the Roman converts to Christianity, changed to the native language of the revisionists. An ecumenical effort to broaden it's appeal satisfying more recent times and contemporary cultures. Its impact was not the same in Rose's judgment. Rose torn between her love of Tasha and her concerns for the occult listened carefully for signs that her husband blasphemed the church out of frustration. A failure in his first effort to be contacted, in desperation elevated a ritual to the heights reserved for religion, advancing it beyond the tolerance of her God. She listened apprehensively, her absorption in silence assaying as he spoke of his experience. Valuing as godly the language of his chants in his appeal, and the use of revered implements of their religion... ameliorating as not blasphemous. Her concerns on hold, she joined the others reluctantly, possibly attributing but not necessarily believing entirely the supernatural and mystical occurrences experienced as the exclusive efforts of surrogates – believing it was Gods direct intervention in guiding Tasha, not to interfere with her destiny – praising God in finding a way of communicating his wishes.

Rose, a guardian of her religious beliefs, was wary of the pagan implications of the ritual setting stage of the campfire. While conceding it as required in making contact with the Shaman, she felt cause for concern and suspicion, fearing her husbands inexperience vulnerable to the implication of idolatry in the fire. Trappings of perfidious irreligious cult followings; advocates of the power of the fire: influencing self-hypnosis, opening doors for aberrations, effectively closing them to all that is holy and reverent. Finding a truth that she could build on: her husband's telling trip to the burial grounds as real, not imagined, that she could easily conceptualize and believe, having read claims of it's existence for years amongst the beliefs of Godly religions. The memorial animal sanctuary of Rainbow Bridge, while not having specific reference in testament writings; Rose Staves reverently aware that St. Francis of Assisi preached of such a place in God's kingdom; could conceive Tasha becoming a courier for St. Francis – empowered with recent mystical spiritual gifts.

Yet her dilemma remained, suspicions abounding: all had occurred in an environment to influence hallucination. Even her husband showing Tasha's torn apart collar and the broken chain of prayer beads did not move Rose from doubt. With much trepidation, she conceded the work of Shamanism as a marginal belief not worthy of deep conviction. Her reservation: what her husband saw, what was imagined by him to see, suggested the influences of mind control, his experiences never really happening. While hypothesizing Rose held her revered necklace cross, as was her reaction for strength in matters of doubt. The substance of her faith: God's omnipotence and intentions no matter how indistinguishable were ever present regardless of circumstance be it secular or religious, persuading her Gods role: contributing the exotic and supernatural surrogates as responding with his cognizance. Conceding, she did so as God's Centurion continuing her guard against sacrilege.

The trips purpose initiated as a last hope, concluding in dejection of all supporters; Tasha conceding her diseased earthly body. The weight of their moroseness easing somewhat when told her sacrifice springing an elevating spiritual emancipation. Still, the prevailing emotion melacholy having taken root at the thought of her death, her demise was irreconcilable. Except George the packs Alpha, who secretly harbored a "one last stand," in spite of his earlier communicarted capitulation to Tasha. He would attempt to engineer a miracles intervention.

Rose welcomed his plans to have Tasha blessed at the church of St. Francis of Assisi on his birthday of celebration, evolving to an animal lover's annual rite of blessing: for pets to continue healthy, those in need of healing, those taken sick and injured, the desperately terminal. The sprinkling of holy water ranging as a blessing for continued good health, or a meaning of anointing, in preparation for entering God's kingdom. Rose was thankful that this religious experience would provide penance, an opportunity to cleanse the residue of possible deceptively encouraged sins by the unperceiving well intentioned. Possible sins of their journey forgiven, reestablishing in her mind the threatened primacy of their religion. In her devotion the only course to follow for Tasha's salvation, here on earth or the hereafter.

George Staves who knowing that Tasha's death was nearing without an intervention; the churches blessing he wished she receive be not preparatory to her death. But as had been written having the opportunity for a miracle making recovery in the offered services with God's oversight, by the spirit of the first renown anthropomorphist: St. Francis of Assisi. He was availed of one last opportunity for divine intervention, encouraged by prayer. Failing this purpose, Tasha would still have been blessed religiously, prior to her meeting her maker.

Tears had welled in everyone's eyes as they looked tenderly at Tasha, knowing this religious exposure, this ceremony, the churches blessing of animals, in Tasha's case, was the sacrament of extra unction in preparation of her death. Except for George and others not yet amongst, the ceremony raising it's bar beyond the blessing; to an adjunct opportunity of miraculous recovery for their pets as had been suggested from reported past experiences,the churches leadership noncommittal, only the churches faithful would speak of the ceremony's credit. Ironically extracting a connection, escaping all others. George strained a parallel between this religious blessing with his search for the hope of Shamanism. Each of it's substance just as ritualistic, the outcome an attempt to intervene in what had already been written.

George Staves, completing his sharing of his experience phoned his daughter Phyllis and son Edward. They too followed their sister and brother-in-law's reaction; voicing awe at his experience,never once retreating from their initial support in spite of the disappointing outcome. What his wounded psyche needed to hear, empathizing with him, they acclaiming in their respective words "all that happened were God's wishes manifested in many ways, in many philosophies." Poignant expressions supporting that his appeal was not irreligious, not alien to God's divinity,"

The oldest of the owners, with their precious pets held tenderly in caring arms or in an obedient proudly displayed heel position, living alone as recent widows and widowers, came seeking spiritual reinforcement. Their faces bearing the heavy lines of emotional strain visiting and settling in their visage. Their partner in lifes death too vivid a memory to face a life unprepared for, one of mistrust and threatening conditions that manifested into nightmarish fear of being alone. Withdrawing, their seclusion perceived as risk reducing, becoming too burdensome to family and friends. In furtherance of their monastic living, sought a continuance or miracle for the mutual need their pets and they gave one another, prayerful that each one of their lives continue; if not, then death taking them together providentially.

A menagerie of the ailing, the hopeful and those seeking a blessing for the continued longevity of their pets, gathered as awaiting parishioners. Expressive were two dogs on three legs, having the one leg taken from them on the operating table. Overcoming the limitation, they moved as freely and happily as if no handicap existed; their owners thankful to God that their lives were spared.

Some came crippled, pitifully dragging their hindquarters when not in a movement enabling sling fashioned by their distraught owners, unable to accept the humane act of letting go.

Within the gathering were dogs and cats colorfully festooned in reversed lampshade collar restraints, purposed to keep them from scratching the healing incision, the aftermath of removing a cancerous tumor from their necks.

The diseased with raging mange came, defoliated to hairless skin, secreting pus succeeding over yet to conquer medication.

They brought their pet birds in shoeboxes, eyes fevered; a damaged wing pinned and splinted to bond the broken bones, positioned to overhang the side wall of the shoebox, necessarily extended as if in soaring flight.

They came hissing in feline travel cases, cats emaciated from appetites lost, constantly wracked by violent vomiting as fevered leukemia destroyed their blood cells and the ability to eat.

The elderly and the young came with framed photographs of their beloved pets that had passed on before this date of observance, seeking a posthumous blessing of their memory and spirit.

Young equestrians, equally committed, equally protective displaying photographs of their treasured riding mount and companion, pictured as a high-strung nervous equine beneath them, asking for a calming blessing for their behemoths in absentia.

Young frisky canines on their way to adulthood, constantly reminded to sit obediently, momentarily successful until once again distracted, noses to the air sifting the abundance of scents, pausing to dwell on those that were foreign, they examples of animal health personified.

They were in line along the sidewalk in front of the church, rivals and traditional enemies; the sickly aware of each others suffering bound them, they shared a kinship without the boundary of species. The healthy influenced by the sick and weak warily tolerating one another. They were an assemblage of infirm and healthy, not as patients waiting to see the veterinarian but to receive the blessings of a holy man, a priest. Todays proxy reaching across thousands of years to connect to the originator, to bless, to comfort, to inspire, to make ready for God's kingdom, or cure if situational worthy.

It was this religious, exclusively named church, this edifice that attracted them, humbling them to seek God's disciple, St. Francis of Assisi, the guardian saint of all God's creatures, where all aspects of creation would be celebrated, where man's relationship with animals is given godly value, publicly.

The parish friar of the St. Francis Church, dressed in a brown robe with a white rope belt cinching his ample waist, came exiting the entry doors, continuing down the steps to the street level to tend to his unusual flock. The muffled choral singing of regular services escaping through the opened doors raised the curiosity of animals that were still fully auditory. There were the psalms commemorating this day, October 4th, the Feast Day of St. Francis of Assisi where the blessing of the pets is offered at the steps of namesake churches. He, St. Francis the Shepherd of all animals, scorned early in his life, tolerated in ridicule, preached to all who would listen: "Animals have souls and are welcome in God's kingdom."

The oldest of the animals weakened with age cowered among the younger more aggressive, panting nervously, anxious of their susceptibility to the younger threat. Their owners recognizing the signs reached down protectively, their touch and words calming their fidgeting pets, seen as reassurance that they would be protected.

The young and healthy waiting their turn, sensing a move to dominate within their midst, the more aggressive recoiling the restrained instinctively, verging on open hostility until calmed by their owners as their blessing neared.

Evolving without being commanded as the thing to do, lines formed headed by the earliest arrivals, in readiness when called upon to approach. The friar stood centered on the church's first step, the steps behind him convenient in serving as his altar, the ceremony beginning with his priestly pronouncement, "God's will, will be served. Come join me in his blessing."

The Friars words began the procession, all to stand before him. Most passed without comment, others passionately and openly pleaded for God to intervene on behalf of their terminally ill pet. The friar, eyes full of pity, would only shake his head in sad understanding, intoning blessings, gently sprinkling the pet with holy water. An acknowledgment that they had a soul and it would be released after death.

Tasha, an early arriver, was part of the first group with Rose and George Staves at her side; slow of movement because of her physical limitations, her personal aura recognized precluding any jeopardy from the other canines. The setting at the steps of the church not feared as a nullification of her new gifted status. She, a practitioner of Shamanism, recognized its power not granted to preempt in this venue. The worthiness of intervention, as it was in her case, the will of the creator.

In obvious pain, with uncertainty shortening her steps, anticipated in the painful extension of her limbs as the friar awaited her patiently. Arriving, she looked up to receive the holy water on her muzzle and body. Instinctively reacting to it as rain, shaking to dislodge the wetness, her action encouraged the friar to smile as he invoked his blessing of the pets:

> "Blessed are you, Lord God, maker of all living creatures. You called forth fish in the sea, birds in the air and animals on land. You inspired St. Francis to call all of them his brothers and sisters. We ask you to bless this pet. By the power of your love, enable it to live according to your plan. May we always praise you for all your beauty in creation. Blessed are you, Lord God, in all your creatures. Amen."

At the end of the short ceremony while most began to leave, some owners remained motionless, reluctant to depart, eyes fixed hopefully on their pets, anticipating something to happen. George Staves among them, a last opportunity in the spontaneity for Godly intervention the last hope for recovery, a demonstrated miracle for the faithful.

Their cause discouragingly ended as the friar returned to the church, he not being assigned this day as hoped with powers of deliverance, effectively ending the ceremonial blessing. The final truth, no cries or shouts of revelation – a miracle occurring… their suffering pets still hopelessly at the door of death. Silent prayers and open pleas for divine intervention, going unheeded; they were disconsolate in failing to reach the miracle enabling source. All their hopes exhausted, their grieving process to continue. The only consolation: their beloved pet had received a blessing from the Creator's surrogate to live out their lives as limited as it may be according to His plan, fulfilling their fate, joining Him spiritually in His kingdom to await their masters to join them.

The blessing completed, the Staveses and Tasha returned home. A somber George called for a family council. He addressed his family with Tasha lying beside him asleep, her anti-inflammatory medicine effective, absenting her position for the moment of pain.

George, in final defeat, said solemnly, "Difficult times are ahead for all of us as we anguish over our impending loss. Declining health during a terminal illness will not be a welcomed experience. We all will be tested. We must be mindful that she is self-aware. Our Tasha senses mood changes, capable of detecting at over one hundred yards human mood swings. If influenced, she'll join us, mirroring our dark and morose moods, a psychological pairing we must guard against. Tasha is aware of her declining health, choosing that outcome as opposed to effecting a self-cure that I believe she has the power to do. In spite of her commitment, she'll be torn apart if we show our true emotions, taking it as a rejection for her decision for her greater good. She would want us to share in that glory. She would not want, as proud and committed as she is of her choice, to see our misery, it would be non-supportive."

His voice cracking, thankful that Tasha was still asleep, he paused to regain control, his wife and daughter who were on the verge of tears, faces contorted in grief.

Staves, steeling himself, said, "she would not want an atmosphere of gloom and despair. She would feel the betrayer for longing to be a spiritual Shaman. This will not be easy for any of us, as close as we have been to her all these years. She is reconciled to her fate as it's her choosing, wanting only our understanding. She will make no effort to delay the eventuality, telling us when it's time to go. It could come at any time; treat each visit as your last contact with her while alive." His words difficult… "in her presence avoid becoming emotional, upsetting in sharing a revisiting of her life… What she has meant to you."

In the weeks that followed his daughter Rosanne and her family came more often to visit. She and her children were expecting the worst, relieved to learn that Tasha was still with them, showing their typical pleasure's not exaggerations or pity while in her company, ignoring her increasing debilitation before their eyes. When leaving, careful to be beyond Tasha's perceptions, they cried in despair at her worsening condition.

Their daughter Phyllis and son Edward, having traveled great distances knowing this would be their last moments with Tasha, spent most of their time with Tasha always in sight. Iron willed to keep their sadness hidden, reliving and recounting for the benefit of all, their shared lives with Tasha, whose attentive ears heard the frequent mention of her name in those colorful stories that pleased everyone including herself. Nothing escaped their revisiting; even the moments held heretofore insignificant were now golden and memorable.

On Phyllis' last evening before returning to California, with everyone asleep, as she had done every evening of her visit, she would quietly join Tasha. She, who enjoyed such a special and sometimes mystical relationship with Tasha, would sit on the carpeted floor of the den Tasha at her side recalling the shared experiences of the past. This visit like the earlier ones was an enabling one, astonishingly, the magic of Phyllis's voice anesthetized Tasha from pain allowing her head to be moved onto Phyllis' lap. Mesmerized by her words, she extended a thankful paw signaling that she wanted to be embraced. Unable to control herself, the unfolding scenario painful Phyllis shed tears, audibly sobbing unashamedly, helpless she couldn't help her as she had in the past. Tasha's circumstances beyond their unique relationship. Phyllis's tears wetting Tasha's coat as the precious moment continued, it telling of the secret way they communicated with one another, expressing that her time was nearing, the illness that debilitated her and brought sadness would end, as another world free of pain, of new responsibilities awaited. It would be the last memory Phyllis would have of her.

George and Rose, as if unaware of each others presence sat in the den, unknowingly orchestrated in common thought. He turned on the television to break the despair of silence, the programming his vain attempt to provide short lived relief, their attention quickly returning to Tasha. George's bearing somber, attempting to compartmentalize his conscience, needing that perspective for recovery. In affect a redemption and absolution, his efforts not a total failure.

His self-exoneration partial, remained angered that Tasha was destined to fall prey to an insidious disease, whose earthly treatment remained stagnant and ineffective, not curative. His devestation, not being able dissuade her, empowered as she was by the paranormal, to enact a self-curing.

He had ranged the grieving process of emotions; denial, shock, and guilt, his scarring not complete, his wounds deep.

His grief distorting rational, anthropomorphizing Tasha, considered natures rate of her species' aging unfair. Its passage toward a life-ending "port of call" catalogued, unaffected by the uniqueness of this extraordinary dog. He had learned, in spite of his efforts, her fatalism seeded immutably in the complexities of her genetic code, in her bloodline, her dividing cells, her tissue structure, all under the control of time ever-moving, consuming, deteriorating. Her life's clock moving unabated, her mortality ending days of light; her tomorrows to cease. A force unleashed at birth unrelenting and overwhelming, a process he thought possible to influence. Without divine intervention the relativity of the species and their separation profound.

When compared to man, the canine life is a mercurial metamorphous, its relative calendar having a yearly birthday every 1.7 months compared to man every twelve months. Its development that much faster.

Selectively he relished her accelerated development – welcoming maturity early in its cycle when measured in human terms, but not it's penalty. To soon would be his judgment with his own life's cycle, the final ticking of her irreversible biological clock – unwinding at the midnight of natural death, her mature life shortened even further by disease while many dawns still awaited him.

Remorse, a reflective heavily weighed stage of the grieving process, now gripped his consciousness as he watched with dread for those final signs of her demise: her refusal to eat or drink. Pitying signs that she no longer sought life sustaining nourishment, her last buoy in continuing life in waters no longer buoyant. The sea of longevity no longer navigable, its forceful current drifting her out to her horizon where the sky meets the sea, easing her ascending, out of the last of the bouys sight and guidance. Their signals no longer her need as she welcomed death, its path sounding position, or it's beacon of light available for destiny's still to be written. Her capacity diminished as her ears deafened to sound, and when her eyes vision lessening, acknowledging little light, it empowered him to provide the final relief of euthanasia, a commission that would haunt him forever.

An irony overwhelmed him: Tasha's diseasing demon proving so formidable, fending off efforts to defeat him, assured of victory. Finding an ally in the very subject it was consuming, its insidiousness gaining the upper hand when Tasha, rather than continuing the fight, relinquished her pursuit of an elixir, fatally turning her back on a remedial silver bullet that would extend her remaining life. Choosing instead to vacate her allotted space among the world's occupants for a newly created being, a new generation, it's genetics and fate to be tested.

He was pledged by oath and ascension as an Alpha. His was charged to honor his duty, to end her last days when comfort was no longer possible. He found himself angry; another stage of the grieving process, lashing out at all, condemning the forces of nature for being indiscriminate toward one so gifted. Tasha's time-dependent biology locked in.

George and Rose continued their practice of turning away to hide their tears from Tasha, her joints stiffened with arthritis, her movement lessening. Her loss of bone density shrinking her once proud physicality. Symptomatic of terminal illness was her incontinence, embarrassing her for her lack of control.

Tasha gave up her moments of privacy. She no longer sought the independence and comfort of curling around the bathroom commode. She no longer wanted solitude. She clearly was troubled being alone, aware of her mortality, but not afraid. Expressing her continued dependency these last days, wakening with a start from short spells of troubled sleep, needing reassurance that George and Rose were nearby before dropping off again. Her wishes: they always be in view within her panorama. Never too far away from responding to her pain-driven yelping; the dosage of her pain relievers having been exceeded, bringing only the Staves's as medicine to nurse and sooth. She would fix her loving bi-colored eyes on them, their images envisioned only in black and white. The sight of her pack members, a mental epidural, sedating, assisting the soothing massaging of her inflamed median points.

The passing days furthered their despair as relief was almost non-existent from her anti-inflammatory medication. Her loved one's words and tender touches, after much time opiating, inducing her to sleep.

Rose and George agreed time was approaching, George to sleep on the couch in the den, Tasha at his side within easy reach of his stroking comforting hands, assuring her he was with her. He would wait for her to fall asleep first before praying in silence that God now excelerate taking her.

"Remember," he said tenderly to her as if language was no barrier, rubbing her neck, "when we were asleep you would jump up onto our bed, nudging me awake, deceptively. Finally when I did get out of bed tricked, you would immediately bury your head in my pillow, rubbing into my scent to become part of you, merging the two of us."

She showed understanding to his words, never moving her eyes from him, smiling as dogs will do, her ears low and back, her eyes half shut, mouth soft and parted, chin held high, panting satisfaction, sharing the joy in traveling his memory lane.

His mind continued to journey as his hand brushed her once luxuriant coat now dulled lifeless by disease. Her loose hairs came off in his hands, remindful of pleasanter days when he, Rose and the children had their first exposure of her blowing her coat. Finding Tasha not receptive to brushing; impatient with the time spent and the frequency in removing her detaching undercoat.

He found participating success in helping her blow her coat when walking, her pauses of curiosity distracting, his hand gently plying her surfacing undercoat from her body, casting the spent "down" to the wind. A treasure lost, regretting never having her "down" woven into a rug or blanket as was being done with lovers of her breed. He then remembered that when her "down" was freed to the wind, he and Tasha would watch as scavenging birds and squirrels quickly plucked it from the ground, flying off or climbing to use it as a nest making component. Nature's answer to recycling he remarked at the time to Rose; conservation, a utilitarian use that would satisfy environmentalists.

Tasha's countenance demonstrating recollection, a participant in his reliving reverie, watched as his petting hand came away full of her loose hair. Perceptively looking toward the patio door, her wishes clear to him: release her bagged blown coat to the outdoors for the birds and squirrels to find. Torments of the past, heirs to what she now willed them – part of her. A Shaman gesture in honoring nature.

Awake they sought connection, eye to eye, she encouraged his hand to touch her head, her body – the direct linkage of continuing their circuitry, his tenderness her comfort – he silently anguishing pain at her shrinking size.

They fell asleep as one. His last thoughts of Tasha digging down through the accumulating snow, sculpting a body sized hole into which she either sat or lay for hours as her wolf ancestors had done; surveying proudly her domain while chilling winds blew churning clouds of snow to overcoat her, hanging crystals of ice from her muzzle and whiskers, playfully flaunting her breed's adaptation to harsh wintry weather. Majestic in her rule.

His troubled sleep shortened as he heard her moaning in pain. Panting frantically as she struggled to rise, yelping at the effort. Her pain growing so intense that it immobilized her in her last resting position. Having desperately moved in search of pain free freedom, was frozen helplessly to distant for him to reach from his sentinel position. Tasha awake, frantic for reassurance, sniffed the air of the darkened room for his familiar scent. Forestalling any further stress Staves quickly came to her assistance, Staves leading her outside to relieve herself, her squatting position given foundation in his willing hands. Returning, with great care delicately positioning her where she could easily be reached. Assured he would now be near enough, she fell back to sleep, secure she was not alone while he, in deep depression, could only find interrupted sleep this night, and those few to follow.

The inevitable words he was dreading to hear would come from him. Nearing the issues threshold, he entrusted to carry out the emotionally dreaded act. It would be exclusively his declaration, solemnly announcing the end had come, knowing affected lives would never be the same, mentally preparing all to grieve. The mourning process about to befall them; shuttering her casting sunlight, the saddening color gray was dominating, veiling all other colors. The colors of the spectrum stolen by the heart-wrenching separation about to take up residency in their hearts and minds. Her waning life's limitation keeping her from being animated in her giving,

Practically immobile, her eyes radiating love being crowded by excruciating pain. They went to Tasha to establish the physical connection she needed, her devotion whether requited or not always her primacy. Now with the opportunity to show physical pleasure her nothing in return willingness to please satisfaction, had been stolen from her. Her illness induced needs: a comforting, careful to the touch appreciation, without solicitation demonstrated in the hours left for her to travel along the path she chose, her only wish. The reversal, conditioning a criteria alien to her bountiful with health earlier days, impossible to forget in the years to come.

George Staves, central to the drama being played out in his tormenting nightmare – staging a masked figure wearing a judicial robe, a juror's box with one seat of the twelve to be filled, a puppet wearing a medical gown brandishing a hypodermic needle whose movement wires and rods were in the hands of a shadowy masked individual. All were symbolic of himself, the connection the role he must fulfill as judge, jury and executioner. His waking hours worse, giving him no piece, real time being consumed more apparent, dreamscape time standing still in the repeating – real time bringing closer the taking of his treasured pet's life. His misery clouding the correctness of his responsibility, as right and merciful. His distraught mind, bringing forth a warped analogy: relieving Tasha of her pain from irreversible disease, as no less than assisted suicide, if not murder itself if a statute existed beyond cruelty to animals. He was a co-executioner, fulfilling her request to end her physicality, not wanting herself exceptionally dimensioned. He was a co-conspirator leaving himself branded with an ignoble act during his consuming melancholy.

Welcoming escapist reprieves, George was quick to find diversion from his approaching duty, exaggerating her good days as a sign of turnaround, proved to be subjective, wishful enthusiasm. A momentary pause of the inevitable not having a clinical basis to be anything more than short-lived. Nonetheless, in desperation, he imagined it a chance, not dissuaded by incalculable odds. Eager to grasp at straws, pushing away from his consciousness her life a fading spark that could not be reconstituted to a full flame. When this thinking inevitably faltered, he moved to again avoid responsibility, the fortuitous escape by an act of God, hoping to awaken to find Tasha had passed on during the night.

No longer ambulatory without assistance; laying down a position minimally tolerable, courageously held her head up, her expressive eyes, with little movement of her head in obvious pain, moved from him to his wife Rose.

"My poor baby," Rose spoke pityingly, "Why is she staring at us?"

"She's talking to us," George answered despairing, turning his head away from Tasha so that she would not see his countenance of misery. Enough of my suppression he chastised himself I'm a man needing to show his feeling for our lives together, that I can no longer hide, my stoicism spent. Turning back to her, his teary eyes a beacon of wretchedness. Her terminal condition his full focus, painfully surging past his reluctance and exaggerations. Her consuming helplessness and wretchedness demanding he spend his range of emotions openly as payment for words said and unsaid of her value to him and his family during their lives together.No longer in the back of his mind surpressed, responding to her mercifully – facilitating her destiny in the afterworld that was now part of her future.

Tasha's every expression, every labored maneuver and declining appetite told them the time was near; that she was ready to leave their side. The physical relationship built over the last fourteen plus years about to end.

Shoulders slumping, having dispatched all hope, Rose sat there watching Tasha disconsolately, her shoulders weighed heavily, slumped in sadness. Knowing the day a future without her was dawning. His throat tightened, difficult to imagine a world without her, never to see her presence again. Her tomorrows ceasing as would all her succeeding tomorrows of dawn and dusk. Her alive sounds stilled, her voice that of the past, traveling in space forever.

He told his wife sadly, "Time is near. I must fulfill my obligation to her."

"We both must," she said reluctantly, joining him. "When will we know?"

"It's almost time," he answered. "She is about to reach a point that would be too cruel of us to allow her life to continue. She'll want to stay as long as she's able to bear the suffering. She'll tell us when she can go no further."

Except for Tasha's panting, no further sound was heard as they shared a common grief. At this moment, not ameliorating her approaching earthly death; her transitioning a spectral inhabitant, commencing the day their longing sorrow begins.

Rose, unable to bear the pain of looking at a Tasha so foreign to what she once was, was so overcome with grief that she moved to leave the room, her tears not to be shared, she sought solitude. Exiting, she paused to carefully stroke her beloved Tasha, a pitying smile on her agonizing face.

"I love you, Tasha," she finally said. Trembling, she left the room.

He was alone, allowing his thoughts to surface parables and truisms that he heretofore gave only tokenism. Their appropriateness now called upon, their full impact dominating his mind.

"Life springs eternal."… "Cup of life runneth over."… "Youth needed for a continuum."… "The clock of life approaching the midnight hour of one's final day." The cutting truth of the words left him bleeding internally.

Although the words succeeded, impacting he be pragmatic in bearing the wounds of his emotional involvement. A final hesitation occurred, never would he be guilty of abandoning her, yet essentially that was what he was preparing to do with euthanasia. Confused, he refered to the insight of a higher source, recalling from the Book of Job verses 33:14–16, just what he needed:

> "For God speaketh once, yeah twice, yet man perceived it not. In a dream, in a vision of night, when deep sleep falleth upon men in slumbering upon their bed, then he openeth the ears of men and sealeth their instruction."

Seeded irreversibly, no longer a reluctant participant, morally and spiritually armed, no longer deterred by the pain he would bear as a participant in ending her life- it's added burden a test in his recovering. An outcome of paradox, Staves told himself, after years of mutual protection placing her in the ultimate of harms way: euthanasia. No longer of a mindset of maintaining unrealistic hope: squeezing out another antagonizing day of life, death being a godsend, any other mindless hope would be tantamount to extreme cruelty.

Expectant of humans, they were the species of the highest intellect, their bonding would not be unusual; but bonding of man and dog with the dog communicating on different planes by a language privileged to understanding by few. George Staves and Tasha were extraordinary by any means of measurement.

The nighttime hours, when sleep was usually welcomed relief for the troubled mind, did not befall them this night, the opportunity to rest ones strained body and mind did not happen; fatigue being resisted to continue to keep her in sight, a portending ominous sign.

They joined each other, he awake with resurfaced condemnation, dreading his grim reaper role. Tasha awake, affected by the falling loss of efficacy of anti-inflammatory medication, moaning as the masking of her pain had practically become non-existent. Her instincts of the wild told her something different was going on in her body; her disease undergoing change from chronic to severe. Her already strained immune system joining her medication was of little consequence to her rampaging disease.

"Tasha girl," he called out to offer her solace to her worsening whimpering. Leaving the couch he went to her to begin his normally soothing massage. But this time she yelped to the worsening pain, stopping him. Aghast, he realized how much weight she had lost.

Rose Staves hearing Tasha's anguish, found them together, he tenderly touching her blanket covered body. "Does she need a blanket? The outside temperature is pleasant."

"Yes," he answered. "She's been shivering all night. Her nose is dry and hot. She's feverish."

Alarmed, calling over her retreating shoulder she responded, "I'll get the baby aspirin."

Nodding in acknowledgement, never taking his eyes off Tasha who just looked at him blankly, her once muscular body now limp and toneless.

Getting aspirin down her gullet proved difficult. Normally she was easily compromised by hiding the aspirin in butter or ice cream. This time she stubbornly refused. Finally he forced her mouth open and shoved the pill as far back as she would allow, holding her mouth shut until she swallowed it.

Within the hour she stopped shivering. To their surprise she painfully rose momentarily, pausing and sniffing at her food bowl. Deterred by her inability to keep her food down, she slumped weakly to the carpet.

"Did you notice how much weight she has lost?" he asked of his wife.

"I've been more aware of it over this past week. We're losing her," she responded tearfully.

He barely shook his head in the affirmative, not normally a superstitious man, nonetheless at that moment dreading her spoken words, a *fait accompli*.

"I'll going to call Dr Kerrigan," Rose said as she walked to the phone. "He might recommend something."

Rose returned within minutes, eyes glistening, her voice cracking, "He agrees with everything we've done. Since her anti-inflammatory medication is no longer providing relief, he did say if she needed additional aspirin to give it to her but to be alert for a toxic reaction," her lower lip quivering at the added threat to Tasha.

Tasha was his passion, making him forgivingly prone to another impossible hope. A tease encouraging his vacillation. Tasha improbably seeming to stabilize, the increased dosage and frequency of aspirin obviously helping. Her cries turning to barks calling for George, her Alpha, to come to her. This time it was his circuitry, not a massage she wanted, to connect telepathy their instincts, wired mind-to-mind, surfacing a mutually shared experience.

They participated in a visualization. Phyllis, sitting in the club chair watching Tasha, after spending many minutes of hypnotically rubbing Tasha's welcoming stomach, completely subduing her; moving gently in brushing with her hands the lids covering her bi-eyes. Tasha's delight drew a shouted pronouncement of how beautiful and magnificent she was from Phyllis who then proceeded to kiss her muzzle, marking it with lipstick. Phyllis's love expression accomplished, she moved to the club chair to watch television, leaving a treat, crowning the pleasure she had brought her.

No longer on the verge of sleep Tasha responded as not being quite ready to end Phyllis' rewarding ministrations. Leaping amazingly from the couch to Phyllis' lap while she was still seated in the club chair, slobbering her with kisses, covering her like an animated blanket, giving life to a bag of popcorn and its contents were sent flying in all directions. Tasha was now throned in Phyllis' lap, defiant in her challenge to those hilarious with laughter and surprise.

As Tasha returned to real time, her eyes brightened and her mouth smiled as only huskies can, her pain amazingly quelled as she savored that mirthful event; a momentary pleasant departure from her present state.

The passage of the days a retreating tide, taking with it a proportion of the depth of Tasha's persona, leaving her the metaphorical equivalent of a eroding coastline. In departure Tasha life's configuration unable to be replenished, only sediment, her last remnants remaining but only temporary, the final destructive act nearby but not immediate, at least that's what they thought, until just prior to dinner time when her circumstances couldn't get any worse.

Staves' supporting hands and arms were no longer able to raise her from her watching prone position. No amount of effort could get her to stand beyond momentarily, slumping to the carpeted floor with a heart wrenching yelp. Suddenly she started to shiver. Rose rushed to cover her with a blanket.

"I'll get the aspirin," she panicked.

Tasha was radiating heat, her nose dry to the touch as he encouraged her to swallow an undisguised aspirin, normally prohibiting, her will to resist non existent. George got her to drink water from his cupped hands as she stared up at him obedient in her response. Moments later she vomited, traces of blood speckling her sputum in a toxic reaction to the aspirin, medicinally her condition declined to untreatable. Her breath was foul; she appeared confused.

The dreaded word of "terminal" was now upon him, Tasha signaling to him that the time was now.

"She's telling us she must go," he said remorsefully, dreading his words of finality, compelled to faintly whisper the same words again, heard only by him. Not a seconding, but a countering final prayer, the time upon us, for the empowered to now intervene upon hearing. A last chance to react to the foreboding.

The hour well past closing time at the veterinarian was not a welcomed situation, foisting upon them helplessness to stem her pain. A quality of life non existent, their faces anguishing that they may have waited too long.

The atmosphere, the anxiety of an intensive care unit waiting room.

Those in wait being told a loved one would expire, a life ending, a greater grieving, commencing with the truth that all hope was gone… prayers for a miracle unanswered. The poignant scenario, that which now gripped the Staves's: called for fulfilling their promise, their obligation, significant of their lives together, nothing more indicative more compelling than spending this last night together watching over her.

"It's important that we spend this last night together," Rose said, desperately trying to muffle her sobbing.

Her husband responded, "She would like that, she knows."

Throughout the night there were few words spoken, other than those to comfort Tasha. Those that passed between them were forced, clipped, fearing additional words impossible without breaking down. Their unwavering attention kept them sleepless, fatiguing them physically and emotionally, bringing forth fitting resignation to the philosophy of acceptance. Messaging: Death is an outgrowth of life that is irrevocable. For Tasha, her passage was ending, this her day of finality, her strained heart approaching its last beat, she would soon die in extreme pain. Climaxing death at their hands would shorten the duration of her intense suffering. In sacrifice: loving her enough to let go."

The odor of amniotic fluid that scented her birth once again in evidence, returning as the odor of death, intermixed with heightened stress chemicals, would be her fading last scent.

Those last hours, Rose and George Staves were always nearby, groggy with deprived sleep, stressed to slowness they still found the energies to respond willingly to her needs, never an imposition.

Awake, they watched pitifully as Tasha's legs failed to respond to her brain's commands. The severe pain short circuited her electronic impulses, forcing her to remain prostrate and anchored to her right side.

Her head, as if weighted heavily, remained stationary, only free for movement was her mouth, opening and closing, tongue lolling to one side, panting in resignation. Her want to eat or drink was nonexistent, refusing their handheld offerings. No longer able to continue a life wracked with pain, she wished for deliverance.

As they had done throughout the night, during those moments when all was quiet, needing assurances, they turned on the lights to see if God had mercifully taken her, sparing them of a haunt they wished to avoid. Tasha's glazed eyes coming immediately into view, her lids blinking repeatedly at the intense pain, tearless, pleading for the relief they could provide. Their consoling words of magic gone, impotent, her only comfort that she was not alone.

They prayed to God for a spiritual blessing, to comfort her during her last night on earth, for strength to perform their merciful obligation.

The early morning brought thunder and rain, the creators voice and tears.

A needed response to a fouled atmosphere, the contaminating industrialized land, the air they breathe holding polutants. "Corrupting man at his advancing finest, yet unable to cure the illnesses of the ages," George said to himself, his bitterness awakened.

"God's spirits also cry for Tasha, this day of her death, not in sadness but in joy as her spirit joins him in his kingdom." The only tears of sadness were to be shed by them, they were mere mortals.

Unlike most canines, the sound of crashing thunder never did frighten Tasha. Alerted, expressing curiosity at the flashing thundering sky, sticking her nose questioningly through the vertical blinds that covered the patio door. This day, incapable of movement, she just lay there, fear still beyond her; Staves knew she had gained a new understanding as a Shaman, theirs and now her use of natures force's.

The weather conditions harvested a procession of unanticipated violent lightening and crashing rain storms, passing through the area. Their unexpectedness in George Staves' mind, the unleashing of the Shaman. Calling forth the power of mother nature, paying tribute to Tasha's corporeal passing, highlighted with pyrotechnics. Celebratory for one of them taking up spectral residence. The Staves lives empty of Tasha, beginning. The stormy weather's suddenness, it's electric start and echoing finish a flashing life before their eyes, as was the life of Tasha who there attention returned to, as if recharged by the disturbances in the sky, beholding her finding unexpected strength after repeated heart breaking failures.Enabled she raised herself from her frozen position, managing with the utmost determination to sit on unsteady haunches whimpering, signaling that she needed to relive herself. Courageous but still in need of George's assistance to walk, to handle the patio steps, to rise from her squatting position. Marveling at her determination as they dried her legs and body wet from rain soaked grass.

Her display giving him momentary pause, until countered by her refusal of the sustenance of food and water, lowering her life's curtain even further. There could be no doubt of her wishes.

Rose Staves' conclusions were the same as his. While he stood downcast rubbing his lack-of-sleep eyes, she was wringing her hands in despair, knowing she was about to hear his words announcing Tasha's death knoll.

"It's time... Time to call Dr. Kerrigan's office," he said almost inaudibly.

"I know," she sobbed, not moving, just staring at Tasha.

"We can't let her continue to live this way," he urged sympathetically, his voice tightening.

"I know it's for the best but I'll miss her so," she said bursting into tears.

George put his arms around his wife to comfort her. "You heard her, you saw her, not eating, not drinking, her pain worsening each day. Her medicines no longer helpful."

"I know," Rose repeated sobbing, her shoulders quaking, her words stuttered. "She's telling us… she had a… fulfilling life, one we were… a very vital part of."

"She needed to get our acceptance and understanding before leaving us, lasting as long as she could… wanting us to provide her passage into her next world," he said.

Released from his embrace, Rose's steps were unsteady as she moved toward the phone. Tentatively underscoring her resistance as if awaiting a last minute reprieve, her husband watched her stand before the phone frozen in a trance-like state. Her hand finally moving, hovering over the phones buttons, her lips trembling, stifling back a cry. Suspecting that she had faltered, he moved to intercede.

Before George could reach Rose in her last minute paralysis, Tasha's piercing high pitched cry of misery penetrated the funeral setting, awakening Rose to the senselessness of her hesitation. She picked up the phone and pressed Dr. Kerrigan's office number, her shaking hands making it difficult. Connected, her voice emotional and fragmented but still audible, he heard her describe the events of the past night and the early morning.

"Yes, I understand, Dr. Kerrigan you've got scheduled surgery… ten o'clock, rear entrance," he heard her say as she softly cradled the phone. She turned showing him a tear-stained face drained of color, pronounced dark circles under her eyes were surrounded by newly furrowed lines of despair. Her sleeplessness, aging her well beyond her years. Recovery would challenge the passage of time.

They decided to call all their children to tell them of their decision, painfully an emotional Rose held the wireless extension phone to Tasha's ears to hear her children's, restraint no longer a needed deception, grieving farewells. Tasha's ears were erect at the sound of her name, her countenance mirroring their sadness.

Rose, sitting next to Tasha, instinctively reached out to pet her cautiously, each touch a reverence: "My dearest Tasha, my beauty, I love you." Tasha responding with difficulty, raised her head panting, her tongue weakly licking Rose's hand.

They sat there transfixed their feeling of impotence mounting; with Tasha between them intermittingly falling asleep, just as alternatively, awakening with anguishing cries, the Staves's damming their helplessness, dreading the passage of the next two hours. Nothing more to be said, bringing separation, opportuning a independence to reminisce and relive the past fourteen plus years: their own individual soliloquy. Their sadness taking temporary leave, travel reflective in their eyes: other times were being visited. Each occasionally breaking their silence sorrowfully chanted her name; "Tasha, Tasha," at each heart wrenching recollection. Their intimate moments increasingly golden, this moment to keep to themselves.

Unable to resist at the recollection, a semblance of a smile appearing as he flashed back to pleasanter times. His first sighting of Tasha those many years ago concealed under his son-in-law's jacket… recalling fondly her independence which he would challenge in their battle for Alpha status… becoming his subordinate, a follower, yet was still dominant and aggressive, always emerging the Alpha among other dogs… her swirling sometimes comical maneuvering within the snow, carving out her "command bunker" in which she would sit or lay reining for hours reliving the lives of her ancestors in the tundra, remembering with pride her regality, her bravery… her intelligence… always there for him… loving to sit for extended periods of time sharing a patio step, leaving only when he left. The composite imagery deepened his smile even further, but that was yesterday, as today's haunting task returned, the interlude too brief.

Rose's thoughts, her pained heart soothed by anecdotal events, hers too a shocked first sighting of Tasha hidden and covered within her son-in-law Bill's jacket. Her initial reaction, she remembered was momentary anger, not ready for another husky to replace Zuni. Tasha's razor sharp baby teeth, affectionately painful, brought her to rebuke, "No, no."… Phyllis' torn nose accident… Rosanne's recovery; a prevented miscarriage… the hide-and-seek game. Her mood changed to remorseful, her smile leaving her lips as she recalled Tasha's false pregnancy… her spaying that would leave them regrettably heirless.

Their vignettes reminiscing times lived where emotions were varying, knowing the next day was a new beginning. Not their present circumstance,the termination of a life, counting the time to finality where the tomorrow of their relationship together ceases to happen.

His words penetrated the heavy silence, "It's a quarter to ten."

Physically weakened, they responded as robots, their movements mechanical, their energy power ebbing, to be further drained, as the count down to the last act demanded of them began.

"I'll take her out back to relieve herself while you get ready," he said, his cracking voice just audible. Rose nodded slowly.

Tasha, as if knowing what was about to happen, with amazing will overriding her pain, stood on weakened legs to await his assistance down the patio steps.

When they returned, she did not attempt to lay down, a last hurrah choosing to stand on wobbly legs, to accommodate as if she knew he would lead her to the car for the final destination of her earthly being.

It proved difficult for George returned stoicism, Tasha proving her readiness, affectionately kissed both of them, bringing new tears to Rose, he bitting his lower lip in despair. Her actions, her message telling them they were not faulted; that she must move on, going willingly to her fate.

Physically and mentally spent they began the final torturous journey, Tasha with their assistance meeting her Creator. A humanitarian act those protectively distanced would say with aplomb. But that was an arms length response; she was family, always near and dear.Irrevocably bonded, bleeding from wounded hearts, returning one less, leaving behind the lifeless object of their grief.

The path to Tasha's eternity, traveling her last mile of streets surrounded by animation. Automatons, their time, their function allowing no interruption, no involvement to wonder the purposes of others amongst them. Making those with depressing purposes, the Staves feel alone by their permeating disinterest, just as well invisible. The Staves wished to shout for their attention. "Don't you sense our misery. We who are about to put a loved one to death, to be open wounded forever. Can you not read our devastation… Slow down to show sympathy of the heart wrenching responsibility expected of us."

Upon arrival they went to the rear entrance as directed, avoiding the sight of others. An assistant to the veterinarian foretold of the circumstances, met them at the door, led them to a treatment room exclusive for the use. The assistant, procedurally competent by her often repeated role, remained deliberately impassive. Her somberness, guarding against expressions of passion filled sympathy, a demeanor encouraged by her profession, it's purpose independence from those about to suffer a great loss, avoiding involvement beyond cursory commiserating. Separation there appropriate professionalism in life or death ministrations. Purposefully distant, an effective medicine in shortening the shock when dealing with emotions under siege, unavoidably perceived as indiffent and cold. For her it was necessary, as there would be others as equally taxing emotionally if allowed to manifest it'self.

With practiced impassivity, the aid placed a blanket on the antiseptically cleansed linoleum floor. With the leash still connected to her collar, Staves moved Tasha onto the blanket where she obediently laid down, sniffing it's scent of death of those that preceded her.

Rose and George were seated on the bench-like ledge of a large window overlooking the parking lot and the path fronting the building. The absence of chairs told them that not too many braved the traumatic task of witnessing their pet being put to sleep.

Consciously aware that these moments would be the last for her earthly presence, Tasha treasured their endearing comforting words while they reached out to pet her, panting under the duress of her illness, yet experiencing internal remarkable calm, the surrounding smell of death of no consequence.

"Mommy loves you," Rose said through trembling lips, her free-flowing tears wetting Tasha's muzzle giving the appearance that she too was crying.

"Tasha girl, my Tasha girl, such a good girl," he said fighting for composure, his hand wiping away Rose's tears from her muzzle.

Compelled as if willed, an authorless prayer suddenly recalled from the archives of his memory bank, finding it strengthening and meaningful commanding he recite it, capturing the moment:

> "And beloved master, should the great master see fit to deprive me of my health or sight, do not turn me away from you. Rather hold me gently in your arms as his skilled hands grant me the mercy of eternal rest, and I will leave you knowing with my last breath I draw, my fate was safest in your loving hands."

The origin of those powerful words, a spiritual prayer speaking to the circumstance of Tasha confounded him with their mystery. If not of St. Francis then who? Where had he first heard them? Read them? He could not recall. Profoundly fitting to troubled hearts and minds in an hour of need. But from whom?

Looking down at Tasha, her visage seemed to be smiling knowingly. Was it possible she was responsible for the recall? He chose to believe she was, stating as much to his wife, The suddenness of the words compelling that he recite them had touched him deeply. It's distinctive message fitting the moment, relieving guilt. It could not be accidental; it was too personal and fitting to come from another source.

Rose agreeing, incredulous as it seemed, she too feeling deeply it was Tasha speaking to them.

Dr. Kerrigan entered the room, his movements without hesitation for the task ahead, neither solicitous nor sympathetic offerings coming from his lips, his professional fortification. His words without emotion in order to render effective ministrations. For the good of all.

"This will happen quickly," he said kneeling as he electrically shaved Tasha's right foreleg exposing her bare skin's injection point.

"Will it hurt her?" Rose asked, her hand to her mouth to smother her deep throated anguish.

"No," he said. "She will be given an injection of Thiobarbiturates, a potent depressive that leads to the loss of consciousness preceding the cessation of the heart function. It will be painless and over in seconds," he said as if reading from the medical book that prepared him for the procedure.

Rose could no longer watch. Crying uncontrollably she rose quickly to rush from the room, leaving George to stay with Tasha.

Dr. Kerrigan, human afterall, his heart saddened by Rose's grief, his prescribed indifference compromised, nodded a sympathetic understanding as

Rose left, biting her quivering lower lip, shameless wails coming from her tortured mouth, the moment too much for her to witness.

Tasha's head lay cradled against George's feet, a position of contact she established right from the beginning. Staves' hand hovered over her mouth in bite preventing caution, not knowing what her reaction would be to the Dr. Kerrigan's pricking her skin. Her reaction was to kiss George's hand, the hand that was assisting her death, wanting nothing more.

Dr. Kerrigan quickly inserted the needle, first extracting blood into the syringe to be sure he had located in a blood vessel, satisfied he pushed the plunger releasing it's deadly contents.

"*Now I lay your head down to sleep*," George Staves whispered, the fatal moment arriving, fighting himself for control, finding the parable appropriate as Tasha slipped into unconsciousness.

Rose, who had been watching from the outside, through the rooms large window, whose open blinds provided some visibility, tearfully burst back into the room, "I should be here. Is she gone?" she asked distraught.

Dr. Kerrigan, pulling away his stethoscope, nodded "yes" arising to leave the room, knowing he could not be part of their bereavement.

George Staves, his hand to Tasha's chest, had felt the slowing and then the last of her heartbeats. Tasha was at peace never to pain again, her torment dying with her.

Rose rushed to drop down to her knees. Reaching down, she reverently raised Tasha's lifeless head in her hands, her name repeatedly escaping from her trembling lips, calling her; Tasha… Tasha, heard only by the living.

Responding, George put a consoling unsteady hand around Rose's arm, urging her to rise with him. Standing above Tasha shaking their heads from side to side, a gesture silently expressing, "No, no" in disbelief that she was gone. Needing each other's support, they embraced one another. A quaking Rose cried unashamedly; he in a continuing struggle to remain stoic.

Tasha's eyes stared back blankly, no longer showing recognition. Her stare from eyes that remained open while all her other organs and senses had shut down, a fingerprint that death leaves behind. He paused before gently closing her visionless eyes, with her life over they were sealed to passage, unable to be penetrated as she had guided him in the past. Offered instead the single-dimensioned reflection seen on stilled shallow lakes. Staves no longer able to probe deeply into her inner being, her mysteries, her consciousness, it's absence a finality.

In death her muscular control ceased. Her succumbing tongue managed to slip from her partially opened mouth as her last breath was drawn. Staves fondly placed Tasha's tongue back into her mouth, it was still warm and wet, he was remorseful that she would kiss no more.

A devastated Rose and George, his returned stoicism leaving him, both at her side tenderly touching her eyes, her ears and her body until all their words of sorrow had been said, their emotional outpouring quieting in exhaustion. Rose's tears having unlocked his sobs became sporadic and then silent, they no longer seen or heard by Tasha. The tide of this fatal day's emotions cresting, receding while looking at her body, silent and stilled, no longer effusing that which had made her so special.

Joining each other silently, knowingly; Tasha no longer to be pitied but to exalt. They, the owners of this once beautiful intelligent animal, a co-habitant as family for all these years, self-commuted their guilt to a blessing of good fortune. They had been privileged. A preservation of her memory would be assured so pronounced was her impact on their lives and the lives of others.

There would be no need to keep in memorial, treasures, symbolic articles attesting to her life. There would be no burial plot no head stone to revere on the anniversaries of her death or any other day; she was always with them in spirit. Fittingly the remnants of her physical being would not be static as it would reposing beneath the ground or in an urn, but mobile and in transition as she was in her physical life. Ironic those very forces of nature that she now could summon, acting upon her ashes over many years as part of natures mechanism, cremated remains turned to dust within the animal burial land.

A photo scrapbook documenting and recording her exploits, moments memorable to the public and those of empirical importance to the family would be their reference in the immediate lonely days that followed.To be augmented as planned with the book he would write was published.

He removed her leash and collar, stipulating with Dr. Kerrigan before they left that she was to be cremated. Specific that she be done singularly, having heard the horror stories of mass cremations and the mixing of remains. They needing assurances that the depositing of her ashes were exclusive.

Since her ashes were to be spread to the four winds, there would be no need for a well crafted retaining urn, the least expensive was all that was needed. Noticing an unknowing Dr. Kerrigan's surprise reaction of disbelief at the incongruity of their frugality, presupposing from their emotional attachment building a shrine to repose her ashes in tribute.

The ride back reduced to two was not without Tasha's presence. Her saliva, streaks now dried, coated her mouth contacting windows. Strands and tufts of her hair; black and white clung to their clothing and the station wagon's interior, both knowing that little signs of her living would be evident or stumbled on for a long time to come; her once existence reminded by surviving races of her being.

Upon returning home the day of Tasha's death,they solemnly began removing all of her belongings and playthings, to be discarded along with her collar and leash at the next refuse pickup. They had agreed on this course as best, withstanding the appearance of cold and dismissive behavior. Preferring the memories of the heart rather than personal properties to impersonal, emptied of the warmth and personality of their once host, their value spent.

They gathered up all of her leftover food and treats, feeling it only fitting that they be gifted to a member of her breed; reflecting as they did so that the rabbits and squirrels would also have been gifted, having free rein over Tasha's backyard domain, learning their daily challenges would no longer be met.

Lacking an appetite, they went to bed earlier than normal, each in need of sleep that was denied these last few days. Long into the night, Rose, in spite of physical exhaustion, could only find occasional sleep, awakening repeatedly by reminding emotional dreamscapes. George, twisting and turning, continued to remain awake, staring into the darkness aware of all the sounds of the night, absent of what he longed to hear.

Laying there fighting sleep, he found a need for space that could only come from being alone. He left his bed without a sign of daybreak, unaware that his wife was also awake, she choosing silence rather than questioning his early rising. His body not relaxed, taut by his continuing lack of sleep, stiffly he descended the stairs to the kitchen, grateful in thinking his wife was unaware of his leaving their bed. Turning the light on in the kitchen, he moved to the refrigerator door adorned with photos magnetically held in place. His mission was to purposefully search for Tasha's photos; finding them easily, he stood motionless in reverence. Suddenly as if a door had been flung open, he felt the rushing chill of dropping temperatures, a storm front bringing change about to be upon him. The remnants of his reclaimed stoicism swept aside as a tidal wave of emotion inundated him, alone freeing him to express the remaining surpressed feelings of those last moments, his anguished voice crying aloud. Unashamed, unable to stop its relentlessness, he could hear his sorrow. Tasha's name escaping his trembling lips repeatedly, questioning whether he had told her often enough how much he loved her.

Tearfully his face contorted by his vented outburst, emotionally beholden he pledged to himself and her spectral being: "Your absence encourages me to recreate and cherish… every sound that you ever voiced, your cries that appealed, your barks and growls that alerted, your whimpers that entreated… I will covet every photograph ever taken of you."

He and his family's diligence had assured photos covered all phases of her life. Photographic possessions now valued as jewels, a history they would view often in the early days of their recovery. Awaiting them, not lessening their devotion: the passing of times curative powers reducing the frequency of revisiting emotions – those moments eventually tempered to fondness. Their final recoveries assent, beginning that first day when the photographs were no longer private, to be proudly shared with visitors, inflating him as he related to the depictions history, saying more than once how fortunate they had been. Thoughts of a written tribute began their repeated visitations.

Upstairs, Rose, still awake, heard his attempts to muffle his cries, deciding it best that she leave him to himself to mourn alone, exorcizing in privacy; she burying her head in her pillow dampened with her own tears.

Recovering from venting his emotions, he sat at the kitchen table quietly staring blankly as though all objects were non-existent or lacked meaning. Prompting his escape from his fixation with nothingness; the spring season conversion of night to dawn, preceded by his finale from stoicism and his torrent of tears for Tasha's demise. Now he looked past that fateful day- moved to the past, a new day beginning with more to follow, the inevitable sequence a foundation to a life with the reality of her absence. Their grief yielding to revering her, they would live with the void, bridged by his fulfilling his promise to her.

~

As is customary this time of the year, the shadowy clouds had occasioned short-lived rainfall. While outside to pick up the days daily newspapers, the cold damp wetness on his face brought a glistening rouging color. His eyes, deeply shadowed by his ordeal, slow in yielding to his former self. As would other breakout signs of Tasha leaving the immediacy of his forefronting mind, slowly easing her memory to a background dwelling, having truly let go, she was no longer positioned in his brains frontal plane occupying the most space, the most notice.

George got into his car, the distance to his destination short as he was soon knocking at the door. It wasn't long before Mr. Corso answered. Immediately upon seeing Staves, he saddened. He was about to offer his hand in condolence, deciding it more fitting to put his arms around a pitying Staves to hug him.

"I'm so terribly sorry to hear that you had to put Tasha down, she was such a magnificent animal," his words torturing him, his eyes misting. "Smokey and Tasha were such good friends for all these many years. A closeness that we both knew could only come from knowing they were of the same breed."

"Thank you for your kind words, Carl. I appreciate them. I know how you feel about dogs. It will be difficult for all of us," Staves responded as he handed him Tasha's remaining food and treats and prepared to leave.

"Can we have a drink in her memory?"

"I don't feel at the moment talking about her Carl. I hope you understand."

"I do," Carl Corso responded, empathizing, "we'll talk another time when things aren't so current."

"Thanks Carl,"yielding, the time to leave nearing "I had her cremated, I've got one more thing to do and that is to spread her ashes in a fitting place."

He paused just as he was about to exit the house. His new resolve still in development, his visage turned melancholy, asking, "Carl, I'd like to say hello to Smokey if it's all right with you."

"Certainly," he answered, understanding. "Come with me."

Carl Corso led George Staves to the backyard of his home where they were greeted by his gray-and-white husky, Smokey. As always, Smokey's recognition was immediate, coming up to Staves and Corso, coaxing to be petted. Within seconds of the mutual greeting, Smokey who had lain on his back curling up his front paws submitting, leaped to his feet with his tail tucked tightly between his legs, whimpering, moving beyond their reach.

Taken aback, looking down at Smokey, George Staves saw some of Tasha's hair clinging to his jacket and trousers, the same ones he had worn, that fateful day. He immediately knew what had affected Smokey's strange behavior; it was unmistakable. Smokey had picked up Tasha's scent from those final moments, distancing himself from the smell of death.

"Do you really think he could know of her death?"

"I believe he did by reading me."

Carl nodded in agreement at the connection.

"Thanks, Carl," Staves acknowledged as he closed the backyard gate,leaving Carl Corso and Smokey behind, feeling his throat constrict as he took measure of Smokey one more time.

Unexpectedly, Smokey who was watching his departure raised his head and issued a mournful howl. A final tribute.

Smokey was fourteen dog years old, as was Tasha, except he remained healthy with not a trace of arthritis affecting his joints. The fortunes of nature, Staves said to himself shaking his head. A miniscule element of jealousy, not lasting long, forced his mind to ask of himself, "Why" as he drove away.

Sequestered, their mourning private, their rite of funeral within the sanctuary of their home. In their missing quiet solitude, indigenous resonant sounds amplified and echoed as if the house were empty of furnishings, unaccustomed and surprising them.

That day and those that would follow, they had received well-intentioned sympathetic phone calls. Subsequently declining to answer, they screened the calls that would resurrect memories, judging that approach best for their mending. Screening prevented well intentioned painfully remindful remembrances, ultimately recalled during expressions of sympathy. Remembrances they had hoped to compartmentalize during their "learning to live with adjustment," pulling apart healing wounds, setting back recovery, necessitating the re-gathering of the resolve of "letting go." They knew their vulnerability to retrograding would continue while their last promise to Tasha remained unsatisfied; her specter unfulfilled until her remains were covering the land of her wishes.

"We won't begin to get closure until we bring her remains to the resting site," he said wearily. "I'm so mentally exhausted that I imagine her. I hear her, feel her touch and smell her scent."

"I know," Rose said sharing, her voice a whisper, "I imagine her everywhere."

George Staves received word that very night from the veterinarian's office; the caller saying Tasha's ashes would be ready for receiving the following morning. He arranged for an early pickup, planning to continue to drive to the chosen site hours away, extending the remaining rite of funeral it's final observance hundreds of miles away, as would the awaiting closure that would set them all free.

"I'll stay in the car," Rose said not wanting to relive her last memory.

Her husband nodded an understanding. His mood somber, he entered the offices of Dr. Kerrigan and returned shortly carrying a mason jar-like container in a plastic bag, silently placing it in the trunk. Returning to the car, he saw from the corner of his eye Rose wiping away tears. He decided not to speak of it for fear of losing himself in her sorrow.

They arrived at the destination within hours of springs warmest part of the day. The stunted shadows that were cast indicated the sun was directly overhead on its trek west. A night falling curtain was hours away, still time for what they had to do.

He remembered the last time he and Tasha had made this trip in the early fall when they both began their mystical search, joined in hope and allegiance. It was the final days of summer with fall in the wings awaiting its curtain call, when the greenery of the towering trees would begin to loose their well fed vibrancy as falling temperatures and shortened days forced the retreating of their life-giving energies.While succumbing presenting it's final mastery in artistry,the spectacular golden and red colors of aging.Ushering in September's equinox to Decembers solistice bringing an end to the seasons, its life cycle.

A death of a season in the making. The dynamics of the landscape somewhat corresponding to his and Tasha's mission: the vernal equinox - her recovery, both given new life… the relationship the dream of poets.He remembered his prayers for the success of the mission they had undertaken-answered positively with a grantee tailoring for sacrifice. With that behind him, sadly the season of birth would bear witness to her physical death.

They drove the final leg of their journey in silence, internally screening their mass of sorrow to a more manageable particulate, sized to allow their lives to continue without Tasha, allowing other subjects interests to filter through and share in their attention.

Here at the site, this day of Tasha's remains deliverance, the scenery was beginning to show rebirth. Remnants of the last snowfall existed only in the land's deepest depressions or shielded by shadows cast by those very trees that were eagerly awaiting transition. The many veined barren branches dismally gray these past months began to show life. Hibernating sap was beginning its upward travel, its birthing power spawning buds and shoots to flourish into a covering of greenery, energized by the warming sun, preceding the bloom of flowering fragrances.

The Irony seized him: returning to where so much hope was first visualized, searching and finding a mechanism to rejuvenate a faltering life, only to be thwarted by Tasha'choice of a ethereal presence, leaving behind the mortal remnants of her spent life inhabiting this land, purposed by God in it's extremes as special.

George the single pallbearer carried the urn bearing Tasha's remains possessively, her weight reduced to nothingness, a shocking contrast to the remembered weight when she was an earthly being.

The alfalfa laced ground beneath their feet was soggy with the spring thaw, their trail boots up to the task stained in wetness.

The steam feeding the lake, while cold, was flowing, seeing the sky again after having been set free of restricting ice days before, the remaining shards to eventually be part of the lake's rising waters.

The abundant fish rippled the lake's surface, having abandoned their role as bottom dwellers during their escape from the cold, searching the still chilled waters surface for food.

The campsite showed the activity of others; ashes left in the stone walled outside "fireplace " he had built, testifying as being used by the outdoorsmen who followed.

As they approached what he had guessed would be the beginning of the path that was mysteriously laid out for him those many months ago, George knew it would be too much to expect to find Shaman artifacts pointing the way. Instead surprisingly the high grass was recently cut, scythe no doubt because of the mower resistant grasses height, providing the path. Taking the compass from his pocket he determined it's direction.

"Who cut this path?" Rose inquired mystified. The distinct smell of cut grass permeated the air around them. "It looks like we were expected but how is that possible?"

Staves, smiling at his wife's uncertainty and distrust for the mysterious, said teasingly, "It's friendly witchcraft. Shamans having fun enjoying themselves with Tasha right along with them."

Rose's believability was further shaken, as their attention was diverted back toward the campsite, amazingly a roaring fire had been started. With her mouth agape in disbelief as yet again no one was in sight, George smiling said, "Another playful act by the spirits."

"Nonsense," Rose responded doubtful. "There has to be another explanation."

"What?" he offered curtly, "Spontaneous combustion?"

Intimidated by his reasoning, she asked nervously, "Are you sure?" The strength and defiance in his answer mellowing her uncertain response.

"I'm sure... They're just having fun at our expense showing off their powers. It's God's will," he said smiling matter-of-factly, hoping to placate her.

They were well along the cut path when another strange incident occurred. A strong powerful roar swept over them. Two fast moving winds at two different altitudes: one carrying debris moving east to west; the other a countering west to east movement propelling small birds in it's path. Their wings extended, not fighting the propulsion, no other option but to be driven. The wind was traveling at levels just above their reach, never touching the ground, twisting and turning, speeding along unimpeded, avoiding them with all but the roar. Having gotten their attention, the twin forces of nature stopped just as suddenly, the debris deposited, the birds flight continuing on their own.

Rose, in wonderment of the strange event remained uncertain, loyal to her convictions, asked skeptically, "Your magicians are having fun at our expense?"

"No question about it, but they never threaten. They're just flaunting their powers. We're welcomed visitors."

Looming in front of them, just as she had remembered his description months before, was a canopied opening cut through the high African grasses, molded woods of manipulated trees presenting an opening. The branches of the trees on both sides of the opening forcefully locked together in unity, providing a tunnel of concealed passage, making it practically beyond detection from all but the familiar, uncut high grass fronted its location concealing it from afar.

"Remarkable," Rose offered no longer wanting to debate, however uncertain she remained as they moved through the significantly cooler passageway. The interwoven branches successfully blocking out the sun creating its own midnight. The only light available was at the entrance and the exit as they moved from one to the other.

Emerging from the tree formed passageway shadowed and chilled by denied sunlight, the expectation of the sight he thought he would share with his wife did not greet them. Unlike his first visit, instead of lavish greenery, mysteriously at odds with the prevailing weather conditions, was freshly fallen snow, up to six inches in depth covering the ground, virgin, undisturbed, and antiseptic. Not a leaf, broken branches, bird droppings or any other adulteration violated its pristine quality. It's stark whiteness in sharp contrast to his original sighting.

"This can't be the place you were telling us about, where you heard but never saw any animals?" Rose asked in utter confusion.

"Yes," George responded stunned, "but not like this. The snows a surprise. "There was no snowfall forecast for this area, only traces at the higher elevation of the mountains where the temperatures are conducive: below freezing, but not here at this time. I've got a feeling this is additional playfulness by our spectral jesters."

Ignoring his assertion Rose said "The view while not as breathtaking as your earlier description has a beauty of it's own. Stark, pure and inviolate," her eyes sweeping the miles and miles of this out of season panorama.

"Whatever it's presentation it still is haunting. My previous experience tells me you cannot mark this beautiful landscape. Watch this," he said to prove his point tossing a crumpled piece of paper onto the snow. No sooner had it landed, the paper disappeared in a puff of smoke. He wasn't surprised; while Rose was wide-eyed in disbelief.

"That consuming mysterious power a guardian unleashed to continue the lands secrecy. Knowing what we just saw; I would guess you cannot photograph this place, denying you evidence that it exists, that you were here, never able to find this place again uninvited."

Rose, skeptical, said, "I brought my camera to photograph the beauty you described to show to the children and for Tasha's photo album. I'm going to try anyway." She aimed the camera at him. He quickly appeared on the viewing screen. Looking closer she saw that the background was non-existent. She then aimed the camera directly at the remarkable snow covered land; the viewing screen remained blank, nothing was visible.

"What does it mean?" Rose asked, becoming frightened for the first time.

"No cause for concern," he said calmly. "It's just that this place is magical. Come, I'll show you more."

As they moved further from the tunnel the suns glare, while not directly in their eyes was intense, amazed he said, "Look at this field and its miles of rolling acreage, not a shadow is being cast by those voluminous clouds and hills; they are not blocking the sun, the snow remaining white in it's reflection. It's not possible except here," he said in wonderment. "It's the magic of the

Rainbow Bridge I told you about. A wintry version. We are safe. You needn't feel frightened. Come there's sure to be more that will confound you."

Rose, remaining wary of the mysterious that preyed upon her in spite of his assurances, clutched her necklace cross for protection.

He offered her his free hand, leading them both onto the snow covered terrain. Their steps strangely silent, equally mystifying, they left no footprints in the snow. The snow remained undisturbed; no evidence that they had come this way, yet here they were. It was not possible they were imagining as they were witness to each other, sharing the same experience, their body weight defying gravity, Staves already experiencing that phenomenon, flaunting the snows magic reached down and grasped a handful of snow which quickly dissipated in his grasp leaving no signs of moisture. The area that his hand had dug showing no signs of disturbance. Rose forced a smile at her husbands playful bravado but remained guarded, her steps cautious, unnatural in its length, mechanical as if expecting the snow covered ground would yield. Confidence and reconciliation coming with each succeeding step, accepting what was happening in this strange environment.

Rose transformed, was no longer fearful of this unknown and its miraculous God-like implications, finally drew courage from his assurances, her trepidations leaving her. Her steps no longer tentative were steady and ground covering.

"Amazing, simply amazing," she commented her anxiety vanquished.

George Staves, knowing what to expect, remained anxious for his wife's reaction in spite of having been forewarned by his description. Wary of her tolerance for the surrounding death as they moved to the burial ground. As they climbed the last of the rising terrain, the land of gray pockmarked desolation. was upon them, it's temperatures decidedly colder; unlike the neighboring land they were leaving. Here moisture laden clouds shielded the sun, yet the barren land was being denied snow. In strange contrast to the nearby land of moderate temperatures, with improbable sunlit snows covering the beautiful greenery – marked differences existing, bordering one another. The sharp line of demarcation was impossible to believe.

Much to his surprise, Rose was up to the challenge, needing no reminder that the purpose of this ground was not for the living. Believing it a sanctified depository for the dead to free their spiritual beings for the afterlife, their eternity.

Rose chilled by the lower temperatures, scanned the bleak panorama, sighting the many caved hills that served as burial vaults, fitting his description. Finally as they drew closer she saw the hurriedly dug burial plots, some remaining covered with loose limestone and silica sand while others, not so fortunate turned her head, not in horror but sorrow for their exposed stiffening carcasses and bleached bones. Death coming too soon as the gravesites were too shallow to hold the wind-blown covering sandy soil and limestone.

While death surrounded them, their sense of morbidity was modulated, mindful that the land for the desperate to find final repose; was a sorrowful but hopeful accommodation. A cemetery without measured allocated spaces, alignment of tombstones and manicured gravesites. The landscape hewn by nature's forces, barren to discourage the curious without it's calling, purposefully deceiving by seemingly offering nothing but barren wastelands, reaching out to guide instinctively the dying, a place sanctioned by God to repose remains in a brotherhood of animal species.

He scanned the landscape, automatically making note of markers among the barrenness and desolation, knowing it unlikely that he may be invited to return.

Drawing a deep breath and then exhaling to modulate his pent up emotions, he opened the wooden box he was carrying and withdrew the tightly lidded Urn containing Tasha's remains, placing it on the sandy soil.

Rose's plaintive eyes, while tearless for what was about to happen, the finality of the act paining her face with disconsolation. The rebirth of her healthy recovering countenance rescued from being drawn and set in sadness, on hold this final moment.

Surprising him she reached out to participate, taking hold of the urn, joining in sharing the actual experience, each contributing in honoring the final commitment to Tasha. A religious experience for both of them, this final act, the two of them parishioners where deliverance and final reconciliation would be their blessing.

They had agreed the funeral service include their religion's prayers, convinced as not blaspheming their church, guided by the beliefs of Saint Francis of Assisi as apropos, notwithstanding the more secular cremation and the spreading of ashes.

The urn empty, the last of Tasha's ashes falling to the ground, the last vestiges of her corporeal being seeded in the secret land as multiple markers for her spectral being, each a headstone facing the heavens she was now traveling. Unexpectedly, a sense of relief came upon them, feelings beyond sorrow and their conscience, freeing their all to long taunt muscles to full range, their attitude expansive, contracting the empty void, furthering closure. Their transformation brought them self-criticism and unworthiness with challenging thoughts of betrayal: the implications of abbreviating the mourning period.

"Never," was their silent chorus, their revering eyes messaging assurances to one another as well as the spirits, Tasha's memory would live on, never to be forgotten as they resumed their lives without her.

They trudged back slowly, reluctant, slowing the return trip as if something more, forgotten at the moment, needed to be done. An unconscious efforts to extend this moment of last contact in the surroundings that would hold her remains, adding additional dimension to this moments vividness,the extended period to be explained in future reflections. A truth, knowing indelible clarity was relative to exposure,to time spent. Their hesitancy, additionally delaying the inevitable recognition that with each retreating step, a step into their future distanced her as a memorable past, as only the living traveled their tomorrows.

Their returning footprints paralleling their arriving ones in the sandy soil of the burial ground as they essentially chose the same route to return; ending as once again they crossed over the divide where physical presence could not be recorded.

While cloudless skies greeted them, the sun continued its strange ambivalence: warming temperatures, while void of casting shadows upon the snow. A new presentation, permitting a more natural, previously withheld, appreciable sublimation of the snow covered undulating landscape. The carpeted snow's guardians continuing their frivolity, allowing the thinned snows surface blades of grass to break the once stark whiteness; the intrusions resplendent in its spectrum, ranging from yellow to blue. Unavailable if they could be seen by plant grazing animals and fowl, the land only for the invited, remaining pristine and unspoiled.

As they approached the forest opening, they paused once more to absorb the breathtaking view; a magnificent still-life painting absent the effective use of shadows. The pigments untracked by brush strokes as if sprayed on, lacking depth assured a motionless image. Inanimate. A stopping of time. They the only continuate of life's being's in this strange un-dimension land.

That imagery was permanently imprinted in their memory, knowing that recall was the only way they could revisit. The splendor of their surroundings shown in their faces was suddenly replaced with astonishing disbelief, shocked to momentary muteness by what was heard.

Instinctively, Rose grabbed her husband's arm tightly, unbelieving the sound she heard.

"What was that?" she gasped. "Could it be?"

"I'm not sure," George replied. "hopeful to hear it again."

Together they waited, alert and sensitized, not daring to speak. They did not have to wait too long. Piercing the quiet again was the unmistakable barking of a dog. Its resonance and voice print distinctly Tasha's. A bark of greeting, of painless joy, bringing to image her romping happily and playfully in the snow, digging and burrowing her muzzle, circling rapidly to build her snow walled den.

"It's her message to us that all is well, that she is now pain free and happy.

To romp about with her playmates," Rose said smiling at the thought, her tears of joy glistening her skin.

"She's sharing with us that she's found her Valhalla, her Rainbow Bridge," George added.

Just as suddenly the communication ended, the surroundings empty to the mere mortal. Nonetheless they remained unmoving, hopeful of another contact. After a few minutes of hearing nothing, they knew the special moment was over, indelibly adding the moment to the past they wished she were not part of.

Their exiting restarted, continuing to move towards the distant canopies entrance, their pace slowed appreciably, unconsciously hopeful of Tasha making another contact from the magical land behind them. Suddenly, the blue sky free of clouds within the miles of their panorama lost it's sunlight plunging them into darkness. Instinctively they reached for one another's security, finding themselves in each others arms just as brilliant colors of natural light predominated. Appearing as streaks of flickering arcs lighting up the skies: green closer to earth, followed by blue, purple, and red at the higher elevation. Astonished George Staves immediately recognized the phenomena as a Aurora Borealis visiting out of season in latitudes usually beyond their perception. Another harmless display of Shaman power directing the raining of charged particles from the sun to enter the local atmosphere between sixty to six hundred twenty miles above the earth. The earth's safety assured by the protective bubble of a magnetic field, the result: the creation of remarkable brilliant lights of various colors visiting the nighttime sky. Inconceivable for this part of the atmosphere, a manipulation enjoyed by the Shamans, a teasing display of their power to command nature to improbable feats, gifted their departure.

It only lasted moments as the day's actual time period returned, the captivation of the flashing lights bringing confusion to their return direction. Quickly referring to his compass he confirmed the troubling extraordinary magnetic activity had rendered the compass useless. Before testing his and Rose's sense of direction, to lead them to the campsite, the tranquil and pristine quality of their wintry greeting card surroundings began to experience change. The typography contouring undisturbed snow in abruption – it was moving. Alarmed by what they first thought to be an earthquake was the snow compressing beneath their feet, knead by unseen forces, something their footfalls were unable to do. The instability forcing them to hold onto one another. Rose, alarmed, screamed:

"Oh my God what's happening?"

Equally apprehensive, George shouted as he stared down at the snow covered ground beneath them, "Look!"

A path was forming for their benefit, a return route undoubtedly provided by the Shaman, the molded path resulting from a change in the snows density, absorbing rather than reflecting the sunlight's spectrum, it's coloring now blue for added distinction. The spectacular messages manufactured for their benefit awing them in intimidation, but being insignificant in a world not their own. Regrouped they hastened their pace. They were about to learn, what was once given, to be taken away. The purpose of the mystical to be served:, other Shaman purposes awaited them in exiting.

Anxious to return to the campsite, with the day ending and time an issue, they didn't stop to share what they had experienced. Would there be more? Anxious, they turned to look backward to view the tree canopy, shocked as the opening in the trees no longer existed. Replacing trees had filled the void with instant growth, as if the void was never there, never part of this earth.

The wave of disbelieving reconstruction, a makeover continued, as arriving at the campsites fire revealed no evidence of having previously burned feverishly, not a trace of heat in the framing rocks, nor the residue ashes. The stilled air attracting mosquitoes and fly's no longer threatened; searching.

Cognizant of Rose's building bewilderment, patiently, on the verge of repeating his explanation of the confounding events taking place, George paused. Suddenly, and silently, the sculpted path with its cut grasses lying where they fell, becoming animated, reversing the domino effect, rising up from the force that began the chain that felled them. The motion so rapid the cut grass returned intact in harmony, as if never severed, the path never there.

Pointing; "Look," he shouted at the spontaneity, "history being recalled in deceptive restoration."

Rose awestruck, troubled, and confused, turned to him after some hesitancy questioning, "Why is this happening? Or is it? Could we have imagined what we experienced? Are we still dreaming?"

"I think not," he responded smiling confidently.

"Why," she asked, her doubts not assuaged.

"All we've seen, all the extraordinary events, the fire that never was. The incongruity of the Aurora Borealis lights in these latitudes lasting minutes. Spectral intervention providing a path when direction was lost, compounded by the compass not functioning, the path having a temporary life, the disappearance of the trees canopy showing no signs of having existed, and now this," pointing to the intact grass. "Once visible as real, their disappearance conspiratorial, making us skeptical and unsure of our magical journey, but I'm not buying it. I've been initiated to their trickery. For sure this a makeover, a mischievous clever ploy, attempting to suggest nothing unusual ever happened. A planned outcome knowing doubts would rise as we returned to our lives without the suggestion of controlled senses of sight and sound, of minds purchased. As is happening right now, our liberation is being counted on to bring distancing, bring doubts, creating ambivalence. Cleverly a manipulation that protects them in it's uncertainty. Giving weight that what we experienced was sharing a selective dream, creating doubts that you and I witnessed a dimension of a surreal world, vulnerable victims as we were to an emotional involvement that was almost disabling. Attempting to capitalize on your voiced doubts of what you said had happened to me during my first visit. Their make over reinforcing that it could have been hypnosis all along. But I remain convinced we co-joined in a mystical experience, not a dreamscape."

She remained uncertain, joining him to casually poke through the cold and wet ashes with a piece of firewood left behind, searching for the fire that had recently lived, confirming ashes of no recent past, no future, feeding her uncertainty.

Countering Rose's residing conflict George Staves said, essentially repeating, "This make over I'm convinced is nothing more than the spectral eliminating physical evidence to secure the secrecy of this secret land.

"It's hard to believe or deny. What I do know for a fact is that we spread Tasha's ashes where she wanted in a place few people have seen, let alone believe. That was real. Look in your hand," she reminded him. "Your still carrying the urn Why hasn't that disappeared, that certainly is evidence."

Before anything more could be said, answering in a familiar howl, initial octaves reaching soprano range crescendo, trailing off as wavering breaks of a deep throated baritone; again distinctively Tasha's voice print, telling of her presence elsewhere, not of their returned to world, answered all questions.

"There's our answer, Tasha telling us."

"How," Rose answered tremulously wanting to believe.

"Think about it," he responded. "Didn't you feel a sense of liberation after leaving the tunnel? Our passage and contact with their world ceasing, now worlds apart, messages and signs no longer in existence by virtue of the makeover introducing the deception of doubt. Planned to assure returning their status as folklore superstition Surely you recognize we are in own world where as occupants heard Tasha independently, defiantly crossing the divide that separates us, gave us proof of confirmation, that it actually happened, hearing Tasha's voice with our minds cleared, verifying her legacy… our experience."

"Of course," she said, even as a Shaman, Tasha displayed her independence, after participating in the non threatening phenomena, differing with her counterparts in message: our experience did take place. Confirmed as we stand free of artificial influences, we could not have been seduced to hear her in our world…Unlike where we visited we could have recorded the miracle of her voice.

Still Rose wished for more demonstrable proof. In silence they knew what had to be done for finality. It had served its purpose.It could no longer be of use. It could not serve as a shrine as it contained nothing. Despairing she took from her husband the urn that bore Tasha's ashes and dropped it inconsequently into the dormant ashes of the fire, improbably it burst into consuming flames, the shock and intense heat thrusting them backwards. The last evidence of Shaman involvement incinerating to ashes – her reluctance to believe ending.

Epilogue

George Staves rose from his patio's beach chair, the journey provided by his transporter over, the selected occurrences in Tasha's life visited now in his copious notes to be recorded in the written word of his book-sharing her esence. The actual moments again traveling in space as energies of sight and sound.

His transporter motionless, receiving no further commands, he was, at the moment satiated, his ability to visit prompting his healing to continue.

Bibliography

The following listing of writings that gave the author acknowledged pleasurable reading throughout, while offering insight and guidance; credited when referenced:

Thomas, Elizabeth Marshall, *The Hidden Life of Dogs*, Pocket Books, 1993

Thomas, Elizabeth Marshall, *The Social Lives of Dogs*, Simon & Shuster, 2000

Pisano, Beverly, *Siberian Huskies*, T.F.H. Publications, Inc. Ltd., 1993

Bass, Rick, *Coulter, The True Story of the Best Dog I Ever Had*, Houghton Mifflin Company, 2000

Katz, Jon, *The New Work of Dogs*, Villard Books, 2003

Maoussaieff, Jeffery and McCarthy, Susan, *When Elephants Weep: The Emotional Lives of Animals*, (Delta) Dell Publishing, 1995

TATE PUBLISHING & *Enterprises*

Tate Publishing is committed to excellence in the publishing industry. Our staff of highly trained professionals, including editors, graphic designers, and marketing personnel, work together to produce the very finest books available. The company reflects the philosophy established by the founders, based on Psalms 68:11,

"THE LORD GAVE THE WORD AND GREAT WAS THE COMPANY OF THOSE WHO PUBLISHED IT."

If you would like further information, please call
1.888.361.9473
or visit our website
www.tatepublishing.com

TATE PUBLISHING & *Enterprises*, LLC
127 E. Trade Center Terrace
Mustang, Oklahoma 73064 USA